NEW YORK REVI

CLASSIC

THE ROOT AND THE FLOWER

L. H. MYERS (1881–1944) was the son F. W. H. Myers, an essayist and investigator into parapsychology, and Evelyn Tennant, an accomplished amateur photographer and famous Victorian beauty. Myers attended Eton and Trinity College, Cambridge, traveled, underwent a transforming mystical experience in a Chicago hotel room, and fell in love with Elsie Palmer, a general's daughter from Glen Eyrie, Colorado, whom he later married. His first novel, *The Orissers* (1922), was followed by *The Clio* (1925), *Strange Glory* (1936), and *The Root and the Flower* (originally issued as three separate books between 1929 and 1935). A final novel, *The Pool of Vishnu* (1940), revisits the Indian setting and some of the characters of *The Root and the Flower* while also reflecting Myers's newfound commitment to communism. Increasingly unhappy in his later years, Myers struggled to write an auto-biography, but remained unsatisfied with the work, which he finally destroyed. He committed suicide in 1944.

PENELOPE FITZGERALD (1916–2000) graduated with honors from Somerville College, Oxford, and worked at a variety of jobs until, in 1975, she published her first book, a biography of the pre-Raphaelite master Edward Burne-Jones. She was the author of two other biographies and ten works of fiction, among them *The Blue Flower*, *Human Voices*, and *The Bookshop*.

THE ROOT AND THE FLOWER

L. H. Myers

■

Introduction by

PENELOPE FITZGERALD

NEW YORK REVIEW BOOKS

New York

THIS IS A NEW YORK REVIEW BOOK
PUBLISHED BY THE NEW YORK REVIEW OF BOOKS

This edition published in 2001 in the United States of America by
The New York Review of Books, 1755 Broadway, New York, NY 10019

Library of Congress Cataloging-in-Publication Data

Myers, L. H. (Leopold Hamilton), 1881-1944.
  The root and the flower / L.H. Myers ; introduction by Penelope
Fitzgerald.
     p.   cm.
  ISBN 0-940322-60-9 (alk. paper)
  1. Akbar, Emperor of Hindustan, 1542-1605—Fiction. 2.
India—History—1526-1765—Fiction. 3. Mogul Empire—Fiction. 4.
Emperors—Fiction. I. Title.
  PR6025.Y43 R66 2000
  823'.912—dc21

                          00-011024

ISBN 0-940322-60-9

Book design by Red Canoe, Deer Lodge, Tennessee
Caroline Kavanagh, Deb Koch
Printed in the United States of America on acid-free paper.
10 9 8 7 6 5 4 3 2 1

March 2001
www.nybooks.com

To Iris

INTRODUCTION

L . H . M Y E R S (Leopold Hamilton Myers, 1881–1944) was born
into a distinguished scholarly family. His father, F. W. Myers, was
one of the founders of the Society for Psychical Research; their
home in Cambridge was a center of hospitality and intellectual
discussion, but it was also rather an odd place to be brought up in.
Frederic Myers was set upon demonstrating the immortality, or at
least the survival, of human personality by acceptable scientific
methods, and his children were half frightened and half fascinated
by the procession of mediums and "sensitives" who came to the
house to give evidence. Leo's mother was passionate and posses-
sive, his father expected rather more of the family than they could
give. When he died Leo had to cut short his time at university to
take his mother abroad; F. W. Myers had made an appointment to
manifest himself after death, and had named a time and place, but
the meeting failed. Leo lost faith, but only in his father's methods.
He saw now that though reason must always be distinguished
from intuition, it should never be separated from it. They must
work together.

He was educated at Eton and Cambridge, and although he was
always as popular as he would allow himself to be, he bitterly
hated both of them. He rejected, in fact, every social structure to
which he belonged, including the literary circles which London

offered him. To Myers, all of these fell grotesquely short. "Just as an individual cannot live for himself," says the Rajah in *The Near and the Far*, "so society cannot live for itself, but must keep a self-transcendent idea before it." In holding this ideal, and in devoting his writing career to it, Myers was unflinchingly sincere, but his life was not consistent with it. He was neither an ascetic nor a revolutionary. Between his seduction at the age of sixteen and his marriage he had a number of affairs, some, he said, "very squalid."* When in 1906 he came into a legacy he moved through society as a generous patron of the arts, but also as a detached and elegant young man, with a taste for racing at Brooklands. Even when, after running through every other political solution, he became a Communist, he still had a part-share in an expensive French restaurant, Boulestin's. Myers, of course, noticed these discrepancies, since he possessed (in the words of his friend L. P. Hartley) "an exquisite wry sense of humor of which he was half-ashamed." But Hartley has also described how, with the close of the 1930s and the threat of war, Myers' self-knowledge darkened into pessimism. A slow and scrupulous writer, he had always depended greatly on the advice of his friends. Now he quarreled fiercely with most of them. As a young man he had asked himself the question: "Why should anyone want to go on living once they know what the world is like?" On the 7th April 1944 he answered it for himself by taking an overdose of veronal.

Myers left his great trilogy, *The Root and the Flower*, to speak for him. Like his other books, it has an exotic setting, in this case sixteenth-century India under the reign of Akbar. He did not pretend to accuracy and indeed he had never been to India, though he visited Ceylon. His motive, as he said in his 1940 Preface, is to give us a clearer view of our own social and ethical problems from the "vantage-point of an imaginary world."

This world, though anything but safe, is a very seductive one. The slow rhythm of the palace, the desert and the river are like an audible pulsation of the Indian heat, but at any moment we may be asked to look at something as small as a mark in the dust or a

---

*Some of these details are from G. H. Bantock: *L. H. Myers: A Critical Study* (1956). Myers began to write an autobiography shortly before his death, but he destroyed it.

dying moth, or stretch our ears for a minute sound. We do not, however, do this for nothing. The descriptive passages hardly ever stand still, they give the sense of something about to happen:

> At the door he paused again; from the roof there hung down wisps of dry, gray moss; ants had built a nest against the threshold and the droppings of wood-pigeons whitened the window-sills. Contrary to his expectations the latch came up when he tried it; the door opened and a curious smell spread upon the fresh air. (p. 69)

> The absence of the moon and stars made the night intimate and earthly; dry leaves, lifted from the ground, were swept across his hands and face. It seemed as if the earth's secret energies were working upon him, and he yielded to a process which he felt to be beneficent. His spirit lay still in a quiet excitement; a sense of expectation gathered; it was like that of a woman who is awaiting the first pangs of her first childbed. (p. 230)

> She showed him the place where ... the young man ... was buried. There certainly were some suspicious marks upon the ground. The soil was cracked, having swollen up in a blister, and this seemed to indicate that the work was not the work of Thugs, for Thugs always drove a stake through the body to allow the gases of decomposition to escape without a sign. (p. 222)

Myers wants us to look at his world of appearances and beyond it. Appearances cannot be dismissed as an illusion, for no illusion can be created except by reason. On the other hand, the life of the spirit is just as real as the pigeon dung and the bloated corpse. "I am" has no meaning without "There is." How can the two be reconciled? On this problem depend the three great questions of the book. First, how can an individual be sure that he has found himself? "If everyone is pretending to be like others," says Prince Jali, "who is like himself?" Secondly, if each individual is a solitary heart, how is he to unite with other human beings? Thirdly, if he does so, how can he be sure that the society he lives in acknowledges "the supremacy of the spirit as the guiding principle of life"?

Reading a long book is like living a long life, it needs an adjustment of pace. Myers is asking us to slow down, and so to deepen the consciousness. At the beginning of the trilogy, a story of war, betrayal, torture and political power, we have to consider what seems a very small incident. The little prince, alone on the palace balcony, sees a snake crawling along the gutter. The wind stirs a twig, and Jali, watching, "entered into the snake's cold, narrow intelligence and shared its angry perplexity." It strikes, loses its balance, and falls to its death on the roof below. The snake shares "the terrible numerousness of living beings, all separate, all alone, all threatened." It could not tell that the twig was not an enemy. It was deceived by appearances. But a little earlier Jali had been gazing at the serene desert horizon, which had looked so different when they made the six days' hot journey across it. "He clung to the truth of appearances as something equal to the truth of what underlay them . . . Deep in his heart he cherished the belief that some day the near and the far would meet."

The first book of the trilogy gives a sense of the imperial war game which will decide the fate of India. Akbar is the ruinous tyrant or "great man" of history. His dream of uniting India's religions—the Din Ilahi—is folly, and he himself is at heart commonplace. His inheritance is disputed between his two sons, Salim, the brutal soldier, and Daniyal, the perverted intellectual. It is the duty of Rajah Amar, in his small kingdom, to decide where his allegiance lies before he withdraws, as he wishes to do, to a monastery. Almost perversely, he favors Daniyal, because he has always disliked him, and he wants to stand uninfluenced by the affections. Sita, the Rajah's wife, is a Christian who prefers, for good or ill, to stay with the rest of humanity. These two, husband and wife, are far apart, and yet they are both searching for perfection. "The gulf is not between those who affirm and those who deny but between those who affirm and those who ignore." The man whom Sita eventually takes for a lover, Hari, is a wild chieftain who relishes life as it comes, but all through the first book we can see him gradually driven, step by step, to concede that he cannot after all live through the senses alone. His love for Sita "seemed to play not upon the nerves of the flesh, not upon the machinery of the brain, but upon the substance of the very soul . . . and he said to himself, 'What is this?' " On the other hand, the Rajah's adviser Gokal, the Brahmin philosopher, is caught in sensuality's trap. He is enslaved by a low-caste girl, Gunevati, who in turn is guided by sheer animal instinct.

Myers, of course, saw the danger of all this. "The impression may come into the reader's mind," he wrote, "that what he has before him is a philosophical novel." This, he knew, would mean neither good philosophy, nor a good novel, nor, before long, any readers. But his characters are not representatives of ideas, they are an invitation to think about them, which is a different matter. And in spite of Myers's detached and elegant manner, they are all human beings. Gunevati, for instance, has been taken, I think quite wrongly, as standing for pure evil. Certainly she resorts to poison, and passively accepts the position of fetish to an obscene and forbidden religious sect. But at other times we are asked to pity her, as Hari does, when he realizes what a low price she puts on herself, in spite of her beauty. Beauty has no particular rights in the world as it is. Jali pities her, too, when she turns pale and ill as a captive in Gokal's house. The truth is that she has no way of knowing herself. To destroy her is not justice.

Book 2 is a *Bildungsroman*, the education of Prince Jali, the Rajah's son. This, in a sense, is the simplest part of the trilogy, and, in terms of action, the most exciting. Jali's ordeals are of the flesh, the mind, and the spirit. As a young adolescent he finds, under Gunevati's tuition, that women are easy enough and he can get into any bedroom he likes. But he wants to understand life, or at least to see it clearly, and his passion for knowledge leads him to explore the secret cults of the Valley and to discover how they connect with the spying and counter-spying of the court. But Jali—for he is only a learner and a searcher—does not know enough, not enough, at least, to outwit his enemies by himself. And after his escape from the Valley he is in greater danger still, as he approaches the neighborhood of the Camp.

Here, perhaps, Myers let his prejudices run away with him. The Camp, or Pleasance, is, as he admitted, a monstrous version of the world of Cambridge and Bloomsbury by which he had once been deceived. It is the stronghold of Daniyal, the artificial paradise of the aesthetes, and to Myers the aesthetes were "trivial," a word which for him meant the denial of life. They were the sterile self-regarders and self-indulgers; sterility leads to cruelty, and self-regard to the death of the spirit. The Camp, then the traveling court of Prince Daniyal and his entourage, entices Jali with the most degrading materialism of all. If we are in any doubt as to how dangerous it is—dangerous rather than merely absurd—we have only to follow, as Jali does, the fate of Gunevati. It is at Daniyal's orders that this girl, who can express herself only through her body and her senses, has her tongue cut out; after that she is forced to learn to write. "She opened her mouth wide. Jali found himself looking into a cavern—black, swollen, horrible." It is this which recalls Jali to himself, so that he will never again be mistaken as to the nature of the Camp.

Jali will be the ruler of the future, but for the present power still rests with Rajah Amar. Book 3 returns us to the problem we set out with. Is the Rajah justified in giving up the near for the far, or is his longing for detachment only another name for the refusal of responsibility? In the face of Gokal's misgivings, he still prepares to withdraw from earthly concerns. But on the very point of leaving he is summoned to the Camp; there the whole nature of evil is brought home to him by another of the book's apparently unimportant moments, the horrible incident of the white cat. Now Amar has to decide, at his own risk, whether in the face of recognized evil a man can ever be absolved from action. The Rajah does not choose what happens to him, but Myers has shown that though there are strict limits to the human will, there are none to human vision. Amar sees what is to be done.

When Gokal brings his fallen body back across the lake, we do not even know whether Amar is dead, or what effect, if any, he has made on Daniyal. Like the relationships of the characters, which have been, all along, subtle and ambiguous, the story never yields a conclusion. "There is no illusory sense of understanding," Myers said, "only the realization of what is." But the trilogy unmistakably ends with a return to life. The thought had come to Gokal that if the Rajah were to die without recovering consciousness, it might be as well. "But he condemned that thought," and as he goes up the path towards the house on the farther side of the lake, he hears Hari, Sita, and Jali talking together on the veranda. With these quiet everyday sounds Myers concludes his strange master-piece, which, it has been said, "brought back the aspect of eternity to the English novel."

—PENELOPE FITZGERALD

THE ROOT
AND
THE FLOWER

BOOK ONE

THE NEAR AND THE FAR

1

LITTLE PRINCE JALI stepped on to the balcony and looked down upon the plain in awe. It was true that from the tower of his father's palace at home there was an even wider view; but that view was familiar, this one was full of mystery. The wall of this strange palace went down and down, until it merged into the sweeping side of the fort; the fort itself crowned the summit of a hill; and the bare rock of the hill continued a precipitous descent down into the River Jumna. The red glitter of sunset lay upon the river; across the water shady groves alternated with sun-swept patches of millet and corn; beyond stretched the desert.

For the last two years of his life—and he was now twelve—the desert had held Jali under a spell. Nearly every evening at home he would climb up into the tower to gaze upon it. Beyond the roofs, beyond the green of irrigated fields, beyond the glistening palms and the dark clumps of citron, cypress, and mango—beyond the little world that he knew there stretched that other world which his eye alone could reach. There it lay, a playground for the winds, a floor for the light of evening to flow along, the home of mirage and colored airs.

It was a region that seemed to promise him a disembodied nimbleness, an unearthly freedom. Its very boundaries were unsubstantial—lines of hills penciled so lightly along the horizon that

5

noonday melted them into the white-hot sky. Only at sunset did those hills become real. Then it was that they emerged, serenely yet with melancholy, out of nothingness into beauty. Cliffs, battlements, ranges, then took on a substance just solid enough to catch the tints of gold and rose that streamed through the air. The watery glitter of mirage was withdrawn from about their feet. They gave, in their remoteness, a measure of the desolate space in between. But this lasted for a few minutes only. Swiftly rising, the dusk submerged them, and what had been hidden day-long under the glare from above was now drowned in a darkness from underneath. Night rolled across the plain, sharp stars pricked the blue; in a moment nothing was left but the twin darkness of earth and sky.

For the last six days Jali had been traveling over the desert and disappointment had befallen him—disappointment, but not disillusion. He clung to the truth of appearances as something equal to the truth of what underlay them. There were two deserts: one that was a glory for the eye, another that it was weariness to trudge. Deep in his heart he cherished the belief that some day the near and the far would meet. Yes, one day he would be vigorous enough in breath and stride to capture the promise of the horizon. Then, instead of crawling like an insect on a little patch of brown sand, swift as a deer he would speed across the filmy leagues; the wind would be singing on his ears, the blood tingling in his veins, his whole body would be a living arrow. Almost, already, in his imagination he could foretaste that joy—of seizing in his grasp, of clasping to his heart, the magic of things seen afar. To fling himself into the distance in one bound, to flash into the visionary scene before it had had time to transform itself—almost he knew how!

Now, however, leaning against the warm marble of the balustrade, he was staring before him dejectedly. And soon the voice of his nurse sounded in the room behind, calling him in to the terrors of a lonely night in a strange room in a vast and shadowy palace. Obeying, he went and stretched himself out upon his couch, and even closed his eyes. She asked if he had said his prayers, and then left him.

Alone, he gave a sigh. His life, alas! was much less simple than she or anyone else supposed. He was a Christian, yes; but those simple prayers to the simple Christian God did not satisfy him.

There were other deities, less gentle. The most exacting he had discovered for himself. It had to be served with secret propitiatory rites. For instance, before going to sleep he had to touch with each of his five fingers each of the four walls of his room, and it was necessary to count up to five each time. This ceremony had to be repeated three times, nor could he allow his attention to stray for a single instant, otherwise sleep would be banished by the fear that he had made a slip. The business was so unpleasant that he always put it off as long as he could. A few minutes after his nurse had gone he got up and returned to the balcony.

There, what at once caught and fixed his attention was a kite balancing in strained immobility, immensely high in the blue. What was the kite thinking about? What held it, motionless and intent, in that particular place? Beneath was the palace with its courts and terraces, a maze of buildings encircled by the prodigious walls of the fort. In a wider circle lay the thronged and intricate city; and beyond the city stretched the plain—enormous, with the Jumna flowing across it, a shining red streak that passed from one veiled distance into another.

Was the kite solitary and speculative as he was, or did its affairs engross it as they engrossed ordinary men? Did the kite notice upon a certain balcony a small boy who was lamentably separate? No, of course to the kite he would not seem to be separate. The loneliness of being the only specimen of oneself was a part of one's own particular secret. Not even one's father or mother could guess it. But often it made him long to fling himself into his mother's arms with the cry: "Let us fly together! Let us die together!" But fly whither? and die into what?

Fascinated by the kite he remained unaware that his father had come into the room. The Rajah stood in the glow that poured in through the balcony arch, a glow that was not the direct light of the sun, but a reflection from the flooding redness outside. It put a flush upon his white tunic and touched with a faint glitter his only ornaments, a jeweled sword-belt and the aigrette clasp on his turban.

Several minutes went by while Rajah Amar continued to gaze upon his son in meditation; what finally distracted him was the sound of steps in the corridor, and the next moment the curtains at the end of the room parted and the Ranee appeared. Standing still upon the threshold, she let her eyes wander about her. The long, narrow room was already dim; but the white marble of its walls distributed what light there was, making visible the delicate floral inlay of agate, onyx, and lapis lazuli, that ran up the doorway and spread across the vaulted ceiling. In this setting, in this dusk that had warmth and transparency, her loveliness was really extraordinary; the Rajah's smile, rapt, tender, and remote, rested upon her as if she were a figure in some pictured scene. The dress she wore was rose-colored, with a fringe of silver, and a veil of pale lilac draped her head and shoulders. Tall and slender, she carried herself with an oriental grace, and yet she was not an Oriental. Her white skin, her dark brown hair that had a ripple in it, proclaimed a Caucasian descent. She was, in fact, the daughter of a Georgian prince, who, exiled, had found a refuge in Persia. There it was that the Rajah had met and married her. It had been the romance of his life and the wonder of it flashed over him now—now in these moments when by some vagary of imagination he found himself gazing at her detachedly with the eyes of a stranger.

At the first sound of her voice, Jali ran in from outside, and presently she took the boy back to his couch. He must be good, she said. He must go to sleep quickly, for he was tired; why, even they were tired after so many long days of travel.

On his bed, Jali lay listening to their lowered voices as they stood talking on the balcony. The sense of their words escaped him, but the sound fixed his mind upon the disquieting world of adult pre-occupations. To begin with, this journey. His father was but one of hundreds of rajahs, chieftains, and grandees, who had been summoned by the Emperor to the Durbar. In this great palace he was actually the Emperor's guest. And this, to be sure, was but one among many palaces that Akbar was putting to use as guest-houses—for he himself was holding court at his new palace-city, Fatehpur-Sikri. The domed and towering outline of that city had been pointed out to him upon the horizon as they were approaching Agra. So many cities! So many palaces! So many noble princes summoned at a word! Grandeur realized upon this scale was inhuman. He had to imagine a world in which even his parents were dwarfed into insignificance. His heart contracted, shrinking before its vision of gigantic, heartless splendors.

After a while the Rajah and Ranee came in again, kissed him upon the forehead, and left him alone for the night. It seemed long ago since the thin, nasal call of the muezzins had floated through the air, but the creak of an occasional ox-cart still rose from the long, powdery roads below, and he could still hear the familiar croaking of the dusty crows preparing to roost. All at once he got up again and slipped out on to the balcony.

A cool breeze was brushing along the palace wall; he noticed it bending a small, wiry plant that grew out of a crack in the masonry below. On the southern or western wall that little plant would have had no chance (not even dry gray lichen could subsist on those scorched surfaces), but here, apparently, it just managed to draw life. Perhaps it was helped by a shallow gutter running along beneath it; perhaps some of its roots spread into the gutter and so could drink deeply whenever rain fell. But all the same, it must be a hard life, and the little plant looked dry enough—and stunted—and, above all, lonely. Jali was sorry for it in its loneliness; he felt the dull weight of the hours, weeks, and months of its solitude. There it would remain all its days, knowing naught else until it withered and was blown away.

With a sigh he looked farther afield, and his eyes widened as they fell upon something strange. Something was moving slowly and cautiously along the gutter—a snake! Yes, possibly even a cobra! The pale-yellow and brown of the snake's body glistened like a stream of flowing metal. By what mistake had the creature strayed into this unlikely place? Impossible to imagine! Yet there it was; and its slow movements betrayed uneasiness and confusion.

As he watched it his instinctive antipathy melted away. He could understand so well what the snake was feeling. He entered into its cold, narrow intelligence and shared its angry perplexity. Its movements were cramped, its advance difficult, it was in constant danger of slipping over the edge. Now and then it lay still in dull reflection, nursing a cold anger that could find no vent.

Meanwhile, the little plant, bent downwards by every puff of wind, was beating its thin twigs against the gutter like a birch. The snake seemed not to see the plant. It moved forward until a light touch from the twigs fell upon its head. At this it stopped and lifted its neck. The little plant was now doing no more than lightly sway and dip. The snake, its head still reared, flickered its tongue and waited. One could feel the angry heaving and straining in its sluggish brain—the dull, red anger waiting to explode. Then came a strong gust sweeping along the wall, and at once the twigs thrashed down upon that furious head—thrashed down and beat it with a movement that seemed to Jali both comic and dreadful. In a flash the head reared itself higher, the neck drew back, and there was a lunge at the twigs and the empty air. O fatal act! To strike, the snake had been obliged to coil, and its coiled body could not support itself upon the narrow ledge. No recovery was possible; it overbalanced and fell.

Jali leaned breathless over the balustrade and saw and heard the falling body strike upon a small, flat roof about fifty feet below. There the creature began to writhe in agony; it could do no more than twist and turn upon the self-same spot.

Jali was trembling, but beneath this agitation there was a deep, troubled wonder. Here was the little plant now waving with a kind of jaunty cynicism! And there was the writhing snake! He remained staring until the darkness was complete, and it was still in a dream that he felt his way back to bed. His chin upon his drawn-up knees, he stared into the obscurity. The world, unquestionably, was a place of mystery and terror. This was revealed in the writhing of the crippled snake, in the jaunty waving of the inno-cent plant in the wind, in the bright-eyed intentness of the hover-ing kite, in the terrible numerousness of living beings, both animal and human, all separate, all alone, all threatened by evil in am-bush. The minutes slid past without his notice. He had forgotten everything, even his defensive rites. When next he stirred it was to become aware of night, deep night. He felt it in the quality of the silence—a silence which, when he listened, became alive with soundless activities. Spiritual presences moved. He was surrounded. Gradually he felt his skin tighten, his heart-beats quicken, his eyes dilate. Slipping to the floor, he crept crouching out of the room. Blessed was the moment when the curtain dropped behind him, and in a corner of the half-lit ante-chamber he perceived his old nurse, curled up asleep. Her serene unconsciousness reassured him; he would not disturb her. Besides, it was not her he wanted. But which was the way to his mother's room? He could not exactly remember.

2

A LONG, EMPTY corridor, lit by small lamps of perfumed oil
stretched away into the distance. Stealing down it on bare feet, he
passed several doorways hung with silken curtains, and from behind them there came the murmur of women's voices. Excitement
carried him on until he stood before an arch which seemed to lead
out on to a small roof-terrace. Here he stopped to peep through the
screen of woven khas-khas grass that stood across the entrance.
The smell of the damped grass roots was delicious; and almost at
once a low music of stringed instruments rose on the night air. A
group of fine ladies were listening, but, as far as he could make
out, his mother was not among them. This, however, was no great
matter to him, for his fears were fast giving way to a sense of adventure. It was something new and strange to be thus wandering
by night in a vast, unknown palace. He lingered until someone got
up and moved towards the screen; whereupon, taking flight, he ran
along several corridors and down stairway after stairway until he
found himself in an ancient and seemingly unoccupied part of the
building. It was solitary here; but, feeling like a ghost himself, he
was not afraid. Going farther yet, and always in a downward direction, he noticed that the walls were no longer of marble but of old
red sandstone. Their surface, polished by the touch of countless
hands, the floor, too, worn by generations of passing feet, informed

him that he was now in the substructure, the ancient palace over which the new one had been built. A further descent would carry him, he supposed, down into the living rock of the citadel; he would find himself at last in that underground labyrinth of which he had heard speak—a region that excited a curiosity which he dared not satisfy. Indeed, a shiver passed over him when all at once he heard, or rather felt, a deep vibration rising from the stone floor beneath his very feet. It took him a moment to realize that this was merely the trumpeting of elephants stabled in some cavern below. He had heard the same sound coming up from the rock chambers beneath his own palace at home. And now, as then, it brought before his mind the scene as he had occasionally witnessed it—the great gray hulks of the elephants, the glistening brown bodies of the men, a confusion of living forms which the smoky glare of the torches could only half illuminate. He imagined the pungent stable smell, sudden outbreaks of sound that flurried one out of one's senses, and the constant dread of being crushed to death.

Turning, he retraced his steps. He was walking faster now, and presently he began to walk faster still, for he had caught the sound of footfalls behind. Luckily the passage had so many turnings that he was able to keep out of sight of his follower. He refrained from running, but it was only from the fear lest those feet behind should break into a run too. Panic was threatening him when all at once he remembered that a little farther on there was a recess where he would be able to hide. Yes; here it was—with a massive pillar in front, which was very convenient. The paintings on the wall showed that this had once been a shrine to Ganpati. The god of luck! he reflected, as he crouched in the shadow cast by a small lamp hanging outside.

A few seconds later a figure appeared. It was that of a man of middle height, well-built and vigorous, who carried himself along with the swinging stride of the hill-folk. His outline seemed to Jali not unfamiliar, and then, to his astonishment, he realized that this was certainly no stranger. It was none other than his uncle, Hari Khan, the man who had married his father's sister. Hari was a borderland chieftain; he lived in the north among the mountains; a fine man, Jali had always thought, and friendly and amusing. To meet like this was really great fun. "How about giving him a start!"

he chuckled to himself; so out he leapt, all of a sudden, with a waving of his arms.

The effect of the joke was not what it should have been. He expected to see his uncle jump, but a cry of the friendliest surprise should have followed immediately after. Instead of this, Hari simply stopped dead and fixed him with an icy stare. True enough, that stare did not last long—hardly more than a second, in fact; but in that second Jali was disconcerted, and his uncle's exclamations, when they came, could not put matters right. Jali! By all the gods, Jali! Now how on earth did he come there! But the shock of that steely regard lingered and had the effect of reviving in his mind fragments of talk overheard on various occasions at home. He had gathered that his uncle was not altogether approved of, a discovery that heightened his interest, adding spice to his private opinion, that Hari Khan was a man whom one did well to like. Well, now—his thoughts ran—it was odd, very odd, to find Uncle Hari abroad in the women's quarters at this hour. And some reflection of his inward mystification no doubt appeared on his face; at any rate, Hari abruptly stopped questioning and began to smile at him speculatively.

"Supposing we sit down for a few minutes—here, on these steps. I should like to have a talk."

They seated themselves, and still Jali could not keep his eyes from expressing the nature of his thoughts. His uncle was dressed, as he now observed, in riding costume; he looked dusty and hot; his expression was singularly alert.

"As for me, you know," Hari explained carelessly, "I've just arrived from up north. A hard day's ride I've had, my dear, and one of many. A few weeks ago I was hunting goat up in the hills . . . Yes, that's what I've been doing—all on my way down from Kabul. I come from the mountains, from the snows, and it's many a long mile, I can tell you."

The sing-song voice and the smile made one uncertain whether to believe him. Hari's blue eyes, too, for all the apparent candor of their gaze, were extraordinarily unrevealing. Nevertheless Jali smiled too, and his heart responded to the comfortable feeling that his uncle's presence always gave him.

During the pause that now came, Hari's thoughts—to judge from that speculative look of his—were sweeping a wide range; and his talk, when he started again, certainly seemed rather rambling. But presently he broke off and began asking all sorts of questions; and then again he stopped to think. "So that's how it is..." he was now musing aloud, "you arrived two or three hours before sunset, and you found quite a crowd at the Great Gate. Narsing was there to receive you all; but I suppose..." and he hesitated, "I suppose anyone really might have slipped in without being noticed?—Yes; and then you were taken up to your rooms. And outside your mother's room, you say there is a terrace—a small terrace overlooking the road by the river.... And you tried to fly your kite from that terrace, and one of your mother's serving-maids was with you. Let me see! Which one was it? Zaghul? She is young and pretty, isn't she? Yes, yes, of course I remember her! And do you know, as it happens, I was passing along that road this evening on my way into the town, and I think I caught sight of you and Zaghul leaning together over the terrace wall...What do you think of that?"

"I never saw you," replied Jali, wondering.

Hari looked away. He was still faintly smiling, and when he turned to Jali again his eyes shone with a secret amusement.

"You can't make me out!" said he.

Jali was silent.

Hari, laughing outright, leant forward and took him by the shoulder. To Jali it was abundantly clear by now that his uncle was alive to the necessity of accounting for himself. Moreover, the significance of his innumerable questions had become pretty plain. He was looking for something—anything—that upon necessity would help him to trump up an explanation of his doings. "You can't make me out!" he had just said; and those words sounded like the prelude to a confession, a confidence, an appeal. Jali's heart bounded with excitement.

"My dear," said Hari, "why don't you ask me point blank what the devil I am up to?" Amusement and good-humor were twinkling together in his eyes. "You think I should answer with some lie. Alas! if only I could find a good one!"

"Well, well!" he went on a moment later, "it is true enough that I have no business here. But this is also true: my only object is to get through into another part of the building without anyone challenging me. I want to get to the Great Terrace, where I shall mingle very respectably with the Emperor's other guests. I also want to see Gokal—you remember Gokal?—I think he is probably there."

Jali, already an accomplice, thrilled. "Do you think I can help you? In any case—I suppose you don't want me to speak of this meeting?"

Hari knit his brows. "I won't ask you to lie, although, to be sure, a lie is easily atoned for by a little offering to Saraswati."

"You forget," said Jali, "I am a Christian."

"No, I don't forget."

At this Jali blushed. He was a Christian, certainly, for his mother had brought him up in her faith; but—good heavens! was there any religion in the world of which he was not, more or less, an adherent? If his mother was a Christian, was not his father a Buddhist, his old nurse a Jain, his teacher a Brahmin, and the companions of his play-hours either Muslims or adherents of some variety of Hinduism? The truth was that Jali was ready to acknowledge every known god as well as others of his own imagining.

"After all, you are your father's son," continued Hari, "and your father's people have lived in this country for many generations. Men cannot live in this country without becoming what the country wills."

Jali was troubled. "Will my mother, then, change?"

"Your mother is an angel," smiled Hari. "God forbid that she should change."

"I don't mind telling lies for you," said Jali, "I tell lies for myself."

Hari shook his head. "I don't want you to lie. And even to keep secrets is a burden. But if it costs you nothing to be silent, then be silent."

"I can easily say nothing," said Jali, after a pause. "You see, I have secrets all the time."

His eyes resting upon the boy meditatively, Hari leant back against the wall. Tranquillity had returned to him; indeed, there was nothing in his manner to suggest that the night was not all before them.

"You have not yet told me why you got up to look for your mother. You felt lonely, I suppose?"

Jali admitted it, and a little later, since Hari was the most understanding of all the grown-up people that he knew, he was telling the story of the small plant and the snake. Hari listened with an attention that was not forced; if he failed to grasp the exact nature of the impression made upon Jali's mind, he did not seem puzzled by the fact that an impression had been made. He pondered; he speculated. "There is too much chance in the world," he said, "and yet, you know, chance is what makes life interesting."

Jali was silent.

"I think life frightens you?" said Hari, smiling.

Jali colored and still remained silent.

"Not to be afraid of this world," said Hari slowly, "you must belong to it."

"Ah, but how?" thought Jali.

"One can always pretend to oneself that one does," Hari went on, looking at him intently. "Didn't I tell you once that in a nightmare the way to escape a pursuing tiger is to turn oneself into one?"

"Yes."

"Pretend to yourself that you are like others," said Hari carelessly. "Everyone is doing it."

"But if everyone is pretending to be like others, who is like himself?"

Hari laughed.

"There is less evil in the world than you think," said he. "At least, that is the best line to go on."

Jali made no reply. What his uncle said was wise and reassuring as far as it went; but what about the evil in the gods? The universe was full of terrifying and destructive forces. There was Kali. . . .

They sat in silence for a time, and in this pause Jali again thrilled to the mystery that enveloped him. To be here, in these soundless vaults, in the depth of night, they two, alone! He pressed his feverish hands against the stone of the step. His gaze rested upon Hari with a dark intensity. That man gave him courage. *His* life, he felt sure, was one long adventure. Well! he, too, would live adventurously. It was a resolve, a sacred vow.

Hari seemed to have gone off into a reverie again, but all at once he gave another little laugh, tapped his companion on the shoulder, and got up. It was time to part, he said. Was Jali ready to go back to bed? Good! A sound sleep, this time, and pleasant dreams!

He stood smiling under the lamp while Jali walked firmly away. The boy's mind was at rest in a sort of exaltation. He found his way back to his room as by a miracle and once in bed fell asleep instantly.

3

SITA WAS THE name the Rajah had given his wife after their marriage; but she had been christened Helen, and as they stood together on Jali's balcony in the fading light, he mused upon the problem of identity, thinking how, under that name, in her own country, amongst her own people, she would have been—would she not?—someone else. Individuality, identity, selfhood, these words, as Buddha said, stood for what was little more than illusion. People were like clouds—changing, melting, mixing . . . But was it right to have married her, to have brought her here? Did it appear right now in the light of the decision that he was taking?

Ten years her senior, he felt himself old enough to be her father. If she had the gift of innocence, he had a faculty for experience; and some men, he reflected, are born with the experience of their ancestors already resting somewhat heavily upon them. He could not reproach her, if, after all these years, in spite of their love, they were still, spiritually, wide apart. In his religion, as he well knew, he stood aloof, not only from her but from nearly all his contemporaries. Buddhism had all but died out of India, and where it survived its form was debased. Many years of study and meditation had at last brought the Rajah to the belief that he had grasped—and even in a certain sense rediscovered—the doctrine of Buddha in its authentic purity. Whole-hearted in his rejection of God, the

Soul, and Immortality, he had a profound contempt for all corruptions of the original teaching. He condemned the Mahayana as a whole; in his opinion, by shifting the emphasis from self-discipline to altruism, it had entirely falsified Gautama's word. Such a concession to human sentiment was disastrous; the truth, in order to be the truth, must be accepted in its entirety. No man could help his fellow save by the force of his example, save by the spectacle of his achieved holiness. The reward of holiness was the bliss of peace—a bliss that you received in this life, and afterwards—well, afterwards your peace was the peace that passeth all understanding. Such had been the teaching of the Enlightened One; it was the truth; and for those who properly understood it, it was the happy truth.

Sita had never been able to understand it. But, although this was a disappointment to him, he did not—no, he did not reproach her. After all, she was blessed. As she walked through the world she found beauty there, and that beauty was to her an assurance that life did, indeed, have the meaning she ascribed to it. Wonderful in her, thought Amar, was the constancy of this accompaniment through all the trivialities of daily living. This it was that kept her gaiety so fresh. Not many minutes ago he had been deterred from entering her room by a babble of feminine talk and laughter, and now she was telling him how amusing the gathering had been. Yes, she had always been popular; she knew how to enjoy the fun of the moment; she and those other ladies were still able to laugh at jokes that had been exchanged for the first time when, as a bride of eighteen, she had arrived in India.

Presently, as they were leaving Jali's room, she besought him to accompany her back to her own apartments. There were some letters to show him, she said; besides, as he well knew, it amused her to overcome his shyness. To his great relief they made their way along the interminable passages without encountering anyone, but, just as he was settling down, the curtains were flung aside and a pretty young woman swept in. Courtly and confused, he at once jumped to his feet. "It is only my husband!" cried Sita, "don't run away, my dove!" But the girl, with a light laugh and lowered eyes, fell back and withdrew. Amar looked into his wife's smiling face and knitted his brows reprovingly. She certainly did not know what he knew; that Ranee Jagashri's husband was the most watchfully jealous man in India—and with good reason.

His thoughts taking a new turn, he looked into his heart and pondered. No; thank God, he could find no jealousy there! Many were the seekers after deliverance, who, when they had reached the age to sever worldly and domestic ties, still hung back. Were he jealous, how could he ever leave this wife of his, so young still and so beautiful, to finish her life without him? In thirteen years she had scarcely changed at all. Her face and figure, like her character, had retained a girlish freshness.

With a sigh he looked again at the two letters he had picked out from the rest. The first was from Queen Miriam, Akbar's Christian consort. She invited Sita to attend service in the little chapel that the Emperor had built for her at Fatehpur-Sikri. Sita would certainly wish to go—and to take Jali with her. But Jali ought not to go; there were political reasons that were obvious; unfortunately, however, Sita would ignore them completely.

The other letter was an invitation from his sister, Ambissa, offering her the coveted distinction of a room in the palace at Fatehpur-Sikri. Of course she ought to accept; but—how bitterly she would cry out against it! The fact was—and the Rajah sighed heavily—she carried unworldliness too far. Life for her remained too simple; she knew but to follow her heart. Not that her head was weak, but it was subject. And while her instinctive charge against him was over-subtlety in the interests of a set philosophic scheme, his against her was that she yielded too easily to the sweeping simplifications of the heart. In vain he reminded her that the children of light were called upon to be as wise as the children of this world; in vain he quoted: "Render unto Caesar . . ."; she would not change her views or her ways.

When he looked up it was to find her eyes fixed questioningly upon him. She was leaning one shoulder against the wall; her head drooped, and he could see that an anticipatory flush of protest had mounted to her cheeks.

He smiled. This pause was charged with memories of long-standing disagreements, nothing ugly, nothing wounding, although sometimes exasperating to both. He could hear her saying: "I believe, I really believe, that in your heart you sometimes wish I were worldly and sophisticated! But even if I tried, it would be no good. And I don't intend to try, for it seems to me that the worldly life is without depth, without richness, without color. People who enjoy competing and making a show very soon get to think that nothing else matters." And, to this, his reply, he could also hear that: his patient, his reasonable, his so-often-repeated reply.

In this moment his mind was made up. Nevertheless, just to try her, he pointed to the two letters and said: "Well?"

"Oh," she murmured, "you know, without my saying it, what I want. You know, too, what I should simply hate!" and she sighed.

"Yes. I know."

"And what do you say?"

"I say: Do as you like."

For several moments after hearing this she looked a little puzzled, a little mistrustful, but gradually a glowing smile of reassurance spread over her face. Her gratitude was altogether delightful, and for the next half-hour, while she was laughing, chatting, and putting order among her things, the Rajah, watching her, had a mind freed from care.

Care returned, however, when he was once more alone. In another wing of the palace, standing before the window in his own room, he looked out at the bats flitting across the stream of his lamp-light, and sadness invaded his heart. Was it his misconception that he understood her better than she him? Or did she really understand him and hide her understanding from herself because it would open her mind to ideas that were antagonistic to her own view of life? Was, therefore, her apparent lack of understanding the evidence of a lack of love? Well; in no case was she to be blamed; perhaps, on the other hand, it was he. . . .

Leaving the window he fell to pacing to and fro. Unquestionably, during the next few weeks, he would have to fight the world with its own weapons. After all, he was a ruler; he had to use statecraft; and without shame he would do it. . . . Diplomacy, finesse, were required in order that his little principality should retain, amidst hungry jealousies, its place and its due. Sita would see him leading a way of life that was distasteful to him and cultivating a society that he despised. But in his own conscience he was justified; and the time for self-explanation—if ever there had been such a time—was past. Nor would he make this the occasion for communicating his great decision—for telling her that her worldly husband with all his worldly activities was engaged in preparing for—what? For the yellow robes of a recluse, and the begging bowl.

It was strange how opportunely this Durbar fell in regard to his maturing plans. It offered an occasion and set him a time in which to make provision, to determine a policy for the future, and lay down a safe course for his successors. Sita, under advice, should hold the reins of government during Jali's minority. At home there were many good men to help her, and at the Imperial Court there would be Gokal.

A glance at his water-clock now told him that in all probability Gokal had arrived and was waiting for him on the Great Terrace. This learned Brahmin was one of the few people with whom he could discuss the subjects that lay nearest to his heart. Gokal was modeled after an unusual pattern; although he had succeeded in capturing the consideration of the world, he was first and foremost a philosopher, a man whose mind was set on eternal things. After dealing with men and affairs—and Gokal would soon post him up on the chief topics of the day—together they would glide off upon the tranquil waters of philosophy, and the night would pass and the stars would grow dim while they drew in a refreshment sweeter than that of sleep.

He was on the point of leaving his room when a messenger presented him with a letter. The envelope, which he turned over and frowned at with great distaste—the envelope was formidably sealed and the handwriting, alas, was his sister's. It was a great temptation to leave the reading until later, for Ambissa's letters were always troublesome and this one was terribly bulky. Reluctantly he broke the seal and took a glance over the first page. Almost at once his brother-in-law's name caught his eye. "As you know," Ambissa wrote, "we have not seen Hari here for over a year, and this prolonged absence of his produces a bad impression. Some months ago he annoyed the Emperor by a foolish attempt to excuse himself from the Durbar, and now some rumors have been started which cause me a great deal of worry. What can have been his reason for keeping company with Mahomet Ali at Kabul? I can't believe that he has begun to interest himself in politics, not even in revolutionary politics. And then where can he have been hiding during the last two months? I cannot help suspecting some new love-affair, and if the injured husband is a man of any importance there will certainly be serious trouble; for the Emperor is becoming more strict in his ideas every day, and takes affairs of that kind into his own hands, although nobody likes it. There have been some terrible scandals here of late, and they have brought him to the end of his patience. Very soon we shall have edicts against immorality as severe as those against meat-eating. After all, if a man can be put to death for killing a finch, he might well suffer as much for adultery. So Hari had better look out. Unfortunately, too, his sins will be visited on me. There are plenty of people here, you may be sure, who would like to hold me responsible for all his failings. A husband, they say, is what his wife makes him. A wife's place is at her husband's side, and so on. How happy these moralists would be to see me packed off into the wilds! And what a reward for all my past forbearance! Picture to yourself the kind of life I should lead in one of those half-ruined castles perched on a barren mountain! But it's not for myself so much that I am alarmed. Consider the boys! Their careers, which promise so well, would be nipped in the bud. Ali, you know, was sixteen last month; he is to be attached to Makh Khan's household for the period of his visit here; and, after the marriage of his daughter Lalita to Prince Daniyal, the Khan will be more influential than ever."

At this point Amar groaned with impatience and looked to see how many more pages there were. Not many, and they could be skimmed, but his attention was held by the postscript.

"I have just this moment discovered that Hari's invitation to the palace at Agra has been canceled. So now you see that I was not exaggerating! For pity's sake ask Gokal what he thinks. I simply cannot imagine what my position will be if Hari fails to appear at the Durbar. Please, Amar, come and see me to-morrow without fail, and make it as early as possible."

The Rajah gave a little laugh of vexation. His own affairs were likely to give him trouble enough, and Ambissa was always immoderate in her demands. To begin with, she had made him late for Gokal.

4

HUGE, DIM LANTERNS stood at the four corners of the terrace, spreading pools of light upon the marble flags beneath them; the rest of the great expanse lay cold and white under the stars. Amar's eyes wandered over the Emperor's guests, who were scattered in small groups here and there. It took him a few moments to distinguish Gokal. His friend's bulky form, draped in white Brahminical robes, would have caught his eye quickly enough had it not been partially hidden by the figure of the man in conversation with him. Who this was, the Rajah failed to make out until he had come quite near, and then, to his extreme surprise, he saw that it was actually his errant brother-in-law. Well! Ambissa, no doubt, would be vastly relieved, but this apparition was certainly no pleasure to him, not just now. It shattered his hopes for an evening of philosophy.

And, as if this were not enough, a drop of pure annoyance was added to his disappointment. His coming—he saw it quite distinctly —was of the nature of an interruption. Hari had been talking and Gokal listening, each with great absorption; and this was hurriedly dissimulated the moment their eyes fell upon him. It was an old puzzle what these two, in character, tastes, and habits, so unlike, found in one another. There the intimacy was, however; and he had just seen it illustrated in their eager confabulation. Not a question but that Hari had been letting Gokal into some exciting secret. Well, Hari's secrets were of no interest whatsoever to *him*; only—and here he gave an inward sigh—he mustn't forget his duty to Ambissa.

Anxious not to give any clue even to the smallest of his feelings, he greeted Hari with more cordiality than was absolutely necessary, and a kindred instinct kept him from asking even the most natural questions. After all, it was for Hari to speak out of his own accord. Let him declare in so many words where he had been hiding during the last two months; whence he sprang; how (since he was not invited) he came to be in the palace at all; in short, let him account for himself. Why, even his dress called for explanation; that tunic of his was very old and scandalously dusty; his turban was torn and his riding boots had obviously not been polished for several days.

In spite of Amar's outward geniality the first greetings were hardly over before a silence threatened to descend. To prevent it the Rajah, eyeing Gokal affectionately, inquired with exaggerated solicitude after the state of his health. This big, sedentary pundit had a talent for humorously exploiting his own foibles, one of which was nervousness about the smallest bodily ailment. Quick to take his cue, Gokal replied with deep gravity that his appetite was not very good and that he feared the position of his present abode was not completely salubrious. He was occupying a little pavilion in the Royal Hunting Grounds, which had been put at his disposal by the Emperor. For this reason it was quite impossible for him to leave it, and thus, as Amar could see, he was placed in a very serious quandary.

While Gokal was talking Hari had looked distrait: and now, turning to Amar with a certain abruptness: "I hear," said he, "that you are going up to the Hills this year."

Amar assented, and he was wondering from whom Hari could possibly have got the news, when the latter went on: "Sita was telling me just now how much she is looking forward to the change. I fancy she sometimes misses her Caucasus."

This time the Rajah was positively taken aback. "Sita told you just now! What do you mean?"

Hari laughed carelessly. "I have just been paying her a little visit."

Surprise kept the Rajah silent.

"Was that too unconventional?" inquired Hari, raising his eyebrows.

The Rajah gave a short laugh. "Of course not; although she must have been rather startled. For one thing, your clothes.... They made me suppose that you had only just got down from your horse."

To this Hari said nothing, and in the pause that followed the Rajah did some rapid thinking. Hari, in his difficulties, must have conceived the notion of enlisting Sita's sympathies, and thought to steal a march by this strangely timed visit. "But I won't have it!" he mentally exclaimed. "I won't have him impose on her warm-heartedness."

Annoyed, he turned away and let his glance wander about him. What a pity that trivial pre-occupations were spoiling the serenity of this hour. The terrace, tinted gold by the lanterns, was itself like a great lantern suspended high in the deep blue air of the night. From gardens far below there rose a dampness scented with orange-blossom. Fireflies were darting their greenish lights about the lower levels of the darkness, and overhead there was the sharp brilliance of the stars.

Amar had withdrawn so deeply into himself that at a touch upon his shoulder he started. It was Gokal; Gokal was pointing to a glow upon the western horizon, and in a low voice he said: "Fatehpur-Sikri!"

The three men walked across to the balustrade, and as they did so a soft plume of light spread out in the distant dark. Others followed; arrows, fountains, and showers, of colored light bejeweled that far-off patch of sky.

The memory of his first visit to the palace-city was revived in Amar's mind. That had been ten years ago, just after the completion of the principal buildings, and a few months before Akbar transferred himself there with his court. He remembered smiling as he stood surveying those walls of fresh-cut stone, uncertain whether he was contemptuous of Akbar or of himself—of Akbar for his confidence or of himself for his doubts. Did the Emperor never question whether the future would justify him? That splendid, unnecessary "City of Victory" raised upon a waterless waste, did he never conceive a later generation moralizing over its ruins? Well! Ten years had gone by since then, and that display on the horizon was Akbar's present answer.

In the meantime, Hari and Gokal had begun to talk about the coming Durbar. The topic was inevitable, although not altogether an agreeable one. There were few among the tributary princes who did not shrink from making a formal exhibition of their vassalage. If, in the ensuing conversation, the Rajah preserved an air of greater indifference than Hari, it was not because his feelings went less deep. The border chieftains were accustomed to the arbitrament of arms; the conqueror in the field was your over-lord by the Will of God. But the Rajah's case was different; his father before him had decided not to throw away human lives in a hopeless struggle; his Principality had lost its independence, but retained an honorable place in the Empire, due to the esteem which the ruling house commanded. It was because he stood aloof from war that the Rajah was minded to regard Akbar as superciliously as the haughtiest of the militant Rajputs. His pride was rooted in ideas of racial, cultural, and intellectual superiority. Akbar might be a great conqueror, but what of that? He might trace his descent from both Tamerlane and Jenghiz Khan, but who were they? Barbarians without tradition, culture, or understanding.

In order to change the subject he at last turned to Gokal. "I understand that the banquet to-night is in honor of the Ambassadors from the East. You, an oriental scholar, how comes it that you are not in attendance?"

"I begged to be excused on account of my health. His Majesty knows that after a State banquet I lie sleepless all night." And Gokal sighed and smiled simultaneously.

"I have reason to believe," said Hari with abruptness, "that Akbar loves me no longer." He threw a glance at his brother-in-law. "I wonder if anyone can tell me the reason?"

"Not I," returned Amar, laconically.

"Well, I expect it's all Ambissa's fault," Hari grumbled this out with a kind of jocular bad taste. "However, I shall certainly not stay in Agra for long unless I find that I am properly appreciated. Now if you were in my place..." He had been keeping an eye fixed upon one of the palace servants who was trimming the lantern in the corner; and, after breaking off, he suddenly called out to the man.

"I think," he said slowly, "I think you have been instructed to spy upon me."

"No, indeed, my lord!" came the humble answer.

Hari compressed his lips. "Present my compliments to the Palace Chamberlain and say I should be glad to have a word with him."

As soon as the man had gone, the Rajah, who had been looking upon this scene with a puzzled frown, shrugged his shoulders and said: "You lose no time in making yourself unpopular."

Hari all at once seemed to recover his good-humor. "Why should I be persecuted by eavesdroppers?" And his eyes twinkled.

"You are talking nonsense," retorted the Rajah crossly. "Even if that fellow was eavesdropping, what of it? You know as well as I do that spies are everywhere. It is part of the established order."

"You may be accustomed to that sort of thing, but I am not," replied Hari, still with a grin.

Amar sighed, leant back against the balustrade, and assumed an air of ironical detachment. "By the way," he brought out, "you should have asked, not for the Palace Chamberlain, but for the Commandant."

"Narsing is the man I want."

"That is the Commandant. The Chamberlain . . ."

He had no time to say more, for a small, dapper figure was already to be seen advancing towards them. Mabun Das was one of those nobodies who attained to positions of power in Akbar's Court. A hint of the subtleness and adroitness that had raised him from obscurity was given in the quick movements of his intelligent eyes and the flutter of his thin, nervous hands. With an elaborate gesture of salutation he stepped before Hari and let flow an elegant apology for failing to meet the distinguished guest at the Gate.

Hari's return of compliments was equally polite; and he added expressions of deep regret at his inability to accept the honor which His Imperial Majesty had done him in inviting him to lodge at the palace. To this the Chamberlain replied with chagrin, but not with much surprise. So far, so good, thought the Rajah; Hari seemed to be mixing a kind of tact with his tomfoolery. Very prudent was his extreme politeness towards this little, dark-skinned southerner, who had the advantage of him, although very much his inferior in rank. Not a word was spoken on the subject of the supposed eavesdropper.

"Having presented my excuses to you," Hari went on, "I have but one other desire before taking my leave; I wish to pay my respects to His Majesty's Deputy himself."

The Bengalee's bright eyes flickered for a moment, then—"Of course!" he cried, with an air of happy alacrity, "I will go and acquaint Narsing Khan of your arrival at once."

As soon as his back was turned, Hari threw a speaking glance at his brother-in-law.

"You have not saved your dignity yet," commented the Rajah. "That little scribe will most likely send word that Narsing is asleep or engaged. Why on earth you came here at all I cannot imagine."

At this Hari's face darkened, but the cloud passed quickly. Hardly had the Rajah finished speaking before the silence of the now empty terrace was broken by the stir of an approaching company. Half a dozen link-boys came forward with lights, and behind them advanced someone whose importance was thus properly illuminated. Here, by a stroke of luck, was Narsing in all his glory. Nor was the big, burly Turcoman difficult to recognize, in spite of his having shaved off his beard and taken on, in place of his usual shabby hunting-suit, a glittering costume to match his recent appointment. It was before this impressive figure that Hari now planted himself, legs apart and head thrown back, with an air that was almost truculent.

"By Allah, the All-powerful!" the great man cried out, "how do *you* come to be here?"

Hari grinned. "And you, old elephant, why were you not at the Great Gate to receive me?"

For a moment Narsing looked as if he might take this amiss, but his good-humor prevailed. Pushing his jeweled turban aside, he scratched his head in perplexity. "I told Mabun Das that, if you came, you were to be brought straight to my private room. The truth is—I have a matter of some delicacy to explain."

Hari continued to look up into Narsing's large red face with amusement, and Narsing stopped scratching his head to pull at a recently vanished beard.

"Proceed without embarrassment," said Hari; "I swear by your beard that I am not a man to take offense."

"Good, good!" returned Narsing, with a certain relief. "Well, in a word, the trouble is this: His Imperial Majesty is seriously displeased with you." The announcement was accompanied by a look in which inquiry and commiseration were evenly balanced.

"Then my invitation to this palace is canceled?"

"I am afraid it is."

Hari smiled. "I thought as much. But what is the reason?"

"There is no reason given."

"But a reason must exist."

"Well, my dear fellow," and Narsing gave a good-natured guffaw, "the reason—whatever it may be—is probably better known to you than to anyone else."

With the air of having said something rather smart, he turned to Amar. "Eh, what do you say, Rajah?"

Hari put on an expression of patient resignation. "Some story of a woman, I suppose. Really, poor old Akbar has women on the brain. And no wonder," he added, "considering that the Royal Palace contains some five thousand of them."

"Hush!" cried Narsing, genuinely shocked by this freedom of speech; and the Rajah, tapping Hari on the shoulder, drew his attention to the approach of Mabun.

Narsing assumed a haughty expression, which did not sit easily upon his genial features. "Mabun Das," said he, "why did you not inform me of Hari Khan's arrival?"

The Chamberlain threw out his hands in a gesture of helpless protestation. Narsing, he explained, had set himself an impossible task in attempting to welcome each guest individually and conduct him to his apartments. Many had arrived at the same moment, and, as chance would have it, Hari Khan had passed through unwelcomed by anyone—not even by his humble self. "For this unintentional rudeness I have already offered Hari Khan my whole-hearted apologies," he added, turning to Hari with a charming smile.

A look of gloomy perplexity appeared upon Narsing's honest face. His responsibilities weighed heavily upon him. He knew that he was but a child compared to Mabun, whose mastery of the intricacies of etiquette was only equaled by his grasp of court intrigues. He was well enough acquainted with Mabun's ways to guess that his Chamberlain wished him to hold his tongue. When they were next alone together some obscure factor in the situation would be tactfully revealed to him. But class loyalty, as well as an old-established liking for Hari, caused him to turn to the latter with a questioning air. His eyes said: "I would infinitely prefer to discuss your affairs with you rather than with him."

There was a slight pause, and then: "The apologies have come from the wrong side," said Hari with deliberation. "My entry into the palace, my dear Narsing, was, I am afraid, very unconventional. I got in—" and he gave a shrug and a laugh, "I got in by a certain secret way."

"By all the devils of Eblis!" exclaimed Narsing, prodigiously taken aback. He stared, then turned in partial illumination to his Chamberlain. "And you had guessed this, I suppose?"

Mabun threw up his hands as one who is casting discretion to the winds. "What shall I say?" he laughed. "Perhaps I had my suspicions! But Hari Khan is Hari Khan. And after all . . ."

Hari continued to address himself to Narsing. "There *is* a secret way. . . . And, although it takes one through the women's quarters, I was indiscreet enough to try it."

"Oh, Hari Khan!" Mabun Das cried out with archness, "in the old days what a scandal such a confession would have made!"

Narsing, who was still staring, pulled at his absent beard.

"I don't like it," he muttered. "I don't like it."

"I saw no harm," replied Hari carelessly. "I was curious to see whether that passage was open, whether an entry was possible for an uninvited guest."

"Humph!" grunted Narsing.

For a few moments no one spoke; Narsing's glance swept round the empty spaces of the terrace and his face was heavy with deliberation. At last he clapped his hands and shouted for cushions. He found it difficult to think clearly while his feet were supporting a weight of sixteen stone.

"Look here, my friend," he said at last. "This is only a trifle, but we must get it cleared up at once. You are not in a position to play pranks of any kind. His Majesty, you know. . . . Besides, some of our guests here might well be scandalized. . . . In short, may Satan take you! I must get to the bottom of this affair."

Thus speaking, he moved to a corner of the terrace where carpets and cushions had been spread upon the flags.

"Bring wine!" he called out to an attendant; "and let it be well packed in snow. My official duties are over for to-night. I shall now hold an unofficial court of inquiry."

Inviting Gokal to be seated on his right and Amar on his left, he sank down upon the softest of the cushions. His return to serenity was being greatly assisted by the thought that the impeccable Mabun had been caught napping at last.

"Now, Hari Khan," he began, after the wine jug had gone round, "I must ask you to make a full confession. In the first place, where is this secret way?"

"You enter it from the old, disused elephant stables."

Mabun nodded. "I know. But I had ordered that a guard should be placed there. It is extraordinary!"

Narsing gave him an impressive glare, and then turned again to Hari.

"How long is it since you broke into the palace?"

"Oh, about a couple of hours, I suppose."

Narsing held up a fat finger. "Not more?"

"Well, make it a little more. But for the last hour at least I have been talking to Gokal on this terrace."

Narsing became still more magisterial. "And before that?"

"I paid a visit to my sister-in-law, Ranee Sita."

Narsing glanced to his left, but Amar's face showed nothing.

"But—but it was an odd time for a visit. When did you arrive in Agra?"

"This evening. At sundown."

"At sundown! And I see the dust of your journey still on you. Am I not right in supposing that you made your way straight into the palace?"

Hari was silent.

"Well, now!" continued Narsing, delighting in his own perspicacity. "It remains for us to find out just why you were in such a hurry to get in."

From this moment, warming to his task, he bombarded the culprit with questions. In a few minutes he elicited the statement that Hari had caught sight of little Jali from the road below. And then came his masterstroke, the illumination towards which he had been struggling; he extorted from the reluctant Hari the admission that Jali had not been alone, that with him had been a maid—a young and pretty serving-maid—whom Hari had perhaps seen once or twice before. When this came out he made a noticeable pause, swept a glance round the assembly, and gave a wink so large and inclusive that everyone present had a share in it. Hari's impulse to enter the palace, his visit to Ranee Sita, the hour or so that could not be accounted for—all was explained. It was a triumph for the cross-examiner, and after Hari had sworn upon his honor that his sister-in-law's apartments were the only ones that he had visited, the good man declared himself satisfied, and the inquiry closed.

This, however, did not mean that he had finished talking. Hari had to receive a reprimand; the Rajah was told that he should advise his wife to be more watchful of the chickens in her charge; and as for Mabun Das—here his tone grew more magisterial— well! he hoped that Mabun Das was as much dismayed as he was to discover that the palace was insecure. Yes, insecure! An opening for scandal and even for crime had been revealed. Was not he, Narsing, answerable for the safety and honor of the highest-born and prettiest women in the Empire to the number of about four score? And what about their jewels? And what about the Emperor's treasure, well known to be lying in the palace vaults?

Color had risen to his cheeks from the heat of his own eloquence; but the snow-cooled wine and the freshness of the midnight hour spread a peace to which he had to yield. Allah, what a night it was! And how good it was, too, to take one's leisure after a toilsome day! Spreading himself out like a fowl of brilliant plumage, he cast his heavy turban aside and gazed up into the sky. These blessed hours of cool and quiet—he was addressing himself to Gokal—were they not intended by the Deity for love, for wine, for conversation with congenial friends and, of course, for religious meditation? To this Gokal gave murmurs of discreet assent. And then Narsing sighed. His kind heart was afflicted by the recollection that the Brahmin could not take wine. That wine was also forbidden to the Faithful was a thought that did not enter his head.

5

WHILE THESE MATTERS were going forward Amar had preserved a detached and faintly ironic air. Nor was this indifference altogether feigned; it was certainly not in order to investigate his brother-in-law's intrigues that he had made the journey to Agra. And yet there was something in this affair that did tease his curiosity. Although he felt almost sure that Narsing was in some way being fooled, he could not believe that any of Hari's downright assertions were false. The puzzle, then, was to conceive what motive he could actually have had for this slinking entry into the palace, and what he could have been doing all the time besides paying that unaccountable visit to Sita. The story of an amour with a serving-maid did not provide a very convincing explanation. There might be something in it, but it seemed too trivial to account for the various peculiar features of Hari's behavior. But never mind; enough and more than enough! The wretched business had already received far more attention than it deserved.

Time for the Rajah passed rapidly in solitude, but slowly in the company of such men as Narsing. Narsing, although beaming with animal vitality, affected him as spiritually non-existent. Nevertheless, as he now told himself, these solid, bustling bodies had their place in the world, nor must he forget that it was his business whilst at Agra to be attentive to the thoughts of others rather than his own.

Narsing's discourse had now turned upon the Emperor, a subject upon which he was well qualified to speak. Springing like Akbar from Central Asian stock, bred in the same customs and traditions, a faithful follower for thirty years in the field as well as at Court, he had known the man in every phase of his career. His eyes had witnessed the building up of the Empire that now stretched over the whole of Northern India, from the frontiers of Persia to the Burmese jungle. The soldier, the administrator, the statesman, the despot, he knew them all. Nor had ample opportunity been wanting, in this stretch of years, to study Akbar's inner life. Only here Narsing had been frustrated by his own temperament. The deep racial and religious drives that carried Akbar along, now hurling him into blunder, now sweeping him on an even wave to success, these forces Narsing was not content simply to find incomprehensible; he had to puzzle and fret over them. More especially he was baffled by the Emperor's attitude towards his sons, and by his unending pre-occupation with religion. This last was surely a very dangerous tendency. Yes, obviously in these two provinces of human life Akbar was a bungler; he had never learnt how to deal with his children or with God. To take his sons first: the eldest, Prince Salim, was now openly preparing to usurp the throne; Prince Murad had just died of drink; and as for the youngest, Daniyal—well, what his father thought of him no one could tell, but he, Narsing, preferred even that rascal, Salim. Then turn to religion; Akbar had been born a good Muslim, but his friends had seen him first questioning, then rejecting, and finally oppressing the Faith. Not for one single day of his life had he known spiritual tranquillity. At Fatehpur-Sikri a special Hall had been built for religious debate, and here he would collect Sufis, Sunnis, Shias Brahmins, Jains, Christians, Jews, Zoroastrians, and crack-brained exponents of every variety of fantastic belief. And then he would make them talk. By Allah! how they talked! And what had come of it all? Nothing! Nothing, unless one was to refer to those clamorous and yet dreary sittings the puny thing that Akbar had recently thrust forth upon the world—a new religion, forsooth—the Din Ilahi, a miscreation that would be negligible were it not so powerfully fathered. The Din Ilahi was by way of containing the valuable constituents of all pre-existing faiths, and its practical purpose was nothing less than to unify the Empire and purify it. What could one say?

Such was the situation over which Narsing was now expending himself in voluble lamentation. He did not need to tell his hearers that the horizon was clouded, but he doubted whether, in the midst of so much splendor and apparent prosperity, they would realize just how threatening the outlook was. Had they heard that the Emperor was on the point of giving his new religion a formal promulgation? Did they realize the extent to which this absurd act would invigorate all the disruptive elements in the Empire? In every province, he told them, the more fanatical of the Muslims were already secretly promising Prince Salim their support, and the rest of the population was preparing to rally under Prince Daniyal. "As for accepting the Din Ilahi," and he flung out a hand at Gokal, "is there, I ask you, a single man of self-respect who will condescend to it?"

Dejectedly the Brahmin shook his head.

"Ah, my dear friend!" sighed Narsing, "you, who have the ear of the Emperor, why cannot you restrain him, dissuade him?"

Gokal said nothing, and his silence convicted Narsing of a want of tact. As a universally respected leader of religious thought, Gokal had grave responsibilities; and these, as anyone might see, threatened to clash with his private interests. For years he had been a special protégé of Akbar's; appointed Court Librarian, he enjoyed a privileged position by the Imperial throne.

Making haste to change his tone and topic, Narsing launched forth into a tirade against Salim. "By Allah!" he cried, "when I think of that man's insolences my blood boils. Can you conceive it, he has actually set up a mint at Allahabad and strikes coins in his own image! Yes, and the other day, if you please, he sent a complete set of his coins to his royal father 'to add to his numismatic collection.'" On the subject of the prince it was not difficult to be entertaining. Salim's character was so freakishly compounded that everything he said or did had its ridiculous side. Sensual, unprincipled, and ill-educated, he, nonetheless, was a man of aspiration. For love he entertained a respect which made him sentimental, for religion a regard which threw him into the grossest superstitions, and for learning a craving that immersed him in alchemy and pseudo-scientific research. Narsing described how he had come upon him one day engrossed in an experiment to extract a special kind of copper from peacocks' feathers. And then, to be sure, there were his literary pretensions! His memoirs! From those stray leaves, carelessly left behind on his removal to Allahabad, court gossips had derived much amusement. For instance, there was the famous description of Akbar: "In his august personal appearance my father is of middle height, but inclining to be tall; he is of the hue of wheat; his eyes and eyebrows are black, and his complexion rather dark than fair; he is lion-bodied, with a broad chest, and his hands and arms long. On the left side of his nose he has a fleshy mole, very agreeable in appearance, of the size of half a pea. Those skilled in the science of physiognomy consider this mole a sign of great prosperity and exceeding good fortune. His august voice is very loud, and in speaking and explaining has a peculiar richness. In his actions and movements he is not like the people of the world, and the Glory of God manifests itself in him."

"As I hope for Paradise!" exclaimed Narsing at the end of his quotation, "what that rogue says there is true! Akbar is more than human!"

His glowing face and glistening eyes were an invitation to his audience to indulge a like enthusiasm, but none of the others had drunk so much wine, and none, certainly, gave the Emperor so unstinting a devotion. Undeterred by their silence, Narsing pursued his theme.

"Gentlemen! had you seen what I have so often seen, the tears would be no further from your eyes than they are from mine now. There, upon his seat on the terrace at Fatehpur-Sikri, night after night, alone, the Emperor sits. Like an image in stone he looks out into the darkness covering this great Empire—the Empire which the strength of his arm and the toil of his brain have built up. And mine, gentlemen, mine has not seldom been the honor of waiting upon him there. I advance across the terrace bearing his jug of wine—the opium wine with which he strives to drown his sorrow. Sometimes the night is dark and I can see no more than his outline. But sometimes the moon is high and clear, and then what do I see? A face of grief! A face of bitter grief!"

Without a doubt the good man was speaking from a heart which, if sentimental, was sincere; nonetheless this ebullition was felt by all to be rather embarrassing; his audience were not sorry when they caught sight of Mabun drawing near.

"Well!" demanded Narsing, his forehead wrinkling with vexation. "What now?"

Mabun sighed sympathetically. "Prince Daniyal! He asks to see you. He is waiting below."

Narsing stared, then emitted a weary groan. "At this hour! Merciful Allah! What does His Royal Highness want?"

"I am not sure," answered Mabun with caution. "But he said something about the hairless cat that you promised to procure for him."

"The hairless cat! You hear that?" He glared round at his circle. "The hairless cat! May he and his menagerie of disgusting pets— But enough! Where is my turban?"

Scrambling to his feet, he began to hunt, with many curses, among the cushions. While he was kicking about, Gokal found it for him.

"I thank you, my honored friend. You see what my life has become. No peace at any hour! Well, my friends, well . . . I wish you all good night. Rajah, do me the favor of seeing Hari Khan off the premises before you go to bed. Go in peace, Hari Khan; may you enjoy tranquil slumbers elsewhere!" With these words he strode off accompanied by Mabun, leaving his guests to smile after his retreating figure.

When talk was resumed it fell again upon the subject of Akbar, but now, left to themselves, the three friends felt at liberty to treat of the Emperor rather differently.

"I believe," said Gokal, when pressed to speak, "I believe that the Emperor's inner life will always remain a mystery. His youth, as we all know, was wild and reckless; he drank to excess and wantonly played with death. We know, too, that he was subject to fits of brooding melancholy, and then—let me remind you of this —in his thirty-sixth year he had what some say was an epileptic seizure, an experience which he, however, regarded as a divine revelation. For a short time he renounced the world; his abdication was even thought possible. In Abu-l-Fazl's words: 'He was nearly abandoning this state of struggle, and entirely gathering up the skirt of his genius from earthly pomp. The primacy of the spiritual world took possession of his holy form. The attraction of cognition of God cast its ray.' "

"For my part," threw in Hari, "I cannot believe that he is an epileptic. I suppose the peculiar strain of mysticism running through his character is somewhat suggestive of epilepsy, but, were he a true epileptic, he could not drink as he does without killing himself."

"I agree," said the Rajah, "and I should even hesitate to call him abnormal. He strikes me as being the average man, but raised to a higher power of manhood. One cannot point to any faults or virtues in the average man which he does not possess. He is sensual, a lover of wine and women; boastful, often cruel, avaricious, cunning hypocritical, and a colossal egoist. He is also an impassioned advocate of abstinence and self-control, humble before God, occasionally generous, simple in his affections, shrewd and credulous in equal degree, and unsparing of toil in the interests of his Throne and Empire. His Majesty is the plain man, I say, raised to a higher power. This constitutes him a natural autocrat. He aspires to make his people great and good as greatness and goodness are understood by him. If his ideas on the subject are a little elementary, that cannot be helped. I am not one of those who make it a grievance that he is great in his own fashion instead of in theirs; although, of course, it is hard for some amongst us, who are men of ancient tradition and culture, to accommodate ourselves to a civilization which is of a cruder type than our own, and imposed upon us from without—a civilization essentially materialistic. It is true that the Emperor himself has idealism; and his idealism takes, I admit, a certain grandiosity from the power that is within him; but all the same . . ." And Amar shrugged and shook his head.

"The Emperor is not a happy man," said Gokal meditatively. "This age is his; he has made it. But he is beginning to realize that he has let loose influences that he cannot stem. When he built up an Empire he did not foresee that its culture would be tainted with a newly born irreligion and vulgarity. When he studied the faith of

41

his fathers he did not foresee that he would lose his belief in it. And when he undertook to supply a unifying creed..."

The Rajah nodded. "After all, he is more than half a Mongol, and the Mongols are a people of prodigious vitality, but they remain, broadly speaking, barbarians. Are you aware that amongst the rank and file the washing of clothes and of cooking-vessels is still held to be a sin? They will also tell you with pride that Tamerlane was born holding in his hand a piece of clotted blood. They still love dirt, honor violence, and believe in devils."

"Whereas we, the civilized, worship cleanliness, honor sophistication, and believe in nothing," put in Hari with a smile.

To this no one made any answer, for, at the end of the terrace, a slender white figure had appeared. "Is that my friend Mabun Das again?" said Hari in a low voice.

After a moment the figure came forward, and Mabun Das it was, but the little man seemed somehow a shade different. Was it the absence of his superior that helped him to impart a greater confidence to his bearing? Or was he temporarily lowering the mask with which he concealed a self-confidence that was always there? Be this as it might, he moved very deliberately towards the three who sat watching him, and stood looking down at them with a smile.

"Well, Mabun Das," said Hari genially, "will you join us in a last cup of wine?"

Mabun declined with a bow.

"What is Prince Daniyal doing here at this time of night?" Hari went on.

The smile on Mabun's face did not leave it, but it seemed to sink inwards and to take on a meaning that was for himself alone.

"The hairless cat..." he murmured.

"And nothing more?"

Mabun shrugged. "The Prince always keeps late hours."

"No doubt, no doubt!" And Hari looked up at the stars.

"He also rises late."

"I suppose so." Hari's regard came down again. Everyone's eyes were now bent upon Mabun interrogatively, for his gentle voice had a strangely mocking note.

"To-morrow, however, the Prince will rise early," said Mabun.

"He will rise to witness the execution of four hundred and nineteen men."

For a few moments no one stirred. Mabun continued to smile, and then suddenly sighed and looked grave. Strangely enough, however, this altered expression seemed just as factitious as the first.

"Yes, gentlemen," continued Mabun softly, "it is so! The Emperor signed their death-warrant a few hours ago. These men and women all belong to one or another of the seventy-two secret sects."

The silence continued. Akbar's recent edicts were well known to all present. They embodied his repeated threats to sweep clean the limbo where religion and lust and every elemental instinct met—met in an obscurity that made their faces all baleful and all alike. A moral and spiritual corruption had set in with the mingling of so many races and creeds. Races copied only each other's vices. Creeds, forced to tolerate one another, learned to tolerate their own decadence. So the Emperor had ordered an inquiry and tabulated the results, he had issued edicts and fixed penalties. But the people had only smiled. The heavens might thunder, but where was the lightning to strike? This sudden bolt, then, might well create dismay. Was it a sign that Akbar had lost his mental balance? Had he not known for years that a subterranean stream of bane was flowing beneath the visible structure of his State? Of course. For years he had known that thousands of his subjects were mysteriously disappearing from the earth. For years he had known that in hundreds of temples and secret meeting-places religious orgies were being held with a frequent accompaniment of human sacrifice. Perhaps it maddened him to be the Emperor of a people whose lives belonged, not to him, but to the Goddess whom he abhorred. In every village, in every city, in the palace itself, he could sniff the sickly taint. Saktism! Thuggee! The worship of the Female Principle! Kali, the Goddess of Birth and Death! Her power, against which Akbar warred, was subtle and diffuse as a pestilence. It had its tides, which were governed by the moon or fate. If the number, four hundred and nineteen, was savagely large, it was also comically small; you could multiply it over and over again with no result except that the people would murmur that their Emperor had gone mad.

With these unspoken thoughts in their minds, Mabun's hearers looked at him and wondered. Seeing that he was known to occupy an important position in Akbar's unofficial intelligence service, there was something a little sinister in his present air of detachment. Yet that detachment did not, perhaps, preclude a judgment; that calm was, perhaps, not cynical.

"So they will die in the morning," said Hari, once more looking up into the night sky.

"Yes. In five or six hours."

"And how?"

"They will be trampled to death by elephants."

"And Akbar will look on?"

"No. Only Prince Daniyal."

Upon this there was another pause. Then Mabun suddenly began to smile his brilliant smile. "Gentlemen," he said in lighter tones, "I am afraid I have turned your thoughts into a rather dismal channel. I offer you my apologies. Before your evening closes, you will revert, I hope, to happier topics." With that he bade them good night, and for a while after he had gone the others sat there, pensive. The great lantern behind Gokal shone down softly upon the dome of his shaven head. Cross-legged and erect like a Buddha, he looked the very image of meditation. Hari, reclining upon one elbow, still kept his eyes fixed upon the shining constellations. Amar, whose gaze had followed Mabun frowningly until he disappeared through the arch, now reached out and for the first time that evening helped himself to wine. When he had drunk a little he looked deep into the bowl and murmured: "Gautama has said that as long as men remain bound in ignorance, so long will there be suffering."

"And evil?" questioned Hari. "What of that?"

"Evil springs from ignorance and delusion. The fires of lust and anger find no fuel when the delusions attached to individuality have been destroyed."

Hari gave a brief laugh and turned to Gokal. "Is it not true that the only religion that was unrepresented at Akbar's debates was Buddhism?"

Gokal made no reply, but Amar answered for him: "Yes. And that is significant."

"Of what?"

Amar's expression was scornful. "In his Din Ilahi Akbar proclaims himself vice-regent of God upon earth. What should he have to do with a doctrine which teaches that there is no God?"

Hari considered for a minute. "Amar," he said at last, "when it comes to choosing between Salim and Daniyal, on which side will you lean?"

For a space Amar remained silent. "That," he said, and his tone was dry, "that I take to be a question of political expediency."

Hari laughed. "Personalities, then, do not count?"

"I know neither Salim nor Daniyal personally."

"But what have you heard?"

"I gather from what I have heard that they are both, in their different ways, ignorant and foolish men."

Hari laughed again. "Is Akbar foolish and ignorant?"

Amar was silent.

"Remember!" said Hari, "they both have the blood of Akbar running in their veins."

Still Amar made no answer.

"And Akbar himself," said Hari, "can neither read nor write."

After this there came a long pause, and then Amar slowly rose to his feet. Hari followed his example, but Gokal still remained motionless with bowed head. Going up to him, Hari grasped him with affectionate roughness by the shoulder. "What is the matter with you, my friend?" he cried. "The whole evening you have been dumb."

Gokal looked up for a few instants, then let his head sink down again; and thus he sat, a monumental figure of dejection.

Hari left him and took a turn down the full length of the terrace. When he came back Gokal was standing by Amar's side.

"Amar," said Hari suddenly, "let me tell you this: Evil is something more than you think."

Amar returned Hari's gaze blankly and said nothing; but, undeterred by this lack of response, Hari went on: "And I will tell you where evil is to be found. In human nature . . . I mean, in the very stuff of life itself. I tell you the word 'human' means, fundamentally, nothing beautiful, virtuous, or intelligent, but something merely—strong. Akbar is very human, very average, very strong.

45

As for you, you want to select. But you weaken yourself thereby. Life! its power is what it is. And to deny it is no deliverance. All that is below—whether in Akbar's soul or in the dark spirit of the masses . . ."

He stopped. He looked from Amar to Gokal, then at Amar again.

"This is my conviction, Amar," he said in a low voice. "What good men resist is not a mere prompting to pleasure, but something that they fear. Am I not right, Gokal?"

The big Brahmin raised both his hands and pressed them wearily to his eyelids. "I do not know. I do not know."

With a frown of sudden anger Hari seized him again by the arm. "You shall stay here until you have spoken."

Gokal dropped his hands and sighed. "What do you want me to say?"

"What you think."

Amar gave an exclamation of impatience. "Enough of this!" he cried, and, making a gesture of invitation to Gokal, he moved towards the archway.

Gokal, however, drew himself up and stepped back from both the one and the other with a resentful movement for which neither was prepared.

"You ask for my opinion? Very well. To me the existence of what we call evil—in its many kinds and degrees—suggests the creative activity of numerous agents which may themselves be our own creations. These agents seem to be striving to embody different kinds of values. In nature there are hostilities—battles with victory and defeat. There is what seems to us regress . . . there is perversion . . . there may be a development in evil as well as in goodness, a movement leading down to Satanic abysses of being."

The Rajah was astonished. Was Gokal associating himself with the vulgar polytheism of the masses? Was he declaring in favor of a Zoroastrian or Manichaean duality? Well, no matter! The tone in which he had delivered himself was petulant. It was not necessary to take him seriously.

Crossing the terrace in silence the three men now passed through the arch and went down the great stairway into the court below. At the Gate they had to wait for a few minutes while Gokal's carriage was being summoned. Beneath them lay the silent city with the moon just rising over the roofs. The night was flooded with a soft, sad light, which seemed to Amar to be like a dawn in the underworld, rousing pale ghosts to another spectral day. His heart was full of a vague unrest, and an unusual longing for companionship came over him. Gokal and Hari were about to drive off together, for Gokal had invited Hari to stay with him at his pavilion. He felt sure that they would continue to sit together, exchanging their thoughts until the day broke, and this idea increased his feeling of loneliness. When Gokal invited him to accompany them he accepted.

6

THE SWIFT LITTLE horses trotted noiselessly along the dusty road, the light carriage swayed from side to side, and each of the three friends followed his own silent thoughts. After passing along the empty streets they went through the city gates, and a little farther on turned off upon a soft track that ran under the trees of the Royal Hunting Grounds. Dry leaves crackled beneath the wheels; moonlight alternated with shadow; white moths and fireflies danced together among the boughs.

In half an hour the carriage drew up in a lane between the blossoming fruit trees of a small enclosure, and here Hari, who had been looking about him all the time as if to take his bearings, sniffed the air and said: "I smell water. Are we near the lake?"

In silence Gokal led the way through a narrow gate and up a path that wandered through the trees. Presently a line of slender tamarisks came into view, and the pale surface of a lake glimmered through their feathery leafage. The path now skirted the lake, which was an oblong sheet of artificial water, upon the stone margin of which were seated innumerable frogs. At each step of Gokal's several frogs leapt up and threw themselves into the water with a splash. Hari laughed immoderately.

A few moments later there appeared a long, low building, somewhat Chinese in style. Behind it stretched a row of dark cypresses, in front was a terrace with a flight of broad steps going down to the water. This was Gokal's pavilion. It was built of a hard wood that had weathered to the same silver-gray as the stone of the terrace. Everything was gray in the moonlight except the shining water and the blossom upon two flowering trees, one on each side of the house.

Gokal led the way up the steps on to the terrace and there halted in a kind of dreamy uncertainty. But an old manservant, who had been lying asleep by the door, unrolled himself from his sheet and salaamed. Gokal bade him bring some fruit and some sherbet.

Standing at the end of the terrace, the Rajah looked out over the water. The moon was now dimmed by thin veils of cloud; and her light, diffused over the whole sky, fell gently and evenly upon everything. Tall, slender trees grew all around the lake in which they stood reflected; but in the center, beyond these shadowy reflections, the placid water made a mirror for the gray clouds drifting past.

The Rajah went down the steps and along the water's edge as far as the corner of the lake. There he stood pensive, wrapped in an unexpected peace. The place seemed to him to be hallowed; it seemed to be watching itself, communing with itself; it seemed to be happy in the contemplation of an unchanging tranquillity. This, thought the Rajah, is a picture of the condition towards which the spirit strives, and with this thought there came over him an intense love of the place. Yes, he loved it with intensity. Some day it would surely be granted him to identify himself with this repose, and to exist, selfless, brooding upon the face of these serene waters.

As he stood there the gross fatalities of the earth, the complications of the world, the uneasiness of human relationships, no longer troubled him. He thought of other men only as kindred creatures seeking—even when they knew it not—the tranquillity that is at the end of all desire.

After a while his eyes turned again towards the pavilion, but Gokal and Hari were not visible from where he stood. Slowly he retraced his steps and, mounting the terrace, found them seated upon a mat of rushes, with a low Chinese table spread before them.

It was to be supposed that they had been talking together before he came, but now they were sitting silent. Gokal's head was bowed, his face hidden.

"Well, Amar," said Hari dryly, and he gave a nod in Gokal's direction, "perhaps you can find out what is the matter with our friend here."

The Rajah stood over Gokal's massive form, which drooped and sagged as if melted by the fervor of an inward grief. Thoughtfully he considered him. He knew that Gokal was subject to fits of profound melancholy, but his despair concerning the destiny of mankind was not infrequently to be traced to some personal mischance. This was a weakness that the Rajah greatly deplored.

He was still considering what line to take when, in a muffled voice, Gokal pronounced the words: "I am mourning for one who has died."

The Rajah was completely taken aback. In silence he and Hari exchanged looks of astonishment.

"A child she was," continued Gokal without lifting his head, "a girl of fourteen . . . the daughter of a gardener . . . A snake bit her . . . her blood was poisoned and she died yesterday. A young girl, very lovely . . . and dead so young."

This confession fell so strangely upon their ears that for a minute neither Hari nor the Rajah could find a word to say. At last Hari shrugged and Amar stammered out: "My dear friend, I had no idea that you had a private sorrow of this kind. I thought . . ."

"Amar!" said Gokal, interrupting, "the favor of the world is nothing to me any longer. The Din Ilahi will fail in the end because it is a folly, and if, in the meantime, it brings about my ruin, what do I really care! My life is a weariness, and I am no longer young. It is true that I have forfeited my caste, and that the Emperor's protection alone stands between me and disgrace. But whether I live or die, here or in exile, it is all a matter of indifference to me."

Hari and the Rajah looked at one another again. Gokal's state of mind was worse than they had thought.

At the end of a painful silence Hari pursed his lips and said: "Obviously, my dear Gokal, you were in love with this girl."

"She was a child—only a child," returned Gokal brokenly. He

had lifted his head at last, and the Rajah noticed the glistening track of a tear that had rolled down his left cheek. "Her father is an old man and his other children are unkind to him. His wife is dead. He had looked after Vasumati from her infancy.... And now he sits all day upon a stone with his head in his hands. Men laugh at him because it was only a girl; but he moans. 'My little love! My little love!' It is a pitiful sight, Rajah, and I hope that he himself will soon die."

A chill ran down the Rajah's spine. He thought of Jali, thankful that the boy was sleeping safely in his bed. But Jali, to be sure, was not very robust.... "Alas!" he sighed inwardly; "alas! for poor human fondnesses! Links in the chain! Fetters! Fetters!" Not more than a few minutes ago he had felt free, a spirit rejoicing in its emancipation. But now his heart was flooded with a tenderness for earthly and familiar things; they seemed to him to possess by virtue of their very lowliness a dignity equal to that of deliverance itself.

Having spoken, Gokal buried his face in his hands, now openly overcome by grief. The Rajah was dismayed and even slightly scandalized. But Hari, with a compassionate smile, patted the Brahmin comfortingly upon the shoulder. The silence dragged on until suddenly Hari seemed to weary of sympathizing; with a muttered exclamation he rose to his feet.

"By all the gods and demons!" he cried, "how comes it that a man such as he can so lose courage? Why is Gokal subject to the common weaknesses of humanity? He has intelligence. He has knowledge. He has wisdom. He should be glorious, but"—and he pointed to Gokal's huddled form—"look at him! He weeps like a woman."

"My dear Hari," sighed the Rajah, "he—he cared for this child."

Hari walked up and down, possessed by an unaccountable excitement.

"Does he not know as well as I that we are all like frogs, like insects—alive one moment and dead the next! We must not mind.... Life is a disgrace to those who mind death."

The Rajah's gaze went out over the lake. "The human affections are the most tenacious of all the chains ..."

"Love," interrupted Hari, "love makes a man contemptuous of

death. That—just that—is what I mean. Does a woman fear her own death or even the death of her lover? No! She fears only the dying of his love."

The Rajah smiled. "You are coming down to another level of ideas," he said rather dryly. "You can hardly recommend that the whole human race should live on the emotional plane of a woman in love."

"I do recommend it!" retorted Hari with headlong impetuosity. "At least I denounce as shameful the emotional plane upon which we nearly all live. We spend our lives fretting over trifles—and running away from death. We live not that we may live, but in order not to die."

The Rajah shrugged. "Anyhow, the remedy does not lie, as you seem to imagine, in taking emotional intoxicants."

Upon this there was silence for a full minute, during which the Rajah and Hari continued to eye one another. Then, laying a hand upon the knee of the heavy bowed figure beside him, the Rajah, too, bowed his head and sat dumb.

With an oath Hari turned on his heel and walked away to the end of the terrace. There a light shelter had been raised against the night dew. In a loud voice he directed Gokal's servant to spread out his couch, then he came back and said: "Amar, your bleak religion appears to satisfy you. So much the better. To me it seems that you are too easily satisfied."

The Rajah smiled as if he had it on his lips to make a crushing rejoinder, but after a glance at Gokal, he said simply: "Let those who can find God take refuge in Him."

Then Gokal stirred; they heard him sigh, and all at once, in a low voice, he quoted the words:

" 'Men flee to God for a refuge from a knowledge that doth not profit, from a prayer that is not heard, from a heart that is not humble and a body that is not satisfied.' "

Hari looked troubled. "Is that true?" he asked after a moment; "that we flee to God for those reasons and those only?"

The question went unanswered; Gokal remained without movement and the Rajah only sighed. After looking from one to the other Hari gave a shrug and announced his intention of lying down for a few hours' sleep.

In silence the other two sat there. The moon, now high, seemed to be hanging stationary over the lake; light clouds drifting around her were reflected upon the still gray face of the water; the night seemed endless and changeless.

In his search for something deeply felt to say Amar was sadly perplexed. His sympathies were complicated by embarrassment and even a slight irritation. What concern had this big, grave man of nearly fifty, this philosopher who stood high in the world of learning as well as at Court—what concern had he with an unlettered girl of fourteen, the daughter of a gardener? Gokal's uncontrolled grief was not only pitiful, but scandalous and rather absurd.

With every passing minute his perplexity deepened and, as it deepened, it generalized itself; he brought his own life under survey and then he thought of life as a whole. Were there no certainties anywhere? ... The lake, lying pale and still before his eyes, breathed a tranquillity that was no longer peaceful, but deadening.

At last he forced himself into speech. "Gokal," he said, "your present grief is no more than a shadow drifting over the surface of your spirit. Wait a little and it will pass."

Gokal's face had a stony pallor in the moonlight; the hollows of his eyes were dark, but Amar felt a deep, empty gaze encountering his own.

"I am grieving for that girl—yes!" And Gokal paused. "But I am also grieving for my lost youth. I am regretting all the illusions I have not pursued, all the follies that I have not committed. Yes; it is for these things that I now grieve."

Amar's heart contracted. Never before had Gokal sounded this particular note, and the words just uttered seemed to rob him of even the strength to sympathize. A voice within him was asking: "Does one, then, come to this?" Gokal was no longer a person, but the small, ancient voice of mankind questioning whether life has any meaning, whether effort is not always vain, whether belief is ever true.

It was time to make an end. There are occasions, the Rajah told himself, when one must simply break off and wait for a change of mood. In an altered tone he made up a few sentences of rather conventional encouragement and then rose to take his departure. In his heart he felt miserable and not a little ashamed, but his chief longing was to get away, and he tried hard to persuade his host not to accompany him back to the carriage. Gokal, however, insisted; and, together, in complete silence, they retraced their steps along the margin of the lake and through the shadows of the little wood. The coachman and the groom were asleep by the roadside, even the horses seemed to have gone to sleep. Amar made his adieux with a dryness that he detested all the more in that Gokal's manner to him was perfect. It had the dignity of sorrow with self-effacement.

After he had driven away Gokal stood gazing down the empty lane. "I have said too much," he reflected, "for why should one's friends be troubled? The things I want to say should be said to oneself alone. Let me talk to myself then in solitude—an old fool addressing an old fool. Gokal, you are reckoned a wise man and learned, but all that you have learned is the simplest and most ancient lesson in the world: it is better to laugh and weep like a child than to follow the wisdom of the wisest. You have traveled down the river of time with a swiftness that you did not see, and the years have carried you unaware into the waste lands of regret. All your life your eyes have been fastened upon the invisible; never did you look up at the fruit trees in the spring, or at the young girls blossoming beside you the full year round. You have studied and pondered—to no profit, gaining nothing but the respect of the simple, who, in reality, are wiser than you. So here, in the end, stands Gokal, with a round back and a round belly and a crushing load of regret."

Unconsciously he had started into movement and was now shambling aimlessly down the road. He saw nothing, heard nothing, was aware of nothing but his grief. But as he shambled along the dawn broke, and when he looked up a ray of light struck upon his face. For a moment he stood still, dismayed, then turned and hurried back towards the house. But the cruel, exquisite dawn was quicker than he. A golden light slanted through the trees, the dew sparkled, the earth rejoiced. And Gokal bent his head and went fast. The beauty of nature in its mindlessness, the beauty of instinct in its thoughtlessness, the beauty of youth in its ignorance —here were the objects of his longing and despair—these were the things that sent him scurrying along to hide like a creature of the night. Stripped of the kindly dark, he glanced shrinkingly from side to side and encountered, all at once, the gaze of two large brown eyes that were staring at him in innocent amazement. It was a little, low-caste lad of ten, who was lost in wonder at the sight of a venerable Brahmin stumbling along with a face bathed in tears.

7

THE SAME DAWN mingled with Hari's dreams and roused him to a sleepy joy. He stretched himself and shivered slightly. A cool air was ruffling the lake, breaking the reflection of the trees, and making the trees themselves rustle and tremble against the emptiness of the sky. The pale yellow light was like coolness made visible; and as it sank through his eyelids, dissipating the sultry dark, he remembered why it was that he felt so happy; he looked back into the past and saw happiness; he looked forward, and there he saw happiness too. In an hour's time he would be strolling along the woodland path to his tryst. The morning would still be in its first freshness, the dew still sparkling, the sky still cool; and in his imagination he could already see the glade where he and his Lalita would meet. He could see her coming; he would hear her telling him that she loved him; he knew the exact tone of her voice, a voice that matched her color, for she was of the hue of gold—hair and skin blending in one glow that made her vivid and warm. This was the girl that loved him; her health and youth went out to meet his passion, and together they lived in a transfigured world.

It was in Kabul, a couple of months ago, that he had first met her. He had been invited to dine with her father, the Afghan chieftain, Makh Khan. A thunder-shower had come down just before he left his house; the air was washed clean; the walls, the paving-stones, everything glistened. How well he could remember standing in the flush of the evening light outside the great nail-studded door of the Khan's palace.

In the hall a table had been spread for six. They were all men there; and the talk—oh, it had been the usual talk; nothing of interest. After the meal they had gone into the inner court, and there had sat beside the fountain, smoking and drinking and eating dried raisins. The trembling water of the fountain threw up flakes of moonlight; the berried branches of the pepper tree made a pattern against the sky.

Then the doors at the end of the court were thrown open and the ladies of the house appeared. The Khan's wife, a big, stout woman, came down the steps with an air of authority. Her three daughters followed; and Hari's first impression of Lalita was that this pretty girl of eighteen must have been badly spoilt. She carried her long-limbed, broad-shouldered young body with a kind of petulant looseness and the tilt of her chin said the company were nothing to her. But that was only a mood; she soon changed; and when she gave her first laugh—ah! then he felt he knew her. For the rest of the evening he watched, he was acutely sensible of her presence, and although hardly a word passed, once at least their glances met.

Returning to his own house, he went straight up on to the roof, and there remained half the night sunk in a deep, sullen abstraction. His life was empty, his energies wasted; he longed to express himself in sudden deeds of violence. All the smoldering disappointments of his life burst into flame; he hated his wife for her conventional ambitions; he hated his sons, whom she had alienated; he hated Akbar, who robbed men of their liberty; he hated Makh Khan and his arrogant wife; he hated everyone—except Lalita.

The girl's smile haunted him; it had the unexpected brilliance of mountain flowers shooting up in the spring out of the stony ground. It changed the current of his thoughts; it reminded him of this and that thing said; it made him remember . . . yes, it had been mentioned that she was in the habit of going for long rides in the morning accompanied only by her groom. With this in his mind he started pacing up and down, and gradually the black cloud of his ill-humor lifted.

Early next day he summoned from his household a man that he

could trust, and after giving him instructions, rode out by himself. About two miles away there was a hill overlooking the level valley bed, and at the top of this hill he dismounted and sat down upon the highland turf. There was a thin wind from the snows blowing past him, and a warmth from the rising sun upon his back. Goat bells tinkled upon the slopes; further down strings of camels moved with grotesque leisureliness along the straight, shadeless roads; human figures were busy about the city gates like bees before the entrance of a hive.

A smile came to his lips and he fell to singing to himself. Pale brown earth beneath, pale blue sky above, and a great silence over all. His song was vague and endless, his mind empty of all directed thought. He was waiting so patiently that his waiting hardly seemed conscious of itself. It was as if he drew upon the patience of the ages, with the sense that it had always been thus. There had always been watching and waiting, and always for the same things.

At last the moment came. From beneath the city wall, and not far from the city gate, something flashed in the sun. His gaze narrowed and he sprang to his feet. In a minute there were some more flashes and then he knew what to do. His eyes gleamed as he mounted and put his horse down the slope.

Not many days later Makh Khan, accompanied by his family, started on a long, leisurely journey south to Agra. The Khan was obeying Akbar's summons with a better grace than most, for it was probable that the Durbar would close with the marriage of Lalita to Prince Daniyal. He traveled with a cumbrous retinue, made short stages and pitched elaborate camps. In some places where the hunting was good he halted for as much as a week.

This suited Hari perfectly. In the guise of a horse-dealer and accompanied by only one servant, he followed the Khan; his modest tent went up every night at the distance of a mile or two from the Khan's site, and stolen meetings with Lalita could be arranged at the close of nearly every day. During the next eight weeks his contentment was complete. He had found romance with a spice of adventure, movement with leisure, a life lived in the present, unburdened and yet rich. All day he would jog along, now chatting with his man, now lost in a happy dream, but always with the thought of his last half-hour with Lalita or of the next to come. Evening brought him the moments of his joy—as ecstatic, as fleeting as the flaming colors of the sky; then, afterwards, he would sit outside his tent in a trance, or perhaps walk along through the dusk to some bit of rising ground, and from there gaze at the lights of the Khan's great encampment twinkling upon the plain.

At night, when he woke to throw wood on his fire, the stillness was infused with another gentler bliss. He watched the flames leap up and shine upon the little pyramid of his tent, or on the trunks of trees and the underside of leaves, or on some jutting rock that cut against the field of stars. As a rule he was awake in time to see the dawn, and one dawn in particular constantly returned to his memory; the sky was of the purest, palest blue, with a few motionless little clouds poised high. It was so unearthly in its silence and purity that he would have been unsurprised if a bevy of angels had flown across it. The essence of serenity was there: a few stars still twinkling through the light-filled air and the grass gray with dew.

Ah! those had been enchanted days; and even now, in this present, with a meeting round the next bend of the path, he could not but cast his eyes backward and stifle a mounting sigh. The first period of the romance was over; the next extended into a most unpromising obscurity. However, to give fortune its due credit, the immediate future looked well enough; the Khan was taking up residence in a garden house of Prince Daniyal's, which was actually on the edge of the Royal Hunting Grounds. For the present, meetings with Lalita could be continued without difficulty.

To while the minutes away he pictured the moment of her coming. First he would hear the thudding of her horse's hoofs, then at the bend of the glade she would appear. Still at a little distance she would pull up, dismount, and throw the reins to her groom. Always she came to him on foot and alone. She would come slowly, looking straight before her and smiling with that deep, glowing smile. During those few seconds the flame of his happiness would soar up to its full height. Anticipation and realization became one and filled him with a double life. Consciousness and self-consciousness, too, worked together, so that he could say of his happiness: "I have captured it! Here it lies in my hand!"

Stretched out beneath a tree he closed his eyes and there

followed an interval during which he was completely lost in his dreams. When he looked at the sun again it was to realize that Lalita was late, and with this came his first twinge of anxiety. From now onwards, he well knew, his disquiet would steadily increase. It would deepen and darken until it became a veritable torment. Was it not strange that only at times such as these did a clear vision of love's miseries come to him? And yet—it was past all question—his happiness during the last two months had been shot through with panics and despairs beyond count. Before him there now lay perhaps an hour of anguish—the time for disappointed hope to burn itself out—then wearily he would get up and go back—dull, spiritless, racked by fears.

To live in one's emotions meant this; it was slavery; he saw it well enough. But was it on that account ignominious? No, he said, no and no! Better this suffering than contentment in the humdrum. It was out of one's subjection to love that love's ecstasies were born. Remember, he said, the sense of lordship over life, the sustained exaltation of days and weeks when you became mindful of ordinary existence only to give it a smile. Think, think again how the world appears to a lover! all those little people down there, ridiculously intent upon the insignificant; look at them, content to let life slip past them, as if there were no such thing as love, that present ecstasy; or death, that onward-rushing night! Yes, to the human spirit thus expanded the common scene appeared for all the world like a piece of make-believe. You couldn't conceive that people were not pretending, not playing parts. Good heavens, it was life itself that they ignored! Couldn't they see that love and death alone had any importance—and death only as being the end of love? Well, no matter! He had seen and been content. He had bidden the seas rise and whelm him. He had bidden the mountains fall and crush him. Overflowing with life he had been joyously ready for death.

For death? Yes, perhaps. But was one ever resigned to *this*? Sullenly he rose to his feet and with a sullen slowness followed his path back through the wood. Why had Lalita failed him? All the elements of hazard and danger in their intrigue took shape before his eyes. Risks that had added zest to his pleasure in the past now looked merely forbidding; after all, they were *her* risks, too. Her misdoing in the eyes of the world would appear far more outrageous than his. For a girl of her race and station it would have been bad enough in any circumstances, but after having been pledged to a Prince of the Royal House . . . An insult to the Throne! that was what people would say. The fact that she was not as yet actually his mistress made no particular difference; no one would believe it, for one thing; moreover, the exact degree of her culpability would be a trifle, if once a scandal arose compromising the honor of the Prince.

Hari's thoughts might have gone on in this fashion for hours had he not turned upon himself in a sudden burst of rage. Fool! Was this the first time that Lalita had failed to keep an appointment? and the obstacles that had kept her back in the past, although insurmountable, had they not always been quite trivial in themselves? Sanely considered, the present case offered no feature that a man had cause to worry about. And yet he *was* worrying; and just because worry *had* to find a point of focus, he had found one.

At their last meeting—which had taken place only the evening before—a slight misadventure had occurred. He had ridden into Agra a few hours after the Khan, and, as previously arranged, had met Lalita just before sundown at a chosen spot in the Royal Hunting Grounds. The meeting had been hurried, for the light was fading and Lalita was not supposed to stay out after dark. And then what had happened was this: he was taking her back to her groom when all at once her horse shied violently, swerving off the narrow forest track. She crashed through some low-growing shrubs, and at the same instant a cry rang out as if someone lying hidden by the wayside had been hurt. He, himself, who was following a few yards behind, quickly caught her up and was successful in seizing the rein of her mount. Upon this she jumped to the ground and was beginning to run back to see what had happened when he called out to her to stop. His tone must have been peremptory, for she obeyed at once. He found it difficult afterwards to remember just what had been in his mind at the time; but, although he had not actually seen anyone at all, he certainly had had an uneasy feeling that several people were lurking in the undergrowth near by. Rather unwillingly he left her to hold the horses and went back a few yards until he caught sight of a crouching figure a little way off the path. It was a woman, and next he perceived that she was bending over a man who lay prone upon the ground. On his nearer approach the woman looked up, and with a quick gesture flung a veil over the man's face. At this he halted. In the dim light little more than the mere outlines of the two figures was visible; but he had already been given a sign that his presence was not wanted, and, for his part, he had no wish to stay. Quickly rejoining Lalita, he told her that there was nothing to be done, and insisted upon her riding off with him at once.

That was the whole episode; and why should his imagination now plague him with the idea that it might in some way be connected with Lalita's failure to appear? On the face of it, nothing could be less likely. The time and place of their rendezvous could not have been known by anybody beforehand; they had ridden away before anyone could have taken note of their appearance; and, lastly, they had not been followed—of that he was quite sure. No; the fancies he was lending himself to were ridiculous.

8

IT WAS JUST at the moment when his thoughts were reaching this turn that his ear caught the patter of bare feet running along behind him. He drew sharply and waited. Round the bend came Lalita's groom, a man whom they could both trust. There was a letter in his hand, and when Hari had cast his eyes over it, his whole aspect became different. All was well; Lalita's absence was explained by her having received a message from Prince Daniyal to say that his visit, which should have been in the afternoon, was to be paid in the morning instead. She gave him a rendezvous for the next day.

When Hari went on again his spirits had swung back to an even greater height than before. He was one of those people who enjoy their foolish happinesses all the more for being aware of the folly in them; and in this case he yielded to his emotion with the abandonment of a drug-taker reveling in his drug. Once again he became negligent of everything outside the ecstasy of his love; he snapped his fingers at Prince Daniyal; he waved aside the problems of the future; he shrugged over the accident in the wood. In a happy dream he followed the path back to the pavilion; still in a dream he mounted the steps, and it was not until he found himself face to face with Sita that he came back from his visionary world.

She was sitting on the little terrace all alone. In her smiling eyes, as she looked up at him, he thought he detected a glint of raillery. She had driven over, it appeared, to spend the day with Gokal, Amar having taken himself off to Fatehpur-Sikri on a variety of affairs, one of which—she threw this in rather pointedly—was to pay Ambissa a visit. At the mention of his wife's name Hari's face darkened and he actually gave a frown. "Well, I see that you, too, are in no hurry to pay visits at Fatehpur-Sikri!" and his tone, unwarrantably enough, seemed to suggest that they were under equally strong obligations. The truth was that confusion was beginning to creep over him at the thought that there was much in his past conduct to account for. Amar could hardly have avoided saying something . . . and she would certainly consider that he had been guilty of bad taste—yes, very bad taste—to make the least of it.

As he seated himself beside her he racked his brains for something to say. Gokal had just sent out word that he was not to be expected for another half-hour; in the meantime here was Sita, looking so charming, and also—he was sure of it now—faintly disdainful.

Although they were old acquaintances, they were not by any means intimate. He could not do otherwise than suppose that she shared Amar's general disapproval of him; but then she was by no means fond of Ambissa; she viewed her sister-in-law's weaknesses far less tolerantly than Amar, he knew that; so it was reasonable to hope that her attitude towards him on the whole . . . Whilst he was thus inwardly considering, the talk fell to her, and friendly as her tone was, it sounded just a shade too even, too balanced, in his ear. When she said something again about her approaching sojourn in the hills, distraitly he answered that Gokal, too, had taken a house in the Khanjo valley, so it appeared that he would be a near neighbor of theirs.

"Yes, and I am simply delighted to hear it!"

"I expect you will see me there as well. Gokal has asked me to pay him a visit."

He said this without thinking; as a matter of fact he had made no plans, his sole concern at the present time being to keep in touch with Lalita. But directly he had spoken he had cause to regret it, for although Sita again exclaimed, this time, he felt, there was little more than politeness behind her phrases.

In a moment his mind was made up. "Sita!" he said suddenly, "I am sure that what you are thinking about me is not at all to my advantage. I want you to let me explain about last night. Yes, please!" he went on, as she gave a little laugh of protest, "I insist upon your listening. Perhaps your opinion will not be very different when I have done, but I do want you to know the truth."

She opened her eyes as if in wonder at his earnestness. "Of course, I will listen, if you like."

"First of all I have to apologize for my visit. It was not the right thing to do."

For a moment she hesitated. "I think you were using me as a blind."

He colored. "Not in the way you think. It is not true that I have been making love to one of your maids. I made use of that suggestion when I saw the opportunity arise; but it is not the truth."

"Oh!" She looked straight at him in surprise. "Then you were lying to Narsing when you said . . ."

"No. For I am not carrying on an intrigue with anyone at all in the palace. Really I can hardly explain even to myself the impulses that came to me that evening and made me act as I did. I can only tell you that I had an instinct to do something peculiar in order to throw people off the scent . . . in order to build up, if possible, some kind of alibi. The truth is, you see, that I had had an accident a little earlier—in the Royal Hunting Grounds—an accident in which I and another were involved. I think we escaped the risk of subsequent recognition, but as a precaution . . ." And his looks asked her to make the best of what was, to be true, a rather obscure explanation.

"But—was that accident a very serious affair?"

He shrugged. "I cannot tell. Probably not."

"Well! Why, then, was it so important . . . ?"

"Who can tell, in this world, what is important and what is not?"

"There must have been something in your mind," murmured Sita, after a pause.

He threw himself back with a laugh. "You are right. You are right. But"—and he laughed again—"God knows what I had in my mind."

She regarded him with a good deal of curiosity, but said nothing.

"As luck would have it," he went on, "my attempt at an alibi succeeded astonishingly well. Dear old Narsing demonstrated to his complete satisfaction that it was before sunset I entered the palace. I believe Mabun Das is convinced of it too. And Mabun being at the head of Akbar's private spy service, I could hardly have done better." He chuckled. "Whatever comes of that accident, no one is now likely to connect *me* with it."

Sita reflected. "It is quite clear that you are afraid something *will* come of it."

Hari shook his head, laughing. "No. That is just a kind of superstitiousness. The small unexpected things in life so often turn out to be the most disastrous. Wherever I look I see chance ruling the world, and I resent it. And yet," he went on, after a pause, "why should I resent it? My purposes are usually ill-judged and chance really does me a kindness in defeating them. Yes, I am lucky; for, after defeating me, chance quite often throws an unimagined windfall at my feet."

If this was an endeavor to engage Sita's interest, it appeared to fail in its object. While he looked into her face she looked steadily out over the sunlit lake, and he was unable to feel that he had done himself very much good. During the ensuing silence his thoughts always came helplessly back to this: "If only I could tell her that I am in love—seriously in love!" But that could not be said.

All at once she smiled to herself, and this he interpreted hopefully.

"Don't judge me harshly!" he pleaded.

"Why do you set me up as a judge? What does my opinion matter? Anyhow, my dear Hari, I don't understand you at all."

"Oh, yes!" he assured her.

"I don't," she persisted, laughing. "I mean I can't make out what you live *for*."

"But do you know what other people live for?"

"Others do seem to have some sort of focus. They have religion, obligations, ambition—or something. But, of course," she added hastily, "I have no right to talk to you like this."

A faint color had appeared on her cheeks; and her eyes wandered; she was going to get up.

Hari leant forward. "Have you considered what is left to a man like me—living in this age, under Akbar? Ambition has been crushed, obligations are out of fashion, and as for religion—well, there is really too wide a choice. I was brought up as a Muslim, but"—and he shrugged—"Allah, alas! has not kept me orthodox. I have a wife and children, it is true, but—their ways, their tastes, are not mine, I once had political responsibilities, but the Emperor has been graciously pleased to remove them. Well, my dear Sita, what is left?"

There was enough truth in this to give her pause, and as for engaging in argument, that would have been to presuppose a foundation of intimacy that was not there. Although strong in her own faith she was not given to proselytizing; on the subject of Hari's delinquencies as a husband she could not have spoken with much warmth of feeling, for her sympathies did not fall naturally on Ambissa's side; and as for his public duties—well, here no doubt there was something to be said. She could remind him that there had been a time when he had enjoyed the Emperor's favor in a quite unusual degree. She could say that he ought not to find it difficult to win back Akbar's regard, and obtain some honorable post in the Imperial Service. But really she had no particular desire to advance anything; why should she? And while she was still hesitating Gokal made his appearance; on the whole, to her relief.

In the talk that followed Hari took a very small share. A veil of pre-occupation descended over him, and Sita, although slightly intrigued, made no attempt to penetrate it. At a little distance, under the trees by the lake, Jali was trying his luck with rod and line, and presently he let out a shout of mingled triumph and consternation, for he had caught a fish. They all had to hurry down to help him take it off the hook and throw it back into the water before it could come to any harm. Whilst this operation was in progress, Hari, who took no active part in it, stood behind looking out over the water, and for a few moments, rapt utterly away, he was with Lalita in another world. Moreover, it so happened that in one of these moments Sita raised her head. He was never to know it, but her glance rested upon him briefly; the next second she was bending down again, deeply busied with the deliverance of the little fish.

9

IN THE AFTERNOON, during the hour of siesta, Hari rose from his couch and quietly left the house. What took him out in the heat of the day was his anxiety to recover a riding-whip, which Lalita had dropped—at least so she said in her letter—close to the scene of the accident. There was just a chance that this whip, if picked up by someone else, might lead to her identification, for, set in its handle was a sapphire of unusual beauty, a present from Prince Daniyal. He set out, accordingly, determined to make a thorough search. But, to begin with, it was not easy to find the place again, and when at last he found it, he hunted for the whip in vain. Vexed, he was on the point of going back when the idea came to him to explore that region of the wood on the chance of coming upon some clue to the character of the mysterious party and their business in the neighborhood. Faint tracks seemed to indicate that they had taken a small, winding path that went off into the very thick of the undergrowth. He followed these traces for about a mile, and then came to a small clearing. In the middle stood a bungalow, not unlike Gokal's, but smaller, and in a condition of decay. He stood staring at it for some time before advancing across the open ground; for although the clearing was overgrown with weeds and the building itself bore every sign of desertion, he could not prevent himself from imagining that someone was peeping at him from behind the closed shutters. At the door he paused again; from the roof there hung down wisps of dry, gray moss; ants had built a nest against the threshold and the droppings of wood-pigeons whitened the window-sills. Contrary to his expectations the latch came up when he tried it; the door opened and a curious smell spread upon the fresh air. Its chief ingredients, to be sure, were rotting wood, decayed matting and bats' dung; but, to his perplexity, there mingled with these odors the sweet scent of a certain flower. He recognized the scent quite well, but could not at the moment recall from what flower it came.

On either side of the entrance hall there was a door. He tried each in turn and found them locked. None of the other rooms, however, were locked and he found them dusty and bare. On his return to the entrance hall he noticed that it was from the room on the right that the smell of flowers came; it filtered through a lattice that ran high up along the wall. Drawing the hunting-knife from his girdle he attacked the lock and in a few seconds the door yielded. The interior of the room was dark, but from the threshold he could see some objects thrown down in a corner, and gradually his eyes distinguished two or three rolls of rugs, several large bundles wrapped up in white linen, and a great heap of dark flowers. As he stood there a moth fluttered out and blundered into his face; it was a big, white moth, exactly like those that had kept flying into Lalita's face the evening before. His eyes following it about in its blind, aimless flight, he fell into a profound muse.

What roused him at last—or so it seemed to him—was the very intensity of the surrounding silence. It was a silence that magnified every little tick of sound that dared to impinge upon it. Outside the house there was, indeed, the vibration of insects' wings, but inside nothing, nothing.

At last he stirred from his place; he went into the dusky room and threw back one of the shutters. He unfolded the rugs and found them to be of the finest quality; the bundles contained food, wine, spirits, silver drinking-vessels, and some sashes of scarlet silk. The flowers, which had looked black, turned out to be, likewise, scarlet. Having finished this examination, he stood up straight; with pursed lips he nodded slowly to himself; a light—a partial light—had dawned upon him.

Several minutes went by during which he stood looking out through the unshuttered window and frowning intently; he stood there until some fancied sound behind caused him to spin round with a start. After this he closed the shutter and left the room, drawing the door to behind him. Across the passage stood the other door, closed, challenging; his eyes rested upon it in dubiety, and then he again drew his hunting-knife and set to work with a quiet but vigorous hand. A few strong thrusts sufficed; the door opened, revealing a room similar to the other and shuttered, but, facing west as it did, the fierce afternoon sun beat in through the broken slats. There was light enough to show him—in the corner opposite—a girl lying asleep, or rather only half-asleep, for she had been disturbed by his forcing of the door. Still, as it seemed, in a dream she lay there, but her eyes were open and staring. His entry, to all appearances, moved her no more than this: that she lifted her lids to stare at him with wonder.

For his part, Hari stared, and there was no further movement on either side, until, leaning back against the doorpost, he gave her a smile and good day.

That smile lingered on during a further interval of complete silence. She was so lovely, this girl, that while his eyes rested upon her he could not help smiling for pleasure. The freshness of childhood was still hers; what her last year had added was softness and bloom and a depth of luminous secrecy behind the eyes—those eyes that veiled—and in so doing betrayed—a consciousness of sex and beauty. As now she moved into a sitting posture, her light garment falling away, revealed a perfect neck and shoulders. At this she looked down and away, but made no other movement, and still she said nothing.

When Hari addressed her again it was to ask what she was doing there, and who she was. But to these, the most obvious of questions, she seemed unready to make reply. With eyes that looked beyond him rather than at him she murmured that she had been asleep; and vaguely, but enchantingly, she smiled.

After her voice had died away a gradual change came over Hari's face. His gaze became shrewder; he could place her; she was one of millions. Millions were like her in all respects save one—they lacked her astonishing beauty. Carelessly did the potter scatter these common vessels over the earth, so carelessly that when one, such as this, chanced to come flawless from his wheel, no notice did he take, no provision did he make. This was a common flower that might blossom on any dunghill and fall to any fate. Moreover, unless beauty had its special rights, who could say that she deserved better?

Abruptly he fell to questioning her, and there was now a certain sharpness in his tone. But his gaze had already revealed admiration and it was from this that she took her cue.

Playing with the folds of her dress, fingering the braids of her hair, she gave answers that told him nothing. She was as baffling as a stubborn child.

It was not long before he adopted another line. "Let me tell you something. I have been into the other room," he said.

For the first time she showed a trace of disquiet; her gaze seemed to darken, although it remained steady.

"I know," he went on, "what you are here for."

Did he? She tried to brazen it out with a laugh. Well; he knew more than she did! She had no idea—no! She supposed she must have been drugged. And her lids dropped again, her lips parted in a delicate suggestion of a yawn.

One might well have lost patience, and Hari was half-ashamed of himself for not doing so. To be sure, she was deserving of pity, but pity could do nothing for her. Her obstinacy made a fool of him, and the answer was to shrug and leave her. But he was not content to do this until he had found out one thing. After casting about for a moment, he made a fresh start.

"How do you know that I am not one of you?" he asked softly.

She continued to fix him with her deep but guarded stare.

"In any case you had better be frank; if I choose, I can denounce you."

"But I've not done anything! Tell me, what have I done?"

"You came here last night in a company of Vamacharis—Followers of the Left-hand Way."

She was silent.

"Are you not aware that the Maharaj, the Shah-in-Shah, His Imperial Majesty Akbar, has ordered that the Vamacharis are to be trodden to death under elephants?"

Oh, it was a shame, a shame! And she shuddered. It was cruel to frighten a girl like that! What should she know of such things? Nothing! Nothing! And there was a sob in her voice.

Hari came up to her, grasped her beautiful arm and drew her to her feet. At the touch of his hand she at once became self-conscious, cast down her eyes and bent her head. He stood over her, very close.

"Lovely one, what is your name?" he murmured.

She put her beads up to her lips, and although her face remained hidden he could guess that she was regaining confidence. This was the kind of approach she knew best how to meet.

"Tell me, what is there to prevent me...in such a lonely place...from plucking this Flower of Delight?"

Her silence gave him his answer.

Compassion again stirred within him. To be so beautiful and to hold oneself so cheap!

"And if I promise not to betray you," he said softly, "will you then not cease to be afraid?"

Drawing her into his arms: "How old are you?" he whispered.

She was fifteen.

Did she live in Agra?

No, her father had a vegetable plot outside the city gates.

How came it that she was not married?

They were poor.

Of her lovers was there not one she preferred?

Rippling with a soft amusement, she shook her head.

"Tell me," he whispered persuasively. "Have you acted as a Yogini before?"

She looked up with rounded eyes. "A Yogini?"

"That's what they call those who represent the Goddess."

"Oh, I thought you meant the other kind—a Dhuta. I thought: 'O, my mother! does he take me for an evil spirit?'" And she laughed quite gaily.

"Tell me, O Lotus of the Dawn, tell me, why were the rites not celebrated last night?"

"Because there was an accident," she replied, but not without slight hesitation.

A smile of intelligence—which she could not see—flickered over Hari's face.

"An accident!" he echoed in a tone of surprise. "What was that?"

Very briefly she told him. "One man was hurt—stunned. The horses knocked him down."

"And those two riders, the man and the woman, did anyone recognize them? Would any one of you know them again?"

She shook her head. "I don't think so. It was too dark."

"Who was the injured man?"

"Oh," she cried out, "I don't know him."

Hari paused. Was it his own arms that had stiffened or her body within them? After a sigh, he said simply: "I wonder!"

That was as far as he got; his further questions elicited nothing—nothing except that her party had brought her here, given her food and wine (the wine was infused with poppy; he could smell it in her breath), and bidden her wait until they came again.

Not long after this he bade her good-bye, and he could see that his going caused her not only relief but astonishment. Without doubt she had expected to pay a price for his promise of discretion. But she had already given him more than she knew. Just as he was leaving, however, he received a slight shock of discomfort. His eye caught the gleam of something bright that had slipped down between the wall and her mattress. Could it be the handle of Lalita's riding-whip? He had to refrain from questioning; it would have been quite impossible to claim the whip; and inquiries might have aroused suspicion. All that he could do was to stumble against the mattress in an endeavor to shift it and give himself a better view of the intriguing object. But the maneuver failed.

Time and again in the next few days Hari's thoughts went back to the girl, and from that starting-point they wandered off along shadowy avenues of speculation. Although he had already taken Gokal into his confidence as regards Lalita, he abstained, for some reason or other, from telling him anything about this encounter. Nor did he say anything to Lalita about it. She, since her arrival in Agra, was showing symptoms of a new nervousness, a new dread of being found out, and her anxieties at the present time attached themselves in particular to the loss of her riding-whip. About that she was superstitiously apprehensive. Had he been able to provide her with complete reassurance he would, perhaps, have spoken out, but the story would be bound to disquiet her and to stimulate her curiosity rather than satisfy it. What could he find to explain to her about the Vamacharis, that sect, the very name of which was not pronounced in polite society? And then she would be sure to ask how seriously the man had been injured, and who he was. This last question was one that he was particularly anxious she should not fasten upon. In his own mind it was troublesome already. When his thoughts went back to the girl's: "Oh, I don't know him!" he found imagination and memory inextricably confused. His efforts to recover her exact look and intonation only added to his uncertainties. Had the significance of that exclamation disclosed itself to him rightly at the time or had it not? He had received the impression that she wouldn't confess to knowing the man because it would be dangerous. Why dangerous? Because he was a personage. She wouldn't *dare* to know him or even to know who he was. No, no! She had more sense than that.

Such was the meaning that Hari gave to her cry, and the reason why it suggested itself so readily was that it went to confirm an earlier suspicion. The injured man, stretching his length upon the ground, had presented what seemed to him, even in that uncertain light, a figure of some consequence. He couldn't have said exactly why, for no detail of the lineaments or even of the dress had been discernible, but the impression had been definite. And now another idea shot into his mind—this time a very extravagant one. What, he questioned, had Daniyal been doing in Agra at that hour of the night when he had called upon Narsing with some ridiculous inquiry about a hairless cat? Might not the Prince have put in his appearance in obedience to an impulse somewhat similar to his own? The theory was so attractive that it took him some time to convince himself that it stood upon no solid ground whatever. Moreover, when he came to think of it, the figure lying prone had almost certainly been that of a man taller and leaner than Daniyal. It suggested Salim rather than Daniyal. But Salim was at Allahabad.

The days went by and he had almost succeeded in forgetting his last adventure, when, looking out of a back window of Gokal's house one morning, he saw the same girl chatting with the women at work over the trough for linen. He was amazed, and not a little disconcerted. What business had that creature here? What did her presence mean? In this land of subterranean connections, in this land of rumors, denunciations, and blackmail, anything was possible. An angry, helpless suspiciousness assailed him. He went off on the spot to find Gokal; he would tell him all he knew and demand to have the girl's presence explained.

After hearing him out with great interest Gokal broke into exclamations. "Why have you kept this from me until now? I believe I can tell you who she is at once. It must be Gunevati, the sister of poor little Vasumati.... Her father told me that he was going to send for her to take Vasumati's place. You say she is pretty? But she cannot be the equal of Vasumati, who was an angel of loveliness. Let me send for her and we shall see."

Vasumati, as Hari remembered, was the girl whose death had so deeply affected his friend, and it was plain that this news about her sister had thrown him into some excitement. He could not help laughing. "Send for her later—not now." And he explained that he hadn't the smallest wish ever to see Gunevati again. "After what I have told you," he went on, "you will, I imagine, find some excuse for sending her away."

Gokal looked a little confused. He mustn't act harshly, he objected. Her father was a devoted servant; the business would not be so simple, for the truth must be kept from the old man at all costs. Hari turned away to hide a smile, and decided to say nothing more for the moment. When Gokal had taken time to think, he could hardly fail to realize that no one of his caste and position could risk keeping a girl such as Gunevati in his neighborhood. And, having an appointment with Lalita, he hurried off.

Of late Lalita and he had not been able to see much of one another; and in other ways, too, the outside world was making itself felt. They found it impossible to ignore the problem of the future any longer; they discussed it by the hour, but no conclusions of any kind were reached. Lalita's marriage was not yet imminent, but its shadow lay constantly between them; the girl could not refrain from bringing Prince Daniyal's name into the conversation at all moments, and this vexed Hari considerably. By nature he was not jealous and his resentment expressed itself chiefly in anger against the pressure of the world; yet, little by little, his feelings towards Daniyal took on the colors of animosity. Four years ago, he had been entrusted by Akbar with the business of instructing the Prince in the art of the chase, and thus he and the youth of six-teen had been thrown into a comradeship that was not one of their own choosing; and, although they had seemed to get on well enough at the time, since then they had fallen completely apart. Hari found it strange that his thoughts should once again be turned upon Daniyal through this particular chain of events. There were moments when he still dallied with the idea that it was, after all, Daniyal who had been knocked down by Lalita's horse, and if this were so, if Daniyal were in truth a Follower of the Left-hand Way, it could almost be counted a duty (as it certainly would be a plea-sure) to denounce him and bring about such a scandal that the match would be broken off.

One morning, as he was actually nursing these thoughts, on his way back from a meeting with Lalita, at a turn of the woodland path his eyes fell upon the slender figure of Gunevati, who was loi-tering beside the way. There was something in her aspect which suggested that the meeting was no accident, and as he came up he looked her sternly in the eyes. She saluted him with a newly found deference, and broke at once into low-voiced entreaties, begging him to take pity upon her father and herself, and not to influence the holy Brahmin against her. The Brahmin was ready to believe in her repentance—and, in truth, she had already renounced all her evil ways. Without the protection of the holy Brahmin she and her father would wither like uprooted plants.

Hari continued to regard her stonily. He was sorely tempted to question her further on the subject of the accident, but caution prevailed. Seeing that his eyes remained unrelenting, the girl at last bowed her head. In sadness she plucked a twig and let it fall to the ground in token of her resignation to fate.

"Your friends of the other night—let *them* care for you!" said Hari with a resolute brutality. "Will they let you starve—you, an incarnation of the Great Goddess?"

She was silent.

Curiosity crept into Hari's fixed regard. That her companions had chosen her was no wonder, but what did she make of that call?

"I know your rites," he continued after a moment. "Your *upa-charas*, I know them." He threw scorn into his voice and watched for her color to rise.

"They are not pretty—your rites!" And he laughed the laugh of disgust.

"The rites are the rites of the Great Mother."

"You believe that? You believe in her?"

"Everyone believes in her."

He shrugged. "Not everyone worships her with those rites."

"They are prescribed."

"Why then are they hidden—if there is no shame?"

She was silent.

"Are you not also ashamed?"

For a moment she raised her eyes to his. "I stand for the Divinity. I am worshiped according to the prescribed rites."

"What of the other Divinities?"

"The Great Mother is the strongest. Kali's is the power."

She spoke as one uttering an obvious truth, and her tone reduced Hari to speechlessness. Perhaps her unconscious cynicism was deep enough to be accounted innocence. Yes, assuredly, she had the innocence of an animal; and yet . . . In perplexity he said: "But surely to you, a girl so young—those things must have seemed strange?"

She lifted her head once more and gave him a sidelong glance. It was almost ironical and seemed to be accompanied by the shadow of a smile.

"Many things seem strange to a girl at first," she replied.

With a gesture Hari left her and passed on.

10

THE DURBAR, WITH a long program of ceremonies and festivities, was now in full swing, and deeply absorbed as he was by
his private affairs, Hari was obliged, like everybody else, to fall
into place and play his allotted part. The calls upon Lalita's time,
too, were certainly no less urgent; her betrothal to the Prince, by
this time an open secret, was soon to be publicly announced, and
she was already enjoying a foretaste of the honors that would soon
be showered upon her. When she and Hari met together now they
brought a host of pre-occupations with them, and the early days of
their intimacy already seemed very remote. There was no falling
off of their passion, but it was beginning to be a cause of constant
unrest and anxiety.

In one respect fortune continued to be kind. Prince Daniyal was
not pressing his suit with any impatience and the date of the marriage remained as distant and uncertain as ever. But what was to
happen in the end? What was to be the outcome of this intrigue,
which was becoming more dangerous every day? Lalita, to be
sure, had no notion, and up to the time of their arrival in Agra,
Hari had been obstinate in his refusal to look the future in the
face. His problem linked itself on one side to the question whether
he had any chance of obtaining a divorce from his wife. There was
not much hope of success, for the Emperor's sanction would be

necessary, and it was to be expected that the rigor of Akbar's present views on marriage would be stiffened by energetic protests from Ambissa herself. She would object with all the weight of her unquestioned virtue behind her, and public sympathy would be on her side. A divorced woman's standing was little better than a widow's; divorced, she would be obliged to retire from Court.

Any compunction that Hari might have felt on this score, had, however, been destroyed by a recent act of hers. He had just discovered that she had not only become a convert to the Emperor's new religion, but had induced his sons, who were still mere striplings, to follow her example. This action overwhelmed him with rage and wiped out his last scruples. He would have made an urgent appeal to the Emperor without another moment's delay, had any circumstances arisen to bring the second half of his program, marriage to Lalita, anywhere within the realms of possibility.

After an interview with Ambissa, in which he gave himself the pleasure of being extremely disagreeable, he came back to Gokal and said: "I am prepared to admit that my wife is in many ways an admirable woman. She has strength of character, a sense of duty, principles—not high, perhaps, but strong—and no vices, at least in the popular acceptation of the word. Seeing her again after a long absence I am forcibly struck by her good points."

"But . . . ?"

"But—our incompatibility of temperament is complete."

"Is she still fond of you?"

"No. In fact, I think she would hate me if her pride would allow it. She was fond of me once, perhaps; but her affection has faded with the discovery that she cannot alter my nature. She is lucky in that her boys take after her. I consider them prigs; and they, no doubt, have a corresponding opinion of me. But Ambissa loves them as no one else in the world. She is without passion, and her manless state has been irksome to her simply because, having married me, she has felt she had a right to me. Her pride has been injured by the thought of what her friends might be saying; if she has wanted me back, it was not for love's sake, but simply for the sake of appearances. There was a day when she was ambitious for me as well as for herself and her children; she wanted me to make myself a position at Court. That ambition dwindled down to the hope that I would at least live decorously by her side, while *she* worked for the family's advancement; all that she now asks is that I should provoke no scandal and allow her a good share of my income."

This was the whole of what Hari had to say about the interview, but to her brother, the Rajah, Ambissa found a great deal more to report. Amar had chanced to come in not many minutes after Hari had made his departure, and he found her still flushed and palpitating. This agitation soon wore off, but she remained perturbed by the threat of divorce.

After listening to her recital the Rajah only smiled. "Not even Hari," said he, "can find the effrontery to present himself before Akbar with the claim that your adoption of the new religion constitutes grounds for divorce. Those may very well be his private feelings—and there may be others who will sympathize with him; but it would hardly be tactful to present that plea to the Emperor."

With these words the Rajah passed on to another topic, for his sister's action filled him with a secret shame. Perhaps it was to be expected that in the course of time a good many among the Emperor's immediate entourage would stoop to this ignoble form of flattery, but only a few had so demeaned themselves as yet. Ambissa, in her own case, had exhibited an undignified haste, an unseemly alacrity, and, of course, in regard to the boys her conduct was monstrous.

With each day that now went by Hari realized more clearly than ever that his past relations with Lalita had been marked by a singular irresolution and that this could not possibly continue. It was actually a fact—and Gokal, whom he had taken into his confidence, was truly astonished when he heard it—that Lalita was not yet his mistress. Could he, then, at this hour, make up his mind to draw her still further into the tangle of difficulties and dangers that beset their intrigue? Past experience had taught him that the fulfillment of his passion generally marked the beginning of its decline, and now less than ever did he feel disposed to sacrifice her to what might well prove to be a passing infatuation. Nevertheless, the time had come when he had to count chiefly upon his own self-restraint, and this was possible only because he had passed beyond the age of wanton impetuosity. But he was also aware that the moment inevitably arrives when to delay makes a lover ridiculous and is apt to cost him not only what he might have had, but what he already has.

It fell to Gokal to be the witness of Hari's tortures of indecision. One day he would say: "I shall go to Akbar and make a desperate bid for divorce and re-marriage. Although I am older than Lalita, our marriage would give us ten years' happiness at least. And who has the right to ask for more?" Then a little later he would declare: "Our love is real enough; but Lalita, like me, is not made for settled happiness. It is perhaps not unfortunate that our marriage is out of the question. My proper course is to run away with her. She is destined for romance, and romance thrives only on adversity. She would be happier with an outlawed lover than with a comfortable husband." And yet an hour after he would very likely be making a great show of reason to explain that, although a life in the wilds would suit him well enough, it would certainly become intolerable to Lalita, who was habituated to all the diversions of civilization.

Against this same civilization and against Lalita's upbringing he inveighed with a concentrated bitterness. "Don't talk to me about her parents!" he would exclaim. "She owes them nothing at all! And I, for my part, have no scruples whatever in their regard. Her father is a big, heavy, arrogant man inflated with pride of birth; her mother is worldly and hard. Lalita's training, from her earliest years, has been calculated to turn out a young female of the greatest possible seductiveness—the idea being that her allurements should purchase her a high place in Society. All her mother's thought has gone to details of dress, deportment, and toilet. The girl has been given the equipment of a courtesan, her innocence, her virginity, being reckoned merely as an added grace. Long before vanity came to lend her patience, she was compelled to give most of her time and thought to the art of arousing men's desire. And now, I ask, has all that been fair to her—or to *me*? A trap was set, and the wrong victim happens to have fallen into it. For victim I am; and as such, why should I be considerate towards my snarers? As for Lalita, it speaks well for her that she has not acquired the heart as well as the arts of the courtesan. It is to her honor that she has been willful, reckless, and defiant, in her sense of wrongdoing.

'We love one another!' she says; and at once it becomes a delicious and justifiable prodigality to give without thought of gain."

Gokal was sparing in reply, having the wit to see that nothing he could say would be of any avail. In the privacy of his own mind he both marveled and pitied, for although by nature inclined to sentiment, his ideas about love had the cut-and-dry cynicism of the pure theorist. It was true that Hari would sometimes cry out in a fury: "What did God make young women for, if not to be seduced?" But he would also spend much time in reviewing the many excellent reasons for going no further. Most of these reasons took their point from the character of the girl herself. "Lalita," he explained, "is under the tyranny of what she calls her conscience. But this conscience, the product of a schoolroom morality, is quite unsupported by true conviction. Instinct bids her obey the promptings of her heart; but her false conscience loads her with fears. It exaggerates in her that dislike of the furtive which is common to nearly all of us and amounts in reality to little more than the dread of the shame of being found out. It is much easier to defy the world with a spectacular gesture than to endure for long the strain and risk of cheating it."

Hari was speaking with a certain bitterness because he could not induce Lalita to shoulder even the smallest share of responsibility for the issue. She used her intelligence to evade every appeal that was made to it. Unconsciously she demanded to be coerced, and allowed every small advance in their intimacy to be followed by an intensification of her scruples and fears. For some time past their meetings had taken place in a deserted hunting-box in the Royal Hunting Grounds, a building almost exactly similar to the one in which the encounter with Gunevati had occurred. He had secretly fitted up one of the rooms with all the things required for their comfort, and in the privacy of this retreat he and she sometimes managed to spend as much as half a day together. What happened on these occasions was that, after sharing a light meal with him, Lalita would yield to his instances and stretch herself out upon the divan for a siesta. The hours they had passed upon that couch together certainly left very little value in her virginity; and now he could not help reflecting that if her surrender had been complete from the beginning they would have been saved many scruples that had worn rather thin and many heart-searchings that were likely to be useless. Even their parting, if it came, would wear an ambiguous aspect; it would come, not because they willed it, but because they had lacked the strength to will otherwise.

In this condition of affairs very little was required to precipitate a crisis. With the exception of Gokal, Hari had admitted no one into his confidence—not even the best of his women friends, Srilata Begum. And yet it was through the agency of Srilata that the crisis ultimately arose. This remarkable woman was a half-sister of Amar's and Ambissa's, but just as they bore small resemblance to one another, so she had little in common with either of them. If, like Ambissa, she had a fondness for the world, the attraction she yielded to was of a very different order. What she looked for was not an enhancement of her own social value, but simply entertainment. If she had early dropped out of the high society so assiduously courted by Ambissa, it was for no other reason than that it bored her. A certain level of culture, a good deal of sophistication and a ready wit—this was what she demanded of her company. The air of the court was too heavy; solid virtues, solid abilities, unrelieved by finesse, did not interest her any more than commonplace stupidity or vice. On the other hand, although, like Amar, she had a consciousness awake to spiritual things, she was entirely lacking in his intellectual and moral fervor and had no other aim than to live lightly. She could endure a dilettantism and triviality that positively nauseated her brother, and she was tolerant of every variety of spiritual corruption. This tolerance of vileness in others stood in singular contrast to the high standard which she set up for herself. Amar did not misunderstand her on this point, but he had no taste for visiting her house, and as for Ambissa, whilst less sensitive to its atmosphere, she shunned it simply because she felt herself to be, intellectually, at a disadvantage there.

The friendship between Hari and Srilata had arisen at a time when Ambissa had pressed her sister into the role of peacemaker. Hari was then living in Agra and the friendship thus initiated had quickly developed into intimacy. In Amar's eyes there was something almost as incongruous about this alliance as about Hari's alliance with Gokal. But there it was!

There would have been nothing unnatural in Hari's turning to Srilata in his perplexities and laying the whole story of his love-affair before her. But this he had not done. Moreover, soon after his arrival in Agra, when Lalita mentioned to him that she had made Srilata's acquaintance, his only response—thrown out in an off-hand way—was that he knew her and considered her very good company. What was not his astonishment, therefore, when now—after many weeks during which Srilata had not been mentioned—Lalita came out with the news that *she* had told Srilata everything, had poured out the whole tale of her troubles and asked for advice.

For quite an appreciable interval after hearing this Hari stared in silence. To have had recourse to a sister of Ambissa's seemed an extraordinary proceeding, but—if Lalita had really known what she was about—it showed a pretty gift of discrimination. There was a queer look in Hari's face as he asked what Srilata's advice had been. Lalita had already said that she had come away from the interview charmed, sustained, comforted; but all she could now find to answer was: "She said it was all very difficult; one had to think . . . and why didn't you come and see her?"

Hari smiled. He recognized Srilata's loyalty, circumspection, and freedom from prejudice. He would go—of course; he promised Lalita that; and then, after they had parted, he retired into a long communion with himself. Or no! It was rather with an evocation of Srilata that he communed, and the results were truly astonishing. Up till now he had cherished the belief that he had given his love-affair a scrutiny from every possible angle. And yet, as he now rehearsed, step by step, the scene of the colloquy before him, he found that more than half his accepted ideas had to be thrown away. Hasty amendments and admissions were needful all the time—explanations that he had never seen any necessity for until now. And so it was that this puppet, animated by his own ventriloquism, became a revealer of the hard truth of things.

When this hour was over he stared aghast at the decisiveness of its results. Unavailingly he took refuge in anger, expending his last energies in an exasperated attack upon Srilata herself. Who was she, after all, that he should defer to her judgment? That desiccated impartiality of hers that awarded to generosity and calculation, to pleasure and self-discipline, to quixotism and expediency, each cynically their due—how was anything valuable to emerge from it? With all the antagonistic elements in equipoise why should the scales tip in favor of this or that? And yet they did—quite definitely, and a conclusion was registered that he could not disregard. It bore the stamp—not of morality, nor of common sense, nor of expediency, nor of good taste, alone; but of an authority compounded of them all. "I will pay Srilata the visit she suggests," he said to himself. "But we shall not find it necessary to talk very long about my private affairs." And so it turned out; for a few minutes only Lalita came under discussion; there was a slight pause, and then the talk passed on.

Not many days later Hari found himself upon his way to what was actually to be the last meeting. Completely worn out in heart and brain he dragged himself dully along. The little house, crouching under its thick cover of trees, seemed to look out at him slyly as he approached it; the room that had been the shelter of his secret intimacy wore a blank face, had a blank silence, that seemed to convey a sneer. A kind of shame mixed with a kind of self-scorn kept him standing there, in the middle of the floor, to survey this and that familiar object with an expression of distaste. At last, however, he sat down and with fixed gaze simply waited.

Lalita's countenance, when she came in, gave him a reflection of his own inward state. The smile she summoned quickly flickered out, and in his arms she held herself stiff and cold, her sad eyes staring widely before her. Yes, her capacity for feeling had run out just like his; so here they stood in the end, without spirit, in the clutches of an unhappiness that had stripped even itself of grace.

He said: "I came prepared, as you know. . . . But is this actually our last meeting?"

Mutely she inclined her head.

"You say it must be?"

"Yes, it must—it must."

A wave of bitterness passed over him. "All the same you will find—when I have gone out of your life . . ."

He could not finish. Her face had quivered into an expression of unhappiness that he could not bear. In silence they drew apart and seated themselves upon the divan; in silence they stared at the truth. What they were submitting to was the inadequacy of their love—that wretched love, which, nevertheless, had such power to torment them. In the face of this spiritual impotence nothing remained to be said—nothing true, at any rate, that was worth saying and nothing worth saying that was true.

"I suppose," he said, "I suppose we shall both get over this more quickly than we think." And when she gave no sign of having heard him he went on: "You will have plenty to distract you at all events. And then this charming marriage.... I hear that your mother is giving a reception for the Prince to-night."

"No. To-morrow night."

"To-morrow? No matter. To-morrow...and then the next day...there will always be something. We won't think about each other more than we can help."

Again he lost himself in his misery. But his eyes fastened upon the sunlight outside. In the freedom of the sky, with the rush of the wind behind them, clouds were flying. Only Lalita and he were imprisoned in misery; shut up in the circle of their insistent memories and the craving of the heart.

All at once her hand shot out, sought his and closed upon it. He returned the pressure of her fingers for one moment and then rose to his feet. The quicker this was all over the better. But he wanted to find something deeply felt first—a word to remember having spoken. Standing a little way back he regarded her intently. With perversity he sought to extract from these instants the full measure of their pain; he revived his most blissful memories; he jeered at himself over his loss.

"Come!" he said at last, and invited her to rise.

She paid no attention to his outstretched hand; she sat looking straight before her.

"I love you," she said in a low voice, "and I am terribly unhappy."

He began a gesture and then checked it.

"Come!" he said again.

She rose and together they left the house. After locking the door behind them, he walked by her side along the narrow path. A few moments brought them within sight of the groom who was holding her horse.

He said: "I think we had better not write."

She winced. "You think not?"

"If we are never to see one another again. . . ."

"We might write just once," she murmured.

After a moment's thought he nodded. Yes; they might write just once—to amend this parting.

The groom was now quite near and their steps, which had retarded, stopped at last completely. "Good-bye, Lalita," he said very low.

She looked at him, caught at her breath, and then turned and ran to her mount. On his side he walked rapidly away.

11

ALL THESE WEEKS Amar had been working diligently in the pursuit of his various ends, and by no means without success. He had settled some troublesome question here, safeguarded his rights there; and now his little principality, he could say, stood as firm and sound outside and in as it was possible to make it. None of this, however, had been accomplished without effort, and it had been brought home to him afresh that he and Akbar were not made to understand one another. Had he been more fortunate in this respect he might have effected in half an hour what had actually cost him many weeks of difficult indirect negotiation. Altogether, he was not sorry that this season was drawing to a close; he had found Imperial Court functions excessively tedious; and the tone of the society at Fatehpur-Sikri was—just as he knew it would be—much less agreeable than that of his own little court. He had been prepared for a good deal of ostentation and even a certain grossness; but it was not the prevailing lack of taste that had displeased him most. Far worse was the atmosphere, heavy and thunderous with intrigue.

At the forefront of his mind during the whole period there stood, naturally, the question of his retirement from the world, and this pre-occupation enclosed him in a secret cell from which he watched, with gathering disquietude, the increasing pressure of rivalry between the two great factions in the Empire. There was a party which, whilst remaining loyal to Akbar, cherished the hope that the Emperor would make concessions to Salim and name him as his successor to the Throne. The other party fastened its ambitions upon Prince Daniyal; it was to this party that Ambissa belonged; and from the first she had strongly, if rather mysteriously, urged her brother to attach himself to it. This, however, the Rajah was not entirely prepared to do. So closely had Daniyal managed to seclude himself within the circle of his own particular friends, so adroitly had he avoided the ordinary run of court functions, that although it had been one of the Rajah's principal objects to make his acquaintance, he found his time at Agra drawing to a close without having done better than to catch sight of the Prince once or twice in the dim distance. Ambissa had promised more than once to bring about a meeting, but somehow nothing had come of it. On the other hand she missed no opportunity of assuring him that Daniyal was charming, that his faults were only those of youth, that he stood very high in his father's esteem, and that he would almost certainly be chosen for the Throne. Amar allowed these words no more than their proper weight; and when, after many weeks, he discovered by chance that Ambissa's acquaintance with Daniyal was of the slightest, he was more irritated than surprised. But, he reflected, her confidence in the young man's future must be strong indeed, if, instead of giving way to pique at her virtual exclusion from his circle, she still obstinately spoke well of him. The explanation probably was that, as a woman of principle, she felt obliged to entertain a high opinion of the man to whose party she was giving her allegiance.

At the moment that this last reflection was passing through his mind, the Rajah became aware of a certain moral discomfort. It sometimes happened thus. After criticizing Ambissa he would be stung by the query whether those same strictures would not, in some degree, apply to himself. Of course he did want to convince himself that Daniyal's was the right side to take, but that was very different from wanting to deceive oneself, surely? Right at the beginning he had admitted Gokal into his confidence and obtained from him the promise that he would watch over Jali during his minority and help Sita with advice; but he had not then been able to speak definitely about his policy. Animated by new scruples, he now went to Gokal again and exposed fully the trend of his recent activities. He supposed, he said, that Gokal would agree that the road he had been mapping out for Sita and Jali was, all things considered, the right one.

To his astonishment, Gokal demurred. And although, when pressed for his reasons, he lapsed into inarticulacy, Amar gathered that he had formed an unfavorable opinion of Daniyal's private character. But Gokal also protested that he knew very little about the Prince and advised Amar to seek information elsewhere. Upon this Amar bethought him of Srilata, and going to her house the next day he discovered, to his extreme surprise, that Daniyal was quite a friend of hers. This fact Ambissa—although she must certainly have known it—had not thought fit to communicate to him; and he began to think that a good deal of the time he had spent in listening to her had been wasted. Once again, however, he made the experience that Srilata's *milieu* was decidedly uncongenial. Her rooms were crowded with people whose appearance and manners he did not much care about, and the only person in the house that he knew was Mabun Das. After arranging to come again for a quiet talk the next day, he left precipitately but with the feeling that he would probably have done better to stay. There was no sense in holding oneself superior to Mabun Das, who was a man of ability and obviously destined to rise high in the world, and as for the empty-headed, affected youths who figured so largely among Srilata's guests, they were very likely members of Daniyal's set, whom it would have been worth his while to study a little, especially as it was too late now to get Srilata to arrange a meeting with Daniyal himself, for the Prince—she had just told him this—was on the point of leaving for the Hills.

The next afternoon, as he was being ushered out into the peach-garden at the back of Srilata's house, he heard a voice under the pagoda and recognized it as Hari's. It was a long time since he had come across his brother-in-law or even thought of him, although his mind had at first gone back occasionally to Hari's unaccountable behavior six weeks ago; and once or twice he had gone so far as to wonder whether Hari might not have been actuated by some mad impulse to make advances to Sita. But that idea had never really formed itself fully, and after Ambissa's complaint of Hari's threat to divorce her it was completely extinguished. He had argued that if Hari were really anxious for a divorce, the reason must be that he wanted to marry again; and that in its turn could only mean that he was in love with some unmarried girl whose favors he could not obtain outside wedlock.

To find Hari here now did not suit him very well because he wanted to conduct his inquiries confidentially, and even, if possible, without making Srilata over-curious as to his reasons for taking so special an interest in the young Prince's character. The first words spoken, however, showed him that his arrival had not been so unhappily timed after all.

"Do come to my aid!" Srilata called out. "Hari is taking me to task for being a friend of Prince Daniyal's."

"Perhaps," answered Amar, smiling, "I, too, should be taking you to task, if I knew rather more about the Prince."

Hari gave a short laugh. "My impression," said he rather dryly, "has always been that you shared Srilata's partiality." And then, turning to his hostess, he went on: "Give him your latest piece of news; I shall be interested to see how he takes it."

His tone was rather surly and he was looking, Amar thought, decidedly out of sorts. The next moment, however, the Rajah's attention was entirely taken up by what Srilata was saying; she had heard that Prince Daniyal was about to make a public and spectacular declaration of his conversion to his august father's new religion.

This came as an unpleasant surprise, but instinctively, Amar dissimulated. "Have you got that on really good authority? As you must know, people for some time have been speculating. . . ."

Srilata nodded to express her certainty and then went on to tell the following story: "One evening, about a week ago, the Prince called at this house dressed in a wonderful flowing robe of white and silver with the words 'Allahu Akbar' embroidered upon his breast. He paraded up and down the room in front of me with great delight—you know what a child he is in such matters—and when I complimented him, he told me that he had designed the costume himself. I then said—quite foolishly, I'm afraid—that I supposed it was intended for a fancy-dress ball. He laughed, and looking at me rather queerly, answered: 'You are right; that's what it is—fancy dress!' And now—just think—I have heard that that marvelous robe is what he has designed for himself in the character of high priest in the Din Ilahi. Apparently he is to be raised to an important position in the new religious hierarchy almost at once."

Srilata was laughing, and Amar pretended to take the matter in the same spirit, but, in reality, he was a good deal put out. He realized that the Prince's decision had great political significance, but even more important to him was the light shed upon the young man's character. The trouble lay here. It was not for himself that he was settling a future policy; it was for Sita. And that made a world of difference. For his part he found little difficulty in sifting out questions of personality from questions of policy, but Sita was otherwise constituted. And once one had recognized that, it became impossible, obviously, to commit her to an allegiance that would be offensive to her own personal standards.

After a little Hari got up and went away, and then Amar took the bull by the horns. "Now listen, my dear Srilata, I am just at the end of my stay here and all my policy has been oriented in the direction of Daniyal. It has seemed fairly obvious to me that Daniyal was to be preferred to his brother, who is an ill-educated, drunken boor and a rebel to boot. It is true that I know Daniyal only by report; but report does not appear to have anything very serious against him. I understand that he is trivial-minded, an amateur of the Arts, and without much sense of the responsibilities of his position; but what is there in that? He appears to appreciate the worth of serious men such as Abu-l-Fazl, Man Singh, and Mobarek, and so long as these stand behind him and make up for his deficiencies, the Empire will not get out of gear. Well, I was saying this to Gokal the other day, when, to my surprise, he began to murmur and mutter against Daniyal. And when I pressed him for his objections he did nothing but continue his mutterings. All I could get out of him in the end was this: 'Prince Daniyal is a leader of fashion.'"

With these last words Amar gave a little laugh, raised his eyebrows, and fixed his sister with a look of patient questioning. Srilata laughed, too, but on rather a dubious note, and as her answer did not come at once, he went on: "Now, what is it that lies at the bottom of Gokal's prejudice? What inspires Hari, too, with such a decided antipathy? Surely you, my dear Srilata, who are by way of liking the Prince, can give me a little enlightenment?"

"I have never said I *liked* him," Srilata protested, after a moment's pause; "but I admit, he amuses me."

"Ah! he amuses you," sighed Amar.

"Yes. Of course he is really trivial in character, as you say, but —well, there must be some frivolity in the world, my dear Amar! And then . . ."

She did not finish her sentence, and for a while Amar studied her in silence. She was thinking of him, he well knew, as a little cramped by prudishness. In his view, on the other hand, her placid overlooking of moral standards simply meant that her taste was one-sided, incomplete. Perhaps even she halted, with most of the world, at that stage where immorality still retains a certain glamour. Nor was she sophisticated enough to hold sophistication cheap.

"If Daniyal is merely trivial," he said slowly, "I don't see how he can be—even amusing."

Srilata disliked argument. "He has, at any rate, a light touch." And her glance was faintly ironic.

"A light touch!" murmured Amar. "He has a light touch. He is a leader of fashion. He is amusing."

Over this he knit his brows with exaggerated concentration. "Should *I* think him amusing?" he asked, with seeming innocence.

"I don't think you would."

"Perhaps not," said Amar, still pondering. "Perhaps merely foolish."

He was hoping to prick Srilata into saying something more, but he failed; and in silence he reflected that her indications, as far as they went, were satisfactory. If Daniyal was a nonentity, he could proceed without scruple along the path that he had chosen. He would explain matters to Sita and she would rest content.

When he next looked up it was to meet Srilata's eyes. They were satirical; obviously she was being reticent. How irritating people sometimes were!

As if not unaware of his feelings she gave a little laugh of apology. "You were talking of Gokal just now; surely one reason for his not liking Daniyal has suggested itself to you? Behind Daniyal there stands Mobarek, and Mobarek, as you know, is far from being a friend of Gokal's. Then, as for Hari's dislike of Daniyal, don't you remember that those two were sent off on a hunting expedition together three or four years ago? Well, I imagine that Hari might very easily have taken a dislike to the Prince then."

This was all very reasonable, and Amar nodded his assent. Perhaps, after all, he was becoming fanciful about Daniyal. In any case, there was nothing more to be got out of Srilata; and yet, just before leaving the house, something impelled him to round upon her and say: "Tell me this, what should *I* think of Daniyal, if I knew him as well as you?"

Srilata's face became thoughtful. "He is not the kind of person you could approve of," she said quietly.

So it was with this, which was just what he did not want to hear, that Amar finally took his leave.

12

ON THE EVE of their departure to the Hills Sita and Jali drove over to Gokal's pavilion to say good-bye. The sky was overcast, the afternoon warm and still. As they trotted along under the trees, a vague sadness oppressed them both; and Sita knew that her depression had very little to do with leaving Agra, but she was uncertain about Jali. Jali had developed a great affection for Gokal, who had been giving him the course of spiritual instruction proper to a boy emerging out of childhood. She reminded him that Gokal would be joining them shortly.

As soon as they reached the little wicket-gate Jali dived in among the trees. It was his habit now, outside the hours of his instruction, to wander away into the woods; and there he would remain hidden until they called to him that it was time to go back. So Sita went on alone up the little path by the lake-side; and Gokal, who was sitting upon the terrace under a large umbrella, looked up from his book and saw her coming, and forthwith took his horn spectacles from off his nose and rose to meet her with a smile of pleasure. She was looking, he thought, more charming than ever, and this admiration was no doubt reflected in his smile. At any rate, Sita's heart warmed towards him and she returned his unspoken compliment with the laughing declaration that his figure, as he sat there on the terrace, had all the dignity and serenity of Buddha.

They had not been talking together for very long before she was tempted to introduce the subject of Hari. She and Hari had scarcely seen each other at all in the last weeks, his confidences had never been renewed, and so she was left with a good deal of unsatisfied curiosity. The question that kept cropping up in her mind was: "Is he really in love? Is he capable of being really and truly in love?" But to ask Gokal for his opinion was not a thing that she could allow herself to do. Almost certainly it would not be possible for him to give an answer without falling into some breach of confidence. Moreover, there was another matter in her mind beside which all others sank into insignificance, and upon this other matter she was fully resolved to speak. For some time past something in Amar's manner had given her a suspicion that he might be contemplating retirement from the world. She had said nothing; she shrank from questioning him about it; it seemed to her that she hardly had the right to question; the first word ought to come from his side. But there was no reason why she should not sound Gokal; it would be easy for him to put her off should he wish to; he could say he knew nothing.

The conversation in the meantime had come round to the Din Ilahi, and Gokal's earlier cheerfulness was clouding over. Did she remember, he asked, that little old man with whom she had seen him talking not many days ago? Well, that was Shaik Mobarek, and Shaik Mobarek had visited him again only the other day in order to bring the news of Prince Daniyal's conversion. Furthermore, this meant that the Din Ilahi was to be publicly proclaimed.

In the pause that Gokal made here, Sita remained silent. She was trying to interpret his words in their full significance. She knew that those who adopted the Din Ilahi had to abjure their former faith and renounce their right of judgment on matters of belief, accepting the Emperor as sole and infallible interpreter of God's will upon earth. But Amar had also told her that in itself, and apart from this, the new religion contained nothing positively bad. It was a Theism broad and simple enough to include everything and signify nothing. Why, then, should Gokal, who was notoriously latitudinarian, take on quite so grave an air? She could not help suspecting that his main concern must be personal; he must be worrying about his own position and the dignities which self-respect might force him to renounce. She sympathized, but her sympathy was tinctured with impatience, for she had always thought that Gokal valued the world too highly. She wouldn't call him a snob—oh no! he would never, for instance, sacrifice a friendship—but in his transactions with the world he must surely have made more than a few little sacrifices of self-esteem. How, otherwise, could he have attained to his actual position at Court? Not through intellectual eminence alone could any man, however highly gifted, hope to stand high in the world.

"Mobarek came to crow over me," continued Gokal sadly. "To him all this is a triumph, while in my eyes it is a disaster. I am convinced that Akbar is committing a terrible folly. And yet," he went on after a silence, "I abstain from condemning him. I know no standard by which such men can be properly judged. The ordinary canons do not apply to Men of Destiny. Such men may be speaking truly when they impute their actions to the decrees of fate. They feel themselves to be the vehicles of a purpose which they do not understand. This is their greatness, if it is also their limitation. In a sense they are puppets."

"But Akbar is not merely a man of action," objected Sita, "he is a thinker, a philosopher, as well."

Gokal gave a smile. "Akbar is a mystic rather than a thinker. Mind you, I do not wish to suggest that mysticism and hard thinking are necessarily incompatible. Thought carried far enough passes beyond its own sphere, or rather becomes aware of its own limitations. It sees the human reason operating in the ocean of being as a special limited kind of activity. But Akbar's inner life is emotional rather than intellectual. He is no thinker."

"At any rate," answered Sita, "he is a seeker after God. Who can doubt it after setting eyes upon the Gate of Victory at Fatehpur-Sikri and reading the inscription over the arch? 'Said Jesus, on whom be peace: The world is a bridge. Pass over it, but build no house therein. Who hopes for an hour hopes for Eternity. Spend the hour in prayer. The rest is unknown.'" There was a thrill in her voice as she spoke, and she added: "Akbar is almost a Christian."

Gokal's hand made a gesture in the air: he smiled and kept his peace.

For a space, during which their eyes rested upon the lake, there was no sound but the cooing of the pigeons in the trees. How lovely the water was with the shadows lengthening over it! Not a breath ruffled its surface; it reflected glassily the faint warm colors of the sultry sky. As her thoughts wandered, Sita's face became dreamy. It was a face, thought Gokal, the beauty of which deepened in tranquillity. It was like the lake. Even so did her beauty shine forth, self-subsistent, an answer that was yet no answer. . . . And he sighed.

"I want you to tell me something," she said, turning towards him suddenly. "For some time past—I really do not know how long—there has been a feeling in my heart that Amar . . ."

No reply came to fill her pause, but Gokal kept his eyes fixed upon her, and she saw them gradually deepen with a grave and speaking sympathy.

"Will it be soon?" she asked, her voice very low.

"Not too soon. . . . No, he will do everything rightly."

So it had come at last! For thirteen years they had been married and it seemed to her now that this was what she had unconsciously begun to expect before half those years had gone by. She was not startled, only saddened. But resolutely she thrust her sadness aside; it was not what she wanted to think about.

"I understand. But it will be difficult for him to leave Jali and—and everything. . . . Yes," she continued tonelessly and with far-gazing eyes, "I understand, and yet it seems to me strange."

"In our country, as you know, men often do this thing. At a certain age, after a man has discharged his duty as a husband, father, and citizen, he responds to another call."

"You are a strange people. But perhaps I can understand."

He sighed, partly from relief.

"And yet, how can God be served," she went on suddenly, "if not in this world—the world into which he has sent us?"

"The value of service," returned Gokal gently, "is recognized by Brahmin and Buddhist alike. The *Upanishad* says: 'In darkness are they who worship only the world, but in greater darkness they who worship the infinite alone. He who accepts both saves himself from death by the knowledge of the former and attains immortality by the knowledge of the latter.' Buddha, too, has said much the same thing. Where we differ from you is in our recognition of the value of holiness. In our minds the relation of man to man is secondary, right conduct following naturally when the relation of man to God is made perfect. Moreover, there is no greater benefit that a man can confer upon his fellows than the example of his own spiritual achievement. We have a saying: 'The perfume of a flower travels before the wind, but the perfume of holiness travels even against the wind.'

"Amar has love in his heart," continued Gokal, speaking low and urgently, "but he believes that love should be indistinguishable from compassion, and that compassion should be exercised through the understanding rather than through the emotions. Love, therefore, should be a recognition of the unity of all consciousness, a comprehension of the goal of all consciousness, and a desire to assist all fellow-creatures towards that goal."

"You can read many of my thoughts," said Sita. "Don't you then also know that I shall never be able to accept Amar's view of life?"

"I, myself, do not accept it," answered Gokal after a moment's pause, "neither do I reject it entirely. I think that you of the Western world should consider carefully whether you have not made an error in idealizing the will to live. Life! The enrichment of life! The intensification of life! The prolongation of life into eternity! Does this obsession have any heartfelt meaning behind it? Do these notions contain a coherent ideal at their core? Buddhism says no! and waits in silence until the intoxication is over, until the commotion has died down."

"So all the world is to turn Buddhist in the end?" And Sita shook her head. "No, I, for my part, shall always affirm what Amar denies. Between us there is a gulf."

Gokal leaned forward earnestly. "The gulf lies not between those who affirm and those who deny, but between those who affirm and those who ignore. Listen!" he went on, "I believe that between your affirmations and our denials there is, in reality, little more than a long difference of mental habit. Fundamentally your mind and Amar's are similar in type; you both raise the same problems and the answers you give are the same in essence, if their substance is not the same. You advocate life's intensification,

Amar its extinguishment; but you both recognize imperfection and you both aim at perfection. Your goal is the same whatever names you give it."

Sita was silent for a moment, then she stretched out her hand. "Gokal, you are very kind to me. I shall turn to you in the days to come."

After the sound of her voice had died away the stillness that fell seemed to hold a particular significance. They sat looking before them, looking at the sheet of luminous water that made a great emptiness at their feet. The dull reddish tints of the sky were reflected in it; the emptiness stretched beneath and above.

At last Gokal drew a long breath that was also a sigh. "I hope I shall be wiser for you than I am for myself."

These words were pronounced in a tone that seemed to mark them for his ear alone. It was in quite another voice that he presently resumed speech. He fell into a discourse on Akbar, on the Empire, on the eternal problems of life and religion. Listening, Sita felt that a little while ago she had done him an injustice. His grave voice carried her into new domains of thought. It was as if he had rapt her up on to some mountain height and were pointing with outstretched arm over unexplored regions of the world.

13

IT WAS NOT until she reached the freshness of the foothills that Sita realized what a dust of weariness had settled down upon her spirit at Agra. Although it was against her intentions she had been drawn further and further into the vortex of festivities at Fatehpur-Sikri, and even her friendships in the Agra Palace had suffered from the rivalries and jealousies that emanated from the Imperial Court. It was depressing to look back on. So much time and energy devoted to formal pomposities or else expended upon small frivolities and trivial excitements into which one had to infuse a gaiety that did not naturally belong to them. However, she could now console herself with the thought that it was not altogether a mistake to give that way of living an occasional trial, for one returned with an even greater content to the pleasures that came to one by nature.

The country through which they were now passing did actually remind her of the Caucasus. Its torrents and flowery meadows, its heavy forests and cool, dewy nights—these brought back not only the memories, but the actual feelings that had been hers in early days. She thought of her parents and their friends, of all the old life that wars and disasters had broken up. It seemed very far away now; and yet that dimness and distance were still home. Memory revived made the civilization into which she had been transplanted seem outlandish again.

Jali was almost the age that she had been when her father had fled from the Caucasus; but how strangely different the type of childhood he presented! What would she have said in those days if he had been shown to her in a dream as the boy who was to be her own son? As she considered this, it struck her that he had changed a good deal during their stay at Agra, but she could not define exactly in what the change consisted. A great part of his aloofness and timidity had gone; he was more boyish now and carried himself with more spirit. But there was something, all the same, in these recent developments that she did not altogether like. "People are changing little by little the whole time," she thought, "but one only notices it at a special moment by a special opening of the eyes."

She was standing before the door of her tent as these reflections drifted through her mind. It was the seventh day of their journey, the plains already seemed to lie far beneath them, and suddenly, against the light of the setting sun, there hobbled up an old woman, hideously bowed and seamed and withered by her years. She held out a shaking hand and said: "Great Lady, may many years and much love stand between you and me!" Sita made no reply, but called to her maid for money and held out some coins in a hand that trembled as much as the old crone's. Yes, the day would surely arrive when for her, too, weariness and bodily decrepitude would stretch a veil over the beauty of the world, making its songs and its flowers and its joys dim and remote. Nor was that all. She would feel that she no longer formed a part of the world's beauty herself. Nothing would be left then but a husk, a shell, a failing old woman, who had once been happy and young.

With a mumbled blessing the old hag shuffled away, and Sita's eyes fell upon Jali, who, a little way off, was sitting cross-legged upon the ground. He sounded a few notes upon a *vina*, and presently, in the thin nasal tone of the people, struck up one of the common songs that he knew:

> Dearest Lord, what art thou?
> Thou art the tiny bundle
> Which thine own
> Little mad woman
> Holds always to her heart.

Little mad woman, I,
And thou her precious bundle, her darling treasure,
Of old torn rags.
On these my head,
When I am wearied by the dusty road,
Rests and I sleep in peace.

Men in the streets point at me,
Laugh at me,
And throw dust.
Some try to pluck thee from my heart;
"Cast him away!" they cry.
Rama! Rama! But how
Could thy mad beggar-woman live without thee?
Little mad woman without her lord, her love?

No. I hurry past.
Hugging thee to my breast,
I go on alone,
Smiling because this mad, mad heart of mine,
Holding thee, holdeth love.

The tears sprang into Sita's eyes, and hiding her face from Jali, she turned and went into the tent. The setting sun sent a dusky glow through the canvas. In the red dusk of the tent she wept for loneliness, while the thin chant of compassionate indifference went on outside. Jali was his father's son; alien like his father; and she longed for her native land and for a people unlike these, whose very tenderness floated upon waters of resignation and sorrow.

Every day their march took them higher into the thin cool air of the hills. From their turning, twisting path they looked down over the heads of dark deodars and huge blossoming rhododendrons. In the early morning, when they made their start, the sun and the mist would still be competing, and then, for half an hour after the mist had vanished, a million dewdrops sparkled on the dark needles of every pine.

For many days after her arrival at Khanjo, Sita did little but wander in the woods, and she found herself taking a delight in them that at times was almost ecstatic. Her spirit melted into an exquisite closeness to the whole visible world; and the visible world she felt to be a garment of God. On coming home in the evening she would find Amar still dreamy from his meditations. In his mind the enjoyment of beauty was not an end in itself, nor even a means of approach to the ultimate goal. It took its place among the higher pleasures, but it was only subsidiary. The Path guided you away from the sensuous world altogether, away from yourself, away from the ardors of earth even at their keenest and purest. Her nature rebelled against this outlook and her companionship with Amar was spoilt by a sense of ceaseless, silent tension.

It was not very long before Gokal arrived, taking up his residence in a house on the other side of the little valley. He arrived in holiday mood, and this cheerful unconcern of his was so marked that one day she questioned Amar about it. How did he account for Gokal's high spirits, seeing that the political situation had certainly not taken any turn for the better and that he himself flippantly declared that his own personal prospects were past praying for? Amar's reply somewhat dismayed her, for she learnt that Gokal was now living in open concubinage with a low-caste girl of fifteen, whom he had brought up to the hills in his train. Such conduct in Gokal was astonishing, but she was perhaps less astonished by the action itself than by the change which it had wrought in his disposition. It seemed pitiful that the whole mental outlook of such a man should be dependent on so trivial a circumstance. After thinking for several moments she asked: "What is the girl like?" And Amar replied that she was quite without character, intelligence, taste, or moral sense. "Then how lovely she must be!" thought Sita, and she sighed, for she was not unlike other women in her inability to decide whether the value which men set on mere beauty was a matter for laughter or tears. Be this as it might, Gokal's love-affair seemed to be dreadfully lacking in the elements of poetry or romance; and yet, apparently, it sufficed to distract him, not only from his personal worries, but from all the higher pre-occupations that had taken so important a place in his life. Weakness like this was lamentable. Intellectually men had a higher vocation than women. But how often men showed themselves inferior to women in their careless profanation of love. A woman saw the beauty of love and instinctively cherished it. A woman saw that in this confused, fragmentary world love was the only power that could fuse a life into a unity and endow it with form and significance. It was wrong of men to profane love in their thoughts and deeds, for all love was in its essence beautiful—even the most passionate earthly love.

A few weeks later, when Hari arrived, his temper presented a decided contrast to Gokal's, and Sita realized quickly enough what the nature of his trouble was. The last time she had seen him in Agra she had made a guess that his love-affair must be turning out unhappily. His moodiness, his somberness, now amply confirmed her suspicions and she said to herself with emphasis that he certainly deserved no better fortune. All the same, her memory of how he had taken her into his confidence soon injected a little sympathy into her ironical view of his plight. Besides, he did present in his gloom a figure of greater dignity, at any rate, than Gokal, whose complacency had become positively distasteful to her since she had discovered its cause. Thank goodness, Hari's love-affair stood on a higher level than that! There was evidence in his present dejection, that he had at least put some genuine feeling into it. She could believe that it had been a romance and not a mere loveless gallantry.

14

NOTWITHSTANDING HIS ABSORPTION in his own private concerns Hari had found it impossible entirely to neglect everything outside; and, rather strangely, it turned out that at the very time when his love-affair was ending its unhappy course, in the eye of the world he was achieving quite a success. First of all, having discovered why it was that he lay under the cloud of the Emperor's displeasure, he had applied himself to putting the matter to rights. The trouble was just what Ambissa had surmised; his visits to Mahomet Hakim Ali at Kabul had been reported at certain high quarters; and when, a little later, it was discovered that he had left Kabul in disguise, suspicion arose that he might be bound for Allahabad with treasonable messages for Prince Salim. The Emperor's secret police had, accordingly, made efforts to trace him. For two months Mabun Das had been searching all in vain, and then, lo and behold! he had turned up on the terrace of the palace at Agra.

Wisely, Hari had lost no time in having an explanation with Mabun Das. There was just enough truth in the suspicion that he was a sympathizer of Salim's to make him anxious to dispel that idea. His story to Mabun was that he had been hunting wild goat in the mountains, and, as far as he could judge, Mabun believed him. Then, some weeks later, he had had a long private audience with Akbar and had succeeded so well in dispelling the last vestiges of the Emperor's ill-humor that he received, the next day, the gift of an embroidered tunic and jeweled dagger. After this his return into favor had proceeded with a rapidity that had created considerable astonishment. The professional courtiers were not very well pleased; but the jealousy he aroused did not go deep, as it was easy to see that he was not an ambitious-minded competitor.

After his parting with Lalita he had no other wish than to obtain a complete change of scene, and he would certainly have indulged this longing, had not his engagements at court been absolutely binding. As it was, he went to the opposite extreme and threw himself into the thick of social activities. There were days when this regime was moderately successful, but efforts made so unspontaneously soon led to exhaustion, and then he would sink back into an even blacker gloom. Whenever he allowed his memories free play, the pain became agonizing. The contrast between his past happiness and his present misery overwhelmed him. How rich and warm and full life had seemed whilst he was in the summer of his love! Now, how completely he was wintered!

He had lost no time in writing to Lalita, because his one idea now was to put the past out of mind. Her reply wakened but little emotion. He read it with a frown, tore it up into fragments and threw them away. He had feared remorse, but this—the most incalculable of emotions—was spared him. He felt none, not even when he got a second letter in which she said: "How long will this misery continue? I don't see how I shall ever manage to live without you. Time seems to do no good."

And yet her pain, he knew, was real enough. He no longer argued that had her love been stronger it would have swept aside the obstacles in its way. No; he accepted the fact that love renounced has a pain that cannot be measured by the motives of the renunciation; and yet he regarded both his sufferings and hers with a certain measure of contempt. She would get over her grief because she was young, and he because he was middle-aged.

Great was his relief when at length he was able to leave Agra, and on his journey up to the Hills there were days when he fostered the illusion that he was cured. Then, very gingerly, he would begin fingering his wounds. He would let Lalita's image float before his eyes just to see whether the old pain had really been stifled to death. Sometimes the stab and sting did not return; and then his heart leapt up at this confirmation of his hope. But an hour later perhaps his eye would fall upon some girl who had a turn of figure, or a gesture, or a look, that resembled Lalita's, and then the sun would darken and the icy chill of bereavement would re-envelop him. Then he felt his spirit shrivel again. All in a moment he became old and weak and sick. When these accesses came upon him he had to rush away into solitude, and later, when the pain had spent itself, he was exhausted and without the wish to live.

In these hours of misery he could not look for consolation from Gokal, for Gokal was in a frame of mind that put him entirely out of sympathy with troubles such as this. Moreover, he could not let his thoughts dwell upon Gokal's position without suffering from self-reproach. It was not until he arrived at Khanjo that he became aware that Gokal had committed the dreadful imprudence of bringing Gunevati with him, and he now saw that, having long ago received some indication of what was afoot, he might well have attempted, before it was too late, to dissuade his friend from slipping into an entanglement that was set about with fearful risks. Having noticed that Gokal's innocent affection for Vasumati was in danger of transferring itself to her sister, why had he not foreseen all the rest? Although it was true that Brahminical discipline had relaxed under the influence of Mongol rule, commerce between a Brahmin and a girl in the position of Gunevati was, by all current notions, an offense of unthinkable heinousness.

Gokal was relying, as he now explained, upon the remoteness and seclusion of the spot. He argued that if ever a rumor should escape into the outer world, time and distance would so greatly have weakened it that his bare denials would suffice. But Hari shook his head over this; everything, in the last resort, would depend upon Akbar, and Akbar was no longer to be counted on.

The Emperor was becoming more and more deeply committed to his new religion; he could not allow it to be a failure without great loss of prestige. His endeavors were now directed on obtaining the support of the Brahmins, and many were yielding to threats, cajolery, and bribes. Gokal had not yet been approached, but it was beyond doubt that the day of his trial would come. If his position had been insecure even before, what did it look like now?

It was curious to observe with what equanimity Gokal was flying in the face of the worst dangers. Moreover, in thus indulging himself in all the pleasures that he had hitherto so rigorously eschewed, he seemed even to be finding a certain spiritual satisfaction. There was more than a little humor and self-directed malice in the commentaries that he passed upon himself and his infatuation. "My dear Hari," he would say, "my alliance with Gunevati, so far from being incongruous, as Amar seems to think, is the most natural and fitting conjunction in the world. In me you find the intellectual weary of his brain-spun cobwebs; in Gunevati the child of nature, a proper toy for a second childhood such as mine. The society of Gunevati is a perpetual refreshment to me. Before meeting her I had no idea how far I had traveled from the simple, the elementary. Sometimes, before making some remark to her, I try to forecast what her response will be, but, when it comes, its glorious and unimaginable crudity never fails to give me a delicious shock. How uninteresting is the educated mind in comparison with hers! Thought crystallizes into patterns of a merely formal complexity; but the instincts, with all the richness of their irrationality, belong to the creative side of life. Animal instinct, embroidered over with the arabesques of the imagination, how can you better me that? I am tired not only of second-rate thinkers, but even of the first-rate. How many there are who think only for the sake of thinking, and what dullards they make of themselves! I shall probably settle down in this spot with Gunevati for the rest of my days, and if I write a book it will be too true for men to understand."

To all this Hari would reply with a laugh and a shrug. There was no use in giving warnings to a man in such a mood. But he prayed that Gokal would tire of Gunevati before she tired of him, for when that happened she would either poison him or run away.

In this quiet upland valley the days slipped by very uneventfully; there was not even much communication between Gokal's house and Amar's, although now and again of an evening Gokal and Hari would stroll over to sit upon Amar's veranda in the moonlight; and then long, desultory conversations would take place to the accompaniment of the hooting owls. Hari, as a rule, said very little, and when he did speak he was apt to be bitter and contentious.

"You talk of loyalty to Akbar," he broke out on one occasion, "but, I ask you, what reason has any one of us to be loyal? That man has robbed us of everything! Independence, initiative, responsibilities, all are gone! And now, it seems, freedom of thought is about to go too! Egoists like Akbar suck up all the virtue in the soil around them; even the lives of their friends are stunted and starved. I have always declared that we should be better off under Salim. He is something of a scoundrel no doubt, but anything is preferable to a full-blooded tyrant."

No one replied to this tirade; but the next day he and Sita happened to be left alone together for a few moments. "I was surprised," she said, "to hear you speak so bitterly about the Emperor, especially after his showing you so much goodwill."

Hari gave a laugh, "Akbar's goodwill is worth a tunic and a jeweled dagger—but no more."

He was staring obstinately at the ground as he spoke, and Sita, after studying him for a moment, gave a sigh and went on: "Surely there is nothing disgraceful in accepting the leadership of a man like Akbar? Independence bought from Salim would be less honorable."

To this Hari made no reply, and the next moment the others returned. Altogether, during these days, Hari showed himself off in a decidedly unbecoming light; but his surliness did him no harm with Sita, for she had her own interpretation of it. Indeed, it rather stimulated her sympathies, making her feel at times that Amar as well as Gokal were both living too contentedly inside the closed circle of their pre-occupations. Gokal's interest was of the senses, Amar's of the mind; but there was nothing that either of them wished to give to the world at large—or to receive from it. Day by day it was being borne in upon her that nothing she could say would move Amar by one hairsbreadth, or put off by one single moment the execution of his resolve. In the depths of her heart she found no condemnation of him, nor even reproach, but superficially she often felt aggrieved. Then, too, there was always some sadness for her in the thought that the goal towards which his face was turned lay so remote from hers. His projected separation from her in this world pained her perhaps not more than his refusal to hope for their reunion in another world. It argued, if not a weakness in his love, a complete absence of faith in the determining power of love.

Gokal's description of the manner in which she had accepted the news of his resolve had filled Amar with admiration and gratitude and he had done what he could to show her what his feelings were. They did not really misunderstand one another; it was not his fault nor hers that a rift opened between them. The rift was narrow as yet; there were still moments when they could walk along side by side and pretend that it was not there. Nevertheless, it went deep, so deep that they now preferred not even to think about it. They felt a constraint in each other's company and the surface of their intercourse was ruffled by many flaws.

All this time Sita was keeping Hari under distant but keen observation; and one day she said: "Hari appears to be recovering from his infatuation. I dare say his unhappiness has been a blessing; in the end, perhaps, his thoughts will turn to God."

Amar smiled rather skeptically before replying, but all he returned was: "For the whole of his life he has been restless and dissatisfied. I take that as a sign that he is possessed by a longing for the Truth."

Whereupon Sita impulsively exclaimed: "Yes, like Akbar, he might well say: 'It is Thee I seek from temple to temple.'"

"Unfortunately," rejoined Amar, "he has sometimes wearied of temples and sought consolation in the harems of his acquaintances instead."

As a matter of fact, Sita's conjectures about Hari were a little premature. His feelings were still embittered and all the world was his enemy. On the other hand, the solitude that he had sought at first was ceasing to be agreeable to him; hours came when he had a longing for human companionship.

From Gokal's garden one could look down through the trees on to a little lawn on the other side of the stream. Here Sita used often to spend an hour with her book, and there were times when the gleam of her dress would fasten insistently upon his attention. It took him several days to make up his mind, but one fine morning he jumped up, resolved at last to join her. After all, nothing peculiar could be found in such a proceeding; and if his presence was unwelcome he would surely manage to detect it.

His path down the slope passed under tall rhododendrons that shut out all the view and, three minutes later, when he came to the moss-grown bridge over the stream, he was disappointed at finding that Sita was no longer there. He went across, however, and sat himself down and began reading a little volume of Persian verse which he found lying upon the grass. He was still reading when Sita reappeared. She looked surprised, but her smile was not unwelcoming, and presently they were discussing the Persian poets together.

When that topic came to an end there was a pause, but the murmur of the stream below and the rustle of the trees overhead gave the silence a peaceful quality. Then she picked up the book and fell to reading her favorite passages aloud, while Hari, outstretched on the warm turf, listened at first absent-mindedly, but later with deep pleasure. After this there came another and a longer silence, and then suddenly he said:

"I wish you could teach me to feel as you do."

"How do I feel!" she asked, surprised.

"I imagine that you feel all the time as though you were living in a fairy tale."

"That's strange!" She looked up at the sky. "You're right. I've always felt that I was part of a fairy tale."

He gave a short laugh. "You haven't changed much, then, since you were a child."

"I've certainly never wanted to," she replied rather hesitatingly. "But one does change." And she sighed.

He raised his head to look at her. "I don't think *you* have—not much. Neither outwardly nor inwardly."

"Why do you speak in that bitter tone?" she asked.

"Because I am bitter."

She didn't want to ask him why, so all she said was: "I'm sorry."

For the first time that day embarrassment threatened to fall upon them. He lay staring down into the miniature forest of grass; her pensive eyes rested upon his bare head. The shape of it was pleasant to her, and she said at last: "I have my moods, too. I feel sometimes that a comet coming to destroy the earth would be a kindly thing; that life is neither tragedy nor comedy, but only a farce—so confused, so self-contradictory, so transient are we. But I don't stay in that mood for long.

"Just now," she went on after a pause, "I feel rather empty of thought. I don't know why—I am content to sit here every day doing nothing."

"You have that book of poetry," he observed.

"Yes. But I haven't been reading it much. I listen to that stream which reminds me of a stream at home."

Hari made no reply; he abstained even from looking at her. She certainly was a charming creature, and he waited, smiling, for her to go on. But the silence continued, so presently he said:

"You seem to inhabit a world of your own vision and making. Don't you sometimes find the prosaic worlds of other people imposing themselves upon you?"

"I did at Agra; but I don't here, and I don't at home. For my friends I can always find a place in my own world—the world which I believe in—the world which you think childish."

"No," he returned wearily, "not childish, only—unreal."

"Why unreal? Look at that butterfly over there." And her eyes wandered around her. "Why unreal? My world takes in everything I see here; this forest and all the life inside it. Isn't this forest as real as Fatehpur-Sikri?"

She broke off, and while she was looking away, he took the opportunity of studying her. Her small head, the lines of her chin and neck—they were enchanting. She certainly was a most flower-like being. She made him think of a flower nodding and swaying in a summer breeze, and yet that pose of hers was erect, it was almost imperious in its erectness.

"You are right, no doubt," said he at last, "and I am wrong. But I was born wrong."

"I'm sorry you are depressed," she returned, in her rather drawling, rather expressionless voice. "You feel, I suppose, that there is no mystery left in anything, that all feeling is stale, that life is an open book which you have read over and over again. And you think that your mood is permanent. Suffering always has, as Feizi says, the nature of infinity."

Very soon after this she got up and wandered away in the

direction of the house. Hari did not offer to accompany her, but seated himself upon the ground again; and while he listened to the liquid sounds of the stream and dry rustle of the breeze, the memory of her parting smile lingered pleasantly in his mind. A peace that he had not felt for many months descended upon him, and the scene before his eyes did more than merely soothe. It instilled into him the conviction that it possessed a value of its own, and in its value, thus deeply felt, there dwelt a power of comfort. For its value was secure and enduring, whilst the value of his own personal happiness—well, that was small at the best. How fortunate, then, that it was open to a man to rejoice in what lay outside himself.

For an hour or more he stayed there; but when he began to reflect upon the problem of conduct he was thrown into perplexity again. What guidance did such feelings and intuitions afford? In what direction did they point? He pondered, but to this question nature made no reply.

15

BY SOME UNACCOUNTABLE turn Hari's spirits the next day were lower than before. It was not so much that his heart ached for Lalita as that his whole being, he felt, was accursed. With appalling clearness he saw a dreadful truth: in addition to the will to live a man needs must have the power to enjoy life. Of these two gifts the second seemed to him the more mysterious, and his loss of it filled him with dismay. Thinking of Sita, he determined to make her bear the brunt of his depression. Her happiness worked upon him like a challenge, calling him to put it to the proof. From the earliest dawn he strove to give shape to the formless pessimism within him, hunting for ideas that would embody it, for words that would drive it sharply into her understanding. Yes, he meant to carry war into her country. Religion, he would say, was nothing more than a refuge—even for those who were not conscious that they stood in need of one. He would tell her that neither courage, nor force of intellect, nor any nameable gift or virtue could be accounted a guarantee against self-deception. Nor could the seeker after truth make any appeal to the authority of wisdom or goodness, for the skeptic of mean character and mean intelligence might—in spite of his meanness or even by virtue of his meanness—interpret the universe more truly than the sage or the saint. There was no evidence that wisdom and goodness had a universal instead of a merely terrestrial significance, and to be satisfied with the latter humanity must be smug, indeed, in its own invented virtue. The plain man had a plain need for some sort of religion, if only as an excuse for behaving decently; as a reason to give himself, for instance, for not breaking the head of the prig, who got on very well (or so at least he would flatter himself) by the light of his own sweet nature. To sum up, a religion was what every honest man wanted and could not, for his very honesty, find.

Sita, of course, was a Christian; she retained very elementary ideas—ideas that had all the charm and naivety of the nursery clinging to them. There was a kind Father in Heaven whose function it was to deal out justice tempered with mercy. There was a system of rewards and punishments, everything, in fact after the pattern of an earthly schoolroom.

Well prepared was Hari at the time of his setting out; but, again, when he got to the little lawn, it was to find no one there. The morning, however, was still young, so he decided to sit down and wait. This time the air was still, the sky pale, but without a cloud; a scent arose from the warm pine needles, and now and then he would catch a breath of fragrance from the moon-flowers in the long grass behind. Those silvery blooms were already wide open and although they faded in the course of a single day there were always others to take their place. Hosts of butterflies hovered over them and when he became tired of watching these a family of water-rats popped out upon the bank. So amusing was the play of the young ones that, for several minutes after Sita had appeared, he and she remained hushed, intent upon not disturbing the game.

This over, it took him a little time to get back into the right vein, but he succeeded in the end and came out with most of his pre-arranged say. Nor was it ineffective. He had the satisfaction of seeing a troubled look spread over Sita's face. "So what I say is this," he concluded, driving his last points home: "Your faith, like your happiness, is simply the expression of a temperament. My temperament is, unfortunately, not hospitable to the delusions of religion. But until quite lately I did manage to bring a certain zest to the business of living. I must recover that zest or give up the game."

"I don't think your zest actually made you very happy," replied Sita distressfully.

"It was better than nothing," said Hari.

"But it had no stability—as you discovered to your cost. Your business now, surely, is to look, not for happiness, but for something deeper out of which happiness will spring."

Hari gave a shrug. "Christianity, I suppose!"

Looking into the distance Sita smiled to herself. "You might do worse."

"I am very well aware that I could not possibly do better," returned Hari. "*Your* Christianity, at any rate, is charming."

"Only you are not, like me, still in the nursery!"

Hari raised himself upon one elbow to contemplate her. Really, it was impossible, whilst lying upon this sweet-smelling grass and talking to someone as pretty as she, to do justice to the blackness of the universe or one's own innermost gloom. But he was not alone in his failure to carry out his full intentions. Sita was missing her aim too. She couldn't find the moment for producing all the serious and compelling things that she had come prepared with. Perhaps homilies would flow from her lips more naturally some other day. At any rate, on this particular morning, the conversation, initiated with solemnity, took its own willful course, grew lighter and lighter, and no attempt was made to alter it.

The next day, too, much the same thing happened, and the next. So, after a while, both she and Hari gave the matter up. The way in which they were passing their time seemed, after all, to be justified in its results. Hari found himself recovering his spirits, and Sita could give herself the credit of bringing this about. Had anyone suggested to them that this was the beginning of a gallantry, they both would have smilingly shaken their heads. It was only by slow degrees that Hari became aware that sentiment was coloring his relationship, and Sita, when this change was no longer to be ignored, slipped into the assumption that his feelings, whatever depths they might reach, would remain without danger for either of them.

Upon this pleasant footing their intimacy grew apace. Although Sita had no taste for vapid flirtation, life without romance was, to her thinking, hardly life at all. She accepted Hari's homage serenely; indeed, it was her very serenity that at last made him restive, so that one day he said: "Are you never afraid of my getting to love you too well?"

117

She gave him a mocking glance. "Can you pass from one love to another as quickly as that?"

"Perhaps!"

Again her glance flitted over him, but she also shook her head, and for the time the subject was not pursued. A few days later, however, when she was talking about her return home, the indifference with which she seemed to envisage their parting stung him once more into speech. "You have grown so accustomed to my adoration," he said, "don't you think you may miss it a little when we part?"

Her answer was made quite lightly. "My dear Hari, I shall miss you very much."

"I was not suggesting that. I said you would miss being made love to."

"Now why," she questioned in a voice completely changed, "why do you go out of your way . . . ?"

He shrugged. "Let us look the truth in the face. I have been making love to you."

"No, no!" she cried.

They were standing beside the little bridge when this was said, for their hour had just run out. A few deep moments of indecision passed over them. They were looking at one another intently. And then Sita turned and took the path up to her house.

On his way home Hari stepped out with a vigor that corresponded to an unwanted stir within. "What do I mean by this?" he questioned. "Am I behaving heedlessly? Do I run the risk of cheapening what would otherwise . . . ?" As his troubled memory touched here and there upon the hours they had shared together, one scene in particular reached forward reproachfully into the present. They were wandering along by the stream and the air was full of white mist that curled up from the wet ground. Every leaf, every twig, every blade, had a bead of water hanging on it; and things close at hand seemed particularly vivid because everything beyond was blotted out by the soft whiteness. They had stopped before a little bank that was crowded with wild flowers. Each flower looked up at them with a color and outline so definite that they felt as if they were children looking at flowers for the first time. How sharp was the sensation—now revived—of standing there, on that little island in the mist, in the presence—so intense —of those archetypal flowers! Was he unregardful of the value of shared moments such as those? Unmindful of their beauty—or of the fineness of restraint? No, no; he must tell her quickly that it was not so.

And yet, although these intentions held, at their next meeting when he tried to carry them out, he was completely baffled, and not a thing took place in the way he had arranged. They came together, he and she, in all the tension of long and anxious heart-searchings—a tension cloaked under a delusive calm. And then, before they knew it, the words they were exchanging were full of a deep agitation; the event carried them away on its own rush; and what he finally said to her was: "You have known for some time that I love you. Nevertheless, everything shall be as you wish. Only tell me what you do wish! Tell me how much I may love you; and I will try. . . ."

She clasped her hands together in the extremity of her disquiet. "You must love me only as you love those flowers, or as a child," she said, "or as a creature of your own imagination; but not—not as a woman, not as a person belonging to the real world."

After this everything went on—or seemed to go on—as before. Sita was apparently determined not to acknowledge any change, and Hari lent himself to the pretense. Nevertheless, his words had recoiled upon him. The question how much their dalliance meant could be ignored (he now felt it all the time) only as long as it had been left unasked. Their loves, while content in the Eden that she had created for them, had been innocent and safe. Why, then, had he stirred up temptation? And why now, just because she showed herself willing to continue on the same footing as before—why was he perpetually haunted by a little laugh of cynical amusement which seemed to be ringing in the air? Why, in spite of his contrition, did he still feel himself spurred on, instigated, assured by some demon within, that he was now free to make love to her with far greater directness than before?

He resisted the enticement; but a good deal of the pleasure that he had formerly taken in her company was lost in the struggle and constraint. Nor was he able any longer to be forgetful of the figure of Amar. Before many days had passed he was saying to himself with groans that there was nothing for it but to go away. He had taken his lesson recently enough; and this time—no, no! there should be no indecision.

A few days more and chance threw him a suggestion which he caught at with a miserable alacrity. He happened to be in the house when an urgent summons came for Amar, whose parents, an aged couple, were spending the hot season on a little country estate of theirs three days' journey westward along the hills. Amar's mother had been taken ill; Amar announced that he would set out the next morning at daybreak; and Hari, giving himself no time for second thoughts, at once made the offer to accompany him.

16

IT WAS RAINING, but not hard. A thin, fine moisture drifted
through the trees, the clouds were lying low upon the hills. All
night it had rained; the hoofs of the horses sank noiselessly into
the sodden leaves, and the heavy boughs above sagged as though
from a weight of despondent thought. To Hari, riding along in silence, Nature herself seemed to have veiled her head in melancholy;
but he was not insensible to the beauty of this her mourning aspect. There was grandeur in the valley depths lost in a clinging mist
and in the darkly wooded mountain-flanks going up into cloud.

With thoughts of Sita pressing incessantly upon his mind, he
strove hard to convince himself that she would understand and approve his going away. The worst part of it was that moments came
when he himself lost all sense of the rightness of the impulse under which he had acted, and then too he had transports of angry
rebelliousness, when he was conscious only of having given his
heart a sudden and very painful wrench. Some of his anger visited
itself upon Amar, who, going along in front, tall, straight-backed,
but with chin sunk upon his breast, presented a figure of the most
profound contemplation. It was impossible to believe that his inward serenity was not flawless. But had any man the right to be
so unaware of the feelings of those near him? How much thought
had he bestowed upon Sita during these last weeks? Was she not,

after all, a woman—and his wife? And could a man withdraw himself from everyday life without suffering the loss of his earthly rights? "You," cried Hari in his heart, "you, who stand in my path, are not a man of flesh and blood but an abstraction. That is what your lofty ideals have made of you. The virtuous man is separated from the rest of mankind by the pedestal of his own virtue; he becomes a stumbling-block—or a figure of absurdity. However," he went on to himself, "I do not condemn Amar's wish to retire from the world, for even if he were to remain in it in order to serve, he would still be far estranged from the human. But then again: how can a man, enclosing himself in the solitude of his own self-conscious will, win freedom from the differentiation of personality? Yet that, precisely, is what Amar is aiming at. Is he not following a road that will carry him farther and farther into the inward maze and tighten the knot of selfhood? And I? Why am I following him?" Once more he lost himself, and then his thoughts came out into the light again: "What I behold as weak and incomplete in myself, what I am now inclined to flee from as from a painful disturbance, or as a sin—can that not be interpreted in a dual way corresponding to its own ambiguous nature? Why is life regarded as either a heaven or a hell? Certainly not because it stands midway between. No, life is both the height and the depth; and filth and cruelty are also joy and strength."

The ride went on, and always in the same unbroken silence. The trees under which they were now passing were taller and also more widely spaced. After a while Hari spurred his horse forward and rode along by Amar's side; but the latter, still deep in meditation, gave no sign of noticing his presence. Hari studied him with sidelong glances, his face wearing a faint smile; and presently, in a voice devoid of all expression, he inquired of Amar whether his religious exercises had been progressing favorably; was he yet within sight of his goal? To bring his mind down to earth cost Amar, clearly, some effort; before replying he fastened upon Hari eyes that were still focused upon thoughts lying far beyond. His answer, however, when it came, was definite enough and delivered with perfect simplicity. Moreover, having once begun to speak, he went on with a freedom from reserve for which Hari was unprepared. Without doubt it was the forest and the grandeur of the forest that wrought upon him. Thoughts that could not have been expressed without a kind of spiritual impropriety in the noise and bustle of the world rose naturally to the lips in a place such as this. Gravely he explained that he had reached a stage on life's journey when worldly things could interest him no longer. But, far from sinking into any tranquillity of indifference, he had been overtaken by a terrible sense of urgency. One half of his life had passed already, and how little he had lessened his distance from his goal! His recent practices in meditation had not been discouraging, but they had shown him that the time for casting off all mundane attachments had arrived. It was necessary that he should enter a monastery.

His gaze had been going straight out before him as he spoke; and Hari, who was looking into his face with concentration, now gave a sudden frown and turned away. As they advanced at a walk under the hush of the wet, windless trees, his thoughts rushed into the distant future. He saw Amar as an old man, sitting under the palm trees of a monastery garden in Ceylon. He saw him in saffron robes, with lined face and shaven head. And then, the next instant, he was seized with an intense awareness of the actual present— the fresh damp scent of this Himalayan wilderness, and the austere presence of the solitary human being at his side. Then again, all at once he traveled in imagination back to the house where Sita, standing by the window with vacant eyes, was pursuing a vision of two travelers upon their way. Into her personality he projected himself with an effect that was like walking into the sunlight out of a sepulchre; and upon his thought of her he lingered until it came to him with a start that he had not yet spoken a word in response to his companion.

"And Sita?" he questioned briefly.

The expression that gathered upon Amar's face was not easily to be interpreted, but there was nothing evasive in his reply. Hari was shown that carefully, conscientiously, everything had been thought out, and every provision made. As he listened, the shadow over his face deepened. Here was a remarkable lesson in the art for which he himself was so signally inapt. He was shown how the wayward vine of this our earthly life could be gently, cunningly, bent to the framework of circumstance, and the spirit, thus acquitted of its mundane charge, be allowed the freedom to soar.

As he considered Amar, envy, admiration, scorn, and curiosity competed in his breast. Currents of sympathy and hostility pulsed through him, quickening the beat of his heart. All at once, and before he rightly knew what he was about, he drew up, and grasping the reins of Amar's horse, brought it to a standstill with his own. Leaning forward in the saddle, he plunged his gaze deep into Amar's eyes, and thus, for at least a minute, held him under a fixed and stern regard. Then, by a curious transformation, that lowering look turned into a smile. The smile said nothing, or rather defied Amar to find a meaning for it.

To this strange piece of behavior the Rajah submitted without any loss of calm. There was no change in his composure; Hari's aggressiveness, if such it was, missed its stroke; his challenge, if it was one, fell to the ground. After another moment he withdrew his hand, and with that the two horses went forward and the ride continued as before.

For the rest of that day, and for the better part of the next, their way lay deep through the same tall ranks of dark-hued, windless trees. The forest was grand and still; not even a bird's note sounded; only at times the sun, breaking through the clouds, shone mistily overhead. For Hari the monotonous hours passed as in a dream. The activities of the world, made to appear at once turbulent and trivial, seemed to be receding beyond hail of memory itself. Like the crash and roar of the waves, as one journeys inland from the sea, they were growing faint, they were now completely unheard. To this sense of isolation he submitted himself; nor was he ungrateful for the numbness that crept over him.

In the afternoon of the second day their ride took them out from under the trees and along the edge of a grassy plateau high up above the great plain. Distance obscured all detail; the eye swept across a limitless expanse over which hung a ceiling of gray cloud. Here and there a bank of storm-rain drifted slowly along, filling the space between earth and sky with a dull purple blur. Even at this elevation the air was hot, damp, and lifeless; the horses moved sluggishly and their riders had no energy to press them on. Hari's thoughts went back to a recluse, beneath whose cave-dwelling they had passed only a few hours ago. Whilst the multitude of human beings swarming invisibly upon the plain offered him, in their close, common life, the likeness of a mildew upon the face of the earth, that hermit stood forth, in his imagination, as a separate and self-subsistent unit. He stood forth, as Hari was pleased to picture him, as an independent center of spiritual life; and that, no doubt, was because he had taken to himself the space for a true individuality to move in. Yet that same principle of individuality was, in Amar's view, delusive; pain and evil were inherent in it, and thus one arrived at the kernel of Buddha's doctrine: wisdom and self-knowledge and self-extinction were one. More than once during that day did Hari feel inclined to retrace his steps to the cave and petition to be received as a disciple. But he had been told that the hermit was a Sakti; and that branch of Hinduism was not the one to which he now inclined. Hinduism in general, however, appealed to him as the broadest and most elastic of all religious systems. He was attracted by its independence of dogma, the smallness of its demands upon blind faith. But these attractions also constituted its weakness, lending point to the criticism made by Amar that Hinduism was not a religion but simply religiousness itself. Upon the spiritual substance it imposed no form, to the urge it gave no certain direction; and although among the uneducated it borrowed shape from the myths, superstitions, and customs, with which the common mind was already richly stocked, in an unencumbered intelligence it remained fluid and colorless, as rarefied, indeed, as any brain-spun metaphysics.

While he was thus meditating they came to another turn of the road that was to take them down from the plateau. At the bottom of the slope there spread a broad valley containing patches of open ground, and as their eyes wandered over it an encampment came into view. After they had moved on a little a closer scrutiny of the clustered tents showed that they belonged to some person of importance, but neither Hari nor Amar was prepared for the information given them upon riding up; they were told that the distinguished traveler was none other than Shaik Mobarek. At this news they exchanged glances; the encounter was not greatly to the liking of either of them, and they shared the sudden idea that perhaps it was not too late to push on. But while they were still halting in hesitation, the curtain before one of the tents was swept aside and Mobarek himself stepped out. Upon seeing them the old man had a movement of surprise, which, however, he was quick to transform into a gesture of welcome. The choice was thus taken out of their hands and a few moments later they found themselves seated as honored guests in the principal marquee. It was a change abrupt enough to be somewhat disconcerting. While Mobarek was playing his part as host with all the manners of an accomplished worldling, Amar was more than a little stiff, and Hari felt hard put to it to keep up an appearance at all. His acquaintance with Mobarek did not go far, nor did he have an inclination to extend it. This little old mystic with his observant eyes, confident manners, and nimble tongue, certainly knew how to make the best of both worlds—and at this time Hari was feeling very little at home in either. Mobarek's gay, quick talk only confused him; he remained more or less in the clouds until a sentence came out that brought him down with a painful jerk. Mobarek had been telling them that he was on his way down from a visit to Prince Daniyal, who was passing the season in the uplands. "And the charming Princess was there too," he went on. "We all spent the happiest fortnight together, and now I am escorting her down to her parents who are attending His Majesty on his way northward to Lahore. Yes, the dear child is with me now; she will be coming in presently. The wedding, I believe, is to take place in about three months' time."

For the next few minutes Hari's nerves were stretched to the limit of his endurance—a condition which he hoped that Mobarek would not observe, or that he would be unable, at any rate, to account for. It was appalling, this idea that Lalita and he might, at any moment, find themselves face to face under Mobarek's inquisitive gaze. Unable to bear the strain he got up at last and left the tent, his excuse being that he liked to superintend the foddering of his horse himself.

Outside he looked about him, desperately undecided what to do. Two rows of tents stretched down the level turf, and behind them on the left rose a dark wall of young firs. He tried to think, but his brain refused its office; with the level evening sunlight pouring into his eyes, he could only blink and peer resourcelessly down the two lines of gleaming tents. Beyond them, not far distant, was the place where the horses were picketed; some grooms were moving about amongst them; but, by some odd chance, there was no one else about; no one handy to send with a message. . . .

Lalita—it confounded him to think of it—she must be somewhere within a dozen yards of where he stood. She might emerge, he supposed, at any moment. Would she be discomposed, would she think he was pursuing her, would she be angry—or glad? As his imagination got under way a new and not unpleasurable excitement flowed through him. Lalita's image, which had grown dim of late, glowed forth again with all the colors of life. That golden skin! That tawny hair of hers! Those strong young limbs whose every turn and movement he had known—he still knew—so well! And then again he quailed; his spirit shrank away. No; he was not ready for this exigency. It was too much.

He had gone forward some thirty yards, and now once more he halted. What he needed was the time to recover self-possession and make up a plan of behavior. His eyes turned to the compact thicket of young firs within such easy reach. Why not—for a brief space—just disappear?

This impulse wheeled him suddenly round into a narrow passage between two of the nearest tents, and at the back of them, before making his dive into the wood, he swept a furtive glance right and left. Five steps more and he would have vanished; but there, in the shadow of the left-hand tent, waiting for him, yes, evidently waiting and expecting—was Lalita herself. What shining eyes, what flushed cheeks! Oh, didn't he know that sparkle and that glow! And she caught hold of him: "Couldn't you hear me? Couldn't you hear me? I was calling you, calling . . . I—" He seized her in his arms. The world disappeared behind the flare of his delight. But it was a madness of two or three seconds only. With unnecessary violence they flung themselves apart; Lalita had gone—disappeared, he imagined, into her tent; and when he came to himself again he was alone—far, far away it seemed from any human stir, deep in the silence and semi-darkness of the fir wood.

17

LESS THAN TWO hours later Hari was seated at Mobarek's table with Lalita upon his right and Amar opposite. Lalita had perfect composure and chatted to Amar with a right measure of vivacity, while Mobarek, although full of attentions for his guests, was prodigal of paternal smiles and sallies in her regard. During the first part of the evening the only person to show signs of preoccupation was Amar, but later he took up his share in the talk, and as time went on Hari became the silent member of the party.

His hour in the wood had seen him through the crisis of his excitement. In that hour he had given himself a loose rein; he had rolled on the ground, shouted his laughter at the skies, shaken his fist at all the four corners of the world. He and Lalita were rebels, they snapped their fingers at circumstance, they defied the powers that be. If they chose they would run away together that very night. Lalita would have no fear; she was ready. Or, if other considerations came in, they would let the spin of a coin decide.

Since then his excitement had died down, but his attitude remained unchanged. Through the long evening hours he made Lalita his study; he could see that, like him, she had learnt more than a little since the miserable day of their parting; but he retained his conviction that he had read her temper aright. It was interesting, it was even a little pathetic, to mark how she had come under the discipline of the world and how its lessons, whether for good or ill, had sunk into her. Noteworthy was her grasp of present requirements and her confidence in her role. She had to present the picture of a happy, self-confident young woman, capable of assuming with ease the brilliant social position that her approaching marriage offered. To this end she had been training herself, and perhaps it even amused her to display before him her newly acquired skill. Fluency in gossip, distinguished intimacies, familiarity with what was fashionable in art, music, and literature—all these she was showing off. But it gave Hari a pang to see her adopting the affectations, the catchwords, the sophisticated inanities, of Prince Daniyal's particular coterie; and still less easy to accept was her pretense that a genuine affection subsisted between Daniyal and herself. It was only a pretense—of that he felt sure—although no doubt she had often hoped that it was going to deceive her too. No doubt she had been making the best she could of her accepted lover. But true worldliness she would never achieve; her character contained both more and less than the necessary ingredients.

Thus the evening wore on until she rose to withdraw. First, she bent her head to Mobarek to receive upon her forehead a benedictory kiss, then she gave her hand to Hari with a formal smile; last, she turned to Amar, and in saying good night reminded him that—if he was really making such an early start next morning—it was also good-bye. It had all seemed very simple, but in truth it was not so. A message had passed in her pressure of Hari's hand; fever had again been injected into his veins. Quickly renewing his conversation with Mobarek, he tried to recover his calm; but his heart was beating out that it was certain—yes, yes, it was certain—that Lalita would be ready to receive him in her tent that night.

Not long after her departure he pleaded fatigue and withdrew. The night was fresh and the sky bright with moonlight, although the moon herself was still hidden behind the mountains in the east. He stood listening to the stillness; the only sound in all the valley seemed to be the lively accents of Mobarek's voice inside the tent. As he walked slowly down the row it struck him that he still was uncertain which was Lalita's. One of them, however, was lit from inside by a faint rosy glow and he marked its position with care.

Sitting at the entrance of his own tent he looked up again into the blue-black sky and presently his eyes fell upon a vision that caught his breath and rapt him out of himself. Hung unimaginably high in the dome of heaven there gleamed a frosted slope, a snow-field which the moon had turned to silver. He gazed at it until his wonder melted into an inexplicable longing and his longing into a biting sadness.

With a shiver he got up at last, but just as he was about to retire into his tent he observed a tall figure approaching over the grass and recognized Amar. As Amar drew nearer it seemed to him that there was something purposeful in his gait; a reluctance, too, in the slowness with which he stalked forward. He waited until Amar stood before him, and then—interpreting the other's silence in his own fashion—he invited him with a gesture into the tent. Inside, a small light was burning; Amar sat down at the little table and he himself sat down opposite. It was some moments before either of them spoke.

"What I have to tell you is that I saw . . ." And Amar knitted his brows. "Good God!" he added with unaccustomed vehemence. "What kind of madness possessed you?"

Hari was silent.

"Mobarek and I came out of the tent two minutes after you left. We were actually following you, and hardly more than a dozen yards behind."

"Did Mobarek see?"

"No. He had stopped for a moment to look into the Princess's tent."

"Lucky!" said Hari dryly.

Amar, still frowning, continued to study him. "I have no wish to interfere in your affairs. . . . That you will surely understand. But all the same . . ." He made a pause. He was waiting; but Hari waited, too, and thus they eyed one another.

At last Hari gave a shrug and a smile. "After all—we make our start at daybreak to-morrow. And that being so . . ."

Amar ignored this; his eyes remained fixed upon Hari's face. There was meaning in that look, and now Hari was the one to frown. A flush, too, rose to his cheeks, nor was it difficult to see that anger caused it.

"Well?" he challenged.

Amar stirred and muttered in the extremity of his annoyance. "Heaven knows," he said again, "I have no wish to mix in your affairs, but it is obvious that Princess Lalita and you are already intimate. In fact, by putting two and two together, I think I can . . ." He broke off. "Is it necessary for me to go on? All that I require of you now is an assurance . . ."

"Of what?"

"That you will commit no follies to-night."

Hari threw back his head and gave an angry laugh.

"You consider me intrusive, perhaps?" And Amar's tone was frigid with distaste. "All the same I must go through with what I conceive to be my duty. The happiness—the lives, possibly—of many people are at stake."

"Very well!" And suddenly leaning forward, Hari drummed with his fingers upon the table. "Very well! Let us thrash this matter out!"

Amar drew back with something like dismay. "Is a discussion really necessary? Surely your good sense . . ."

"No!" said Hari. "And to tell you the truth, I have no good sense at my disposition—at any rate, not to-night."

Amar was silent; and looking straight into his eyes, Hari went on: "I am tired of expediency. Do you understand?"

"Expediency?" Amar gave a weary sigh.

"I see no reason why I should respect other people's petty conveniences. I have never much regarded my own."

There was no reply.

"Lalita feels as I do." Hari laughed and snapped his fingers. "She is ready. Very well!"

At this, with a muffled exclamation, Amar threw himself back in his seat. The light of anger shone in his eyes, and he said: "You may treat yourself as you please, but common decency forbids that you should risk . . ."

"Oh, I know what you mean, my dear Amar!" Hari's eyes had now caught the spark. "You mean that I ought to bear in mind that you have been busily currying favor with Lalita's father—and that the person responsible for bringing you two together was Ambissa —and that the whole trend of your policy is towards Daniyal. You want me to bear in mind that your future relationship with Daniyal might be prejudiced if it were to happen that I, your brother-in-law, whilst in your company, made off with his betrothed."

Amar, visibly, had to struggle to control himself. "These taunts are undeserved. But I am not here to defend myself. If you choose to think that I am actuated merely by self-interest, you may do so. I shall be satisfied if I succeed in dissuading you. . . ."

Hari was not listening. A singular agitation had taken possession of him and he interrupted with violence.

"Amar! Have you the cynicism to approve of that girl's marriage to Daniyal? And are you going to have the cynicism to attach yourself to Daniyal's party? Answer me plainly, for worldliness should have the courage of its convictions."

"You are mixing up things that do not belong together." And Amar stiffened. "The choice between Salim and Daniyal is a political one. I am not interested in Daniyal's private affairs. What business have *you* to concern yourself with them? And as for the kind of interference you appear to be contemplating now . . ."

"What about love?"

"I see, you are smiling," replied Amar, "and your smile answers you."

Hari shook his head. "No. Nor do you understand." He got up and poured himself out some water. "I have come to such a pass that I cannot measure my feelings at all."

These words were followed by silence. Amar was scrutinizing him in some surprise; Hari was in the grip of an emotion, the nature of which was obscure to him.

"Listen!" Hari went on with a kind of somber impetuosity, "your mind is too reasonable for me, and believing, as I do, that reason itself is delusive, I prefer to take my delusions from nearer to their source. Since man needs must be mad, I prefer to be mad in a simpler, easier way. I will tell you why you don't believe in a God, Amar. Your reason tells you that if there is a God He must certainly stand outside reason Himself. To begin with, no God, sane after your pattern, would have constructed a world on such lines as this. Look about you! What is there in nature that your reason can understand or approve? The rising of sap in the trees, the unfolding of flowers, the swarming of bees, the mating of beasts, everywhere birth and death with a little interval of wantonness and waste in between. All this you condemn, and perhaps rightly. But what if I prefer to let my life flow as unreasoning Nature wills?"

A thoughtful look had come into Amar's face and his eyes were now bent upon the ground.

"I think I begin to understand you better," he pronounced after an interval.

"Do you?" Hari shot a sidelong glance at him. "What do you understand?"

"This: the world presents itself to you as alien and even antagonistic, and you intend your acts to be acts of rebellion. But that attitude is vain. Could you, but for one moment, see yourself and the world in their true relation, you would be ashamed at your absurdity. You would see that you are separated from the whole by delusions only—the delusions clustering about the Self. Ah! then you would see that liberty is not the liberty to rebel, and you would cease to be a child who beats at the stone over which it has just stumbled."

Hari smiled as he made his reply. "No; my rebelliousness is less simple than that. You see, I am without your absolute confidence in a particular scheme of values. You are a good Buddhist; and life, you hold, must of necessity be uneasiness, distressfulness, vanity, and vexation of spirit. Perhaps I agree so far; but with you it follows that life as a whole is an evil which might well be brought to an end. With that I disagree. Life stretches illimitably before us as well as behind us, and we possess no standards by which to judge its worth. Not in terms of reasonableness, or of happiness, or of any accepted good, can it be judged. Life, taking it in the large, gives us one hint only—I should say, only one single command: Live!"

Amar looked at him searchingly. "I am no hedonist. But I respect wisdom, and if wisdom brings happiness in its train, I see no reason to reject it. There is no glory in continuing to flounder through the miseries of sensuality, ill-will, and ignorance."

He paused; for a space the two men considered one another; then Hari said:

"I think it is you who are the rebel, Amar; and a more desperate one than I, for what you are rebelling against in yourself is more powerful than either reason or morality."

133

Having spoken these words, Hari moved to the tent entrance and stood looking out into the night. As Amar considered the outline of his head and shoulders, his earlier fears melted away. The atmosphere had strangely altered since the beginning of their colloquy. He heard the intake of Hari's deep breaths and saw him shiver from the chill of the air; then Hari returned and threw himself down upon his seat.

"Well?" He smiled wanly. "And what do you say now?"

Amar was silent.

"You have gained your point. I suppose that is enough?"

"You have decided well," murmured Amar.

"The spirit rises in one, and the spirit dies down. . . ." His regard had become ironical; and after a minute he went on: "But what of her? Has it died down in her too?"

"You have given her up once before," said Amar. "This—all this—has been her doing. And it is sheer folly."

Hari eyed him with a certain curiosity. "Are you actually—a little bitter against her?"

"Bitter? No, no!"

"My friend," said Hari in a tone of rather dreary raillery, "I am not sure that in one branch of self-knowledge at least I have not outdistanced you. You have made no terms with the feminine in yourself, and of that we all partake. Some day it may wreak vengeance upon you."

Amar smiled enigmatically. "The feminine has its own path— but to the same goal. Women, too, have their special gift—which I leave to them."

"I envy you your certainties."

"There is one which, by itself, is enough."

"And that?"

Amar had risen from his seat. "Above all doubts there rises our intuition of the moral law. Nor have you forgotten it, Karma, the noblest intuition of our race."

Hari made no reply. After waiting a moment Amar went slowly outside, and together they stood looking up into the vault of the night.

"I know," said Hari in an undertone, "I know that the sun will rise in the east; would to God I felt equally certain that evil bore with it its inevitable expiation."

"It does."

These words fell with a heavy stroke, but Hari's face did not change.

"Know this," continued Amar, "there is a distinction between causation in dead matter, causation in the organic world, and causation in the animate world, where the operation of moral law is superimposed upon the natural. This is Karma; it is the chief force in the universe inasmuch as it controls life's gradual progress towards final deliverance."

Hari, whose eyes had been lifted to the night sky, now fixed them once again upon his companion.

"You must tell me more about these things," he muttered after a pause.

Amar inclined his head.

"Thoughts like those came to me in the forest," said Hari slowly. "But there were others, too."

18

THE VALLEY WAS full of mist when Hari and Amar set out in the dawning of the next day. A pale, unfriendly light filtered down from overhead; the damp air seemed to blow chillingly against them as they breasted it, and yet there was no stir in the endless ranks of tall, dark trees, and the mist coiled and uncoiled after its own lazy will. In the course of the morning they traveled up into a mild sunlight; the afternoon found them ranging along the shoulder of a hill; and before the sun had sunk far they were able to look down into the little valley of Ravi which was their destination. Amar could now point to the gray shingle roof of his father's house. It had been built on a small spur running out into the flat valley-bed, which was nearly all occupied by a shallow lake. The lake was fringed with willows and other water-loving trees; large stretches of it were covered with what looked like rushes and water-lilies; and flocks of birds kept rising and settling upon its surface. A cloudy sky hung above, but now and then a few watery beams would stray along the valley, silvering the water and lighting up the silvery green of the willows.

In this scene there was one feature that arrested Amar's attention, a group of gaily decorated tents close to his father's house. As he looked at them it dawned upon him that the encampment must be Prince Daniyal's; and, although Mobarek had prepared him for the Prince's presence somewhere in the neighborhood, it was a surprise to find him so near as this. Why had Daniyal not pitched his camp upon the usual ground on the other side of the lake? The reason did not become apparent until they were half-way down the slope, and then they saw that recent heavy rains had flooded the whole valley, turning the level water-meadows into a wide marsh. But surely, thought Amar, the Prince might have gone to some other place altogether, for it was obviously unfitting that a house where an old lady lay dying should be surrounded by the bustle of a royal encampment.

Upon reaching the house he committed Hari to the care of his father and hastened to his mother's bedside. Rajah Bihar was hardly known to Hari, who remembered him just well enough to perceive how greatly he had aged since their last meeting. A profound pity for the poor old man seized upon him at once, and this sentiment was dominant in his mind during the whole of his stay. For the next few days he had to spend his time almost uninterruptedly in the aged Rajah's company, for a heavy storm which broke out in the night continued without a single break. Day and night the house resounded to the rush and rattle of the gale, and, although he would gladly have passed the hours tramping about the wet hillsides, he saw himself obliged to sit in the semi-darkness indoors in order not to wound the feelings of his host. The house was an old-fashioned building, picturesque in the fashion of a bygone day, and no doubt pleasant enough in sunny weather, but inexpressibly gloomy when the rain came down like this. Its would-be quaintness and coziness then revealed themselves as nothing better than ugliness and dark discomfort. But it was the atmosphere of the house that oppressed Hari most; it breathed a stale breath of decrepitude which seemed to stifle the heart. And then too, alas! at all times and everywhere, hovering feebly and solicitously about him, was the tremulous figure of the old Rajah.

In his youth Rajah Bihar had been dapper and he retained a certain spruceness even now. Every morning he went through the ritual of a careful toilet and presented himself to the world with as soldierly a bearing as he could. His code bade him not only hide his feelings, but pass hurriedly over all his personal concerns. His daily reports on his wife were curt and, as it were, apologetic, giving place quickly to topics of more general interest. To make talk, to keep up appearances, was absolutely essential to his self-respect. Deep as his devotion to the Ranee was, sometimes in the midst of his talk he would actually forget to obey a summons to her bedside. His grief was the grief of the aged; buried under the ash of so many burnt-out years, it had no strength to flame; it smoldered, it smoldered; and how should it do more?

At times, as he was sitting stiffly in his chair opposite, Hari could see the swelling sorrow mount up into his watery old eyes. But then, clearing his throat and smoothing his white mustache with a fine silk handkerchief, he would launch out upon an ocean of commonplaces, and the sound of his own voice seemed to have a miraculous power to comfort him. The truth was that although able to keep up his self-respect and courage, these were the last qualities that he retained. So empty was his intelligence that Hari could not help hoping that it had never, even at its best, been anything more than mediocre; and how cynical, in any case, was the work of time; to leave self-respect and courage so naked that they —even they—appeared almost ridiculous. But perhaps—perhaps the old Rajah's stoicism was not so poignant after all. Perhaps it had its roots sunk deep in the knowledge that he could, and in the end he would, welcome Time's ultimate robbery, Life's ultimate consolation, the loss of the power even to suffer.

After the first few days Hari and Amar began to see a little more of one another and in these novel conditions each gradually discovered unsuspected elements in the other's character. Gratitude mingled with Amar's surprise at the surpassing patience shown by Hari towards his father. There was something in this, and in the whole of his present disposition, that the Rajah would have liked to understand better. Why did he prolong his stay in this house of discomfort and sadness? It looked almost as if he were deliberately subjecting himself to a new discipline; and the story came into Amar's mind how Buddha, when in the pride of youth, had gone forth one day and chanced to meet a woman stricken with disease, a man infirm with age, and a corpse. Legend had it that this incident marked a crisis in his spiritual development; and what if it should turn out that these days at Ravi were to make a similar turning point in Hari's career? In their talks together Hari showed that one side of his nature was deeply responsive to the Buddhist doctrine, but it was equally clear that there was another side that rebelled. In some of his arguments Amar was quick to observe the influence of Sita. For instance, what excellence, he would say, could one attribute to the ideal of self-extinguishment—more especially if it was sought merely as an appeasement of life's unrest? If pain and evil were inherent in individuality, happiness and goodness were also inconceivable apart from it. The true condition of blessedness must be one in which individuality was not extinguished but refined, intensified, and enlarged. Perfected selves, then, might be expected to continue their own existence—not primarily as enjoyers of happiness, but as centers for the radiation, the absorption, the interaction, of the world's ultimate goodness and beauty.

Amar remembered having heard this before and he could only answer now as he had answered then. Those were theories which experience could neither prove nor disprove; Buddhism was satisfied with another task; it would not choose to call itself a philosophy, or a religion, or even an ethic. It was not properly a philosophy, inasmuch as it dismissed most of the questions raised in metaphysics as entirely devoid of meaning; it was not a religion, inasmuch as it rejected dogma and made no concessions to desires that were vain; it was not an ethic, because it did not regard morality as the highest category; right behavior, it said, was not an end in itself, but merely one of the conditions that a man must satisfy in order to reach his goal. Buddhism did not profess to explain the world or to justify it; it did no more than teach the way of deliverance. The truth of its pronouncements was not susceptible of logical proof, because the truths of logic were truths in and for logic only; they were not truths in and for reality. The truths of reality were ultimate; and, although partially expressible in terms of conceptual knowledge, were not fully apprehensible in that sphere. They had to be felt as well as heard. They had to prove themselves in the immediate inward experience of the initiate. The teacher said: "It is thus!" and when the learner had learnt to see that thus it was, he rested upon his immediate intuition. "Knowledge," said Amar, "and by that I mean conceptual knowledge—propounds two riddles for every one that it solves. By standing outside the world to judge it, you create the subject-object relation which is a condition of knowledge, but an obstacle to the grasp of ultimate truth. The highest function of knowledge is to adjust itself to wisdom. And wisdom I define as the possession of ultimate truth. Wisdom does not answer all the riddles that knowledge propounds; it dissipates them."

This and much more did Amar explain in the semi-darkness of his father's inhospitable guest-chamber, with the rain obstinately hissing and drumming upon the roof, and the old Rajah, as often as not, dozing in a corner. Sadly, bitterly, did Hari contrast this wintry doctrine with the summer radiance of Sita's beliefs. And was it not something of a paradox that she had brought him an experience that lent weight, not to her view of life, but to Amar's? He was flying from her because this world was so ordered that the good here below could not be realized positively; it could only be shadowed forth in the ghostly shapes of abstinence and renunciation—earthly images of the ultimate Nirvana.

In these talks Hari and Amar drew together, but in a sphere far removed from everyday life, and it could not be said that they made any advance in real intimacy. If, covertly, they were giving each other a more interested observation than ever before, the cause of this lay elsewhere; it arose through the agency of Prince Daniyal. The position had been taking shape in this wise: the old Rajah had been naively excited and even flattered by the Prince's choice of a site, by the mere circumstance of his propinquity. In the first days this had been his staple topic; it inspired him with endless reminiscences of Court and camp; he took immense pride in having been on terms of intimacy with Akbar when the Emperor was a young man. It was plain that he hourly expected the Prince to make some sign of recognition of this, to show him a little more than the bare bones of civility; and while common courtesy enjoined a visit, the Prince, he made sure, would show him some small extra attention. It was lamentable, therefore, to count the days going by without this visit taking place, and to observe how a veil of chagrin thickened over the old man's earlier anticipations. First at one window and then at another he would watch with a brooding eye the activities of Daniyal's retinue; but while his feelings were hurt, his pride still held out. He did his best not only to ignore the Prince's neglect but to extenuate the unseemliness of the commotion that was made around the house.

Every day, every hour, added to the smart, and although he spoke hardly a word, one could see what form his bewilderment and pain were taking. The behavior of Akbar's son must mean that ever since his retirement from active service he had been living under a delusion. It had been a delusion that his name was of good report, that he was remembered at Court with respect and even—by some—with affection. This was all a dream; he had been forgotten; he was nothing. But, no! it was more likely that evil tongues had been busy about him and that his fair fame had been besmirched. Either one thing or the other; and now—well, there was no redress, it was too late to do anything.

With the spectacle of Rajah Bihar's distress constantly before one's eyes how was it possible to avoid having the Prince's presence outside the gates on one's mind all the time? And yet Hari had very soon found that the subject was not to be mentioned to Amar. Well, he thought at first, Amar no doubt did right to pass over Daniyal's unmannerliness with scorn; but later he could not rest in this opinion. Amar's obstinate silence, the air of complete indifference that he affected, became intolerable and threw Hari into an irritated mystification. A man needs must be either more or less than human not to foster some resentment at such behavior. There was no doubt that Amar found himself in a sorry predicament; he had to choose between being a bad Buddhist or an inhuman son. But why couldn't he be more open about it? For whose benefit was he wearing this mask of unconcern, which in truth, only drew attention to the feelings that it hid. It looked as if Amar was being disingenuous with himself, as if he was unable to judge this episode on its own merits. One suspected him of taking glances into the past and into the future; of feeling that the miserable little affair made—or threatened to make—complications. The arrangements he had just completed, the course he had mapped out—was everything to be upset by—well, just by this?

But enough! Hari went on to himself. Putting Amar out of the question, what of his own temper, his own attitude, in regard to the Prince? The moment had come when he was obliged to look closely at the matter, because, at last, the expression on poor old

Rajah Bihar's face had become too much for him and he was determined to take the affair into his own hands. In the first flush of his
resolve he told himself that while Amar, not being acquainted
with the Prince, could not very well take the initiative, it would
be a perfectly simple thing for *him* to do so. But—was it? The more
he thought about it the less he liked it. True, at the end of that
hunting trip four years ago, he and Daniyal had parted on perfectly
good terms; but mightn't Daniyal have changed in the interval—
just as he himself had? Of course, in his own case, there was Lalita; and he hadn't the shadow of a reason to suppose that Daniyal
wasn't innocent of all knowledge in *that* direction. But he honestly believed that his altered attitude towards Daniyal was not so
much due to jealousy as to one of those changes that arise from a
reinterpretation of character in the light of after-experience. Well
then! the approach was not one that he could make so confidently
after all. He would make it, but he would contrive to give the
meeting an accidental appearance; nor could he feel quite happy
about the manner of his reception.

19

AMAR SPENT MANY hours at his meditations. Sitting alone in an inner chamber, his back to the window, his eyes fixed upon a blank wall, he struggled daily with an exercise known as the Bramah Vihara. "Let thy mind," so the charge ran, "pervade one-quarter of the world with thoughts of love, and so the second, and so the third, and so the fourth. And thus the whole wide world, above, below, around, and everywhere, thou shalt continue to pervade with heart of love, far-reaching, grown great, and beyond measure. And just as a mighty trumpeter makes himself heard, and that without difficulty, towards all the four directions, even so of all things that have shape or form there is not one thou shalt pass by or leave aside; but regard them all with mind set free and deep-felt love." This exercise was to be repeated, substituting for love first pity, then sympathy, then equanimity. It was a meditation designed to break the fifth fetter, that of Ill-will. The first four fetters in their order were Delusions pertaining to the Self, Doubt, Reliance upon the efficacy of Good Works, and Sensuality. Until quite recently Amar had believed that his freedom from these shackles was won, and that he was therefore entitled to consider himself fairly launched upon the Path. But that confidence had now vanished. He had been smitten with an agonizing uncertainty whether the whole structure of his spiritual life was not in jeopardy. A seam had suddenly appeared upon the smooth wall of the edifice, a flaw which seemed to proclaim that the actual foundations were at fault. Ill-will had taken a hold upon him; and ill-will, he knew, can only subsist in a mind still obscured by self-love.

In this secluded chamber of his he had already wrestled for many hours and days, and his distress had steadily increased. He felt like a man who sees his life threatened, not by the blow of a sword, but by the prick of a pin. For his trouble in its external origin was paltry—a trifle of the meanest sort. But its very paltriness, by exasperating him, added to its venom. Deep was the humiliation of the thought that while his mother lay dying he had a mind to fret over a small piece of discourtesy on the part of a thoughtless young exquisite. That the slight was put upon his father and that his father took it so hard—no extenuation was to be found there—no, nor anywhere else. At such a time as this—no, no! To be pettily distracted at this moment of life; now, when it was his privilege to bear his mother company through her last days, her last hours, upon earth—God help him!—nothing could palliate the sorriness of such a self-betrayal. Some hidden smallness of character was coming to light; a concealed debility, a rot—and a rot that was progressive.

Every day the poison of his self-preoccupation was spreading further and further through his system. He was fast becoming a spiritual hypochondriac; his will, strong for any other task he set it, balked before this: he could not put away that particular knot of trivial concern; his pride was roused; he could not achieve inattention to self. And the fact that he saw this, understood it, admitted it: this was the last link in the vicious circle of his self-bondage.

One morning, when he was sitting in his mother's room, there came a veritable crisis in his sufferings. His nerves had just been put on edge by a meeting with his father in the passage. In that offhand manner of his that was so pitiful as a pretense the old Rajah announced that an application had just been made by Daniyal's chief cook: the man begged for the loan of some kitchen pots and pans; they were wanted for a supper-party that evening, which was to be a specially grand affair. Of course, said the old Rajah, he had replied that he was delighted to be of any service to His Royal Highness, delighted and honored—of course, of course. . . . And rather guiltily, rather defiantly, he had shuffled away, bleating with a laugh that had no sense, and mumbling through his gray hairs.

It was with the flavor of this encounter on his palate that Amar sat by the window, reading aloud from the *Mahabharata*; and the magnificence of the thought and language served only to sharpen his self-disgust. Never had he felt more keenly the distinction between the essential and the trivial, the sacred and the petty; never had the wings of his spirit beat more frantically to reach the upper air; but never, alas! had his mortal nature responded more dully, never had his sense of frustration been more acute. He knew this passage so well that he had no need of the book; nevertheless, he kept his head bent over it, for he feared to meet the eyes that he knew were fixed upon him. In the last two days his mother had become so weak that it was plain the end must be very near. Those eyes that gazed with such a mysterious intensity, those lineaments that he loved above all others—not much longer would they belong to the world of material things. Memories! very soon they would be that. And this sunny morning in this quiet room— that, too, a memory, a memory! O bitterness of time, with love such a trifle in its immensity! And those last moments of closeness, passing, passing, passing; in how many hours would they be over and gone?

He heard his voice reading in the quiet room, he smelt the jasmine upon the air, his spirit struggled. There was no haven where it could find rest. The images of the world haunted him; his old father, Hari, Daniyal . . .

In the same voice he continued to read on, but presently his gaze wandered out through the window and swept the shining landscape. It fell upon three human shapes standing in a field of emerald grass, whilst around them in a circle there caracoled a piebald stallion held on a long rein. In spite of the distance he could see everything clearly, and his ear, suddenly extending its range, caught the sound—and even the intonations—of those far-away voices. One of the men was a groom, the other two were Hari and Daniyal. They were following the horse with their eyes, and some joke had just passed between them. He could tell from their movements and gestures alone what the tone of their intercourse was. Daniyal was flinging himself about, pirouetting, and kicking up the turf at his feet. Evidently he was in high fettle, and Hari, too, seemed . . .

Abruptly Amar averted his eyes, recalled his attention, and heard again the splendor of the verses that were falling from his lips. But what a new surge of emotion ran, hissing, over the uttered words. That meeting—he could not believe it had been wholly accidental. Hari was risking a snub to do what he himself, pocketing his pride, should perhaps, for his poor father's sake, have done. The perspiration broke out upon his brow; a hundred different ways of envisaging the case, a hundred conflicting modes of feeling, rushed forward to be examined in the gray north light of his self-mistrust. And all the time this was going on, a part of his mind was outside with those two men upon that sunlit field; another part was downstairs, in the shadows, companioning with exasperated pity his poor, foolish father; and yet another part was here, here in this room, seeing, hearing, feeling—every sense alert.

Above all, he was conscious of his mother's mysterious regard. Whether those eyes of hers saw, or into what plane of existence her blank, dark vision penetrated, that he could not tell. Her eyes so deeply sunk in that emaciated face, were like two holes through which a man might look into the darkness beyond life. To her, he imagined, nothing now remained but a sense of human mortality. She did not guess his anguish. No, no! She still believed in his security. She heard only the sound of his voice, which to her was tranquillity. Perhaps she had passed beyond everything now—even love. Love, which last of all would surrender its claim to life, love itself, had closed its eyes, murmured its own blessing, and died out of her heart. Certainly she was a very old woman, and very sick, and it was blessed that she should die. Blessed had she been in her simplicity; and even so—very simply, without doubt—without mistrust—let her pass out of life.

He would leave her now. He would leave her at this moment while he had the courage to look steadily into her face. Her lids had just dropped; but she was not dead—only asleep. He could still see the pulse beating in her neck. "Your mistress is sleeping," he whispered to an attendant, and without a sound he was gone.

Back in his own chamber he made no attempt to follow a course of prescribed meditation, but threw himself upon his couch and let his anguish lead him where it would. Gradually it abated. In the afternoon he found his mother able to speak. She was at peace, as he had forced himself to continue to believe. When he left her he was happier than he had been for some time. And so the day wore on.

In the evening, as he was sitting with his book, news came that Prince Daniyal was below. Yes, only a moment ago His Royal Highness had been ushered into the guest-chamber (the servant was all a-tremble with excitement), and the Maharajah, his father, urgently besought him to come down at once. Amar inclined his head, and for a little while after the man had gone remained sitting in his place with a countenance upon which there dwelt a smile. That smile had many shades of meaning; as a comment it fell most scathingly perhaps upon himself.

Downstairs he found Daniyal seated in the place of honor with two of his gentlemen in attendance, whilst the old Rajah was bowing out his ceremonious speeches. To these manners (which had been out of date for some time) Daniyal responded with sufficient amiability, although it was evident that not the whole of his attention was engaged. His glances wandered, and in his eyes there was a veiled gleam of amusement. No doubt, thought Amar, this distant twinkle had helped to earn for him the reputation of a man of humor. He looked as if he might be holding a witty thing up his sleeve. This, however, would hardly be an occasion for producing it.

When everyone was seated refreshments were handed round and the exchange of civilities continued, the principal speakers being the old Rajah and one of Daniyal's gentlemen, whose special function it seemed to be to save the Prince unnecessary trouble of this kind. Now, at last, for the first time in his life, Amar had the opportunity of studying Daniyal at close quarters. He saw a good-looking young man of medium height, a fair-skinned, smooth-fleshed youth, who gave an impression of perfect physical well-being. Perhaps Daniyal was a trifle broad at the hips; perhaps he was a little too plump for his twenty years; his chin and mouth, maybe, were a shade too full in their modeling. But these imperfections might be considered insignificant; and perhaps it was some other and more inward blemish that reminded Amar that Daniyal was the son of Akbar by a slave. That thought, whatever its origin, was very prominently before him now, filling him with speculations about the girl whom he had never seen—that beautiful creature, who had died at Daniyal's birth—died after less than a year of notoriety, leaving her parentage and provenance unknown. Her beauty, by all report, had been of the kind that can only arise from an unusual mixture of blood. There was little doubt in many minds that she had taken from somewhere a strong Persian strain; but the more knowing in these matters let that pass as unimportant, and insisted that her most marked characteristics—the wonderful surface, the close texture, of her flesh—gave unmistakable indications of a possibly remote, but still prepotent, Chinese ancestry.

Amar's eyes rested upon Daniyal gravely, benignly; and no one (except possibly Sita or Hari) could have guessed how diligently the work of appraisal was going on behind that smooth brow. Daniyal, unquestionably, had comeliness and ease; he wore an air of negligent authority; he was as handsome a young prince as anyone could wish to see. All the hues and curves of youthful health were there; flawless the whites of his eyes and the enamel of his teeth, fresh the skin, and the hair as glossy as the coat of a well-groomed horse. Amar's attentive smile, the gentle side-tilt of his head, might well have been taken as tokens of approbation, of regard, of pleasure in the royal condescension. And it was true, and more than true, that Amar was pleased; only his pleasure was not of that sort at all, it was the pleasure of well-satisfied disdain.

How exactly had this come about? Amar himself would not have been able to say. Although he was observing Daniyal very carefully, his sentiment was not built up on any conscious assessment. It was too quick, spontaneous, and assured, for that. The scrutiny was merely confirmatory. And again, Amar's standards were so completely a part of his heritage that he was never really conscious in his application of them. All he knew was that in the presence of the Prince he got an immediate impression of vulgarity—or of something, at any rate, which for want of a better word had to be called vulgarity. It was a pity no other term would fit, because the defect was reflected so shadowily on to the external man; it was a defect of spirit, of the innermost spirit—something that betrayed itself primarily to the moral sense.

Further than this Amar did not care to go. It suited him to rest here; to feel what he felt, to see what he saw; with that he was more than content. The only thing that troubled him now was the sense of his past foolishness. Good heavens! To think that he had allowed his pride—even the surface of his pride—to be ruffled! Well, let this be a lesson; let him mark well that he was still liable to be impressed by a name, to be imposed upon—just like all the world—by the world's own rumor. As long as the object itself kept out of sight, he could still be fooled by its prestige.

After a few minutes the Prince rose to his feet and—much to his host's surprise and gratification—asked to be shown round the room. True, the old Rajah set no great store by his possessions, but the house stood as his parents had made it, and this gave it a certain place in his esteem. So the round began, and it was not long before Amar perceived that Daniyal was genuinely interested, only his interest was not at all of the kind his father imagined. The old gentleman had remembered that Daniyal was an amateur of the arts, and from the way in which the Prince paused before this object and that, he was led to believe that his house must really contain specimens of rarity that were fit to give pleasure to a connoisseur. Very soon, at his orders, dusty old lumber was being pulled out into the light; furniture, cumbrous and grotesque in every conceivable fashion, was dragged creaking from its corners; and Daniyal did, indeed, eye each piece as it came with an enjoyment that rose higher and higher. Throwing lively glances over his shoulder at his two companions, he loudly declared that never would he rest content until he had fitted up a room in his palace exactly similar to this. And he was speaking the truth, for it was one of his diversions to illustrate the sophistication of his taste by caricaturing antiquated modes.

Amar, in the background, followed this scene with an air of grave and yet smiling detachment. To see his father as ridiculous would have been to bring himself down to a plane within measurable distance of Daniyal's. No, what he saw was the Prince cutting so lamentable a figure that he was almost able to pity him.

When the tour of inspection was over, the Prince made ready to leave. He was in good humor now, and quite graciously he expressed his regret that the Ranee's state of health forbade him to hope that either his host or Amar would wish to attend his supper-party. To

Hari, however, who at that moment came into the room, he offered an invitation.

After he had gone, the old Rajah, even more tremulous than usual, but also far more alert and erect, began strutting about the room with his most soldierly air. A fine young man, he swore; oh yes, you could see at a glance whose son he was. And this went on until it occurred to him to hurry upstairs, hoping that he might find his good wife able to share his satisfaction in the proud event.

His departure left the two others burdened with a good many small embarrassments. To get rid of one of them, to let Hari see where he stood, Amar put warmth into his tone and said: "I know whom I have to thank for this visit; I caught sight of you this morning out of the window. Really, my dear Hari, that was a crowning act of kindness."

Hari actually colored. "I can't think why I didn't do it before. The Prince showed himself perfectly amiable."

After this they went on talking about Daniyal, and although the talk had a fair appearance of naturalness, there was considerable strain beneath the surface. Nothing said was more than a half-truth; to go further in any direction would be, each felt, a dangerous and difficult venture. But contact with Amar's mind (even of this gingerly sort) had the effect of concentrating Hari's attention upon the "vulgarity" in Daniyal. His sense of it in the past had remained floating in suspension; a drop of acid from Amar's particular fastidiousness had been needed to precipitate it.

But if he got something from Amar's sensibility, did Amar get nothing in return? It seemed not. Amar was satisfied with what he could see out of his own eyes. He was careful not to say—but he implied—that after seeing the Prince for himself he simply could not imagine how anyone should find the slightest difficulty in describing him with a single word. But there, never mind! Perhaps other people had a vision that pierced deeper than his. This unspoken comment Hari found exceedingly irritating; but he could not very well retort to what had not been said.

Just as they were about to part, however, the atmosphere suddenly changed. They dropped into what seemed by contrast a pronounced bluntness.

"I don't think I shall go to Daniyal's supper-party to-night," Hari announced without warning.

"Oh!" Amar looked his surprise. "Why not?"

"I am not definitely committed."

"But why not go?"

"Because I don't like that young man."

Amar gave a little laugh. "Like him? Of course you don't! How should you? Why should you? It is merely a question . . ."

Hari interrupted with a bark of impatience. "Oh, I know your views."

"It would seem," remarked Amar blandly, "more polite to go."

A little ashamed of his outburst, Hari laughed. "Very well then! I will."

About an hour before dawn in that same night Amar was roused from sleep by Hari's manservant, who burst into the room with the news that his master had been seized by Daniyal's guards and placed under arrest. It appeared that Hari was accused of having behaved in a manner insulting to the Prince.

Amar's emotion was one of extreme annoyance and even of dismay. He was alarmed for Hari; something serious might lie at the back of this affair; the spleen of jealousy—dangerously disclosed—on Hari's side; or the animosity of an aroused suspicion on Daniyal's. And then he had his own position to think about. An unpleasantness of this kind would be apt to strain the relations of all concerned. It would certainly do him no good to fling himself in on Hari's behalf, and that was what he now had to do.

While making ready to go across to Daniyal's camp he racked his brains with profitless surmises; the thought that the Prince's rudeness to his father might have helped to bring the disaster about only served to inflame his annoyance. Without loss of time he presented himself at the Royal Tent, and although the Prince did not decline to see him, he refused all discussion, referring him to two of his gentlemen-in-waiting, with whom he was marched off. Throughout the whole length of the ensuing negotiations these two young men acted as go-betweens, and very incompetent and self-important and silly did they show themselves to be. A long, tedious comedy of recriminations, explanations and apologies (the apologies were all invented by Amar, for Hari remained sulky and obdurate) unrolled itself during the course of the morning. Hour after hour went by, at last noon came and went, and still the case remained undecided. It was illustrative of the absurdity of the proceedings that Amar never discovered how the trouble had actually arisen, nor did he even get it perfectly clear in his mind in what manner precisely Hari had offended. Nevertheless, in the end, his good offices were crowned with success; he was able to inform Hari that the Prince had relented so far as to agree to his being sent under escort to Agra, there to be detained during a further consideration of his case. "You are getting off very lightly," Amar went on, "because although still technically under arrest, you will be lodged in the palace and your jailer will be our good friend Narsing. Besides, I have been given to understand that at the end of a couple of weeks you will be told that Prince Daniyal has graciously accepted your apologies and granted you a pardon." He spoke in a tone of weariness and exasperation, and Hari, although he had scowled at the word apologies, had the grace to express himself grateful. A few hours later he set out under escort for Agra.

20

NOT MANY DAYS later Hari found himself once again leaning over the balustrade of the Great Terrace at Agra. During his sojourn in the palace before joining Gokal in the Hills, he had become very familiar with the wide, heat-stricken prospect stretching away below; he had spent hours gazing over it, while his heart was aching unendurably for Lalita. The countryside looked different now under its veil of green, and his feelings for Lalita had changed their color too.

Day after day, on his journey down from the Hills, he had ridden along deeply engaged by the changing company of his thoughts. They held him in an unbroken reverie from which not even his arrival in Agra had as yet sufficed to rouse him. Vaguely he had noticed that the bazaars, so thronged and noisy before, were now comparatively quiet; the place evidently had lost half its life with the departure of the Emperor from Fatehpur-Sikri. Then, too, the wet season had commenced, but without doing much to abate the heat; in the streets people were hanging about their doors listlessly; and at the great gate of the palace, instead of the usual crowd, there was only the gatekeeper and his guard.

His reverie continued until a step sounded behind him and Narsing's voice rang out. The tone was round and hearty, but, thought Hari, unless the evening light was deceiving him, the man's face

153

had grown haggard and old. This hardly seemed possible in so short an interval, and yet—yes, weariness was dragging at those heavy features; and presently, as if giving in to the truth, Narsing let his tone change; he heaved a great sigh and said: "You won't find much gaiety left here, I am afraid; nor will you find me a very cheerful companion. No, Hari Khan, I am out of sorts. I am dull. Dull"—he added in the manner of an aside—"but not peaceful."

While they were standing there the sun went down behind clouds and a roll of thunder came out of the distance. Hari was expecting to be questioned about Daniyal, but either from discretion or indifference Narsing left the subject alone. His mind, like his body, seemed to have become flaccid. He mopped his forehead; he drew difficult breath; his comments upon current affairs were gloomy and confused. After a while Hari interrupted him to inquire after Mabun; and at that Narsing threw up his hands and hunched his shoulders expressively. Mabun—let no one make any mistake!—was now a personage, a man of high dignity; honors had been showered upon him, so that he now took his place amongst the great ones of the land. "Ah, that little fellow's cleverness!" he exclaimed at the end. "He seems to know everything. He makes me feel like a child."

They were still on this topic when the man himself appeared. There was a beaming welcome in his face, his voice was as crisp as ever, his gestures had lost none of their alertness. Hari was pleased by the cordiality shown him, for he had taken a liking to Mabun during his last stay in the palace. Without a moment's hesitation the latter began to question him about "that little affair with the Prince"; but Hari, remembering that Mabun was by way of being on very good terms with Daniyal, was laughingly evasive in his replies.

During the next few days the rain was incessant and he mooned about the palace a prey to restlessness and self-dissatisfaction. Neither Narsing nor Mabun made their appearance, Narsing being in bed with fever, and Mabun—so the message went—busy with urgent State affairs. At last, upon an afternoon of dull, sullen heat, Hari ordered a horse, and, having been given his parole, was permitted to go out riding by himself. Instinctively he turned his horse's head in the direction of the Royal Hunting Grounds and, upon reaching the wood, took a path in the direction of the deserted hunting-box where he had first met Gunevati. As he rode along memory and imagination grew busy with the scene, and his curiosity to see the place again grew stronger every moment. What a dreary aspect the house would wear under these gray skies! He could see it in his mind's eye standing wet and forlorn in the center of its tangle of weeds. By now the weeds and vines would, he imagined, very nearly have submerged it.

After twice losing his way he came to what he took to be the place; and yet it seemed to him still that somehow he must be making a mistake. If it was the same clearing, what had become of the bungalow? Several moments passed while he stood staring; then he urged his horse forward until he came to some blackened stones with pieces of charred timber lying here and there amongst them. This, evidently, was all that remained of the building. After walking his horse up and down to scare away the snakes, he fell to searching the ground. It seemed reasonable to suppose that something—some scraps of metal, for instance—might still be there. Perhaps at the back of his mind there was the fantastic notion that he might come across the remains of Lalita's riding-whip. But he found nothing at all; and after a little while he gave up, remounted, and went on again.

It was not long before he was passing by Gokal's pavilion, and then he entered the little path that he had so often followed with so eager a heart only a few months ago. Those days now seemed very distant, and the rains had changed the aspect of every bush and tree; but the little bungalow itself looked just the same, except that its wooden sides had been stained dark by the rain, and the branches of the now leafy trees seemed to hug it around more closely. It had a secret air. After tying his horse up to the broken fence, he tried the door and succeeded in pushing it open without difficulty. The room which he and Lalita used to occupy had, at his own orders, been dismantled, and it was now bare. He felt no emotion whatever as he looked about; in fact, he could not help wondering what impulse had brought him here. Noticing some marks upon one of the walls, he walked across the creaking floor and found that someone had outlined in ochre the figures of a man and a woman. The drawing was obscene, and as he examined it the thought struck him that possibly there had been an intention of portraiture. Flushing hotly with anger and disgust, he turned away and walked out of the house.

On his homeward path he was occupied with dream-like musings which had for their point of departure the burnt-out hunting-box and the obscene drawing. What hand had done these things? And was any significance to be attached to them? Probably not. And yet every man was walking through a world of unheard voices and unseen eyes; every man was dragging along with him through life an unperceived web of observation and comment that sometimes decided his fate.

Without noticing what he was doing, he reined up in front of Gokal's house, dismounted, and sat him down upon the terrace steps. His eyes stared out, unseeing, over the lake. When he next became conscious of his surroundings it was to observe that the air was uncannily still; not a leaf moved anywhere; there was a peculiar absence of all sound. His horse seemed to feel this strangeness as well as he; it stood without a twitch or a quiver, hanging its head low.

"I am alone in the world," thought Hari, "and every man is for ever alone." His sense of solitariness was overpowering, and all at once the words of the sage sprang into his mind: "Religion is what a man does with his solitariness." At this moment he could do nothing with his solitariness; it was too overpowering. So he started up, flung himself upon his horse, and went on again.

The next day it was too wet to go for a ride, and in the afternoon he decided that pride should not prevent him from taking the initiative and paying Mabun a visit. Making his way over to the distant wing which was reserved for the State official and his activities, he obtained admission to Mabun's small private suite; and there his host, notwithstanding the pressure of his affairs (Hari could now see for himself that the excuse was real enough), entertained him so cordially that he was encouraged to go again. He followed this visit up with several more during the course of the next two weeks; but he still remained uncertain how far he could trust Mabun and became impatient for Srilata's return to Agra in order to question her about him. He did not have very much longer to wait, for Srilata, who had no love of rusticity, always came back to town some time before anyone else. They met, as usual, in the garden behind her house, and she confessed immediately that she was full of the greatest curiosity to hear what had actually occurred at the unfortunate supper-party. He could trust her, she said, not to gossip; and of course it was of the greatest importance that stories should not be spread abroad, lest Daniyal, feeling that his dignity was touched, should become really vindictive.

Never had Hari been better pleased to find himself in Srilata's sympathetic company, but the supper-party was not a subject that he wanted to talk to anyone about. "For heaven's sake," he exclaimed, "let us leave that miserable affair alone! What do you want me to say—beyond making the admission that I lost my temper?"

"But *why* did you lose your temper?"

"I really don't know."

"Oh, nonsense! And, anyhow—what did you *do*?"

"Well"—and he shrugged—"the moment came when I could stand that company no longer. So I got up to leave the room—but, unfortunately, two or three foolish people stood in my way."

"I see," said Srilata blandly.

There was a pause during which Hari seemed to be consulting his memory; but nothing came of it; all that he finally said was: "Anyhow, it will soon all blow over."

Srilata looked troubled. "I gather that you took a violent dislike to Daniyal."

"I confess I did."

Srilata said nothing; and her silence told him quite plainly what it was that she was thinking: he was jealous of Daniyal; that had been the trouble.

Well, it suited him to leave it at that. Nevertheless, he must not, he felt, remain entirely dumb. "It is a question of personality, I suppose." He threw this out with a somewhat grudging air. "Or you might call it a question of taste. Daniyal and his friends happened to offend my taste. It doesn't sound very important, I know; but you can see, I'm sure . . ."

What Srilata did see was that he was not inclined to go into details, and she had no idea of pressing him. Perhaps he had resented some reference (it might have been a slighting one, for she knew her Daniyal) to Princess Lalita. Whilst respecting his reserve, she was also somewhat disquieted by it. When a man is reticent about his past follies the reason often is that he nourishes the intention of repeating them. Before taking his leave, too, Hari added another shade to her misgivings; he asked her for her opinion of Mabun: "Just how far is that nice little fellow to be trusted? That's what I want to know," he said.

"Not so far as me!" she answered smiling, and a rather significant pause had preceded her reply.

"Of course not; I know that. But still—within reason, I suppose?" For a second he seemed to consider deeply. "Is he really—at bottom—such a friend of Daniyal's?"

"Yes, certainly. At least I have no reason to think otherwise."

She said this with great decision, and it seemed to her that Hari was allowing her words their full emphasis. But, with him, you never knew.... What, she wondered, could he be meditating now? After he had left, she raised her eyebrows and sighed.

To get a view of Mabun divested of his charming manners, a view of him in workaday dress, that had been Hari's ambition for a long time. The way to do it occurred to him the next morning; so he put on some very old clothes and went round to the back of the palace buildings, where there was generally a small crowd waiting for an audience with the great man. Mingling with the rank and file he was duly admitted into a waiting-room, and from there, when the porter's back was turned, he slipped into the immense hall at the far end of which Mabun was transacting business. Standing among some men who were being called up, one by one, for examination, he stared across the room at what was going forward. The spectacle fascinated him. Those quick little gestures of Mabun's, the narrowing eyes, a glance that darted, an intelligence that you could see pouncing on its point. At what a pace that mind went! There was never a moment when Mabun's thought was not obviously far in advance of everybody else's. It was doubly clear now that amongst his social equals he habitually did his best to hide his advantage; but here he was ruthless; he cut his interlocutor short; his least word had a terrible trenchancy. Two or three minutes, as a rule, sufficed for each man; when the interview took longer he was weighing not merely the speech but the speaker, and then sometimes he would become leisurely, almost suave; his head nodded understandingly, his eyelids drooped. But after an interval this manner would be whisked off; he would straighten himself, and the few words that were rapped out sent the man smartly about his business.

At length, having seen enough, Hari pushed his way through the front line of onlookers and waited for the moment when Mabun's eye should fall upon him. It happened soon enough, and with a sharp movement of surprise the examiner paused; then presently, after dismissing the creature before him, he hurried down the room. "Hari Khan, what brings me this unexpected honor?" Hari laughed and murmured nothing definite, but in the long, smiling look that he fixed upon Mabun something significant was no doubt conveyed. At any rate there came a pause, a brief interval in which Mabun seemed to be registering a new intimation. His manner, which in coming forward had had all its usual gay urbanity, again tightened, but with a difference. Hari had before him neither the man of society, nor the man of business, but yet another.

"Let me see"—his glance swept the room—"I think I can break off now. Yes, if you will excuse me for one moment, Hari Khan. . . ."

He beckoned to an assistant and gave orders. "There, I am ready now. Follow me, if you please. I am at your service." And he led the way out of the hall by a side-door.

They went down several passages in the direction of the suite where Mabun had been in the habit of receiving him. Mabun's manner was grave, with a particular gravity that Hari had never seen him wear before; furthermore, he appeared to be revolving some very difficult thoughts. After they had gone a little way he stopped. A decision seemed to have ripened; he halted beside a window and by its light subjected Hari to a friendly, but probing, scrutiny. "Yes," he pronounced at last, "I think we might as well have our talk in here." Taking a few steps down another passage, he unlocked a small door, and, smiling a little, he bade Hari enter. "I will join you," he said, "in ten minutes."

The room in which Hari found himself was small, comfortably furnished, but not well aired; and this at once drew his attention to the fact that the windows were so high above the ground that no one could see in from outside. The moment the door closed he began looking about him. He was conscious of an excitement which went deep, but was well under control. He knew that he was about to disregard Srilata's warning. After all, one had to follow one's own instincts about a man; and the sight of Mabun at work had, somehow, brought him to a determination. As he looked around, Mabun's rather deliberate choice of this little room was a stimulus to his curiosity. Books and musical instruments were lying about, and in one corner there was a hookah with some charred tobacco still in the bowl. (That was odd, perhaps, for Mabun did not smoke.) On a table in the opposite corner there lay an object wrapped in silk. Before this Hari paused, and then suddenly snatched it up. His fingers ran along the silk, feeling at what was underneath; then he untied the silken cord, pulled off the covering, and brought to light just what he had begun to expect—Lalita's riding-whip.

For a minute or two he stood there, looking straight before him and smiling to himself. Then he swished the whip through the air and laughed gently. It had certainly been very tactful of Mabun to give him ten minutes in which to think matters over. But ten minutes, ten days, or ten years—it was all the same! Was Mabun the man he took him for? Everything hinged upon that.

21

"WELL!" SAID MABUN, entering briskly, "I hope, my dear
Hari Khan, you found something to interest you during my absence? Ah!" he exclaimed, his smile expanding, "I see you did."

Hari was still standing on the same spot and the whip was still
in his hands. Swishing it through the air once more, he gave
Mabun a long, level look; and the smile, on his side, was a questioning one.

"A very fine gem that—in the handle," Mabun remarked with
the gentlest of malice.

"Oh, very!"

Amusement was reflected on both faces, and it was with a particularly friendly shade of courtesy that Mabun invited his guest
to be seated. He himself sat down on the same divan, facing and
quite near.

"My dear Hari Khan"—and his delicate hand fluttered out to
give a reassuring touch to Hari's knee—"I am going to explain
everything as quickly as I can. You must on no account be disconcerted. Your secrets are quite safe in my keeping."

Hari nodded. Although he certainly had every reason to be disconcerted, what he experienced for the moment was rather a feeling of elation.

"Incidentally, I shall have to tell you a good many secrets of my own," Mabun continued. "It is fortunate that we can trust one another, because, as you will see, our paths have met and we are destined to travel along side by side. Now, first of all, listen to this: Prince Daniyal is no friend of mine."

At this—so prompt and unequivocal a confirmation of his suspicions—Hari almost started; at any rate, he revealed his feelings sufficiently to cause Mabun to smile and say:

"Yes, that is important, is it not?" A slight pause underlined the words before he went on: "And now, something more, my friend: for the last three years I have been busy weaving a net in which to snare the Prince; and at last my net, I think, is strong enough to hold him. For the last three years, Hari Khan, I have studied my man; all his goings-out and comings-in have been watched. The task has not been easy because it would have been fatal if the Prince had formed suspicions. And he is cunning. . . . Oh, always taking precautions! Never off his guard! For example, on the evening of your arrival in Agra (Ah, how well, you and I, we remember that evening, Hari Khan!) he gave my agents the slip. When they picked up his traces again he was recovering from a slight accident—a slight accident, Hari Khan, a slight accident!"— and Mabun's eyes twinkled gaily.—"He had been knocked down by a horse and stunned. As you can imagine, I made every effort to probe into the affair, and I finally discovered on what errand he had been bound. My dear Hari Khan, let me confess that I was overcome by blank astonishment! The Prince as a Vamachari, it was unthinkable! As we know, he has no taste for women; still less is he to be suspected of religious fanaticism. And yet—there was no mistake! One explanation alone offers itself: he was seeking a new sensation. It was a flight from ennui, from the boredom in which he is everlastingly imprisoned. Ah!" murmured Mabun, after a moment of apparent musing, "may you and I never know to what an inferno of boredom a man may descend!

"This discovery was the most important I had yet made. I continued to push my inquiries in every direction; I re-examined all the witnesses I could lay my hands on; I left no stone unturned. Nothing more came to light until one of my men brought in to me that whip. He had found it in the thatch of the cottage inhabited by that girl, Gunevati. When I saw the gem in the handle I knew at once from whose hand the whip had fallen. I gave orders that Princess Lalita should be watched, and a few days later of course I knew everything." Mabun laughed gently. "I knew then what kind of goat you had been hunting in the mountains; I could follow the movements of your mind upon that fateful evening five months ago. Oh, you were very clever in putting us all off the scent! Allow me to congratulate you, Hari Khan, on that; and still more—if I may do so without impertinence—on your love-affair—for, indeed, the Princess is very charming—but most of all, most of all, my friend, I want to congratulate you on *this*: fate, through me, is putting great power into your hands; you and I, between us, we can bring confusion upon Prince Daniyal; we can destroy your rival and safeguard the future of the Empire."

Laughing gaily at the flourish of his own rhetoric, Mabun sprang to his feet; and an unfeigned excitement sent him tripping lightly up and down the room. Opposite there was an alcove, and it was characteristic of the man that, even in this dance of exultation, he stopped to take a look behind the curtain hanging over it, as if one could never make too sure of one's privacy. Never had Hari seen him in any aspect even remotely resembling this. Here was the real Mabun, the delighted machinator, the ardent plotter, the enthusiast for intrigue.

After a minute he was back again, and in a voice hushed by its own intensity he proceeded to expound and explain. Everything went to show that Akbar's rage against the secret sects was reaching its culmination; with great pomp and circumstance he had just elevated the Prince to High Priesthood in the Din Ilahi; the explosives were ready; so now for the spark, the spark!

Hari was listening, attentive indeed, but apparently half dazed. The minutes passed; another hour passed; and still Mabun's fluency was the same. It was curious that in all this time Hari's demeanor did not change. He sat there heavily and hardly said a word.

At last, after a truly magnificent peroration, the display was over; the flashing, sparkling torrent of Mabun's eloquence had run itself out, or rather—so abrupt was his descent into tranquillity—the appearance was given of a tap being suddenly turned off. With a sigh—not too deep a one—the orator relaxed, seemed to take stock of his results, and his gentle smile admitted that they were not wholly satisfactory. Well, no need to be discouraged yet! He gathered himself together again, but obviously for an experiment in another line. He laid a hand once more upon Hari's knee, a small brown hand that greatly resembled a monkey's, and in a quiet voice he said: "Hari Khan, I see that you are still mistrustful. But why, I ask, do you not rely a little more upon your insight into character? Am I so difficult to understand? For my part, I trust my insight, and that is why I speak to you without fear. Oh yes, how should I not know you, when five minutes with a man is all I ever need. Let me point out this, Hari Khan: there is all the difference in the world between the judging of a character and the judging of a lie. All men lie; and almost any fool can lie well enough to take in even a clever man. But with character it is different. It is very difficult for a man to conceal what he really is. Oh, *I* know *you* well enough, my dear Hari! And when I say I know a man I mean that I know what kinds of things he is prepared to lie about, what kinds of people he will lie to, and what kinds of reasons he will have for so doing. Few people lie entirely without reason, and in most cases the reasons are good. So many people ask to be lied to and deserve nothing better. You see, it takes two to make a lie; and it is the stupidity, or the prejudice, or the self-conceit, of one party that makes the lie necessary. Hari Khan, you are a man to whom certain lies would be most repugnant. But there are more important things in the world than truth-telling, my friend! And sometimes it is a sin to be squeamish. Is that not so?" For a brief instant only he paused. It was evident that he did not really wish for an answer. "Are you waiting for more evidence of my confidence in you? Well, well; you shall have it! You shall have it! But is it not time that you opened your mind to me—just a little—in return?"

At the end of this strange dissertation Mabun laughed softly, looking deep into Hari's eyes as he did so. Nothing could well be more engaging, and Hari smiled and stirred uncomfortably as if only too conscious of his churlishness.

"Mabun Das," he said at last. "Ask me what questions you will. I will not refuse to answer them."

Mabun sketched a light gesture in the air. "Why should I want to catechize you, my friend? Are *you* not the best judge of what I should be told? There may be things I should like to hear; there may be things I have no business to hear. You are not a fool, Hari Khan. You guessed that I was no friend of Prince Daniyal's; else why did you come to me this morning?"

"Yes. I guessed that."

"Exactly."

Hari pursed his lips. "Forgive me! I take no interest in politics."

"My friend," said Mabun slowly, "if you are involved you are involved. But why trouble yourself about the political aspect of the affair. Leave that to me. Let this question stand in your mind as a personal one." He paused. "Let it be simply a question"—he paused again and leant forward with very bright eyes—"a question of planting your heel upon the neck of the cobra."

Hari considered and finally gave a nod. "Very good. What then?"

"First of all," said Mabun decisively, "there comes this quarrel of yours with the Prince. You must let me know how you stand."

Hari got up and stretched his cramped limbs. "I don't know if you will understand me," he said in a quiet voice; "but even now I am quite uncertain what my feelings about Daniyal really are. When I say I detest him, does that cover the whole ground? The Prince, even as a boy, commanded my admiration. And the other day I found that his personality worked upon me like a challenge. I know him to be courageous. He is prepared to follow his wickedness wherever it may lead him."

Standing in front of Mabun, he looked down into his face and frowned thoughtfully. "I suppose you want to hear about that supper-party?" There was an inflection in his voice at which Mabun inwardly smiled. He, too, like Srilata, knew his Daniyal well, and with a ready tact he set about helping his interlocutor out. That brilliantly lighted tent and those twenty or thirty young men, for the most part powdered and scented—how well he could imagine it, he mused aloud. He, in his time, had assisted at more than one such gathering. But no doubt for Hari it had been a new experience —and not an agreeable one? Oh no, in fact really rather nauseating. . . . That chatter, those finicking manners, those airs of *petit maître* and *petite dame* combined. The sniggering delight they took in one another's mean little immoralities! Yes, yes, he could well see how Hari's impatience, his disgust, must gradually have reached boiling point; but—how had the crisis come? What, actually, had happened?

The blend of curiosity and sympathy in Mabun's manner was really intensely droll; and Hari laughed out loud; it was a laugh made rough by the memories evoked. "I will tell you exactly what happened, and you shall judge whether I had any excuse for losing my temper. Late in the evening a certain fair-haired youth, who was sitting next to Daniyal at table, left the room and presently returned dressed in a girl's clothes. Sitting himself down by Daniyal again, he proceeded to mimic Princess Lalita in her speech and manners. Daniyal was evidently prepared for the entertainment, for he played up. He completed the scene by fondling the creature and addressing him as 'Lalita darling.' "

Having spoken, Hari waited for Mabun's comments; but none came. For once in his life Mabun was experiencing disgust—or, at any rate, he had the tact to make it seem so. For a decent interval he turned his head away; then, after brushing the displeasing images aside—"The report," he said in a studiedly level voice, "the report stated merely that you had acted in a manner insulting to the Prince. I should like to ask: What did you actually do?"

Hari repeated what he had said to Srilata. "And that's the whole story."

"You spoke no word to anyone?"

"I said nothing at all."

Mabun nodded and closed his eyes. "What we have to consider is whether Daniyal acted with the express object of making you reveal yourself. I mean, has he any suspicions? I was a little surprised, I confess, on your arrival here, not to receive a private letter from him. You must remember that he looks upon me as a personal friend."

The silence that followed was a heavy one. Mabun's eyes were fixed upon Hari intently, but even in their steadiness they seemed to scintillate. Hari began to walk slowly up and down the room.

"Well, we shall see!" Mabun brought out in the end. "The order for your release is a little overdue already. If it does not soon come . . ."

Hari gave a brief laugh and continued his march up and down.

He had no idea how long Mabun and he had been closeted together, and his eyes wandered to the door. Without waiting for a further hint Mabun rose to his feet, and briefly they arranged for a renewal of the talk next morning. Quite unaware that he was still holding Lalita's whip in his hand, he was on the point of leaving the room when Mabun laid a detaining hand on his arm.

"Are you taking that whip with you, my friend?"

Hari broke into a laugh.

"Oh, Hari! Hari!" And Mabun with a head-shake drew him firmly away from the door. "Tell me! since your arrest you have not, I hope, had any communication with the Princess?"

Hari colored. "Yes. I sent her a word of warning. How could I refrain?"

"Of warning?"

"Certainly. I said: 'Marry the Prince if you will, but know this . . .'"

"It was rash."

"I took every precaution."

"You cannot even count upon her destroying your letters."

"I think I can."

Mabun made a gesture of impatience. "If we are to be fellow-conspirators, my dear Hari . . ."

"Fellow-conspirators is rather a strong word, isn't it, Mabun?"

"Why do you pretend to be half-hearted? I know you to be a man of spirit."

Hari fixed Mabun with intensity. "What exactly are you expecting of me?"

"In the first place, discretion, circumspection."

"And then?"

Mabun smiled and shrugged. "Oh, merely your testimony, your testimony. Nothing more 'political' than that!"

Hari paused and considered. "I wonder," he said reflectively, "I wonder why you dislike the Prince so much?"

"Your wonder is not very flattering," laughed Mabun; "but, in point of fact, the Prince is nothing to me. I am working for the welfare of the Empire."

Hari received this in silence.

"Akbar will die soon. The astrologers have foretold it. It is undesirable that Prince Daniyal should succeed him. Can you doubt it, Hari Khan?"

Hari shrugged. "For my part, I don't profess to be unbiased. But this question of our future ruler is an important one; and I should have thought that a man like you, immune from personal prejudices, might well have given the preference to Daniyal. He, at any rate, has intelligence; whereas his brother is likely to set the whole Empire by the ears."

At these words Mabun took a few steps away and surveyed Hari with eyes narrowed in an effort of the deepest deliberation. Then suddenly he began talking with extraordinary earnestness and fluency. "I will explain. Listen to me carefully, I beg. These are my reasons for preferring Prince Salim to Daniyal. Daniyal is in league with Mobarek and what Mobarek stands for is not good. That little Persian is called a mystic"—and Mabun snapped his fingers in derision—"but he is also a typical ecclesiastic. He has a vision of the unification of temporal and spiritual powers in this land. His mind has been dazzled by the splendors of Byzantine sacerdotalism at the height of its glory. He is an authoritarian; his ideal is a rigid hierarchy. He sees in the caste system, in the privileged position of the Brahmins, machinery ready to hand . . . and in the Emperor he finds a man endowed with the prestige, the potency, and perhaps the ambition, to give feasibility to his scheme. That is Mobarek! And if any man can make that dream of his come true, Akbar can do it. But Akbar will always be Akbar, a living man, an individuality, not the impersonal figure-head, the impassive symbol of an all-powerful Church. After Akbar there must be Daniyal, because Daniyal is ready to lend himself to those designs. Imagine a Holy Indian Empire with an Emperor-Pope at its head! And imagine the Emperor-Pope to be Daniyal, a debauched youth, surrounded by eunuchs and catamites; a living idol with painted cheeks who would be exhibited with ecclesiastical pomp before his prostrated subjects once or twice a year. The position would amuse Daniyal; it would appeal both to his cynicism and to his love of all that is meretricious and spectacular. The best part of his time he would spend in a seclusion of incredible magnificence, entertaining himself lightly, in the fashion of his set, with music, art, literature, and—sodomy. Everything much in his present style, but without any restraint . . . and without wanting for money."

Hari looked at Mabun dumbly; the rush of his words had been completely overpowering. Mabun stepped back a few paces and gave him a malicious little smile.

"Before you go," said he, "let me make my position absolutely clear. I am a secret supporter of Prince Salim's."

Hari's look continued to question.

"I mean," said Mabun with another touch of impatience, "I mean that I am plotting with Salim for Akbar's dethronement— should it prove necessary. I fear that it may, and that before long. There is the danger that Akbar will crumble the Empire to pieces in his own hands before he dies, or that at his death he will hand it over to Daniyal. Neither of these disasters shall occur if I can help it. Unless Akbar returns to his senses, unless Daniyal and Mobarek are disgraced and banished, Salim must take the throne. Now there you have my position in a nutshell; I have confessed all; I have confided in you without reserve. Please think my words over, Hari Khan, and to-morrow we will go on with our talk."

22

HARI SPENT THE remainder of that day pacing up and down the Great Terrace with bowed head or halting to stare vacant-eyed over the balustrade. At times he still felt a certain elation, even a kind of gaiety; and yet reason insisted that his position was, in reality, a most anxious one. He was not so simple as to look upon Mabun's confidences as merely flattering; no, they were not that; and still less were they reassuring. First and foremost, they provided him with a measure of Mabun's sense of power; they opened his eyes to the degree of his own entanglement.

In all this affair it was the element of entanglement that he chiefly objected to; the sense of being caught, of being pressed into the service of a cabal. Of course the fact that Daniyal was already his enemy and that he was already disposed to support Salim did materially ease the situation. But, unfortunately, it was in his character to turn obstinate at the least hint of coercion, and although Mabun had been tact and consideration personified, he found it hard to overlook the fact that Mabun had the upper hand. If he was going to work against Daniyal in favor of Salim he would do it in no other way than his own way, and by his own will, and at his own time. All his life he had stood clear of parties and factions. It seemed absurd that a trivial accident should plunge him into a life and death partisanship.

What manner of man was this Mabun who claimed him as a fellow-conspirator? The question posed itself with greater urgency than ever. To get a comprehensive view of Mabun's character, to knit all the disparate elements together into an intelligible whole: this was his task. There was perceptiveness and sensitiveness in Mabun, there was ambition (probably in excess), and, above all, there was a ruthless devotion to purpose. Of the minor egotisms, personal frailties, and petty vanities, he could find but little trace. It was as if the man had grown tired of himself as a person and preferred to be simply a machine. In his hunt for clues Hari went over everything that he had ever heard about Mabun's private life. The little there was came to this: he had started in life as a petty scribe, his quick wits had carried him rapidly upwards, intelligence and industry seemed to be the sole secret of his success. At sixteen he had married a girl of about his own age, and she had died less than twelve months later in childbirth. This was the only chapter in his life that stood out in detachment from the rest. Not many weeks after his wife's death he had attempted suicide and for the space of one year he had walked the world like a ghost. Then suddenly all had changed; his life had resumed its flow; very soon he took another wife, and then concubines by the score; at the present time, in fact, he was reputed to keep about a dozen separate establishments and to be the father of thirty or forty children.

Now, did that history, put next to the living present, throw any illumination upon the inward life of the man? Hari was seeking desperately to get a notion of the mainspring of that existence; he wanted to know what were Mabun's underlying emotions, his compelling beliefs, and what part they played in his life. Well, perhaps he *was* able to form a sort of idea. Perhaps the plain truth was that Mabun was taking the world simply as a gymnasium in which to exercise his abounding energies. Probably it was a waste of time to look for ultimate motives, spiritual allegiances. Anyhow, taking Mabun for just what he seemed to be, Hari liked him—liked him increasingly—and his respect kept pace with his liking.

And now, to come right up to the actual issue; his co-operation was wanted by Mabun, and something quite definite in the way of co-operation. Could he bring himself to do what was wanted? Mabun considered that the evidence of his honorable friend Hari

Khan would be of immense value in bringing about Daniyal's disgrace. Nor was there any fault of reasoning here. In a country where nine hundred and ninety-nine people out of every thousand were ready to perjure themselves for the price of a bowl of rice, the character, the quality of a witness, was everything. There were very few men, even in his immediate entourage, whose word Akbar would respect; and one of those few Mabun believed his friend Hari to be. Exactly. And it was, therefore, particularly unfortunate that were this same trusted and trustworthy Hari to stand up before the Emperor and speak as Mabun wished, he would be perjuring himself and bearing false witness.

That was the crux, the hidden, distracting heart of the affair. That was what had been oppressing him, holding him in a kind of semi-paralysis, from the moment that Mabun had come out with the statement that Daniyal was the victim of the accident in the wood. Hari knew it was not so. Upon seeing Daniyal again at close quarters he had been obliged to reject the idea quite definitely. And although Mabun's story had thrown him momently into a daze, as soon as his mind had cleared he had not only seen the lie for what it was, but had measured its use and its purpose. In the first place Mabun had thought it not impossible that he, Hari, might in all innocence be able to conjure up a false memory in support of a story told with such calm assurance. Failing this, however, the lie, even when detected, might, Mabun would suppose, be a very pleasant one to accept. Moreover, his dear friend Hari would, he trusted, accept it in the spirit in which it was offered—accept it, that is to say, as a tribute to his delicacy of feeling. The kind intention was to make the necessary piece of perjury as easy as possible. He hoped so to arrange things that no one—not even he himself—need ever know whether his friend Hari was wittingly or unwittingly bearing false witness. It was considerate, it was exquisitely tactful, it was just like him. The better you knew Mabun the less unpleasing did the sinuosities of his mind appear. The little man had done his best; and when he saw that his story about Daniyal had not gone down, when he saw that Hari was in danger of blurting something out, how adroitly he had pleaded for silence! That little dissertation of his about lying—it had had a hundred different meanings, but primarily it had been intended of course as a gentle nudge, as a hint, as a prayer that Hari would at least take his time to think, to consider, to weigh carefully. . . .

Yes, little by little, the elements in Mabun's character were falling into place, and with the effect of making Hari feel that the man was—in spite of so much—worthy of trust. You were not to misjudge him simply because he was considerate of your pampered conscience, of your snobbish adherence to a certain code. His own whole-heartedness, his own single-mindedness, lifted him far above all such indulgences. What he saw was the magnitude of the political issue, the great things at stake; and one had to admit that the disproportion between these and one's own small scruples was pretty large; one's own private and personal distaste for perjury was not an impressively weighty factor in the opposite balance.

When the time came for continuing his talk with Mabun, Hari had made his mind up definitely upon one point. He intended to have the truth exposed in all its nakedness; and if he had grown not a little ashamed of his scruples, he would, nonetheless, spread them out before Mabun's reproachful eyes. Strung up to a high pitch, he was starting along the passage when a messenger stopped him with a polite but hurried note begging him to defer his visit to the afternoon. The intervening hours dragged unendurably; what in the world could Mabun find worthy to take precedence of their affairs?

At last he was marching once again along the endless corridors to the suite where all his talks, excepting the last, had taken place. A servant was posted at the door; and this man, instead of admitting him, led the way farther along to the same little room as last time.

Whilst waiting for Mabun he wandered restlessly about and finally explored the curtained alcove behind which Mabun had glanced. At the back of it he found a door; and, putting his ear to it, he fancied that he heard someone moving on the other side. As he was debating whether to try the door or not, Mabun came in; and on that he emerged from behind the curtain, looking, no doubt, more than a trifle self-conscious. Mabun, on his side, seemed to him to be less composed than usual; he had the air of bringing with him harassing pre-occupations. It was with a rather satirical smile that he said: "Have no fear, Hari Khan. That door is locked, and I hold the key."

Without further comment on either side the two men seated themselves on the divan as before; and as before Mabun took the lead. Confidently assuming that Hari was ready to follow him, he began at once to develop and elaborate his theme.

Hari tried to be patient. There could be no harm, he imagined, in letting Mabun talk as much as he liked; nevertheless, after a while, he began to grow restive, and finally he made—or tried to make—an interruption. By his air Mabun could see what was coming—that face of discomfort, that frowning and fidgeting—oh, it was clear enough! And poor Mabun, with a look of agonized supplication, went on talking faster and more urgently than ever. He refused to give up hope; when Hari broke in, he tried to drown his voice; and when Hari spoke louder, his accents grew shriller still. For a minute or more this ridiculous contest went on. It ended with a sudden extraordinary seizure of nervousness on Mabun's side; he grasped Hari by the arm; "Less loud, my dear friend; less loud, I beg!" and his gaze fastened anxiously upon the curtain opposite. Really it seemed ridiculous that they should be exposed to any risk from eavesdroppers; and Hari exclaimed loudly in his impatience. Nevertheless, the next moment it appeared to him that the little Bengalee's face had turned an extraordinary color. How was this? Had Mabun any reason to suppose . . . had his ear caught some sound . . . ?

He was still leaning forward and frowning perplexedly when the outrageous, the unbelievable thing happened. From behind the curtain there resounded the clatter of a piece of furniture overturned, and this was followed by the mutter of an oath.

Hari drew back; he and Mabun looked at one another; there was silence. Two or three seconds passed thus. Then another oath sounded, and this time it rang out with the violence of passion let loose; the curtain was viciously pulled aside, and a tall, gaunt man lurched into the room. This person's appearance—to say nothing of the mode of his apparition—was somewhat alarming and at the same time somewhat ridiculous. From between his eyelids, much inflamed by drink, his small, wild eyes shone with the light of fury. "Enough!" he shouted out hoarsely. "Chatter, chatter, chatter! By Shaitan, you are both accursed!"

Hari and Mabun had instinctively sprung to their feet; and

Mabun, who a moment ago had been tense and livid, now began dancing up and down from the ferment of his emotions. But to speak he had no chance; for the newcomer, sweeping the glare of his frenzied exasperation from the one to the other in turn, continued to hold the field with the splutter and bellow of his rage.

In these moments it dawned upon Hari who he was. It was Salim. Impossible as it seemed, it must be Salim. Strangely accoutred (no doubt he considered himself in disguise), half-drunk, and bursting with ineffective irritation, he nevertheless managed to offer an imperious, if not a wholly dignified, figure. Staring, Hari began to revive a definite memory of those features; and when he glanced round at Mabun for confirmation, the latter, throwing out his hand in a gesture of despair, said in a strangled voice: "His Royal Highness Prince Salim."

At this Hari saluted with all due ceremony; and Salim, letting himself drop heavily down upon a chair, made acknowledgment with a scowl.

"Permit me . . ." began Mabun. "If only Your Royal Highness will deign . . ."

"Sit down, monkey!" roared Salim. "Haven't you chattered enough already? Sit down and be quiet! Merciful Allah!" and he went on cursing through his beard.

Mabun obeyed, but Hari remained standing.

"Sit you down, too, Hari Khan," Salim growled out after a pause. "I am coming to business with you. You'll find me a different customer. Yes—and now that you are talking to *me*, perhaps you will talk better sense."

Hari inclined his head. "I will do my best, Your Royal Highness."

Salim grunted. The tone of this somewhat puzzled him, for he was accustomed to browbeating; he liked to play the bully, and although his bark was notoriously worse than his bite, it was not often that anyone dared to stand up to him.

"Look you! I am tired of hair-splitting. I am going to come straight to the point. We are talking about that accident in the wood. You recognized my brother well enough, and that's an end of it. I advise you not to try my patience too far, Hari Khan."

"I beg Your Royal Highness's pardon, but . . ."

"Nonsense!" shouted Salim, mightily slapping his thigh.

175

Hari smiled and kept silence. He had recovered his composure, and although his spirit was roused, he had his temper well under control. As for Salim, if he, too, kept silence for a minute, it was because his accumulated irritation was simmering and seething without finding an adequate vent.

"You know who I am," he cried out at last, "so take warning! Collect your wits, my good fellow, before it is too late. I know you for the scoundrel you are. I hold your life in my hand. What I say I say, Hari Khan. You recognized my brother, Prince Daniyal. If you deny it, you lie. And then . . ."

Swaying about on his seat, he let his small eyes, glittering wickedly, finish his sentence for him.

"Again I beg Your Royal Highness's pardon," said Hari. "I think you must have heard me just now, when I was saying—or trying to say—to Mabun Das . . ."

"Permit me! One moment!" interjected Mabun, springing in despair from the divan. "It is no use going back over old ground. No, no! Let us start afresh, let us forget! The subject must be approached from a new angle. To be sure, there is some way out of the difficulty. Only let us leave it until to-morrow. A little time for reflection, a little patience, a little . . ."

"A little money!" broke in Salim with a snarl. "The fellow wants money, I suppose, or honors—or Allah alone knows what? Otherwise he must be stark staring mad."

So speaking he turned upon Hari a look that was intended to be offensive—and so, indeed, it was. A little of Hari's temper slipped past his self-control; a slight flush mounted.

"Up to now," he pronounced deliberately, "the trouble has been that I could not honestly identify the man, who, Your Royal Highness declares, was Prince Daniyal; but now . . ."

At these words a look of blank horror spread over Mabun's face, and Salim—almost unable to believe his ears—leant forward with a strange growl.

"Well, now," continued Hari, "I really believe I can identify that man with some confidence. It was Your Royal Highness himself."

Salim made a noise in his throat; and his hand fumbled after his dagger. "Idiot!" he brought out, half-rising from his seat. "Idiot and . . ."

Hari sat firm and fixed him with a level look. For two or three seconds he felt that he had been an idiot indeed. Salim, every inch a swashbuckler, swayed now forwards, now backwards, and perhaps it really was nothing more than chance that finally dropped him backwards into his chair again. With a bark of forced laughter he flung out a hand: "Look at him!" he called to the quivering Mabun; "Hark at him!" and he shook his fist. "That—that is the man you said would be of use!"

Mabun appeared to have exhausted all his emotions. "In any case," he said dully, "Hari Khan is a sympathizer, I am prepared to answer for him personally."

Salim shut his eyes for a few moments and pursed his lips. When he raised his lids again it was to study Hari with a resentful, baffled curiosity. "The fellow really seems to be a lunatic, a half-wit!" he commented to himself. "What does he want? How does he hope to save his wretched skin?" Suddenly he swung round at Mabun, thrusting his face at him with a sneer. "You answer for him, do you? Well, I should advise you to take care. What if I were to inform the Emperor about his little intrigues? What would my father have to say about that, eh? Or my brother either, for that matter? He and his Princess! He and his Princess! And yet—look at him! He has the impertinence to sit there and contradict me. Bah! Get me some wine, Mabun Das. All this talk has parched my throat;—besides, it is my hour."

Mabun got up, hesitated for a moment, and then disappeared through the alcove into a room beyond.

"You will find the doors all unlocked," Salim called after him, chuckling. "And next time you try to shut me in . . ." He slapped both his thighs, laughed, and turning to Hari—"A good little man in his way, but fussy! Thinks he can treat me like a child. He loses his nerve, you know; it is always the same story, every time I pay him a visit. But I come disguised, as you see. I know what I'm doing. It wouldn't do for my father to catch me, that's true enough. Not that I should get much more than a scolding, but poor Mabun would be thrown to the elephants. Oh, yes, he's on tenterhooks, I can tell you!"

Hari smiled politely and remained silent. Salim, who was evidently craving for his wine, pressed his hands wearily over his eyeballs and blew out his lips. "This is the hour at which I allow myself five cups," he informed Hari. "Five cups and no more."

"Your Royal Highness is temperate," returned Hari pleasantly.

"My brother Daniyal drinks in secret. Did you know that? You mark my words, he will end like poor Murad."

Hari found nothing to reply, and after a moment Salim began humming to himself. It was fairly evident that his abstraction was feigned.

"By the way, Hari Khan," he said all at once, "there is something I have been meaning to ask you. What has become of that girl Gunevati?" He paused, then leant forward, and after sending a glance in the direction of the alcove, said in a lowered voice: "If you want to do me a service, Hari Khan, you will find that girl and send her over to me at Allahabad. This is between you and me, mind you; for Mabun Das, although a good little fellow in his way, is no use in an affair of this kind. I tell you he is as nervous as a cat . . . always afraid of betrayal. He thinks the girl is untrustworthy . . . tells me he has hunted everywhere and can't find her. Says she has disappeared—been murdered! All lies, of course! Curse him, I always know when he's lying to me. But if you will find that girl, Hari Khan, I will overlook all your damned impertinence. Do you see?" With these last words he got up, went and peeped cautiously behind the curtain and tiptoed back. Giving Hari a grin and a wink: "Just coming!" he whispered.

When Mabun reappeared, it was with a wine-jug and some glasses. Salim was sprawling in his chair again and humming abstractedly to himself. As soon as the jug had been set down he seized it and poured out a glassful. "Good stuff!" said he, and after tossing off three glasses in quick succession he looked around him with benignity. "This is what my royal father used to drink when he was my age—only he drank twice as much. We are very much alike, he and I. I love him. And his love for me is beyond all bounds. But there it is! He is old. He has lost his wits and persecutes true believers. You, Hari Khan," and he raised his finger at Hari, "you, a good Muslim, will understand that my duty towards Islam comes first. And after that comes my duty to the Empire. To the Empire!—why, even this unbelieving dog, Mabun Das, is able to understand that. Allah and the Empire! It is for them I strive. It is for them I am here now; I risk my life—but what of that? It is all done gladly, gladly!"

Another half-hour slipped by while he continued in much the same vein, and in the meantime seven glasses, as Hari counted, went down his throat, although he repeatedly declared that he was taking but five. Mabun sat opposite, very watchful and collected, licking his lips from time to time like one who has many words to repress. As for Hari, he was longing to take himself off, and directly a suitable occasion arose, he exchanged glances with Mabun and got up. Salim, who by now was considerably fuddled, made no attempt to detain him, and his withdrawal was ceremonious but rapid.

23

ON HIS WAY back to his room Hari could not help smiling broadly to himself. Poor Mabun! How many and various were the difficulties he had to contend with! All this multifarious human material—what foolish, mulish stuff it was! For a man who knew his own mind, saw his goal, and had the will, the wits, and the heart, to make for it—for such a man what a spectacle his common fellow-creatures must provide! Ordinary human nature, compact of inconsistencies and prejudices, inconstancies and irrelevancies—what must it appear in his eyes! And what a life's task to be continually humoring, cajoling, and threatening, the infinite waywardness of mankind! No wonder Mabun's hands fluttered, no wonder his eyebrows sometimes twitched! A hundred times a day no doubt he had to remind himself that just this was his business: to compensate with his own brains for the stupidity of others, to make up with his own care for another's carelessness, with his own foresight for another's short-sightedness, with his own untiring industry for the almost universal indolence of men. It was his business, day in, day out, to manipulate a thousand fragile threads and never let one snap, to pick his way through mazes of intricate detail and never lose his grasp, to be tripped up by every form of sublunary folly and never relax his smile.

Besides, this was to say nothing of the freakishness of blind chance. It could only be by some quite incalculable piece of ill-luck that this last episode had occurred. But was the mischance really a serious one for anybody concerned? His own feelings, Hari reflected, remained exactly the same. He was far from harboring any resentment against Salim. The Prince was a perfect specimen of a boor; but that he had always known. If Mabun was feeling distressed and apologetic, he must take haste to comfort him. His conscience still sided with Mabun; and if he obeyed it, the fact that Salim would think he was intimidated or actuated by self-interest, ought not to matter to him at all. Salim's opinion of one was not a thing to be considered.

Towards sunset on the same day, as he was sitting with Narsing on the terrace, Mabun made his appearance. There was no change in his demeanor, his step was as brisk and light as ever; he joined in the conversation with all his habitual deftness and urbanity. In the course of the last three weeks it had become abundantly evident that Narsing was seriously out of health. It was his habit now to spend many hours upon a couch in a corner of the terrace; but as soon as the sun dipped below the horizon he would drag himself wearily indoors. On this occasion, no sooner had he withdrawn than Mabun turned upon Hari a rueful, sardonic regard. Together they went and leaned over the balustrade; and after gathering reassurance from the few words that Hari let fall, Mabun made a rapid plunge to the heart of his subject. It was Salim he now had to talk about.

"Yes, my dear Hari," he was presently explaining, "Salim's passion for Gunevati, although less than two months old, introduces another tiresome element into the situation. He became completely infatuated after the last meeting of the fraternity—a meeting that took place only a few days before Gokal carried the girl off to the Hills. Since then Salim has been clamoring for her and giving me a lot of trouble. Of course I have the best reasons in the world for disapproving of this connection. Just consider what Gunevati is! Could anyone be more dangerous? Were Salim to take her into his harem, Daniyal's spies would begin ferreting into her history and it would not be long before Daniyal would be in a position to bring against Salim just those accusations that we are arranging to bring against *him*. But you have seen for yourself what Salim is like! His demand for Gunevati is in character with the rest of his behavior. My dear Hari, these visits of his to Agra in disguise! This hiding in the palace! These religious orgies in that hunting-box under his father's very nose! All these are follies that imperil the cause and drive me to the verge of distraction. And then he persists in trying to bribe or bully me into giving up to him a part of his father's treasure lying in these vaults. In fact that was his object when he made the first of these secret visits, which are the curse of my life. Oh, I assure you, Salim is a very unwelcome guest here! But what can I do? He sends word that he is coming; he comes; and I have no choice but to take him in."

Mabun's looks were really pathetic; he threw out his hands helplessly; but the pause he made was not a long one. "Thank God, my dear Hari, I find in you a man of common sense. I hope you understand that ever since I got to know you (I mean when you were staying here two or three months ago) I have been acting as your friend. It was a lucky chance that threw us together at that time, for it was in those weeks that Gunevati betrayed you to Salim, who at once requested me to put you out of the way for fear lest you might have recognized him in the wood and be minded to denounce him. I had to convince Salim that you yourself were too heavily compromised to be dangerous, and I pointed out at the same time how useful you might be in lending weight to an accusation against Daniyal."

Here Mabun paused and seemed to be waiting.

"So, even at that time," said Hari, "you already had your designs."

"Exactly!" smiled Mabun, "and now I am coming to that. Daniyal has no alibi, because he was secretly closeted with me at the very time that the accident in the wood took place. He was successfully persuading me to yield to him what I have consistently refused to Salim—a part of his father's treasure. And presently, my dear Hari, you will see why."

An hour had already gone by, but the evening was warm and still, and accordingly they arranged to sup on the terrace together. During the meal the talk turned on indifferent topics, and Hari was glad of the opportunity for a little further reflection. No sooner had the servants withdrawn, however, than Mabun started off again.

"My dear Hari, there must be a great deal in my scheme which still remains ambiguous to you. A great deal, too, that sounds almost fantastical. Now let me anticipate your objections. You are not tired? You are prepared to listen a little longer? That is excellent!" And for the next three hours Mabun's talk flowed on with hardly a single break. His discourse opened with an analysis of Akbar's relationship to his sons. Salim, in spite of all his insubordination, was still the favorite; there was a natural bond of affection between these two, whereas of Daniyal the Emperor had no understanding whatever. Daniyal was cunning, pliant, outwardly full of respect, and exceedingly adroit in keeping his father in ignorance of his true character and disposition. Through his friends, notably through Mobarek, he instilled into the Emperor a false picture of himself, and at the same time, naturally enough, everything was done to blacken the character of Salim. Of his two sons Akbar really knew little but what came to him through the mouths of others; it was a situation that gave intrigue its fullest scope, and unless the question of the succession were to be resolved by force of arms, the envenomed arts of calumny and intrigue would be paramount up to the very end.

The battle-ground was the mind of Akbar, and the peculiarities of that mind conditioned the tactics to be employed. "Listen to me very carefully, my dear Hari, for here I begin to deal with what is probably your first and most obvious objection to my scheme. 'Why,' you ask, 'why go to the pains of bringing up against Daniyal a charge which is comparatively trivial and completely false, when there are doubtless many weighty and true offenses that might be preferred against him?' Well, let us examine the offenses that you have in mind and let us see how Akbar would regard them. In the first place, there is the taking of human life. But this, when done by emperors—and what I say holds good for royal princes as well—goes by the name of secret execution, and is regarded, if not as actually permissible, at any rate as excusable. Akbar, who has resorted to secret execution on many occasions himself, would certainly not be roused to any great anger against Daniyal on this score. Consider next the charges of robbery and blackmail. Those actions when committed by princes go by the names of forced loans and private fines. It is quite true, of course, that Daniyal is in the habit of extorting enormous sums from his friends by threatening to charge them with conspiring with Salim, but Akbar must already be aware of this, and he certainly would not make it a cause of quarrel with Daniyal; anything, in his opinion, being preferable in a son to the asking of money from his father. There remains, then, the suggestion, my dear Hari, that Daniyal should be arraigned for the form of immorality to which he is actually addicted. But here again the proposal will not bear examination, for, although it is quite true that Akbar would object very strongly to Daniyal's vices were he to see them as they are, there is not the smallest chance of his doing so. In his mind sodomy is associated with stories of youthful Greek heroes bound together in death-defying friendship; it reminds him, too, of his own early days and of rough, manly loves amongst the young warriors of the Steppes. Sodomy, in his view of it, is at the furthest possible remove from effeminacy or perversion. It is an excess of virility; it is merely the young fighter's peccadillo. Then, too, how could Akbar, even if he were so minded, publicly take exception to sodomy? Why, such an attitude would be regarded by those of his own race as an insult not only to the country of his birth but to the memory of his illustrious ancestors. And in this country, too, amongst us Hindus, sodomy, you must remember, ranks only in the fourth degree of misdoing, it takes an inconspicuous place with 'dissimulation, looking disrespectfully at a Brahmin, and smelling any spirituous liquor, or anything extremely fetid and unfit to be smelt.' No, my friend, if you consider my scheme far-fetched and my way of going to work devious and unpractical, you are falling into a common error. One cannot build straight roads in the country of the human mind. You must not regard your own standards and opinions as universal. We must take Akbar as we find him. We cannot make him see Daniyal through *our* eyes; to reach our ends we must paint Daniyal in colors that will make him odious in *his* eyes, in the eyes of the actual living Akbar.

"This being conceded," Mabun went on, "the merits of my scheme become patent. For Akbar all offenses fall into two categories; offenses against God, and offenses against himself; and the matter is again simplified by the fact that in his mind these categories very largely overlap. He has always looked upon a king as 'a shadow of God,' and recently he has made the belief, that he is the actual representative of God on earth, the corner-stone of his new religion. Well then! the situation speaks for itself. In accepting one of the highest offices in the new priesthood Daniyal has played into our hands. If we can show that at the very time when he was making these public professions he was also indulging in secret ceremonial orgies as a member of one of the sects that Akbar holds in greatest detestation, if we can do this, Hari Khan, then Daniyal is lost."

After a few moments of impressive silence Mabun began again. "Akbar is about to preside over another Court of Justice; he will sit in judgment upon those accused of offenses of this sort, and he has sworn an oath not to consider rank, dignity, or position. Now, I have arranged that his investigations shall show that the thing he hates is not only in the ranks of the base-born but close to the Throne itself. Thus, step by step, and in circumstances of the greatest publicity, he will be led on in the direction of Daniyal, until at last an indictment becomes inevitable. Then, and not till then, Gunevati and her associates will be produced, and they will say what I have ordered them to say, because their lives depend upon it. Someone, no doubt, will raise his voice to protest against taking the testimony of the base-born against the word of a prince, but that objection will be met by the call that I shall make upon you."

Hari was silent, and perhaps it was to prevent the utterance of the protestations that he saw gathering behind his frowning brows that Mabun ran hastily on into speech again. "The evidences against Daniyal will not only be unimpeachable, but various. There will be found in Gunevati's possession jewels traceable to him, and amongst these Akbar will recognize some as belonging to his own treasure. Offenses against his purse, as you know, drive the Emperor to madness. In hot haste he will order my arrest and examine into the extent of his losses. At this juncture my life will be in danger, for his messengers will find a part of the treasure gone. But I shall recover it for him; my agents will find it in the cellars of Daniyal's palace, and then..." At this point Mabun waved his hand airily, smiled, and fell into silence.

The look of gloom upon Hari's face did not seem to be lifting. "I am afraid I am wearying you," Mabun said softly. "Why should I trouble you with details? My own object is to convince you that I have been careful and painstaking in my arrangements."

With this he ceased and remained quiet, but obviously not without great effort. While his lips remained closed, his eyes dwelt upon Hari's face with an eloquent anxiety. "Can you refuse," they seemed to say, "the little thing I ask, when I have already given—and am still ready to give—so much?"

Hari sighed, brushed his face over with his hands, and even groaned aloud. These methods were natural and proper to Mabun; in Mabun they were not unbecoming. A born intriguer, and conscious of the excellence of his cause, he could go forward dauntless and unashamed. Besides, he was the leader; his was the detached intelligence—impersonal, disinterested, manipulating its instruments. But what of the wretched tools themselves, and in particular that base instrument, Hari Khan? Allah! What a sorry charge was being laid upon him! Could he ever humble himself sufficiently to play his allotted part?

At last, after having left Mabun's side and taken one or two moody turns up and down the terrace, he came back and said: "Would to God I had killed Daniyal on the night of the banquet! Would to God Salim had persuaded you to destroy me out of hand! I tell you, Mabun, those courses would have suited me better than this. I can give you no promises, no assurances of any kind. I detest public affairs. Your machinations weary me. I hope I may succeed in persuading myself to do as you wish, and that is all I can say."

Mabun laughed gently and grasped him confidingly by the arm. "Say no more, my dear Hari Khan. I shall never forgive myself if you continue to fret. No, no, you must on no account worry. I dare say we shall manage well enough by ourselves—Salim and Gunevati and I." At the conjunction of these names he laughed merrily. "If I think you are a little foolish, that doesn't prevent me from entering into your feelings with deep sympathy."

Hari faced round and looked him up and down with an eye that was full of liking. Mabun was all smiles and gentle mockery now, but even so, one could detect the fire and fixity of his purpose behind. Mabun against Daniyal! The mongoose against the cobra! Yes, he liked this little mongoose well. And how vividly he could visualize the nimble, gallant little creature, coat bristling, eyes like sparks, crouching tensely for a spring at its coiled and watchful enemy.

He was silent, until, after a while, his thoughts took another turn, "Mabun!" he cried, "not many days ago I was almost ready to renounce the world altogether, and that was before you had begun to plague me!"

The look of amusement upon Mabun's face deepened. "I don't see you in a cloister yet awhile, my friend."

Hari looked up into the starless, moonless sky. Heavy clouds could be felt moving across it. A few big drops of rain splashed upon the marble flags.

"No, perhaps a cave in some mountain-side would be better." He smiled, and then went on inconsequently. "If a man like Akbar is to be cast aside after a few years like a worn-out shoe, what are the uses of ambition, energy, and valor?"

Mabun emitted a long-drawn sighing breath. "God grant that Daniyal and Mobarek may fall and that Akbar will continue to reign for many a long year. Is not that precisely my object? Is it not *that* I am working for?"

"But Salim—in his impatience for the throne . . ."

"Bah!" and Mabun snapped his fingers. "If necessary, I would betray him into his father's hands. No harm would result."

Hari threw up his head and laughed. "Forgive me, Mabun, but in my ears all this sounds a little glib. History does not take its shape like a clay pot—even when the potter is Mabun Das."

"I do not pretend to omnipotence—but I am practical."

"Too practical. Your ends fall within the range of man's vision. The world is not governed by men with their definite ends, but by fate with its unintelligible purpose."

"Unintelligible indeed!" scoffed Mabun, but with the greatest gentleness.

Hari continued unabashed. "If the day ever arrives when men gain control of their worldly courses, that will be a sign that the end of the world is at hand. It will mean that men have taken the wrong turning and committed spiritual suicide without even suspecting it. Having encompassed their limited perfection, there will not be one human being left whose life is worth preserving, and God's thumb will descend and crush the whole.

"I seem to be assuming the mantle of the prophet," he went on after a pause. "I must have borrowed it from Narsing, who surprised me this afternoon with many solemn utterances. He maintained that Akbar, in spite of all his follies, was the fountain of our spiritual life in this age. He prophesied that after Akbar's death the Empire would crumble into corruption. I listened respectfully."

They were both standing by the balustrade, and Mabun's eyes continued to look steadily out into the thick, sultry darkness.

"Poor Narsing!"

"Is he so foolish?"

"I mean: he is dying," Mabun replied softly. "And for him death is hard."

"Dying? Are you sure of it?"

"Quite sure. I know his disease. He did not tell you that he was dying—no? Nevertheless, he knows it as well as I, only he will not accept the truth."

Hari turned away from Mabun, and as he once more fronted the darkness Narsing's recent looks and words floated back into his mind invested with new and pathetic shades of meaning. When he next spoke it was to inquire whether Narsing would live long enough to see Akbar again on the latter's return to Fatehpur-Sikri.

Mabun shook his head doubtfully, and then fixed upon Hari a look which the latter was at a loss to understand.

"Akbar will never return to Fatehpur-Sikri. I do not mean that he, too, is to die. What I mean is that Fatehpur-Sikri is already dead."

Puzzled, Hari knitted his brows.

"It is so," continued Mabun, now again gazing tranquilly into the night. "Fatehpur-Sikri is as dead as if the grass were already growing among its stones. In fact, grass *has* already sprouted in the pavement of the Great Court; I myself saw it when I went there a few days ago.

"No city should ever have been built upon that spot," he continued after a pause. "Akbar chose it because it had been the abode of the saint who promised him the birth of a son. Nevertheless"—and Mabun's inflection was very delicate—"Nevertheless, it was an ill-chosen site. The reservoirs upon which Fatehpur-Sikri depended have all cracked; the water has escaped; the ground in that region is brittle and hollow; and now the city is doomed. Of course it is being given out that all can be made good, but—I tell you this in confidence, Hari Khan—that is absolutely untrue. It is impossible to construct reservoirs on such ground. Waterless the city will remain. Soon it will be a ruin."

Hari made no reply. With his eyes turned in the direction of Fatehpur-Sikri he followed the memories that drifted across his mind.

After a pause of some length Mabun straightened himself, gave a smile, and said: "I hope I have not depressed you, my friend? Alas, the truth is the truth, reality is reality, and there is no escaping it. At least," he corrected himself, "there is no escape for a man like you."

Hari gave a laugh, and together they strolled towards the entrance arch, for it was time to part.

"What do you mean by reality, my dear Mabun?"

"Oh, I am no philosopher. By reality I mean Maya—the phenomenal world, Illusion, if you please to call it so. But for us illusion alone exists; we live in it; it is our life; let us accept it! Hari Khan, if there is a God, it is our Hindu God—Shiva, the dancing God—Shiva, the sportive God, who out of the super-abundance of his energies has created the world for his play. Do not be depressed. After Akbar another will arise. Individuals are nothing. Shiva dances on!"

24

IT WAS LATE that night before sleep put an end to Hari's meditations, which were of a gloomy cast, being chiefly concerned with the vanity of earthly ambitions and desires. In the darkness of his room he saw again the soft, silent blossoms of light that had unfolded upon the sky-line over Fatehpur-Sikri five months ago; and in the great span of the ages the blossoming of empires seemed scarcely less brief. Then, too, there was poor Narsing, upon whom his thoughts lingered with a more intimate melancholy. He wished he could resemble little Mabun, who knew how to watch time's flight unregretfully and without awe.

When he awoke the next morning, however, his disposition had entirely changed. It was in a spirit of ribald indifference that he regarded the fate of Fatehpur-Sikri, and thinking of Narsing he said: "At the age of sixty a man has lived long enough. It is death no less than birth that keeps the world fresh and young. There must not be too many old eyes to look at it."

He was taking his first turn upon the terrace when two letters arrived; one was from Mabun and the other was handed to him by a messenger who came direct from Amar. Tearing open Mabun's letter first, he learnt with a surge of thankfulness that the order for his release had arrived. This matter, as he now realized, had been weighing upon him more heavily than he had cared to admit.

Amar's letter was less cheerful. That the old Ranee had died he was quite prepared to learn, but Amar went on to say that his father remained so stricken by her death that he had found it impossible to leave him. He had, accordingly, written to Sita to suggest that she should join him at Ravi; but Sita had replied with the distressing news that Gokal was dangerously ill and that to leave him all alone was not to be thought of. "Since then, however," Amar went on, "I have heard that the worst is over, and by the time you get this letter Sita will be on her way to me, bringing Gokal with her. He is still very weak, I fear, but we are all agreed that the change of scene may hasten his recovery. A little while ago, when he thought he was dying, the idea that you were a prisoner and unable to come to him was a burden upon his mind. Now that you are free to come and go as you please, you will, I am sure, wish to visit him here; for, although out of danger, he is by no means himself again."

Hari read this letter over several times. Then, without being unduly perturbed—for, after all, Amar said that Gokal was on the road to recovery—he determined upon an immediate departure. He was glad that his discussions with Mabun would be cut short; glad, too, that he would be spared another meeting with Salim. The thought that Sita would be at Ravi he did not dare to dwell on; but it was in the most joyful mood that he made ready for the journey.

Although Amar's letter had provided him with a good reason for sudden departure, he was a little nervous of what Mabun might find to say; but the latter raised no difficulty. On the contrary he was helpful in providing horses and equipment, so that at noon Hari was ready to set off.

Great was his satisfaction at putting Agra behind him. While his horse ambled along over the wide, open country, he gazed about with continuous delight. The road was lively with village folk, for the rains had just passed by, and a mild sun was drawing up the moisture from the rice-fields that glittered through swathes of white mist.

Weary of himself and his personal affairs, every detail of the outward scene was pleasant to him. With his freedom he had regained a sense of leisure, and this remained with him during the whole of the journey. On the tenth day he reached the mouth of the little valley of Ravi. The evening light was behind him as he gazed over the familiar water-meadows towards the distant roof of the old Rajah's house. It was flushed by the sun when he first caught sight of it, and stood bright against its background of trees. There was an exquisite freshness in the air, a smell of wet grass and the bell-like tinkle of the small green marsh-frog. A flock of wild duck eddied up from the reeds a few yards away, flew round in a circle, and settled down again. Their movement lent an even greater tranquillity to the scene, and he dropped the reins of his horse, letting it wander here and there cropping the rich grass. So deeply did this valley stir his emotions that he was seized with the impulse to turn round and fly from it. He was reminded of the old Ranee who had died, and for some reason that he could not understand he thought of the dead with envy. What greater blessing could any man look for than to fade out of individuality into the wide peace of such a scene as this? What could be better than to feel the knot of selfhood loosen and one's spirit flowing over those luminous spaces between the tranquil level of the earth and the brightening stars? Ah! then would one learn what it was to breathe, not with the quick, hot breath of humanity, but with the long, slow rhythm of the earth herself.

As he rode forward again he noticed a change in the landscape; Prince Daniyal's encampment had been transferred to the other side of the lake and in its place there stood a humbler group of tents, presumably Gokal's. On arriving, it was to them that he directed his steps, and very soon he came upon Gokal himself lying upon a couch in the shade of a great tree.

Anxiously did he scan his friend's features and it seemed to him that they had not only grown thinner but acquired a new sternness of cast. The impression made upon him in the first hour of their intercourse was that Gokal was wrapped in a profound calm, but as the evening wore on he saw that this calm was unnatural—or, rather, that it covered a feverish unrest.

In its main outlines the story that Gokal had to tell was simple enough. It was barely three months ago, as Hari now remembered, that he had jokingly warned him of what might easily happen if he persisted in keeping Gunevati by his side. But Gokal had paid little heed at the time, and later, as his infatuation deepened, he had become still more thoughtless. If he continued to see the girl as she was, he never drew the practical conclusions, never anticipated the probable results in life as it went on from day to day. Because her smiles were always ready, because she had the indolence of an animal and never seemed to notice time slipping by, he imagined that all the desires of her nature were fulfilled. Why should she grow bored, when she could amuse herself the whole day long with the tinting of her lips and eyelashes, or the trying on of this dress and that? Was she not enjoying comforts and luxuries that she had never dreamed of before? She appeared to be without ambition; and it was not for a long time that she gave a thought to money, wanting only to gratify her small, passing whims when they came. Later on, when she began to value an ornament for what it was worth, Gokal paid no heed to the change. He did not notice that after a day or two her costlier adornments would be discarded and were never to be seen again. He missed the significance of the fact that at this time, too, she became variable in her moods. The fits of petulance that alternated with her childlike gaiety only made her more attractive in his eyes. Thus it went on, until one day, not long after his evening meal, he was seized with violent sickness. The sickness persisted; his condition grew worse and worse, and finally he fell into a coma. In the early morning Sita received a message from his frightened servants to say that their master was nearly dead. She hurried to his side, and found him unconscious, with a pulse that could hardly be felt. By great good fortune it shot into her mind that there was an old herb-woman living in the neighborhood. The woman was summoned, she got to work, and after four hours of her ministrations Gokal was out of danger. His first inquiries were after Gunevati; where was she? had she been stricken down in a similar fashion? If not, how came it that she was not at his side?

Courageously Sita decided to take upon herself the dismal task of telling him that Gunevati had mysteriously disappeared. She and Gokal had been in each other's company much more frequently since the departure of Hari and Amar. She had become completely tolerant of his infatuation, and although Gunevati was never mentioned between them, he knew well enough what her attitude was. It was thus from the standing of a friendship which had become very close that she spoke out and broke the news. For a minute or more there was complete silence, while Gokal looked at her with an uncomprehending stare. Then, gradually, as his mind adjusted itself, a faint flush colored his ashen cheeks, and at length letting his lids sink he turned his head away. Not until two days later did Gunevati's name pass his lips, and then it was to ask if Sita would mind looking in the girl's room to see if any letters or papers throwing light on her departure had been left behind. Sita found paints, powders, and dresses, all thrown about; the room was in confusion, but no papers were to be seen.

On a broad general view Gunevati's behavior was intelligible enough; but the case, when looked into more closely, presented certain rather mysterious characters. A plan had certainly been made out beforehand and with the aid of abettors from outside. This much Sita saw clearly; but for her part she certainly had no inclination to probe deeper, nor did Gokal express any wish (he certainly lacked the means) to set regular investigations on foot.

For nearly a fortnight his physical prostration was complete. Later, as his strength returned, he seemed to be trying to forget; and it was his greatest pleasure to listen while Sita read aloud to him. In the talks that followed from this reading their intimacy sank its roots deeper still. Sita found herself opening her heart to him as she had never done to anyone before. One day she confessed that she no longer loved Amar. It was true that he remained her dearest friend upon earth: "But friendship"—she said it with a sigh—"is not the same as love. Amar," she went on, "has withdrawn his heart from the world. I am left behind, but I do not complain, because I know that he must follow his Path. Love to him does not mean what it means to me, and I truly believe that this difference in our ideals puts us further apart than if he were actually in love with somebody else."

Gokal looked grave when he heard this. It would be the saddest thing imaginable, he reflected, if Sita and Amar were to allow a real coldness to settle between them now. Unless they were to part with a perfect understanding on both sides, how could they bear to part at all? In their separation each would be haunted by remorseful thoughts. Nothing more tormenting for her nor more distracting for him could be conceived; his progress would be fatally impeded;

and she, guessing it, would feel in great measure responsible. The dread of such a calamity Gokal might have dismissed as fanciful, had not Sita's words made him feel the prick of another sharper anxiety. He asked himself—and not for the first time—whether Sita and Hari might not be in danger of falling in love. Hitherto he had taken reassurance from the openness with which she would talk about both Hari and Amar; she seemed to have nothing to hide. And now, one day, by way of a test, he told her that in a letter written from Ravi, Hari had declared that he was growing weary of the world and that when he next went back to his own country, it would be to immerse himself in the study of Buddhist philosophy. Sita took a moment's thought, then she smiled and said: "That only shows that Hari does not yet understand himself. This world will always be real to him; he finds value in the actual moment. His character in this respect is very different from Amar's." And then, when Gokal pressed her: Amar, she went on to say, was more conscious of the past and future than of the present itself. Amar was concentrated upon what was to come, and to that extent even his most unselfish actions were interested, for they were steps on his way to his goal. Hari's very egotism had a disinterested quality, which it took from the fact that he was at the mercy of emotions that were not ruled by his individual will. "I have that in me which deeply sympathizes with Amar," she concluded rather helplessly, "but another part of me rebels against him."

Gokal frowned. He was perhaps fonder of Hari, but he felt that it was to Amar that he owed his deeper allegiance. "You must remember this," he replied, "to Amar the moments really worth living are moments of inspiration—moments when life's profoundest problems become sharp in outline and an answer is half-seen. To Hari inspiration is something different. His inspiration goes, as you say, to light up the actual minute; it shines upon the stuff of life; but does it, I ask, go so far as Amar's towards the up-building of his spiritual being? Amar's inspiration is a deep inward fervor, in the heat of which the fine gold of wisdom is melted out from the dross."

"When Amar speaks of wisdom," said Sita with a smile of melancholy, "he means something different from me, something tending away from life. As for me, I simply cannot think of wisdom and the poetic spirit as things apart. Surely poetry is wise?

and poetry requires the whole of life, all the senses of life, all that you teach and hear and see, for its material."

This conversation was one of many that took place on Gokal's veranda with the afternoon sun slanting through the garden trees. Gokal's strength was slow in returning, and if his weakness took the edge off his mental distress it permitted his melancholy to spread far. Hour after hour he would meditate despairingly upon the anomalies in his character. He was able to see Gunevati as she was, and yet he still craved for her, and found himself constantly trying to extenuate her misdoing. In his despair he veritably longed for death, and yet his bodily condition was a perpetual anxiety to him. So solitary was he in his mind and in all his mental habits that society had never afforded him any true pleasure, and yet he found solitude unendurable. Contemplating the world from a height and truly despising its vanities, he, nevertheless, was awed by worldly greatness and remained a respecter of persons.

Many of his thoughts he confided to Sita, but there were others that he was ashamed to confess. One day, for example, when she asked for the meaning of the sardonic smile upon his face, how could he confess that he was thinking how all night he had lain awake tormented by memories. He had remembered how one morning upon his journey up to Khanjo, he was buying Gunevati some trinkets from a wandering peddler, and being put out at last by her lamentable want of taste, he let fall a slighting word and a sneer. It was the memory of her wince and blush that now haunted him. It filled his nights with remorse. Remorse! No wonder his smile was sardonic!

This being the general tone of his mind, he not only found comfort in Sita, but was astonished by her power of consolation, which went far beyond anything that he had thought possible. For the first time in life he realized the full possible value of loving-kindness as a factor in human experience. Up to the present he had been held aloof from Christianity not merely by its dogmas but from an inability to accept its fundamental principle: he could not allow to Love the importance given to it in the teaching of Christ. In other words, Christianity had presented itself to him either as a system of theology which he could not accept, or as a species of Humanism—and Humanism he detested as being simply an ethic from which the highest spiritual values were omitted. But no one could accuse Sita of losing sight of those elements in religion which elevated it above any merely altruistic doctrine. She had a sense of poetry that matched his own; she had an understanding for the heroic, the sublime. Of set intent, accordingly, he surrendered himself to her spiritual effluences, letting the balm flow, and awaiting, passive and yet attentive, whatever revelation might emerge.

To Sita herself, however, he was very sparing of his admissions. He had it upon his conscience to say nothing that could possibly reinforce her prejudices as a Westerner against the oriental outlook. To her he would often maintain with uncompromising rigor that the tendency of Christianity was to exalt the ideal of social duty at the expense of the ideal self-illumination. It flavored with an unwholesome sweetness the pure springs of idealism; a slightly materialistic, and at the same time slightly sentimental, element was introduced. The intellectual part of religion was subordinated to the emotional, or else thrust aside altogether, truth being handed over to science as the only domain in which the idea had any meaning left to it. And thus the ancient and unmatched conceptions of wisdom and holiness were driven from men's minds, and metaphysics was neglected as unnecessary.

At other times, however, he liked to allow himself the luxury of sounding the full, rich chords of philosophic despair. He would quote from Ecclesiastes, and on one occasion he said: "Sita, more than four thousand years ago there lived in Egypt a fellow-creature of ours who wrote these words: 'Lull thy heart to peace in oblivion; so long as thou livest follow the call of thy heart and be happy. Never weary of following thy desire and vex not thy heart while thou sojournest upon earth. It is not given to man to carry his possessions with him. None that have gone have ever returned. Tears cannot refresh the heart of him who lieth in the grave. Therefore do thou make holiday and have no care.'"

"Yes; that is the first word in wisdom," replied Sita, smiling, "but Gokal, is it the last?"

On this afternoon, as it so happened, he was sensible of an undercurrent of peace, so after a moment he returned her smile and went on: "Do you remember, I once said that the riddle of the universe would be solved only when men had reached a state of consciousness in which the riddle, as such, did not exist? Well; you might say to me now that the beauty in life would be triumphant, if men had the eyes to see it. Could they but see around them the outward and visible signs of an inward and spiritual grace, that grace would be there. You love the world of appearances because it is the world of poetry, and it is possible that you are justified. It may be intended that after the ascent into communion with the One there should be a descent once more to the Many— but with the knowledge of Oneness retained. This is the doctrine of Plotinus and of Dionysius the Areopagite."

These days came to an end when Gokal was well enough to make the journey to Ravi. He seemed to bear the discomforts of travel well enough, but on his arrival he suffered a relapse, and then he ceased to reproach himself for having hinted to Amar by letter that nothing would please him better than that Hari should return.

2 5

THAT NIGHT HARI and Gokal sat up to a late hour watching the moon spread its light over the lake. The evergreen oak under which they sat stood upon a small promontory and threw the shadow of its dark, thick foliage on to the silvered water. A light breeze was blowing from the opposite shore; it brought with it a just perceptible strain of music that came from Daniyal's encampment. One could almost believe the old legend that moonlight playing upon water once made a harmony audible to Lakshmi's ear. In the long pauses that fell between them the two friends felt that the bond of their union was close indeed. They shrank from spoiling the beauty of this hour with difficult and painful topics.

To-morrow, thought Hari, would be soon enough to tell the story of Salim's passion for Gunevati. Unfortunately, to withhold this intelligence altogether was out of the question, if only on account of the light it shed on the mystery of her disappearance. It looked more than probable that the Prince's agents had taken a hand in her flight and had carried her off to their master's palace in Allahabad. On his side Gokal was thinking that he must not delay too long in speaking to Hari about Amar and Sita; he would tell him how anxious he was that their approaching separation should not be marred by any failure of understanding and sympathy. Hari would be quick to take this as an admonition, if anything of that nature was needed.

It was after midnight when they parted, Hari betaking himself to a tent that Gokal had prepared at no great distance from his own. The same gentle breeze was ruffling the lake and the moon was still clear in the sky; nevertheless, at dawn Hari was awoken by the violent flapping of his canvas and the beat of heavy rain upon the roof. A fierce squall was driving down the valley; and after a while he rose, fearing lest the tent should be torn away; but before he had finished dressing the rain had passed; the sun was shining; and the wind, although it continued, was much less violent.

Stepping outside, he looked about him and never in his life had he seen a morning lovelier than this. The massed clouds were flying away before the sunrise that gilded their rolling whiteness and suffused the uncovered sky with a pale greenness that melted into pale blue. Flocks of wood-pigeons were hurtling through the air, the lake was bright with hurrying wavelets, and all the trees around the camp were flinging leaves and raindrops upon the wind.

No one was yet about, and presently he wandered into the garden of the Rajah's house. In its old-fashioned way this garden was pleasant to the eye. The Persian style had not yet come into vogue when it was laid out, and so the designer had been content with a naive imitation of the Chinese. Little streamlets and ponds had been arranged here and there, with dwarf willows hanging over them, and in the background clumps of heavy-flowered magnolias, flame-leafed azaleas, blue hydrangeas, and feathery bamboos. A few exotic trees planted by the old Rajah's father were certainly rather out of place, but there was something pleasing in the very simplicity of the taste that had put them there. Hari sat down upon a bench, and at last the thoughts of Sita which he had been suppressing for so long crowded irresistibly into his mind. He wondered what their meeting would be like; but even now, with his heart beating at the thought of it, he was afraid to give his imagination rein, and starting to his feet, he began wandering again along the narrow, winding paths.

In a little while he was halting beside the largest lakelet, which had a Chinese bridge flung over it, with the usual willow trailing its light green foliage on the water. As he was looking down at the pink lilies he realized all at once that the wind had dropped; everything had suddenly fallen into a complete tranquillity, not a leaf was now astir. Three huge blue and white butterflies appeared and began tumbling about over their own clear reflections. From where he stood the house was out of sight, although it was not more than a few yards away; and presently voices were to be heard in that direction. His heart began to beat once more as he listened for Sita's voice, and in a minute, sure enough, it rang out quite loud in the still air. To his amusement it sounded the note of temper; and, smiling to himself, he made a cautious approach until only a thin screen of shrubs separated him from the open window at which— to judge by the sound—Sita must be standing. She was talking to Amar, whose replies came muffled from the room behind. Her tone continued to be exceedingly cross, and Hari's smile broadened as he realized that he was overhearing a regular domestic quarrel. It was strange, perhaps, that he stayed to listen, especially as he had a horror of the revelations that spring from certain changes of voice or manner when people are carried away. In his time he had heard more than one fine lady lose her temper and always to his disillusionment. Yet now, he stood his ground, and, listening, fell into a positive enchantment. Sita could let herself go as much as she pleased, she could storm and rage, but no harm would ensue. Nor did the unfortunate Amar lack dignity, although plainly he deserved his scolding. What he had done was to leave the shutters of the adjoining room open with the result that Sita's best dresses had been soaked through by the rain in the night. Hari's amusement increased every minute; indeed, a quite extravagant joyousness took possession of him. As he stood there amongst the flowers and butterflies the world seemed to him a place of extraordinary beauty. Living appeared to be a wonderfully simple thing after all. You had but to throw away the trouble and worry of taking things unto yourself, and then all the earth would be yours to enjoy in a disinterested ravishment. The striving between man and man would have vanished; Paradise was as simple as that.

Pushing his way quietly through the shrubs, he crept up to the window itself. Sita was no longer there, but as he peeped into the room he caught a glimpse of her sitting at table with Amar. She showed her profile, whilst Amar was presenting his back. There were tea-things before them and a plate of Kashmiri biscuits. Now and then a sigh came from Sita, and her eyes kept wandering over her dresses, several of which were hanging out near the window to dry. Hari waited for her glance to fall upon him, and after a minute she turned her head, gave a slight start, and opened her eyes wide. He had put a finger up to his lips to enjoin silence, and she obeyed the signal. Smilingly he motioned to her to join him in the garden, and, although evidently a little mystified, she nodded her consent.

Waiting for her at the corner of the house, Hari was conscious only of an immense, unhoped-for happiness; and he said to himself: "What is this? What is this?" His feelings sharpened into a sense of agonizing sweetness; his being was invaded by an anguish that was delicious and seemed to play not upon the nerves of the flesh, not upon the machinery of the brain, but upon the substance of the very soul. In another moment Sita appeared and they went down together in silence through the trees until they were beyond sight or sound of the house. Then he stopped her and looked into her eyes; and her face, which had been smiling when she joined him, was now grave, as if a veil of secret wonder had descended over it. She seemed to be marveling inwardly, her eyes were deep with divination, and she waited. What he said he hardly knew, but the color deepened in her cheeks, and the long breath that she drew seemed to be shaken by an inward tremulousness. For a brief space they stood thus, and, while he continued speaking to her, her eyes wandered from side to side, but her hands lay quiet in his. At last she closed her eyes, in order, maybe, to shut out the sound of his voice, or, maybe, to hear it yet more clearly. Did she understand what he was saying? Had she really caught a breath of the wild, spiritual fragrance that was working a miracle upon his heart? A smile had dawned upon her upturned face, and it seemed to him to be full of a tender mockery; but, when she answered, her voice was trembling. "Oh, it is wonderful to be loved...." She spoke dreamily, as if to herself. "But one should be wonderful to deserve it.... To be loved one ought to be above all change. One ought to be perfect in body and spirit. One ought to exist but for love alone—no matter how short the time. One should be perfect —and then one should die."

She laughed a little after saying this, and presently he saw that tears were shining in her eyes. While they stood thus together with his arms about her, time no longer existed for them. It was only when the increasing stir of morning broke in upon their ears that they remembered where they were or how they had come to be there.

After watching her go back along the path to the house Hari stood for a long while in a daze. The two butterflies were still tumbling about over the lily-pond, the shadows across the path seemed to be almost the same; but Gokal probably was beginning to wonder what had become of him.

For the rest of that day he felt himself strangely disconnected from all his past, and many days went by before he recovered from bewilderment at what had happened. He understood better now the character of the sudden change that sometimes overtook people, making a saint out of a sinner, or turning a modest woman into a wanton. When he asked himself whether his present disposition was likely to be enduring he could not see the smallest shadow of doubt. Time might work its changes upon the substance of his love, but that love was firmly rooted, and he would carry it, for good or ill, down to the grave. So incontestable did this appear in his own mind that he was quite unreasonably surprised not to find the same confidence in Sita. That misgivings had overtaken her became evident in their next meeting. Starting out together from the garden gate, they climbed a little hill at the back of the house and sat down under a solitary pine. It was not until then that Hari noticed that beneath the glow of her happiness there was a deep disquiet. At first she was abstracted and would hardly speak, but after a while she said: "I have been thinking about Amar... and not only of him but of myself. Hari, I am trying as hard as I can not to love you in a human way, only to think of you as something outside ordinary life. You won't think this cold and cowardly, will you? I want what one can get only in dreams. If life is not a dream, it ought to become one. It is like a dream to me that you should love me. What joy it gives me! But now I ask you this: Why should you, who have had many human loves, want just another one? Why not leave this in its own world? You won't think ill of me, will you? But I know how I should want to go deeper and deeper into the heart of things. And then—all the doubt! All the pain!

Fresh pain at every turn. . . . Amar tells me that I am an extremist, and that is true. So love must remain a dream for me. In dreams one can give everything—be everything—but ordinary life is not made for that."

Hari was very little troubled by these words. His happiness in the present was so great that he made no demand upon the future. To be with her, or even to be aware that she existed, seemed to be enough. He took little account of her fears, and although he succeeded in allaying them temporarily, in the intervals between meetings they would spring up again.

"This still seems so strange to me," she would say, "half unreal . . . And yet if I found it unreal I could never be proud again, I could never believe again that my world was true." Often she fixed upon him a gaze of troubled intensity. "I wonder if you can understand? It is dreadfully important to me. You must not break the course of my life with something that is not deep. I could not bear it. It may sound foolish, but my world is very precious to me. You are seeking to break into it. You have broken into it. And now . . ."

When she spoke in this fashion Hari would look anxiously into his heart, but still he could find nothing to shake his self-confidence. Calling Lalita back into mind, so dissimilar did that experience and this seem to him that no points emerged even for comparison. And it was the same when he looked further back. What did puzzle him at this time was his complete change of feeling as regards Amar. His former scruples had entirely vanished; but he could not manufacture scruples to order, so he shrugged, and without probing very deeply into the matter, told himself that his conscience was exceedingly erratic.

2 6

AT THIS TIME the only shadow upon Hari's happiness was that cast by the figure of Gokal. It was becoming more obvious every day that he was not making a good recovery, and Hari anxiously debated whether the cause was primarily physical or mental. The news that Gunevati was probably in the hands of Salim had affected him very strongly; during the conversation his face had alternately flushed and turned pale, his manner had become more and more agitated, and in the end he had fallen into a strained silence. Hari perceived that he was in the grip of jealousy; and, after this, the subject was left alone. It lay between them, occupying their thoughts, but offering no aspect upon which anything could be said.

And it was the same with the subject of Sita. Gokal had begun to speak, but desisted almost at once on perceiving that his warning came too late. His mute sadness made Hari look into his heart again, but still his conscience remained without voice. What had happened was fated, a thing beyond cavil or repining. As regards Amar, both he and Sita were fully as anxious as Gokal that he should not carry away with him into his retreat pre-occupations that would hinder his progress; and it was for this reason principally that they were determined to keep their love secret. For the rest, the immediate effect of the happiness in which they lived was to make everything outside their love seem insignificant. In the course of their talks together Hari gave a brief account of his quarrel with Daniyal and of the development of his relations with Mabun at Agra. But all that seemed very far away; he could not give it much importance, and it suited him very well that Sita should take his story in the same spirit. All she asked was that he should not make any important decisions without her knowledge. She felt confident that when it came to the point he would be unable to bring himself to lie to Akbar. Her own loyalty to the Emperor was unshakable, and it led her into tirades against Mabun, whom Hari laughingly defended as one of the cleverest and most single-minded men in the Empire, and a loyal friend as well. This he really believed, although he felt tolerably certain that Mabun would sacrifice him should his purpose require it. "Mabun," he insisted, "is a man of feeling. He rises above his own particular temperament. Never would he display a contempt for religion, parade cynicism, or even indulge in irony."

Endless were their talks together during these days. Sita's alarms were gradually quieting down, and the happiness she embraced rested on a gathering confidence that Hari's love would endure. But did she imagine that he would remain content for ever with the position as it now stood? Would she, indeed, have been quite content herself, had she truly believed that his passion was so easily satisfied? No doubt it pleased her to remonstrate with him over even a kiss, but there was that in her manner which seemed to say: "And yet I should be disappointed, I confess, if you had no wish to kiss me. Were that the case, our love might become dull to you; it might even become a little dull to me . . . On the other hand, if you could kiss me without protest, might that not become dull too?"

For a time Hari submitted to these conditions without vexation and even when he began to suffer from them he made little attempt to break them down. Nevertheless, one day he felt impelled to speak bluntly. "How long," he asked, "do you imagine that you can go on playing with love?"

"Am I playing with love?" she asked thoughtfully, then added: "Yes, I suppose I am."

He said nothing more on that occasion, but his inward disquiet increased. If she, on her side, was now certain of him, could he be so certain of her? She could not be happy without the assurance that his love was serious, and yet she had the wish to make a light thing of it. That was because she was ashamed of taking real love without giving everything in return. She wanted to give her love, and yet she wanted to withhold it. How long was this contradictory humor to be indulged?

When next they met, his manner was as gentle and smiling as ever, but she was not slow to detect a touch of grimness beneath. They were sitting in the woods that went up behind the house, and it was she who first broke the silence that presently fell between them.

"I can see that you are angry with me," she murmured, "and I also know why."

Hari kept his eyes fixed upon the distance, and in a moment she went on: "You make me feel it wrong to be as I am. You make me feel mean-spirited. And yet—can't you leave me outside the world, outside ordinary life? Couldn't you take me more lightly? Couldn't you"—she hesitated—"couldn't you play with love—instead of letting it be a sad, craving thing?"

Although he now turned and looked at her steadily, she could not make out what was behind his eyes. She grew more troubled. She hesitated again; and at last, as if in answer to the words that he would not speak—"Surely," she said, "the heart and mind of man, divine and deep, are always unappeasable?" And in a lower voice still she added: "Whatever I gave it would never really meet your need."

In the secret depths of his being Hari was shaken. Was it true, what she said? Was it better thus? Was fulfillment always imperfect?

On that occasion again the subject was broken off, the issue left undecided. For an hour afterwards Hari mused in solitude, and later in the evening, sitting beside the lake, he continued his reverie in the company of Gokal, who was plunged in silence too. When next he raised his eyes the moon was up, and his gaze dwelt for a moment upon his companion's meditative face. "Gokal," he said, "I have been thinking for some time that I ought to visit Khanjo." And he went on to explain that although he had written to Mabun to inform him of Gunevati's disappearance, his report had, perforce, been very scrappy. He felt he owed it to Mabun to make some personal investigations on the spot. The whole journey, he supposed, would take little more than a week.

For a minute after he had spoken Gokal looked startled; then he seized upon the idea with an eagerness that caused Hari some secret astonishment. It looked as though Gokal were not yet resigned, or had, at any rate, allowed the elements of mystery in Gunevati's disappearance to take an undue hold upon his imagination.

Was it by design that Hari set out upon this journey without having any further talk with Sita in private? Perhaps he himself could hardly have given a definite answer. Regarded simply as a piece of strategy the move was not remarkable for artfulness; nevertheless, the abrupt manner of his departure disquieted Sita—it disquieted her, although she could not help suspecting that it was intended to have just this effect.

His second day's travel brought him to the hermit's cave under the cliff. It was situated at the top of a rough slide of rocks, the cave mouth making a black hole in the face of the precipice that towered on above. The evening sun was shining upon that great wall of stone and the hermit himself was visible as a small, naked figure against the darkness of his lair. From the road below Hari gazed up and debated within himself; it would be a hot and dusty climb; but he was curious, and the fact that the man was a Sakti no longer discouraged him. As he scrambled up amongst the tumbled boulders he hoped devoutly that the hermit would not retire into the cavern at his approach, as such men often did. It was a relief, upon reaching the stone platform, to find him still there; and he made haste to salute him with every sign of veneration, taking the dust from his feet in the approved manner. The hermit, seated cross-legged upon the ground, looked down at this somewhat ironically. He was small and wizen, and had the air of being prematurely aged. After bidding his visitor be seated, he waited, examining him with watchful, beady eyes, the pupils of which were jet black and the whites strangely yellow. There was a striking contrast between the mean appearance of the recluse and the grandeur of the scene about him. From this high place one looked down the full length of the great, empty valley. At its end the sun was sinking after a day's travel through a burning sky. Glorious was the emptiness beneath, falling westward into the haze of the evening's fullest glow. And in that ocean of sunlight, washing the steepness of the cliff, soaring eagles, like flecks of gold, hung or plunged, and in their descent snatched an invisible prey.

"Why have you come?" asked the hermit.

Hari hesitated. "To hear whatever you may vouchsafe to say."

The hermit smiled. "I am a Sakti of three bars"—he pointed to the mark on his forehead—"and when men come to me it is to talk of love."

"So be it!" replied Hari. "Of love, then, we will speak."

"Love," said the hermit with a sneer, "is the chief of the fictitious values of Prakriti or Nature. A man assigns value to the beloved and to her love; he also assigns value to his own. Thus he gives himself and his concerns an imaginary importance and flatters his self-esteem."

Hari nodded gravely, making an effort to conceal the antipathy with which the hermit inspired him. After some reflection he said: "You are speaking of the love between a man and a woman, but there is also brotherly love and the love of a man for the Divine."

The hermit opened his mouth in a silent laugh. "What I have said applies to all love. Behind love is the craving for self-aggrandizement. Man has invented God and deified love in order to give himself greater importance—at any rate in his own eyes."

"If man is the measure of all things," said Hari, "then he is as great as he believes himself to be."

"Unfortunately," returned the hermit, again smiling his unpleasant smile, "he cannot believe himself to be great on his own merits. He is always driven to relate himself to the Divine."

Hari was silent, and for a minute or more his attention was distracted from his companion. The golden haze had deepened; the crags, the precipices, the darkly wooded slopes melted away from the deepest blue beneath him into filmy transparencies above. Only this cliff and this small rock platform upon which he and his companion were seated glowed still as if in the heart of a furnace, the sun's heat and brilliance still striking there.

Then, as he was still gazing down the valley, he became aware that the hermit was studying him, and he turned to meet those eyes that held a crafty gleam.

"What is your scheme of things?" he inquired, again looking away.

"The world," said the hermit, "is ruled by a number of irrational forces, which constitute Prakriti; and we, ourselves, *are* Prakriti. The external world is not mirrored by us, passively, in our sense-perceptions, but created as a magic lantern creates the images that it projects."

"I have been taught," said Hari, "that Prakriti is identical with Maya, the principle of finitude or delusion."

"How can that be called delusive which alone exists? The Infinite, the Absolute, the Real—call it what you will—transcends the categories of existence and non-existence. For us, therefore, it is not, and never will be. Finitude is essential to existence, and we are finite centers creating the world."

"And we create love as part of the world," said Hari, "yet you began by discriminating against love."

At this the hermit gave Hari an evil look, but after a moment he said: "I did not deny the existence of love. I denied the legitimacy of the value attached to it."

"But your philosophy provides no criterion by which to judge values or even to distinguish between truth and error."

"And what philosophy does more?" The hermit's evil look had returned, but presently it faded into a weary mockery. "Underlying all philosophies are a set of beliefs that can neither be justified nor rejected; the instinct to philosophize is but one of the minor activities of Prakriti; no philosophy is anything more than an index to the character of its exponent."

As he spoke these last words he was again smiling, and it appeared to Hari, although he could hardly believe his eyes, that the man actually gave him a wink. For a minute or more nothing was said. Hari was thrown into bewilderment. Was the man really as petty as he seemed? Or did the very enormity of his pettiness redeem him? So dazzling was the yellow radiance in which they were now both enveloped that it contributed not a little to his mental confusion; so majestic was the great bowl of the valley filled with a swirling haze of fire that he could only blink and wonder. When he glanced at the hermit it was to encounter the same watchful smile; and the miserable thinness of the man and the weariness that was reflected in his yellow eyes filled his heart with pity. But it would never do, he felt, to let this appear.

Assuming, therefore, an air of discomfiture, he rose slowly to his feet. "Your thought is beyond me," he muttered. "I must confess that I am no philosopher." There was an awkward pause during which he kept his eyes fixed upon the ground. Then with an abrupt farewell salutation he took himself off down the slope. The hermit had not ceased to smile, but the scorn in his smile seemed slightly forced, and Hari had the uncomfortable feeling that perhaps his pity had not been successfully concealed. On the other hand, it was possible that he was doing the hermit an injustice. It was possible that the hermit saw everything, including the meanness of his own character, and was sufficiently detached not to care. Was that what the hermit's wink had meant? Was his essential ego so far withdrawn that it took no greater interest in the meanness of the man who happened to be himself than in the meanness of any other?

This state of mind—and he knew it to be not uncommon—perplexed Hari as he considered it. Was character, personality, everything? or was it nothing? In many ways he agreed with the hermit; but he would have liked to go further and to believe that the truth was conditioned by character no less than by sense-perceptions. He would also, however, have liked to think that no human being would ever accept any system of belief that was not in harmony with such feelings as those, for instance, just inspired in him by the setting sun. In a properly appointed universe there should be a God with an absolute standard by which human standards were to be judged. If value lay at the heart of things, then objective truth—as reason attempted to frame it—could offer at best but an unimportant aspect of the whole. Realists were apt to disparage value as an all-too-human concept. They were apt to believe that the reason could humanize itself; and then they would prostrate themselves before it with the most abject religiosity. Unfortunately, of all human attributes the most obviously all-too-human was discursive reason itself. For reason was the instrument of man's conscious purposes, and these were the instrument of his unconscious purposes, and these again were but a small part of the activity of Nature or God. Was that activity purposeful, too? Analogy, a poor guide perhaps, but our only one, would say yes.

Having brought these reflections to a comfortable conclusion, he allowed his thoughts to fly back to Sita, and with Sita they remained during the whole of the rest of his journey. The haze of his pre-occupations dimmed even his first hours at Khanjo. Upon the little lawn, where he and Sita had once sat together, he stood in a trance, staring down at the red and brown carpet of fallen rhododendron blossoms that now covered it over. It was very silent here in the wilderness of trees; indeed, the whole place was wrapped in a silence which he felt to be slightly uncanny. All the servants excepting those of the lowest caste had gone; and these, in addition to their usual air of apathy, seemed to him to wear a furtive look. Dusk fell while he sat in the veranda of Gokal's house trying to fix his mind upon the business before him.

It was early next morning when he walked across the yard and threw open Gunevati's room, which had been kept locked since Sita's visit to it. The windows were closed; the sun beating on the roof had heated the air inside, which was heavy and heavily charged with scent. His search took him some time, for he went over every inch of the room. When he had finished he was in a sweat and threw himself down on the bed, yielding to an unaccountable exhaustion. So vividly had this scent and all these intimate belongings brought the girl before his eyes that her actual physical absence was like a kind of self-contradiction in nature. She was here and yet she was not here; and his heart seemed to ache for her. But perhaps it was for Sita that his heart really was aching? or perhaps it was out of sympathy for Gokal? In any case, he was in the grip of a new and overwhelming compassion. "Did Gokal come into this room? Did he see those dresses lying about and smell this familiar perfume? Alas!" he cried out within himself, "what hideous pain!" And after this there came the thought: "Shall I ever stand bereft of Sita?"

As he lay there with closed eyes he was gradually overcome with shame at his earlier lack of imagination. Within what narrow limits his self-absorption had confined him! His perceptions, his intuitions, his understanding—how much further they might have gone! The extent of his negligence revealed itself to him now. The longer he stared into the past the darker and deeper became the vistas of his speculation.

Two hours passed by before he got up and prepared to leave the room. The only objects of any interest that he had found were a few scraps of paper inscribed with charms; and these were only interesting in that they raised the question: Whose hand was it that had penned them? Gunevati herself was, of course, illiterate; the script had a degree of refinement that put the village scribe out of consideration; and the handwriting was certainly not Gokal's. Following an idea that had come to him in the course of his musings he took the path across the valley to Amar's house. Before the door there squatted two or three wretched-looking women who watched him without even turning their heads. Again it entered his mind that they had a secret, and he was glad that he had thought of sending two of his men on ahead. He had selected two lent to him by Mabun and had given them instructions to enter the valley from the other direction in the guise of pilgrims on their way to the Banassi shrine. These men were to mix with the people of the place and pick up all they could. But he was now afraid that they would not find out much, for his own arrival so soon after was evidently putting the people on their guard. No doubt they had jumped to the conclusion that Gokal had succumbed to the poison given him and that his friend had come determined to wreak vengeance upon someone at any cost.

After wandering round and about the house, he found what he was looking for: the place where the rubbish had been thrown. It had occurred to him that some relic of Jali's lesson-hours should surely be discoverable, and his object was to compare Jali's handwriting with that of the Tantric charms. It was not long before he succeeded in unearthing a page of manuscript, some verses from the Septuagint translated into Persian. This exercise could only be Jali's, and he saw at a glance that his conjecture had been correct.

It was in an even more pensive mood that he went back across the valley, and for the rest of the day he sat in meditation in the veranda of Gokal's house. Had there been any doubt in his mind as to what this association between Gunevati and Jali implied, it would have been dispelled by the gross obscenity of many of the

Mantras—especially those designed to capture a man's love. And to think that this had been going on under his eyes week after week! What blindness! What stupid incuriosity regarding other people's thoughts and feelings! He recalled his night meeting with Jali in the corridor of the Agra Palace and was filled with contrition at having neglected ever to give the boy more than a passing thought since that day. He had known very well that Jali must be leading an intense inward life, and yet he had never troubled himself to think about it. Had his sympathies been a little more alive, many things might have turned out differently. . . .

The silence and solitude of the place were filled with vanished presences, and his musings took their color from the deep-hued forest that spread its cloak over every fold of the ground. One day followed another, and his sojourn at Khanjo was drawing itself out much longer than he had expected; but he could not permit himself to leave until he had talked with the herb-woman who had attended Gokal; and she was away gathering roots on the high hills. A hope that he might obtain some fresh light upon the nature of Gokal's poisoning had really held the first place in his mind from the outset.

27

IT SEEMED TO Sita that she had begun to love Hari on that misty, rainy day two months ago, when he and Amar had ridden away from Khanjo. But her love, she supposed, would have lain dormant for ever had Hari not returned and made a call upon it.

One could not know oneself. Although she had sometimes felt that it might happen to her to fall deeply in love, now that the thing had come to pass she was confounded. Could somebody else have foreseen her future better than she? Ambissa, for instance? Even in the old days Ambissa had shaken her head when she saw that the duties of a wife and mother had not absorbed all her sister-in-law's energies. Ambissa, on her visits, had extolled the selfless Hindu women (whom she resembled little enough herself) and had deprecated her taking so lively a part in the social and intellectual life of Amar's court. And there had been other women, too, who, being inclined to light conduct, interpreted her freedom of spirit in their own fashion. Well, they could now say they had been right; but the world's way of being right was such a shallow way! The world was incapable of understanding what was in her heart now; and in those old days she had been blameless indeed.

Thinking of Jali, she was glad, instead of sorry, that he was spiritually so detached. He loved her no doubt, but she could see that her ways of thought and feeling affected him as strange; and although he was lonely, he seemed to cherish his loneliness with passion. Once when she was teaching him her religion, he looked at her gravely and said: "Yes, you create Christ; but I create devils." Jali did not need her, she now said to herself with mingled sadness and relief, neither did Amar. And then she wondered again whether all that had happened could possibly have been foreseen or averted. Not that she wished that it had been averted; she preferred to love, even if loving meant suffering.

The last time, when Hari had ridden away, it had been quite different. She had let him go then without any anxiety. Perhaps she had felt sure that he was taking with him memories that he would be unable to cast off. At any rate, the thought of him had been a warm, steady glow at the back of her heart, making her feel life to be rich and deep. That season had been like the spring, a season of promise and expectation. She had been without her present sense of self-committal, of unsafety, of a hunger for a happiness that might easily be snatched away. Now, with each day of Hari's absence, her uneasiness increased. As the warmth of his presence faded, loneliness and misgiving took possession of her heart. She was living with intensity, but that intensity was painful. Hari was the ghostly companion of her solitary walks, and passionately did she argue and plead with him. "Do not mistake me!" she cried out in her heart. "Do not imagine that I was born to be a nun. No, I am alive to all sides of love. But, although I need you, I also need to wander in the lands of my own mind—solitary and free. I do not want to be your captive . . . although it could be— it would be—wonderful. You—who are free, too, really—you must let me be free. Don't draw me into any depths however sweet. . . . For I should not be able to emerge whole again; and you—perhaps you would!"

The more deeply and irretrievably she felt her heart to be engaged, the more poignant became the terror lest he should one day fail her. She said to herself that if she could be sure of dying at once she would accept her present risks with a light heart. But one did not die: that was the horror of it. One lived to see the world turn into a waste. And with the memory of the magical world of yesterday, one moved, stiff and frozen, under the cold light of ordinary days; only they were not ordinary days now, but days of agony. "I could not face it!" she said to her invisible companion. "For, you see, my dreams and imaginings would have gone too! They would have been lost to me—perhaps for ever."

Sunk in a deep abstraction she would walk, swift and unseeing, for many miles through the dark woods, and then, stopping suddenly, look round like one aroused from sleep. Her being was saturated with the spirit of the forest through which she had come —the moist, peaty earth, the solemn pools of brown water, the trees with gray lichen hanging down. She would look up at the tall pines standing quiet around her—very quiet, as if concentrated upon their silent growth. She felt the strength of those age-long, patient lives, and throwing herself down and pressing her fingers into the loose, cool mold she lost the outer trappings of personality altogether; she was no longer the young Ranee, nor the wife, nor the mother, nor even the woman who loved. She lost herself completely; she was no longer anything but an emotion, so still, so profound, that there was no name by which it could be described.

Two weeks and more went by, and Hari's return was overdue. She began to lose her sleep and she found it harder and harder to rouse herself from long daydreams that were full of pain. Again and again she reconstructed their talks together, and in each one of his words she read a dire meaning, in each one of his silences she found an implication that froze her heart. No doubt he was angry; he was disappointed; he felt that his love had been misprized.

And then, yet once again, she would look into herself and search. Was she really divided in spirit? Was she timid, ungenerous, lukewarm? A good Christian she was not (God forgive her!), but was she not even a woman capable of love? Why had she not been able to yield to love in all simplicity? Why could she not accept that inspiration and live it unafraid? She thought of Christ, and so closely was her religion interwoven with the tissue of her life that she could not now tear the two apart and isolate a moral code by which to judge herself. How could it be wrong—indeed, it could not be wrong—to love? How could it be wrong to do that which was so joyful—and which gave one so much pain?

But what of Hari, as day after day still went by? What could have happened? Was he ill? Was he dead?

And then, to bring her distress to its climax, she was pierced by pangs of jealous suspicion. It came into her mind that Hari might have met with Lalita once again. Was it not possible that his love for that girl had never really died, that the old passion was ready to leap up into flame? These thoughts came to her one night as she lay sleepless; and bitterly did she regret not having made more sure at the very first. She ought to have studied him more closely; she should have been able to read his heart more clearly than he could himself. The torment of these thoughts drove her from her bed; she threw open the shutters and sat by the window in the bright moonlight. Ah, now, she thought, it was too late, too late! And yet what beauty still adorned the world! What peace in that dark night-sky! A gleam of silver shone from the lake where the setting moon just fell upon it. Owls were hooting from far-away trees behind the house. She remembered how often she had sat beside her window like this in old days, and what a cool, fresh happiness had then been hers, how smoothly her spirit had slid out into the night. All that was over now. The beauty and the peace were remote from her. So bitter was the contrast that a flame of anger leapt up in her heart. It was Hari, not she, who was answerable. Hari's were the blame and the shame! All that she had ever meant to give him was friendship; had she not resisted every step upon the fatal road leading to this?

But her anger flickered out very quickly, and for a space she laid her head on her arms. Then, getting up, and moving with great quietness—for Amar was asleep in the next room—she lit a candle and sat down to write. The trembling of her hand almost prevented her. "Will you tell me why you stay away, and why you went away without saying a word to me? I was happy before and now I am unhappy. I am frightened—because I did trust you and let myself depend on you. I found in life an added richness and loveliness, but now I feel that life is perhaps going to give me the lie. But it cannot be you who would do this to me? And yet—you went away without speaking a word. I think of the times when I said that I was afraid of becoming dependent on you, and you answered that you would never fail me. But perhaps I am being foolish. . . . I know that I am liable to fall into panics—thinking of change and chance and time that waste this fleeting, transitory world. And the stars, they terrify me. Love is the only fire at which we can warm ourselves when the great spaces look down on us, and the empty coldness of them settles upon us. Up here, under the huge, snowy mountains, I feel remote from the ordinary kindliness of life. Yesterday I walked to the edge of the valley and looked down into the pearly distance towards the plains, and I thought that nothing could match the loveliness of the earth except an exquisite love in the hearts of men. But the thought of you was mixed with a dreadful fear. When shall I see you again? Perhaps you are staying away because you wished me to be lonely and to make this appeal? But that thought frightens me too. Must love be like that—instead of confidence and peace? I only know that I am not used to such suffering, and that not long ago I put all my trust in you."

This written, she closed her eyes and sat still. She felt more tranquil. It would not be difficult to send the letter off secretly the next day. Having hidden it under her pillow, she sank into an exhausted sleep.

When morning came the letter was hidden again, this time in her dress, and she carried it about with her all day. She could not bring herself to send it. There was a thought in her mind that gave her the calm of resignation. She knew that if the worst was true, no letter, no appeal, would be of any avail. One had to wait in silence —if need be, for ever. One had to take one's suffering in secret.

All the morning she sat before the house with a white face and her hands folded in her lap. Would it be possible to retire from the world, she wondered—to become a nun? And, thinking of St. Teresa and Lady Julian, "Oh! what joy it would give me," she cried out in her heart, "what joy, if I could follow in their path!"

Later she went out for another solitary walk. It was a dusky afternoon and the air was gentle and warm. For miles round there was nothing to be heard but the uneven soughing of the wind. She went through a belt of forest, and at its further edge a flock of pigeons were flying in and out of the trees. For a long time she stood watching their quick, strong flight. They seemed unable to make up their minds, but at last they took wing and did not return. Straight on through the wet sky they went, and disappeared into a rainy distance.

She loitered for a while on the outskirts of the wood; sometimes brushing through the damp bushes, sometimes leaning against the

219

trunk of a tree. The wind was coming up from over the hills opposite, with clouds and gloom in its wake. The idea came to her that Hari might be traveling along under that obscurity and she longed to warm her heart with this fancy on the way home; but she resisted; and later she was glad, for when she reached the house Hari had not yet arrived.

2 8

HARI'S LAST DAYS at Khanjo were spent in a fever of unrest, and his impatience to rejoin Sita was exasperated by a failure to make any good use of his time. The herb-woman, when at last she returned, assured him that Gokal had been poisoned by fungi alone, but he could not help doubting her. There was nothing to be done beyond giving her money; but not even for money was she likely to incriminate herself; and if, as he suspected, the fungi had been used to conceal another poison which she herself had supplied, nothing, not even the most earnest assurances of pardon and immunity from punishment, would make her confess it. Some people would have ordered that she should be tortured, but that went against his nature. So it might well be that the issue whether Gokal was to live or die lay in the decision of this cynical old woman; but nothing that he could say or do would influence her.

In elucidating the mystery of Gunevati's flight he was scarcely more successful. His men got some evidence that a party of strangers had arrived in the district a few days before the girl's disappearance; and the reluctance shown by everybody to say anything about those strangers made one suspect that they had been persons with full power to intimidate. The people of the district, however, were so base-born that it was unnecessary, perhaps, to look for any reasoned cause for their sullen secretiveness; or possibly they were nervous about the recent murder of a young man from a neighbor-ing village. Gunevati, it appeared, was indirectly responsible, and for some unknown reason the villagers seemed extremely anxious that the murder should not be investigated. Hari would never have heard of it but for the herb-woman, who evidently thought it only fair to make some return for all the money she had been given. She showed him the place where, according to her, the young man (who had been Gunevati's lover) was buried. There certainly were some suspicious marks upon the ground. The soil was cracked, having swollen up in a blister, and this seemed to indicate that the work was not the work of Thugs, for Thugs always drove a stake through the body to allow the gases of decomposition to escape without a sign. Nevertheless, there was good cause to believe that many of the men in the village were Thugs; at any rate, as the herb-woman significantly observed, they had very quickly estab-lished relations with Gunevati, in whom they had without doubt recognized one of Kali's secret devotees. To sum up, the scraps of information obtained were merely confusing; all they revealed was that evil things had been taking place. Hari left Khanjo with thankfulness, determined to forget it as soon as he could, for that little valley held secrets that he could not hope ever to penetrate.

After putting the forest behind him he was able to ride fast, and he certainly made the most of his opportunities. What would he not have given to know whether his prolonged absence had caused Sita a single moment's unrest or anxiety! He could very easily be-lieve that she had remained perfectly serene. He could see her di-viding her days between the old Rajah, Gokal, and Jali. She would have listened to the old Rajah's maunderings with delightful pa-tience; she would have played chess with Gokal; she would have gone boating on the lake with Jali; and thus her days would have sped peacefully by. Well! if she had really been like that, what was he to make of it? How could he escape the conclusion that her feelings for him were very different from his for her? Had any woman, who was herself in love, ever before begged her lover to take his love lightly? Ah, no! he said in sudden agony. And her at-titude to him during all their days together, was it not consistent with the theory that she was simply a romantic, a little in love with Love—nothing more! With these thoughts obsessing him,

Hari rode fast, indeed; but he could not outride his doubts and misgivings which deepened every hour.

The shadows of the alders were drawing out over the meadows as he urged his tired horse along the last mile. He had a foolish hope that he might come upon Sita sitting beside the lake-path, and as he dismounted before the old Rajah's house he gazed up at the windows with the same causeless expectation. It was thus that Amar found him, and there by the gate they stood for a while, before he went on to his tent, but not without having accepted an invitation to come in later on. During the interval he had no thought but this: "I shall know how I stand the first moment I set eyes upon her." In his mind the idea had become firmly fixed that this meeting would reveal the turn of his fate. Her face, her attitude, the manner of her greeting—he trembled in anticipation; and it was with a still more profound inward tremor that he entered the room. The sun had set not long ago, and the whole party were seated by the window that looked upon the lake. A soft twilight, reflected up from the water, mingled with the yellow shine of the lamps that had just been lit. Some game was being played in which everyone took a part; Sita's laughter was ringing out as he came forward, and it seemed to him in that instant that he was looking upon an ideally happy and contented family group. His eyes sought Sita's, but he could not capture her regard; even as she rose to give him her hand she was still laughing; it was impossible to believe that she had lost her peace of mind for a single moment.

The next few minutes were the most painful in the whole of Hari's life. Again and again he searched Sita's face; it was serene and gay; she seemed not to notice the anguished looks, which—regardless of the others—he could not refrain from fastening upon her. Either she was too indifferent to observe them or she was pretending not to, and he did not know which supposition was the worst.

Very well then! The blow had fallen, and all that mattered for the moment was to keep up appearances. Taking himself sternly under control, he directed his conversation to everyone in turn and abstained from looking at Sita except when actually addressing her. Every moment of that dreadful visit confirmed his first impression, and as soon as he could he brought the ordeal to an end.

Not for one instant did it enter his imagination that the whole fabric of his hopes and fears had been spun out of nothing at all. The simple truth was that his return had swept Sita's misery out of existence in one instant. From one of the windows she had seen him approach; she had overheard his conversation with Amar; she had noted the strain in his eyes, the anxiety in his voice; and then she had rushed to her room to give way to tears. Happiness had come back to her, a happiness tired and tremulous at first, but afterwards triumphant. Once again she could enter into Jali's games with spirit, once again she could offer to those about her an appearance that was not odiously and miserably deceptive. "He loves me!" she cried out within her heart, "and if he does not love me enough, I can make him love me more." From the moment she had seen him coming she had known that she would give herself to him wholly. The struggle was over; her conscience troubled her no longer. So great was this relief from inward conflict that she went about the house singing and laughing to herself.

During the whole of Hari's visit she was divided between amusement and compassion. Not all, but a little, of what was passing in his mind she was able to guess. "Ah, when I undeceive him!" she thought to herself, and the knowledge of the joy she could give doubled her own.

It was in a condition of dreadful calm that Hari walked back to his tent. "No doubt I deserve this!" he said to himself, and from that thought he endeavored to extract comfort. Sita had discovered that her heart was, in reality, bound to her husband and child. Could he blame her, if a woman's instinct to color her life with romance had carried her for a few steps off her true road? Oh, but it was not kind of her to have acted like this! She should have set a watch upon the path from Khanjo and let a messenger intercept him with a letter. She should have spared him this meeting. But how should she—not being ensnared by passion herself—how should she conceive what he was feeling? To understand madness one must oneself be mad.

Presently he got up and stood at the entrance of his tent. A few faint stars behind the clouds gave great profundity to the sky; but the human misery within the insignificant compass of a man's mind could be, he thought, as deep. Yet when he looked back into the tent again and when his eye fell on two or three withered flowers that Sita had once given him: "A little earthly happiness," he thought, "is what man craves. Give him that, poor wretch, and the stars may all go out."

A small light shining through the darkness marked Gokal's tent and told him that its occupant was still awake. He hesitated, feeling that if he joined Gokal it should be with the object of bestowing sympathy rather than of seeking it. Poor Gokal's unrest had been aggravated instead of assuaged by the brief account already given him of the investigations at Khanjo.

While he was still undecided, the light from Gokal's tent was obscured, but a few moments later he observed that there was still a faint glow coming through the canvas. This showed that the tent door had been closed; and he could not help asking himself what that meant, for Gokal was accustomed to leave his door open all night. After a few moments he stepped quietly through the darkness towards the closed tent. The canvas was everywhere fastened up, but in a minute he found a chink to which he put his eye. Without any shame, and with a good deal more curiosity than he could account for, he set himself to spy into the tent. Nothing appeared to be out of the ordinary. Gokal was sitting on his couch staring down at something beside him; his face was turned away, but before very long he seemed to catch some sound, for he lifted his head and looked all round about. It was a long, searching look that had something furtive about it; it gave Hari the impression that he was meditating an act that he felt must on no account be overseen. For a moment, fearful of detection, Hari drew his head back; but his heart had begun to beat with a vague, painful anxiety, and after a minute he stooped again to his chink. Gokal's face was now wholly visible, and to Hari's horror, his expression was almost that of an idiot. His eyes were staring widely, unseeingly; his chin had dropped; there was no intelligence, but a terrible, remote concentration of thought depicted on his face.

Hari felt his limbs beginning to tremble; he straightened himself and after a few moments of desperate hesitancy moved quietly away to a distance of several yards from the tent. Then he turned and walked back again, this time making as much noise as possible.

"Still awake?" he cried, and pushed at the flap which was tied over the entrance.

A few moments passed before any answer came, and in the meantime he managed to get another peep into the interior. Gokal appeared to be thrusting something hurriedly away out of sight behind the couch; and his manner, as he admitted his visitor, was awkward and confused. Hari explained that he had just come back from the old Rajah's house, and on seeing a light still burning thought he would step in for a chat. He found the greatest difficulty in giving himself a natural demeanor, for his suspicions were deepening all the time. Gokal, who had again seated himself upon the couch, averted his eyes, swallowed, and said nothing. The small oil-lamp on the table beside him was burning smokily; and it was obviously in an attempt to give himself countenance that he leant forward and made as though to trim the wick; but the shaking of his hand prevented him.

"Gokal," said Hari, "I am afraid you have fever to-night."

"That may be," the answer came huskily. And he added: "Yes, I am feverish."

All at once Hari put aside all pretense. Dropping down on a seat opposite, he fastened upon Gokal a gaze of profound anxiety.

"For God's sake," he said, "what were you doing before I came in?"

"Doing? Nothing."

With a gesture Hari brushed this aside. "I ask: what were you doing?"

Gokal stared at him warily and in silence.

"I was standing outside," said Hari. "I have been watching you for these last ten minutes. Do you understand?"

A frown of perplexity appeared upon Gokal's face.

Hari drew a deep breath and it was with throttled utterance that he said: "Very well. But I shall not leave you. I shall remain here."

The two men regarded one another intently, and for a while there was silence in the tent. Hari's gaze was fixed and searching, but Gokal's was unsteady, and to Hari it almost seemed as if he could see—behind the darkness of those shifting pupils—a headlong rout of thoughts. At last, however, Gokal blinked, sighed, and gently shook his head.

"Dear Hari," he said with a transient smile, "you are making a mistake. I am not thinking of suicide—not at this moment, no."

At first Hari's expression hardly changed; then gradually his tensity relaxed. "You frightened me," he murmured. He was still scrutinizing Gokal with a painful concentration. "And even so—there is still something you must explain—there is still something I do not understand."

The smile on Gokal's face had been replaced by a look of agony. He struggled with himself, but the agitation that had been discernible in him from the beginning was no longer to be held down. All at once he started a sentence and then cut it short; he began a gesture and left it uncompleted; in the end, with a sort of moan, he leant backwards, he felt with his hand on the floor, and brought up some object that was lying hidden behind his couch.

"There! Do you see that? And that?" Down upon the bed he flung a muslin dress, a necklace, some silver bangles.

Bewildered, Hari bent forward and examined them. "These were Gunevati's?" he asked hesitatingly.

"*Were*? You say *were*? You think, then, she is dead?"

"No, no. Why should I mean that? Why should she be dead?"

Gokal took up the piece of muslin, spread it out on the bed, and gazed at it for a full minute with a look that baffled Hari completely. But his perplexity was soon submerged by a rising tide of compassion.

"So that is what you were hiding from me?" he pronounced with sadness. "My poor Gokal, what, in God's name, shall I say? You know as well as I do that you are in bondage. You are obsessed. You are possessed. You are mad. Have you not taken that girl's mortal body? Have you not seen into the miserable emptiness of her mind? All that she has or is you have already made yours. What more, then, do you desire? What is it possible to obtain? Companionship, affection, love—they are not in her to give. You know all this. You know your madness. You know . . ."

He stopped. Gokal was neither listening nor pretending to listen; he had a look of agonized intensity; his eyes rolled as if he were seeking some way of escape from the turmoil of his own brain. "Do you *wish* she were dead?" Hari asked suddenly.

Gokal said: "I think she is dead."

"Why?"

There was a pause. Gokal's manner was now so odd that Hari began to fear for his reason.

"Those"—and Gokal pointed—"those were the things she was actually wearing when she ran away."

"But," stammered Hari, "but how, in that case . . ."

"Someone thrust those things into my tent—just now—in the darkness—about an hour ago."

"How can that be? You are making some mistake. Gokal, you know, you have fever. . . . You have imagined. . . ."

Gokal lifted his arms to heaven and groaned. "No, I am not mad. Someone is mocking me! Someone is mocking me with her death!" And he covered his face with his hands.

29

IT WAS ABOUT two hours later that Hari stepped out of Gokal's tent. The night was dark, with a warm, fitful breeze that blew into his face as he stumbled over the rough grass. The light in his own tent had gone out; on all sides it was dark.

In the course of his talk with Gokal an idea had taken shape in his mind, and after a little while he had felt that he must communicate it. So far, in his account of his doings at Khanjo, he had omitted all reference to Jali. The boy's association with Gunevati was a matter, as he well knew, that Gokal would take very deeply to heart. Poor Gokal would stare aghast at the picture of the evil that he was responsible for.

And yet a complete revelation had now to be made, for it was his present conjecture that the perpetrator of this odious trick was Jali himself. True, he had no theory to explain how Jali had come by those belongings of Gunevati's, and everything behind the actual incident remained as mysterious as before. Nevertheless, his intuition held firm; he was convinced that Jali knew a great deal more about Gunevati than either he or Gokal; and in this piece of wanton mystification he saw Jali's hand.

The pain of the stroke was intensified for Gokal by his affection for Jali and by his previous confidence that his affection was returned. Hari made haste to assure him that he need not think

229

differently now. There was a common propensity in children to indulge in freakish acts of this nature, and it was impossible in the
present case to believe that the boy had meant any harm.

After Hari had left him Gokal continued to sit upon his couch
before the open doorway through which there flowed the damp
night air charged with the scents of grass and sedge, and filled with
a thousand rustlings and murmurings, and the creaking of boughs
rubbing together in the wind. After a while a gust blew out his
lamp, but instead of relighting it he rose and seated himself outside the open door. As the warm wind blew about his limbs he felt
his fever leaving him. The absence of the moon and stars made the
night intimate and earthly; dry leaves, lifted from the ground, were
swept across his hands and face. It seemed as if the earth's secret
energies were working upon him, and he yielded to a process
which he felt to be beneficent. His spirit lay still in a quiet excitement; a sense of expectation gathered; it was like that of a woman
who is awaiting the first pangs of her first childbed. Little by little
he lost the feeling of his body and his consciousness diffused itself
over the night. "Can this be death?" he wondered, and his answer
came as a vanishing of the question's significance. The rustle of
the leaves grew fainter, the darkness deepened and became absolute; at last his spirit, completely isolated, spoke to itself and
said: "I am aware only of being aware." What now remained was a
consciousness that was not Gokal's, because it knew nothing of
Gokal; nor did it know anything of the world, or of time, or of
space. It knew nothing but itself.

The duration of this state was immeasurable for as long as the
state was changeless, but it was still without a break of consciousness that the flow of external sensation returned. He became again
aware of the rustle of the wind and of time passing; then he recognized the sound of the wind for what it was. In dormancy his
memories of the world returned, but long before he evoked them
he was active in thought. He said to himself: "I have had an experience of the possibility of pure self-consciousness. In that state
subject and object are one; awareness reflects awareness like two
mirrors placed opposite, and that unity in duality seems to constitute self-consciousness, which is also selfhood."

And then it seemed to him that he was explaining these things to Amar, who shook his head and said: "The attribution of self-hood is unjustified."

"But self-consciousness," he replied, "is selfhood. It is a closed circuit."

Amar shook his head again. "Pure consciousness is conscious-ness of *its* self, which is not the same thing as consciousness of one's self. Where there is no remembering personality there can be no selfhood."

As he was considering this, Gokal's eyes began to see again and he noticed a few dim stars in the sky above the hill top. Whereupon it struck him that in the blankness of pure self-consciousness there were no stars; in fact, the whole phenomenal world remained unaccounted for. And on that there followed the conviction that pure self-consciousness was not the final state of spirit, and that his experience was only interesting as a direct personal revelation of the falseness of Amar's last statement. Pure self-consciousness might, he considered, be a suspensory condition between rebirths. And this was what he next said, adding that no consciousness which did not comprehend in a static and perfected unity all tem-poral processes from the beginning to the end of time could claim absoluteness or godhead.

And again Amar frowned and replied that ideas of personality, even of consciousness, were null when applied to the Absolute. The Absolute, as Buddha constantly implied, was simply that of which nothing could be predicated.

But at this point Gokal felt himself possessed by a keen and ir-recusable sense of the reality and significance of the phenomenal world as a feature of the Absolute. "To philosophize at all," he said, "is to postulate that the process in Time calls for explana-tion. An explanation of it must be explicit or implicit in every sys-tem of thought, whether you call it a philosophy or no."

He would have gone on, but all at once his mind dropped to an-other plane; his thoughts changed, his attention was fixed upon psychological actualities. Looking into Amar's mind he saw jeal-ousy there and suspicion and yet other shadowy forms of evil. Amar now seemed to him to be standing by the door of the tent with the light of the lamp shining upon him, and the austerity of his countenance and the rigidity of his bearing inspired Gokal with deep misgivings. He thought of Tche-Sing and another Chinese priest whom he knew, both Buddhists of a school kindred to Amar's. These two were far advanced in wisdom, and what was remarkable in their bearing was its easiness, and upon their countenances a smile that bespoke a benign suppleness of mind. A terrible doubt seized him whether Amar was not misdirecting himself entirely; and when he looked at Tche-Sing for an answer, the latter to his surprise bent down to his ear and quoted from the Christian Scriptures: "If therefore, the light that is in him be darkness, how great is that darkness." And again yet lower he whispered: "Base things of the world, and things which are despised, hath God chosen, yea, and things that are not, to bring to nought the things that are." Gokal's heart sank, for he knew that Amar would be unable to make anything of these words, his mind, stiffened by logic, being obtuse to the awful paradoxes of the world of spirit. Yet was it possible that this devout seeker after truth should fail absolutely? In great anguish he cried out: "Amar, your love for me has been one of the greatest supports of my life and for a twofold reason. I have felt that you were able to love me for myself only *because* I was your brother in aspiration. Now consider this well, Amar, and the quality of your love shall show you a truth that has hidden itself from your intelligence. Upon what does your love rest and unto what does it address itself? You will see that it is more than human and seeks what is more than human. It rests upon an intuition that for you a man is lovable inasmuch as he partakes of the divine essence. You will see that your love addresses itself to the divine. There is no other explanation of the highest love; it has one object and one only. Such love is in you and it testifies to your unacknowledged recognition of God."

Having spoken, Gokal waited anxiously for a reply; but for a long while Amar remained dumb; and when at last he answered there was anger in his tone. "Is this how you would help me?" he said. "Would you tempt me back into doubt? Love is the last of the imperfections to fade before the white radiance of Nirvana is reached. I know who has corrupted you. But, unshakable, I take my stand upon the wisdom of the Enlightened One."

Gokal lifted his eyes to the heavens, and behold! the night-sky was ablaze with constellations that the earth had never seen before. He was filled with ineffable awe, but he knew that Amar could not share his vision, and he said:

"Where is the doctrine that is absolutely pure? And where shall a man seek truth except from the light within? Listen to the divine Plotinus: 'Let us call upon God himself, not by form of words, but by the lifting to him of the soul in prayer. And the only way to pray is to advance solitarily towards the One who is solitary.' "

At this point the vehemence of his emotion roused him from his fantasies, but he continued to sit where he was; and, while the day broke and the dawn brightened, his eyes still remained fixed, as if he was unaware of the passing of the night.

A little later, the camp servants, rising to their tasks, looked with surprise at their master sitting there, but although they whispered among themselves, they forebore to approach him. Warm and still was the radiance that flooded the valley, and presently Sita, the sunlight falling upon her eyes, was awakened and went to her window to look out. She saw a flock of wild geese wheeling in the sun. She saw Jali talking to two boatmen who were showing him some kittens taken from a wild cat that had been shot the day before. A little later she saw Amar going down the path towards the lake, and remembered that he had told her he had to pay a visit on Shaik Mobarek, who was now in Daniyal's camp.

Whilst dressing with a happy, leisurely care, she went again and again to the window to smell the jasmine that blossomed just beneath the sill. And then it came into her mind that she possessed a tiny bottle of a very ancient essence distilled in Persia from the Five Flowers of Love. Her grandmother, who had given it to her, used to say that the flowers had to be plucked by the light of the full moon when it is as yellow as a jackal and its nether rim still touches the horizon. This bottle she now unsealed, and from the thick amber drops there rose a perfume that was exquisite indeed, but which did not please her half so well as that blowing in upon the fresh air. Those amber drops breathed of loves dead and embalmed, of loves that had been young too many weary years ago. The moon since then had traveled too many weary leagues and seen too many lovers grow old and die. Then her thoughts turned to the poor dead Ranee. Not many weeks ago, as she was bending over a chest of precious silks, another perfume, very sweet but older and sadder yet, had floated up out of a past less far. The memory made her sigh; she put the stopper back into the bottle and went down into the garden. Jali was sitting on a bench overlooking the lake, but he did not seem to hear her when she called; and so, because it was still early, she lingered by the side of the lily-pond where she and Hari had stood together on that day. She recalled how the blue butterflies had been playing over the water, and how clear their reflections had been. Then she went on down the path and through the gate towards the group of tents, and all at once she found herself in the presence of Gokal. Heavy and unmoving as a statue he sat there with the cool, golden sunlight pouring over his white robe and gilding the pallor of his face. She faltered for an instant, for it almost seemed to her as if he was sitting there in the expectation of her coming. His eyes rested upon her with an indecipherable tranquillity, and the idea of accounting for this early visit of hers vanished from her mind. She stood before him in silence and returned his gaze. If he could see into her heart, if he could pierce her outward calm and see the fountains of radiance within, it was well. By him she had the wish to be known fully.

They sat together for a while; and presently, although the words they exchanged were without significance, she felt that he was aware of what she would have him know. But this did not bring him back from his remoteness. His eyes resting upon the lake, his face set in a stony calm, he looked like the sculptured image of himself, and his spirit seemed to be communicating with her from another sphere.

After a space they fell silent, and then she rose quietly and stood before him once more.

"Is Hari still sleeping?" she asked.

"Yes, he must be still asleep. When he comes, what shall I say?"

"Tell him to join me up there." Her gaze was fixed upon the wooded knoll behind the house. "He will know where to find me."

BOOK TWO

PRINCE JALI

1

A COLORED SAIL upon the lake caught Jali's eye, and before bending down again to play with the kittens at his feet, he fixed a long deep look upon the opposite shore. There, across two miles of milky-blue water, shimmered and glittered the pleasure-houses, kiosks, and pavilions of Prince Daniyal's encampment. Seen through the haze of the early morning they looked scarcely real—hardly more substantial than their inverted image that trembled upon the lake's pearly surface.

Three months ago, Jali reflected, nothing had been there; that mushroom cluster had not yet sprung up; he would have looked across at a bare, green stretch of marsh, with a clear view to the hills rising behind; and everything would have been different then,—yes, very different.

He sighed and wondered; and well indeed he might. For was it not a remarkable caprice that had prompted a sophisticated young Prince to build a standing camp—a small town, in fact, with all the urbanities and frivolities of a fashionable watering-place—in this remote spot, the charm and beauty of which were nothing if not modest and unspectacular. Nevertheless that façade of light, gay tints displayed itself not inharmoniously across the water; the domes, cupolas, and minarets of Daniyal's baroque architecture soared up, jauntily perhaps, but not unpleasingly against the virgin slopes beyond; and this camp, of course, was devoted to the arts of peace, not of war; so that it was admirably fitting that those thousands of tinsel flakes, floating in the air above it, should actually be flocks of white doves, which it had been the Prince's fancy to dip into vats of gold and silver paint.

At a respectful distance behind Jali stood two boatmen, who were waiting for their young master's orders. They waited deferentially, but not without exchanging an occasional glance—a glance that had its meaning. At last, with a nervous twitching of his brows, Jali came out of his muse, and began once more to roll the plump gray-striped kittens over and over with his foot. Absorbed by this play he smiled, and as his face relaxed he looked again like the boy who had left home six months ago. But the change was brief; in another minute he drew himself up, and it was with a hard look that he turned to his two attendants. "Very well, then!" he said. "The next time I go, I shall go alone."

Both the men immediately broke out into apologies and protestations, but Jali never even gave them a hearing. "Leave the boathouse unlocked," he ordered; "I might want to go over to-night."

With these words he sauntered away along the path and presently sat down on a bench overlooking the lake. The garden was now empty save for him; the house behind stood sunny and silent in the slanting golden light; a few bees hummed among the flowers and flowering trees.

As he sat there a breeze came up with the strengthening sunlight; the lake's glass was ruffled and lost the sleepy reflections of the dawn. Jali sat motionless, staring; and such immobility was unnatural in one so young. His childish face had the heavy look that rests upon old faces when unobserved; that youthful body— now well grown, for he had gained much in strength and stature during the last six months—you saw it held rigid with a tensity that obviously corresponded with an inward tension of the mind.

And an hour later, when his mother came out of the house and called to him, he was still sitting there. She called, and you might have seen his eyelids flicker; but by no other movement did he show that he had heard. For a minute she waited, perplexed, then turned and moved away, a figure strolling pensively along under the checkered sunshine of the garden path.

Cold and black and heavy, cold and dead as a stone, does Jali's heart lie within him at this hour. The sun pours its golden warmth along the valley, and he feels nothing of it; those who love him may call to him, but he feigns not to hear; he sits cold, untouched; a blot of darkness, a stain of evil and misery, upon the earth. Peace and beauty serve only to send his thoughts back to happier days; he sees himself again in his father's Palace at home; he sees himself in the morning sitting in his study, its cool walls flecked with a dancing pattern thrown up by the splashing fountain of the court; he sees himself at noon in the white glare of the bathing pool, leaping and diving with his friends; at picnics, laughing; in the dusk of the cypress avenue, day-dreaming; upon his couch at night with the moonlight streaming across the marble floor. Always and everywhere he sees himself as happy.

But—it was his mind that made this sudden jump—but yet all this was half-illusory. These pictures were misty and inexact; memory had sentimentalized them. He saw it clearly in the contrast afforded by another kind of recollection that came to him now. For this was the kind that carries one right out of the present to make one not merely remember—but seemingly *re-live*—a moment of past time. For a few instants, then, Jali stood once again on the balcony of the Agra Palace; once again the wide, unfamiliar plain stretched away beneath him in the evening light; once again the kite was balancing high overhead; once again the little plant was waving in the wind that brushed along the palace wall. The resuscitated moment died again, the strangeness passed, but it left him with a solemn sense of predestination. The forebodings of that small boy on the balcony had—alas!—been amply justified; he had looked into the future with a great fear—and rightly, rightly had he been afraid. Life was not less dreadful than you imagined it: it was far worse. If one survived, if one remained alive in spite of all, it was because one could get accustomed to anything. One had more strength than one knew.

To understand Jali better it is necessary to throw a brief look backwards at his parentage and earlier life. The small principality over which his father ruled stood alone, like a green island, in the sands of the central Indian desert. The oasis governed by Rajah Amar was green and pleasant with the palm and the fig, the mango and the cypress; and not with these only, for it was also the garden of an old-established culture. Whilst the whole, or nearly the whole, of Northern India had seen its native refinements submerged under the wash of a robuster but decidedly cruder habit of life, this unimportant little Court had been left practically untouched. Thus it had been given to Jali to grow up in a community where tradition survived, where manners were still in their golden age, and hardness, coarseness, and ostentation had not yet taken root. And, if his environment was a civilized one, so, too, was the blood that flowed in his veins. Only that civilized blood of his was a mixed blood as well. In him the conflicting spirits of the East and West were both alive, in contact, but not in unison. It is tempting to ascribe to this duality the peculiarities of his nature, in particular that precocity which made him realize—earlier, certainly, and more fully than most children, how starkly each one of us, in his self-consciousness, stands alone. As soon as Jali could reflect at all it was upon the points of dissimilarity between himself and others; and as his individuality developed—rapidly, but secretly—into its own pattern, he recognized its uniqueness and regarded it with gathering dismay. Very early and quite instinctively he studied the art of dissimulation, and, since secrecy is a powerful upbuilder of the inner life, he soon had a good deal to hide as well as the skill to hide it. The child that could and would tell you all that passed through its mind would live under no tension, there would be little of that interior fermentation which generates speculative thought. What is told is spent and done with; and that, perhaps, is one of the reasons why an instinct for secrecy is nearly always to be found in children that are thoughtful. It is prudent, it is interesting, and it is certainly not difficult, to hide one's true self; one hides it behind the ready-made figure of the child that one is believed or expected to be; one adopts the suggested appearance, and lives, undivined and undisturbed, behind the mask. No doubt it was the mixed blood in his veins, which, although it did not deprive Jali of the natural affections, held him so far aloof from his father and mother alike. At the age of thirteen his thinking self was deeply ensconced in a retreat that he was determined not to betray.

For two or three years already he had been firm in the belief that he differed gravely from the rest of mankind. First and foremost, to his thinking, he differed in being full of fear. Long before his journey from home fear had already established itself as the great principle of his secret life. Each increase in his power to reflect had shown him more clearly than before that the present moment of any creature's happiness was balanced upon a knife-edge with abysses of calamity on either side. Nor was it only the undisputed evils of life that he feared: the mere business of living seemed to him to call for a succession of efforts, audacities, and endurances, that were truly appalling. This idea was strengthened by observation of others—in particular, of his father, whose routine of self-discipline and activity he watched with secret awe. But his mother, no less—how wonderful, how incomprehensible, she was! And the same lesson was impressed on him when he cast his eyes outside the Palace gates, where the poverty-stricken, the diseased, the altogether luckless, swarmed and endured their fate. What a front humanity presented! What pluck, what spirit, in high and low alike!

To be fair to himself, however, he had to add this: there were signs everywhere that other people didn't mind the things he minded—or at any rate, not half so much. They didn't even notice a great many things that turned him sick with pain. They were different; he was always brought back to that. He saw it in everything: they didn't think the things he thought, nor wonder at the things he wondered at, nor like the things he liked. They were utterly different. But if this was comforting as an excuse, in another way it was exceedingly depressing; it made one feel so lonely.

To himself, Jali felt, and to himself alone, could he look for the explanation of things. Other people's interpretations of the world might do for them, but they would not do for him: his problems presented themselves differently. Thus, at this early age, he was already engaged—and more or less wittingly—in a single-handed endeavor to relate himself to the world; and by the world he meant sometimes the world of men and their affairs, and sometimes the world of the gods. A feeling that might with equal fairness be called pride or humility told him not to expect much enlightenment from outside.

With all this, however, he was eminently teachable. His masters

found him quick and receptive; and in the matter of spiritual illumination each of his parents was delighted by his ready understanding. Rajah Amar believed—and was right in believing—that
his son's grasp of the Buddhist doctrine was as complete as could
be expected in a boy of that age. Sita, similarly, made no mistake
in believing that Jali's nature was responsive to the truths and
beauties of the Christian faith. What neither the one nor the other
suspected was that his eclecticism covered a peculiar kind of unbelief. He accepted the things told him as true for the teller, but
he could not believe that they were true for himself. Most often,
indeed, whilst listening he was unconscious of this unbelief of
his; it was only afterwards, in a moment of meditation, that he
became aware of his own skepticism. But so it was with him: until
an idea had received the stamp of his own private endorsement, it
remained a stranger in his mind, however hospitably he might
entertain it. And thus the truths of Buddhism and Christianity
were comfortably accommodated there; they lived at peace in his
guest-chambers, but to the inner places of his personality they
had no access.

His parents knew as much about him as any parents were
likely to have known about such a son. Their love for him and his
for them only sharpened his capacity for deceiving them and theirs
for being deceived. It was true that besides seeing what he showed
them, they saw a little of what he did not mean to show; but it was
precisely with that little that he deceived them most. For he almost always knew when he had betrayed himself and would instinctively set about turning that piece of self-betrayal to good
account. Thus, when they told him that they proposed to take him
to Agra, he simulated pleasure; but his pretense was not good
enough, and at once he knew it. Instinctively, therefore, he set about
providing them with a misleading clue to the nature of his reluctance, pretending, first of all, that he was distressed by the prospect
of leaving his boy friend Nazim, and secondly, that he would sadly
miss his polo lessons. As a matter of fact he had little affection for
Nazim, who bored him; and as for polo, he detested it. But these
dispositions of his were pretenses of long standing; and they served
him well at this juncture as a means of disguising the truth.
Actually, what he experienced was the stab of a complex and al-

most indescribable anguish. For months and months he had been awaiting this, or something like it; and in the now decreed journey to Agra he saw the hand of an inexorable fate. To look at him, you would have said that he found the idea of leaving home exciting, perhaps even a little awe-inspiring, but only when he took the trouble to think about it; and it seemed equally plain that he did not think about it very much. Really, his parents would say to one another, although Jali was precocious in many ways, in others he remained distressingly backward. When would he learn to take a *practical* interest in the world about him? or show a desire for the actual *experiencing* of life?

The actual experiencing of life! Now this of course was exactly what Jali was brooding over—with terror—every hour of his existence. Hence that air of childish unconcern, a labor of instinctive shame and cunning. He offered the appearance of being engrossed in the present, because the present was nothing but a continuous dread of what the future held in store. The future, his fear of it, and his deepening conviction that he was unequal to facing it, were never out of his thoughts. The view he took of his own case was certainly far graver than that of his parents. It was his conviction that his incompetence, his timidity, his want of buoyancy and self-reliance, were symptoms of a predisposition, which, unless defeated, would lead to his utter destruction. He felt this, he knew it. He opposed himself violently to his self-confessed cowardice. There was a stern mentor within him, a tyrant who strove to drive him to all the courses that his nature hated most. The more he quailed, the more he had to dare; the more he shrank, the more he must some day undertake. His being was shaken to its utmost foundations by this inward conflict.

Such had Jali been in the days of his home-life. His eyes then had been fixed in terror upon the moment when he would be obliged to emerge from the deep, dark solitudes of the self in which he had lived hitherto so intensely and with so much hidden fear. The heroic resolutions that he was building up would then have to be translated into actions; one day he would be storming the invisible barriers that separated him from the world of men.

Well! The decree had gone forth at last, and as the day of departure drew nearer and nearer he felt that this good-bye to his old life constituted a veritable death. If a boy named Jali came home again, it would be a different boy. He was committing suicide, only not by sliding into peaceful death, but by violent metamorphosis. Not for one instant could he envisage the possibility of enduring failure and returning unchanged. The desperation into which he had gradually been sinking forbade any thought of that. To return to the solitary island of self, after having failed to effect a landing on the busy continent of mankind? To listen, as an outcast, to the great seductive murmur of real life in which one could take no part? To submit in tameness to one's enduring impotence? No! that never! He must change, and change completely, before he would consent to come home again. If necessary, he would run away from his parents; he would disappear into the unknown.

At night, with these thoughts, he shivered from terror; and often tears of self-pity would trickle down his cheeks. Why was he predestined to so hideous an ordeal? Why could the love of father and mother do nothing for him? Why could no one ever understand or share his secret burden? Examining his parents he saw them as strangers; he loved them, they loved him; but they were themselves, and he was himself; to each man his burden; there was no sharing, no relief. The blackness of such reflections was like the blackness of the solitudes between the stars.

On the eve of the great day he was calm. Towards sundown he persuaded his father to accompany him to the top of the tower and point out the route over the desert. For the last time he fixed his gaze upon the visionary line of hills that had been his horizon until now; and the thought that he would soon be treading that ground with his feet and touching it with his hands, threw him into a strange bewilderment. His father directed his eyes to a faint, purple streak upon the belt of gold; that was a crevice in the mountain-side, a shadowy gorge through which the cavalcade would pass. And beyond—but Jali was no longer listening; his thought had stopped to hover over that spot. How could that mystic *There* ever become a *Here*? It could not—without changing. It existed only in its thereness. No one ever got *There*—unless, perhaps, in the impossible Heaven of the Christians.

While he gazed, the vaporous gold melted, the mystic range

was lost in the hot browns and purple of the desert night. He descended from the tower with a melancholy that was benign compared with his long-accustomed anguish; a breath of indifference that had been wafted from those distances that were after all unattainable.

2

AFTER THE JOURNEY came the Agra Palace, and at once these long, absorbing days of travel disappeared into the background; he parted with them abruptly—just as he had already parted with nearly everything that belonged to his former life.

Here, at last, he was in the great world. Pomp and circumstance surrounded him, brilliance and bustle pressed close on every side. Great ladies and their flocks of attendant maids filled the air with cries and scents; the flutter of their raiment was a perpetual breeze; they surged up and down the stairs, they ran into you at every corner; and then they were always laughing, always, it seemed, in a condition of happy excitement. This was the Great World with a vengeance, and Jali clenched his teeth. So long as no one paid any attention to him, it was endurable; but unfortunately, quite often he was noticed. The smiling girls that pushed past in the corridors would fling a word over their shoulders; a great lady, as he peeped out on some terrace, would beckon him to her side. Sometimes, even, two or three of these alarming creatures would cluster familiarly about him, and then there would be questions and sallies, and it would be for him to play the game, to show what stuff he was made of.

In this extraordinary place how much at ease, how casual, everybody seemed! He found himself flattered and petted one moment, and dropped out of mind the next. Nobody knew, or cared, who he was; no one was self-conscious or shy. Any day, through a doorway carelessly curtained, he might catch sight of some beauty at her toilet. The things he saw did not shock him, though they often astonished him not a little.

Well, here he was!—and perhaps the strangeness of it would wear off. He was resolved to shirk nothing, to welcome every experience. He would do his best, albeit a timid, blushing best it was bound to be. Most important it was, too, that he should hide his deep, inward agitation; for what, others might well wonder, what was there here to be so agitated about? To another doubtless these new experiences would not seem to be of any particular moment; and how could he explain that for him they were terrific, that his ability to cope with them was for him almost a matter of life and death? He had put himself on trial; he had set himself a desperate task; it was for him to become one with the world instead of remaining an oddity and a stranger. More than once in his self-communings he called into mind the words that his Uncle Hari had spoken to him in that strange midnight colloquy of theirs on the very first night of his arrival. "Not to be afraid of others you must be like them, and in order to be like them, pretend to yourself that you are." And Hari had also said: "People are much better than you imagine." That meeting with Hari had surely been a sign from Fate; it was meant to set the seal on his resolve.

At the close of each one of these anxious days, Jali would review his course and wonder if he was getting on as well as he should. Was he finding his feet like the two or three other boys—slightly younger than himself—who already seemed quite at home in their surroundings? After a week or so, when his first perturbations had worn off, he took stock of his position, he gave it a colder and more searching scrutiny than he had dared to do before. The result was chilling. A terribly discouraging fact took shape before his eyes: he was not—no, he was not a success. Impossible to remain blind any longer: here he was in the world, the world was all round him, he was struggling to amalgamate with it—but it was no good. Instead of feeling less alien, he was feeling more so; and all these strangers, he greatly feared, were feeling the same thing about him too. Neither his anxiety to please, nor his good manners (he couldn't help knowing that his manners were quite good), nor anything in his whole equipment, was of any avail. Not even his aptitude at pretending to be other than he was. He knew of course how to put up an appearance that suited his parents, but as for these new people—he simply could not find any fashion of making himself pleasing to them. Without a doubt they had an instinct that he was not one of them; they could see through him, even when he was most artful. And what made this perspicacity of theirs the more extraordinary was that these people were not clever; in fact, they were extraordinarily crude and imperceptive compared with the people at home. This inferiority of theirs struck him at once; but it didn't make his want of success any the less bitter. After all this was the world, and he had to take it as he found it; this was the world, and he was much too anxious and overawed to assume the office of critic. No, for the time being his mind dwelt only on the astounding merits of these people—their self-assurance, their knowingness, their nonchalance and gaiety. How amazingly well, too, the happy creatures understood one another! Oh, they knew the world in and out! In that vast region of acquaintance where he was a stranger, they moved about at their ease. So little was Jali tainted by priggishness or snobbery, so completely was he out of conceit with himself just now, that he would gladly have bartered a whole bushel of his own wares for a few pecks of their robuster merits. A stout heart and a thick skin, a knowing eye and a ready laugh—these, these were what he admired and coveted.

It was not until later, not until he had been reduced to despair—and then only in the moments of his despair—that his natural taste asserted itself; but when these rare transports of revolt did seize him, scathing indeed were the judgments that he passed. Then, in solitary storms of fury and contempt, he would contrast the women of the Palace with the people of his father's Court at home, and—good God!—how uncultivated, how tasteless, how deep-seatedly vulgar they nearly all appeared. Crude they were, and stupid, whenever they touched upon a matter outside the sphere of their particular worldly competence. If these people were offering him a fair sample of the world, the world was not a very fine place. His father had warned him, it was true, that Akbar's

guests, gathered together on the sole principle of worldly greatness, were likely to vary considerably in other respects; he had
been warned, too, that smartness and vulgarity often went hand in
hand; but, good heavens! those gentle forewarnings had hardly prepared him for this! And yet he despised, he fought against, his own
fastidiousness. What was the use of blushing and wincing and
being ashamed on behalf of others who were not ashamed of themselves? "Why must I be such an infernal prig?" he asked himself
more than once. However, there were some aspects of this life that
he did savor in a quite unpriggish fashion; like all children, he
could take a pleasure in being scandalized; and if the vulgarities
remained an offense, the improprieties that he observed were an
excitement and a pleasure.

But none of this was of any consequence—nothing mattered except the dreadful, outstanding fact that he was a failure. And now
it was his problem to discover the cause. Hour after hour he brooded
upon this agonizing mystery. Why was he different? In what particulars did he displease? Why was he in the humiliating position
of having to overcome indifference that verged upon dislike? And
why were his best efforts of no account? It was beyond his power
to make it out. One or two of his mistakes he did discover and correct, but this was not enough. For instance, having grasped the fact
that good manners are an offense where the general level is low, he
did his best to copy the prevailing mode. That helped; but after
that? What else could one do? Poor Jali! if he had been fairly quick
to learn that those who do not possess any natural refinement bitterly resent that quality in others, he did not yet fully realize that
refinement is the hardest thing in the world to dissimulate. His
new acquaintances detected evidences of it in his very endeavors
to disguise it. His very humility was humiliating them.

But against all these discouragements he persisted with the
doggedness of a growing despair, and it struck him that by observing his parents he might pick up some hint. In a sense his father
and mother stood mid-way between him and the alien world; although they remained detached, they were not like him, hopelessly out of touch. Well! very soon he decided that his parents and
the world entirely misconceived one another, and were in contact
only by virtue of their misconceptions. His parents took a view of

their Palace acquaintances that was comfortable and convenient to themselves; and the world similarly made up for itself a comfortable work-a-day conception of his parents. Why couldn't he and the world come together on the same lines?

He bent his mind to this problem with intense concentration. Of course the reason why his parents didn't see the world as he saw it, was that the ladies and maids of the Palace were careful that Rajah Amar and Ranee Sita should not. (*He* was only a child, before whom anything could be said.) His parents positively invited the world to deceive them; they called for certain appearances, and other people instinctively acted up to expectation in just the same fashion that he did. Yes, and the other side of the matter was this: by calling for certain appearances, you expressed yourself as a type, you exhibited certain recognized features, a stock personality; you gave people a plain, straightforward reading of your character. The view that the Palace people took of his parents was ridiculously superficial, but that didn't in the least matter. The point was that his parents and the world each presented the other with something intelligible, they presented stock-in-trade figures between whom a stock-in-trade intercourse was possible. When he came to think of it, was not his own communication with his parents conducted through the agency of a fictitious personality? And had his parents been more penetrating, had they been discerners of reality instead of instigators of pretense, wouldn't they have seen through his disguise long ago? And, if they ever had, wouldn't they have been dismayed by the emptiness behind? For the real Jali—who was he? What was he? One really couldn't say. Anyhow he didn't seem to be taking part at all, when it was a question of human intercourse. The true self seemed to be isolated by its own inalienable nature from other true selves. It was appearances that formed the bridge between person and person. Moreover, his true self, the real Jali, was emptiness—was nothing at all. Yes; even to himself he was an emptiness, a nothingness. And didn't it emerge out of all this that what he was inclined to call real was nothingness itself?

Having pushed his thoughts thus far Jali halted somewhat breathlessly. It seemed to him that he was at last gaining light. To live in and for reality was to dwindle and fade, to accept appearances was to wax fat and grow strong. It was by cultivating the appearances and illusions belonging to the outer man that you not only offered to others but obtained for yourself a substantial and intelligible being. A man should give and take generously in the false coin of appearances. You possessed a character, solidity, force, by virtue of your unawareness, your obtuseness, your incapacity to perceive the inward hollowness of things. Was it not obvious for instance that his father was only able to be a Buddhist by ignoring everything that told against Buddhism? And was not his mother with her Christianity in exactly the same position? People had to chose between *seeing* and *being*. The more of reality you saw, the less of being you possessed. He, Jali, *saw* things as they really were, and *was*, in consequence, practically nothing at all.

With this it seemed to Jali that he had come out into the full light of a great truth. He was laying hold of verities that had been incubating darkly within him from the beginning of his life, and, as his ideas took shape, he trembled with excitement. What he was discovering was of sovereign importance to him—a scheme of the world, a system of thought. For days he continued to brood over his constructions and test them in the light of remembered experience. He found their truth exemplified everywhere. Take the case of that big, jolly man, Narsing Deo—no one could be more vital, positive, and substantial than he, and no one assuredly could be more imperceptive, farther away from the heart of things. Then look at all these noisy, childish, excitable women in the Palace—were they for a moment to realize their own hollowness and vanity, what would happen? Why, they would collapse—collapse into something as lifeless and colorless as he himself. Consider again that little boy of eight who lumbered about the corridors on all fours, playing at elephant, a great favorite with everyone, although he was very much in the way:—if the women all took to him so kindly, it was chiefly because they all knew exactly where they were with him: his limitations made him definite and intelligible, so that one could smile indulgently as he lumbered by. Well, now! it was in exactly the same spirit that his parents and these people accepted one another. In an exactly similar manner these people smiled at his father and mother with their Buddhism and Christianity; while the latter, on their side, had an equally benign smile for the characteristics of their Palace acquaintances. All that anybody wanted, or needed to offer, was something graspable; and it was odd, but established beyond doubt, that what was graspable could not be spirit—it must be illusory—in short, Maya.

So Jali had come back to a position that lay inside the philosophy of his father's race, although his road had been all of his own finding. And since the translation of intuitions into ideas always brings exhilarations, these ideas, although not in themselves very exhilarating, did much to raise his spirits. He had been born—he felt it—for speculation; and whereas the ready-made speculations of others could not, unfortunately, take hold of him, now at last he was on the way to building up his own body of truth. There was something rather grand in that, and it was not lost on him. His sense of inferiority was balanced by an equal sense of power. If he *was* nothing, on the other hand he *saw* everything. He stood in an isolation that was at once contemptible and splendid.

3

EVER SINCE HIS arrival at the Palace Jali had mixed with its inmates as much as he could, for that had been an essential part of his self-discipline. Mercifully, however, this Palace life had been broken up by days spent at Gokal's pavilion in the Royal Hunting Grounds; indeed, without these excursions he could hardly have supported the strain of his present mode of existence. After the chatter of crowded rooms, the turmoil of thronging corridors, after his incessant unsuccessful efforts to "catch on," to look happy and alert—after this torment, the peace of the woods was Paradise.

Loitering alone along the leafy paths or sitting dreamily by the lake-side, he found something akin to resignation. In this mood he took a quiet pleasure in reflecting that all was vanity: everything that other people thought was vain, and all their zest foolish. Just as the women of the Palace were noisy and excited about nothing, so also his father was grave and intent about nothing, and his mother eager and happy in a world tinted rose-color by her dreams. All these people had personalities; they were able to entertain the illusions that endow one with a personality; they became opaque, solid, comfortable to themselves and others. But he couldn't do it; he was doomed to remain as weak and limpid as water. Something in one ought to darken, he supposed, a nucleus ought to form, around which one's own illusions, and other people's illusions about one, grouped themselves—until one developed substance —until one became, if one was really lucky, "a character"—for instance, a great jolly mass of vitality and nonsense like the lovable Narsing Deo.

This peace of course was not very far from despair, and yet Jali had not yet entirely abandoned his purpose. After all, having succeeded in making up an appearance that satisfied his parents, why should he not find one in the end that would satisfy the world? For the moment he was drawing breath, casting around for fresh expedients, trying to recover strength. And now, in the desert of his dejection there was revealed to him a stream of spiritual sustenance along which he could direct his steps. His parents had persuaded Gokal to take up their son's instruction at the point where his earlier teachers had broken off. In inaugurating these lessons Rajah Amar had been quietly confident that Jali would emerge with a mind quickened to the truth of the Buddhist doctrine, and Sita was equally confident that nothing in Gokal's teaching would loosen his grasp of Christian principles. The boy was well aware of what his parents thought, and, in consequence, extremely reticent concerning his own thoughts. The truth was, of course, that he had never been able to bring either Christianity or Buddhism into any relation with the problems of his inner life. Christianity elucidated nothing for him; on the contrary, it insisted upon a set of beliefs that seemed to him so arbitrary that he could only wonder how they had ever arisen in anybody's mind. How could anyone believe that a soul sprang into existence on this earth and then continued to live for ever after? Surely if there were such things as souls, their existence must stretch back into the past as well as forward unto the future? And then, was it reasonable to think that "being good" during one brief earth-life was a matter of such importance as to determine the whole everlasting future of an immortal soul? And this idea of goodness as something quite independent of knowledge and understanding, what was the sense of it? Why was so much importance attached to it? Only to a few departments of human life did the idea of goodness have any application. Goodness, in his mother's sense of the word, did not apply to a poem or to a truth, or to most of one's daily behavior. Moreover, why was it "right" to regard life itself as a blessing and to believe in so many things that were obviously not true? The Buddhist attitude towards life seemed to him much more reasonable; but alas! it was singularly uninteresting. You were forbidden to speculate on any of the matters that most invited speculation. You were told neither why nor how the world came to be the extraordinary place it was. Jali took an interest in life that was commensurate with his immense fear of it; he had a very lively sense of the power and reality of evil, which Buddhism made nothing of. The truth of the matter was that if his mother's religion was too fanciful for him, his father's was too fanciless.

But what was Gokal's religion? He did not know, and he suspected that Gokal did not know. Yet through his teacher's utterances there breathed a spirit of infinite refreshment. Gokal's personality captivated him entirely, lifting up his mind, not only out of the heated, noisy atmosphere of the Palace, but also out of the haze of his own immature theories. He was lifted into an air that revived his blood, and reanimated the flame of a spirit that bewilderment, self-depreciation, and failure had reduced to an anguished flicker. Whether his teacher was engaged in expounding the central beliefs of the Vedanta, in drawing comparisons between the doctrines of Christ and Buddha and Plato, or in considering the arguments for and against pre-existence, Jali's whole being was vibrant with response. During these distressful days his intercourse with Gokal kept his self-respect alive. The idle chatter of the Court ladies and their maids was generally quite above his head, but this man he could always understand. The world despised him, it shouldered him aside; but this sage treated him as an equal, giving him speech worthy of the gods. Upon Gokal's terrace, under a huge blue umbrella with golden dragons sprawling across it, Jali would lie at full length, his eyes fixed upon his friend's face, deeply intent and never wearying. His attention was all there, even when the other delightful components of the scene were present to his tranquilized senses—the glitter of the lake, the birds calling monotonously in the trees, the monkeys scuffling over the shingle of the roof. Those hours upon the terrace had a healing influence of which he stood in sore need. In his despair he had begun to despise everything that he found in himself, even those qualities which he shared with his parents, and had been inclined to admire in them. But now, dimly, yet not uncertainly, he detected in this man's nature a strain even more intimately sympathetic to his own hidden and despised self. And the extraordinary thing was that, if such a weakness existed in Gokal, it was continually converting itself by some miracle of self-transcendence into a strength that was superior to that of the strong. Gokal, he liked to think, might actually both *be* and *see*: in him vision might be combined with power.

Already he loved Gokal, yet not even to him was he willing to confide the secrets of his inner life. A natural privacy surrounded your central spirit, making it indecorous, as it would certainly be futile, to attempt to share the ultimate burden of self-consciousness. Nor did Gokal ever question him, he was content not to press too close. He gave, however, abundantly; he was not reluctant to expose, even before this small boy, his deepest meditations, or to ruminate, as with an intimate friend, on the problems suggested by his own life. Sometimes frowning with confessed frustration, sometimes smiling in self-mockery, but always with a perfect singleness of mind, he would pore over the special subject of the hour, examining into its mystery with slow, careful words, and, as it were, turning it over with expressive movements of large, beautiful hands.

Then, after he had gone back into the pavilion for his siesta, Jali would wander away into the woods behind the house. For a while his face would remain eager and his eyes brilliant as his thoughts continued upon their set course. For a while they would wing their way in the high air to which Gokal had transported them; but little by little the spell would wear off, the climate of his mind would change, and he would find himself once more wandering despairingly round in the old labyrinth of his perplexities and fears. That was a region that none of the saints or philosophers in history seemed to have any knowledge of. Not one of them started with a spirit as drearily skeptical as his.

Thus, once more in the company of his own loneliness, he would creep about under the thin shade of the parching trees. The hot noontide hush would be lying upon the land—upon the plains, the deserts, the forests, upon the whole of India and beyond, if only one's fancy could picture it. In that hush he moved and loitered and halted; he listened to it and felt it engulfing him in a vastness that was without bounds. He looked up into the thirsty foliage, he listened, he peered, he followed with his eyes the irresolute fall of a leaf. Flimsy and tattered was all the shade that these poor branches could now give; and alas for the green and sappy things that had trusted to their protection! Alas for the mosses and grasses and cool-veined plants, alas for the delicate bushes, huddling vainly in patches of ground that had once been moist, in crevices that had once looked safe! The furious sun, by sheer persistence, had broken through to them, turning them suddenly into skeletons; and it was these beautiful silvery skeletons that now invested the wood with its air of magical desiccation, and by the clinking of their fairy bones filled it with its peculiar silky rustle. That rustle!—hark to it now!—rushing past, like a flight of ghosts, upon the hot wind's breath.

Here and there, it is true, a tree of stouter foliage had resisted, its shining leaves still strong to throw the sun's arrows off. All round its trunk there would lie a pool of darkness, a small sanctuary of comparative cool. Here one could stand and think. But at this hour of the sun's full might how could one really think? The white silence and blazing mystery of noon roused one to an activity that spent itself in sheer entrancement; it could not be turned to any knowledgeable purpose. In the silence and mystery of the night thought was free, but now you halted, you waited, you listened and peered; you were filled with expectation—and that was all.

In the course of these long scorching days Jali grew familiar with a dozen narrow tracks, so invariably deserted, so aimlessly meandering, that at first their existence was a puzzle to him. But presently he discovered that most of them brought one in the end to a small dilapidated Hindu shrine that stood by itself in the midst of the wood. You could hardly call it a temple, for it was so small, but it had its own enclosure which was separated from the jungle by a low mud wall; and it had a group of sacred fig trees at the back of it. In days long ago its squat sun-baked walls must have been gay with paint, but the colors had nearly all peeled off. The low, round, whitewashed dome sheltered an altar upon which stood a primitive lingan. So it was really a temple, although a very humble one; it still was the home of a god.

Jali came here quite often, attracted by the subtle and benign character of the godling whose presence pervaded the whole grove. There was a mystic harmony in the pattern made by the twisted branches of the sacred trees. There was a mystic beauty in the shadows they threw on the dusty yellow ground. Often and often he would stand on the fringe of the wood, considering the place and yielding to its influences. He never met anyone here, but it was evident that the temple had not been completely deserted. Fresh offerings of marigolds and bilva leaves appeared nearly every day upon the altar; and well did he understand this continued fidelity of the few.

One afternoon—it was certainly the hottest of the year—he made his way through the dry, bleached grass, under the dry, rustling trees, and stood surveying the temple in the abstraction of profound thought. But this time there came to him, after a while, the feeling that he was not alone. Perhaps, he reflected, it was the company of the gray monkeys that he was sensible of, for, after squatting asleep upon the pipal boughs, they had begun yawning and stretching their arms. "The shade of the pipal spreads peace, the shade of the pipal spreads peace," these words repeated themselves in lullaby fashion in Jali's mind, and presently he sighed, and, like a monkey himself (they had once more become torpid), squatted down upon his haunches and let the lids drop over his eyes. But a little later he opened them again, and his attention was at once caught by a patch of color that had appeared beside the temple wall. It was a woman's dress; and when the figure rose to its feet he recognized Gunevati. Once or twice already he had seen the girl in the yard of Gokal's pavilion, and each time her beauty had struck disquiet into his heart, leaving an ache that had been slow in fading away. For this reason he had unconsciously avoided going into the yard of late. But now, from his lair in the dry grass, he looked out upon Gunevati with an interest that was less uneasy. His gaze sharpened, his pulse quickened, but the peace of the benign godling was upon him, and he remained collected.

In and about the temple doorway Gunevati drifted, loitering, halting, and going on again, her lovely body as lazy as a water-weed swaying in a stream. Overhead the sun's eye glared intolerably and the weight of noon lay upon her like the heavy waters of a deep sea. It seemed to Jali that in her dreamy dawdlings she was at one with the unhurried earth: she was like a lotus unfolding upon a mere, she was an evening cloud, she was a down-fluttering leaf, she was the slow yawn of the golden tiger drowsy in his cave. And the present moment—usually as sharp as a knife-edge ripping between the past and the future—the present moment, as he watched her, expanded into a great lake of peace.

After a while her eyes turned in his direction, and as her gaze settled upon him her movements died into a pause. With great intentness they contemplated one another; time's leisurely progress was suspended altogether; the world waited, or so it seemed, in a little interval of complete rest.

Bright, fixed, and expressionless as those of a mouse, Jali's eye stared at the girl over the stalks of the jungle grass; and her eyes were expressionless too, until a slow smile spread up to them from her slightly parted lips. At last, without changing his posture, Jali beckoned, and after a moment she came. Leisurely, confidingly, she squatted down beside him; and then they began talking together in the special, muted tones imposed by the majesty of high noon.

Above them, all about them, was silence; only, somewhere in the blazing distance, a kokila-bird was sounding its single, inexpressive note; and the monotony of that sound was like an audible pulsation of the heat. While Gunevati's soft murmur ran on, an occasional puff of wind made the shade flicker and the grasses waver; and the monkeys on their perch opposite once more fell to searching in one another's fur. Jali's eyes dwelt deeply upon her. Deeply he studied the slender arch of her eyebrows, the small delicate nostrils, the exquisite curves of mouth and chin. "She is like a gazelle," he thought. "One becomes like an animal or a houri when one is as perfect as that."

He was attending to her words very little, but presently she became earnest and he had to listen more. She had just been making an augury, she told him; it was for a girl friend, who, after two years of marriage, had remained childless. What one had to do was to make up a ball of the combined excrement of husband and wife (but it was no use unless you knew the appropriate charms; and they had to be recited without a single slip!); and then the ball had to be left for a week in a carefully chosen spot inside the temple grounds. Well, she had done all this; and to-day she had broken the ball open and found, to her great satisfaction, that it contained animal life. That meant that her friend need not despair; sooner or later a child would be conceived. "And will it be a boy?" asked Jali. She sighed. Perhaps some clever person might be able to foretell even that, but her lore did not go so far. Anyhow there would be a child; and if her friend prayed regularly at this temple the god would in all probability make it a boy.

After this she went on to other things; she told him many curious tales to illustrate the godling's character. He had, apparently, a vein of puckishness in his composition; for instance, one woman, who had once bought him lettuce in the place of bilva-leaves, subsequently gave a birth to a rabbit. She was still defining the peculiarities of this and of her other favorite gods when Jali noticed that the sun was slanting in under the boughs and the evening already come. Now, too, from time to time, a bearer of offerings would go by and enter the temple to lay his tribute on the shrine. And, whether it was a man or a woman, each passer-by would turn to look curiously upon that pair. And every time this happened Jali was conscious that the meeting of the stranger's eyes with Gunevati's was different from their meeting with his—something occurred: the meeting was not just blank. At that his thoughts turned again upon himself, and his old-standing misery fastened upon him. Such loneliness as his must, he imagined, be quite unknown to Gunevati; for, assuredly, in a single moment she could establish contact with anyone in the world; and when she was by herself she enjoyed the watchful and interested company of at least a hundred gods.

4

THE PROFOUND CONTEMPLATION under which he had held
Gunevati in this their first meeting, prolonged itself into musings
which were filled with the desire to see her again. That gaze of
his, so dreamy and yet so intent, had been instinct with a two-fold
wonder: wonder at her loveliness, and wonder at her outlook on
the world. His spirit, in her presence, felt comforted and sustained.
Looking into her eyes he looked into profound depths of animal
serenity; it rejoiced him to sit peering into the warm dusk of that
mind, where fancy unfolded and bloomed like orchids in the
jungle-swamps of her native Malabar.

He never argued or contradicted or seemed to raise a doubt. It
would have pleased him to believe all that she believed, even at its
most absurd, even when her recitals became grotesque or horrible.
Hers was a mind that one could take one's ease in, a veritable
paradise of indolence and sensuous unrestraint. She had her guiding rules, it was true: one should do this; one should do that:—
but they were splendidly irrational; there was no sense in them,
nothing but arbitrary belief. No principles of any abstract ethic, no
needfulness of self-government, did she know; and he could well
imagine with what reproachful eyes she would look at anyone who
should attempt to instruct her. Why this harshness, they would
ask? Why go out of your way to make life vexatious and difficult?

If she was very unlike his own people, she was also very unlike the snobbish ladies of the Palace and their knowing maids. These, mistress and maid alike, were too much wrapped up in the world to spare time for the gods. Gunevati's religion, if you could call it that, permeated her whole existence, keeping pretentiousness and vulgarity right out of her range. She lived in the companionship of mystery. No detail of her life could be trivial or tiresome, since the present moment had the interest and importance of being so mysterious in what it was. Taking life simply, she found it to consist almost entirely of religion and sex. These by prescriptive right occupied the center of her consciousness, and to her they were almost as one thing. But they were a unity with two aspects, one of which was terrifying and the other delicious. To his astonishment, and at first to his great consternation, Jali found that she took certain proclivities in his nature for granted. As early as at their second meeting, in fact as soon as she was quite at her ease with him, she became unblushingly enticing; she smiled up from under her lashes; she moved herself up close; she laughed and confided, she beguiled and insisted, until he could hold back no longer from what was, after all, the thing that he most greatly desired. Then, how entrancing she became! She was lascivious with the playfulness, the gentleness, and the modesty that only the truly lascivious know how to affect.

Later, when Jali had collected himself again, he returned to his first astonishment. How, he wondered, had she been able to divine his secret mind? Gunevati was much diverted by this perplexity. She made no mock, but the soft amusement that she betrayed was more illuminating than words. At first, indeed, in the matter of talk there was a great deal that went beside the mark, because Jali's vision of the world was quite as extraordinary to her as hers was to him. Soon, however, he saw that in the field of their present discussion she undoubtedly had the truth and the knowledge nearly all on her side; so that gradually his incredulity was overcome, and he arrived at the astonishing conclusion that, although she was without question, a very ill-educated, ignorant, and superstitious girl, yet her comprehension of human nature was a good deal deeper than his. Gunevati knew little, perhaps, but what she did know lay at the very heart of things; and then at last it dawned on him that he had been looking into the sky for plain truths that were lying on the ground at his feet. The veil of decorum that society habitually spreads over the instinct of sex was not after all so opaque but that he might have recognized what lay underneath. Then, too, he saw presently that Gunevati's version of things was not likely to be more fantastic or cynical than it need be. For the girl was not cynical; indeed she was positively naive. The world's conventions imposed on her; its formal distinctions, its pompous decrees, commanded her unquestioning respect. But, while prostrating herself in all humility before social greatness, she could not help remembering that even Rajahs and Emperors were males, and that as males they were simply complementary to her own lowly self. Great ladies, too, were women and as such had no secrets from her. Admittedly Gunevati was ignorant and unsophisticated; but the things she knew—and here it was that Jali paused and pondered and held his breath—the things she knew were marvelous and signified much.

It was not easy to reconcile this new knowledge with the body of his previous experience; but he did a great deal of thinking, and one day, after much hesitation, he approached Gunevati with an idea. Why shouldn't he, he asked, put the truth of some of her pronouncements to the test? He couldn't help thinking that the Palace ladies offered an uncommonly promising field for experiment. Wouldn't it be interesting . . . ? Wouldn't it be possible . . . ? What did Gunevati think?

Gunevati burst into laughter, clapped her hands, and thought the idea splendid. It was with the greatest goodwill in the world that she set about coaching him up. She discoursed with high enthusiasm, and Jali listened with deep attention; she was very encouraging; what she said seemed too wonderful—almost unbelievable; nevertheless he took heart and believed.

This was by far the most heroic task that he had yet imposed upon himself. The courage with which he went to it was the courage of desperation; he was delivering his ultimate assault upon the disdainful world. The last few moments before his ordeal saw him pass from shivering terror into a mood of delirious audacity. The victim of his experiment was one of the prettiest serving-maids, who had attracted him from the first. Nothing could have been more dashing than the attack he delivered, and he acquitted himself so well that the astonished girl was almost swept off her feet. Back in his room again, although now trembling and exhausted, he could not but see that his trial, although not conclusive, had been highly encouraging. The next day he followed up his advantage, and this time his triumph was complete. Nor was that enough; one victory did not suffice him. Inebriated by success, he determined upon another and a more ambitious venture. And again triumph was his!

These experiences were critical in his career; and a thoroughgoing readjustment of his ideas had now to take place. He was not yet quite sure—but he made bold to suspect—that the barrier between himself and the rest of mankind was at last laid low. He almost dared to believe that the cure for all his troubles, the magic password, was his at last. His respect for Gunevati's wisdom and his gratitude for her instruction soared to the utmost heights. He reported everything to her with exactitude, and together they laughed and rejoiced. Flattered by his extravagant esteem the girl became quite conceited and was almost ready to agree that her knowledge of human nature was unrivaled in the world. She continued to shower advice and instruction upon her pupil; and Jali, after drinking in every word, would hurry back to the Palace in order to prove her infallibility, and develop a new feature of his technique.

It would be difficult to exaggerate the change in his mental outlook. Not only did he find himself transformed, but everybody else seemed to be transformed as well. He lived in a state of ravishment; and it was the very excess of his self-confidence that carried him along without any serious check. The women of the Palace saw a tongue-tied, self-conscious boy most piquantly transformed into an impudent but charming young rake. They could not make it out. Amused glances and titters followed him. Scarcely more than a week ago, he had been unwanted and mis-esteemed; now he was a scandal and a delight.

When Jali found time to examine into what had occurred, he saw that just as in his relations with his parents he had developed an outward personality and a mode of behavior that satisfied their requirements, so now he had chanced upon another mode of behavior that his new audience could understand and appreciate. He had associated Gunevati's teachings with certain memories of a boy at home, who, for his age, was of a most enterprising ill-conduct, and, although he had only seen this boy once or twice in his life, he now suddenly found himself inspired to present a very good imitation of him. Thus, in a moment, he leapt into possession of ways and manners exactly suited to his chosen part.

These were splendid days. But the apex of his ambition, the summit of his glory, was not yet quite reached. Very soon after his arrival in the Palace he had been hopelessly captivated by a pretty, flighty young Ranee, who had not been slow to notice the effect she produced on him. It had amused Ranee Jagashri to slip him a few inviting smiles behind his mother's back; and more than once in her apartments she had encouraged him to be a good deal more enterprising than he knew how to be. But this had not lasted long; to his humiliation she had soon lost interest in him. Well, it was only to be expected. And those few drops of bitterness had not counted for much in the ocean of his misery at that time. Now it was different. Now, now he was not the man to sit down tamely under such a slight. So it was a very much altered Jali—a Jali flushed with conquering impudence, who presently laid siege at the lady's door. The little Ranee was wonderstruck; then greatly diverted; and finally, more out of amusement than anything else, she let him have his way.

For a period Jali simply didn't know himself any more. His old nature had suffered a complete eclipse. But, although gratified vanity and sensuality no doubt accounted for much in this change, their roots did not drive down very deep. More important in his present exultation was the belief that he had discovered the necessary bond between himself and the rest of mankind. No longer did he need to walk in fear of man's hostility or of woman's contempt; and thus, no longer oppressed by his old anguish, he believed that his old difficulties had vanished for good and all. By a natural reaction he now turned against most of his earlier opinions; the world was not a bad place after all; its grapes were not sour; to despise it was ridiculous; to fear it unnecessary.

He thought a great deal about Gunevati and the advantages of a simplified vision of the world. Not only was Gunevati's outlook much more easy and comfortable than his father's or his mother's, but it had brought him out of isolation into communion with the kindly race of man. Of course, when he looked at Gunevati through his father's eyes, he saw her as absurd. But surely his father in scorning Gunevati held nearly the whole of our ordinary human nature in scorn? Yes, for was it not the avowed aim of Buddhism to take all the color out of life? But he was against this; he preferred life to be simple and highly colored.

Apart from taste, too, Buddhism had never appealed effectively to his reason. Illusion, even as illusion, had to be accounted for; things were not imagined, that is to say, invented, or created, without there being some reason behind it. The things you found in the world were the creations of gods working through the imagination of men. If his father appealed to the effective force of disbelief in order to annihilate the world, Gunevati and her like preferred to use the effective force of belief in maintaining and extending the work of creation. Kali informed her and she informed Kali; it was all the same thing; and her Kali was assuredly as real as any of his father's abstract ideas. Wasn't it rather ingenuous of his father to put such faith in merely intellectual constructions? His father would find it very easy, no doubt, to make mock of poor Gunevati; but he, Jali, felt certain that she was the less simple of the two; she was merely simple-minded; his father was simple-natured.

Gunevati stood nearer to the heart of things: this again was the burden of his thought when he compared her with his mother. In Gunevati there was no question of resorting to religion in order to find a meaning and justification for life, and still less was it a question of giving reality to religion by bringing it down into the homely business of the day. Every moment of her existence was charged with a superfluity of interest, which called and accounted for its religious significance. But in what, exactly, did that interest reside? In the body, in sex; and sex and religion were one. This position established Gunevati very firmly on life's bed-rock. It grounded her on the Actual, and made many of his mother's beliefs look far-fetched, many of her exigencies fanciful. Gunevati had no need to look into the past for a Savior, nor into the future for Heaven. She lived in her body, and her body was her present sufficiency.

There had often been moments in the past when Jali had nourished resentment against his parents for what he considered their unseeingness. Unreasonably enough, whilst taking infinite pains to delude them, he had resented their capacity for being deluded; and now, after emerging from his first intoxication, his feelings against them waxed strong. How completely they had ignored his spiritual development during these last few weeks! His fears and miseries, his efforts and despairs, his discoveries, his daring, and his triumphs—of all these they remained unaware. Moreover, were he to attempt to describe the course of his life to them they would not, he felt sure, understand it. And as little would they be able to understand Gunevati. They might imagine that they were capable of putting their prejudices aside and entering into her intelligence, but they would be mistaken. The imagination of adults was delusive; adults raised a thin intellectual ghost of comprehension, but further they could not go.

His parents' vision, Jali told himself, was just as limited as Gunevati's, but whereas hers was limited by ignorance, theirs was limited by an unconscious will to ignore. It even seemed to him that the actual experiences of a man's life were largely determined by his ingrained preconceptions. Certain things might happen to his uncle Hari, for example, which simply could not happen to his father. Fate fitted your world to your expectations—whether in a spirit of irony or of kindliness, it was hard to say. And so, too, in his mother's case. He and she might live together side by side in the Agra Palace for years, but the worlds they would each be living in would be leagues apart. They would be different, not merely different in color and atmosphere, but in the very events they contained. And here was an apt instance of what he meant. Not long ago his mother had missed an emerald ornament, a cross that had been given her by the Katholicos of Tiflis at the time of her baptism at home. Now, he had recently seen that cross in a drawer of Ranee Jagashri's dressing-table. And yet his mother believed (and, no doubt, was fated ever to believe) that Jagashri was a charming lady and her devoted friend. There, then, was a single example from among a score.

From all this a certain truth very plainly emerged: everyone living lived in a particular world of his own. There was his father's world, and his mother's world, and Gunevati's world—there was also, he supposed, the world of a tiger, and of a cobra, and of a little plant. And who was to say that one world was truer or more real than another? Some were richer than others, but all were equally real and true. The only creature in existence that lacked a vision, a personality, and consequently, a world of its own, was himself. But there was a compensation for this; his lack enabled him to see through the eyes of others. He could look at the world through Gunevati's eyes as well as through the eyes of his parents. Other people were limited by their own personalities and had not got this power.

5

FOR A TIME, then, Jali's life continued to be one of intense excitement—an excitement sometimes ecstatic, but never approaching very close to happiness. As soon as he became capable of collected thought he began to understand that his old problems, instead of disappearing, had only changed their shape. The trouble was that at bottom he remained exactly the same. Granted that if he was able to envisage the world as Gunevati envisaged it; still, he was quite unable to *feel* and *accept* the world as she felt and accepted it: that, he saw, would never be within his power. Her temperament was what it was because she had no other self behind; but, when he adopted her vision, he did it of set intent, and his own self lay behind, remaining absolutely unchanged.

Another aspect of the essential difference between him and her was brought out whenever he attempted to make her understand his parents' outlook on life. Their inborn tastes and distastes—for instance, their distaste for sensuality, their dislike of unreason and disorder—these were unintelligible to her; and although her purely intellectual deficiencies did not particularly vex him, he was unable to accept with the same equanimity her lack of moral taste. She had no appreciation of nobility of character; there was no poetry in her, nor anything worthy of the name of romance. If he could find beauty in her spontaneous aptitude for enjoying the gift of life, he couldn't give her much credit for that; it was a natural endowment for which she was not even grateful.

His attention was sharply directed to these shortcomings by her attitude towards Gokal. In accordance with his custom he was concealing from his parents the deep affection that he had conceived for his teacher, but he had not taken the same line with Gunevati. He had imagined that she must be responding with an affectionate gratitude to Gokal's continued kindnesses to her father and herself, and that she would be very ready to join him in love and respect for her benefactor. To his surprise, however, when he spoke admiringly of Gokal, Gunevati was unresponsive; she would look away through half-closed eyes and the curve of her lips seemed slightly derisive. Then again, in another matter she caused him decided annoyance; she showed an inclination to speak disrespectfully of his parents. He could see that she took an unworthy pleasure in considering how grossly they were being deceived as regards the conduct as well as the character of their son. Nor was it worth his while to attempt to explain to her that there was something fine in such unawareness, something fine in the incapacity to suspect deceit. On these occasions he turned away from Gunevati with disgust, and some of that disgust would settle upon his opinion of himself as well. There were times now when it would have been easy for him to go further in this direction and become sentimental, indulge in repentances that would be only half sincere, and make confessions which he would afterwards regret. He had to remind himself that, although it was given to him to admire his parents for the quality of their vision, that vision was not his by nature's right. It was impossible for him to become like them, just as it was impossible for him to become like Gunevati. He was himself, unique—at once abject and sublime.

As, little by little, he descended into this self-analytical way of thought, his former loneliness crept over him once more. He contemplated the unchangeableness of his inmost self and was appalled. Then, too, a kind of tidal wave of nostalgia for his lost innocence would sometimes sweep forward out of a serene sky and break over him with devastating effect. Never, never could you go back a single step on your way! Forgetting was no use; by forgetting you only wiped out the things that had happened; the *effect* of the things that had happened could never be wiped out.

The melancholy accompanying these reflections was accentuated by a very tender sentiment which he conceived at this time for a maid of Ranee Jagashri's. This was a humble little person with nothing in her appearance to distinguish her from many others, unless you were observant enough to notice the quality of her gaze. To Jali, at any rate, her eyes seemed to express a deep and intelligent wonder. In his fancy she became a counterpart of himself, the possessor of just those feelings that had haunted him from his infancy, making the world a place of marvels and terrors. To make advances to her never entered his head; that would have been a profanation; for his sentiment required only the lightest and most ethereal of sustenance. He watched her covertly day by day. She went about her business in the bustling, shrill-voiced throng with a shrinking quality which Jali ascribed not to timidity, nor pride, but to a natural fastidiousness. Around this unassuming figure he wove a veil of sentiment, unconsciously endowing her with all those traits in his own character that were being outraged by his present mode of life. It shamed him to be offering her the spectacle of his amours with her mistress. Before long he decided to break off with Ranee Jagashri; for the truth was that ever since his discovery of that lady's theft of his mother's emerald cross, he had disliked her, and hated himself for continuing the relationship.

In the natural course of things he informed Gunevati of his project, which included the stealing of the cross from Jagashri in order to put it back among his mother's jewels. After he had spoken, Gunevati slowly shook her head; she declared that what he proposed would never do; in the first place, the Ranee would be incensed by his breaking off; secondly, as soon as she saw the cross in his mother's possession once more, she would suspect his part in the affair. Her rage then would be terrible. No woman—certainly no great lady—would submit tamely to such an insult. Jali was very much put about; he argued a little, but without any confidence; and not for worlds would he have let Gunevati into the secret of his sentiment for the Ranee's little maid. At last he asked her mournfully what he was to do, and received the discouraging reply that he must wait until Jagashri tired of him.

271

At their next meeting Gunevati took up the subject again; there would be no objection, she said, to his stealing the cross and giving it to *her*—why not punish Ranee Jagashri by doing that? "To you!" cried Jali, unspeakably outraged by the suggestion. But the next moment he blushed at his impoliteness and entered into evasive explanations. The question of Jagashri and the cross focused his malaise. He suffered both from a sense of disloyalty and from the feeling that he was trapped. Yes, he had entangled himself; and although his relationship with the Ranee (which, Gunevati assured him, might well come to an end any day) was bound to terminate with his departure from Agra, he took little comfort from this thought. The point was that his life was now set along a road of unconquerable habitude, with an endless series of snares, entanglements, and deceits upon the way. He appreciated, as he never had before, the beauty and enviability of his father's detachment and his mother's singleness of nature.

Soon, too, his relations with Gunevati became less smooth, for just as she was losing her awe of his social position, he was ceasing to be so greatly impressed by her reading of the heart of man. Nor was she slow to grasp this change, which caused her to resent all the more his modest attempts at improving her. A streak of common spite was apt to crop up in her now and then, a tendency to sneer at what she couldn't understand and to disparage the qualities she lacked. He had been prompt to check her tendency to speak slightingly of his father and mother, but she made up for it in another direction. One day, when he was snubbing her for the same impertinent attitude in regard to Gokal, she turned upon him and administered so paralyzing a blow that his powers of standing up to her on this particular ground were lost to him for ever. She assured him—and her assurances were circumstantial—that Gokal had been importuning her for some weeks past; and after his indignant incredulity had been overcome, she continued, out of sheer malice, to torment him with laughing descriptions of the actual scenes in which the Brahmin's infatuation had declared itself.

Jali was distressed beyond words. Was he shocked at the indignity of this behavior in the man he so deeply revered? Was he jealous of Gokal? Or was he jealous of Gunevati? For hours and days he brooded, angrily probing his persistent pain. To his credit it may be said, however, that his loyalty to Gokal remained unshaken; he altered his conception of his friend no more than was necessary; his regard was not lessened, it was even enriched by an indulgence springing from a more sturdy love. Had not the truth that all men are human already been well driven into him by Gunevati herself?

Then, too, although the girl insisted that she had neither enticed Gokal nor yielded to him, Jali was shrewd enough to pass these protestations over with contemptuous disbelief. Gunevati's way was to declare that all men assailed her and that nearly all were scornfully repulsed. She was a liar, he knew. Quietly, therefore, and privately he accommodated himself to the idea that he and Gokal were now actually sharing her favors; and the fact that he was aware of this, whilst Gokal was not, began to inspire him with a new feeling of protective intimacy, a kind of secret complicity which was tinctured with compassion. For how unworthy of Gokal this wretched girl was! A positive hatred of her would seize upon him when he pictured the wise and gentle Brahmin being tempted and beguiled. No doubt she had employed all her most shameless, shameful arts in order to drag him down.

About this time an evil mood hung over Gunevati, and day after day she gave herself the pleasure of angering him by making mock of Gokal. When this happened, such rage would seize upon Jali that he would fly from her presence and spend many hours vainly looking for a plan to expose her—without, at the same time, exposing himself.

As a natural consequence, too, his feelings for Gokal now became passionate, and often, while reclining at the Brahmin's feet, he would sing to himself a voiceless paean of adoration. For him every fold of Gokal's robes was majestic, and his massive frame like a buttress of the earth. The lights and shadows of thought that played over Gokal's features were like movements of sun and cloud across the eternal hills. In that face each line had meaning; godlike was the intelligence that looked out at you from beneath the overhang of those brows. Gokal's eyes were filled with starlight; yet a network of delicate wrinkles bound them in common kindliness to the world of men. And then, conjuring up the lithe, smooth-skinned loveliness of Gunevati, he found it vacant and null. *Her* countenance with its purely surface beauty seemed emptier to him now than the pathetic animal faces of deer or gazelles. No longer could be read into it the appeal of wild and gentle mindlessness; he understood Gunevati's mind too well, and now at last he knew that he disliked it.

The violence of his hostility did, however, moderate in a little while, and the two continued to meet on terms that seemed unchanged. But Gunevati realized that she had a whip in her hand; and ever after this it pleased her to flick at him occasionally in order to assure herself of her power. As for Jali, he locked his anger away deep in his heart, where it went to feed the flame of his devotion to Gokal. It was with a strange mixture of emotions that he contemplated his approaching departure from Agra. He would feel, he now realized, an intense relief upon putting behind him all that complex of excitement, effort, and agitation that constituted his present life. But wouldn't he also feel dull? No! For Gokal was going to join him in the Hills; and there he would have Gokal all to himself—Gokal without Gunevati.

He was not yet properly aware of it, but the strain of his present mode of life had already begun to tell upon him seriously. This was proved by an incident which nearly brought about his undoing. His mother had long wanted him to attend a service at Queen Miriam's chapel at Fatehpur-Sikri, but for one reason or another that event had been put off until now. And whereas, a few weeks ago, Jali would have had no objection to joining with his mother in her worship of the Christian God, the idea of doing so now filled him with the greatest discomfort. In the first place, he was afraid lest he should fail in devoutness. His mother had always insisted that her God was exceedingly benign; but Jali had it from other sources that He was keen-sighted, exacting, and jealous almost beyond belief—jealous to the point of not tolerating the worship of any other gods beside Himself! Might not the Christian God, then, piercing the secrets in his heart, look upon his attendance in the chapel as a piece of sheer impudence? Nor was this all: another misgiving assailed him. Doubtful of his powers of self-control, he feared lest he should make some dreadful self-betrayal. What if he were to break down and confess everything?

Anyhow, there was no way of avoiding the ordeal. So it was with as cheerful an air as he could muster that he accompanied his mother to Fatehpur-Sikri and entered the chapel at her side. For the first few minutes he felt very hysterical, but scarcely had the music begun before he forgot himself, his spirit being caught up in a sense of worship so spontaneous and complete, that no consciousness of guilt or hypocrisy remained. No longer did he think of the Christian God as prone to anger. He yielded himself to an ineffable longing for the peace of beauty, and the beauty of peace. The beauty of Mary's Heaven, the beauty that lay upon the line of desert horizons—the beauty of sanctity and the far ideal—all this, this that he had forgotten, returned to him in a surge of emotion which was only endurable for as long as he kept the thought of himself, as he now was, out of his mind. But he could not keep that thought at bay for ever. All at once regret assailed him with overpowering force. He beat it down, he strove not to listen to the passionless voices of the choir, nor to understand the cold beatitude they expressed. And yet the music that was tormenting him must also have been a support; for, when it ceased, he dropped into a pit of despair. The light by which men live seemed to abandon him entirely; a black wave of faintness rushed upon him, and he yielded to it with thankfulness.

For the next two days, lying almost without movement upon his bed, he exaggerated his sickness of body, and by this means concealed the sickness of his mind. The temptation to make a confession was very strong, so that at moments he was within an ace of yielding to it. And yet, through all this rending conflict, one thing above all others remained certain, he, Jali, was an isolated consciousness, and as such must fight his spiritual battles by himself. He couldn't or wouldn't accept either his father's or his mother's lights; upon that he set his teeth, and from there, too, he went on to another declaration. He was not ready to sacrifice the so-called evil in him to the so-called good. The temptation to be so good was often more insidious than the temptation to be wicked; often it was more demoralizing to be good than to be wicked. The longing for goodness and purity had its reverse side, which was a longing for relief from responsibilities, effort, and danger. One had one's self-respect to consider. Let him, then, adhere to his resolution to sever himself from parents, childhood, and all. Besides, there was no real *possibility*, even, of going back. So he hardened himself to suffer in solitude, cultivating scorn for family affections that had always proved blind and unavailing. Just as his love for his parents had been rooted in weakness, so theirs for him had been rooted in self-deception.

6

AT FIRST THE interest of the journey and the novelty of the
scene at Khanjo did much to distract Jali from his pre-occupations.
It was now his wish to put Gunevati out of mind altogether; and
in this he was fairly successful, in spite of her having announced
to him, just a few hours before his departure, that Gokal actually
intended to take her with him to the Hills. But she had spoken
teasingly, and he refused to believe that there was anything behind
what she said. So he waited for Gokal with an impatience that was
unspoilt by any uneasiness; and this was his frame of mind until,
one night, shortly before Gokal was due, he woke up to reflect
how dreadful it would be if Gunevati actually did reappear. Her
presence would not only completely alter the flavor of his life in
this place—it would destroy all his dreams of unspoilt companionship with Gokal. Might she not, too, infect him again with the
excitement that he had so thankfully thrown off? Since leaving
Agra he had come to see that his attitude towards his parents had
been growing more and more unfair; the Jali they believed in had a
real—or, at any rate, a half-real—existence; so that his view of
himself as completely "different" and of them as completely "unseeing" had been on the whole more distorted than theirs. When
he told himself that he had contempt for them, it was himself that

he was in reality despising. The truth was that he had been quite unlike himself at Agra—in fact almost mad.

Very soberly he reviewed his recent career, and, although he could not for a moment believe that he would fall back into his former condition of mind, he felt that his present tranquillity was threatened. His parents had given him a pair of cat-bears, charming creatures that were exceedingly tame and would follow him about the house and grounds. Much of his time was now devoted to these animals; the fact that the female was about to have a family inspired him with the deepest interest; in some odd way these two cat-bears symbolized for him the peace and security of his present existence.

Then Gokal arrived; and when he learned that Gunevati *was* in his company, a strange emotion made him catch at his breath. His heart sank, but one might say that it gave a leap at the same time. At any rate his excitement at that moment was not wholly unpleasurable: it was not until later, when he was lying wakefully on his bed at night, that every feeling except anxiety faded out of his mind. Then, then, indeed a thousand fears assailed him. He had no confidence in his ability successfully to conceal from Gunevati his dismay at her coming. His fear of her and his desire of her would doubtless conspire to make him return to their former relationship. The idea came, too, that she might succeed in poisoning Gokal's mind against him. With these thoughts working feverishly in his brain, he got up and stood for a while looking down upon the golden-brown bodies of his two friends, the cat-bears, who were lying asleep in their basket. His heart ached just as if he were being unexpectedly compelled to take leave of them for ever.

The next morning he went into the yard at the back of Gokal's bungalow, and there he found Gunevati sitting on the steps of an outbuilding that had evidently been prepared as her quarters. She was brushing her hair and drying it in the sun. On the other side of the yard was Gokal's cook, busy before the cook-house, and it was to him first that Jali discreetly went up. Whilst exchanging greetings with the cook he examined Gunevati out of the tail of his eye; and very soon he felt over his whole body the glow of a sensation that he recognized only too well. In vain he turned his back; desires that had lain dormant since his departure from Agra flooded his brain with images of the girl's beauty and ready wantonness. But his sensuality was now embittered by a deeply rooted dislike. Nevertheless, while he cursed her in his heart, his desires were also prompting him to suppress that dislike; thus whilst pretending to listen to the cook, he was filled with a deep interior agitation. A strange and rather suspect gentleness began to suffuse his thoughts of Gunevati as he reflected upon the pleasures that she afforded Gokal,—pleasures that he could intimately appreciate. Gunevati was a subtle, secret link between Gokal and him; the gestures, glances, tricks of behavior, that charmed him—these all charmed Gokal too. And so a kind of fragrance was infused into his desire, and again a protective feeling entered into his understanding of the Brahmin's infatuation. Alas! if only Gunevati were not so unworthy! If only she could recognize nobility when she met it! But she was neither intelligent nor trustworthy; he had just overheard his father saying that it was madness on Gokal's part to have brought her here.

The sense of her dangerousness grew upon him as he stood there. She was a thing of allurement and danger—not only to Gokal and to him, but to all the world. In so far as she was unconscious of being a peril she was more evil still. Yet—why should a pretty, unthinking girl inspire these sentiments? Was it fair to her to interpret her thus? Would not a good Buddhist see in her only a link in the long karmic chain, and a Christian only a sister in God? Oh, but those conceptions of her, how far-fetched they seemed! how flagrantly they ignored the immediate, blood-stirring reality! She had no life, no being, no reason, except in sex; and she herself felt it. She was a living bait—a bait of the dark, merciless Kali.

He walked across the yard, acutely conscious that the cook's eyes were fixed upon him. The old man's presence compelled Gunevati to rise deferentially and give him a proper salute. He was pleased, and waited a few moments before motioning her to sit down again. But there was a smile in her eyes, which the cook could not see, and the humility of her attitude did not disguise her pride in her lovely body, her glowing consciousness of its beauty and of its lure.

"You never believed the Brahmin would bring me," she murmured. "But now you see!"

He was silent.

"The Brahmin loves me more than ever. Look!" and she held out an arm covered with bracelets.

"Very pretty," said Jali, turning his face away.

Her slender figure arched in a backward pose, she smiled up at him, and her braceleted arm shielded her eyes from the sun. His gaze was drawn back to her, but he could find nothing to say.

"When have I ever lied to you?" she went on. "Perhaps you would like to believe that the holy Brahmin loves me as a father? But, I tell you, the loves of old men are the most unholy of all."

"Our house," said Jali, "is on the other side of the little stream. One can see it through the trees."

"I know," said Gunevati.

"Half a mile above it there is a place where three paths meet." He paused and gulped. "I will meet you there to-morrow at noon."

Gunevati said nothing. She was looking down at the delicate skin on her own shoulder, and it seemed to inspire her with a kind of mournful tenderness. Her tone, when she spoke again, was petulant. "By my mother, this country is lonely and horrible beyond words! These dark trees! And the air, how cold! Who but *rishis* or demons could endure to live in this place! All others who come here of their own free will must indeed be mad."

In his heart Jali was inclined to agree with her, but he was also angered, as she intended he should be. And his anger seemed only to increase his desire. Her eyes, as she looked at him, became mocking.

"I know you," she said. "You are longing to take me in your arms"—and her laugh rang out.—"Only, like a child, you are ashamed to say it."

Flushing hotly, Jali took a glance at the cook, who, crouching over his brazier, pretended not to have heard that laugh. Had the cook not been there, thought Jali, his anger would assuredly have broken out. As it was, he turned and walked quickly out of the yard.

On the morrow they met; and, after this, secret meetings in the forest became customary; but, whilst yielding to his desires, he tried to persuade himself that he might still avoid falling back into the old intimacy. If Gokal was able to use Gunevati for his pleasure, and yet preserve (as Jali supposed he did) a tranquil independence of spirit, why should not he do likewise? The unreflective arrogance of this reasoning was balanced by an equally unreflective modesty; it did not occur to him that Gunevati might set some store by their former companionship and be piqued by his new attitude. In point of fact she was piqued. Her ascendancy over the young Rajah had been flattering to her, and it annoyed her to see that, while her spell over his senses still held, her former influence was quite gone. If great men and powerful could be totally enslaved through their senses, why not this child? She pondered over the riddle until the answer came. She had won her ascendancy over Jali by opening his eyes to new aspects of life, and it was only by perpetually ministering to the hunger of that youthful, restless intelligence that she could hope to hold him in thrall. How tiresome it was! Was the boy worth the trouble? She swore that he was not; and yet she began to scheme how to get him back. As a first measure she made a trial of denying him her favors; and then, when this did no good, she came to realize that he lived less in his senses than in his heart, and that his heart was less swayed by his senses than by his thinking mind. With resentment, if not with jealousy, she awoke to a full understanding of the importance of Gokal in his life; and she was angered to a degree that she could not easily account for. This fat old man and this silly boy, what were they to her? Nothing, less than nothing! Yet the next time she and Jali met she sharpened her tongue, and was more spiteful in her mockery of Gokal than ever before. The result was highly significant; Jali turned livid with rage and finally went so far as to assure her that the pleasures he found in her arms were as nothing compared to the deep happiness of his hours at the Brahmin's side.

This was much the most serious quarrel they had yet had, and its consequences, although indirect, were decisive. Gunevati made up her mind to play her trump cards. She knew that she could tell Jali things that would reawaken all his former interest in her, and more than restore her lost prestige. If she had abstained until now, it was because her story was not one that could be lightly told. It involved the revelation that she was a Vamachari, a Follower of the Left-hand Way, and at this time, when the Emperor's rage against the secret sects was in full flame, no more dangerous

disclosure could possibly be made. But it was also just this revelation that would raise her to heights of wonder and interest in
Jali's eyes.

Once or twice already, when she had hinted at an unusual
knowledge of forbidden things, his response had showed her where
her best opportunities lay. She understood that knowledge, and especially the idea of hidden knowledge, fascinated him. Never had
she met anyone before so sensitive to the underground murmurs
and stirrings of the passion, half-religious, half-erotic, which dominated the spirit of her race; and that sensitiveness seemed to have
been accentuated rather than diminished by the refinements of his
character and upbringing.

The next day she made him accompany her farther than usual
into the forest, and when they were seated together in a remote,
sunny glade, she made her first beginning. On the purely material
side, her tale, as she was well aware, could hardly fail to thrill him.
He had often spoken to her about his uncle Hari, a figure who
evidently had touched his sympathies. Well, wouldn't it interest
him to hear how Hari had run across her and the other members of
her confraternity as they were stealing along, one evening in the
summer, to their appointed meeting-place in the Agra Woods? and
wouldn't he be excited at hearing that Hari had had a companion,
and that his companion had accidentally ridden down a certain
member of her group? Yes! and the rider had been the Princess
Lalita, the betrothed of Prince Daniyal! And the man knocked
down and stunned had been no other than Prince Salim himself!
Oh, the story in its barest particulars would be thrilling.

So here they now were; and she had not gone far before she saw
Jali's eyes light up and fix upon her with breathless intensity. His
rapt stare told her that she had not over-estimated her powers. On
that afternoon, and over a long sequence of afternoons, Jali did indeed hang upon her words. The method she followed was one of
hints, broken sentences, and long obstinate pauses; but every now
and then she would come out with a little rush of succinct, definite information, allaying his irritation and binding his interest
once more. Many were the hours they spent in that glade, and
Gunevati, basking upon the warm pine needles and smiling mysteriously to herself, was now fully content. The hunger of those

two dark eyes fixed upon her was more flattering to her vanity than that other hunger with which she was already a little wearisomely familiar.

It was not long ago that Hari Khan had arrived in Khanjo, and Jali had noticed at once that he was not in his usual spirits. Gunevati provided an explanation: the Princess Lalita, she said, had broken off her affair with him and he was suffering from heart-sickness. Explaining this, she laughed unkindly; she had no love for his uncle, and gave as her reason that he had not scrupled to take advantage of her defenselessness after discovering her in the deserted bungalow. But one day she also murmured something about his having spoken evil of her to Gokal; and then later, she came out with the astonishing remark that it was probably Hari Khan who had reported her to Mabun Das.

To Jali the conversation that took place between them on that afternoon was of particular importance, because it arrested a spirit of incredulity that had been gathering in him, and forced him to recognize Gunevati as actually playing a part—obscure, but nonetheless influential—in the affairs of the great world. She had already told him that Prince Salim was in love with her and that this infatuation greatly exercised the mind of Mabun Das; but these statements had left no impression on him at the time. The occurrence of such imposing names in Gunevati's narrative had done little more, so far, than spread an air of unreality over it; he hadn't been able to accept it as true that the busy Mabun Das knew or cared anything about a girl like this. But here she was reaffirming the fact, and this time he meant to probe a little.

"I used to see Mabun Das very often at the Agra Palace," he said slowly. "I don't think I liked him very much, although he was always so polite. He never seemed to be really listening to what anyone said—not even to my father."

"He listened to *me*!" said Gunevati with a low laugh.

Jali again was amazed. Was she actually claiming to have had an interview with the great man himself? He fixed upon her a deeply mistrustful gaze.

It happened to be one of Gunevati's more communicative days, and perhaps Jali's silence piqued her. At any rate, she presently raised herself upon one elbow and gave him a little grimace. "You doubt me," she said. "You doubt whether I really ever saw Mabun Das. Well!" and she gave him a peculiar smile. "Do you remember the marks on my back?"

"I do."

Sitting up, she gave her shoulders a twitch that caused her light muslin dress to slip down to her waist. "Look at those old marks," she went on craning round herself, to examine the amber-colored smoothness of her skin. "Don't you remember asking me how I got them?"

Jali bent forward. "The marks are quite gone now."

"But you remember them?"

"Yes. You told me it was your father who did it."

"You know my father. How could you believe that such a mild old man would beat me like that? No; those marks were the work of Mabun Das himself."

Jali knitted his brows in silence, while she laughed with a queer, soft complacency. "It was like this," she told him. "One day, when I and my father were out, Mabun Das's spies came and searched our cottage; and they found Princess Lalita's riding whip, which I had hidden in the reed thatch of the roof. But I knew nothing of their visit; and the next day, when Mabun Das summoned me before him, of course I denied all knowledge of the whip. And then, all at once—O my mother! I could have died!—Mabun Das drew forth the whip and flourished it before my eyes. And when I shrank away he bade me come quite close. And then he struck me three times. And with the first blow he said: 'This is to teach you there is one man on earth that you must never lie to.' And with the second blow he said: 'This is to make you remember that your life is in my hands.' And with the third: 'This is to warn you that for the rest of your life my eye will be on you and my ear listening to everything you say.' "

Whilst she was speaking Gunevati's eyes had changed; and now Jali saw in them a darkness that he had never seen before. With an intake of breath the girl swept her glance round the enclosing circle of trees. Jali's gaze went round too; and there was a pause before he said: "I think—I think you had better keep those words of Mabun Das's well in your mind."

This was a chapter in Gunevati's life that left Jali thoughtful, but it did not engage his interest for long. Affairs of the great world, affairs social and political, he felt to be quite outside his competence. So, although he vaguely conceived that the incidents related by Gunevati were such as might interest Mabun Das (for instance, it wouldn't do, of course, for Akbar to find out that Prince Salim was a Vamachari, nor for Daniyal to find out that Hari Khan had been conducting an intrigue with his betrothed)— although he realized that these scandalous secrets were potentially of political importance, this aspect of them remained indifferent to him. What, first of all, fascinated him in Gunevati's story was its revelation of the essential secrecy of the human mind. In his egoism he had been prone to fancy that he alone possessed vital secrets. But this clearly was a mistake. Here was his uncle Hari, living an adventurous, hidden life! of which the world knew nothing, a life of which Gunevati probably only knew a part, and that only because chance had made her hidden life cross Hari's at a certain point. How astonishingly secret most human lives in all probability were! Here were his father and mother, and Gokal, and Hari, and Gunevati, and himself, all living closely together, all participating, as it seemed, in an open, common life, and yet without doubt each one of these minds contained profound secrets. Each contained a small and partial knowledge of a single body of fact, which in its entirety was known by no one on earth.

A few days later he expressed some part of these reflections to Gunevati; but, as always happened when he generalized, she failed to show an interest. In order to come down to the particular: "Do you suppose," he asked, "that my father and mother, for instance, know things about you that you would never imagine possible, or other things about Hari Khan which you do not know? And what would happen in the world if people could see into one another's minds?"

Gunevati laughed, and gave a small shrug.

"Tell me!" persisted Jali.

The girl yawned. "I can tell you one thing that your mother knows and that Rajah Amar does not know," said she, suddenly looking amused.

"What is that?"

"That Hari Khan has become her lover."

"Oh!—What makes you think that?" said Jali, taken aback. "Besides," he added a moment later, "what of Princess Lalita? I think you must be joking."

"No. I am not joking. Don't you know that they have been meeting every day down by the stream?"

"Yes," said Jali. "But . . ."

He broke off. It would be a waste of time to set out to convince Gunevati that the relationship might be innocent. Besides, it was not a matter he would care to hear her discuss. Not that he was particularly angry or shocked; he had accepted the possibility that what she said was true. Only, oddly enough, he was not very deeply interested; and the reason for this was that, having grown up to think of his parents as beings apart, he was unable to look upon the things that happened to them as having the same kind of significance that they would have if they were to happen to him. In matters affecting his parents he could not conceive that ordinary human feelings were involved, or human standards applicable. Whenever he was forced to recognize in his father or mother feelings similar to his own, he experienced a certain discomfort. If he was learning to regard other adults as humanly akin to himself, he was still unconsciously reluctant to do the same for his parents, and this because his sense of responsibility towards them would thereby be increased.

So the principal effect of Gunevati's allegation was to heighten the feelings that her other disclosures had given birth to. The world was an extraordinarily mysterious place; the lives of men were secret; and the deeper you dug down the more strange and alluring the arcanum of Spirit became.

7

GUNEVATI'S EXPECTATIONS WERE justified, and better than she knew. After Jali's first excitement was over, he retained an intense curiosity to penetrate into the dark background of religion and passion against which her characters moved. Moreover, his imagination, working upon the material offered, drew not a little of its inspiration from sources of which she had no knowledge.

A little more than a year ago he had accompanied his father on a journey through the steamy jungle-lands of the South, and that experience had made a lasting impression on him. In particular he now recalled the dark, the time-worn, the blood-stained temples of the region, temples that were the true homes of Kali. And was it not from the South that the golden-hued Gunevati herself came?

So this pretty girl stretched out at his side in the cool Himalayan shade was seen by him as an incarnation of a dark and dreadful power; a power that, whilst secretly ruling over the whole earth, preferred not to reveal itself in its mighty nakedness to any but the initiates of its ancient home. While she sang to herself, and yawned, and played with the fir-cones, he would sit apart, gazing at her fixedly, from out of a cloud of thought.

In what rites had Gunevati not participated? What ecstasies, what savage deliriums had she not witnessed? What mysteries had she not gazed upon with her childishly cynical eyes? Alas! he could not make her mind yield up its secrets, secrets which she herself probably only half-understood. Now and then, in the night-time, it seemed to him that he might yet of his own strength, enter into direct communication with the demiurgic forces that were haunting him—forces whose colossal forms he felt heaving against the unsubstantial veil of the visible world. Unceasingly he was obsessed by the thought of a secret knowledge that it was his destiny to make his own. He must learn, and learn, and learn; he must learn not only the things that his father knew and the things that Gokal knew, but the things that Gunevati knew; and then more, much more—all that still lay beyond.

Before long he was beseeching Gunevati to make arrangements for his initiation into her secret sect; and in the end, for the sake of peace, the girl went so far as to introduce him to some friends that she had made in the village. These people, although not Vamacharis, were adherents of a similar cult. Amongst them was one who excited Jali's particular curiosity, because he also belonged to the infamous brotherhood of Aghoris. But after this creature had shown himself off by eating a mixture of putrid offal and dead insects out of a human skull, Jali's stomach proclaimed itself weaker than his spirit. To state the case frankly, there was not one of Gunevati's new friends who did not strike him with spiritual, if not physical, nausea. These people might be traffickers in the mysterious and the unhallowed, but they were certainly very squalid as well. Nor did Gunevati herself appear to any advantage in their society; her complete want of fastidiousness became manifest; and when he and she and her friends were together, it became all too plain where the true affinities lay. For him and for his people she had no instinctive sympathy at all; it was to the villagers that she turned, and they were truly detestable.

On her side, it was not long before Gunevati saw that she had made a mistake in allowing reality to interfere with Jali's imaginings. But how could she have managed differently? And what line was she to take now? Abruptly her mood changed; impatience with Jali flared up in her; all the boredom that she had been staving off assailed her with redoubled force. Was she to waste all her youth in this wilderness, bereft of all admirers excepting a fat old man and an exacting boy? Besides—and this was what really piqued her—between the man and the boy there was a friendship in which she had no place.

It had now become a rule for Jali to spend his morning hours with Gokal in the veranda, and before long Gunevati saw that this offered her a new method of offense. She succeeded in making Gokal think that she was developing an interest for serious things, and thus inveigled him into admitting her to these sessions whenever she chose to come. To Jali her presence was intolerable; he rightly saw it as intended to be outrageous and insulting to both. From the first day that she put in an appearance his peace of mind was gone. He could never tell when she might not come gliding softly round the side of the house, to seat herself with an exaggerated demureness upon the veranda's lowest step. He would pretend to take no notice of her arrival, and as a rule Gokal would do the same. His eyes would remain fixed upon the Brahmin's face, and the latter would make no pause in his speech. But oh! the mockery of it! How lamentably self-conscious they both were! In agony Jali would wait for a stumble, a faltering, a change—however slight—in the speaker's voice. Very rarely, if ever, did Gokal succeed in passing successfully through the ordeal. Besides, what was the use, when the victory was bound to go to Gunevati in any case? For, if Gokal did succeed in ignoring her silent presence, she had a dozen different devices at her command for exposing his secret disarray. It was enough that she should raise her bosom in a sigh, or sway to one side in pretended alarm at the buzzing of a wasp. Any trick sufficed: Gokal would interrupt himself and turn to her with a caressing look, and speak some friendly word. To Jali the slightest incident of this kind was tremendous in significance. The tumult in his breast continued to rage for long after the Brahmin had resumed his discourse; and well Gunevati knew how it was.

In these days the antagonism between the two rapidly deepened, and although Jali never fully revealed his feelings, his meetings with the girl became less frequent and their relations increasingly strained. If he still occasionally yielded to his desires, and if Gunevati was still cynically complaisant, that physical intimacy counted for nothing.

There had been a moment not long ago when Jali had thought

seriously of taking his uncle into his confidence. It was true that
he had sworn to Gunevati not to betray her; but he argued to himself that his loyalty to his own people should come first. Was it fair
to Hari not to report to him upon matters in which he was closely
concerned? He felt strongly that it was not. Then, too, the idea of
making a confession was now less unpleasant to him than before,
for his own personal secrets were, in some sort, balanced by the
secrets that he had learned about Hari. His strongest inducement,
however, resided in the fact that Hari's attitude towards Gunevati
was by no means friendly, and he was disposed to think that his
disclosures might lead to Gunevati's being sent away.

The decision before him was a momentous one, and he was
still weighing it in his mind when the girl herself unknowingly
tipped the scales. Her careless, confident assertion that his mother
and Hari had become lovers drove all idea of a confession out of his
head. Without fully believing all she said, he could see for himself
that those two had drawn very closely together; and that, by itself,
when he considered it, was enough to change his mind. Hitherto
his uncle had occupied an exceptional position in his thoughts as a
grown-up person with whom it might be possible to stand on
terms of confidence. Hari's love-affair with the Princess Lalita had
not altered his conception of him, for the Princess (he had seen her
once or twice at Agra) was just a pretty young woman with whom
anyone might well have an affair; but to have an affair with his
mother was quite a different matter; it snatched you up and away
into the remote realm where his parents belonged.

Nevertheless, it was not without regret that he abandoned
his plan; and after that, as the evil traits in Gunevati's character
grew more conspicuous every day, the loneliness of his position
came to press with increasing weight upon his mind. Not content
with spoiling his lesson-hours, Gunevati now went back to her old
habit of abusing Gokal to him, and what roused his especial disgust was her present tendency to select, not the Brahmin's weaknesses but his goodness of heart, and even his very affection for
her, as the target for her spiteful shafts. Latterly, too, she had got
into the way of questioning him about his parents, and her tone
was never pleasant. For them, for Hari, for Gokal, she evidently
nourished distinct strains of active dislike; these were the senti-

ments that he saw flickering up, like summer lightning, out of the gloomy boredom of her life at Khanjo.

A powerful longing to escape from this remote valley now obsessed him, just as it did her. The Himalayan scene had never had any charms for him, and his aversion to it was fast becoming intense. He could not endure these confining mountain-slopes muffled in somber trees, the meager sky-space, the absence of a horizon. The people of the valley, too, were filled with the dull, instinctive malevolence of an inferior race. This was brought home to him by a small adventure that befell him at about this time. He was returning from a ramble by himself through the woods, when a low whimpering struck upon his ear; and, while he stood still, trying to discover whence the sound arose, the conviction gained upon him that a woman or child must have met with an accident, and was now lying helpless somewhere under the dark trees. Frantic to bring aid, he called out and began running hither and thither. At last he came upon a pit; and looking down, saw a bear-cub lying wounded below. It was not the kind of bear that would eat the garden produce of the villagers or do them any harm; yet, as he was staring down at it in helpless pity, a large stone was dropped from above striking the poor animal on its side. Moreover, the ground all round the bear was strewn with similar stones, not one of them heavy enough to have killed it. And now, lifting his head, he saw for the first time one of the village women with two or three children about her, grinning at him from the other side of the pit. With rage in his heart he shouted out at them, and asked how long the bear had been in its present plight. The indifferent answer came "About a week." At this his anger knew no bounds, and, after driving the bear's tormentors away, he made straight for Gokal's house. But his uncle Hari, whom he was looking for, happened not to be in when he got there, so he plunged headlong into Gokal's private room. The fact that Gunevati was lying on the couch, and that his sudden entry had thrown Gokal into obvious confusion, did not suffice to arrest him. Describing what he had seen, he begged that men should be sent out in all haste to put an end to the bear-cub's miseries.

As soon as Gokal had grasped the situation he showed no lack of feeling; but for a few moments Jali's breathless incoherence had merely bewildered him, and unconsciously he had turned to Gunevati with an air of appealing to her for help. The girl's response had been to raise puzzled eyebrows and shake her head; but, not a moment before, Jali had caught her eye, which was fixed upon him with a look of the most malicious amusement. This behavior goaded him to frenzy. "As for you!" he shouted at her in a voice of undisguised hate: "You are playing the hypocrite again! You must have known about that bear all the time. It was your friend, the lame boy, who threw down the rock."

This outburst was followed by a silence, and Jali realized that the tone in which he had just addressed Gunevati must have struck Gokal as decidedly odd. But before anything further could be said, a servant came into the room, and to him Gokal now gave the necessary orders for the bear-cub's immediate destruction. While this was going on, Gunevati, from behind Gokal's back, continued to eye Jali with the same looks of wicked amusement; but, when the servant had gone, she came forward, and in a tone of meek distress protested that she had been quite innocent of the knowledge that had been imputed to her. Then, after inclining herself before the young Rajah with dignified humility, she quietly left the room.

As soon as she was gone an embarrassed silence fell. To Jali's relief it was broken by the coming of another servant, who was bringing him some lemonade to drink, and a basin in which to wash his hands and face. This done, he waited with averted eyes for Gokal to speak. His heart was beating hard, and he knew that, should an opportunity be given him, he would be unequal to resisting the temptation to make everything known. Obstinately he kept his face turned away, but he was aware that Gokal's troubled gaze was resting heavily upon him. A few critical moments passed, moments in which the future course of affairs might have been wholly changed. But it was not to be. The Brahmin hesitated, and the reasons for his hesitation were numerous and complicated. Some were less creditable to him than others; but it was certainly not the less creditable alone that formed his ultimate decision. What he did was to ask his pupil whether it was not true that he had latterly taken Gunevati in aversion. His voice was very embarrassed, and further than this he could not force himself to go. Jali replied curtly: "Yes," and then, after another painful silence, Gokal went on: "Very well; if that is the case she shall no longer join us in the morning."

Shortly after this they parted, and the cloud of their discomfort had not yet lifted, but neither of them was seriously disturbed about it, for they both knew that their amity remained unspoilt. On his way home Jali felt a certain elation; for had not Gunevati suffered a reverse?

That reverse turned out to be less complete than it should have been. On the pretext of picking flowers for the decoration of Gokal's room, Gunevati would often saunter out into the sunlight of the garden while Gokal's discourse was going on. Now stooping down, now reaching up, she was able to display the grace of her young body more provocatively even than before. Her beauty traveled like a poisonous perfume into the shade of the veranda where master and pupil sat.

Such was Jali's position when fate gave another turn to the wheel, a turn which he at once felt to be menacing. Quite unexpectedly Rajah Amar was called away from Khanjo to attend his aged mother's death-bed; and, to everyone's surprise, Hari elected to accompany him. It was a gray, autumnal morning upon which the two rode off, and as Jali watched them disappearing under the trees, a new cloud of apprehension settled down upon his heart. From this hour onwards a vague fear, a sense of gathering evil, scarcely ever left him. What exactly he was afraid of he would have been unable to say; but he could not forget the bear-cub in the pit, and he knew that in just the same spirit the villagers would welcome any misfortune that might befall the strangers within their gates. They would refuse the ordinary offices of mercy; gloating, they would hold back. These were the people with whom Gunevati stood in instinctive sympathy, and even perhaps in some kind of secret alliance.

Under the stimulus of fear his insight was sharpened. He began to understand much better the nature of Gunevati's discontent. Each one of the brief days of her youth and beauty was to her a priceless treasure, and in handfuls that treasure was being thrown away. An old saying, recently quoted by Hari, cropped up in Jali's mind: "A woman measures her beauty by the evil that it works

293

in the world." Where were the rich and handsome lovers, and with them the dissensions, intrigues, and murders, that Gunevati had a right to see enlivening her path? For long hours Jali sat upon his bed and meditated. It was disquieting to recall the expression of disdainful boredom that was habitual to Gunevati when Gokal's eyes were not actually resting upon her. It was dreadful to remember how Gokal's face would light up with tenderness whenever she passed by.

8

AMONGST GUNEVATI'S FRIENDS in the village lower down
in the valley was a herb-woman, whose position among the na-
tives was remarkable, for although they looked upon her as little
better than an outcast, she dominated them by the force of her personality. Her offices were sought for at childbirth, in sickness, in
affairs of the heart, and at death. No doubt her intelligence was
very superior to that of the others, but this did not seem to excite
their hatred; perhaps they considered that she atoned for it by
the unusual repulsiveness of her appearance and habits. Her hut,
which she had been compelled to build at some distance from the
village, emitted a stench that was different from theirs, and which
even they found unpleasant.

Jali had some difficulty in understanding what made Gunevati
associate with this woman, for she did not naturally incline towards the poverty-stricken, nor was intelligence any special rec-
ommendation to her. Once or twice out of sheer curiosity he
questioned her about Mujatta the Cockroach as this woman was
called, and rather to his surprise she betrayed a slight, but unmistakable, embarrassment. She took the line of denying the intimacy, yet he had no doubt in his mind that it existed. Not only
had he overheard the village women coupling her name derisively
with Mujatta's, but, one day, as he was wandering by himself in

the forest, he had come out unexpectedly into a clearing which he recognized as the herb-woman's, and had seen Gunevati standing by the door of the hovel, deep in conversation with someone inside. Not wishing to be seen, he had watched her for a few moments from the shade of the trees and then slipped quietly away.

This was some time ago, and meanwhile he had not given Mujatta more than a passing thought, yet now it happened that, waking one night from a deep sleep, he was seized with the sudden conviction that Gunevati and this woman were hatching mischief together. Moreover, as he lay there, staring into the dark, his dread rapidly took a more definite form; it seemed to him that the village women had used the word "poison"; and then he suddenly remembered that very soon after Gunevati's arrival at Khanjo she herself had laughingly told him that Mujatta was a noted poisoner. In a very few minutes he was entirely possessed by the dreadful idea that Gunevati was making up her mind to poison Gokal.

No more sleep was possible for him that night. Hour after hour he lay rigid in his bed, his body frozen and shivering, while his mind strained and labored in a torment of anguished conjecture. His task was to collect, review, collate, and interpret every detail that might have some bearing on the affair. Each one of Gunevati's looks, words, and actions during the past weeks had to be considered and weighed. And then he had to penetrate her mind; his speculations must carry him to the truth, and the certainty that he had found the truth.

At some point in the midst of this brain-racking labor he got up and went to the window; and when he next became conscious of his surroundings it was to find himself standing there, in a patch of moonlight, with his friends, the cat-bears, roused from their sleep and snuffling at his heels. Automatically he put them back into their basket and returned to bed. Dawn glimmered into the room, and he was still in the same condition; but, as the day brightened and the household stir began, his fears lost their first panic intensity. He no longer felt that instant action was obligatory; he could allow himself time to deliberate—say, twenty-four hours—before doing whatever had to be done.

And what might that be? In God's name, what? Were it in his power to kill Gunevati by a mere act of will, she would be dead, he told himself in the very next second; and not one scruple or misgiving would he have. Well! wasn't it, then, mere cowardice that prevented him from taking the necessary steps to bring about what he desired. "I must think!" he muttered. "I must think!"

Having given out that he was suffering from a headache, he continued to lie on his bed; and, as he wrestled with the dreadful decision that was gradually imposing itself upon him, his teeth once more began to chatter with cold and fear. The action before him called for a violation of his instincts more cruel than any he had yet attempted. It was even worse than setting out to make advances to the women in the Palace. To bring about Gunevati's death—even with the expert assistance of the herb-woman—was going to be an agony, a torture. Each step of his plan, as he pictured himself in the performance of it, filled him with a sickening horror. But he saw no real difficulties in his way. Mujatta was ruled solely by the love of gain; it was well known by everyone that there was nothing she would not do, no one she would not betray, for the sake of an extra coin. And, although Gunevati might, thanks to Gokal, be in a position to pay her well for her services, he, Jali, could without question pay her far better. He felt sure that as soon as he had made the foul creature see what was in his mind she would put herself at his disposition with a shameless alacrity. After all, too, some danger attached to doing away with a Brahmin, but no one (unless it were Gokal) would make much ado about Gunevati's death.

As the morning wore on he fell into an uneasy sleep, and, awaking about noon, found himself much more collected. Twenty-four hours was the period that his father allotted to himself for solitary meditation before confirming a sentence of death, and he determined to follow his father's example. Stretched out motionless in the green twilight of his shaded room, he strove hard to reach the detached, dispassionate firmness that he desired. The cat-bears, considerably perplexed by their young master's unaccountable behavior during the last twelve hours, padded gently about on the matting, occasionally putting their forepaws upon the bed in order to take a look into his face. Jali found his thoughts ungovernable. Instead of concentrating on the question of Gunevati's deserts, he lost himself in wonder at the appalling change of outlook that had overtaken him in the night. Yesterday at this hour he had been, comparatively speaking, serene. And what, he asked, had happened—actually happened—in the meantime to throw him into this walking nightmare? Nothing! Absolutely nothing! He had merely opened his eyes and seen things in a new light. Something had taken place in his mind comparable to the breaking of the monsoon. For some time past his mental weather had been dull and lowering, and now had come the thunderclap. In all this, what was truth and what was illusion? Which view of the situation was the right one?

A sudden mistrust of himself and all his most careful reasonings swept over him. Was it possible that he was losing his mental balance? Was he going mad? He began to picture what would happen if he were to attempt to make an explanation of his present fears to his parents. Could he find anything to tell them that would carry conviction? Or would they, with gentle expostulatory voices, and quiet incredulous smiles, apply themselves to soothing him down? The very thought filled him with rage, making him grind his teeth in a frenzy of anger and suffering. Yet perhaps, perhaps, they *would* be in the right? Perhaps, perhaps, he *was* nearly mad? Well, be this as it might, he would rather die, he would rather let Gokal die, than open his heart to them at this hour. This was his affair. He had involved himself with Gunevati; he was, in a sense, in league with her. Very good, this terror under which he labored was the price he had to pay for his truck with her and her friends. Moreover, single-handed, he would outwit and defeat her! If he stood alone, it was because he was disloyal both to evil and to good. It was inevitable that he should stand alone. In grudging his mother and Gokal their unsuspectingness and freedom from care, in pitying himself for the horror of these hours, he was falling to the level of Gunevati—or even lower, for Gunevati was at least happy in her vileness. His path in life was destined to be solitary—had he forgotten it? It was the path of knowledge, of experience; and if it was in the nature of things that knowledge should mean defilement, he must not complain. The world had done nothing but defile him since the hour of his birth; or, to put it more truly, he was condemned by some inexplicable law of his own nature to do himself unceasing outrage.

On these reflections he again fell into an exhausted sleep. Awaking calmer, a new thought dawned upon him. Here, at Khanjo, Gunevati couldn't poison Gokal without drawing suspicion on to herself in a quite marked degree. Nor was there any place in the world less easy to hide in or make an escape from. If she had any ordinary prudence she would hold herself back until Gokal was once more on the road and passing through some town in which one could, without trouble, disappear. Of course the question presented itself why, if running away was so simple, she should go out of her way to poison Gokal at all? She knew that Gokal wasn't the man to have her pursued or nourish thoughts of revenge. Why not make the simplest assumption, which was that she would have the patience to wait until Gokal left Khanjo, and then take the first good opportunity of joining Prince Salim at Allahabad? Why suppose that the idea of poison had ever entered her head?

Exactly! So here he was again at the beginning of all his reasonings. He could have laughed aloud at himself, had he not been so weary and so profoundly penetrated by fear. The questions he had just been asking were the questions of common sense; but—what had common sense to do here? Its only legitimate function was to abdicate, to acknowledge itself out of place. Of this Jali was completely convinced. If he mistrusted his intuitions, he mistrusted far more the common-sense arguments by which they could be shown to be silly. Gunevati was a creature of impulse, mixed with cunning. Her calculations, starting from irrational premises, would work to irrational conclusions; to show that it would be both pointless and dangerous to poison Gokal at Khanjo was not to show that Gunevati would not do it.

This line of thought, unconsoling as it was, did, however, lead him to another idea. Why should he not arrange with Mujatta for Gunevati's flight instead of for her death? If it was merely a question of money (and with Mujatta everything came to that) the obstacles could easily be overcome. He had quite a respectable sum of his own, in his chest, and, if necessary, he would find some more somewhere. Why shouldn't he and Mujatta launch Gunevati forth at once upon a journey to Prince Salim at Allahabad? Gunevati had told him repeatedly enough that the Prince was frantic to get hold of her. Why shouldn't he, Jali, pay for a messenger to be dispatched in all haste to the Prince, who, one might reasonably suppose, would then see about her abduction himself.

One objection to the scheme did, indeed, cross Jali's mind at this point, but he brushed it aside. If Gunevati were to be believed, Mabun Das had a strong desire to keep her and Prince Salim apart, and he had even given the girl his ironic benediction when she had told him that Gokal was proposing to take her off to the hills. Well! Deep as Jali's respect for Mabun Das was, this, he felt, wasn't the occasion for considering him at all. He was much too desperate, and he believed that Gunevati's impatience would make her equally willing to risk Mabun Das's wrath. Once in Prince Salim's harem she would presumably be safe enough. Here, then, was a way out! Here was a ray of light, here was hope, at last!

Shaking all over with excitement, Jali sprang to his feet and fell to pacing the room. The thing to do was to find Mujatta and win her confidence and complicity; he must get her to reveal to him what was in Gunevati's mind. It was absolutely essential that he should discover from Mujatta whether Gokal was in peril; he could not, he would not, take chances; he could not tolerate a situation in which Gokal's life actually hung upon the spiteful impulses of an utterly conscienceless and unreasoning girl.

Drawing a deep breath he halted before the window, and for a stretch of perhaps five minutes he stared frowningly and unseeingly at the bushes outside. This wonderful scheme of his, this heaven-sent solution of his problem—could he accept it? Was it really safe? If he hadn't really cared—that is, if he hadn't cared as desperately as he did—how splendidly it would have satisfied him! For it was a good scheme; there was nothing against it, except that it involved delay, and—Gokal's life was at stake! He couldn't take chances; he couldn't allow himself to be soothed by fair words from a creature such as Mujatta; whatever she were to say, he wouldn't be able to feel absolutely safe. How could she answer for Gunevati from one moment to another? Didn't he know much better than she the nature of Gunevati's feelings towards Gokal? And as for her feelings towards him, Jali—well, they wouldn't be improved by his desperate anxiety to see the last of her; and in providing her with a means of escape, wouldn't he be actually removing what was perhaps deterring her more than anything else from administering poison?

What finally emerged as a result of these anxious deliberations was the resolve to visit Mujatta without delay and to be guided by the outcome of that meeting. Late in the afternoon he slipped out of the house. But after he had gone a little way through the forest he came across the lame boy, who was the constant attendant of Mujatta, and from him he learnt that she had gone away to assist a woman in childbirth in a neighboring village and would not be at home again until the next day.

That night his sleep was very profound, but he awoke at dawn just as he had intended. Mistrustful of the lame boy's statement, he was determined to make an early visit to the clearing to see for himself whether Mujatta was there. The change from the peace of unconsciousness to the misery of his waking life was almost more than he could bear. Dressing in the chill of a gray dawn, he could not help weakly hoping that the herb-woman would not be there, for he was feeling particularly unequal to his undertaking. Although he had come across Mujatta several times, and although she had always been servile and ingratiating in her odious way, he had never yet spoken more than a dozen words to her. She filled him with unspeakable disgust.

The valley was still full of mist, as he hurried furtively along through the dripping tangles of rhododendrons, and then out among the tall straight columns of the forest trees. Self-coercion, he reflected grimly, could go no further. To be deliberately seeking out this woman, to be entering into confidential relations with her, to be forcing himself to tolerate her physical proximity—could anything be more horrible?

On reaching the clearing he paused for a moment to collect his wits and look round. The hovel stood about fifty yards away across a stretch of rough, weedy ground. It stood surrounded by dirt and rubbish, it looked indescribably squalid and desolate; but a thin plume of white smoke was going up from the roof, and Jali felt almost sure that the herb-woman herself must be there. Clenching his teeth, he walked resolutely forward. He went up to the door which was closed; and it was his intention to call out. But he felt his voice to be too unsteady, so he picked up a piece of wood, and knocked with that, for he could not bear to touch the filthy door with his own hand. His knocking produced no immediate response, but he could hear someone moving about inside, and presently an obsequious voice cried out: "One instant, Great Lord! Great Lord, deign to forgive! Your slave is hastening . . . hastening. . . ."

It was *her* voice; and since she said "Great Lord," she must, he supposed, have seen him coming, though how, he could not quite make out, for there was no window on this side of the hut.

Then the door opened, and he noticed at once that as her eyes fell upon him her expression underwent a slight change. He noticed this, but his mind at the time did no more. "Come out!" he said, backing away from the hut. "Come out! I have something to say to you."

Mujatta the Cockroach was a woman of sturdy build and slightly inclined to corpulence. She habitually wore a dirty black cotton dress which went down from her neck to her ankles. Her most remarkable physical traits were, first, the shortness of her arms, and secondly, the length of her neck. This immensely long neck of hers was slightly goitered so that her almost chinless face and tiny head seemed to be little more than a prolongation of it. The result was a conformation, the snakishness of which was accentuated by her habit of undulating her neck and protruding her head at you; for she was one of those talkers who like to discharge their volubility at short range.

As Jali now backed, she came forward, and when he backed farther she came forward again. In spite of his previous self-preparation contact with Mujatta's personality was proving too much for him. His thoughts began to flutter wildly about in his head like a flock of frightened birds.

"I have come to talk to you about Gunevati," he brought out in a loud, unnatural voice. "Do you understand? I want you to tell me . . . all about Gunevati . . . about her plans. . . . I am sure you know everything . . . and I have money here. . . ."

Mujatta's habitual expression was one of the most villainous ingratiatingness. Her little beady eyes seemed to be offering an eager yet treacherous welcome to all the turpitudes in the world. In these first moments curiosity—a very natural curiosity, no doubt—was legible upon her features, but after he had spoken it seemed to him that her curiosity became tinged with an impudent amusement. It almost looked as if she found his all-too-visible disgust and loathing of her a matter to smile over. However, after his stammerings had become a little more explicit, her expression underwent, he fancied, another slight change. He got the impression that she had been put on her guard.

These signs were not auspicious. Already he felt a slight disappointment. She was talking hard now, and, whilst hiding her mind behind a screen of empty words, she seemed to him to be reading his thoughts. Faithful to his intentions, he raised his voice again and resolutely shouted her down. He had his little store of prepared sentences; and these he now brought out. They came from his lips very much at random, it was true; but still they ought to have given Mujatta pause. Instead of this, however, whenever he stopped to draw breath, her meaningless, irrelevant flatteries poured forth again. A presentiment of failure seized him. As each moment passed it was becoming more unmistakably clear that something in his calculations had gone wrong. The woman actually didn't seem to want to hear what he had to say, and, although it was impossible that she should not be taking in the trend of his speech, those eyes of hers, bright and unblinking as a serpent's, continued to be utterly unresponsive. The light of greed and complicity, which should have been kindled long ago, was not there.

Jali felt that he could do no more. What his actual words had been he hardly knew, nor was he afterwards able to recall more than a phrase here and there; but he had carried out his intentions, he had finished—and he had been defeated! Looking round, he found himself now standing by the edge of the clearing. Nor was it only with the repulsiveness of her physical presence that the woman had been pressing him back; it was rather with the strength of a superior will. For some reason, incomprehensible to him, she was eager that he should be gone; so here he now stood routed, with not a word left in his head. The thing that had happened was inexplicable. Mujatta, servile, greedy of gain, had driven him away.

He was staring at her in voiceless bewilderment when a loud whistle sounded from somewhere behind the hut, and at this the woman's head swept round on her long neck with a movement that might well have been accompanied by a hiss. Then the lame boy appeared, jogging towards them with all the speed of which he was capable. As he came he called out and pointed excitedly behind him.

Mujatta turned to Jali again; in a torrent of words she explained that a band of miserable outcasts, the very sight of which would pollute him, were on the point of paying her a visit. Poor wretches! they were suffering from an infectious disease, and she in her charity was going to cure them. Had she but known that the young Maharajah was going to honor her with his presence, she would assuredly have kept them away. But alack! it was now too late; they were already upon her! So the young lord must fly, must fly!

Jali was nothing loath. All his other feelings had given way before an overmastering longing to be gone. Nevertheless, before losing himself in the shade of the trees, he took one swift look behind. That Mujatta had been lying he had not for one moment doubted; and now her mendacity was well proved. His backward glance showed him a well-dressed figure moving with leisurely tread towards the hut. It was certainly not the figure of an outcast.

9

HEEDLESS OF WHERE he was going, he hurried away down the woodland track. The early sunlight was now falling in patches of gold upon the red-brown tree-trunks, and already a scent of warm pine-needles rose from the damp ground. After a little he stopped and looked absently about him, then threw himself down by the side of the path. He had dressed, that morning, in fine clothes, with the half-conscious object of imposing upon Mujatta. Certainly his white turban with its jeweled plumelet had been meant to impress her with the wealth at his command. He now tore it from his head with rage and flung it on the ground.

After sitting there for a while, he clasped his hands over his face and tried to arrange his thoughts. This proved impossible, and yet something exciting was taking place in his brain all the same. Out of the dark turmoil within ideas flashed forth of their own accord. And they were wonderful, dazzling; they made his heart beat fast.

Mujatta had certainly been expecting that important visitor; the reason she had been so unforthcoming was that she had some plan already in hand. She had been suspicious of him because she didn't know how much he knew, or whether he approved. And her plan—what would it have as its object, if not the abduction of Gunevati? Who could that stranger be, if not an emissary of Prince Salim's? Yes! here was the truth of the matter: Mujatta and Gunevati had forestalled him; they had already thought of his plan and set it afoot.

Hadn't it been quite natural, he went on—in fact almost inevitable, that Mujatta should misinterpret his manner of approach? Wouldn't she naturally be thinking that he was in love with Gunevati (which was undoubtedly what Gunevati would have given her to believe), and wouldn't she imagine that he was visiting her with the idea of preventing the girl's flight? This strange, early morning visit of his, and then his begging her to "betray" Gunevati, and his promise of a bribe,—wouldn't she read her own mistaken meaning into every word?

Jali leapt to his feet, and then threw himself down again. Never in his life before had he pursued his flying thoughts with a more frantic excitement than now. How wonderful his thoughts were! They showed him that everything was going well. They promised him an end to his torments. It looked as if Gunevati were actually on the brink of flight; and, if this were so, why should she go to the trouble of poisoning Gokal? Oh, no! she wouldn't poison him now. Not just for the satisfaction of a groundless grudge. She wouldn't complicate her plans and incur the risk of pursuit: it would be ridiculous to suppose that.

Once more Jali's joyful excitement spurred him to his feet, and he fell to walking distractedly up and down. Everything seemed to fit in with his newly born surmises: Gunevati's intimacy with the herb-woman was adequately accounted for without recourse to the idea of poison. Thank heaven! he hadn't used the word poison in his talk with Mujatta. But—was he quite sure that he hadn't? Terrible doubt! What exactly had he said? He had spoken a good deal about his power to pay her more generously than Gunevati. He had asked her quite definitely to betray Gunevati's secrets. He had made it very clear that he might call upon her to take some action against Gunevati, but—he had never hinted—even remotely —that he . . . No, no, if he had used the word poison, it had been earlier—when he was inviting her to betray Gunevati's confidences. He was almost sure of that. But all the same . . .

So violent was the sudden access of this new anxiety that he felt himself trembling like a leaf. He was in a fever to rush back to Mujatta and do away with all her possible misconceptions. But,

God help him! he must first regain some measure of calm. Fool, blunderer, that he had been! Wasn't it more than likely that just now he had done nothing but harm? And if he were to rush back now—very likely breaking into the interview between Mujatta and the stranger—wouldn't he be probably doing yet more mischief? He pressed his burning face with his hands. He *must* see Mujatta again soon—before she got a chance of repeating his words to Gunevati. But not at once—not until he had collected himself, not until he had managed to think, to think.

Putting forth his utmost powers of self-control, he sat down once more by the path. No doubt there were still a hundred contingencies for which he was quite unprepared. For instance, Gunevati might have been already there, in Mujatta's hut, all the time! *That* might have been the reason why Mujatta was so circumspect, and why she kept edging him away; or, again, Gunevati might have arrived at the hut since he left it; and what would he do or say, if, upon arriving there, he were to find Mujatta and Gunevati and the stranger, all three together? How would he explain to Gunevati this early morning visit of his?

As he surveyed his former scheme for poisoning the girl a cold sweat of horror broke out over his whole frame. That scheme which had looked so simple and commendable a few hours ago —it now struck him as monstrous and perilous beyond all words. Other people—people who were at home in the world—*they* no doubt could contrive and carry out such things. But oh! not he, not he!

He was sitting on the ground, the palms of his hands pressed hard against his eyes, when these thoughts raced through his mind, and the distress they caused him was such that he uttered a stifled groan. Extraordinary was the shock he received upon hearing that groan, as it were, answered; for there came to his ears a very faint, very brief, little laugh. Raising his head with a quiver of dismay, he saw before him Gunevati, who was standing at a forking of the path, not more than ten yards away. Her pose suggested that she might have been there for a minute already, perhaps more. He stared speechless, and her eyes met his with a gaze that seemed to him dangerously cold. In these moments it was quite beyond him to hide his discomfiture; he couldn't cease from staring, even though he felt that his stare was saying: "How much can you guess? How much do you know?"

She was standing at a forking of the ways. Had she come from Mujatta's hut or was she going to it? Had he but raised his head a minute earlier, had he but caught a sound of her footsteps on the path, he might have known. But he did not. Gunevati, like him, was dressed in her best clothes. She was wearing cherry-colored silks, and on her arms and bosom were silver bangles and precious stones. She glowed like an idol against the dark forest shades. Haughty and alien did she seem to him at this moment. Very different from Gunevati, the gazelle, who had come, docile to his beckoning, in the Agra wood. In those fine clothes and with that look in her eyes her proper place was, in truth, the harem of some royal prince—a harem where she could recline all day upon cushions of golden tissue, breathing an air of sandal-wood and musk.

"Gunevati!" he brought out at last, and with smiles and accents horribly forced he exclaimed at the earliness of her rising. "Where are you going?" he faltered.

The girl looked at him—not searchingly, but with a contemptuousness that he found even more alarming.

He rose to his feet, and stood waiting. But Gunevati remained silent, and with lowered eyes began plucking the petals from a blue poppy that she had been wearing at her waist. That poppy, thought Jali, must have come from Gokal's garden, and it looked fresh. Assuredly, then, she was on her way *to* Mujatta; but the next instant he decided no. She would not be pulling her flowers to pieces unless the interview with Salim's messenger were over. It was terrible, not knowing from which direction she had come! Did this chilling manner of hers mean that she had overheard some part of his conversation with Mujatta? He shuddered inwardly. These conjectures were like so many dagger-thrusts, and he was defenseless.

Poison! he thought, poison! Had she overheard that word on his lips? Or had it, perhaps, been repeated to her? And what was he to answer, if she asked *him* what *his* business was at this hour? She had him at every possible disadvantage. He couldn't even decide in what tone, in what manner, he ought to address her. Several days had gone by since they last met, and it seemed to him now that not a shred of their former friendliness remained. But perhaps that was only what *he* felt? No doubt the vehemence of his secret thoughts about her had confused him; there was no reason why her feelings about him should correspond to his about her.

He said: "I was on my way to see you." This did not contain a denial of his visit to Mujatta; he might have been intending to come to her after that visit.

"Indeed?" her eyebrows went up. "You wanted to see me? I wonder what about?"

He wished that she would lift her head, but she was still intent upon the blue poppy in her hand. "For some time past," he said, "I have had the idea that—that you were planning to go away."

She smiled. "Why should I want to go away? When did you get that idea?"

He was silent.

"What were you wanting to say to me? Were you going to try to persuade me to stay?"

He remained silent. She looked up, and her dark eyes, although wide open, seemed to him like windows shuttered and barred. "Anyhow, you are quite wrong," she continued in the same even tone. "Why should I want to leave my Brahmin? Shouldn't I be a fool to run away from a man like that? A man who dotes on me and gives me all I want? What does it matter if he is old and fat and stupid? I can take other men as lovers when they please me. The Brahmin is too stupid to notice anything."

"But here you are bored, you are wasted. There is no one here," stammered Jali.

Gunevati gave a little laugh. "Is that all you know? Haven't I told you about the young charcoal-burner down the valley, who is as beautiful as Krishna when he appeared among the cow-maidens. Were I to say to him: 'Kill the Brahmin!' he would kill him. For the sake of my beautiful charcoal-burner I am content to stay here."

Her malicious intention was obvious; but that did not necessarily mean that everything she was saying was untrue. Jali looked at her helplessly, and all at once he was seized by an irresistible impulse to make a bid for her candor. "I will tell you the truth," he cried out. "I have just been to see Mujatta."

"It is pleasant to speak the truth sometimes," observed Gunevati unmoved.

But Jali was determined not to give up. Wasn't it, after all, certain that she *was* on the eve of flight? That dress of hers, put on for the distinguished stranger, wasn't it almost a proof?

"Why should we lie to one another?" he went on with rising ardor. "I went to Mujatta to ask her whether it was true that she was helping you to join Prince Salim."

"Tell me, then," said Gunevati, with an ambiguous smile, "why are you so anxious that I should go away?"

Jali had no reply ready. There was something terribly cunning, something terribly obstinate, and also something terribly unintelligent, about Gunevati. That smile of hers was making his heart sick.

"Are you longing for me to leave you alone with your Brahmin?" Gunevati asked smoothly. "Would you like that? Please tell me."

She was teasing him. But why? And behind that smile was there not something more than mere idle mischief? Desperately did he regret having flaunted his love of Gokal before her eyes; desperately did he now cast about for some flattery with which to placate her, for some dust to throw in her eyes.

"You see!" said Gunevati, "you don't know how to answer me! Nor have you explained why you went to Mujatta instead of coming to me. Mujatta is *my* friend—not yours."

"A pretty friend, by Shiva!" exclaimed Jali in a gust of bitterness.

Gunevati was silent for a moment; and to his astonishment he saw that he had angered her.

"Yes. She is my friend. I was not born a Ranee."

"I meant she is not worthy to be your friend. You have better friends than that, Gunevati."

"The fat Brahmin, I suppose?"

"Yes."

"And *you*?"

"Yes—me."

Did he pronounce that last word falteringly? Be that as it might, there was a moment's silence, and then Gunevati gave a little laugh. She laughed! She was looking at him strangely. Again, although he felt as if his eyes must be betraying him, he was unable to detach them from her face. How much did she suspect? Did she suspect and yet laugh? It was terrible. As he looked into her

310

face he thought of it, as it would have appeared cold and fixed in death. And he had schemed how to bring that face and that lovely youthful body down into the grave. It was not remorse that he felt, it was horror. The world was too stark and ruthless a place for him; its passions and issues too harsh; he was not made to endure in himself, nor even to see others endure, the terrific ordeal of life. For a moment he thought of his mother and marveled at her spirit. Was it blindness, or insensitiveness, or courage, that enabled her to walk smiling through the world? But *she* was not treacherous, she was single-hearted, whereas in his heart and on his lips even now there was treachery and guile.

"Gunevati," he murmured, "why are you like this?" His lips were quivering. "Can't you see that I should prefer to be your friend!"

She laughed again, and inwardly he shuddered. There was something inexorable about Gunevati; that soft and lovely creature had all the inexorable hardness of the world. But sometimes there was justice in inexorableness. And there was justice in Gunevati now. Only—she was also cruel; and she had the stupid persistency of a child.

"Why do you want me for a friend?" she asked. "Is it not enough for you to have the Brahmin as your friend?"

He felt that she was worsting him. He had not yet discovered whether she was on her way to or from the herb-woman; he had discovered nothing. But she, on the other hand, seemed to be playing with him, and he was becoming quite distraught.

By a great effort he steadied his voice. "You have often told me that you were longing to escape from Khanjo. I am sure that you have a plan for joining Prince Salim. And Mujatta has helped you to arrange it. Gunevati! Why won't you tell me the truth?"

Gunevati pursed her lips as if tempted to make a cutting reply. But the next moment she flung her scarf over her head; to his dismay he saw that she was making ready to move on.

"Wait! Gunevati, please wait!"

"Wait? What for?"

"I think—I think it is to-night—that you are going away?"

"To-night!" She smiled a little. "You seem to be in a great hurry to have the Brahmin all to yourself."

311

"I . . ." and he stopped, his voice failing him.

"How should a poor girl like me go and come as she pleases? Have I the money to do everything that I want?" And she shrugged.

"Gunevati!"

But, without paying heed, again she made as if to go upon her way; and her way—Jali's blood ran cold when he saw it—her way was back towards Gokal's house.

"Wait, Gunevati!" he called out in a suffocated voice. "O God! Why are you leaving me like this? Gunevati! why have you turned into an enemy?"

At last he had forgotten completely his previous designs against her. He was conscious of nothing but his appeal and her hardness. He rushed up and seized her by the arm. "Look, Gunevati," he cried. "Here is money! Take it! Take all you need!" He had drawn out his purse and was thrusting it upon her. "Take some money for your journey. You will need it, and I have plenty here. Can't you see now that I want only to help you? Why don't you speak? Why don't you say you understand?"

At the clutch of his hand on her arm Gunevati stood still, but in the look she turned upon him there was little comfort to be found. She seemed not surprised, nor vindictive, but simply unmoved. On the other hand the sudden appearance of the purse did, perceptibly, surprise her. She looked into his face, and then back at the purse—the purse that he had produced so unexpectedly. It was now dangling before her—almost like a bribe. The purse seemed to awaken a train of thought. But she made no movement to accept it; and after a few instants a change passed over her face, her eyebrows went up a little, and very quietly she drew herself away. Very quietly she moved away from him, but this time it was in the direction of Mujatta's hut.

10

UNTIL SHE HAD completely disappeared, Jali stood where he was, staring. Then he flung the purse on the ground, and, leaning his head against a tree, broke into painful sobs. He was finished. He could do no more. Although he retained the belief that, after all, Gunevati *was* going away, that thought failed to take any hold upon his mind, or to bring him the comfort it should. He was completely subjugated by a sense of weariness, humiliation, and defeat; his spirit lay in the dust.

An hour passed; and then he realized that he must hurry home. During this interval his brain had been empty; now he must apply himself to the business of turning back into the boy he was supposed to be. He must pick up again the threads of his home-life, that remote, trivial, happy existence which was supposed to be his only one. But, as he stumbled blindly along, another spell of sheer bewilderment overtook him. He became suddenly aware of the bird-songs and the sunlight and the sweet-scented air. Here all about him was a world of reality which he was living in and yet ignoring. What a contrast between it and the world of his secret preoccupations! This was the world his mother lived in, and wasn't it more real—this world of sunlight and serenity—than his own world of darkness and fear? With such force did this question grip him that he stopped for a few minutes in a frowning concentration of thought. Wasn't he perhaps becoming mad like those beggars one saw wandering along the road, muttering to themselves, with a far-away look in their eyes? Let him try to stand outside himself and examine his case sanely. It was like this: ever since Gunevati's arrival at Khanjo, he had sunk into greater and greater distress of mind; he had been oppressed by a gathering sense of entanglement and dire responsibility and helplessness, a sense of guilt and hidden danger. And this had gone on until, in the end, he had reached the hell where he now stood. But what had actually happened in the outside world to account for this inward change? Nothing, or practically nothing! And didn't this show that he was losing touch with reality? Didn't it prove that he was in the clutches of a nightmare? And couldn't he wake up from this nightmare and find happiness again?

These reflections, although they brought him to no conclusion, fortified him a little for the part he had to play, and after reaching home and spending an hour with his mother, he continued to argue with himself in the same vein. What could he point to in the actual visible world to prove that Gokal's life was, or had ever been, in jeopardy? Why! to assume just for the sake of argument that all his conjectures were well-grounded, didn't those very conjectures themselves now lead to the happy conclusion that Gunevati was on the eve of flight? And didn't this save Gokal from any possible danger?

In the afternoon he accompanied his mother to Gokal's house. It was curious that, although Gokal was the center of his agitations, the man himself had hardly occupied his thoughts. And now, as he walked along by his mother's side, he positively dreaded setting eyes upon him again. Nor was this dread ill-founded. As soon as they were all seated together in the veranda with the sun shining down through the hanging flowers of the convolvulus, and the talk flowing peacefully along—ah then! a dreadful anguish seized him; the tranquil security suggested by the outward aspect of things was altogether too poignant to be borne. But he managed, without betraying himself, to get up and stroll away.

Having turned the corner of the house, he stopped, and it was not long before his self-control came back. He had decided, before setting out, that he would make himself an opportunity to spy upon Gunevati, or even to pay a surreptitious visit to her room. So presently he dived into a tangle of shrubs and crept noiselessly along under them until he got to the back of the outhouse in which Gunevati was lodged. Her window was not so high up but that he could peep in; and at once his eyes fell upon the girl herself, who was bending intently over some small bits of paper which he recognized as the charms that he had written out for her in days that now seemed very far away. She was so engrossed in what she was doing that he was able to straighten himself up sufficiently to look farther into the room; and what he saw there made his heart leap for joy. On the ground beside the door two or three bundles were lying, and the room itself had been cleared of its customary litter. Without a doubt Gunevati was preparing for flight.

Breathless, his heart pounding against his ribs, he moved cautiously away, and a few minutes later he was once more on the veranda. Here, sitting upon the step at his mother's feet, he listened dreamily to the conversation going on above his head; he listened also to the humming of the bees and the sighing of the wind in the pines; and an ecstatic relief, a thankfulness deeper than any he had yet known, swept over his spirit. At last he felt convinced that all was well; he need not rack his brains any more, he could put away his anxiety. In a few hours Gunevati would be gone, and here was Gokal, serene and in good health! The dreadful nightmare had ended.

It was too much! Again he felt a hysterical emotion overwhelming him; he had to get up and go away. This time he ran wildly down the slope towards his own house, but before getting there he plunged into a thicket, sank down upon the ground, and let himself weep his fill.

An hour passed, an hour of exquisite relaxation; yet, empty as his mind was, towards the end of this time he became aware that there was a tiny flaw in his serenity. There was something that pressed upon his attention. It was like a small thorn, which, when his mind made certain movements, gave it a just perceptible prick.

He got up and walked home with a sober gait. Going straight to his room, he stood staring out of the window; suddenly he noticed that the brief minutes of his happiness had already come to an end. Secretly, as it were, and without his authorization, his brain had sprung into activity again; it was now working uneasily round and about the figure of Gunevati. Presently, as he walked up and down the room, he was lost in an obscure but powerful anxiety. And suddenly a vision sprang up before his eyes—a vision of Gunevati and the parting look she had swept over him, as he had stood there, poor wretch! offering his purse. She had looked at him strangely. Then she had gone back to Mujatta. He walked up and down. Beneath his knitted brows his eyes were fixed and staring. Gunevati had looked at the purse strangely, and—instead of going home—she had gone back to Mujatta. God! why wouldn't his brain leave him in peace! Why must it for ever torment him? He saw the truth plainly now! He saw it with deadly lucidity. Everything that he had done was a mistake. And his last and most fatal mistake had been the offering of that purse. Gunevati had guessed that the money had been intended for Mujatta; she had gone back to Mujatta to question her about it; and the two between them— heaven help him!—what conclusions would they not have reached?

Before this last mistake of his Gunevati might have been content to fly without taking her revenge; but, after this, flight alone would assuredly not satisfy her. How persistently she had harked back to his love of Gokal! Didn't she feel by instinct that this love was a measure of his detestation of *her*? Would she permit his hatred of her, his treachery towards her, to pass without punishment? Would she be content to take herself off, leaving him to unspoilt happiness with Gokal?

Jali staggered to his bed and let himself sink down. Perhaps he was exaggerating; perhaps his judgment was upset. Gunevati was rancorous, but she was also indolent. Not even in rancor was she likely to be consistent. Just now, as he had watched her through the window, she had been poring over those ridiculous charms of hers as if nothing else in the world were of consequence; she was probably trying to make some augury for the success of her journey. Wasn't it quite possible that after parting from him in the morning she had hardly troubled to give him a second thought?

And yet again, how could he tell? How could he hope to read the mind of so alien a creature? Oh, the mystery of human minds! Those secret engines at work on every side of one! Those secret centers of energy, manufacturing love and hate. Could one see into the depths of *any* human mind? No, even the simplest and friendliest had its core of coldness, darkness, and indifference, if not actual hostility. As for him, Jali, he was no better than any-one else.

What had Gunevati been thinking about as she sat in her room, packing up her scents and cosmetics, intent over her foolish charms, busy with a hundred small details of her private life? Was there any means of reckoning the likelihood of her possessing a little box of powder, a little vial, that had been slipped into her hand one day—perhaps weeks ago—by the vile Mujatta? Was she considering that little box now, as it lay half-hidden in her palm? Was she fingering it, and saying to herself: "Shall I? Wouldn't it just serve them both right?"

The day wore on; and Jali continued, of necessity, to play his double part. In his mother's presence his manner was as usual, but no matter whether he was with her or by himself, his secret tor-ment went on. As evening approached, there loomed up before him the menace of a critical hour, the hour of Gokal's evening meal, the hour of Gunevati's last opportunity. What could he do? Surely this last risk could be obviated?

As the light in the west began to turn golden, he slipped once more out of the house. Quietly and quickly his feet pattered along the path which was already growing dark under the ceiling of the trees. To think that it was only twelve hours ago that he had made his first expedition to Mujatta's hut! Twelve hours! And it might have been twelve years. Time had become without meaning to him. He was living in a present that was made timeless by its un-bearable intensity. Halting for a moment, he laid his hand upon a tree-trunk and turned his face to heaven. "O Brahm!" he suppli-cated. "Let there be a long peace before my next rebirth."

At last he arrived at the clearing. A cloudless evening sky looked down into it, and the trees all around were motionless walls of darkness. Mujatta's hut through the gloaming looked small, solitary, and mysterious. The ground in between, with its littering refuse, made him think of a deserted battle-field. White wisps of smoke drifted up from a hole in the roof.

Presently a figure, which he made sure was Mujatta's, appeared in the open doorway. For a moment longer he remained motionless under the trees. That solitary figure fascinated him. What were the thoughts that moved inside that skull? What was the meaning of that life—to itself? or to the world of which it formed a part? He drew a deep breath and stepped forward towards the hut; this time he was not going to fail; Mujatta should be made to feel that he was desperate; by threats, cajoleries, or bribes, he would arrive at the truth of what she knew.

As soon as he moved the woman caught sight of him: he could tell that from the sharp turn of her head. And having seen him, she stood still, waiting. He forced himself to come up close enough to look well into her face, which wore its habitual smile—a smile that expressed nothing except a vacuous, crafty eagerness.

"You see, I have come again," he articulated; and she nodded and clucked in answer. This second visit of his did not seem to surprise her, and she lost no time in launching forth upon a stream of meaningless flatteries.

He was ready to cut her short. Imitating the voice and manner of the usher at his father's court, he shouted into her face.

"Be silent, woman!"

Mujatta stopped; if not intimidated, she was at any rate somewhat taken aback.

Then Jali began. "I know everything!" he said. "I have been talking with Gunevati, and she has told me everything."

Mujatta was silent. For a few moments the two peered at one another through the dusk.

"Listen!" continued Jali, and he went on. There was no reason why she should hide anything from him any longer. He had seen Gunevati, he had watched her making her preparations; he was favorable to her flight. His reason for coming here now was that he feared lest she might be meditating some mischief before she went.

Having brought this out, he paused; and once again Mujatta let flow her senseless verbiage. And once again he shouted her down. Let her not dare to hide anything! Let her speak out, and speak the whole truth! Candor would be well rewarded, but should she hold anything back . . .

He stopped, suffocating, and now as he peered yet closer into the woman's face he suspected that he was failing again.

"Aie, aie, aie!" she cried with a great deal of ducking and mouthing. What was the little lord saying? What was this thing the young Maharajah wanted of her? Aie, aie! his words came so fast and furious that she was completely overwhelmed. What had she, poor old Mujatta—the Cockroach as they all called her—what had she to do with Gunevati? Gunevati was under the protection of the holy Brahmin. She was a grand lady now. She could not be expected to give her confidence to poor old Mujatta.

Shaking with rage, Jali interrupted, he had seen her visitor of the morning, and he knew well enough what the visitor's business was. By Shiva, unless she wished to die the death of a dog . . .

"Aie, aie, aie!" The shrill, hypocritical plaint rose above his voice, which, for all his blustering, was husky and weak. Aie, aie! the Lord Krishna have mercy upon her! Was the Maharajah angered with his slave?

Jali was almost speechless. What was the barrier between her intelligence and his? There seemed to be something hidden in her mind that took the meaning out of everything he could possibly say; she seemed to be cunning and stupid in a manner that he could not hope to comprehend.

"Listen, woman!" he cried. "I have told you that I have money with me, and I mean it. Look at this purse! The money is yours, if . . ." and he thrust the purse into her face.

Mujatta's expression changed; for the first time she looked greedy, and a new ray of hope sprang up in his heart.

"Money," he repeated. "Gold!"

"Aie, aie, little lord!" A greasy palm shot out. Let the bountiful Maharajah but give her a coin or two in token of good faith and she would lay her heart, her whole heart, bare before him.

"Have you ever sold poison to Gunevati?"

"Poison! By Shiva, never!"

"Listen! From here I am going to the holy Brahmin's house, and unless you succeed in convincing me . . ."

"Gracious lord! Gracious lord, I swear . . . !"

"Has Gunevati ever spoken to you of poison?"

"Never, beneficent lord! Never, never!" And, hastily stowing away the coins that he had shaken out, she extended her palm for more. "Just one more," she whined, "just one."

"Speak, devil!" gasped Jali.

She pushed her face into his and began to whisper. Just a few more coins and she would tell him all. For she knew everything, everything. Everyone confided in her. Gunevati had no secrets from her—oh, no! Why then, the very first week after her arrival, Gunevati had come into her hut and said . . .

Jali's hands were trembling; his whole body was trembling; clumsily he shook out more coins; he had nearly come to the bottom of his purse.

There was a pause; Mujatta was stowing away her money; it was obvious that her whole interest lay there. And then her hand went out yet once again.

The pause lengthened: both were silent; at last a sudden perception of the futility of his proceedings struck Jali like a blow in the face.

"Unless you speak," he said on a low voice, "I will kill you. Do you understand?"

The woman's countenance was beaming with triumphant satisfaction. "Aie, aie," the whine of thinly disguised falsity broke out afresh. Verily, the young Maharajah was to her as a god! Unworthy slave, what would she not do to show her gratitude! But when he asked her to tell him about Gunevati, what was she to say? Gunevati had come to her, in the first instance, to be cured of a wart on her foot. The holy Brahmin had said to her: "Go to the old woman and be cured of your wart." And so . . .

"The poison! You sold her poison!" whispered Jali dementedly.

The woman threw up her hands. "Young Maharajah! How should I come to possess poison?" and she glanced furtively over her shoulder towards the door of her hut.

Jali was beyond speech.

"Beneficent lord! Beneficent lord!" And still bowing and nodding and muttering in her usual style, Mujatta backed with uncanny speed towards the black doorway behind her.

A scream burst from Jali's throat. "Foul hag!" he cried. "Stop! I command you: stop!"

But she did not stop. With a frightened, yet triumphantly evil, glance over her shoulder she turned for a final scurry into her lair.

Another howl of rage and execration broke from Jali's throat, and, snatching up a stake from the ground, he rushed and struck at the woman's head with all the strength of his arm. The wood was half rotten and broke at the blow, but Mujatta fell in a heap. For a minute, while she lay there faintly moaning, he looked down at her, and even raised his arm to strike again. Then he threw the stick from him and moved a few steps away.

The woman was silent now. All was silent in the clearing, and over the whole forest. He looked around him. The sky overhead was dark blue and powdered with stars; the tall, straight trees stood without movement; a thin stream of white smoke still went up from the roof of the hut.

All at once he gathered himself together and began to run. He ran swiftly through the gloom of the forest in the direction of Gokal's house. All thought of Mujatta passed out of his mind. The hour of Gokal's evening meal was not far off—and he must be there.

The interval between his leaving the clearing and his arrival at the back of Gokal's yard seemed hardly to form a part of his waking life. He was vaguely conscious of bruising himself against an occasional tree-trunk, and once, on catching his foot in a root, he fell sprawling to the ground. When he reached the door of the yard his breath was coming in gasps and the sweat was pouring down his face. He looked cautiously in. Firelight shone upon the seamed countenance of the old cook who was squatting before his pans. Somebody was moving in the darkness at the back of the yard. Smoke from another fire, burning somewhere outside, showed that Gokal's servants were also preparing their meal. There was no sign of Gunevati; and the door of her house was shut.

Jali waited for a little in order to wipe his face and recover breath. His violent run through the wood had done him good; and the everyday tranquillity of the scene now before his eyes had the effect of further steadying him. He continued to stand there and watch. How conscientiously the old cook applied himself to the task. "What can I say to him?" he asked himself. "He will think me completely mad." A yellow firelight mingling with the afterglow of sunset and with the brightness of a rising moon, the smell of wood-smoke, murmuring voices out of the dusk,—these were things that he remembered from his earliest childhood; they were familiar and friendly and safe.

Slowly he moved across to the fire, taking care not to startle the old man, nor to step within the area of purified ground. The face lifted up to him was grave; and brief, though courteous, was the return made to his salutations. He stood by and waited; provided that you did not distract him, the cook would be willing to talk. And, sure enough, presently the old man launched forth upon one of his sententious discourses. The burden of it was that the valley of Khanjo and its inhabitants were accursed; thieves these people were and liars, and bearers of parasites—not innocent, like those at home, but poisoners, firing your blood with disease. Blessed would the day be when his master saw the wisdom of quitting this vile country of darkness, rains, plagues, and necromancers of the baser sort.

All this Jali had heard more than once before; and with all of it he heartily agreed. Now, however, he had his own word to put in; and as soon as a pause came he formally cleared his throat. "What you say, O Madhuradan, is true. But listen! for I have something to add thereto."

The cook lifted up his patient, wrinkled face; whereupon, looking deep into his eyes, Jali said:

"Although this valley does indeed contain enough evil in itself, your master—may he rest in Brahm!—imported evil into it."

So unexpected was this speech that several seconds went by before the cook made answer.

"Blessed is the moment when the eye of wisdom is opened," he murmured; and then, bowing his head, he went on: "The son of Rajah Amar has spoken out of the ancestral heart."

Jali was profoundly stirred. For a minute more he remained there in silence, then slipped away into the shadows and left the yard. The old man was, assuredly, shrewder than he believed him to be. Slow-minded he had always seemed, and garrulous and overflowing with facile emotion; but there was more in him than had appeared.

It was with a new sense of reassurance, a newly found calm, that Jali made his way back to his own house. But in point of fact his exhaustion was so great that he would hardly have been capable of any further emotion in any circumstances whatsoever. A little later, as he went to bed, he told himself that all was well; but he knew that he would have had to tell himself this in any case; for, in truth, he could do no more—he was at the end of his strength.

11

WHEN HE WOKE from his sleep, his waking was sudden and complete; his mind was perfectly clear, or so it seemed to him; and if he felt a certain bewilderment—that was simply because he could not make out what time of day it was. A few seconds later, however, he realized that the light in his room was not daylight at all, but very bright moonlight; and the next moment he heard the voices of men talking excitedly and understood that it was they who had woken him. In a single overwhelming rush his memories returned; and almost in the same instant he guessed what the situation was—Gokal had been poisoned after all: Gokal was dying or dead.

He lay quite still in his bed and listened. That voice with a sob in it was the voice of Gokal's cook. Weak and garrulous the old man now sounded, and his mother was sternly questioning and chiding him. Other agitated explanatory voices broke in; a group of Gokal's servants were talking to his mother through the window of her room. And the servants in the house were hurrying about in a turmoil. He heard someone being sent off to fetch the herb-woman, whose skill in medicine was accounted great. "I wonder if I killed her," thought Jali. The fact that she was being sent for showed that Gokal was not yet actually dead.

He lay in bed, very calm, resolved to pretend that he was

still asleep. His agonies were over; he noted it himself without surprise. At the back of his mind the same thought was repeating itself over and over again: "This is the end. I shall try to find Gunevati, and kill her. But in any case, this is the end."

For the time being all he had to do was to lie still and keep his eyes closed. He felt sure that his mother was making ready to go over to Gokal's house; and he had hopes that after looking in at him she would give the servants orders that he was not to be disturbed. Everything happened as he expected. Before very long his mother and the others moved off, and the house became quiet again. For a little longer he lay still, listening to the subdued but excited voices of the group, who were moving down the path that went across the valley. Then he got up and dressed himself. Taking his dagger to the window, he examined it carefully in the moonlight, and felt its edge. There was very little hope of finding Gunevati, he supposed; most likely she was already well on her way out of the valley; but all the same he was not going to let any chance slip by.

In these intentions there was certainly an element of make-believe; if his thoughts were concentrated on Gunevati to the exclusion of Gokal, it was because he was seeking to make revenge serve as a refuge from grief; in revenge, real or factitious, he could forget himself. Vengeance, then, was his inspiration and support, as presently he crept out of the house, dagger in hand, upon a quest that he liked to regard as murderous. Noiselessly he sped along the path that his mother and the others had taken a few minutes ago. The full, bright moon cast an air of unreality over everything. It made a new kind of day, an unearthly day, a day in which unearthly things could happen. This was the kind of day in which he would henceforth live; for him there should be no more accounting to humdrum reality. He was a new, mad Jali; he was raised above fatigue and fear, above all the everyday feelings of ordinary man. Turning his face up to the moon's enormous disc, he dazzled himself with its light, and drank deeper and deeper of the reckless indifference it instilled into him.

Before very long the lights of his mother's party appeared on the pathway in front. His pace had been much faster than theirs, and it would have been easy to join them. But instead of this he hung a few yards behind, dodging in and out of the shadows. It pleased him to follow thus, unseen, like a stalking beast, and he imagined himself springing out upon the hindmost man, stabbing him in the back, and vanishing into the bushes.

A little later, when the house came in sight, he left the path in order to work his way through the tangle of rhododendrons up to the back of Gunevati's hut. Again he looked in through the window, and this time, seeing that the room was empty, he swung himself in over the sill. The moon, full and round and red, was pouring its light into the room. He stood by the window, staring about him, his shadow lying in a black streak across the floor. Gunevati had gone; her bundles had gone; there was nothing left of her but a faint perfume in the air.

After a minute he went to the door, opened it a crack, and peeped into the yard. A group of Gokal's servants were gathered together outside the house, talking in tense undertones. He strained his ears to catch what they were saying; and presently one man raised his voice in his excitement, as he described how he had seen Gunevati walking away into the forest soon after nightfall. Well! said another contemptuously, there was nothing very unusual in that; and these words raised a brief, significant laugh.

Jali closed the door again, and suddenly a flood of anger swept over him. What fools people were! All this talk and excitement after the event! People never foresaw anything, were never on their guard against anything, and then they would lift hands and voices in idiotic consternation when disaster befell. It was because they did not really mind about anything. It seemed to him that he was the only person in the world who really minded things. Trembling with rage and despair, he swore to himself that he would mind no more. He would outdo the others in their shallowness, their irresponsibility, their gross indifference.

As he looked round the room, the idea came to him to make a search. Pulling open chests and cupboards, he examined everything that Gunevati had left behind and flung all her belongings in confusion on to the floor. What his object was he could hardly have explained; but a malevolent curiosity animated him; and perhaps he cherished the hope that he might come across something that would help him to bring retribution upon her. Forgetting that

326

the girl could neither read nor write, he searched particularly for letters or scraps of paper. When, however, he came upon the charms that he himself had copied out, he threw them away without a thought.

Having finished, he made a pause. He stood still in the middle of the disordered room and stared about him with a face of despair. What next? What could he do next to save himself from thought? The moon shone full into his face, and he stared at it wildly; again he tried to hypnotize himself with its brilliance; why couldn't he lose himself in the reality with which that flood of blue light was inundating the earth. "I must become mad or unconscious," he said to himself. "I must sleep. Why not sleep, and sleep, and sleep?"

With a sudden bound he ran forward, sprang through the window, and went tearing and fighting his way through the bushes down the slope. In a few minutes he was home again; and at once he threw off his clothes and flung himself upon the bed. "I will be ill," he thought. "I will have fever, delirium. I will lose myself somehow." Yes, he would rave, he would go mad; if necessary, he would die.

Towards morning, when his mother looked into the room, she found him tossing and moaning. To his secret astonishment and satisfaction, he was in truth feeling decidedly ill. He complained of high fever, and was given a cooling draught. A little later he fell into a doze, and when he woke he was sick. He told his mother that without a doubt he had been poisoned like Gokal. This fiction gave him great comfort; not long after, he sank into a profound sleep.

For the next few days he protested that he was ill and refused to rise from his bed. His mother informed him that Gokal had been made very ill by a dish of mushrooms, and had nearly died; but now he was making a good recovery. Jali received this news dreamily; and although he listened to her daily reports with deep attention, there was nothing to show that Gokal was much in his thoughts.

The truth was this: he had managed to transport himself in imagination far away from the hated valley of Khanjo. In dreams at night and in reveries by day he lived through scenes chosen from his earlier years; and, curiously enough, the memories that most pleasantly and incessantly haunted him were those of his journey with his father to the wet jungle-lands of the South. The dreams that took him back to those days were strangely ecstatic, they spread a haze of rapture over the daytime hours. One, in particular, recurring night after night in various patterns, had such an entrancing sweetness that he would lie still all through the day after it came pursuing—as though it were some floating scent or sound —the elusive delight with which it tantalized him.

This dream always opened with the same scene. It appeared to him that he had been traveling for many hours along a moist, green tunnel through the jungle, and was emerging at last into a small open space that was bathed in a pink flush of evening light. In front of him there rose a gray hillock of stone, a smooth gently curving mound of bare rock; and as he stood before it he could feel upon his face its heat, and upon his eyeballs its glare. The low sunlight, sweeping over the breathless jungle-top, struck full upon that ancient, naked slope, making it shine and roast; and nothing grew upon it but gray, leafless, twisted, yet virginal, temple-trees, their roots clutching the barren rock, their arms lifting snow-white blossoms into the air. Those trees were impassioned priest-esses,—priestesses crowning with a strange beauty and perfuming with the scent of paradise, this jungle-island that was either sacred or accursed.

A door, a little door, painted a dull red, stood before him in the slope of stone, and on one side of it was another smaller door leading into the chamber where the sacred cobras had once been housed. Gunevati was with him; it was she who told him this.

And now the dull red door was opened, and candles were lighted; and their flames, which were pale green in the sunlight, turned yellow as they were taken into the dark. Before going in he turned his eyes once more upon the crystalline blossoms of the temple-trees; and that crystalline whiteness, sun-gilt against the blue, brought Mary, Mother of God, into his mind. Yet the blue of the sky—hot, hot, beyond the thin, gray branches—was not the cool blue of Mary's robes; nor was the sun's gilt a pious gilt; nor were the white flowers faint-scented lilies, but blossoms so drugged by their own sweetness that they would drop, whilst yet unfaded, to the ground.

The dark closed about him like water, making him throw back his head and hold out his hands. At first he breathed and stepped gingerly, but the air, although heavy and sweet like a syrup, was without the smallest taint of staleness, and the floor was clean and smooth to his bare feet. Presently the guiding priests halted and when they held up their candles, he found himself in a broad chamber in the heart of the rock. Of the sun he could now see nothing more than a small rusty patch of light upon the stone of the distant doorway. But, although the sunlight was far away, this chamber was very hot. For, whether blazing in mid-heaven or sunk under the sea, the sun was here—here in this belly of rock, here in this womb of earth; here the sun reigned supreme—reigned in a darkness that was unutterably charged with its demonic energies.

By the glimmer of the candles Jali gazed upwards into the faces of the carven gods; and they, vacantly ferocious, glared and gnashed their teeth at the emptiness before them. Thus, century after century, in the stifling dark they had gnashed their teeth and glared. And Jali considered them thoughtfully, without derision and without fear; these symbols of godhead impressed him as both suitable and august.

Then his dream would change, and it would seem to him that he was stepping out into the cool night air. The priest who accompanied him was Gokal—but an older, fatter Gokal, a sardonic Gokal; this man it was who always locked up the small red door; then bowed low and disappeared. After this, exhausted and yet happy, he would drag himself up the flight of shallow steps cut in the gray rock-ground. Motionless and fragrant round him stood the temple-trees, their thin arms uplifted, offering white blossoms to the moonlight. In the east the sky was now green, with a copper-colored moon hanging behind the motionless fronds of a tall, distant palm. Low clouds rested upon the western horizon like huge crocodiles sleeping in a pool of blood. The moon, as she rose, played strangely with the wisps of jungle-vapor that were sailing over the green-black trees. Fruit-bats were dancing silently and madly in the middle air.

The daylong reveries induced by this dream had the allurements of sensuality and poetry combined; they tantalized Jali with a rapture that was both intimate and remote. The moments that he dwelt upon with special ecstasy were, first, that of his emergence from the jungle when the mysterious mound broke upon his sight; and then, the timeless period of his final contemplation, when, standing on the summit of the mound, he looked over the jungle darkening in the night.

During these days his attitude towards his mother was one of obstinate aloofness. He told her that he would never get well at Khanjo, and that it was necessary that the whole party should leave without delay. She answered that as soon as Gokal was well enough to travel, they would all set out together to join his father at Ravi; and she begged him to take his food properly and get up from his bed. But he refused; the most she could prevail on him to do was to recline in a hammock in front of the house.

This went on until the actual day of departure arrived. When that joyful morning came he was up at dawn and as active as any one could be. The start was made early, with the sunlight slanting through the dew-drenched rhododendrons and the birds still loudly singing. Jali was the first in the saddle, and there he sat, before the house, beside himself with eagerness to be off. Meanwhile the people of the village were gathering to see the cavalcade set out, and their presence added more than a touch of anxiety to his impatience. In particular he hated the sight of the herb-woman, who, ever since the night of Gokal's seizure, had been enjoying the glory of having saved the holy Brahmin's life. That vile creature was much in evidence now, for she actually had the impudence to stand forward from amongst the shivering, sullen-looking crowd and make great demonstrations of devotion and respect. Jali watched her with fear and rage.

At last Gokal's train arrived and the combined party was ready. Gokal had slept well and was in good spirits, he seemed to share the general view that this change was going to restore him to complete health. It was a supreme moment for Jali when the word was given to start. Riding on, he threw back his head, closed his eyes, and offered a prayer of ecstatic thankfulness to all known and unknown gods. Never had sunlight and bird-song seemed so exquisite to him as now; never before had life offered him such a moment of heartfelt rejoicing.

At the first turn of the road, when the detested spot was about to pass out of sight, he drew up in order to let the train go by. Although he scorned to breathe a parting malediction upon the evil little valley where he and his had suffered such ill, he vowed to himself that he would erase the memory of it from his mind for ever.

All day they rode along through the tall, dark trees, and after a while Jali realized that not until open ground was reached would he feel really safe. He looked at the straight trunks rising on either side and frowned at them in contemptuous distaste. Their ridiculous weight of sagging boughs was like the bedraggled plumage of a half-drowned fowl. And the little ice-cold brooks that ran across the path, the little mountain meadows with their starry flowers —they were one and all made in the same pattern of petty prettiness. Give him the dirt and broken potsherds outside a desert town! Yes, by Shiva, dung and potsherds on the desert, with the wind and sunlight streaming over them, they were pleasanter to him by far than the sweetest Alpine field!

The caravan moved slowly, its pace being set by Gokal's heavy palanquin, and it was accordingly not until the morning of the third day that open country was reached. When this happened Jali's sense of escape was complete, and every circumstance ministered to his delight. The weather was bright and warm, the party were all in good spirits, and Gokal, instead of being exhausted by the journey, was showing distinct signs of added strength. When at last the whole of the procession had come out on to the great rolling expanse of sunny turf, Jali sprang from his horse and began to dance madly about, shouting and behaving in a fashion so foreign to him that his mother came near to alarm. Then next, remounting in a flash, he galloped on ahead, guided his horse up to the summit of a knoll, and there stood gazing over the plains in a transport of joy. In his imagination he saw himself sliding like an eagle through the air; he was sliding down over the intervening hills to alight in the glorious heat and dust of the brown Indian plain.

From now on, after so many nerve-racking weeks, he dared to cast aside all care. Once every morning and afternoon he would ride ahead of the others, and so find time to pick berries and flowers, or stand and gaze his fill over the hills that sloped downward into the west. And always he would take with him the basket that contained his family of cat-bears and give them an airing on the grass. The past, he felt, was done with; in a few days Gokal would be well again, and then nothing would remain to remind him of evil times gone by. Everything in fact would be better than ever before—better because trials and dangers survived had changed the old Jali into another man.

It was in the first hours of a mild and sunny afternoon that the travelers reached the brow of the hill above Ravi, and here they found Amar waiting to welcome them, for he had been informed by a runner of their approach. Gokal's palanquin was put down, and as there was plenty of time to cover the last few miles of the journey, they called for an hour's halt. But the talk and the tea-drinking in prospect offered Jali no particular attractions, so presently he announced his intention of riding on by himself. As his horse picked its way carefully down the mountain path he sang out loud in his content. The warmth of the sun upon the slope brought out the scent of the thyme; bushy-tailed rock-rats were scuttling in and out of their holes; the lake glittering beneath him promised pleasures that he had always longed for, and never yet been able to enjoy.

Upon reaching the floor of the valley he found himself in a loose thicket of brier and blackthorn, the bushes of which were intertwined with raspberry canes covered with ripe fruit. About two hundred yards away the lake shone behind a fringe of alders and willows. Jali tied his horse up to a tree, and, before going down to the water, fell to eating the berries which had an unfamiliar but delicious taste.

12

IT WAS WHILE he was thus engaged that he received a shock of surprise, for all at once he heard his name called out from quite near. Starting round in bewilderment he beheld his cousin Ali, Hari's eldest son, stretched out at his ease under the shade of a tufted alder. How Ali came to be in this place he could not imagine. The last time he had seen him was at Fatehpur-Sikri, when Ali had been in attendance upon Makh Khan. Jali had not taken to him much at that time, for his cousin, who was seventeen, and older by nearly four years, had treated him with more patronage than he liked. But in the unexpectedness of this encounter his former impressions passed out of his mind, and he returned Ali's hail with a shout of astonished pleasure. The latter, without changing his position, smiled quietly as he ran up, his composure implying that he could hardly be expected to exhibit an equal excitement. No, Ali was not a young man that life could easily take aback. Not that he had the air of being conceited, nor even of possessing more self-assurance than one should at seventeen; but he did somehow convey the impression that he knew where he stood in the world; and there he took his place, ready to look anybody straight in the eyes, modest, amicable, but possibly just a trifle smug.

For a while the two boys exchanged questions, Jali chatting

quite eagerly; but of a sudden his eye caught the gleam of something white behind the screen of willows, and incontinently he broke off.

"Is that a sailing boat?" he asked.

"Yes. My boat."

Jali's eyes widened. He had a passion for sailing that he had never been able to indulge. There was something in the lean of a tall mast, and the bellying of a full sail, that gave him a thrill akin to his thrill from the desert.

"Perhaps you would like to have a look at the boat?" continued Ali, and with these words he rose and lazily brushed the leaves from his well-cut tunic. His face, his manners, his general deportment, were all beautifully of a piece.

Together they went down to the small creek, and there Jali beheld by far the most elegant little boat that he had ever seen. While he was staring, silent with admiration and envy, Ali examined the sky. "Not a breath!" he grumbled; "nor any chance of getting one. I shall have to row myself back."

Jali sighed profoundly. He had just been hearing that his cousin was now in Prince Daniyal's suite, having joined the Prince in his lake-encampment about three weeks ago. Compared with himself, Ali was an accomplished worldling; and here, staring him in the face, was one of the magnificent prizes the worldly life had to offer. The Prince had given Ali this boat for his very own; with several others it had been brought to the place overland, at immense cost, strapped to the back of an elephant. "I," thought Jali, "I shall have to rest content with one of the clumsy local craft."

Naturally, the talk went back to Prince Daniyal, and although Ali was not at all the man to boast, he did allow a few illuminating rays to fall upon his present course of life. Existence in Daniyal's circle was made to scintillate magically before Jali's eyes, and the sight of that boat converted him into a very respectful listener. However, even without the boat he would have been curious to hear anything that Ali could tell him about Daniyal. Half the ladies in the Agra Palace had been infatuated with the Prince despite the fact that not one in ten could boast of even a slight acquaintance. Lady Jagashri had been among the most ardent and at the same time one of the most favored, for the Prince on several occasions had thrown a smiling word in her direction. Jali remembered that even his aunt Srilata had confessed herself to be interested and amused by Daniyal; and for his aunt Jali cherished a deep, if somewhat puzzled, respect. Thus, although not attaching too much importance to what these ladies thought, Jali had become impressed with the fact that the Prince enjoyed a certain prestige over and above that conferred upon him by his rank; the Prince stood out in his mind as an intriguing personage; and now he thought it quite interesting, as well as not a little strange, to find Ali serving as a link. For the Prince was eminently artistic and intellectual, a patron of the Arts, whilst Ali had never seemed to have the smallest leaning in that direction. The Ali he knew was a promising polo-player, an enthusiastic sportsman, a youth whose good looks, good manners, and out-of-door aptitudes, commended him quite adequately without his needing to trouble about the things of the mind. It was very difficult to picture him as a member of the sophisticated company surrounding the brilliant young prince.

Before he had finished admiring the boat, however, his cousin laid a hand upon his arm. "We haven't much time left," he said, and his eye traveled to the mountain-slope down which the rest of Jali's party could be seen making their leisurely way. "And there are one or two things I ought perhaps to explain." On the "perhaps" he paused; he was giving his young friend a look as who should say: "To a man of the world not many more words would be necessary. Surely you can guess . . . ?"

But Jali could not guess; and, as he continued to show a blank face, Ali pursed his lips and went on. Had it not struck Jali as odd that he should have joined the Prince's retinue just at the time when the relations between the Prince and his father were rather strained, his father being actually under arrest, by the Prince's orders, at Agra?

Jali blushed and felt small. The thought *had* come into his head, but the sight of that marvelous boat had driven it out again. Besides, he always found it so hard to bear in mind that Hari Khan and Ali were father and son; they were so ridiculously unlike one another.

For a few moments his companion continued to fix him with a steady regard. That level look of Ali's was a noteworthy characteristic of him. It was not impolite, it was not appraising, it was certainly far from penetrating. It seemed merely to say: "See how steadily I can look you in the face." But there was, as Jali now understood, a particular point in that look at this moment, for Ali's position certainly was rather questionable.

Then the young man went on to explain. The betrothal of Makh Khan's daughter, Lalita, to Prince Daniyal had naturally brought the Khan and the Prince together, and equally naturally he, Ali, who was then in attendance on Makh Khan, had come under Daniyal's notice. His mother, too, was already a friend of the Prince's, and when the latter proposed that he should be transferred to his suite, she had had no reason for withholding her consent. For the quarrel, Jali must understand, between his father and the Prince, had not yet taken place—or at any rate she had not yet heard about it. And as for canceling the appointment afterwards—well, the Prince might very well have been the one to do that; but he had not done so. On the contrary he had been charming. And although he had felt obliged, as a matter of form, to keep Hari Khan under arrest for a little while longer, he certainly bore him no malice.

Here Ali paused; and, when he went on, his tone was more confidential. His father—God bless him!—was, as everyone knew, not an easy man to deal with; everyone knew, too, that his faults lay wholly on the surface. What a pity it was, then, that he had—well, such a confoundedly difficult character? Of course, having long ago given up all responsibility for his children, he had no right to object to his son's present appointment. He was not in a position to interfere. But—and here Ali sighed and gave a little laugh—with a man of that temperament you never could tell. So the situation was—a little delicate.

"Has he said nothing yet?" inquired Jali cautiously.

"He doesn't yet know," was the answer.

Jali, somewhat astonished, kept silence. For one thing, the way in which Ali spoke of his father seemed to him rather preposterous. He looked at Ali and then he thought of Hari Khan. Surely Ali was not quite of the stature to speak of Hari Khan in a tone of indulgent superiority.

His face must have reflected some part of these thoughts, for it was with a frown of rising impatience that Ali went on. The time was fast approaching, he said, when his father would be released from Agra, but it was unlikely that he would come back to this place; and, even if he did visit again the house on the other side of the lake, there was no reason why he should not still remain in ignorance of where his son was. Indeed, he undoubtedly would remain ignorant—unless some busybody were to inform him.

"I see," said Jali, who by this time had grasped what was expected of him. "I see," he repeated thoughtfully. "But," he blurted out after a pause, "but what about *my* father? Hasn't *he* found out yet that you are here?"

Ali shook his head. "Your father has only visited the camp once since I arrived, and then—well, I kept out of his way. He knows nothing."

Again Ali's eyes were making it very plain that he was finding his cousin difficult to deal with, different from a true man of the world. With an effort Jali pulled himself together: after all, Ali's affairs were no business of his; Ali's self-importance was insufferable; what on earth did it matter where Ali was? Ali could go to the devil. Having reached this conclusion, he raised his eyes and said simply that he understood. "I won't mention your name at all," he added.

The other's face at once became serene again. "The longer the time that goes by," he observed complacently, "the more difficult my father will find it to raise difficulties or to make an unpleasant scene. As I began by saying, the situation is really rather a delicate one; it calls for tact; I am glad I have made you see that."

This, evidently, was meant as a compliment; and a little later, when they were taking leave of one another, Ali gave expression to his amiability by suggesting that they should meet again. Why should they not meet next time upon the waters of the lake? Jali could easily step across from one boat into the other, and then he could test the *Eaglet*'s sailing powers for himself.

During the next few days Jali was busy examining his new surroundings, and when his mind turned to Ali it was merely to think of him as the possessor of the most beautiful boat in the world. The old Rajah's house and garden were quite unlike anything he had ever seen before; the house struck him as astonishingly ugly and odd; even the garden he considered rather ugly; but

337

in spite of this he was far from disliking the place. The atmosphere here was completely different from that of Khanjo; and if the house itself was without beauty, the valley and the lake amply made up for it. The lake was pale in color, an opalescent sheet of water that melted into an air that was often slightly misty. Nearly every day the sun was reflected upon it, as a pale, distant disc, a moon-like sun that floated quiveringly upon its smooth milky waters. Almost at once Jali became fond of the valley, the friendliness of which encouraged him in the belief that here Gokal would quickly regain his strength.

His hired boat, when it arrived, was of course not to be compared with Ali's. On the first morning that he took it out there were several of Daniyal's fairy craft scudding about under little flaws of wind; and he wondered if his cousin's was among them. It was to be hoped that Ali would prove to be nicer and more interesting than he had seemed to be at Fatehpur-Sikri. "Perhaps," he thought, "I was too young to see the best of him then. God knows that I have altered since! And, maybe, Ali has altered too." But when he considered their last meeting he felt dubious. The tone in which Ali had spoken of Hari Khan stuck in his mind as having been ludicrously smug. But then—he might have seen this before! Ali's voice had not, of course, been his own; it had been merely an echo of the world's voice; for the world, which considered Ali a very promising young man, did, sure enough, regard Hari Khan as an eccentric. Ali was obviously much more adaptable than his father. Look at the way in which he had picked up the manners and fashions of the Court! "But that is just what I don't like about him," thought Jali, and then he corrected himself by saying: "I suppose I am jealous. Anyhow, I have no right to think of Ali as a fool; he succeeds where I should certainly fail."

It was in no very sanguine spirit that he set out that morning to search for his cousin on the lake. Nevertheless the meeting, which took place almost at once, went off unexpectedly well. He made the astonishing discovery that Ali was not only quite agreeable, but also most interesting to talk to. Yes, it was extraordinary! It showed you how little you could tell. Ali was intensely engrossed in literature and art; he displayed a familiarity with the books, pictures, and music of the day that made one positively blush for one's ignorance. Moreover, the audacity of his opinions was often startling.

Jali went home very much impressed and not a little exhilarated. Here were new vistas opening before him, and this just at a time when his young intelligence was eager for a fresh kind of adventure. For too long already he had been suffering from over-tension of the spirit. The time had come for him to throw off material cares, to enjoy, in complete detachment from practical life, the enthusiasms proper to adolescence—enthusiasms which, whether wise or foolish, are as different from those of childhood as from those of maturity. Hitherto, although far from insensitive to beauty, he had not approached the Arts with any independence of mind. Hitherto life itself had absorbed him; life and the meaning of life had been problems instant and all-engrossing; the difficult business of living had allowed him no freedom, no self-confidence, no ambition to attend to superfluities or cultivate the luxuries of the spirit. Docile in accepting the aesthetic judgments of others, it had never occurred to him to consider whether he had a personal taste of his own; and of the pleasures of heresy, of the glories to be found in revolt, he was, of course, even more profoundly unaware.

Ali was soon to bring about a change. Ali, who had formerly seemed so wooden, so conventional, such a blockhead, now appeared as an angel of intellectual freedom and light. With the prestige and brilliance of the Camp behind him, his lightest word carried weight. Listening, Jali felt that he was listening to the voice of Prince Daniyal himself. And could anything be more exciting than that? Not for anyone in Jali's present case; not for anyone living in this neighborhood, where the Camp attracted your attention all the time. Every day some new rumor of the Prince's doings spread round the valley; every day you saw some new building springing up, or heard about some new marvel that was being imported from the outside world. That extraordinary community of Daniyal's, the Camp—the Pleasance of the Arts, as it was called—shimmering at you from the other side of the lake, at once so conspicuous, so provocative, and so far removed—it was the talk not only of Ali but of all the servants, of the fishermen, everyone. Even his father and mother discussed Daniyal—in a vein of persiflage, it was true; but that, Jali knew, was the tone people often used to disguise more serious consideration.

Ali's tone in describing the brilliant society in which he now moved was naturally quite different. He had no wish to pretend that his admiration for the Prince was not overwhelming. Daniyal, in his judgment, was almost a god. With this, however, he was anxious to make it clear that his head was not in the least turned by Daniyal's worldly greatness; his admiration was not for the Imperial Prince, nor for the Darling of Society, but for the Poet, the Artist, the enraptured Lover of Beauty.

Jali was in no mood to question or dissent. He read feverishly all the books that his cousin lent to him—books that were in vogue in the Camp. He vied with Ali in composing verses in the manner favored by the Camp; he theorized with Ali by the hour. All this was exciting in a new and delightful way. He lost the sense of being a helpless child. At a time when he was actually becoming more puerile every day, he gloried in an expanding sense of sophistication.

13

IN THIS NEW phase of his existence, Jali succeeded in putting his past miseries out of mind, or rather he thought of them only in so far as they added to his newly found self-esteem. This they did by reminding him that he was a person of experience and suffering. Of Gokal, the unwitting cause of his suffering, he still saw very little; and, although his feelings for his former teacher remained unchanged, he did not wish, for the time being, to be in his company, nor even to give him much thought. The truth was, of course, that his spirit needed relaxation, and was eagerly going forth to its new interests on the other side of the lake. Most of his time he now spent on the water in the company of Ali, and a splendid holiday this was. How delightful to escape from one's self and the tyranny of things that really mattered. But didn't art, then, really matter? Were art and literature less important than the miserable cares of our material life? Certainly not! They mattered infinitely more, he would have told you; but, fortunately, in another way; impersonally, instead of personally, pleasantly instead of unpleasantly. Oh, the glorious freedom of the mind, when (as Ali said), casting off from dreary actuality, it spreads sail to the winds of the imagination, and steers for Perfect Beauty. This was the voyage upon which Prince Daniyal was set, and his inspired crew!

It was not long before Ali had to draw rather heavily upon the prestige that came from being a member of this crew. If, as sometimes happened, he said something that sounded quite incredibly foolish, there was nothing for Jali to do but pass over the remark in silence and suppose that he had not properly understood. And yet, and yet, in after days he was never willing to admit to himself that he had been completely taken in. Somewhere at the back of his mind his earliest impressions of Ali had—oh, most certainly!— still lingered. His first astonishment at finding Ali admitted into the Prince's circle had never been completely wiped out—not even by that marvelous self-assurance of Ali's, not even by that casual omniscience, nor the unfailing up-to-dateness of his information. Even in these early days his strongest argument in favor of Ali was apt to run like this: unless Ali really was what he pretended to be, one found oneself obliged to regard him as an almost unimaginable compound of fool and impostor. And if in very truth he was just that, how on earth was his presence in the Camp to be accounted for? These questions were unanswerable; and, outwardly at least, Ali's pontificate remained unquestioned. But a growing impatience provoked by his heavy patronage stimulated Jali's impious doubts. A certain common sense, too, was ingrained in him; he refused to believe that the Camp was as silly in its ideas as Ali frequently made out. According to Ali, for instance, the Camp taught that thinking for oneself consisted in nothing more than in reversing established opinions, that the newest thing was necessarily superior to one that came before, and that the ultimate test of the worth of an idea was its capacity to startle the Philistine and annoy him. If Ali was to be believed, there was no independence in the Camp; the Camp had its own inverted orthodoxy, and was as bigoted as any of the old schools; opinions changed often, but always unanimously; they changed, as fashions change, on the stroke of the bell.

So Ali's prestige began to go down, and presently a fresh and still more damaging light was thrown upon him. One day, as the two boys were sailing idly along, Ali (who liked to recount in much detail his conversations with distinguished personages) opened out with the remark that he had just been having a singularly interesting discussion on Persian prosody with a lady who was perhaps the most brilliant and fascinating of all the women in the Camp.

"And who might that be?" asked Jali.

"Lady Jagashri," returned Ali complacently.

For a few moments, after hearing this, Jali found himself bereft of speech. That Lady Jagashri should be among the Prince's chosen guests was past all conceiving, and so was the notion that she and Ali had been talking solemnly together about Persian prosody. His silence was so full of astonishment and confusion that Ali, anxious though he was to get on with his discourse, paused to give him a smile. "It almost looks as if you knew her?" he observed shrewdly.

Jali, reddening still further, murmured something about having seen the Ranee once or twice in the Agra Palace. His companion, after eyeing him teasingly, laughed. "Pretty, isn't she?" was his comment; and with a flow of banter he made it plain that he could guess well enough what had happened: Jali had conceived a small boy's romantic passion for the lady and worshiped her from afar. Well, she certainly was pretty enough! But to go back to Persian prosody. . . .

While he was holding forth Jali struggled to restore order in his mind. It appeared that Ranee Jagashri had already been in the Camp for two or three weeks, and that she and Ali had made great friends. Ali and Jagashri friends! And discussing Persian prosody together! What on earth did it mean? Jagashri—Heaven help her!— was completely brainless, and to his certain knowledge her true tastes did not lie in the direction of literature. If he was sure of anything he was sure of that. At Agra, in her attempts to ingratiate herself with Daniyal, she had incurred a good deal of ridicule. Was he to believe that both her intelligence and her character had become quite different since then? As he gazed at his companion, he pondered. Ali, after having finished with Persian prosody, was returning to his jocular vein. It was his habit to show himself off as a man of the world now and then, and on these occasions he would speak of women with a certain license, as a man who regards sex as *une bagatelle*. He liked to show Jali that he could joke on the subject; but he would always draw himself up in good time out of regard for his young cousin's tender years. On this occasion, whilst listening to Ali's pleasantries, Jali was thinking hard. Could it really be true that during the last three weeks the handsome Ali had seen nothing better to do with this very pretty little Ranee than to talk literature with her? And had he really considered her conversation worth listening to? It was nothing short of incredible, and yet—there it was!

In the course of the next twenty-four hours Jali gave the matter still further thought. What was he to make of Ali, if his worldly pretensions turned out to be as hollow as his literary ones? What was he to make of those competent and disabused airs of his? Was Ali's manner, in its whole range from modest self-assurance to lofty superciliousness, simply a façade of fraud? It seemed as if it must be so; but then what was Ali doing in the Camp? Was it conceivable that he and Ranee Jagashri succeeded in taking in that sophisticated community? And, if not, what did the Camp see in them?

A few days after this, as he and Ali were cruising about together on the lake, the latter made a very startling proposal: he offered to take him for a visit to the Camp. Never had this suggested itself to Jali before even as a possibility; and it was astonishing to hear this invitation thrown out as if it were the most ordinary thing in the world. Casualness of manner in Ali, however, was no sure sign of absence of premeditation; so Jali, although he demurred at first out of sheer timidity, soon allowed himself to be overborne. The boat was accordingly brought round, and Jali was still far from having recovered from his attack of nervousness when he found himself actually arriving before Daniyal's glittering water-front.

From a distance the Pleasance of the Arts had always looked singularly attractive; and now, on a nearer view, it seemed to Jali that the caprices of Daniyal's taste had justified themselves completely. The effect produced was that of a stage scene—a scene that would suit a gay performance of marionettes. Yes, it was a setting for creatures, half doll, half god, the exquisite descendants of the figures he had often seen upon rude stages at village fairs. There, in those simple surroundings, it was old legends and fairy stories that were enacted; but the living actors upon a stage such as this would fitly be illustrating tales of an elegant and sophisticated frivolity. It was the frivolous character of the Camp's informing spirit which at once captivated and slightly astonished him, for Ali's talk of Daniyal's revolutionary ardors had prepared him for something more earnest and severe. But this *mise-en-scène* was charming, and he at once accepted it. With the memory of Akbar's conventional magnificences in his mind, especially did he enjoy the absence of the over-ornate, the avoidance of cloying richness, the rejection of even the most time-consecrated commonplaces of design. Newly in love with the new, he was unwilling to reject any of Daniyal's novelties, if he could possibly help it. A novel silliness, springing up in protest against an old silliness, was surely the better of the two? Besides, one was entitled to suppose that it had amused the Prince, here and there, to make fun of his own innovations; he credited Daniyal with quite enough humor for that.

From the landing-stage Ali conducted him down a wooden promenade that ran along the lake-front. The whole of the Camp, in fact, was built on a platform that stood in part over the water and in part over the marshy ground behind. All the gaieties of a popular pleasure-resort were to be found here, but they had all been slightly parodied and, as it were, denatured, to suit a subtler taste. Music was sounding in the air; a bright-looking throng were strolling or sitting about; some, under fantastically decorated awnings, were drinking snow-cooled beverages, some were watching jugglers and mountebanks, many were flocking to an arena where combats between various kinds of wild animals, including even snakes, had been announced. Everyone wore the brightest and most daring costumes; so much so, that on his arrival, Jali had imagined that some mask or carnival must be in progress; but Ali took satisfaction in informing him that these gaieties were of everyday occurrence, and that it was not until after midnight that the true revelries began.

Thus, from astonishment to astonishment Jali wandered on, until presently, in an open place, which formed the heart of Daniyal's architectural design, he stopped, wonder-struck, before a flight of fancy, which, by its very childishness, fascinated him more than anything else. It was a group of six trees in the center of the square. But what unbelievable trees they were! They were golden—trunks, branches, leaves, all had the glister of gold. And in these trees were perched Daniyal's silvered doves, and amongst them were scarlet macaws, green parakeets, pink and green parrots and cockatoos, and two or three pelicans of a snowy whiteness.

Ali, who was thoroughly enjoying himself, took the entranced Jali by the arm and led him up to the nearest tree; each one of the leaves he showed him was artificial, and attached to its twig by wire. The trees themselves were as dead as the planking into which they were fixed! Moreover, the whole square, Jali next had to observe, was in fact built over a piece of the lake; and down one side of it there ran an imitation canal, showing a frontage of houses designed by an Italian architect in the Venetian style. It was all marvelous indeed; and not less marvelous, now that he found time to examine them in more detail, were the human beings for whom this *mise-en-scène* had been provided. What dresses! What jewels! What brilliance of lip and luster of eye! Who were they, what were they, these doll-like, artificial creatures? In some cases you couldn't even tell whether they were men or women! To give an answer to the question in Jali's silent, roving stare his guide complacently explained that here, in the Pleasance of the Arts, everyone was, so to speak, *somebody*. Here you might come across people of every variety—except one, the commonplace. Dull, conventional people—people who weren't lit by the divine spark, had no chance of gaining admission here. Daniyal had thrown away the shackles of ordinary prejudices and cant. Originality of mind, intellectual merit, poetic fire, these alone counted with him; and on this basis all were equal. Here you might meet Princes of the most ancient line hobnobbing with poets, acrobats, and artists. Much, however, as Daniyal honored superiority of the mind, he was not—you could see it for yourself! —an intellectual snob. Pedantry bored him; he liked to be amused; the art which he recognized as Art had to be for ever young and new and gay.

Jali nodded, listened, stared, and was so dazed by the diversity of his impressions that his feet stumbled as he went along. Some of the things his companion said did, occasionally, send a ripple of impatience over his wonder; some of the sights he was shown he could not in strict honesty admire. But these little points of dissidence were quickly submerged under the general flood of his enthusiasm and excitement. What a wonder and a marvel life might be turned into! How necessary was revolt, revolt against old-established prejudices, dull custom, and, above all, the bullying, nagging, disposition of Nature! In artificiality the spirit found its true life. It was proper that a light self-intoxication should carry you along like thistle-down upon the wind. Jali felt ashamed as he reflected how pitifully he had allowed Nature to tyrannize over him up to this date.

With a hundred half-finished thoughts of this kind in his head, he was quite unable to make of himself a satisfactory companion. At first his hebetude had gratified Ali, but by this time he was beginning to find it tiresome. So, after walking his speechless friend about for a little while longer, he took him down to the lake-side, and put him into a boat. On his side, Jali was nothing loath; it was a relief to him to be alone with his excitement. Wonder and enthusiasm held him spellbound, as he sat in the stern with his eyes fixed upon the receding shore. His enthusiasm became, indeed, almost devotional in character, while he gazed and gazed across the glassy water into the falling shadows of the hills. Against those misty blues and greens the Camp, like a carven moonstone, shone palely in a subdued light of its own. Pink and yellow, orange and violet, the paper lanterns made dim dots of color on a frontage that was otherwise spectrally faint. In the midst of Nature's wilderness the Pleasance of the Arts lay perfect and complete, a little paradise of artifice and art, a small gem-like thought in an unthinking world.

14

FROM THIS DAY forward Jali was overflowing with an ardor for some cause that he could not clearly define; although Daniyal stood forth as the champion of it, and the Camp was its visible embodiment. As for Ali he preferred not to think about him, nor to grant him any significance. Regarded as a satellite of Daniyal's, one had to suppose that he was revolving in a very undistinguished outer orbit. Ali's conversation, which he had once found so stimulating, he now felt to be pretentious and silly. He couldn't do away with the sense that however daring Ali might be in his opinions, at heart—unknown to himself—he remained conventional and a prig. The satisfaction of holding advanced views was quite lost when an Ali was sharing them with you. There was little glory in being in the van, if an Ali was marching by your side. Sometimes, indeed, in order to avoid finding himself in agreement with his cousin he would stifle an opinion of the most enticing originality and deliberately support in its stead one that Gokal, or even his father, might not have disowned.

In his further visits to the Camp, which now followed as a matter of course, it was not long before he made the acquaintance of a good many of Ali's friends, young men of about the same age, good-looking and superciliously urbane. They disappointed him because he could not find in any one of them an ardor matching his own. Like Ali they were one and all wedded to the Arts; but their minds, unfortunately, were, one and all, like Ali's too. He found it just as difficult to account for them as for Ali; in fact, the community as a whole was presenting him with more puzzles every day. The small doubts and uneasinesses that he hoped would disappear, still dogged his admiration of the Prince. Yet there must be, he felt, a recondite intellectual position, from which, once you reached it, everything would be seen to fall into place. Those features of the Camp which, so far, had refused to look other than willfully silly, vulgar, or trivial, would then be seen to be not really amiss, or at the worst, aberrations of no importance. After all, was it to be expected of any band of spiritual adventurers pressing forward into new territory that they should follow no false trails, or never lose their way? Thus, in a spirit faithful but still inquiring, Jali continued to seek for more light. To his discomfiture, however, he found that as often as he screwed up his courage to question, he was met with a cold stare. Ali and his friends were shocked. Was he, their looks asked, after all, a Philistine at heart? It almost looked as if he had no right to be in the Pleasance of the Arts at all.

During this time he did his best to avoid meeting Ranee Jagashri, but in spite of all his precautions one or two meetings did occur, and each one was more unpleasant than the last. An obscure instinct had warned him, it was true, against expecting any great show of cordiality on her part, but he had not prepared himself for a manner so exceedingly uncivil. Why was it that, whilst putting on her friendliest airs for Ali, she treated him to the most crushing snubs? Time and again he had to sit by—looking, and indeed feeling, like a small sulky boy—whilst she and Ali talked art and literature above his head. Their absurd airs of connoisseurship made him inwardly fume with rage. Well! he would say to himself afterwards, although the ambitious Ranee had succeeded in worming her way into Daniyal's company, the fact that she still considered Ali good enough to talk to was clear proof that she had not penetrated very far. Ali and Ranee Jagashri made him feel bitter, but his bitterness did not spring wholly, nor even chiefly, from pique. It pained him to think of Daniyal as surrounded by people of such little worth. Why did the Prince tolerate this scum, this fringe of frothy second-rateness? Wasn't it rather hard on his genuine admirers that they should have to stand in the midst of such a crowd? It was not that he, personally, had any wish or ambition to approach closer to Daniyal; he would have felt terribly out of place anywhere near the center of that glittering company; but sometimes he was taken with a longing that the elect should know that he was with them in spirit; he would have liked them to be aware that there was one by whom their gay and gallant pursuit of beauty was really and truly appreciated, one who veritably understood where others only pretended to understand.

Then came the day when he had a great experience: he actually exchanged words with the Prince himself. It happened in a newly erected picture gallery where the Camp's first exhibition of paintings was taking place. Ali, who, like everyone else in the Camp, was as great an amateur of pictures as of books and music, was kindly showing him round, and as they were standing together in the big, nearly empty room, suddenly an arm descended across Ali's shoulders, and a friendly hand came down at the same time upon his own arm. He looked round, and there was Daniyal himself! He was staring up into the handsome, smiling countenance of the master of the Camp. It was an overwhelming moment; indeed, the whole experience would have been overwhelming in the last degree; had not Daniyal's easy, reassuring manner quickly taken the edge off his alarm. Actually he was able to recover himself, more or less, even in the short breathing-space allowed him, whilst Ali was explaining who he was. In these moments, too, he had an opportunity of observing what charming manners his cousin had when addressing those who were his elders and superiors. His diffidence expressed itself winningly, with a flush and a hesitancy that broke up the heaviness of his habitual exterior. But Jali's attention was really fixed on Daniyal. It seemed to him that for a moment after his name had been pronounced, the Prince's countenance took on the blankness that masks a rapid movement of thought. The next instant, however, that face recovered all its former liveliness. "I see! I see!" said the Prince laughingly. "So you are the son of Rajah Amar, and the cousin of my beloved Ali! You are staying in that deliciously quaint old house on the other side of the lake! Dear me, how amusing!"

Jali could not understand exactly what the Prince found amusing, and had no idea what to reply; but Daniyal saved him by going on. "What responsibilities I am shouldering, to be sure! What sins I have taken on my head! Here is Ali living with me without his father's knowledge! And now you—you visit me on the sly. What would your father say to it, my dearest child? Are you sure that he quite approves of me?" Daniyal's eyes, which were light blue, were dancing, and it seemed to Jali that they must have some quality of Akbar's, which he had heard described as "vibrant as the sea in sunshine."

"Tell me, Ali!" the Prince continued, swinging round. "Tell me what kind of a boy is this little cousin of yours? Is he as demure as he looks, or will he be getting into trouble here? With those great brown eyes of his . . . I shouldn't wonder. . . ."

He was now fixing a half-mocking, half-questioning gaze on Jali, and the meaning behind it was not easy to make out. Daniyal's manners bewildered Jali; if they had quickly dissipated his awe, they had put a peculiar discomfort in its place. The Prince, he felt, was *over*-mannered, and his elegance far from patrician. But these impressions were fugitive. He was too confused to hold fast to them, and afterwards it was the Prince's amiability alone that occupied his mind. After all, here, in his private retreat, Daniyal might well be permitted to throw stiffness and formality aside.

"I have something to tell you," said the Prince, once more addressing Ali. "Your father has been released, and I should not be at all surprised if he were already on his way back here." He paused and gave a little laugh. "Does that trouble you, my dear? I see no reason why it should."

Ali had flushed, but he made all haste to agree, and the next instant Daniyal turned to the picture before which they happened to be standing. Eagerly, enthusiastically, he began pointing out its merits, and Jali tried hard to listen to what he was saying, although, in truth, it was the man and not the picture that interested him. How, he was wondering, how could one ever tell what a man like the Prince was really thinking about? The only thing you could be sure of was that he had a lot of things in his mind at the same time. For instance, even now, while he was talking and while his fingers were hovering expressively over the picture, you could see his eyes wandering about the room. His tongue might be busy with one thing, and his eyes with another, and his brain would be attending to half a dozen matters as well.

With abruptness Daniyal came to a stop, and his gaze swept over Jali absently. "Visit the Pleasance of the Arts as often as you like, my dear! As Ali's friend you were welcome before, and now you are welcome on your own account."

These were his last words to Jali; but before going he bent down to Ali's ear in order to whisper something that was for him alone. While that murmur went on his arm was round the boy's shoulders again, and then, giving him a parting squeeze, he strolled off to his waiting attendants.

This meeting with the Prince had an unforeseen result. The next day Jali learnt that he was the recipient of a signal favor: the Prince invited him to be present at the opening of the great wooden theater that was by far the most important building in the Camp. The occasion was to be celebrated by the first performance of a burlesque composed by the Prince himself. Jali was amazed, enormously flattered, and not a little alarmed. The slightly distasteful elements in his recent impression of Daniyal were entirely wiped out of his mind. For some weeks past he had been nursing a secret project which he now felt encouraged to carry out. This was to present to the Prince, with a suitable dedication, a small collection of verses that he had recently composed.

The intervening days were made feverish by his anticipations. From morning to night he was absorbed in polishing his verses and dreaming of the great occasion. If he had any reasons for feeling uncertain whether the play would be of superlative merit, he put this possibility entirely out of mind. It was not until the day and the hour had actually arrived that a sudden access of nervousness seized him. Shrinkingly he took his place in the great hall amongst Ali and his friends; the bright artificial light, the hot scented atmosphere, the color and glitter of the bejeweled assembly, these stirred him to an excitement that was made painful by misgivings. It was a relief when the lights were extinguished, and the play began. Apart from a few poems and a few paragraphs of prose, the world had seen nothing of the Prince's own work as yet; this burlesque stood out as his most ambitious venture.

Ten minutes went by; and then Jali took his eyes off the stage and lifted them anxiously to Ali's face. How was Ali feeling? Was he satisfied? Was there really nothing wrong? Assuredly not! His friend's fixed complacent smile was completely reassuring. Good! With a sigh of restored confidence he turned his attention once more to the scene.

Another ten minutes elapsed, and now again he sent a glance at his companion. It encountered the same smug smile upon Ali's face; yes! Ali's eyes remained fastened upon the stage, and his expression was still one of fixed and inane gratification. But this time Jali was not satisfied; he frowned, and turned anxiously to examine the other people near him. Their expressions resembled Ali's; they all wore the same mask-like smile. But, said Jali, to himself, this is horrible! This is like some evil dream. Setting his teeth, he once more gave ear to the play; clearly there must be something in the performance that he was missing, there must be another angle of vision, there must be some subtle twist of the intelligence upon itself, which, once achieved, revealed this string of seeming vulgarities and ineptitudes as something else, as something utterly different.

Poor Jali! He waited, he struggled; but it was of no avail. His case was hopeless. He was beyond all help. In this large, glittering congregation of the elect he was an outsider, he stood lamentably and degradedly alone. What seemed to him to be spiteful, tasteless, and pretentious beyond all words—this very thing was being received by others with every mark of amusement and pleasure. What, then, became of his faith in a shared enthusiasm? What of his belief that he and these people were linked together by a common understanding? What of his splendid ideas for a youthful and regenerated art? And, above all, what became of Daniyal as a leader?

Well, he had made a mistake! But—what a tremendous mistake! Its magnitude so confused him that for the moment he could feel little more than blank consternation. For the first time in his life it was being given to him to view the full breadth of the gulf by which our human nature can be sundered in its estimate of what is pleasant and admirable in this world. His experience of the women in the Agra Palace had been no preparation, nor even his commerce with Gunevati. The Palace women had been trained in a different convention, and as for Gunevati, she belonged to a different natural order. But here, in this vast hall, were gathered together people that he had been led to regard as creatures belonging to his own kind—nay, he had been disposed to consider them superior, a chosen few, a little band, who, already first in the order of the world, preferred to put away pride of rank in order to labor in the open field of art. What did it all mean? His bewilderment was as ingenuous as it was complete. He was innocent of any idea of passing a moral or aesthetic judgment; there was no taint of arrogance, nor even undue self-confidence, in his condemnation of that which, seemingly, was good enough to win the approval of those who should know better than he. He was merely responding after the law of his own nature: other stomachs might accept this fare, but his rejected it. Daniyal's intentions—he saw that well enough —were satirical; but it seemed to him that personal ridicule, when addressed by young men in the Prince's position to those who were obscure and unpretentious, needed, to say the least of it, a great deal more humor and literary skill than Daniyal had at his command. And when, on the other hand, famous characters in religious history were taken by the Prince as his butts, a reverse, but equally unfortunate, disproportion between the satirist and his victims stood out. The objects of Daniyal's mockery then, indeed, appeared wholly out of his reach; they towered above him like Colossi carved in the face of a cliff; no attempt of his to belittle them could possibly result in damage to anyone but himself.

Had the performance been specially designed to prove to the Prince's young admirer that he had been an arrant fool, it could hardly have been bettered; and as the performance dragged on, he became more and more distressed, in particular by a sense of humiliation. And yet why, he asked himself, why should he blush and glow and sweat in such a furnace of shame, when he was in no wise responsible for anything he was seeing or hearing? Finally, he resorted to the expedient of keeping his eyes tight shut and repeating poetry to himself, or working out sums in his head.

The end came at last, and he stumbled out at Ali's heels, too dispirited to care what his cousin was thinking or what he himself would be expected to say. With Ali at his side he walked dismally down the gaily beflagged street, waiting with sardonic indifference for the inevitable flow of praise. He was let off more easily than he had expected. Ali was by nature cautious. A suspicion that the play had not quite come up to the general expectation had filtered into his brain, and he had decided to hold his hand until the Camp's verdict had been pronounced. So he confined himself for the time being to playful comments upon minor points. Had Jali noticed this? Had he appreciated that? Hadn't he been more than a little scandalized now and then? Really Daniyal was dreadful at times! When he gave rein to his delicious flippancy, there was no telling what might not slip out! But of this one could always be certain: nothing could come from him that was not redeemed by wit, by savage irony, by mordant satire.

By now they had reached the lake-side and Jali looked desperately round for his boat. It was being rowed in; but a few minutes would have to elapse before it could reach the pier. In a dream he heard Ali's complacent voice going on. The play, Ali considered, had been no food for babes. Strong meat it emphatically was. But then Daniyal knew that he was addressing a select audience. "What did you think of his Lakshmi?" he asked suddenly.

"Lakshmi?"

"Yes. The girl who played Lakshmi in those last scenes. Did you ever see a more marvelous figure?"

He was now being the man of the world, and Jali knew the proper, bashful response. He admitted that Lakshmi's figure had seemed to him very good.

"For a long time," Ali went on, "Daniyal could not find anyone fitted for the part. Face and figure, you see, had to be perfect—absolutely perfect. And then this girl, Gunevati, turned up out of the blue. It was a great stroke of luck."

Jali moved sharply back; he felt as if Ali had dealt him a blow in the midriff.

"Gunevati, did you say? Did you say the name was Gunevati?"

"Yes, Gunevati."

Jali was silent for a few moments; he kept his face turned away; then—"Gunevati is a common name," he mumbled. "Where—where did you say the girl came from?"

Ali shrugged. "Heaven knows!"

"What is she like?"

"Like?—Well, you could see for yourself."

Jali groaned faintly. "She didn't speak, surely? I didn't hear her voice."

His companion stared at him with impatience.

"Naturally. She hadn't a speaking part. I am talking of the girl who was carried in, naked, on the golden lotus-leaf. I think you must have been asleep."

Jali had no reply. The boat was there, and his one idea was to escape. Hurriedly he bade his companion good-bye, and took his seat in the stern. Again it was a windless evening, the lake was like a sheet of glass; and while his two men plied their oars, he looked back, his eyes fixed upon the receding shore.

All at once he started to his feet and nearly fell overboard; he bade the rowers stop.

"I want you to take me back," he brought out in a strangled voice. "I find I have forgotten something."

The boat returned and he sprang on to the pier. "Wait for me here," he said. "I shall not be long."

15

IT WAS SHE: there was no mistake. A few moments after he had reached the door at the back of the theater, she stepped out, and he had to hide himself hastily among the loitering crowd. The sight of her set up a trembling in all his limbs; he peeped from behind men's shoulders, and then drew back, and then peeped again. In God's name, what did it mean, her presence here? He was aghast, feeling himself confronted with the workings of some agency supernatural and malign.

She went away with a group of her friends, all gaily chattering. He followed them with his eyes down the street until they were lost to view. The crowd was dispersing, and with an effort he pulled himself out of his daze. Furtively, by back-alleys, he hurried down again to the lake-side. The things that had been happening to him that day seemed to form no part of real life; on one level his mind was alert, and yet he was also lost in a dream.

There was a wonderful luminousness and tranquillity on the water over which he was presently gliding, and he was reminded of the evening upon which he had been rowed home from Daniyal's Camp for the first time. The little lanterns on the dusky shore were glowing with the same tints of orange, violet, and green; there was the same mildness in the air; and the rowlocks made the same monotonous creak as his two rowers bent to their stroke.

Presently, too, as before, strains of music came traveling over the water; and that evening and this mingled still more closely in his wondering thoughts. The mystery of time and human destinies overwhelmed him.

But beneath the level of this dreaminess his mind, without doubt, was the scene of a great activity. Just as the temporary extinguishment of lights at a play covers a rapid alteration of the stage, so, one must suppose, his present dreaminess was not without its purpose. A change in his mental landscape had to be effected; he had to accommodate himself to a new conception of Prince Daniyal and his Camp. While his eyes were still resting absently upon the lake, while parts of his mind floated detached in the mild evening air, there passed, at the back of his consciousness, a procession of disquieting images. Ali and his complacent young friends, Daniyal and his sleek ornate audience, the lady Jagashri, and now Gunevati—what a strange collection they made! By what law had they come together? They must, he imagined, have something in common, apart from being in his opinion one and all detestable. Again and again, in blank bewilderment, his mind returned to the apparition of Gunevati. If she had gained in mysteriousness, the Camp had gained no less.

His boat touched the opposite shore; automatically he jumped out, and began to walk up to the house. The sky was now starry, the earth quite dark, and falling dews had put a chill into the air. Of a sudden it came over him that he had been living in a state of foolish intoxication ever since his arrival at Ravi, and that now at least he was making a return to the real. But why must reality be so drab, why must it cast such a chill? And why was he obliged to come back to it? Was there no means by which one could maintain oneself in dreams? A flash of memory took him back to his hours of madness on the night of Gokal's poisoning, those strange hours when he had been drunken with blue moonlight and fantastic ideas of revenge. But no! he knew of course that it was impossible to keep one's madness up.

He sighed, and, halting for a moment on the path, looked long and steadily at the yellow lights of the house shining down at him through the garden trees. Standing there, he experienced another change of heart. His love, his true respect, for the human beings on this side of the lake seemed to him to offer something trustworthy and admirable amidst all the shifting sands of the world. Why should he ever visit the Camp again? Why ever? The Camp was odious to him; he would give it up, he would bury his memories of it, just as he had buried his memories of Khanjo. But before this idea had fairly taken hold of his mind, he turned and cast his eyes backwards over the water. The lights on the far shore were twinkling behind a thin veil of mist, and while he looked at them, the voice of a secret knowledge told him that he would certainly go back. Fear clutched at his heart; he felt himself coerced.

For the next two or three days he never went out on the water at all, and during this period his uncertainties and indecisions left him not a moment of peace. If he had to go back, where would he find the patience to bear with Ali, or to suffer Ranee Jagashri's snubs? And if—if it really was his intention to seek out Gunevati —where, in God's name, would he find the courage for the ordeal? If this was yielding to temptation, how unattractive temptation could be! The more he pondered the less he could understand himself; for it would not satisfy him to put everything down to the instinct of curiosity. What was curiosity? Wasn't it the very energy of thought? Wasn't it even the very energy of life? Even animals were curious; and perhaps plants too. Certainly if a man were to lose his curiosity entirely he would very soon fade away into death.

By this time he was willing to admit to himself that what drew him most powerfully of all to the Camp was his desire to solve the mystery of Gunevati's apparition there. And he also argued that this curiosity was not idle, since it was his duty to investigate the girl's present disposition, and find out whether she was likely to work mischief with her tongue. Since she had it in her power to do harm to both Gokal and Hari, it was greatly to be hoped that her wholesome respect for Mabun Das persisted.

This train of thought, by which he sought to justify himself, did not, however, succeed very well in its object, for it inevitably suggested another and a more effective line of action. Why didn't he make a confession to his uncle Hari? The latter had just returned; and his presence in the house made Jali dislike more than ever being involved in a conspiracy of silence with Ali. Up till now he had done his best to excuse himself in his own eyes by nourishing a

personal grievance against his uncle. Never had Hari followed up
the offer of friendship which had seemed to be implicit in his attitude on his first night in Agra: Hari had shown neglectfulness and
indifference. Then, too, there was the question of Hari's relations
with his mother: that raised the same barrier as before.

But wouldn't it, he now asked, wouldn't it be very wrong of
him to leave Hari in ignorance of Gunevati's presence in the
Camp? He put himself this question over and over again; but always shirked a plain answer. If he realized that he was no judge
of the situation, he also realized that it would be impracticable
to tell Hari a part, instead of the whole, of his story; so that actually the first syllable of his confession would be as critical and momentous as a dislodged pebble that starts an avalanche. Deep in
his heart he suspected that the information he was withholding
might have very wide bearings; but that suspicion he was going to
ignore. Affairs "public" or "political" were no concern of his; he
didn't understand them. For him the question was simply one between himself and his own people, a question of personal relations. Was he in duty bound to open the eyes of Hari and his
parents to facts and conditions which they had no excuse for not
apprehending for themselves?

At Khanjo the idea had gradually formed itself in his mind that
human beings, one and all, lived in fictitious worlds which they
arranged to suit their comfort. (Since then he had seen this truth
exemplified in himself; for hadn't he, during all these past weeks,
deceived himself with regard to Gokal's health? Hadn't he persuaded himself that Gokal was gaining strength every day, whereas
in reality he was making no progress at all?) It was like this: just as
the veining on a slab of marble in your bathroom might be seen by
you for years as making a picture of a man on horseback, and then
one day would appear instead just like a flock of birds on the wing;
so, any day, something might happen inside you (or a slight jolt
might come from outside) that would completely change your
view of your whole situation in the world. And it was your duty,
when that happened, to examine the new pattern, not to push it
hastily out of mind. Well, none of the people he knew seemed ever
to be willing to do this. His father and mother, Hari, Gokal—he
saw them all living in blinkers, and this spectacle had brought

him, in the end, into a state of cold, contemptuous rage. Let calamity befall! he now said. Those who chose the pleasures of ignorance must accept its dangers as well.

It was in this spirit that he finally made up his mind not to confess. He would go back to the Camp instead, and keep watch as best he could. Surely he had learnt something since his days at Khanjo? Surely he would make a better match for Gunevati now?

This was a vainglorious mood, but when he bethought him of his earlier vows that Gunevati should be made to pay for her iniquity, shame stabbed him to the quick. He realized that his anger had lost its effective heat; he regarded her now with wonder and repulsion, but dispassionately. She, Ali, Jagashri, and the others, they had taught him that human beings are not what you begin by thinking they are; it was a mistake to regard them as naturally guided by reason and goodwill. No, no! they were incalculable; in fact they were monsters. But—could one honestly say that there wasn't something rather fine in being a monster? Even nice people probably had a monstrous side without knowing it. And perhaps— this came suddenly into his head—perhaps each one of those monsters, even Gunevati, looked upon itself as a kindly-disposed, reasonable creature, and marveled at the monstrousness of others. Very likely he, Jali, ranked as a veritable monster in the estimation of someone!

To his surprise he began to discover in himself a vein of admiration for Gunevati's monstrousness. The gratuitousness of her evildoing endowed it with a certain magnificence. And most of her modes of thinking and feeling might be seen—by those with an eye for such curiosities—as marked by a similar lurid distinction. She was interesting with an interestingness which his own type, the type governed by moral fastidiousness, by sensitiveness, by generosity, must of necessity lack. Regretfully he recognized this, and his sense of loyalty to his own kind, although not diminished, was slightly dimmed.

It was curious that while his intention to seek out Gunevati was gradually gaining strength, he made no attempt to prepare himself for the actual event. Sometimes, indeed, in his reveries he would conjure up pictures of the meeting, but these were always absurdly fanciful. He would imagine himself admonishing the girl with such fire that at last, humble and repentant, she would throw herself on the ground at his feet. Very rarely did he call to mind how gay and serene she had actually looked as she was stepping out of the theater door.

His first move, he decided, must be to seek out Ali, although unfortunately it was improbable that Ali would be very well informed. When Ali took interest in a woman it was not on account of her beauty; and when he expressed admiration for a woman's beauty, it was really her social position that he was thinking about. He had an eye for very inconspicuous charms when rank and fashion set them off; but to beauty unadorned he appeared singularly indifferent.

It was accordingly with a good deal of anticipatory impatience that Jali went to look for his friend on the lake; especially as he foresaw that Ali would be overflowing with talk about the Prince's play. He was right; but he should have accounted it a mercy that he was not called upon to go into ecstasies himself. In point of fact the badness of the play (quite apart from its vulgarity) had been glaring enough to throw the Camp into a predicament, and they were making the best of it by telling one another that, although lacking in the finish which the hand of a practiced playwright would have given it, its sheer brilliance carried it off. Ali was at pains to explain this; and, thought Jali, never in his life before had he been so wordy and dull. It was in vain that he tried to bring the conversation round to Gunevati; Ali invariably dismissed her with some brief, supercilious jocularity. The temptation was great to let something drop that would startle his companion out of his tedious course; but good sense just prevailed.

For an hour they sailed up and down the lake, Jali becoming more and more impatient all the time. He would have suggested landing at the Camp, had he seen how, upon getting there, he was to shake Ali off. The wiser course would unquestionably be to wait until the next day, when he could visit the Camp by himself. He was still hesitating, when the decision was made for him, Ali declaring that the wind was too light to make sailing amusing and that they might as well go ashore. So ashore they went, and Jali presently found himself strolling at Ali's side without any idea what to do next. Indeed, a kind of mental paralysis had seized him, rendering him quite incapable of coherent thought. Automatically, however, he was steering his companion towards the western quarter of the Camp where Gunevati was most likely to be found. The painstaking Ali was still discoursing on Daniyal's play; clearly he was determined to make it perfectly plain to his young cousin (although he could not say it in so many words) that the Prince's admirers were far from being disappointed.

By this time the condition of Jali's nerves was such that, whenever the trend of Ali's speech reached him, he could not help grinding his teeth. His presentiment that he was about to meet with Gunevati was becoming more and more overpowering with each step he took; nor was he blind to the desirability of saying something to prepare his companion for the occurrence. At length with a ghastly sprightliness he managed to articulate: "I wonder if we shall run across that girl Gunevati; I happen to have met her once or twice before. In fact I—I—" At this point words failed him; but it made no difference, because Ali was not listening. Either his voice was too weak and uncertain, or Ali was too much wrapped up in his theme; anyhow, his pitiable sentences went unheard.

Their stroll was bringing them to the outskirts of the Camp. On their left the lake glittered and rippled, overhead the sun shone bright; a scattering of bungalows ran along among the alders and willows, with here and there a tea-garden gay with the lively youth of both sexes who ministered to the artistic diversions of the community. Here—Jali felt sure of it!—Gunevati would presently be found. His eyes roved about wildly: that pink dress over there—was that she? No!—but what about this other girl under the tree? or that one with her back turned? "Perhaps," he thought, "I shall catch sight of her before she sees me, and then there will still be time to swerve aside and escape. But why—why am I coming here at all? And what, in God's name, am I to do with this accursed Ali?"

His consciousness of folly deepened until the expected shock came. At last in that array of strange faces there appeared a face that he knew. Moreover Gunevati had the advantage: she first had seen and recognized him. Now—could he believe it?—she was actually sending him the friendliest of signals. She was smiling, she had jumped to her feet! This complete absence of embarrassment on her part deprived him of his last shreds of self-possession; from this moment onwards he was a creature dazed. In a dream he saw Gunevati leave the two girls between whom she had been sitting and run down through the tea-garden to where he and Ali stood. And the next moment he was responding—sheepishly to be sure, but still not otherwise than friendly—to her greetings, which were those of an old friend. There was no insincerity in her either; not only was she without the smallest trace of a guilty conscience, but her pleasure at seeing him was obviously genuine. So complete was his disarray that for a few moments he even lost sight of the fact that Ali was standing by his side; it was Gunevati who reminded him of it by throwing beguiling glances in this young man's direction. Hastily he murmured an introduction, and as he did so, he noticed that his cousin was not by any means less taken aback than he had expected. Ali, in fact, was stiff and staring, his fresh complexion was showing a vivid scarlet.

Events moved rapidly. Before either he or Ali found time to realize what they were doing, still less to demur, they were incorporated in the tea-party under the trees. They were seated on mats laid on the close-cropped grass, with small porcelain cups in front of them, and the chatter of three young girls buzzing in their ears. Jali was gazing at Gunevati, wonder-struck; and the longer he looked at her the greater was his stupefaction. Never before had he seen her so animated, so full of the joy of health and life. There was no pretense in it at all; nor did he even need to wonder over the warmth of her welcome; she was happy, and therefore ready—out of the abundance of her self-content—to give any familiar face an equally joyous greeting.

While she and her companions chattered on, busy with the tea-things, busy at the game of making themselves as charming as they could, Jali managed to recollect himself a little, and it was with dismay that he surveyed the extent of the ground he had already lost. His prepared positions (if he ever had had any) were gone, never to be regained. And this had happened without his putting up any fight at all! Whatever the proper tone with Gunevati might have been, never, never, after this, would he be able to assume it. As he stared at her, he couldn't help asking himself whether the situation was really what he thought it; wasn't it possible that Gunevati was innocent? Mightn't Gokal's poisoning have been accidental after all?

These doubts were transitory; he couldn't but discard them. Wasn't it significant enough in itself that the girl made not a single inquiry after Gokal? No reference to the past fell from her lips. Nor did she even ask him about himself; and from this he concluded that she was already aware of everything; she knew perfectly well that he and his family and Gokal were now living together on the other side of the lake. Rather strangely, too, she seemed to know all about Ali, although she had never met him before. She and the two girls with her had unmistakably taken an interest in him from the first; their manner towards him showed that they were delighted to be making his acquaintance. Surely Ali should have felt this to be flattering? surely it should have put him at his ease? But it did not. Ali, that man of the world, was making it lamentably obvious that he was quite out of his element. He was gauche, he remained—even after his first surprise was over—inordinately stiff and uncomfortable. Was he in terror lest any of his smart friends should see him in this company? That hardly seemed likely, for smart people did not come this way. No, it looked as if he were simply suffering from shyness—and suffering excessively, for he didn't yet dare to look his amiable hostess in the face. This was bad; for unless Ali soon managed to become better pleased with himself, an enduring rancor would result. It was necessary, therefore, to do one's best to help him to appear to better advantage; and this Jali strove to do; but no doubt he was clumsy, and no doubt mortification and anger were making Ali unusually perceptive; at any rate he soon saw what his young cousin was up to, and became in consequence more self-conscious and more envenomed.

From now on Jali was entirely taken up with his concern about Ali; and this concern developed into a nervous dread of the consequences that might result from his having brought Ali and Gunevati together. Of a truth it was highly unlikely that Ali would seek to improve his acquaintance with a person of Gunevati's social standing; but Gunevati on her side might quite well take the initiative; and was Ali the man to resist persistent blandishments?

Unhappy and bemused, Jali now lost all power of speech. In a condition of helpless passivity he continued to sit in his place, whilst the light rapid chatter of the three girls flew backwards and forwards over his and Ali's heads. And then, all at once, almost as suddenly and disconcertingly as it had begun, the tea-party came to an end. Everything in a moment became flutter and confusion. With shrieks of dismay the girls recollected that they had a re-hearsal to attend. Yes, actually! and when Daniyal himself was to be present, they had forgotten it! and now they were going to be late! So there was a scramble, a whirlwind of flowered muslins, and before their two guests had fully grasped what everything was about, they found themselves alone.

Most uncomfortable was the stillness that followed. Whilst they were getting ready for their own departure, Jali was hard put to it not to appear sheepish, and Ali was visibly struggling to re-cover his habitual manners that had so completely deserted him. His conversation in the meantime was most inauspiciously polite; it made Jali feel sure that sooner or later he would have to suffer the full weight of his accumulated wrath. Before taking leave of him on the pier, he could not refrain from muttering a few words of self-exculpation and apology. It was a mistake. Ali's brows dark-ened into a scowl, nevertheless he was quick to declare that their little adventure had amused him beyond all measure. Oh, he wouldn't have missed it for anything in the world!

16

IT WAS AN anxious and discouraged Jali that stepped back into the boat. But as soon as he was by himself again, and able to see things in better perspective, his predominating sentiment was one of outrage. The callousness and frivolity illustrated by Gunevati at every turn disgusted him beyond measure. On his way back across the lake so bitter was the rage that gathered within him that hot tears sprang into his eyes. Not once had Gunevati given a sign— not even by a look or a silence—that her wickedness was weighing upon her conscience. Had she no sentiment even of curiosity about Gokal? Had she no wish for direct news of him? He searched his memory in vain for a single sign that she was waiting for some future opportunity to talk to him alone. There had been nothing in her manner to suggest it; on the contrary, he had distinctly received the impression that her friendliness was conditional upon his agreeing that the past should be buried. And he, for his part, had appeared to accept these terms—yes, and without demur! Rage at his own tameness was mingled with his detestation of her, and a longing to punish her sprang up once more in his heart.

Yet, when he asked himself how, in the circumstances, he could have behaved differently, no answer was forthcoming. Nor did further reflection prove of any avail; its only result was to damp his fury down into a smoldering bitterness. He couldn't help seeing Gunevati's callousness and frivolity as the natural outcome of her overflowing health and happiness. She was thus constituted; her moral nature was thus conditioned. And could he, in all honesty, regard her as very singular in this respect? If health and happiness normally bred indifference to others, it was a pity; but these qualities possessed a remarkable power of self-justification no matter how they were manifested. Thus, whilst feeling outraged, he also was conscious of a check. He could not allow his moral indignation all the freedom and exuberance it craved, and a descent into more sober thinking was the result.

Surveying his recent actions, he had to admit that they had done nothing but add to his perplexities. If, in his foolish day-dreams, he had ever cherished the notion that he might bring home to Gunevati some sense of her iniquity, that illusion had received its death-blow; nor did it seem likely that the watch and guard that he proposed to keep over her, was going to prove very effective. The Camp had already wrought a considerable change in her. To describe that change superficially, one might say that she had taken on the Camp manner. And this manner, the meretriciousness of which was not too conspicuous in those to whom it came naturally, displayed itself at its worst in Gunevati and her friends. No degree of awkwardness or constraint could have been less attractive than the gay unself-consciousness that the three girls at the tea-party had been so proud to flaunt. How much better it was, he reflected, to be lacking in self-assurance than to possess it without sufficient justification! With her new airs Gunevati unconsciously parodied the affectations of the smart, and to his surprise Jali found persons as apparently unlike one another as his virtuous aunt Ambissa and the flighty Ranee Jagashri, brought together in his purview as creatures spiritually akin. In aping her social superiors Gunevati betrayed them much more damagingly than herself.

Then, too, with her new manner and her new assurance she had picked up a veneer of sophistication; and one could see that she was very pleased with herself on this account. The fumes of the Camp had gone to her head like wine, and it made Jali grow hot with shame to recall how recently he had been in the same case. Thank God, he was sober enough now! Heaven be his witness, that folly was left behind.

Well then! Seeing that further visits to the Camp promised him neither profit nor pleasure, would it not be reasonable to stop going there? To this the answer was, unfortunately, that his curiosity was too strong to allow him any choice; he would go back because he must.

When next he set out it was with the firm intention of avoiding his cousin at all costs; and he accordingly ordered his boatmen to take an indirect course across the lake and to land him at the pier that was farthest removed from the one Ali habitually used. When he thought of Ali, when he conjured up a picture of that young man's steady eyes, well-chiseled lips, and general air of modest self-esteem, he felt an uncontrollable surge of exasperation and contempt. His nerves, that day, were tightly stretched; he knew it; he had keyed himself up for a talk with Gunevati, and was determined to weigh his every word. But he was without confidence in himself. In the past he had always done badly; was he likely to do any better now? Already he had weakly allowed her to determine the footing upon which they were to meet. The truth was that he had no capacity for dealing with Gunevati, or Ali, or anyone else; the world had to be fought with its own weapons, and these were not yet in his armory.

Sunk in gloomy thoughts he stepped out of his boat on to the pier, and, lifting abstracted eyes, the first object that met his gaze was Ali, who was leaning against a post and watching him with a faint smile. No choice was left but to approach, whereupon Ali at once inquired what had made him choose this particular pier. The encounter was unfortunate, nor did this opening promise well. Ali seemed to have his mind made up, he fell into step at his young cousin's side, and they had not gone many yards together before battle was joined. He had chosen for his subject "those tea-shop friends of yours," and he very soon showed that he had prepared a great many slighting things to say. A disdainful amusement curled his lips as he spoke, and he made careful choice of his words. To have such "poor, tawdry creatures" as friends argued, he feared, a certain lack of taste; but no doubt it was just as well that some people should be less fastidious than others. The thing that chiefly troubled him was Jali's extreme youth and inexperience; no doubt he prided himself on being an extremely precocious young rake, but in his, Ali's eyes, he looked merely foolish. How in the world had he made these lamentable acquaintances? Or, to put it a little differently, where exactly had Gunevati picked him up?

"I met her in Agra!"

"In the Agra Palace? I suppose she was in the service of one of the ladies there?"

Jali looked down and said nothing; he was hoping that his silence would pass as an assent. But his companion was disposed to be suspicious. "I warn you," he said peremptorily, "you had better answer me."

"Oh? Why?"

"Because, unless you make a clean breast of it, I shall have to take steps. . . ."

At this Jali laughed; and had he been content with that, all might have been well: what "steps" could Ali possibly take? But he was boiling with rage, and Ali's curiosity offered him his chance. He set about teasing his questioner with hints and partial disclosures, and then, when he saw that nothing could annoy him more than the naked truth, he looked Ali mockingly in the face and made a bare-faced avowal.

The result far exceeded his expectations. Ali gasped and was still. For a minute or two they walked on together in complete silence, and then Jali began to feel nervous. Glancing furtively upwards, he observed that Ali's face was pale, very pale; his eyes were blinking, his lips quivering, altogether his looks suggested that he might be on the verge of some seizure. At this, consternation fell upon Jali; the violence of his companion's emotions completely bewildered him; they were extraordinary, abnormal in fact. He felt that they revealed a great deal—but what? He could not imagine.

At last, in a husky voice, Ali resumed speech, and now matters moved forward with great rapidity. An exchange of insults took place in regular schoolboy style, the climax being reached when Jali, in reply to something particularly offensive, declared that always, from the very first, he had looked upon Ali as a prig, a snob, and a bore.

On this they parted. Ali's fist was tightly clenched for a blow, but a lingering and perhaps mistaken regard for decorum restrained him, so he merely turned on his heel and walked away. Jali, too, moved off in another direction; he was pale and trembling, but strangely elated withal.

After going blindly along for some minutes he stopped in the shade of a little open pavilion fronting the lake. Hardly had he sat down, before a band of musicians struck up a lively tune not far behind. These strains were far from agreeable to him, but he remained where he was. As a matter of fact, it was by no means easy, in the Pleasance of the Arts, to escape from the sound of music, just as, on certain days, you could not escape from a sweet, sickly smell that hung over the whole place. This smell came from the marsh over which the flimsy structure of the Camp had been erected. Both smell and music were present to Jali's senses now, and hardly less unpleasant to him was the glare thrown up from the sunny lake. But these small physical discomforts were noticed by him only as exaggerations of the wide mental discomfort by which he was possessed. It seemed to him, as he sat there, that the Camp, taking it all in all, was a place of garish nightmare. And the fact that it wasn't impressively dreadful made it all the worse. He wasn't yet prepared to say that it was as horrible as Khanjo, but—well, he hadn't done with the Camp yet; and who could tell?

The brief elation of combat had completely died out of him, and he was soon lost in painful endeavors to give shape to his formless fears. Without doubt he had made a bitter enemy of Ali, and it wasn't pleasant to recall the violence of Ali's rage. That rage had seemed positively maniacal in its intensity. It had revealed something dark and unintelligible. Hitherto he had imagined in his conceit that he could read Ali like an open book, but now he saw Ali joining Gunevati in the ranks of those whom he termed "monsters."

And then his thoughts wandered to the others that knew—to the Ranee Jagashri, and those strange young friends of Ali's, who seemed to have none of the pressure of life behind them, no speculation, no ambition, no zeal of any kind (unless you could count as zeal their pre-occupation with Art, which seemed to be rather presupposed than expressed in the elegant nonchalance of their lives)—none of these people did anything to redeem the community, or even to make it more intelligible, in his eyes. As he looked out over the lake towards his grandfather's house, a longing to fly back to it seized him. Safety and goodness lay over there. But he could not, it seemed, embrace the good single-heartedly—no, not yet! He must first taste other experiences, so that, when he did reject the world, it should be with the disdain bred of complete knowledge and competence. Before embracing the good, he must be assured that he was doing it out of knowledge and strength. Or was this quibbling? If he was now justified in his present course, why should he feel such shame? When he looked back at his association with Ali, a wave of humiliation passed over him. His truck with Ali and the Camp already seemed to him more ignominious than his truck with Gunevati and Mujatta. Why was this? He could not make it out.

No not quite! But, as he examined his heart, he realized something more. It was his very sense of the Camp's sinisterness that bound him to it. He was drawn here in order to watch, and circumvent, and even propitiate, the malign powers that might otherwise do him harm. This was at the bottom of his present anxiety to find Gunevati and discover the state of her feelings towards him and his friends. His recent quarrel with Ali had sharpened this anxiety; he was actually possessed by a ridiculous fear lest he should find Gunevati and Ali already together; and it was the prick of this fear that now made him get up and begin walking hurriedly in the direction of the tea-garden. When, from some little distance, he espied the girl sitting by herself in the same place under the flowering acacia, he experienced a glow of relief.

But how was she going to receive him now that he was alone? Again he felt greatly relieved when she greeted him with a friendly smile. He did, however, presently detect a defensive glint in her eyes, and this made him very careful both in his manner and in what he said. His caution was rewarded, for when she had gauged his attitude, she took the initiative herself.

"I suppose you are waiting to hear what happened to me after— well, after I left Khanjo?"

Jali murmured an assent.

Her face, while she looked him straight in the eyes, showed that she had previously decided what line to take. "I see you are as inquisitive as ever!" And she laughed carelessly. "But I don't mind telling you about it. Why should I?"

For a moment she paused, pursing her lips; then suddenly, nervously, she gave a look all round. That look reminded him of the glance she had sent round the forest glade at Khanjo, when first she had breathed out the name of Mabun Das. A wave of reassurance passed over him. She was still afraid of that man—even here, and Mabun Das was his best guarantee of her discretion.

Well! she began, some little time before her disappearance from Khanjo she had found a means of acquainting Prince Salim of her whereabouts, and the Prince, who was still furiously in love with her, had at once taken steps to secure her abduction. A lieutenant of his had appeared in the neighborhood, and with him a small body of men who were to escort her to Allahabad. Everything went off as arranged; and for three days all had been well. Then, on the evening of the fourth day, as they were journeying through a desert-place sudden disaster overtook them. They found themselves surrounded by armed men; the six horsemen who rode at her side were set upon and all killed except one. On the next day this poor wretch was castrated, and dispatched to Salim with insulting messages from his brother. For it turned out that they had been betrayed into the hands of Daniyal, who had spies even in his brother's court and took pleasure in playing such tricks as this upon him whenever it was possible. So now she was kept prisoner in a small clay hut for what must have been nearly a fortnight, pending the arrival of more particular instructions regarding what was to be done with her. Fortunately, her beauty had now been reported to the Prince in such terms that he was taken with the desire to look upon it himself. Accordingly she had been brought to the Camp. But during this journey she had lived in a state of terror. What was she to do if Daniyal submitted her to cross-examination. Mabun Das had bidden her be silent on all matters under pain of death; Daniyal, had he reason to suppose she could tell him anything interesting about his brother, would certainly threaten her with torture. Her position seemed truly terrible. But directly after her first interview with the Prince this nightmare was lifted, and she found herself raised from hell into a veritable paradise. For Daniyal had no thought of questioning her; the moment he set eyes upon her he stood gazing spellbound. She looked, he declared, a very incarnation of the goddess who was to appear in his play. So he bade her strip, and at the sight of her body, he actually pirouetted with delight. Thus, in a few seconds, her fortune was decided. After patting her cheek, tilting up her chin, and laughing into her eyes, he dismissed her; and since then her life had been a dream of happiness, for she was turning into a great actress.

Towards the end of this narrative Gunevati's eyes had begun to sparkle again, and it was with a charming zest that she now launched into a description of the honors and splendors of her present mode of life. As he looked and listened, Jali underwent an unexpected change of feeling; he became conscious of a small stir of compassion. The plain truth was that she had been miserable under Gokal's roof; the pale, but lovely, listlessness of her air in those days was now replaced by an animation that made a different creature of her. At Khanjo she had languished, she could not help it; here she found an atmosphere that suited her; she was happy and she could not help that.

Presently, tired of talking, she lay back at full length on the grass and gave a contented sigh. Thank heaven, there was no rehearsal that afternoon, she said; she had been working very hard of late on a new play of Daniyal's in which she had a speaking part. She loved the theater passionately; she was like the Prince in that, for he, too, preferred the dramatic art to any other. How wonderful his play had been! Oh, the Prince was an intellectual giant; there was no doubt about it. Jali said nothing; he had already discovered at the tea-party what her views were about the Prince and his play. Besides, not to argue with Gunevati was an old-established principle of his.

There was a slight pause, and when she next turned to him, he could see that a fresh topic had come into her mind. Raising herself upon one elbow, she gave him a lovely, coaxing glance from beneath her lashes; it was a glance the meaning of which he understood; it said: "Now we will talk about something really exciting: we are going to find the most thrilling and confidential things to say to one another." This look in her eyes took him back to the little Hindu temple in the Agra woods, and again a contemptuous pity stirred within his heart. When she looked like this her vulgarity fell away from her, she seemed childlike. Still smiling, she drew herself a little closer towards him and whispered: "You must—you simply must—tell me everything about Ali."

Jali was considerably surprised. "But what can there be to say about *him*?"

"Oh, you know! Everything!"

"About Ali?" He eyed her in perplexity. This, surely, would not be her manner if she had fallen in love? No, she seemed rather to be begging for an amusing piece of scandal. "I can tell you that Ali is a perfect fool," he said, a reminiscent flush rising in his cheeks.

"A fool!" laughed Gunevati appreciatively. "Yes, isn't he!—unless," she added, reflectively, "unless, you know, he is really very, very cunning."

"I don't understand," said Jali.

"You don't understand?"

"No."

"But you must! I am talking about Ali and the Prince."

"What about Ali and the Prince?"

She became impatient. "Ali and the Prince! How much is there really between them?"

Jali was silent. He was now keeping his eyes fixed on the lake and trying not to let his expression betray him. He did not yet understand fully, but he had the feeling that a light had dawned, and that at last he was going to understand Daniyal and the Camp much better. If only he could get Gunevati to go on talking . . . and if at the same time he went on thinking hard. . . .

"Tell me first what *you* know," he suggested.

Gunevati was not unwilling. She went off at a great pace in a very confidential tone, and with knitted brows Jali concentrated upon the implications that lay underneath the froth of her speech. She, of course, was far from realizing how illuminating she was. And indeed it seemed to him, as the light in his mind increased, that his blindness hitherto had been almost willful. He was still confused; he was still far from grasping the whole breadth of the meaning that underlay her words. But surely it was significant enough that her gossip was that of the whole community, and her tone the tone of the entire Camp.

With all the adroitness at his command he hid his ignorance; he even pretended to join her in speculations which seemed to him perfectly fantastic. He simply could not conceive Ali in the character that she imputed to him; indeed, as he now realized, Ali had unwittingly stood as a screen between him and the truth about the Camp. She might be right—she certainly was right—in her view of the Camp, but about Ali, surely, she was quite absurdly wrong. However, it was not Ali that he was now interested in; it was the Camp. While Gunevati was pestering him about Ali, his mental gaze went far beyond to take in the whole prospect offered by Daniyal and his extraordinary community. At this panorama he stared fascinated, and presently, finding that Gunevati's talk was merely distracting, he got up and took leave of her. But not before they had arranged to meet again the next day.

17

OH YES, HE had been very dull-witted! He could now think of a hundred things that might have opened his eyes—not merely things seen and heard at the Camp, but chance comments, shrugs, and silences, on the part of his father and others. He remembered in particular one occasion when he had heard Hari and Gokal discussing the Camp. They had agreed that it owed its existence to the Prince's need of a pleasure-ground—a place well removed from the Emperor's eye, where he would be free to conduct life after his own taste, without fear of observation and censure.

How completely, too, he had failed to come to an understanding of Ali. Indeed, his cousin's character still puzzled him greatly. Granted that Ali had an inborn instinct to shut his eyes and turn away from all knowledge that was inconvenient, did that make him a fool? If Ali had the art of avoiding experiences that were likely to teach him what he didn't want to know, was he the less intelligent for that? If he used his counterfeit knowledge of the world as a protection against deeper understanding, if his pretensions were primarily of service in deceiving himself, was that attitude necessarily a stupid one? Assuming that it didn't please him to probe down to the heart of things, what then? Or, to shift one's ground a little, if he *was* a fool, wasn't it all the same very wily of him to be a fool in just the way he was?

These reflections carried Jali far; but they were of no use to him the next day, when Gunevati reopened her topic. He had hurried to his rendezvous with eagerness, greatly hoping that he would be able to appear less unsophisticated. He felt this important, because there were numerous points on which he wanted more information; and in their last talk Gunevati had shown herself rather impatient of his naivety. It disappointed him, then, to find that he was still quite unable to answer her questions about Ali in an intelligent manner, and when she repeated that Daniyal was very much captivated by Ali, and that the attention of the whole Camp was fastened with breathless interest upon those two, he could still do no more than gape. But, while she was talking, there flashed into his mind a recollection of the eager, inquisitive looks that the three girls had bent upon Ali in the tea-garden. There had been a mixture of curiosity, envy, and reluctant admiration, in that scrutiny, which did, when he came to think of it, seem to bear out what she said. And then, another idea occurred to him: Could any part of Ali's persistent self-consciousness have been due to a guilty conscience—or at least to a glimmering suspicion of what those looks meant?

The day before, he had insisted very sincerely that Ali was a fool, an innocent and uninteresting fool, and nothing more. But now strange doubts presented themselves. He remembered Ali's face of maniacal rage at the time of their quarrel; he remembered the scene in the picture-gallery when the Prince's arm had rested so lovingly on Ali's shoulders, and Ali had blushed coyly at the touch. And finally he remembered a certain belt—a magnificent belt—that Ali had recently displayed; he remembered that, when questioned about it, instead of boasting that it was a gift of Daniyal's, Ali had revealed the donor's name with a good deal of embarrassment.

As a result of these reflections Jali lost some of his inward assurance, but he continued to assure Gunevati that Ali was a prig and a prude. Hadn't she noticed his manners at the tea-party? How could she reconcile manners like that with . . . ? But no! Gunevati was unmoved. Ali guileless and unsuspecting, good heavens, what an idea! Had he not been living in the Camp for weeks, even months? As for his uneasy manner with young women, that had struck her as a very suspicious sign; it was precisely among youths like Ali (you could call them prigs and prudes, if you liked) that people like the Prince found their most promising material. She wasn't arguing that Ali had already been seduced, but how could he fail to know that he had been taken in the Camp as a candidate for seduction? He was being studied, he was there on approval, he had to grow up in the way he should go, or eventually he would get his dismissal. Daniyal didn't want to hurry him: that was evident: the Prince was being unusually patient, and Ali was making unusually pretty play with his prudery. It was absurd to maintain that Ali didn't know what he was doing, quite absurd.

That day, before they parted, Gunevati was pestering him to bring Ali to see her, and after a little prevarication he saw nothing for it but to tell her the story of their quarrel, and even to let her know that Ali did not consider her society good enough for him. To his astonishment she not only took this in perfectly good part, but let him see that she held Ali in greater esteem than before. Not only did his story strengthen her in her view of Ali, but he was compelled to recognize the strange fact that homosexual proclivities inspired her with genuine respect. This attitude of mind was the more remarkable in that she herself had, confessedly, none. She was simply accepting the standards of the Camp, accepting them with a docility and whole-heartedness that contrasted strikingly with her resistance to the influence brought to bear upon her by Gokal.

From this time forward not a day passed without his spending an hour or so in her company, and he found her irresponsible gossip far more illuminating than Ali's disquisitions had ever been. When not talking literature Ali had occupied himself mainly with questions of social position, polite usage, and fashion. Gunevati, on the other hand, gave him intimate details about the private lives of the outstanding personages in the Camp. In tone and subject-matter his two instructors could hardly have been more unlike, and yet it often struck him that fundamentally they had much in common. To each the voice of fashion was absolutely peremptory: what fashion enjoined, that they were eager to accept, repeat, believe, and practice, without ever a thought of dissent. In Ali's case, it was true, conformity was not always quite easy, for there was a good deal in his present surroundings that his earlier upbringing had not prepared him for. On the other hand, Gunevati had no moral pre-possessions to confuse her, she could accept the Camp's view of itself without any blinking or turning aside. For her, homosexuality was at once a delectable piece of naughtiness, a badge of intellectual distinction, and the leaning natural to sensitive and superior personalities. In the course of her talks to Jali all these attitudes were illustrated in turn: sometimes her eyes would dance with the delight of scandalization, sometimes they would grow large with respectful admiration, sometimes they would darken with indignant sympathy, as she cited some instance where the elect had suffered from the misjudgments of a coarse and prejudiced world. It was one of her pleasures to sit with Jali in some quiet corner of the promenade from which they could watch the crowd that paraded up and down; and as this or that notability went by, she would nudge her companion and produce some new titbit out of her store of scandal, and the uglier the story was the greater the zest and pleasure revealed by her flushed cheeks and sparkling eyes.

Proof, if anyone could be, against the smallest infection from her enthusiasm, Jali would listen with deep attention; but, when she was not looking, he would fix upon her a cool and wondering gaze. Particularly strange did it seem to him that this girl, who had taken part in the ceremonials of the Vamacharis, should find it possible to take such pleasure in the small self-conscious immoralities of the Prince's sleek friends. Perhaps those past experiences of hers had meant nothing to her? Perhaps her nature could vibrate only to the notes sounded by the Camp? This remained a puzzle to him; but through her he learnt a great deal nevertheless. He came to comprehend that the pleasure which the Camp took in regarding itself as scandalous was actually the chief source of its inspiration, its principal well-spring of energy. It was true that, for the appreciation of the finer shades of their own meanness and malice, Daniyal's friends had to look to themselves and be their own audience—they had to depend upon the clack of their own tongues; upon their own giggles and shrieks, for the applause due to any particularly subtle stroke in the game; but, broadly speaking, what sustained them, what carried them along and inspired their activities, was the belief that they were attracting the attention of an outraged outside world. The Camp was withdrawn because it had to be, moreover, the idea that they were sufficient unto themselves was very necessary to them; but it was nothing else than the truth, that they depended basically upon a solid, shockable world of decorum and common sense. They had to believe that a great ox-like eye was fixed upon them in horror. Without this their lives lost their point.

It required no great perspicacity in Jali to make this discovery, for most of the Camp's weaker members were constantly betraying themselves. And it was not only in regard to sex, but equally in discussing art and letters, that Jagashri, Ali, and nearly all Ali's friends, would succumb to the temptation to sit down to a long bout of gloating and chuckling over the supposed scandalization of the old-fashioned and censorious. This was a form of self-indulgence that had always filled Jali with embarrassment; and now at last he understood quite clearly that, although art might be an end unto itself, the Camp was decidedly not. What the Camp needed, it needed as imperatively as his father needed the truth of Buddhism and his mother the love of God. Was it not strange? Some people in order not to faint by the wayside had to postulate a moral law, some had even to have recourse to the notion of a loving God. For such exigent persons nothing would do but to find a meaning in the universe as a whole—a meaning that would link the courses of the farthest stars to the smallest movements of the human heart. How much more reasonable, how much more modest were Daniyal and his friends! Accepting this world as a stage, they asked only for a little finery in which to dress up and an audience easy to shock.

And yet, although he despised the Camp with one side of his mind, Jali was still fascinated by it. The glamour that formerly invested it had not faded out, but had turned into an evil glamour. The Prince, too, continued to be a very intriguing person in his eyes. If he surveyed him with disgust, that disgust was accompanied not by indifference but by curiosity. The heights that he had looked for were not there; but undoubtedly there were depths to explore.

So his visits continued; and he now took to crossing the lake at night. This was done largely out of bravado, although his ostensible reason was that Gunevati's rehearsals occupied her during most of the day. He had no difficulty in slipping out of the house after everybody had gone to sleep; he would steal down through the garden to the little cove where his boatman would be waiting, and in a few minutes he would be sliding over the still water towards the colored haze and the music that marked the position of the Camp.

Very little pleasure did these night excursions give him. Ali's friends (who now used to cut him dead) had been uncongenial, but Gunevati's were no better; their manners jarred upon him; their high spirits, whether genuine or pretended, were very noisily expressed; and their diversions soon palled. He would leave the crowded dancing- and gambling-halls with aching limbs, seared eye-balls, and a throbbing head. On his way back across the lake in the chill of dawn his thoughts would turn sadly upon the contrast between these people and himself. Although he despised them, he envied them. What was it that enabled them to drag themselves up, morning after morning, from the ashes of last night's revelries, ready to paint their haggard faces with the hues of health, and to begin all over again? Such zest, no matter how aroused or how directed, did them a good deal of credit. In a world so full of the drab, the tedious, and the terrifying, it was after all rather fine to remain trivial-minded and to enjoy one's trivial-mindedness.

In this mood of his a shallow world-weariness was no doubt masking unconfessed pleasures of self-admiration; but he was not to be allowed to indulge himself in these for very long. His first intimations of an approaching change came one evening when he was sitting with Gunevati and a little Persian actor, who called himself Mansur, at a table outside one of the big pavilions where she and her friends had been dancing. It was a hot windless night, and the hour was late; the noisy party had dispersed, leaving the long table empty save for these two who were sitting together at one end under the light of a large paper lantern, whilst he, alone at the other end, had pushed his chair back into the shadows and was watching them with that dreamy, yet fixed, attention that extreme lassitude sometimes brings.

Earlier in the evening he had noticed that Gunevati was not in good spirits, and he could guess the reason why: people were beginning to say that she would never make a good actress. Mansur, on the other hand, had a small, neat talent which he never over-strained; he was secure in the Prince's esteem, whilst she ran some risk of losing her part in Daniyal's new play. Would the flatteries that she was lavishing on Mansur induce him to help her, or to put in a good word for her? Jali doubted it.

Mansur was a stocky little man with a long body and short legs. Although Gunevati was doing her utmost to entertain him, his flat, vacantly arrogant face was not even turned towards her. In the task of pleasing him she was handicapped, as she well knew, by his being completely indifferent to women; moreover she lacked the particular kind of finesse which, of all human qualities, alone commanded his respect. Now and then—without meaning to—she would say something that did have the effect of amusing him, and then his eyes would twinkle and he would look round for someone with whom to share his sense of her absurdity. Gunevati was not thin-skinned; but her animation had not been very spontaneous to begin with, and it did in the end succumb to this treatment. She fell silent; she looked round the deserted terrace and sighed.

The cessation of her talk made Jali suddenly aware of the si-lence about them. Only the musicians and dancers in the pavilion were still lively, still pouring their confused clamor out into the night. Mansur yawned. He was not tired, his face was fresh, his expression complacent; but most unmistakably he was bored. He sipped at the glass in front of him, and after a little while a thought came into his mind and he began to smile. "My dear, I must tell you," he chuckled: "this afternoon I changed my religion. I joined the Din Ilahi." With twinkling eyes he rocked gently in his chair, and, for want of a better audience, looked round at Jali. "I took the oath before the Prince, who was dressed up in his white robes. Daniyal is now my High Priest."

Gunevati sighed. She had been fondly hoping for some vague promise, or encouragement, or consolation, but evidently Mansur was intending to ignore all her former efforts. Quiet laughter was shaking him, and, servile, she did her best to look amused.

"Why don't *you* join the Din Ilahi, my dear? Think how pleased the Prince would be!" and he turned his face to her for the first time. Its large, flat expanse was broken by a beaklike nose and small unrevealing eyes which Gunevati did not care to meet.

She laughed uneasily. "I shouldn't mind joining, if I thought it would make any difference." Both Jali and Mansur knew that superstition was holding her back. She was afraid of offending the many gods to whom she owed allegiance.

Mansur's fat little fingers again began to tap upon the table, and Jali suddenly felt certain that never in the course of that man's life had a single generous sentiment entered his heart. Not long ago he would have puzzled over Mansur; he would have looked for the hidden spark; but now he knew better—or he thought he did; and although his nature shrank from Mansur with unconquerable dislike, his mind surveyed him coolly. On the other hand, when he looked at Gunevati, he was moved by a certain compassion. Dimly he felt that she lacked something—the kind of flair—necessary to become a successful member of this community; in these moments there came to him his first presentiment that here she might, perhaps, meet with her destruction.

Mansur's eyes began to twinkle again, and he threw Jali a glance that invited him to share in the entertainment. "I hear that the Princess Lalita is to arrive quite soon. She is going to take a part in the Prince's play."

At these words the blood rushed into Gunevati's face. "The parts are all filled. I don't see where she can come in. Besides, who says that she can act?"

"Oh, I expect she can act well enough. She wouldn't, I suppose, be given an important part."

Gunevati's silence was piteous; but at last she rallied a little. "Mansur, why shouldn't there also be a private performance of the play as the Prince originally wrote it? About half a dozen scenes have been completely cut out, apparently. And I have heard . . ."

"No, no no!" Mansur lifted his hands from the table in horror.

"But . . ."

"No, no! Quite impossible!"

"But the Prince doesn't think so."

"*I* do. And what is more, I have told the Prince I won't have anything to do with it."

The little man spoke with an air of disdainful finality. Nevertheless, after a pause, he took up the subject again. He embarked upon a long rapid speech to which Jali found it impossible to give attention. The gist of the matter, as he already knew, was this: in the first version of his play Daniyal had introduced certain scenes in which the chief Ministers of State, and even the Emperor himself, were put upon the stage and held up to ridicule. One or two of the more reckless spirits in the Camp were encouraging Daniyal to get up a private performance of these scenes; but the idea was rejected by the community as a whole as imprudent in the last degree.

Gunevati sighed regretfully. "The Prince promised me one of the best parts in that version of the play," she murmured.

Mansur gave her a quick look. Her head was bent over the table, and she was tracing a design on it with the tip of her finger.

Silently he began to laugh. "And you accepted?"

"Yes."

Mansur turned his face deliberately round to Jali, and nothing could have been more eloquent of contemptuous amusement than the lines of his pursed lips and narrow eyes. Jali stared into that face, fascinated, but his tired brain was dull in making out the message it conveyed.

"Dear, dear!" ejaculated Mansur, and suddenly the whole expanse of his countenance creased into a hundred wrinkles; he shook his head gently, and gently rocked in his seat.

For at least a minute nothing more was said. Gunevati raised her head, and, after glancing at Mansur she actually winced; indignant, a muscle in her throat began to quiver, and Jali guessed that she was not far from tears.

Mansur picked up his glass, drained it, and put it down with a finished gesture. "I must be going," he said negligently, and his dangling toes felt for the ground under his chair. "If you take my advice, my dear, you will join the Din Ilahi before you think about accepting a part in that play." With indifferent familiarity he patted the girl's bare shoulders. "Nothing dangerous in the Din Ilahi!" he laughed. "Quite the reverse! Ah, here is someone coming to tell you your fortune, or are you afraid of that too?"

Gunevati turned her head sharply, and the look she threw at the approaching figure was one of undisguised aversion. It was an attendant of the establishment, whose business it was to go round telling fortunes, distributing favors, or playing clownish tricks, for the amusement of the guests. These creatures were dressed in fantastic costumes and had their faces painted so extravagantly that they ceased to look human. After executing a few comic dance-steps, the clown came up and handed to each a little object taken from a basket on his arm.

"Why not have your fortune told?" suggested Mansur teasingly.

"No," replied Gunevati, and, turning to the clown with angry eyes, said in a loud voice: "Go away."

Opening his packet, Jali found three little paper bags of tinsel dust, which, thrown at passers-by, would burst, leaving a bright splash of gold or silver upon the victim's dress. Mansur had been given a fan, and Gunevati a large gilded walnut. These nuts usually contained a slip of paper inscribed with amorous and complimentary verses. When her walnut was handed to her, Gunevati's hand closed upon it quickly, but she made no movement to open it. She continued to look up at Mansur, who was standing at her side, and her expression was anxious and appealing.

"Would it really please Daniyal if I were to join the Din Ilahi?" she faltered.

Mansur shrugged. "Look in your nut," said he, grinning over his shoulder. "Perhaps that will give you a piece of good advice."

And now, to Jali's astonishment, Gunevati, who had taken all Mansur's previous gibes so tamely, threw him a look of undisguised rage, and seemed about to make a vicious retort. Mansur ceased grinning, and began to walk away. Still staring after him, Gunevati retained for several moments an expression that seemed to Jali quite extraordinary. What had there been in the man's last words to rouse her to this extent? They had sounded like a harmless little joke.

For a few minutes longer he and she sat there in silence. When they got up, she said she was going home, whilst he dragged himself down to the lake-side to be taken back across the sleeping water.

18

HE FOUND HE had a good deal to think about. To begin with, it had become clear that Gunevati must really be regarded as "in love" with the Prince. To be sure, he had, in a way, known this before. How could he have failed to know it, when she had often confessed it to him—prided herself upon it in fact. But he had never taken her seriously: her admiration had seemed too preposterous, her infatuation too fantastic. Besides, he could see that it had been, in part, her object to shock him; for she had caught from the Camp its irresistible craving to scandalize. This had come to his notice in one of their earliest talks together, when she had made the barefaced confession that she was bitterly envious of the attentions Ali was receiving from Daniyal. What wouldn't *she* give, she had said, for a single one of those glances and smiles that the Prince lavished upon that miserable ninny! And a little later, when he had allowed himself to express his own abhorrence of the Prince, she had insisted upon declaring her admiration for just those characteristics of Daniyal's that were most proper to excite disgust. Since then, too, she had consistently gloried in the Prince's vileness, asseverating that it was *that* that endued him with his special charm and glamour in her eyes. Surely a good deal of this was affectation? Had Daniyal's vileness been exemplified on a grandiose—or even a dignified—scale, had she been able to point to spectacular villainies, Jali would have suspected her less,— would have been able to enter into her feelings, if not with sympathy, at least with a certain understanding. But when he inquired of her what crimes the Prince had committed, what great lusts or cruelties were attributable to him, she had nothing to reply. Her stories were of meannesses, trickeries, and deceits, all of a most contemptible pettiness.

Her conversation with Mansur provoked in him a fresh curiosity and uneasiness. It contained allusions that were mystifying; for instance, what had Mansur meant by saying that there might be a message for her in the walnut. The more he thought about it the more certain he became that Mansur's remark had not been simply an innocent little joke. It had thrown Gunevati into the kind of rage which he knew to be a symptom of alarm. The incident reminded him that for some time past she had been subject to sudden fits of nervousness. In the middle of a lively party her manner would change, her gaiety would drop, she would become absent-minded, her eyes would wander. What did these things, taken together, point to? A child of his age, Jali was at no loss for a reply. Her pleasure was spoilt by a sudden consciousness that she was being watched, that she was under the eyes of a spy; in fact, with his knowledge of her circumstances he might well conclude that she felt the shadow of Mabun Das fall upon her. After all, wasn't it almost certain that Mabun Das did have spies in the Camp, and wouldn't Gunevati be an object for their special surveillance? As this idea took shape in his mind he was filled with satisfaction. His recent fears lest she should be sliding into a dangerous path were greatly relieved; it reassured him to reflect that she was receiving constant reminders of the spiritual presence of Mabun Das.

The next day, in accordance with a carefully thought-out plan, he invited her for a row on the lake, and took the oars himself, leaving his boatmen behind. Although the sun was hot, and she preferred to dawdle along under the shade of the alders, he rowed obstinately out into the lake, nor did he stop until there could be no question but that they were well out of earshot from the shore or from any other boat. He had noticed that these were the conditions in which Gunevati was most likely to be communicative.

Dropping his oars, he let the boat lose way, and very soon Gunevati's trailing hand made not the faintest ripple on the glass-smooth water. The sun was lightly veiled in a white haze overhead; it was not long after noon, and the whole earth seemed to be taking its siesta. After looking all about him, Jali brought his eyes to rest upon Gunevati, who was stretched out on the bottom of the boat. For a minute their looks met, and he could see that she guessed what was coming. Without further ado he questioned her about Mansur and the walnut, and besought her to confide in him.

Gunevati sat up; she, too, cast a swift glance all around; then, hanging her head and shoulders over the side of the boat, she appeared to be taking counsel with herself.

He said: "I think you have a suspicion that you are being watched."

She gave a nod.

"Mabun Das has spies in the Camp?"

He could not see her face, which was turned to the water, but she made a small sound of assent.

"Tell me about it?" he urged.

Without any change of position, she began, after a while, to speak. She told him that he had guessed rightly in attributing her nervousness to Mabun Das's spies; but, as her story developed, he soon found that his surmises had hardly carried him far enough. Her watchers had a mode of procedure that was truly extraordinary; he could only suppose that the wily Mabun had a variety of methods, and that he had chosen for Gunevati the one which he considered the most appropriate. It appeared that on the last night of her journey, when her kidnappers were bringing her to the Camp, a mysterious voice had spoken to her out of the dark to deliver words of warning. Let her not forget, it said, that in the Camp, as elsewhere, the ears of Mabun Das would hear every word she spoke, and that the smallest indiscretion on her part would be visited with terrible punishment. Then the same voice issued instructions; it prescribed what answers she was to give to the questions that Daniyal was likely to put to her. Three times the warning and the instructions were repeated, and then all was still in her tent. Ever since that night, however, a reminder had been placed, at intervals, before her eyes. A few days after her establishment in the

Camp, a little picture of a human head with the tongue protruding, and a dagger thrust through it, had appeared upon a piece of paper on her dressing-table. And regularly after this the same warning would crop up, only, by progressive simplifications, the drawings had become an ideograph that would be meaningless to anyone excepting herself. It was reduced to a sign consisting of an oval with a line cutting into it and another line at right-angles to the first. Week after week this sign continued to appear—sometimes beside her plate at supper, sometimes in a letter slipped under her door; she might even find it inscribed in the dust of her path as she started out for a walk.

All the time she was speaking her head remained bent over the lake, her hand dabbled idly with the water, and her voice sounded quite calm. But in that calm there was more than a hint of weariness; nor did Jali fail to suspect that this mood might very well be the reaction from quite another. He could easily picture her rolling upon her bed and sobbing and biting her nails in an ecstasy of nervous rage and foreboding. His own heart, as he was listening, had certainly hastened its beat. There was something rather sinister in the treatment that was being meted out to this girl, whose life had appeared to him, a short while ago, completely irresponsible and carefree. He was stirred, excited, filled with a sense of the extraordinary; and these feelings were suffused with a satisfaction, which poor Gunevati was certainly not in a position to share. In his view a little intimidation was by no means out of place; he was not sorry to learn that Mabun Das preserved a sense of his responsibilities.

These sentiments, however, were private; and he was careful not to appear lacking in sympathy. Indeed, the droop of her figure, the bowed head, the lifeless tone of her voice, did awaken his pity. Not only was she despairingly in love, not only was she falling from success to failure, but Mabun Das's treatment was, evidently, beginning to tell upon her nerves. Presently he began to ply her with questions.

Her replies were inarticulate, almost inaudible. She shook her shoulders peevishly, she begged him to desist. Sitting up in the boat, she pressed her cold wet hands over her eyes and gave a deep sigh. "Take me back into the shade," she said.

Without stirring, he continued to gaze at her.

"Gunevati!"

"Yes?"

"Aren't you tired of the Camp yet? Wouldn't you like to leave it?"

She gave a small, contemptuous laugh, that was like a sniff. "No."

"But . . ." He lacked the confidence to finish.

She looked out over the water with melancholy eyes and repeated her little sniff. "Oh, I know. Princess Lalita is coming. That poor fool! What does she come for? He can't bear the sight of her. But I don't mind. Let her come!"

This was not what Jali had been thinking about. "I don't mean that," he stammered. "I was wondering . . ."

"If I should lose my part. Oh yes, that may happen."

"If I were you, I should hate the Camp. I should detest it!" exclaimed Jali with sudden vehemence.

She shook her head, and with her eyes fixed upon the distance, smiled sadly. "Oh, you don't understand."

"Gunevati! Can't you give up loving Daniyal when you see that it is so useless, so stupid?"

The smile lingered about her mouth; then slowly she brought her gaze to bear on him, and in its melancholy it was almost tender.

"You don't understand," she repeated in a murmur. "All that makes no difference."

"Daniyal!" he exclaimed with bitterness. "Daniyal of all people!"

Her expression remained unchanged. "Do you think one falls in love with a person because he is 'nice'?" she asked very gently.

Jali had no reply. After a moment he picked up his oars, and in silence they rowed back to the Camp.

The next few days went by quite uneventfully, but his thoughts about Gunevati continued to be perplexed and uneasy. Not long ago, he remembered, she had seemed to him to be without a care in the world; now he knew that beneath the frivolous surface of her life two strong currents of emotion were flowing: one was the fear that Mabun Das had laid upon her, the other was her feeling for Daniyal and the Camp. The expression of her eyes, the tone of her voice, haunted him. She had said to him once before: "I *love* the Camp!" and he remembered now that she had said it in such an accent that he had been startled.

His uneasiness had the effect of making him more observant, and he became more attentive to the rumors which at this time were flying about the Camp in great profusion. For some time past he had been dimly aware that a spirit of unrest was abroad, but he had attributed it to the jealousies aroused by the approaching fêtes—more especially the production of Daniyal's new play. It now became clear to him that there was something more in the air. One day he heard it reported that the Emperor was threatening to pay Daniyal a visit, another day it was said that, hearing that his son's play contained offensive material, Akbar had issued a peremptory order that the theater should be closed forthwith, and the Camp broken up. A third and still more fantastic report was to the effect that the Emperor himself had actually visited the Camp in disguise—with consequences that were going to be disastrous not only for the Prince, but for everyone there. Certain it was, in any case, that no one talked any longer of Daniyal's producing— even in the strictest privacy—the scurrilous parts of his play. And when some of the audacious spirits who had egged him on disappeared from the Camp, their departure was made the subject of lurid conjecture. Not but that other ways were to be found of explaining these disappearances, and of accounting, in general, for the crop of rumors that had sprung up. The amount of money that Daniyal was dissipating day by day reached an enormous sum. And inevitably; for this luxurious community, luxuriously entertained in a remote corner of the hills, was of necessity very expensive to support. From whom did Daniyal obtain the required funds? Certainly not from his father. And if from his young followers, how long would their complaisance, or their purses, bear the strain? How long could the process go on before they were all ruined, or before the scandal burst before the throne of Akbar himself? Gunevati was proud to declare that never a week went by without the suicide of some princeling, whose fortune had passed into Daniyal's pockets either at the gaming table or in some more mysterious and less reputable manner. Thus did it please *her* to account for the gaps among Daniyal's friends; and, if Mansur would smile and shrug at words such as these, even he—complacently cynical, as he was—confessed to a considerable uncertainty regarding the future. It was generally felt that Daniyal's prolonged absence from Court must be telling unfavorably against him; no doubt he was hoping to make up (in the Emperor's esteem at least) for his lack of interest in public affairs by advertising a great enthusiasm for the New Religion. According to Mansur, in his letters to his father, he represented the Camp as constructed primarily as a sort of Holy City or Mecca for pilgrims of the Din Ilahi, and in the same spirit he described his theater as a temple of the new faith. But it was unlikely that these distortions of the truth would serve for long; there were not a few who considered that Daniyal was over-reaching himself, and predicted that sooner or later the Camp would provide his enemies with a powerful weapon against him. Jali listened and tried to give these things their due importance, but actually they did little more than supply a colorable background to his own personal intimations of insecurity; they suggested that not for himself alone, nor for Gunevati alone, but for everyone, some important change was impending.

He felt this at home, too, as if not even here was the course of life to continue as before. In one respect conditions were already slightly different. A week ago a spell of inclement weather had caused Gokal to abandon his tents and take up residence in the house. This had brought the two into one another's company again; and the discomfort that Jali now felt in Gokal's presence forced him to recognize that he was suffering from a sense of guilt. Once or twice the Brahmin had looked at him with a question in his eyes, and Jali had been constrained to turn his face away. It argued, indeed, no great delicacy of conscience in him that he should be feeling this self-disgust. To himself he frankly admitted it. First of all, he had given up Gokal's society in order to spend his time with Ali; then (taking a step from the ridiculous into the ignoble) he had resumed a kind of friendship with the very person who had done Gokal cruel harm. No wonder he could not go straight from the one to the other without a sense of shame.

19

AND THEN AN incident took place that gave shape to his vague disquiet.

One evening, not long after he had gone to bed, the sound of oars on the lake caused him to sit up in astonishment; and a little later he distinctly heard a boat bump against the landing-stage at the bottom of the garden. In the dark he got up and went to the window to look out. His father had been sitting on a seat underneath; and now he saw him rise and move slowly down the path to the lake. In the direction of the landing-stage a lantern-light was visible through the trees; and presently this light began to move up towards the house. It was not long before he heard his father's voice raised in the greeting of some visitor, and at that his heart began to beat faster, for there was nowhere anybody could come from excepting the Camp. After a few minutes his father reappeared in the company of an old gentleman, whose head was wrapped up in a white shawl. Moving in a leisurely fashion, the two went indoors, and a moment later he heard voices in the guest-chamber which was beneath his own room. By leaning right out of the window he was able to catch a few sentences now and again, enough to inform him that the old gentleman was Shaik Mobarek, and that he had come over from the Camp. What did this visit portend? It wasn't as if his father and Mobarek had ever been very great friends—although his father, he remembered, used always to speak of the Shaik with a good deal of respect.

For several minutes he strained his ears; but most of the conversation escaped him. Then, all at once, he heard his own name pronounced—or was it Ali's? They were talking about Ali or Jali—he could not make out which. This brought him to an immediate decision. He made his way stealthily down the stairs and out into the garden. His mother, he knew, had already gone to bed; there was nothing to prevent him from standing outside the open window and eavesdropping.

To his surprise the voices had now ceased, but presently a rustling sound suggested an explanation: Mobarek, he imagined, had brought some papers, which his father was now reading. After a minute he heard a short, dry laugh. "She has plenty of excuses—or reasons—for having sent Ali there, but I doubt whether they will carry much weight with Hari. Did you say that Ali is now being called back?"

"Yes, he will be leaving the Pleasance within the next few days."

"I hope he will be gone before Hari returns."

"My dear Rajah, so far you have read only a part of Ambissa Begum's letter. Please go on with it. I know what it contains, for she has been very open with me."

After this, for a minute or two, there was complete silence, then the Rajah said: "Really, she has been presuming too much upon your patience, your good nature."

"Certainly not, my dear Rajah, certainly not! She felt that she could rely on my discretion, and naturally I feel honored."

"But this"—and the Rajah's fingers could be heard tapping the letter—"this deals largely with my affairs."

"I know. And I therefore run the risk of appearing intrusive. However..." The speaker went on talking for some time, but Jali could not make out what he was saying.

Feeling stiff and cramped, he now moved away, but presently curiosity brought him back to the window again, and for a moment he ventured to peep in.

His father was standing by the table. "Can I give you a little more sherbet—or some fruit?"

"Sherbet, please." The Shaik paused to take a few sips. "Rajah, I am afraid there is something on your mind."

"Only this: it is quite plain that my sister wishes me to commit myself."

Mobarek laughed airily. "On the contrary, what Ambissa has asked me to do is to persuade you that in the eyes of the world you have been—and still are—committing yourself."

"How?"

"My dear Rajah, I know, and she knows, that it is a mere accident that you and the Prince are here together as neighbors in this remote spot, but the world does not understand that. At a time when everyone is taking sides with either Salim or Daniyal, you are *here*. People will regard that as significant."

"I think you exaggerate."

"What do I exaggerate? Rajah, you have now been out of the world for some months. You are ignorant of the actual state of affairs. Please take it from me that a man in your position cannot stand aloof."

There was a note of hesitation in Amar's voice as he replied: "I have no wish to disassociate myself publicly from Prince Daniyal —especially if that implies sympathy with his brother."

Mobarek gave a gentle little laugh. "Rajah—tell me frankly!— have you never been conscious of any awkwardness in your position here? Have you never found it embarrassing to be living close to the Prince and yet avoiding nearer acquaintance?"

The Rajah was silent.

"It is not as if you and he had had an easy start either," Mobarek went on with gentle persistence. "I am referring to that trouble between the Prince and Hari Khan, when you were called in to act as go-between."

"I hope that my attitude on that occasion . . ."

"No, no! Daniyal is far from feeling unfriendly; I am only wondering whether he has not been suspicious of unfriendliness in you." The old man paused, then added suddenly: "Did you know that Mabun Das was on his way here?"

"No."

"Didn't you? He will be here in a week or less. All things considered, I can't help regarding it as unfortunate that Hari Khan should once again be living under your roof. Gokal, too, is a person whom the Prince has no reason to regard with great favor."

After a moment's silence Amar said: "What has Gokal done to incur the Prince's displeasure?"

"Well, I think he can hardly help feeling that Gokal's attitude to the Din Ilahi is not very flattering—either to himself or to the Emperor. Then, too, Gokal's influence with the Emperor has been considerable in the past, and I think Daniyal feels that Gokal has never used it to bring father and son to a better understanding of one another."

To this the Rajah made no answer.

"Yesterday," Mobarek went on, "I heard something that will, I am afraid, cause you a good deal of concern. Gokal's recent indiscretion—you know what I am referring to—is not so safely hidden from the world as—as he perhaps imagines. Daniyal has knowledge of it."

Amar's reply was a little delayed, but his voice, when it came, was even enough. "I am sorry to hear this. Do you suppose that others besides the Prince . . ."

"No. Daniyal was speaking to me in strict confidence. I think you can rely on his discretion."

There was a long silence, and the sound of Mobarek's voice, when he next spoke, showed that he had risen and gone over to where Amar was standing. "I want you to believe that I am going to use all my influence with Daniyal in Gokal's favor.—And now, my dear Rajah, I ought to be taking my leave. But I hope you will pay me a visit on the other side of the water before long. To-morrow the Prince should be starting on his journey to Kathiapur to meet Princess Lalita. Will you come the day after?"

It was to be heard that the speakers were now moving in the direction of the door. Two or three minutes later they appeared in the porch in front of the house. "Oh yes," Mobarek was saying, "your sister and Lalita have become great friends; and, seeing that poor Lalita was already rather over-tired, Ambissa thought it might be a good plan. Life at the Pleasance is not exactly restful, you know. Daniyal's vitality is inexhaustible."

"I much regret that it cannot be managed," Amar replied quietly. "My father is a very old man, and I must tell you that since my mother's death—which took place only two months ago—he has been wandering in his mind." While speaking the Rajah was closely watching Mobarek's face. "Without a doubt," he went on, "Ambissa has failed to realize how matters stand. And that must be largely my own fault. In my anxiety not to distress her overmuch, I may have disguised the truth. Anyhow, circumstances make it impossible for me to offer the Princess hospitality, much as I should . . ."

"Of course, of course!" broke in Mobarek in a tone of warm understanding. "Are you going to accompany me down to the lake, Rajah? That is very kind of you. Now let me see . . ." The rest of the sentence was lost to Jali, although the old man's voice continued to reach him for some time.

After the two had gone, he came out from his hiding place, and stood looking at the lights that were again moving here and there on the little pier. The upper windows of the house behind him were dark, but the idea came into his head that someone might be watching him all the same. He turned and crept quietly up to his room.

20

HE GOT INTO bed and there lay still, staring into the dark with wide, excited eyes. The strain of the last hour had been great, and now he felt tired, but able to enjoy a sense of relaxation, and the refreshment that follows a period of complete engrossment. First of all his mind went back to the news of Ali's near departure. That had given him a great surprise, and he smiled as he recalled how terrified he had been lest his own name should be pronounced next. The thought that Ali was to leave the Camp caused him deep satisfaction, not only because he was afraid lest Ali should do him some bad turn, but also because his complicity with Ali had never ceased to be a source of discomfort to him. Surely he could now regard himself as having done with Ali for ever? And with regard to Gunevati, surely he would be able to say the same thing as soon as Mabun Das arrived? These reflections were very comforting. Moreover, the effect of the conversation as a whole had been to show him that the small field of his secret anxieties was not cut off from the rest of the world, as he was given to imagine, but existed as part of a much larger situation—a situation in which such important personages as his father, Shaik Mobarek, and Mabun Das took their place.

It was on these thoughts that he dropped off to sleep. The less agreeable features of his newly enlarged horizon had not yet

claimed his attention; if he managed to put off thinking about
Gokal, that was due partly to the composure with which his father
had received Mobarek's disclosure, and partly to the fact that the
danger threatening Gokal was not immediate, nor one that he
could visualize clearly.

So he went to sleep undisturbed, but the frame of mind in
which he awoke the next morning showed that his brain had in reality taken other aspects of the case. The excitement of the night
had all evaporated, leaving him with a mind illuminated by very
cold, gray light. For a time he lay quietly in bed, while the sounds
of the house came to him familiarly, announcing the routine of the
day. He could hear his father taking his usual turn on the terrace,
his mother going over to the apartments of the old Rajah to see
how he had passed the night, and the servants pattering about at
their various tasks. Certain sounds from Gokal's wing reminded
him that the Brahmin had decided, with the return of good weather,
to give up his present quarters and go back to his tents.

It suddenly struck him that for the many weeks he had been
living in this house he had been singularly unmindful of the
thoughts and feelings of those around him. Day by day he had seen
his father pace the terrace, and then withdraw into his private
room, there to spend long hours alone—but not once had he been
moved to speculate regarding what was going on in that mind. Day
by day he had seen Gokal reclining on his couch, but he had
merely glanced and turned away; he had never even fairly envisaged the question whether Gokal was moving towards health or
the grave. Day by day he had been in the company of his mother,
and into some dim region of his consciousness there had filtered
the perception that she and Hari were undoubtedly in love. But
what that meant to her (or to Hari) he had never concerned himself
to imagine. This was the way his mind worked; and yet he was
always ready to be astonished at the "unseeingness" of others. It
was true that his father seemed to him just now quite unusually
imperceptive in failing to see that his mother and Hari loved one
another; but wasn't he, possibly, just as blind to something of
equally vital import to himself?

At this he paused, deeply considering; and then again something struck him. In regard to Gunevati he had been strangely ob-

tuse. Little as he could understand her so-called love for Daniyal, he might have realized before now that it would vastly intensify her chagrin at not becoming a better actress. Being unable—owing to Daniyal's indifference to women—to make effective use of her customary wiles, she must have struggled hard to improve herself. And when her want of success became apparent, how could it have failed to occur to her that she could, if only she dared, draw his attention upon herself in quite another way?

The question this bore upon was of course that of Gokal's betrayal. Had the Prince obtained his information from his spies or from Gunevati herself? The first seemed the likeliest conjecture, but it was also possible that not even her fear of Mabun Das, not even "the warnings" had sufficed to keep Gunevati from using her tongue. Yes, the betrayal of Gokal might well have been her work, her first step on a very dangerous path. She might, Jali conceived, have argued that Mabun Das did not interest himself particularly in Gokal, whereas Daniyal, on the other hand, would be vastly amused to find that he was in a position to blackmail so eminent and respected a personage. Daniyal's delight in scandal was noteworthy even in the Camp where scandalmongering was the principal pastime. The Prince spent a great deal of his time in the theater; he was in the habit of strolling about the stage during rehearsals, and not infrequently he would chat with anyone who happened to be in the wings. There were days when Gunevati would come out of the theater, radiant, to boast that Daniyal had stood talking to her for at least five minutes.

Jali's thoughts had now narrowed themselves down to a definite problem, but he deliberately put it aside in order to return to a consideration of his father and Mobarek. It would be a mistake, he felt sure, to write Mobarek down as nothing more than a crafty old statesman with schemes in his head, which his father was reluctant to support. His father, he knew, had a real respect for Mobarek in spite of the latter's allegiance to Daniyal. Here was a very interesting problem: Mobarek tolerated Daniyal, and his father tolerated Mobarek; indeed his father's attitude suggested that he himself might be persuaded to tolerate Daniyal in time.

A little later, Jali took a solitary walk by the lake-side. He was feeling exceedingly puzzled. Was it possible that Daniyal and his friends were different from what he thought them? Did they possess compensating virtues that he was unable to see? Or, assuming that Daniyal was indeed what he thought him, was it necessary to look upon such a character as vile? Weren't all people very much alike when you got to know them? Wasn't it rather naive to consider some people very good and others very wicked? Was he, Jali, competent to judge of the pleasantness or unpleasantness of other people? When he came to examine his own character, it certainly did not strike him as particularly pleasant.

There was some comfort in the thought that he himself might be almost as odious as Daniyal, because then he would not be so hopelessly out of place in the world, nor suffering misery that was undeserved. On the other hand, the world did certainly contain *some* unquestionably nice people. He came back to that with a conviction that was unshakable. His father and mother, Hari and Gokal—they *were* superior to the inmates of the Camp. And what about their position?

It suddenly came over him with impassioned feeling that nothing else mattered so much. He had reason to believe—everything was still leading him to believe—that nice people were exceedingly scarce. Was the world made up of people like those he had seen at Agra and people like Daniyal and his crew? If that was the case, if "nice people" constituted only a handful—a poor, ineffective, inarticulate handful—then nothing was left but despair. Here, here, he realized, was the core of his present unhappiness. And comparing himself as he now was with what he had been at Khanjo, it seemed to him that his present unhappiness, if less violent, nevertheless threatened to penetrate far deeper. The cloud that had enveloped him at Khanjo had been local and temporary: his present gloom threatened to stretch in a darkening pall over the whole of his life.

In the afternoon he went down to the boat-house. The weather had turned dull and heavy, so that he had to order his boatmen to bring out a rowing-boat.

They rowed with a sluggishness that was due partly to the languor of the day, and partly due to their unwillingness to take him to the Camp; for they were beginning to be afraid that their young master's increasing recklessness would lead to his being found out, and that a part of Rajah Amar's wrath might be visited on them.

Jali sat in the stern with a set face and absent gaze. He was thinking hard. How was he to extract from Gunevati what he wanted to know? He felt that he must set about his task with great caution, for it was possible—quite possible—that Daniyal had *not* obtained his information about Gokal from her, and that she was not yet even aware that the Prince had been told. Of course Daniyal was sure to question her on the subject sooner or later, but, if he delayed until after Mabun Das's arrival, the danger would be greatly reduced; for then Gunevati would certainly not dare to be indiscreet. The critical period was *now*, and danger would continue until Daniyal left the Camp.

What he feared more than anything else was that she would yield to the temptation to talk about Hari. The fact that the Prince was on the point of setting out to meet Princess Lalita and bring her back to the Camp might just tip the scale. Gunevati knew well enough in what spirit Daniyal would receive the news that Lalita had not scrupled to carry on an intrigue with Hari even after her official betrothal. He would be delighted; it would amuse him immensely; he would laugh. How should he not laugh upon suddenly finding himself able to evade a marriage for which he had always been disinclined? How amusing for him to be in a position to disconcert the Emperor, create a tremendous scandal in the Imperial Court, and bring shame and disaster upon Hari and the Princess.

Under the stimulus of this anxiety Jali racked his brains to find a scheme for getting Gunevati to reveal herself. In the event of his failing (which was only too likely), he might, he reflected, have recourse to Mansur. From Mansur it might be possible to find out at least whether she and Daniyal had been seen talking together more than usual of late; if Mansur was in a position to expose or betray Gunevati in any way, he would probably enjoy doing so; everybody in the Camp was always ready to do a friend a bad turn. Only he mustn't appear too much in earnest, for neither would Mansur be desirous of doing *him* a *good* turn.

His boat was now nearing the opposite shore; already he caught a whiff of the aromatic gums and incense that were being burnt in braziers here and there about the Camp. This was done in an attempt to mask the smell of the polluted marsh, which was becoming more unpleasant every day. A canopy of sweet-smelling smoke hung over the gabled and domed roofs, framing the Camp from above—just as the gray water framed it from below. Jali eyed the approaching façade with loathing; each jerk of the oars that was bringing him nearer tightened the oppression of his heart. Upon reaching the landing-stage he noticed that the lake-front was deserted, and as he stepped out he remembered that this was the day fixed for a spectacle of unusual interest in the open-air arena at the back of the Camp. For a few moments he stood still, grinding his teeth with annoyance; Gunevati, who never missed any festive occasion, was sure to be there; nor was she likely to come away so long as any part of the entertainment remained to be seen.

For nearly an hour he wandered forlornly round and about, and during most of this time was lost in a deep abstraction. From the depths of one of his reveries he awoke to find himself halting before a large brazier that was sending up a dense, brown column of smoke to thicken the pall overhead. Over this brazier stood one of the negroes that Daniyal had imported into the Camp, a man of great stature and girth, jet-black, and possessed of a countenance that fascinated Jali by reason of its immense animal gusto. The negro was poking the charcoal with an iron bar, and when a glowing coal of any size fell through the grid he would pick it up and play with it, tossing it high into the air and catching it again. Out of a doorway near-by there stepped a young girl whose extravagantly painted face and bizarre dress showed her to be prepared for the stage. As she came running past, with flashing teeth and glinting eyes and a joggle of her full breasts, the negro reached out an arm like a gorilla's, and caught her half-naked body against his own glistening flesh. For a moment she hung suspended in his clasp; but he forgot that he was holding a live coal in the other hand, and a second later with a howl he dropped coal and girl together, to hop up and down on his toes, his head thrown back in a grin of mingled amusement and pain. With shrieks of laughter the girl ran on.

Roused from his pre-occupation, Jali made the sudden decision that he would go to the house where Gunevati was lodged and wait for her there. Up to this time he had avoided visiting her in her own quarters, but a certain curiosity to see them now seized him, and he had grown weary of wandering about the streets. As he went along there came into his mind a memory of the night when he had ransacked her room at Khanjo. That had been a terrible period in his life; he had often assured himself that he would never suffer so much again; but now he was not so sure. When he came to the house he found an Arab doorkeeper squatting before the entrance. It was a large building in which the Prince lodged a considerable number of the entertainers in his employ. Jali had heard talk of this Arab, who was given out to be a eunuch; everyone said that for a small bribe he would admit anyone. This report proved true enough; and the next minute, following the man's directions, he was proceeding down a long, empty corridor. Some of the doors he passed stood open; but although the whole house was seemingly deserted, he went by them with hurried, furtive tread. It was not only the leer of the doorkeeper that made him shamefaced; the feelings that had hitherto kept him away from this place, now returned in strength, giving him a sense of being engaged upon a squalid and dangerous errand. The door of the room which he took to be Gunevati's was shut, but, fearing to find himself mistaken, he stood outside listening, and a minute elapsed before he could muster up courage to raise the latch. On his first view of the room, he was surprised by its size and the elegance of its appointments. It was in half-light, produced by screens of fretted cedar over the main window; spreading branches of Persian lilac and roses and sprays of jasmine stood in the corners; and the furniture was of old Kashmiri make. It occurred to him that this apartment must have been assigned to Gunevati soon after her arrival, in the days when she was winning easy triumphs in the voiceless role of Lakshmi. The next thing that caught his attention was an enormous pile of water-lilies in the middle of the room. The heap was so big that it spread over nearly the whole floor, and the sweet, but muddy, smell of the blossoms was overpowering. This smell had always been very unpleasant to him, and now the scent of the thick white flowers was mixed with the still muddier smell of the wet stalks and leaves. It made an atmosphere that seemed to him almost unbreathable. He was on the point of retreating when the couch at the other end of the room gave a sudden creak, and someone who had been lying down sat up to look who had come in. To his satisfaction he saw that it was actually Gunevati.

405

21

THE LOOK OF pleasure that came into his face was completely unfeigned, so nearly had he given up hope of seeing her that day. He kept this pleased expression as he advanced across the room; smiling shyly, he was conscious of the hypocrisy of his smile. Gunevati looked as if she had been crying, but instead of alluding to that, he asked if she was ill. She had a headache, she told him; she and her friends had been out on the lake all the morning, bathing and picking water-lilies, and the sun had been too much for her. "How did you know you would find me here?" she asked.

"I didn't know. I thought you must be at the Circus. But I got tired of wandering about the Camp, so I decided to come here and wait for you."

She was eyeing him with a certain curiosity. Sitting up a little, she arranged the cushions behind her head; the thin, yellow silk of her robe left her neck and arms bare; her hair hung in two braids over her shoulders. Seeing that she had left the foot of the couch free for him, he sat himself down on it.

Her manner of looking at him increased his self-consciousness; turning his head about, he examined the room with a pretended interest. Amusement seemed to gather behind her eyes as they continued to rest upon him, and he suddenly guessed in what fashion she was interpreting his shyness.

"Did I wake you up?" he asked.

"Yes. But it doesn't matter. What did you want to talk to me about?"

He had his answer ready, but he kept it back. He explained that he had forgotten this was a great day at the Circus, and asked what was going on there.

"But what made you come to my room?" she persisted.

He pretended to hesitate. "Well, as I was walking about, I suddenly realized that I was just outside your door."

She laughed gently.

Again for a moment he gave himself the appearance of hesitating, then in lowered tones he said: "I also saw *the sign* written in the dust just outside."

This lie, he fancied, was quite a useful one: whilst accounting, in some sort, for his visit, it also turned the conversation in the direction he desired. He had the satisfaction of seeing Gunevati frown.

"Did Ahmed notice it?" she asked.

"Ahmed?"

"The doorkeeper."

"No, I don't think he could have noticed it. He seemed to be half-asleep. I rubbed it out with my foot as I came in."

He knew her to be very sensitive about the sign, which she seemed to regard as a disgrace. While he studied her surreptitiously, a sudden wave of self-disgust swept over him. How tired he was of deceits and trickeries! Whether at home or at the Camp, he was always acting a part. His true self seemed to be incapable of honest relationships: it was condemned by some deep defect of nature to everlasting treachery.

After a moment she stretched out her arms and gave a yawn that was also half a sigh. "Hand me that mirror, will you?" And she began examining herself.

A little disappointed, he went off an another tack. "I had a piece of news yesterday. Just as I was leaving the Camp someone told me that Ali was going away. Is it true?"

"Yes, he is going." She spoke absently; she was applying some kohl to her eyelashes.

"Really going?" Jali leant forward with exaggerated eagerness. "But why? Is the Prince sending him away?"

Gunevati continued to study her reflection in the glass. "Oh, his mother wanted him, I suppose. But he'll come back. That affair is not over yet, my dear. We shall have our Ali back again before very long." She spoke distraitly; she was without the interest in Ali that she had once had.

Half to himself Jali murmured: "The smell of your water-lilies makes me feel quite sick," and closing his eyes, he leaned back against the wall at the foot of the couch. Beneath the surface his sense of strain and discomfort was great, but he was bent upon giving himself a natural, peaceful air. A sudden vision came to him of Gunevati sporting naked on the lily-lea with her friends. He could imagine the shrieks, the laughter, the splashing, the ruthless tearing at the long slimy stalks and the tossing of the booty on to the bank. The shallows must have become quite turbid before the naked, panting, muddied girls had thrown themselves down on the grass under the sun. How enviable to be like Gunevati, to hold but one thing before your mind at a time, to be hungry and eat, sleepy and sleep, to be laughing and screaming one moment, and then to come back and indulge in a fit of tears. What did tears matter? They would soon be over, and then one was ready for the next thing. No overlapping, no inward confusion or conflict.

Presently she embarked upon a theme which, he knew, might well occupy her for an hour on end. It was the story of her relations with Ranee Jagashri , the earlier chapters of which he had already listened to often before. At the time when she was at the height of her glory (her glory, poor thing, being in reality, merely that of having been a "discovery" of Daniyal's), the Ranee had made advances to her in the most overt fashion, her object evidently being to advertise "an affair." Gunevati had felt flattered, and although it was not long before she realized that the Ranee was merely seeking notoriety, she saw no reason to reject the offered liaison. If it would help to make the Ranee interesting in the Prince's eyes, it would do the same thing for her. Her feelings for Jagashri at this time were not unfriendly; whilst she looked down upon her somewhat for not being a true Lesbian, she could not but admire the determined way in which she pretended to be one. When Jali had expressed his surprise at finding Jagashri in the Camp, she had told him that at Agra the Ranee, in her anxiety to attract

Daniyal's favorable notice, had bribed a lady who was well established in his coterie to flaunt an amour with her before the Prince's eyes. It was accordingly certain that Gunevati was no dupe, but that did not prevent her from being furious when Jagashri dropped her—as she presently did—on the first signs of her falling out of fashion. All this was an old story; what Gunevati now had to recount was a prospect of successful revenge. Jagashri she averred, had been taking her pleasure with a male lover in the Camp all the time; and this man had betrayed her to Mansur, who in turn had passed the news on to *her*. Well; she had at once set about seducing Jagashri's lover, and had succeeded so well (at least so she said) that he was now ready to blackmail Jagashri, who had had the folly to send him love-letters, which, if circulated, would make her the laughing-stock of the Camp.

Jali pretended to be listening and to be amused, but in truth he hardly took in a word of what Gunevati was saying. He had heard too many stories of this kind before; his mind was far away; he doubted whether Gunevati was telling the truth. All her story did was to awaken a faint flicker of pity in his heart, for he saw in her virulent hatred of Jagashri a measure of her consciousness of her own decline and failure.

When she had finished, she lay back, her hands clasped behind her head, and there followed a silence in which she seemed to sink into her former listlessness. Jali felt far from listless. The silence oppressed him; it reigned not only in this room, but over the whole neighborhood, and the faint sounds of cheering that floated in through the window were embarrassing, for they drew attention to the gaieties in which Gunevati was taking no part. Not until this moment had he asked himself with sufficient seriousness what it meant that she should be shutting herself up here in this room by herself. Was she merely indulging in a fit of childish petulance, or had she been so slighted that she dared not show her face in public?

As he watched her, a new detail caught his attention. Although her eyes were half-closed and her attitude appeared to be one of relaxation, her foot, which was hanging down from the couch, had a rapid, nervous movement. This observation wrought upon him most singularly. His mind, which had been in a state of tension, was now also caught up in an agonizing suspense. His physical discomfort, too, caused by the scent of the lilies, was turning into a languor akin to faintness. He looked with longing at a small window at the other end of the room, the only one that was without a screen. What did these white flowers, what did this languor, remind him of? Something that had happened long ago; something that was now happening all over again. But how could things happen over again? And what was it that he remembered? Ah, yes! it was the blossoms of the temple-trees upon the sacred mound. . . . But that had been a delight, and this was a kind of torment.

Although he refrained from looking at Gunevati he knew that her eyes were upon him. She was looking at him fixedly, and behind her eyes there was a smile. He heard her move; she was swinging herself into a sitting position. She came and sat close beside him on the edge of the couch. A curious passivity held him motionless; he remained looking straight before him, while Gunevati's laughing eyes and laughing mouth came closer and closer to his face. Then suddenly her arms were upon his shoulders; the weight of her body threw him backwards, and she was lying on him, her lips pressed against his. Almost at once he began to struggle; and with so much real determination that in another moment he was on his feet. Trembling, bathed in sweat, he stood by the couch and looked down at her. There she lay, upon her back, laughing. She lay with her feet trailing on the ground, her arms outspread, her whole body indolently relaxed. He stood looking down at the lovely curves of her upturned chin, her throat, and her breasts. Her laughter was so full of insult that the blood rushed to his head; he turned and walked round the heap of water-lilies to the open window.

The air felt fresh, and it quickly restored him. Outside was a little grass-covered court, shaded by two or three birches. From tree to tree there hung a clothes-line covered with gay muslins. The scene looked pleasant, until he noticed two rats nosing in a heap of garbage in one corner.

His mind was now working again with complete lucidity. "I mustn't let this interfere," he thought. "I must keep my object steadily before me. I shall have to be tactful for a while; for she must not feel offended." He had little doubt that he understood her; but that again must not be allowed to appear. He mustn't give signs of guessing how hopeless and humiliated she felt. He must behave boyishly; he must appear embarrassed, angry. He must let her laugh at him; it would not be difficult.

He waited. But no sound came from the dusky room behind him, and presently he felt that a catastrophe might be brewing in the silence at his back. Intently he listened; he could hear nothing but the buzzing of a blue-bottle that had been attracted by the smell of the water-lilies.

"Jali!" Her voice, when it came, was full of mockery. "What are you doing over there? Come back! I want to talk to you."

His face cleared, but, quickly remembering his part, "What do you want?" he said surlily.

"Come here!"

"I can't bear the smell of your water-lilies. They make me feel sick."

"Nonsense!" She was laughing. "I want to talk to you."

"What about?"

"Tell me, my jewel! Does your Brahmin know that I am here?"

This was the first mention of Gokal that had passed her lips since their dreadful parting at Khanjo. Jali's heart began to thump against his ribs; he remained facing the window.

"No. I think not," he replied after a silence.

"Why don't you tell him?"

"Why should I?"

"Because it might interest him to hear it."

He made no answer.

"You are afraid that he still loves me," she mocked.

Jali's lips moved to curse her silently. "No," he said after a moment; "Gokal doesn't think about you at all."

She gave a little laugh and murmured something that he failed to catch. Turning, he saw that she was sitting up against a pile of cushions in her former place. He went back across the room and took his seat once more at the foot of the couch.

Again a dreadful silence, a nerve-racking silence, settled down upon them. Moving impatiently from one flower to another, the blue-bottle buzzed loudly by fits and starts. The cheering from

411

the Circus had stopped, but all at once there came through the open window a distant, deep-toned roar. So deep was it, so vibrant, that, although very faint, the sense of power it conveyed was extraordinary. Gunevati drew a long breath. "That is one of the Prince's lions," she said. "Have you seen them? They were fetched all the way from Africa."

Jali made no reply. He was still leaning back against the wall, with an absent gaze fixed upon the water-lilies, and all at once he found himself looking into a tiny eye that was staring straight into his. At first he thought it was a snake, but suddenly the creature gave a sharp movement which showed it to be a large newt. The scent of the lilies was again sending him into a lethargy, and again he felt as if Time were halting in its course. He thought of those moments when, in the terrific blaze of noon, he had watched Gunevati idling beside the little temple in the wood. Now, as then, he felt the Present expand, and stagnate, and reflect everlastingness; only there was no foretaste of beatitude in this experience; it was rather an initiation into a state of living death. In this stand-still of Time something seemed to be maturing, but with a slowness that gave every moment the value of eternity.

Thus strangely stricken he sat there, until once more Gunevati's foot attracted his attention. He felt that she was going to speak.

"You have no idea how the Prince laughed when I told him about Gokal."

"You told him about Gokal?"

"I did."

"What did you tell him?"

"Everything."

"You told him, then, how you . . ."

She sneered. "It was just that that amused him so much."

Jali made no answer. A deathly calm spread over him. Between this and instant murder there was no middle way. Besides he wanted to hear more.

"I knew you had told the Prince," he said after a pause.

"Oh!" She showed some surprise. "How did you know that?"

"Shaik Mobarek visited my father yesterday evening. I heard them having a long talk together."

She kept her eyes fixed upon him; she was slightly disconcerted, he thought; though whether by this piece of news, or by his equanimity, he could not tell.

"Did they talk about me?" she asked.

"No. At least your name was not actually mentioned."

"What did they talk about?"

"Many things. But why should I tell you, when . . ." He broke off. "You had better be careful," he added.

She was gazing at him hard; her foot now had a very rapid swing. "What do you mean?" she said.

"Well—in the first place, I was thinking of something Mansur said not long ago."

"What was that?"

"He thought that you had been growing rather reckless lately."

"Reckless?"

"With your tongue."

A sharp cry of anger escaped her. "What nonsense! And what does Mansur know about it? Besides, as for Gokal, what does Mabun Das care about *him*?"

Jali paused for a moment, then he said: "Mabun Das is coming. Did you know?"

"Yes. I know."

"And Mabun Das is very friendly with Hari Khan. Had you forgotten?"

She stared back at him, frowning. "Forgotten? No. But what has that got to do with it?"

He kept silent.

"We are talking about Gokal," she continued scornfully. "And Mabun Das cares nothing about *him*. He isn't in love with the old fool, like you."

"No. But with regard to Hari Khan. . . ."

"Hari Khan!" she cried in a voice shrill with exasperation. "Why do you drag Hari Khan in? He has nothing to do with it."

At these words Jali felt satisfied, and rejoiced in profound thankfulness. Looking calmly into her eyes he replied: "What I mean is that Hari Khan is very fond of Gokal. He has been feeling angry with you already, and he will be angrier still if he hears that you have been talking."

Gunevati's face actually suggested that she had overlooked this.

There was a silence during which she seemed to be wrestling with her emotions. "I am not afraid of Hari Khan!" she pronounced at last with great passion.

Jali determined to add one more stroke. "It seems to me that the sign of warning has been coming to you more often of late. Isn't that because *they* know that you have become reckless? Almost anyone can see you—and perhaps even overhear you—as you stand there in the wings talking to the Prince."

Gunevati's nostrils twitched and her eyes flashed; then she sprang from the couch and stood over Jali, as if longing to do him physical injury. He looked up into her face curiously. It was strange to see features which, in their soft and subtle delicacy seemed designed to express only the gentleness of love, actually illustrating an extreme of hate and fear.

"I curse the Brahmin!" she cried. "An old fat man, a fool—he should have died the death of a pig! What does Mabun Das care about him? Why should he listen to Hari Khan? He has plenty of other things to attend to. And as for the Prince—he laughed, I tell you! The Prince laughed!"

Having spoken, she made a sudden turn, went to a small cabinet, and drew from it a bundle which she flung at Jali's feet. "These are the only things of his that I have not sold—rubbish! I give him back his rubbish and spit in his face. Take these things to him and tell him that from me!"

Jali had risen from his place, and now he bent down automatically to pick up the bundle. It was the dress that Gunevati had habitually worn at Khanjo, and he noticed that some cheap bracelets were threaded on to the piece of string that tied it up.

His brain was now dull, his senses all deadened. This is the end! he thought; and as he looked into Gunevati's rage-distorted countenance he wondered if she also felt that something decisive had taken place. For a minute they stood there facing one another; and then he saw that for her, too, this day and this moment were critical. Only it was not with Gokal, nor with Hari, nor even with Mabun Das, that she was primarily concerned; in the center of her being stood the dazzling figure of the Prince; if she was contemplating her failure as an actress, her desertion by her friends, their ridicule, and her probable dismissal from the Camp—this was merely the outward shape of her great interior tragedy. Looking into her face—as he thought for the last time—it was borne in on him that she had neither the heart, nor the mind, nor the will, to escape her fate—whatever that might be. Her perversity and triviality were as stubborn and fateful as any of the virtues of wise and saintly men. There was no more to be said in the way of warning or appeal. He regarded her with an embarrassment into which there entered an element of awe. For while she stood for so little in herself, she represented so much in the world.

22

IN THE AFTERNOON of the next day he crossed the lake again, but instead of taking his boat to the Camp, he put in at a point two miles below it, and, after telling his boatmen to wait for him there, started off through the tangle of young birches and willows that clothed this part of the lake-shore. His object was to assure himself that the Prince had started on his journey, and this he proposed to do by making inquiries upon the road along which the Prince had to pass.

A few months ago this road had been nothing but a narrow track; it was now a well-trodden highway, provided with halting-places for the constant stream of porters that passed along it. Jali had about a mile of rough, boggy ground to cross, and it was with a peculiar mixture of nervous concentration and absent-mindedness that he picked his way along. He had slept little that night, and now was so tired that his thoughts drifted to the promptings of every chance association. For the moment he was thinking about the valley of Ravi, and taking comfort in the reflection that in a few months, or at most in a few years, it would return to its natural state. For Daniyal's Camp was certainly not permanent, and after its desertion the light wooden structures that composed it would very soon rot away. He could see them in his mind's eye, flimsy ruins without any beauty in their decay; in the end mosses and creepers would spread over everything, willows and alders would sprout up, the site would disappear completely.

In those days, he supposed, the Prince would be reigning as Emperor over the land; and, with a dozen country palaces at his disposal, why should he ever waste a thought upon the valley of Ravi? But it was wretched to picture Daniyal lording it over the whole of India!—wretched to think of him and his friends as wielding authority, setting the tone of society, and giving India its name among men. Even should he, Jali, choose to retire to his lovely valley and live as a hermit in his grandfather's house, he would still be a subject of Daniyal's. At these reflections his brow clouded, and he was astonished at the violence of the hatred he found in his heart.

In about twenty minutes he came out on to the road, and inquired of a group squatting by the wayside whether the Prince had yet passed. It was not often that anything in the Camp took place in accordance with previous announcement, so he was somewhat surprised when the answer came in what seemed to be the affirmative. But it was doubtful whether these people had properly understood him, for they spoke in a dialect that he himself was hardly able to make out. Proceeding farther along the road in the direction of the Camp, he asked again. This time the answer came crisp and clear: the Prince had passed about an hour ago. Although greatly pleased by this news, he went on; he knew better than to consider the matter as put beyond all doubt. The next three persons that he met all assured him that the Prince had not yet started, and as one of his informants was a member of the Prince's own guard, he felt obliged to accept this intelligence as reliable. It was a disappointment, although far from unexpected. Gloomily he turned off the road, and, choosing a place out of sight of the passers-by, sat down to take counsel with himself. Although his disinclination to go forward into the Camp was very strong, the anxiety that pressed him on had an almost equal intensity. He knew that there would be no peace of mind for him so long as he had not done all that was possible to discover how matters stood. Whilst thus at conflict with himself, his gaze wandered over the mountain-slope down which he had first come into the valley of Ravi on his journey from Khanjo, and suddenly he became aware that a party of five men on horseback were descending by the same path. His mind turned at once to Hari: he seemed to remember that Hari had taken four men with him. Shading his eyes, he strove hard to identify the leading horseman; nor was it very long before he did actually convince himself that his surmise had been right.

Excitement stirred within him; whilst his gaze remained fixed upon that distant figure, his imagination was actively at work. He visualized Hari at Khanjo; he pictured him conducting his investigations; and, as one scene after another passed before his mind's eye, he saw in a flash that the only thing Hari was really likely to have discovered was what his, Jali's, relations with Gunevati had been. One of the villagers, if not Mujatta herself, would—almost certainly—have given him this information. The moment he thought of this it seemed to him as plain as anything could be, and he was staggered by his stupidity in not having seen it before.

In a kind of daze he began walking up and down. Here at last was the end of this dreadful period of his concealments and deceptions. Taxed with having carried on an intrigue with Gunevati, he would conceal no vestige of the truth. A grim satisfaction possessed him; much as he dreaded the ordeal that lay ahead he also welcomed it. His heart was beating hard as he watched Hari and his four horsemen coming down the slope. Their path would take them round the end of the lake without bringing them any nearer to the Camp, and, as the loop was a long one, a couple of hours must elapse before they would reach the old Rajah's house. Jali noted this with relief, for it gave him time to think.

The exultation that had seized upon him a moment ago was already beginning to evaporate. When he looked to see what it was built upon he could find nothing—nothing except a weak relief at having done with his concealments and responsibilities. The situation remained the same in every other respect. His confessions would do nothing to extricate Gokal from his difficulties, nor relieve Hari from the dangers that threatened him. Moreover, owing to the Prince's delay in starting, these dangers loomed up more imminent than ever.

A minute ago, in his first excitement, he had vaguely assumed that everything would now be cleared up and that his elders and betters would lose no time in putting matters right. But, to picture the future a little more closely, how far was he likely to succeed in conveying his meaning to persons whose minds were so unprepared and so different from his? To explain the bare facts of the case would be possible no doubt, but bare facts were often misleading; and when it came to communicating subtle shades of feeling, conjecture, and intuition, how hopeless the undertaking appeared! If, for a few instants, he had imagined himself putting an end to his spiritual isolation, that had been a very foolish dream. How could he ever explain what he had been in the old days, or what he had gone through, or what he had now become?

Nor did his discouragement stop here. Suddenly he discovered that his childish confidence in his elders had disappeared. Hitherto it had been an article of his faith that in all those matters where he himself was incompetent, they were of godlike capability. Something had recently happened to undermine that belief, so that now, when he thought of his father, Hari, and Gokal taking the situation in hand, he felt no pleasant glow of reassurance, but a sinking of the heart. Of himself he already despaired; his failure to foresee the almost infallible consequences of Hari's visit to Khanjo had destroyed his last hopes of ever being able to make an intelligent use of his intelligence. But his elders now appeared no better. In one respect they were even worse, for whereas he was aware of his stupidity, they were quite unaware of theirs.

In a sudden revulsion of feeling he stamped up and down the glade, whilst tears of rage and hopelessness streamed down his cheeks. He saw fools, fools everywhere! Nothing but fools! Look at Hari, coming back, smug and jaunty no doubt, from what he considered a very successful investigation! How hopelessly his cheerful self-conceit, his appetites, and his sentimentalities blinded him! Look at Rajah Amar! If his unawareness of his wife's feelings did not label him clearly enough, you had only to consider his life: not only had he been consistently humbugged by his dependants, not only was he continually deceived in his friends, not only was he quite ignorant of the true character and behavior of his son, but he entirely failed to understand his own nature, and his moral code was merely a glorification of his own temperament. Look at Gokal, doting on a vile creature, who ridiculed him, and finally attempted to take his life! Was there anyone in the world who was not either odious, or a fool, or both? Mabun Das, might one say? No, him least of all. What was he but a poor little man who shut his eyes to the stars, concentrating the whole beam of his narrow intelligence upon the things at his feet, and yet, there he was, the person chiefly responsible for the disasters now impending!

Worn out at last by helpless rage, Jali threw himself on the ground and sullenly wiped the tears from his face. In a few moments he was calm enough to be taken with a certain surprise at the turn of his own feelings. Why this fury against his own people, in particular his own father? He swerved aside from the question, but not before observing that what rankled in his mind was the even tone in which his father habitually spoke about Daniyal and the Camp. His open-mindedness had vanished completely; he now knew that he hated Daniyal and his company with a hatred so violent that it would listen to no arguments on the other side. His rage against his father and Hari sprang from the knowledge that he would be unable to kindle in them a flame of hatred equal to his own. That really was what he had had in his mind when telling himself despairingly that he would be unable to "explain." His secret desire was to make use of his father and the others as instruments of his vengeance, to set them upon Daniyal like a host of avenging furies. This momentary glance into his own heart filled him with astonishment, and then he turned his thoughts away.

The time had come to make a move. His final decision was to go home, so as to be there when Hari arrived. Gloomily he got up and made his way back to the boat. There was little likelihood that Hari would say anything that day, but his looks and manner might, he thought, show him how the land lay. In any case, it would be better to put off going to the Camp until the evening, when Mansur and the other people he wanted to question would be more easy to find.

The night was warm, dark, and gusty. Little rapid waves slapped the sides of the boat as Jali set out, and the wind made progress slow. His thoughts were no longer concerned with Hari, who had given him no sign of what was in his mind; but in truth it

mattered little how much Hari already knew, since he felt bound
to make a full confession in any case. To guard against any weakening of his resolution, he acted upon a freakish impulse that had
seized him only a few minutes ago. Before coming down to the
boat, he had crept through the darkness to Gokal's tent and thrust
Gunevati's dress and trinkets under the flap that hung over the entrance. His idea was that Gokal should find the things there when
he woke in the morning.

Now, as his boat pushed its way through the moist wind and
ruffled water, it was neither with Hari nor with Gokal that he was
occupied. He had returned to the perplexed and feverish thoughts
that had kept him awake through the previous night. Gunevati's
image haunted him; her personality obsessed him; not for a moment since their last meeting had she been entirely out of his
mind. At first he had tried to argue that she was insane. Had he
been able to look upon her merely as a "case," he could have denied her half her significance. But, comparing her with others in
the Camp who were unquestionably unbalanced, prone to hyste-
ria, or addicted to drink or drugs, he could find no points of resemblance. Mentally as well as physically Gunevati exhibited herself
as sound; the evil in her was not a disease. Her nerves, too, were
good; he could not help admitting that her nervous stability was
far superior to his.

In the long hours of the night he had been quite unable to prevent his thoughts from flying up into regions of sheer wonder. He
saw the girl under two aspects, the contrasts between which threw
him into bewilderment. In the first she appeared as a creature both
undeveloped and ill-developed, a being low in the scale of human
worth: her second aspect showed her as one who had gone beyond
him into a sphere where larger powers moved and issues were
more dire. How came it that she seemed already to have fulfilled
herself? whereas he still stood, vacillating and terrified, upon the
threshold of life. Thinking of her body, so soft, so youthful—a body
not more than two or three years older than his!—he was overawed by the ruthlessness of the forces by which she was carried
along. In operation those forces were enormous and implacable;
in essence they were trivial, haphazard, and unworthy of respect.
For this reason he refused to dignify her infatuation with the name

of love. Love! No, no, that would be to flatter her too much. Her infatuation might be all-important to her, it might have important consequences for others, but it remained a spurious and contemptible thing.

The lights of the Camp were dancing on the broken water as his boat drew near; the smell of the place and its everlasting music came to him with a familiarity that made him feel as if he had known it from the beginning of time. The force of his loathing was so intense that he fell into a fit of trembling. Was there nothing that anyone could do to bring destruction upon this nest of snakes?

Before landing, he braced himself for his task; chiefly he wanted to ascertain whether Gunevati had had any conversation with the Prince within the last twenty-four hours, and whether there was any likelihood of their meeting before the Prince made his start. This he hoped to find out from Mansur. To seek *her* out again was impossible. Wandering about along the lake-front, he began by making inquiries among the boatmen and others regarding the Prince's movements; but only to meet the usual evasive answers, which were prompted partly by ignorance and partly by an instinctive disinclination to be obliging. There was a good deal of stir in the streets, and many strange faces were to be seen; placards announced that the festivities were to open in six days. Keeping a sharp look out for Mansur or anybody else who might be of use, he made his way by a devious route towards Gunevati's house. It had occurred to him that Ahmed, the doorkeeper, was a person to question, and he had provided himself with plenty of money to induce the man to speak. Out of the door of the building, when he reached it, there was issuing a troupe of girls, evidently on their way to the theater for a rehearsal. Lamps threw a strong light over the scene, and had Gunevati been amongst them, he could not have failed to see her. Until they had moved away he stood by a booth making purchases of sweetmeats and rice-spirit. The spirits might, he thought, be acceptable to Ahmed, whose scowling face showed that he was sober, and was finding that condition a very disagreeable one. Unable to muster up courage to accost the bevy of laughing girls, Jali gave himself the excuse that nothing they might have told him would have been worthy of belief. Waiting until the last had gone, he sauntered up to Ahmed and offered him a glass of spirits. But the man refused it, and, after peering at him and finally remembering his face, he went and placed himself squarely in the doorway.

Jali explained that he had no wish to go in.

Then what did he want? asked Ahmed.

He replied that, having heard Gunevati was unwell, he had come to inquire after her.

The doorkeeper eyed him suspiciously, then mumbled that she was still ill and could see no one.

Jali expressed regret, and, whilst talking, pressed some money into the man's hand. The effect of this was good; Ahmed became willing to converse upon general topics, but, whenever Jali led round to the subject of Gunevati, he grew taciturn. In a short time it became clear that something was wrong, and that in some way or other Ahmed himself must have come in for a certain amount of blame. The nature of Gunevati's malady remained, however, a mystery; indeed the man spoke in a fashion that made Jali doubtful whether she had been ill at all; and yet Ahmed was so emphatic in his assertions that she had not been out of her room for the last thirty-six hours that it was impossible not to believe that that at least was true.

Feeling anxious and disturbed, Jali lingered as long as he could; and before going he drew his bow at a venture. "I will tell you why I am so curious about Gunevati," he said in a confidential tone. "The fact is that not many minutes ago I heard some people saying that the Prince himself was taking a great interest in her condition, and was even thinking of coming to pay her a visit."

The effect of these words upon Ahmed was very unexpected. His face, pale and haggard already as a result of abstention from liquor, turned to a ghastlier hue, and he poured forth a torrent of curses, most of which were directed at the Prince. As a means of gaining further information, the ruse had failed completely; wherefore, hastily bidding him good night, Jali turned and made off down the lane.

His mind was now in a turmoil. It appalled him to reflect that Ahmed had actually regarded a visit from the Prince as within the bounds of possibility. His sole desire on the moment was to question Mansur, who at this hour was generally to be found at his supper in a small eating-house on the lake-front. He hurried on, and was fortunate enough to come upon him just as he was stepping out of the house. Mansur looked slightly flushed with good cheer; his little, twinkling eyes surveyed Jali shrewdly.

"Who are you looking for?" he asked.

"Gunevati," returned Jali with boldness.

Mansur's face was, as usual, inscrutable. "Well, you won't find her here."

"Is she rehearsing?" Jali inquired innocently.

A gleam of amusement came into Mansur's eyes, and he shook his head.

"Well, but—can you tell me where she is?"

Mansur looked down his nose, deliberated, and finally put a hand on Jali's shoulder. "Look here!" he said laughingly. "I don't think this Camp is quite the place for you. There are things going on that you don't understand. If I were you, I shouldn't come any more."

"But what has happened to Gunevati?" asked Jali with trembling lips. "Is she dead?"

Mansur laughed silently, looking round in his usual fashion for an audience with which to share his sense of his interlocutor's ridiculousness. And an audience happened to be there—in the shape of three young men who had just strolled up. The four of them surveyed Jali smilingly.

"No, no! she isn't dead. At least, not so far as I know. I haven't seen her for two days."

"Then what is she doing?"

"Sulking. She has been turned out of the cast. And it was high time too. Poor thing, she will never act. It was ridiculous to try to teach her."

"Is she ill?"

Mansur shrugged and turned away a little, drawing down the corners of his mouth. "I don't know anything about her," he said shortly.

"But, please—please tell me!" Jali implored. "I am sure you really know what has happened."

Mansur was already moving away, but he stopped to shrug again; and now, as he surveyed Jali, his eyes began to twinkle more than ever. "I *don't* know," he said, "but I think I can guess."

"What?" faltered Jali breathlessly.

"Well, I think—I think she is going to have a baby. That's what's the matter with her."

"A baby!" Jali gasped.

"Yes, yours." And, still radiating merriment, Mansur, with his three companions, went on his way.

Dumbfounded, petrified, Jali stood still where he was. The idea presented by Mansur horrified him so much that he was quite incapable of considering the degree of its verisimilitude. A child of his and Gunevati's! a being in which a part of his nature would be mingled with a part of hers! That would be the acme of horror! the last ignominy that life could inflict! A child of his and hers would be a spiritual monstrosity. He didn't believe Mansur—oh no! But his disbelief was merely a frantic rejection of something too abominable to be true.

After recovering from his first stupor, he turned, and, like one demented, ran back by the way he had just come; but instead of making for the front of the building where Gunevati lived, he plunged into a dark, narrow alley that ran along the back of it. The building was of irregular shape, and the alley full of corners, which made it hard for him to find the point he wanted; his object was to gain access to the small yard that he had looked into from the window of Gunevati's room. Deciding at last which was the most likely spot, he hoisted himself over the palings without much difficulty. But the enclosure he dropped into was not the right one; it had no birch-trees in it. Cautiously he looked about him, and in a minute he saw the tops of his trees quite clearly against the night sky. There was another paling between him and them, but this was no more formidable than the one he had already scaled. A minute later he was creeping softly over the grass towards Gunevati's window, which was unshuttered and showed a dim light.

He looked into the room. A solitary candle stood on a table in the center, and at the other end he could make out the form of Gunevati, lying upon her couch, with her face turned to the wall. His eyes stared; they stared as if by sheer intensity of vision he could tear her secrets from her. Once or twice she moved a little; once with a sigh, she threw out an arm.

Supporting himself against the sill, he stared and stared. For him that human form was the focus of all life's mysteries and horrors. Sweat poured down his face, as he stared across the silent room, and wondered.

The minutes went by, unchanging and terrible. His legs were trembling so violently that had he not been able to rest half his weight on the window-sill he would have sunk to the earth. And still he lacked the courage to make the smallest sound.

Then Gunevati stirred; she turned herself round, and a moment later sat up on the edge of the bed. Her face was pale and wore a fixed, heavy look. She gazed straight at him with dark, wide-open eyes. Not for a moment did she appear startled or surprised; she merely frowned, as if wearily resentful of this intrusion on her privacy. For a minute or more the two looked at one another; then with the same slow and heavy motion of her body she turned again and took up her former position with her face to the wall.

Jali made no movement whatsoever. The room turned black before his eyes. Sometimes he could see nothing but the candle; at other times he could make out Gunevati's form in the obscurity beyond it; and then again a veil of darkness would come down and he could see nothing at all.

After an interval—he knew not how long—Gunevati turned her head again, looking to see if he were still there. She considered him somberly for a few moments, then rose with heavy deliberation to her feet. She picked up the candle from the table and advanced slowly across the room to the window, and there stood, with knitted brows, looking into his face, which was nearly on a level with hers. In his eyes there was anguished interrogation; his lips moved in an effort to question; and this she must have seen. A curious expression came into her face, as she continued to gaze at him. Then slowly she raised the candle until it shone full upon her, and opened her mouth wide. Jali found himself looking into a cavern, black, swollen, horrible—without a tongue.

After a moment she closed her mouth again; she lowered the candle; she turned and went back to her bed, and stretched herself out as before.

23

SO HERE WAS Jali now! Here he was, sitting upon a bench outside the old Rajah's house in the morning sunlight, with the lake rippling before his eyes, and a light breeze blowing about him, a breeze filled with the rustle and sparkle of the new-born day.

In his mind there was no sunlight; the darkness of the night still remained there—a darkness that was not of that night only, but of the whole long night of humanity's suffering and evil-doing. Taking the last turn of events by itself, he might have found relief in the thought that Gunevati had been rendered incapable of working any further harm; he might have reflected that the fate which had over-taken her was not undeserved. But he had not yet discovered with any certainty the extent of the harm she had already done; nor could he contemplate her punishment, however well deserved, with any other sentiment than horror.

He had been sitting on this seat for an hour or more in the vague expectation of a summons from Hari or Gokal. But no summons came; and at last he felt that he must act for himself. Well, he was ready! He thought: I will wait until that flock of ducks rises again, and then I will go and speak out.

Half a minute later the signal came, and at once he got up.

BOOK THREE

RAJAH AMAR

INTRODUCTION

HITHERTO RAJAH AMAR has not played a very prominent part in this chronicle; now, however, he moves to the center of the stage, and I count myself fortunate in being able to carry the story forward by quoting passages from his private journal. It is true that, judged purely as a record of events, the Rajah's journal is not entirely satisfactory. Writing only to please himself, he gives his thoughts and feelings a good deal of space; but, since the character of the man now enters as a factor of importance in the development of the general situation, I believe that there is a distinct advantage to be gained from letting the Rajah speak for himself, and reveal himself in his own way. Even his digressiveness is, in a certain sense, illuminating, and in his very sententiousness I often find a faint but pleasing pungency, a flavor of self-mockery. Perhaps I am wrong, but I suspect the Rajah of being a man whose humor it is to pretend that he has none. When I am made to smile by his solemnity, he, I strongly suspect, is secretly smiling too. And when, quite suddenly he comes out with something positively laughable, I cannot believe that this highly self-conscious and self-critical gentleman is unaware of what he has done. For instance, in an opening to a long and rather dull disquisition on racial characteristics he smoothly remarks, "It has been said that human affinities and antipathies are determined very largely by the sense of smell ... In my opinion even more important is the religious sense." And in recounting a conversation with an important personage he says, "The reply I made was long-winded and slightly pompous," and again, "I was beginning a vague and rather insipid reply, when ..." What, I ask, are we to make of this? Well, for my part, I credit the Rajah, first with a sense of humor, secondly with an eye for some at least of his own foibles, and thirdly with a taste for making fun of himself.

Of this, however, enough. I must beware of laying emphasis on a trait that is, in any case, unimportant. My words would be misleading were they to prepare the reader for flippancy. No, this journal is nothing if not the expression of a mind in a state of high tension, the revelation of a spirit serious and sincere. The Rajah is possessed by a grave sense of the critical nature of the times, and if he is pre-occupied—as well he may be!—by the difficulties of his own particular situation, this pre-occupation is not petty, nor selfish. In one passage of his journal he says: "Akbar still occupies the Imperial Throne, his figure still looms gigantically in the background; but he gives the impression of having been stricken into semi-petrifaction; if he is a figure of Destiny, it is of Destiny brooding upon Predestination; and while this inscrutable colossus stirs no finger and makes no sign, we, a swarm of lesser creatures, weave helplessly our intricate dance at his feet."

To me, who am familiar with the earlier chapters of this journal, which are chiefly concerned with his religious life, it is curious to observe the change that takes place not only in the tone of his writing, but even, it would seem, in his personality, as soon as he plunges into the world of men and affairs. At first, I must confess, I found this change rather disconcerting, for I did not like the Rajah so well in his new character. Little by little, however, I came to understand what had happened: Amar was conscientiously endeavoring to be untrue to himself. That was the trouble, and I recognized it as dating from the time, when, still a boy, he had become the ruler of a little State. Born a contemplative, well did he know that nothing could ever make him of the world nor for the world,—worldliness, he knew, was even farther from him than the saintliness to which he aspired;—and yet, since he was in the world—and occupying, indeed, a not irresponsible position there,—it behooved him to acquit himself properly in his mundane part. To render—gracefully and in exact measure—unto Caesar the things that are Caesar's; that became his ambition! Poor Amar! His earlier diaries contain passages which show how much effort went in this endeavor; and, if he achieved any kind of success, it is still open to us to doubt whether the effort was not misapplied. For we cannot help suspecting him of over-valuing the qualities in which he is deficient, of over-estimating accomplishments that are worth acquiring only at a lesser cost.

By a curious piece of good fortune a portrait of the Rajah is extant. It is the product of a rather poor Persian artist, working without imagination within the limits of a strict convention. He shows us his royal subject standing stiffly in full dress uniform in what is probably a deer-park. The park is full of innocent animals,—we notice in particular a lamb prancing in a little patch of flowers in the background. The Rajah faces us with a look of supreme detachment,—he seems, indeed, completely absent from the earthly scene; and yet in one hand he holds a piece of sugar— or is it salt?—which he is offering to a doe. This creature the artist has succeeded in investing with an air of extraordinary respectfulness—so much so that she seems to be on the point of dropping a curtsy. A picture of more skill and sophistication might well have been less revealing. Convention has forced the artist to make Amar superbly upright, voluminously sashed, hugely turbaned, and encased in a tunic that sticks out all about him like a ballet-dancer's tulle; but it has not stood in the way of a very painstaking and no doubt accurate delineation of feature. We look fairly and squarely into a long, narrow, clean-shaven face. The chin is firm, the mouth expressive of purpose, the eyes deepset. This would be the face of a man whose vision is narrow, did the eyes not reveal a character critically watchful of itself.

PART ONE

1

RAJAH AMAR SAILED across the lake just after dawn. He stepped out of the boat on to the pier and drew the folds of his white cloak about him. A fresh breeze and a level light were streaming down the valley, tipping the ripe meadow-grasses with gold and the wavelets with silver. At this early hour the promenade of the Pleasance of the Arts was empty save for a few sweepers who were brushing away the litter of a festive night. The dust that went up from their brooms was gilded into beauty by the sun; it rose like the smoke of incense before the shuttered pleasure-houses behind.

And the Rajah said to himself: "For many months I have been like a messenger who sits upon the outer step and waits. He watches the passers-by, he dreams, he smiles to himself. He is waiting.

"When in the spring a mountain river is dammed up by a wall of ice, a still lake forms; the silent water leans and leans; day after day the valley rests in quiet; but one day the break comes."

Turning northward towards the high mountains, he fixed upon the mists that were veiling them a long and frowning look; and slowly, as he gazed, there emerged a phantasmal glitter, a vision that hung so loftily above the morning haze that his imagination could not join it to the solid earth. He gazed, and it was as if his spirit sailed from out of him; it sailed like a cloudlet amongst those icebound peaks. Closing his eyes, he conjured up a vision of the peaks at night. His spirit drifted as a vapor through black, frost-deadened night, amongst ice-slopes lit only by their own whiteness and the scintillation of unnumbered stars.

O silent dark! Cold, silent, bediamonded dark! Not the jungle-dark, full of violence and stealth; not the recurrent, red dark of life-blood; not the restless, blue dark of the sea; but the dark of the heights—Nirvana!

(*Here the Rajah takes up the tale in his own words.*)

The sound of a step behind caused me to turn my head. A big, swarthy, fleshy man who was approaching, hailed me genially by name. "Rajah Amar! What an early visit! I suppose it means that you are anxious to catch the Prince before he makes his start. Well, there is no hurry. Daniyal certainly won't get off before noon."

I replied that I had come to see Shaik Mobarek, not the Prince.

"But what makes you think he will be ready at this hour?"

"He has often told me that he wakes at dawn, and that he likes to receive visitors as early as possible."

"Extraordinary! At his age too! I am told he is nearly eighty. A most remarkable man." The newcomer broke off to gaze intently at the rippling water. "Do you know, but for this cold wind, I think I would take a dip. In fact, that was my intention in coming down here."

At last it came back to me that I had run across this man—his name was Churaman—two or three times before: once at my sister's house in Agra and then at some court function. On these occasions I had not taken to him particularly; his manner had seemed to me rather too free and easy,—as if he were trying to make up in self-assurance for what he lacked in breeding.

"If you like," Churaman went on, "I will show you the way to the Shaik's house; and perhaps you won't mind if I come in with you for a moment. The Shaik always interests me. A wicked old man, perhaps; but a remarkable personality! The last time we met, I remember, he had a bad toothache; and with his head muffled up in a shawl he looked like a very clever, very malicious old dowager—and he talked rather like one too."

435

Churaman chuckled as he spoke but I did not respond. To be without respect, or to pretend to be without respect, for those who stand high above you—this is to be guilty of either an unintentional or an intentional stupidity.

As we proceeded along the lake-front, my eyes wandered over the outward scene; I looked, in a kind of trance, at Daniyal's fantastic house-fronts aglow in the slanting sunlight; I looked at our far-flung shadows moving before us over the frayed flanking of the vulgar promenade; I looked upwards and saw huge masses of white cloud rolling before the wind. For a few seconds my old doubts returned; I thought of Sita, and my intended withdrawal from the world seemed to me both selfish and unjustified. But the next moment I reminded myself that Sita was no less religious than I. She would remember that her own prophet has said: "Everyone that hath forsaken wife, or children, or lands, for my name's sake shall receive an hundred fold, and shall inherit everlasting life." I bethought me once again that he who waits upon the world to release him waits till death. Worldly affairs drag on; one entanglement transforms itself into another. However long I were to delay, the moment must inevitably come when I should have to do violence to my own feelings and those of others. Well! that moment was here now. Here I was with my feet upon the road!

These meditations were interrupted by a strange spectacle. Coming up from one of the jetties, there appeared a group of men with one in their midst who seemed to be without the use of his limbs. He was urged along by two boatmen, whilst others followed behind. The young man thus attended presented a pitiable appearance; water dripped from his clothing, his sodden turban had been clapped on to his head all awry. His face was ashen, his eyes vacant and wild. I halted, and my astonishment was increased when I observed that, although the young man's dress was indicative of high rank, his rescuers were treating him with scant ceremony—hardly, indeed, with ordinary consideration. When his turban fell off, those behind kicked it along with gibes, and although the half-drowned wretch was begging for a moment's halt, his escorts continued to hustle him forward without an instant's respite.

I was about to intervene when Churaman laid a hand upon my arm, and in a low hurried voice begged me to pay no heed. The young man, he assured me, was "all right"; the boatmen, too, knew quite well what they were about; this was not the first time that such a thing had happened. Churaman spoke with such evident understanding of the case that I complied. But, as the young man passed, I received another shock of surprise. "Surely," I said, "that is Prince Dantawat?"

There was a pause before Churaman answered, and I saw his expression change several times. When they did come, his words were spoken in that candid and confidential tone of voice that at once inspires mistrust. Poor Prince Dantawat, he explained, had had "various troubles," as a result of which he was now "slightly unbalanced." The strain of living in the Camp had been too much for him. "Yes, that's the truth of the matter. It is sad, very sad; for Dantawat is really such a nice fellow. A little neurotic, of course; and then—well, Daniyal has been rather inconsiderate to him lately, and I am afraid he has taken it too much to heart. However, Dantawat will soon recover, if—if only we can get him away. All he needs is a change."

"You mean that Prince Dantawat threw himself into the lake?"

"Well—yes!" The admission was made reluctantly.

"And this has happened before?"

Again Churaman's expression presented an interesting study. I could see that, although he felt a genuine pity for Dantawat, he was amused; and I suspected that amongst his own friends he would very soon be treating the whole affair as an excellent joke.

"Well, to tell the truth," he replied at last, "Dantawat *has* behaved like this before. You see, he wants to attract Daniyal's attention. Daniyal certainly is rather unfeeling at times."

At this point I laid constraint upon myself. Knowing that Churaman had arrived at the Camp only a week or so ago, I decided to impose on him a little, if I could. I began talking about Daniyal and his friends as if I were more familiar with them than I really am; and these tactics were successful, for presently Churaman fell to speaking with a good deal of freedom. It evidently pleased him to let me see that he had known Daniyal quite well in early days. This intimacy had arisen out of the circumstance that Churaman's foster-mother and Prince Salim's had been sisters; and the three children, thus brought together in infancy, had kept up a certain companionship during boyhood. In age Churaman came mid-way between Salim and Daniyal, and his friendship had gradually transferred itself from the elder to the younger brother, for Salim had grown up rough, hectoring, and unintelligent, while Daniyal had been good-looking, well-mannered, and extremely precocious. All three boys, however, had remained fairly good friends, until Salim, in the beginning of his seventeenth year, suddenly developed a violent hatred of his brother, who was then about twelve. The reason for this hatred Churaman at first professed himself quite unable to define, but a little later he said in his rapid, off-hand way: "Oh, it was jealousy, of course! Pure jealousy! At the time when Salim was a big, shaggy, rough-looking youth, Daniyal was really quite beautiful. He had dignity, too. Such a contrast to Salim, who had nothing but bluster and swagger! Even at the age of twelve, Daniyal was much the more advanced, much more of a man of the world. Salim thought of nothing but polo and hunting. Daniyal was interested in—well, in lots of things."

"What things?" I asked.

"Oh, in—in people and everything. I mean he revealed an artistic nature; he was in fact exceedingly knowing for his age. Not that he was much of a talker in those days. No, he was very silent, very reserved. Not shy; but—for a small boy—extraordinarily self-contained. For one thing, he had no mother, you must remember. There was no one with whom he was intimate. Salim's mother, who brought him up, was as kind as anyone could be; but he never took to her."

Here Churaman broke off—rather abruptly, as it seemed. But I showed such a flattering interest in what he was saying that he started off again. Daniyal, he said, at this time had become a great favorite with the grooms and men of the royal elephant stables. "Oddly enough, although he was no horseman, he got on with the men much better than Salim. This made Salim jealous, and then it was that they had—well, it was a dreadful affair."

Again Churaman stopped. Nor could I get him to tell me what "the affair" was. I could see that he was thinking over what he had said and wondering how much I could read between the lines. As a matter of fact I was quite in the dark. Perhaps my expression revealed it, for presently his own interest in what he had to say carried him forward again.

"Really," he exclaimed, "it was extraordinary, the relationship between these two boys! At times Salim's brutality was almost unbelievable; yet Daniyal never seemed to avoid it. There is no doubt that he fascinated Salim, and that he knew he did. Salim couldn't forget him, couldn't ignore him, as he longed to do. For weeks at a time he would pretend to be unaware of Daniyal's existence, but this pretense always ended in a scene of unusual brutality. And Daniyal, even while he was being knocked about, somehow kept his air of superiority; it was as if he knew that he was really scoring off Salim all the time. But I must say that when Salim was sent away Daniyal felt it to be a relief. In a short time he became quite changed. He gathered round him a circle of friends,—clever boys that Salim would never have got on with."

"Since then," I observed, "he and Salim have of course met very little."

Churaman nodded. "I shall never forget the one occasion when I witnessed a meeting between them. Salim flushed and glowered, and could not find a single word. Daniyal, on the other hand, smiled and was perfectly amiable. In the end it looked as if Salim was going to knock him down."

A little later we were speaking about the present rivalry between the two brothers and the question of taking sides. "Thank heaven!" exclaimed Churaman, "I am nothing but a poor artist. Politics simply don't concern me at all."

"But your sympathies," I said smiling, "are obviously with Daniyal."

"I am an artist," Churaman repeated, "and I naturally have more in common with Daniyal, to whom art means something."

I paused; I was thinking that were Churaman a true artist, he would hold Daniyal's clique in particular abhorrence—just as to me the self-deceiving and the self-righteous are more odious than confessed cynics.

"Yes," I replied at last, "you are fortunate, but, all the same, I doubt whether there is a single man in the Empire who can say that the question of the succession is a matter of no interest to him."

Churaman smiled and said quickly: "At any rate, I am not one of those who run the risk of being beheaded, if he finds himself on the losing side."

I joined him in his laugh. "Nor I. At least I hope not. But now tell me: Which, in your opinion, will be the losing side?"

Without a moment's hesitation Churaman replied: "Salim's."

"You feel so sure?"

"Yes,—and I can easily explain why."

"Tell me."

"First, Daniyal is the cleverer; secondly, he has the cleverer friends; and, thirdly, his friends have the ear of the Emperor. Daniyal has Mobarek and Mabun Das on his side; surely that by itself ought to assure him the victory."

I looked at Churaman and said nothing.

"Surely," he went on in a tone of irritation, "surely Akbar has enough common sense to realize what is best for the Empire? Of course neither Salim nor Daniyal are all that he could wish; but he sees that Daniyal's faults are his own private affair, whereas Salim's are of the kind to work public mischief."

I shrugged. I was not going to argue the matter with Churaman, who to my thinking was simplifying the problem quite unwarrantably. Was it possible that he did not know it? Was he incapable of grasping either the subtleties of Akbar's character or the complexity of the forces that govern the course of the world's history? The Emperor combines naivety, cunning, and idealism. His cunning is naive, his naivety is cunning, and his idealism is both— as well as something more. If I could define that something more, I could define the character of Life itself. I believe Akbar's idealism to be of a kind that will never throw him off the road that leads to worldly success. This sounds like a sneer at Akbar, but it is rather a comment upon the world. Never have I met an idealism that I have felt to be wholly pure, never have I met a heart that I have felt to be wholly honest, but that it has proved a handicap to its possessor. Were it not for the examples provided by Christ and Buddha, I should say there is no greatness, no generosity, no graciousness, in man or in woman, that can win worldly recognition on its own merits alone. In general the virtues and graces that are famous are those that are heavily alloyed. When Mobarek says that Akbar's choice will be utilitarian, and that expediency points unmistakably to Daniyal, he is, I repeat, grossly simplifying the problem. I, for my part, feel certain that Akbar will be guided by

440

his idealism, but, Akbar's choice once made, I shall say: "*That* was ultimately expedient. For such is Akbar, and such is the nature of the world."

We were now approaching a house of some importance that stood inside an enclosure of its own. Among the men standing by the gate several were wearing the uniform of Mobarek's household. When I announced myself, I was at once admitted, and Churaman followed me in. A few minutes later a secretary appeared, and, after asking me a few questions, bowed and escorted us into the Shaik's presence.

Mobarek was occupying a large room on the ground floor. Glancing round, as I came in, I recognized many of the tapestries, curtains, and rugs, as being his own property. Some of the furniture, too, was his, notably the throne-like bed at the end of the room, with its canopy of embroidered Chinese silk. In this bed the Shaik was now reclining, propped up with cushions, a fur tippet over his shoulders, and papers spread out on the counterpane. Secretaries and attendants stood on either side. As we advanced, with a sweep of his hand he pushed the litter of papers away from him, and his voice rang out in greetings—greetings which to my mistrustful ears sounded too amiable to be sincere.

2

STUDYING THE SHAIK in the clear light of morning, I was struck by his freshness in old age. I could not help comparing him with my own father, to whom the years had brought not only infirmity of body but also decay of mind. *His* years seemed to have stripped him of nothing but youth's weaknesses and inconsequences. Left with a frame from which all the heavy humors of the flesh had long since been dried out, he made the slenderness and saplessness of old age seem actually no disadvantage. Against his canopy of crimson and gold this little old man shone with a silvery brightness; he convinced you that with only dry pith and a few tendons to call his own, he was far better equipped than you for the struggle of life. His eyes rested on us smilingly, brilliantly, and while he spoke, his hands, pale and light as thistle-down, waved upon the air a delicate accompaniment to his speech.

"My friends," he cried. "You find me really at my wit's end. As you know, the Prince should have started for Kathiapur at least forty-eight hours ago. It was most important that he should be there in time to meet Princess Lalita and his future father-in-law. He promised me yesterday that he would make an early start this morning, yet now I hear that he is still in bed—in bed and chatting to his friends! He even tells about conducting another rehearsal this afternoon."

Although Mobarek spoke laughingly, it was to be seen that he was really perturbed. I seated myself in a chair that had been brought forward for me, whilst Churaman, wrinkling his brows, paced to and fro on the other side of the bed. Mobarek followed him with his eyes, and presently added softly: "The Prince has that play of his on the brain. He can think of nothing else."

Churaman nodded.

"You were with him at the last rehearsal?"

"I was."

"My dear Churaman," said Mobarek, and his voice was soft as silk, "I think the Prince suggested not long ago that you should conduct the rehearsals in his absence? He has the very highest opinion of your knowledge in these matters. Well, for heaven's sake, go and see him at once! Inspire him with confidence! Persuade him that you will conduct these last rehearsals even better than he could himself! Do you think you can manage it?"

For a moment Churaman maintained an impressive silence. Then: "Yes!" he said, "I will go now."

"Excellent!" said Mobarek with a charming smile. "You will be a public benefactor if you succeed."

"I will do my best," returned Churaman, and with that he strode out of the room.

As the door closed behind him Mobarek turned to me. "I owe you a thousand apologies, Rajah. You expected a quiet talk, and instead . . . But you see what a predicament I am in. Imagine the Khan and Princess Lalita waiting hour by hour, day by day, for Daniyal who does not arrive! You know the Khan, Rajah. He is not the man to endure such things patiently. Trifles, do you say? Ah, but such trifles tell! They mount up—and they tell. The Khan is not finding Daniyal very satisfactory. Nor is the Emperor. And as for Lalita herself—well, I don't disguise from you that the Prince makes a rather poor lover. With him, I am afraid, Art comes first."

These last words issued from the old man's lips with an effect that struck me as peculiar; the tone in which they were pronounced gave me no clue how to take them. I looked at Mobarek hard, but the Shaik's face so often wears a smile of quiet interior amusement that his expression at this moment was quite unrevealing. With his chin on his breast he appeared to be sunk in an ironic contemplation of Daniyal's wayward personality; nevertheless his eyes were alert; I felt sure that I was being studied; and my response was cautious. "I have been told," I said, "that Daniyal is not particularly anxious to marry."

"Perhaps not. Perhaps not. You see, he is already wedded to the Arts."

The note of humor was quite clearly sounded now, but I still felt it wise to ignore the lead given me. "Princess Lalita," I said, "shows, no doubt, a sympathetic understanding of his character."

"Yes; fortunately the dear Princess makes allowances. I give her great credit for it. She is a clever girl, although, as you know, impulsive."

My face remained wooden. The truth is that at the time I did not perceive the meaning that might be lurking behind those last words. It was not until I began thinking them over afterwards that there flashed upon me a remembrance of the moment when I had caught sight of Hari and Lalita in each other's arms. Was it conceivable that Mobarek had seen what I had seen?

At this point I must jot down a reflection which I wish to impress upon myself by way of warning. One habitually forgets that much may be learnt from a conversation long after that conversation is over. Speaking for myself, I can truly say that my best critical faculties do not come into play until retrospection begins; and I believe that I am not peculiar in this: I believe that many apparently capricious changes of heart or of opinion are in truth based upon new perceptions that have been tardy but just.

To go back to Mobarek's last words, he may have been deceived by the unintelligent look on my face. If, indeed, he was testing me, he very likely concluded that *my* eye had missed what *his* had seen. Thus, if my mind moves less nimbly than his, it is possible that this inferiority has some small advantages as well as its obvious disadvantages. My slow-wittedness may make him think me more stupid than I am.

"I suppose," I brought out at last, and my accent was rather uncertain, "I suppose the Princess, also, is of an artistic temperament?"

Mobarek appeared not to hear. "Did you see the Prince's last play?" he asked.

"No, I was not invited."

"Perhaps it was just as well!" And he laughed gently. "You might not have thought very highly of it. In fact, I can't be sure that you would find much to admire in anything the Prince has yet turned out. Tastes differ; I leave it at that. Certainly it is not for an old man like *me* to pronounce on these things. When I say that the Prince is an artist, I mean only that in his life Art takes the first place. And surely, Rajah, an ardor for beauty, even if crude or bizarre in its manifestations, is not a thing to be discouraged or despised? I hope you feel that you can sympathize with Daniyal's enthusiasms, even if your taste and his do not always coincide. The young are less fastidious than we are in some respects, Rajah. I must confess that not a few of Daniyal's companions in Art jar on me a good deal. Companions in Art! There you have it! Art, like necessity, makes strange bedfellows, eh? Take our friend Churaman, for instance,—a nice fellow, quite a nice fellow, and clever, I believe, in his own particular line. Daniyal is genuinely fond of him—thinks he has a real sense of the stage. Ah me! What will our friend Churaman have to say when he comes back, I wonder?" And the Shaik gave a sigh.

I confess I was completely at a loss. Never had the old man's smile been more elfish. It was impossible to believe that his air of listening to his own voice with a detached amusement was wholly feigned. As I watched him, however, his face swiftly changed, and it was in quite another tone that he went on: "Rajah, the breaking-off of the engagement between the Prince and Lalita would be a calamity of the first magnitude. Is it possible that you don't realize that? Oh, Rajah, you have been out of the world too long."

He sighed again, and again I kept silent.

"Perhaps," he said, "you imagine that the Khan must be just as eager for this alliance as the Emperor? Well, I won't deny that the Khan is flattered; but—but there is another side to this affair. As you know, the Khan is the lion amongst the Mahommedan tribesmen of the North; and, as you should remember, he was also at one time a great personal friend of Prince Salim's. They are both true believers, and they share the reputation of being the foremost champions of Islam. Now, if the Khan marries his daughter to Daniyal, he will not only be making himself very unpopular with his own subjects, but the neighboring chieftains may well turn upon him as a traitor to the Faith. It is a nice question whether his prestige on the frontier can bear the strain that he is about to put upon it. He evidently thinks that it will; but Salim is trying very hard to persuade him that it won't. The present moment is critical—not only for the Khan but for the Emperor as well. An armed insurrection in the North timed to coincide with a movement of Salim's armies up from the South would be"—he shrugged—"well, pretty serious."

I was bound to say that I was not unimpressed. Mobarek might, for his own ends, be giving me a somewhat one-sided account of the situation, but I felt sure that he was not making any serious departure from the truth. I was beginning a vague and rather insipid reply when three loud strokes, sounded on a gong outside, interrupted me. This was followed by an intoned call, not unlike that of the muezzins at the hour of prayer.

"I am afraid we shall have to continue our talk a little later," said the Shaik, "I have to prepare myself for worship."

Without fully understanding what was afoot, I retired to the ante-chamber, where I was presently joined by Mobarek's major-domo, who explained that his master was to rise, perform certain ceremonial ablutions, and then proceed to a small temple that had been raised in the garden. There for a quarter of an hour he would hold solitary communion with the Deity.

Whilst he was speaking, his face suddenly became very red, and after a moment he broke off and rushed to the door. In subdued, but forcible tones, I heard him giving orders to the servants outside that they were to disperse a group of children who were shouting and laughing by the lake. When he returned to me his color was still high. "The gong that sounded a few minutes ago was a signal that absolute silence should be preserved round and about the house. That is one of the commands laid down by His Majesty. He has said: 'The Emperor is the vice-regent of God; the chief Priests are the vice-regents of the Emperor. When their prayers arise, let no man shake the air with any sound louder than his natural breathing.' "

I answered this with a grave nod, and, feeling dispensed from further conversation, drew away, sat down, and followed my own thoughts. These were concerned with Mobarek, whose character puzzled and interested me exceedingly. Its dominant note has always seemed to me to be a passion for organization, and for the discipline that organization both requires and enforces. I respect this trait. In the individual it betokens self-respect, and in the race it makes for civilization. But Mobarek is too much set upon grading human worth, and the standard which he uses is not a good one. I do not say that he leaves ultimate values out of account, my complaint is that they are not accepted as supreme; they are given a place on a scale that is essentially worldly. Of course the Emperor presents a figure that does not fit very conveniently into Mobarek's scheme of things. Akbar has many characteristics that he is obliged to regard with humorous indulgence. But then I have noticed that occasionally (perhaps, in order to give his reverence more luster) he likes to speak of even God upon a jesting tone; and similarly, when he makes fun of the Emperor, it is always with the implication that in Akbar even absurdities become august. From first to last he is incapable of disloyalty to the caste spirit. Confronted with the necessity of conferring upon either Salim or Daniyal the advantage of his support, he did not, I imagine, hesitate for one instant. No! Salim he would regard as a reckless and intractable boor. Daniyal may offend his taste in many ways, but he sees in him a useful tool. In Daniyal he finds a disposition not too ambitious to be dangerous, and a cynicism of which he knows he can take advantage. This in addition to a figure the flashiness of which imposes upon the vulgar world of to-day.

I imagine he had no difficulty in persuading Daniyal to adopt the new religion, upon which his heart is set. This vague, bodiless creed is the ostensible rationale of the all-embracing hierarchic order which it is his ambition to establish. Bent upon the welding of secular and sacred authority, he finds in our caste system a framework round which to build. But nothing can be done without reconciling the Brahmins and inducing them to take their place in his scheme. It is this that has focused his interest upon Gokal; and here—as I now begin to see—here it is that I, too, make a claim upon his attention. Gokal's is such a commanding figure that his acceptance of the Din Ilahi would bring in the great majority of the Brahmins who are now in fact hesitant. *I* take my importance as the person most likely to be able to persuade Gokal to give them the lead. Yes, I believe this to be the explanation that I have been seeking, the motive at the bottom of Mobarek's overtures. It is strange, perhaps, that the idea did not come to me before. The truth of course is that for the past months my mind has been occupied with matters of a very different order, and I find it hard to set in motion again the machinery of worldly calculation.

But I must return to my narrative. I was gazing meditatively out of the window, when my eye fell upon Churaman, who was striding along the road at a great pace. The next minute I heard him shouting to the servants outside; and a moment later he burst into the room.

"News!" he cried. "I have some really exciting news!"

"You have had a talk with Daniyal?"

"Yes."

"And you were successful?"

"Well, not exactly. But—the whole situation has changed." He paused, looking round the room. "Where is the Shaik?"

"Here." And, turning round, I saw that Mobarek had returned, and was inviting us to rejoin him in the larger room.

Churaman pushed past me with impetuosity. "Shaik!" he cried, "I have great tidings."

Mobarek smiled at him composedly.

"Perhaps you have already heard? Prince Salim has made a move! Civil war has begun!"

I did not take this announcement very seriously. As for Mobarek he threw out his hands with a shrug.

"Yes, Salim has made a move," repeated Churaman, still with gusto.

"You mean . . ." I began.

"I mean," interrupted Churaman, "that he has marched out of Allahabad at the head of his army, and is making in this direction."

"His army is not quartered anywhere near Allahabad," I murmured; and Mobarek added: "These rumors have been running over the Camp for the last month."

Churaman drew himself up. "I am telling you what I have just heard from Daniyal himself, and what he believes to be true. Salim is said to be heading straight for this place. He is at the head of seventeen thousand horsemen, his express purpose being to cut us off."

A look of impatience passed over Mobarek's face, and he replied rather coolly that "Salim's move" portended very little. It could not be anything more than a demonstration made for political ends.

Churaman, feeling slightly snubbed, turned to me. "I mentioned to the Prince that you were here, and he said he was delighted to hear it. There were one or two matters that he particularly wanted to see you about."

I felt some surprise, but said nothing. The prospect of a meeting with the Prince was not particularly agreeable to me, but I tried not to let this be apparent.

Churaman addressed himself to Mobarek again. "Daniyal asked me to tell you that he would be here in another hour or so. I could not persuade him...." He broke off because Mobarek had moved to the window, and was looking out with a frown on his face. We joined him and saw an altercation going on at the outer gate. It was the unfortunate Dantawat, to whom admittance was being roughly denied.

Mobarek turned to Churaman with a rather chilly suavity. "It would be a kindness on your part, if you would go out and take poor Prince Dantawat away. And will you come back again a little later when the Prince is here? Then perhaps some arrangement can be made about the rehearsals."

Churaman bowed and took himself off, whereupon Mobarek looked at me, smiled, and said: "Come! We will continue our talk."

3

HE LED ME into a little room at the back of the house, in the middle of which there stood a Chinese tray covered with light refreshments. His dress, I noticed, was now very superb, and his manner seemed to have become more lordly; but beneath these airs I observed a new friendliness of disposition. Laying his hand upon my shoulder, he smiled into my face—rather strangely, I thought—before bidding me sit down.

"Rajah," said he, seating himself opposite, "we look at life from different angles, you and I, but that does not mean that our immediate political views and aims are bound to be antagonistic. I think you are inclined to agree with me on two important points: first, that a compromise ought to be possible between the Brahmins and the Din Ilahi, and, secondly, that Daniyal's succession to the Throne is, on the whole, preferable to Salim's. Here then—and these two questions cover nearly the whole field of practical politics at the moment—we do not disagree."

Leaning forward across the low table, he smiled into my face, and again I was conscious of a certain sympathy between us. Nevertheless the reply I made was long-winded and slightly pompous. I adopted this tone because I wanted to show Mobarek that I was not afraid of being a prig; and I ended up by stating quite explicitly that I was anxious to find out whether Daniyal's intellectual and moral defects were such as to make it impossible for me to join his party.

Mobarek's answer was splendid in its implied self-commendation. Daniyal's chief fault, he said, was irresponsibility, and this would cause him to lean upon his advisers; thus his very defect would indirectly minister to the welfare of the Empire.

A little later I said something about Daniyal's equalitarian ideas, and at this Mobarek pursed his lips and became astonishingly, but by no means unpleasingly, sententious. "Between man and man," he pronounced, "there is more difference in spiritual worth than between man and the beasts of the field, for to us God has bestowed the power greatly to exalt or to debase ourselves. Looking around me, I see some men who are as animals, others who approach to angelhood. The theory of the equality of men is too absurd to affect practical politics. What, I ask you, is society, if not the systematizing of the natural inequalities between race and race, caste and caste, and man and man?"

"That may be so," I replied, "but all the same the Prince . . ."

"The Prince," interrupted Mobarek sternly, "has accepted the Din Ilahi, and such ideas as are inconsistent with that faith he must discard. Only the other day I pointed out to him that the law of society is but an extension of the law of God. Upon this earth we see an ordered hierarchy of creatures from the lowest to the highest, and beyond our vision there exists an enormously elaborate and magnificent hierarchy of Spiritual Beings." He looked up, heavenwards, for a moment, then went on slowly: "Yes, and again, beyond these there dwells, in dazzling and impenetrable mystery, an incomprehensible and sublime Power, of whom the Sun may be regarded as the physical symbol."

I had not realized before how the influences of childhood had persisted in this old man. Mobarek evidently has an adoration of, a reverence for, the sun, fire, and light, after the Zoroastrian manner; his Sufi doctrines have suffused the Din Ilahi with a coloring derived from generations of primitive Sun-worshipers.

"Rajah," he continued, "let me remind you of the verses in which Jalal Ud-Din Rumi, four hundred years ago, expressed God's divine law:

> " I died from mineral and plant became;
> Died from the plant, and took a sentient frame;

451

> Died from the beast, and donned a human dress;
> When by my dying did I e'er grow less?
> Another time from manhood I must die
> To soar with angel-pinions through the sky.
> As angel also must I fade away,
> Since everything shall perish save his Day.
> Let me be Naught! For all things do proclaim
> That 'unto Him do we return again!'

"This is the evolution of spirit in passage through material and semi-material worlds. Jalal Ud-Din's words are inspired. No doubt they will receive useful certification in a later age by those who move upon their feet instead of using wings. Personally I believe that one day science will make much of this divinely ordained progression of life;—nor will science neglect the study of *light*. When I speak of light as the source and seed of life I am using no mere figure of speech. The rays of light from the sun may be regarded either as a very tenuous form of matter, or as energy, or as angels from the mind of God. The Emperor by divine inspiration is powerfully imbued with this truth."

He was looking at me fixedly and I suppose my face was not sufficiently responsive, for his gaze suddenly became severe, and he went on: "Is it possible that you are unaware that at noon of the day when the sun enters the nineteenth degree of Aries, the whole world being then surrounded by his light, the Emperor causes a round piece of a white and shining stone to be exposed to God's beams? A piece of cotton is then held under it, which catches fire from the concentrated rays. This celestial fire is committed to the care of proper persons. The lamp-lighters, torch-bearers, and cooks of the royal household use it for their offices; and when a year has passed away, they renew the fire." He paused, then added: "The sun is the torch by which God's sovereignty is illuminated for our eyes."

I gazed at Mobarek with the deepest interest, and my heart warmed towards him. While I was considering my reply, he took up speech again—this time in a different tone.

"I think you are critical of the Prince." There was a light of amusement in his eyes. "Well, I am not uncritical of him myself. I see his faults as well as anyone."

"They are the faults of youth?" I suggested.

"Yes, but he will never outgrow them."

"No?"

"No."

For a moment we were silent; then Mobarek gave a shrug. "We speak of the faults of youth as if they belonged only to youth, but as a matter of fact most men never learn to do more than dissimulate them. Those faults, if they are faults, spring from a fundamental principle, the instinct to rebel."

I was a little surprised, and I let him see it.

"Everyone," he went on decisively, "contains within himself the impulses of the rebel, the revolutionary, the enemy of order and discipline."

"The instinct to destroy?" I added.

Mobarek gave me a quick look. "That is possible. All change involves destruction. What we see in the young is a revolt against two tyrannies: the tyranny of the Past and the tyranny of Nature. I expect you, Rajah, as a much younger man, to be less intolerant of Daniyal's faults than I am. My age cramps me. Much of what Daniyal wants to destroy seems to me better than anything he has to put in its place. However, he and I will counterbalance one another."

"You speak with remarkable detachment," I said.

"As for the revolt against Nature," he continued, "that, too, has its uses. If it conduces to the cult of the stylized, the conventionalized, the artificial, just for their own sakes, it also, more broadly, makes for civilization."

"Civilization?" I echoed. "At what point between barbarism and decadence does civilization reign? If a civilized community be defined as one where you find aesthetic pre-occupations, subtle thought, and polished intercourse, is civilization necessarily desirable? Aesthetic pre-occupations are not inconsistent with a wholly inadequate conception of the range and power of art; thought may be subtle and yet trivial; and polished intercourse may be singularly uninteresting."

Mobarek smiled, and remained silent for some time; then—

"The point I want to emphasize," he went on, "is that the rebellious instinct is in reality constructive; it only appears destructive in its more naive and superficial manifestations,—that is to say in its attacks upon what the young man feels to be outworn, cumbersome and restrictive. The past—and the actually passing—are the fulcrum against which the lever of youth must press. Daniyal's attitude to the Emperor and the whole of the old school is, in my view, quite foolish in many respects. I am not particularly interested in Art, so of that I will not speak; but his social and political ideas often seem to me ridiculous."

"His attitude at present," I murmured, "is not very helpful to you. I mean in regard to the Princess and her father. May I ask whether Lalita herself is anxious to come to the Camp?"

Mobarek pursed his lips.

"Forgive me for speaking discouragingly," I went on, "but I am wondering whether you are not going to find it difficult to bring off this match. The Princess's own inclinations might—in the circumstances—just turn the scale."

"You are quite right, Rajah." There was a humorous gleam in Mobarek's eyes. "You are quite right. And that is why I have just decided that I must go to Kathiapur myself. I shall start tomorrow. The apologies and excuses I shall make for the Prince will be better than any he could make for himself. It will not be my fault if Lalita doesn't return here with me."

I admired the old man's energy and self-confidence. "The Prince has good friends," I said. "I hope he will prove to us all that he deserves them."

Mobarek smiled; he was looking at me fixedly. "I want you to come with me, Rajah."

This suggestion did not surprise me overmuch. Mobarek of course knew that Ambissa had been begging me to come to Kathiapur. "You want me to accompany you?" I said slowly. "Well, after all, why not? I am much flattered by your invitation."

"Then you will?" said Mobarek quickly. "Excellent!"

"And yet . . ." I hesitated.

"I think that when you crossed the lake this morning . . ." said Mobarek, looking at me with a smile.

454

I could not help stiffening. The old man was showing almost too much insight. "I had no fixed plans," I said.

"No. But you were determined to let yourself be guided by the play of events. So, if I press you . . . ?"

I laughed. "Yes."

Mobarek leant across the table to lay a hand on my arm. "That gives me the greatest pleasure. And now"—he rose with briskness to his feet—"we must rejoin our friends. The Prince may be here at any moment."

I followed him into a large reception-room, where we found Churaman with several young men of the Prince's train. Their heads together, they were chattering and giggling like schoolgirls; but as soon as Mobarek appeared, the conversation changed its tone. After a while, having separated Churaman from the crowd, I succeeded in bringing him back to the subject of Daniyal. In Churaman's opinion the fact that Daniyal's mother was a slave-girl has exercised a powerful influence upon the Prince's character. This is interesting. Interesting, too, is the information that Daniyal cannot endure the sight of physical pain. He declares that at the mass execution of the Vamacharis, about six months ago, the Prince actually fainted.

Finally we got on to the subject of the Prince's marriage; and here Churaman went further than he can have intended in the way of self-revelation. In describing the series of incivilities that Lalita had received at Daniyal's hands, he allowed a considerable satisfaction to appear. My first supposition was that at some time or other the Princess had slighted him; but when it presently came out that the two had never met, it became clear that Churaman was using the tone of the Camp—a tone for which Daniyal is himself no doubt responsible. Now, my own opinion of Lalita (formed upon very slight acquaintance) is not particularly favorable; but that does not alter my judgment upon Daniyal in this matter, nor did it help me tolerate Churaman's tone. I rejoined Mobarek, and remained with him until the Prince was announced.

4

THE MOMENT HE entered the room I was seized with dismay. On our previous meetings, certainly, I had found him unprepossessing enough; but never—no, never before—had he affected me like this. His appearance, his gestures, the inflections of his voice—in short the whole presence and personality of this young man were infinitely displeasing. With a sinking heart I asked myself whether I should ever find it possible, in any circumstances, to range myself on his side, or to propose to Sita that she should do so. Wonderingly I glanced at Mobarek. His face of smiling urbanity was a lesson to me.

For some time after Daniyal had made his entrance, and while he was deploying himself with a distressing superabundance of speech and gesture, we stood about him, proclaiming with courtiers' smiles that our eyes and ears were entranced. "Oh my dear Shaik! My beloved Guru!"—to give an example of his style— "Isn't this too atrocious! My dear, can you conceive it,—two hundred of my wretched guests have run away already! Yes, two hundred of them, including at least half a dozen members of my cast! Members of the cast, mind you! And some of them had quite important parts. Tell me, what am I to do? Isn't it just like Salim to play me this trick? The rumors spread round the Camp yesterday evening have all been traced to his spies. You don't believe me!

But, my dear, the Camp is swarming with them! Why, I know many of them quite well by sight! I went up to one the other day and said: 'My dear good man, I know you mean well; I know you want to do what you can to earn the money that my excellent brother is paying you. Pray go where you like, and do what you like, and report what you like! Only, I implore you, don't interfere with my actors! Don't interfere with my play!'—But Salim, I imagine, has already been told that I am putting him in as a comic figure. And here is the result! In his fury he is doing all he can to stop the performance."

Of this kind of thing the Prince gave us full measure; and all the while he was spinning about on his heels, gesticulating, and making his pale blue cloak billow out behind him. For a while I thought he was exaggerating his customary frivolity out of bravado, but a little later my impression changed. I now believe that the face has melted away behind the mask, that the posturer has swallowed up the man. Daniyal, I swear, has become in fact no more than what he makes himself appear.

After a while, when the effect of his entry had worn off, he made a pretense of catching sight of me for the first time. This gave him a fresh impetus, and he saluted me with an effusiveness so unmeasured, so obviously artificial, that I became not a little embarrassed. I am, I may say, an exceptionally unsuitable subject for the exercise of charm. The moment I suspect anyone of making a conscious effort in this direction, I am seized with discomfort. Without question, to respond rightly to such manners as Daniyal's is an art in itself—an art in which I have not—thank heaven!—had occasion to take much practice. For this reason, when I look back upon the scene, I am seized with misgivings. I can't be sure that I was successful in concealing what I felt. It is true that Daniyal's manner did not change, his egregious affability did not abate, but I should be unwise to take reassurance from that. Daniyal may very likely have been too astute to alter his manner by a single shade, even though he *did* see what effect it had on me.

Before long he was back on the subject of Salim. "That big brother of mine, Rajah, has two hobbies: war and religion. Both of them, you see, give him an excuse for killing people; and that is what he most enjoys. For political reasons, too, his religious life is becoming very beautiful just now; I am told that he turns his face towards Mecca and lifts up his behind in prayer at least four times a day."

This sally was meant for all to hear, and after everyone had duly applauded it—"I do think," he added, "Salim is getting too big a boy for that sort of thing, don't you, Rajah?"

"Alas!" he continued a little later, "the piping days of peace are over. At any moment Salim may come rushing into my theater—to find us, probably, shaking our sides at his counterpart upon the stage! Heavens, what a massacre will follow! And what a glorious day it will be for him, the dear man! In one fell swoop he will have cleared the country of everybody of any intelligence. Yes, India, after that, will become a perfect paradise for our rulers; and all the other governments of the world will turn green with envy."

It is a serious failing of mine that I cannot endure this kind of thing with patience. But worse was yet to come. After dismissing his suite, the Prince called me to him, thrust his arm through mine, and led me out into the garden behind the house.

"My dear Rajah," said he in a confidential tone, "I want to have a word with you—a word about Ali."

The mention of Ali at this moment gave me a small shock of surprise. The Prince, I thought, had subjects of greater importance to give his mind to. But no! I was mistaken, and he proved it by descanting for at least an hour upon the merits of the Camp as an institution for forming the youthful character. "I want you to explain this to Hari Khan," he concluded. "It would be so tiresome if he were to object to Ali's remaining with me. It might lead to all sorts of trouble, you know."

No doubt I looked rather dubious about my mission, for after a pause he went on: "It is really rather important that you should bring Hari Khan to see things in their true light—I mean for his own sake. It would be a thousand pities, if a trifling misunderstanding were to throw him into the arms of my brother Salim. We should none of us like to see that!"

The appearance of Mobarek now brought our talk to an end; but, before withdrawing, I received an invitation from Daniyal to join him presently at luncheon. As I followed the servant who had been told to show me to my room, I considered the Prince's last words about Hari. Although spoken lightly, they were more than sufficient to give warning. The subject of Ali had more in it than I had at first realized.

And now I have to record an incident which produced a profoundly disagreeable impression on my mind. As I was going along a corridor on my way to my room, a strange noise came to my ears; the next moment a door in front of me burst open with great violence, and a girl flung herself headlong into the passage. She was evidently running away, but before she could recover her balance a man dashed out after her and succeeded in grabbing hold of her arms. While the two were struggling there before me, I recognized her:—it was Gunevati!

No words can describe my astonishment. I stared, dumbfounded, while a breathless tussle took place. The scene was rendered the more unpleasant by the fact that the man was a young negro. He was trying to drag Gunevati back into the room, but she resisted him with the strength of a maniac. Except for a gasping and panting and the shuffling of feet, no sound came from either of them. Then Gunevati's eyes chanced to light upon my face, and for an instant she stopped struggling. The man, too, looked up; and in that brief interval Gunevati made an odd sound in her throat. In consternation I called out her name; I was, indeed, about to make some intervention, when the struggle broke out afresh. This time the negro had a firm grip. He picked the girl up bodily from the ground, and lurched through the doorway into the room. I approached and looked in. Near the window, looking sour and annoyed, was a little man whom I recognized, having seen him in the Prince's train not half an hour ago. A big, flat, brown face on the top of a thick, short-legged body gave this fellow the appearance of a large baked crab. I had gathered below that his name was Mansur and that he played a part of some importance in Daniyal's play; but this did not help me to understand what he was doing here at this moment. In his hand were writing materials and something that looked like a school copy-book. The room, I observed, was bare except for a table and two chairs. On one of these the negro now attempted to make Gunevati sit down; but she succeeded in upsetting it, and with a vigorous kick sent it flying across the room.

Blinking nervously, and with an expression of disgust, Mansur waddled after the chair and brought it back. This performance was gone through once more before Mansur caught sight of me. With an expressive smile he stood still, shrugged, and threw out his hands. "You see how it is! It is ridiculous! What can I do?"

I gazed at him in silence. I also looked at Gunevati, who, still pinioned by the negro, was breathing hard and had the same demented look in her eyes. My speechlessness prompted Mansur to say something more.

"The Prince has told me that I am to teach her how to write. But how am I to teach her to write? It is perfectly ridiculous. How can I teach a girl who behaves like that? She is mad."

He spoke with a strong Persian accent, and from his tone, which was both insolent and querulous, I recognized his type. To the negro he said: "I wash my hands of the whole business. I shall tell His Royal Highness that she is a dangerous lunatic. Is there a lock on the door?"

He came and examined it. "Yes. You had better lock her up— and keep watch outside the window as well. Now I have warned you. It is your responsibility, not mine."

He joined me outside in the passage, continuing to grumble in the tone of a servant who has been asked to do something outside his usual task. "I am an actor. It is not my business to be a schoolmaster. Certainly not a schoolmaster for lunatics." So speaking, he mopped his brow with a silk handkerchief that was strongly perfumed, and adjusted his turban, which, I suspect, Gunevati had recently knocked off. Then, without another word, he walked away.

In the meantime my guide, who had disappeared, returned to me, and was profuse in apologies for having taken me the wrong way. We reached my room without further adventures, and there I fell at once into uneasy speculations. Where had Gunevati come from? How long had she been in the Camp, and what was she doing here? Her presence filled me with the blackest suspicions,— suspicions that attached themselves not only to Daniyal but to Mobarek as well. It looked as if the Prince had gone to the pains of getting hold of Gunevati in order to use her as a witness against Gokal. And Mobarek, who had said nothing to me about Gunevati's presence here, appeared to be party to this.

Next I began puzzling over certain peculiar features of the scene I had just witnessed. Why had Gunevati been so frantic? And, if frantic, why had she struggled dumbly—without crying out? There was something amiss with her that I could not understand. And, finally, why did Daniyal want her to learn to write?

An hour later I went down again and found a luncheon table laid out very simply in the arbor at the end of the garden. We sat down to our meal without any formality. At the head of the table was the Prince, with Mobarek on one side, and I on the other. On my left was Churaman (who arrived breathless just after we had seated ourselves), and on the other side of Mobarek sat a certain Prince Jara.

The conversation that was going on when I came down showed me that Daniyal had agreed—and evidently with the greatest satisfaction—to Mobarek's proposal that *he* should be the one to take the journey to Kathiapur. For the rest, Daniyal had the air of a man who feels he has earned the right to relax. Most of his conversation was addressed to Churaman, who had been superintending a rehearsal, which he, poor man, had been obliged to miss. I had an opportunity of observing how tactfully Mobarek handled his royal protégé, for during the course of the meal there appeared from time to time discreet secretaries with papers which they slipped into Mobarek's hands, and Mobarek had to persuade the Prince to run his eye over them before appending his signature.

At first I imagined that the meal would soon be over, for Daniyal ate with negligent haste, almost giving one the impression that he might at any moment get up and walk away. Laughing, drinking, eating, and talking, all at the same time, with his chair tilted back and his eyes sliding from one face to another, he gave an unpleasant impression of restlessness. Twice in the next hour Prince Jara was called upon to get up and parade before him in order to show off some fancy costume. Once it was a cloak that the impersonator of Salim was to wear, and once a robe that Prince Jara himself had designed for a new order of sub-deacons in the Din Ilahi. Taking this poor youth and Churaman as his audience, Daniyal was soon displaying himself at his worst. Not content with Salim as a butt, he fell upon the dignitaries of his father's Court, mocking and disparaging them with a spitefulness that went in excess of anything I should have imagined possible. A group of conscientious, energetic, and for the most part very able men, engaged upon the thankless and difficult task of government, Daniyal sees—or pretends to see—as a collection of stupid, cruel, and ridiculous scoundrels. Occasionally I glanced at Mobarek. His expression betrayed nothing, and I was impressed with a sense of his detachment and power. Without a doubt he despises Daniyal, but I must allow it to be possible that his contempt is qualified by perceptions that I lack.

When at last Churaman and Prince Jara got up and went about their business, the atmosphere very sensibly changed. Daniyal's animation dropped, he became absent-minded, and I felt that his own departure was imminent. Without waste of time, therefore, I described the scene I had witnessed upstairs, and my tone was eloquent of inquiry.

Daniyal and Mobarek exchanged glances; then Daniyal threw back his head and laughed.

"Does your Royal Highness give me leave to explain?" said Mobarek with a smile.

"Of course, my dear Shaik," replied Daniyal, and he began slicing a mango on his plate.

Mobarek accordingly turned to me, and the story he had to tell relieved my mind of a considerable weight.

"Prince," he added after a moment, "the Rajah no doubt finds it strange that Gunevati should have found the courage—or rather the impertinence—to pour out her tale into your Royal Highness's ears. Have I your permission once more to explain?"

Daniyal shrugged and nodded.

"She is in love with his Royal Highness." Mobarek made this announcement with a smile. "Her object in revealing her scandalous relations with Gokal was simply to make herself interesting."

Daniyal leant back on his chair and wiped his hands delicately on a napkin. I waited. Nothing had been said as yet to throw light on the scene upstairs; but I felt the explanation to be about to come; and I also felt that it was going to be unpleasing.

"Rajah," said the Prince, "yesterday—or was it the day before? —word was brought to me that Gunevati's tongue had just been cut out."

I stared with a frown of horror.

"Someone has cut her tongue out," the Prince repeated, and he looked me straight in the eyes.

"Someone? Who?"

Daniyal's face darkened and his eyes narrowed. "Friends of Gokal's perhaps."

I started back in anger.

"No, no!" interposed Mobarek. "His Royal Highness does not mean that."

Daniyal gave a little laugh. "At any rate her indiscretion was quickly punished,—but by whom?"

I was silent.

"By Salim's spies," cried Daniyal. "Who else could have done it? Yes," he went on, "Salim's hand is quite plainly to be discerned in this affair. Salim has been moved by fury at the girl's capture and by fear lest she should betray his secrets."

For some moments after pronouncing these last words, he remained lost in thought, and his expression struck me as particularly disagreeable. Then, coming out of his muse with a shrug, "That girl," he exclaimed, "is really dreadfully foolish, and—what is much more important—a very poor actress. As Lakshmi she merely had to show herself naked on the stage, and that was not beyond her. In my new play I gave her a better part; I had hopes for her; but alas!" He shook his head. "She is unteachable."

My reply was a vague murmur. The Prince sighed again, and went on, "It has come to my ears that she is suspected of having been the cause of . . ." A flush slowly spread over his face. "In fact it has been suggested that she put something into Gokal's food. Can that really be true?"

"I am afraid there is no doubt about it," I answered.

Again Daniyal's expression became most unpleasant, and, as I looked at him I remembered having noticed that our meal had been served in such a fashion that it would have been impossible to poison him without poisoning the whole lot of us. We had all helped ourselves from one and the same dish, and never had he begun eating until we had almost finished our portions.

After a moment, throwing his napkin down, he began speaking with great vehemence and rapidity. "A poisoner! Good heavens, what an abominable girl! It is strange how easily women seem to turn to poison. I find such callousness and savagery really beyond conception. Upon my word, she and Salim are very well suited to one another. I think I could do no better than to send her back to him at once."

After this outburst he fell silent, frowning and drumming his fingers on the table.

"Shaik," he said at last, "please send for Mansur. I must have a talk with him. Afterwards I shall perhaps have a few words with the girl herself."

5

WE WAITED FOR Mansur in silence. I reflected that nothing had been said about Daniyal's reason for wishing Gunevati to be taught how to write, nor about her reason for refusing; but here, at any rate, there was no mystery. Daniyal was obviously annoyed with himself for not having got more information out of the girl while she was still in possession of her tongue; and she, poor thing, was terrified lest acquiring the art of writing should bring further calamity upon her.

Presently, when the servant returned, it was to say that Mansur was nowhere to be found; he seemed to have left the house without a word to anyone. This was an uncomfortable moment for us all, the little actor's unauthorized departure being a piece of unconscionable insolence. A look of extreme rage appeared upon Daniyal's face, but it gave way almost at once to an expression of disgusted boredom. He half-closed his eyes, and the next minute, to my surprise, he was actually yawning.

Just as a drug addict is suddenly seized with a craving for his drug, so was he now craving for the stimulus of his noisy, gesticulating crowd. Neither Gunevati nor Salim—no, not the Throne itself!—was of any importance to him for the time being.

"Shaik," he said carelessly, "I shall go into this affair later. Just now I really haven't . . ."

He was on the point of getting up, when an agitated secretary was to be seen hurrying over the lawn. "Your Royal Highness," the man gasped, "a terrible calamity has occurred! A letter from His Majesty has been lost! The messenger was swept away in a flood! He is drowned. And the letter to Your Royal Highness has disappeared with him."

The poor man (it was one of Mobarek's secretaries, not Daniyal's) was quivering with emotion. His eyes moved anxiously from the Prince's face to Mobarek's; he wrung his hands to illustrate his personal sympathy.

But the effect of this news on the Prince was not what he expected. After staring with an unmoved face for half a minute, Daniyal closed his eyes and smiled a beatific smile.

"A calamity indeed!" he pronounced at last. "Good heavens, to think that an inspired message from my august father has been swallowed up by a vulgar mountain-flood! How could Almighty God allow such a thing!"

Mobarek gave a quick frown, and with a gesture bade the confused secretary begone. As for Daniyal, his good-humor had incontinently returned to him. Lying back in his chair, he surveyed Mobarek with a smile of malicious amusement. "What do you say to that, Shaik? Could anything be more providential? Without being sure what that letter contained, I shrewdly suspected it was nothing good. But the letter is lost! It is lost! And so all is well."

Mobarek frowned again, making me think that perhaps I had better retire, to leave him free to remonstrate with Daniyal as he pleased. But at that moment some men and women appeared on the other side of the lawn, and the Prince, when he saw them, jumped up with a cry of delight. To the newcomers, for the moment at least, belonged the center of the stage, and they took up their parts in approved fashion by launching forth upon a humorous account of their journey. In the interests of facetiousness all verisimilitude was sacrificed; but that did not matter, as the conversation was merely an exhibition in the art of creating social appearances;—nothing mattered except that there should be the requisite amount of noise and laughter. This fashion of acting up to an agreed standard of elegance is to my mind a very tiresome business. It is this, precisely, which on a lower social level produces the genteel. Of course in Daniyal's group just the opposite effect is created. Here the genteel is given altogether too wide a berth; you are reminded of it by its opposite—a naturalness too good to be true, an exaggerated *sans-gêne*, a daring which pretends to be unaware of itself. What is this, if not a double-distilled vulgarity? Indeed, it seems to me that just as it takes all the cleverness of a clever man to make the perfect fool, so it is the special privilege of the sophisticated that they alone are able to produce vulgarity's richest, rarest fruits.

But here I must check myself, for without a doubt I am becoming uncharitable. The fact is that, after living for several months in seclusion, I am not in the best humor for company. I should remember, too, that my nature is lacking in geniality. Nor is this fault easily corrected. In order to be genial it is not enough to be willing—nay, anxious—to overlook other people's shortcomings; more important is it to be unaware of one's own. Nothing makes others more uneasy than to feel that their companion is self-critical. A great deal can be forgiven to the fatuous.

But to return to my narrative. Prince Jara and Churaman now joined us, and the company settled down to discuss with much gusto the jealousies of Daniyal's friends who had not been invited to the Camp. From this they went on to the moral indignation which the Camp aroused in the ranks of the prudes and philistines; they scoffed at the bad taste of everyone except themselves,—in particular at the badness of the art which was receiving official patronage. Daniyal was witty about the costliness and ugliness of Fatehpur-Sikri. "God, in destroying it," said he, "has agreeably surprised me by showing that His taste is at any rate a little better than my father's."

From this it was an easy step to the Emperor's lost letter, and he was making the most of it as a subject for humor, when Mobarek's secretary—the same that had appeared before—once more came over the lawn; and again, poor creature, he looked very unhappy in his mission.

"Your Royal Highness . . ." he began timidly.

"Well?" said Daniyal, impatient at being interrupted.

"Your Royal Highness—the letter . . ."

"Well!" said Daniyal again.

"It—it has been recovered. Forgive me, Your Royal Highness, I have it here."

This time the joke was against Daniyal, but he carried the situation off not too badly. Throwing the letter down on the table, he eyed it with an expressive grimace; then, turning to Mobarek— "Shaik," he said, "in spite of all evidence to the contrary, this letter has *not* been recovered! Believe me, what you see here is nothing but a poor ghost! The letter remains lost, lost! By heaven, I am not to be cheated so easily out of that convenient flood."

While the company laughed their approval, Daniyal picked the letter up again, tossed it into the air and caught it with the dexterity of a juggler; then he examined the great blue seal. "I think I shall open it," he said carelessly; "it will be interesting to see . . ."

If he had half intended—and I am inclined to think he had—to read the letter aloud, this intention was quickly changed. I noticed his face darken as his eyes skimmed the lines; evidently the Emperor's letter contained matters graver than any he had expected. After a moment he thrust it into his pocket and broke out into an indignant tirade. What it was exactly that so outraged his feelings we were not told, but the sympathy of his audience was not the less prompt, nor their cries the less loud, for that. Persiflage and cynicism disappeared, submerged for the time being under a wave of fine moral indignation. I confess this took me aback. These people had given me to understand that moral indignation was a silliness characteristic of the philistine. Besides, who would have expected that those who spent so much time in trying to wound the feelings of others, would be so unreasonable as to cry out when their own susceptibilities were hurt?

Long evening shadows were stretching over the grass before Daniyal made a move, and then it was only to drag us after him to his theater. Yes, busy as he knew Mobarek to be, he kept him—and me—dawdling about in his theater for nearly two hours more, while fitful, muddled attempts were being made to rehearse certain fragments of his play. Truly the worldly life calls for a self-discipline which the common man may well be thankful to escape. More especially as this discipline is often petty in intention and act. The world is too much like a theater, where, in order to look lordly and bear yourself with pride, you have to give all your private time to the painting of your face, to dressing up, and posturing before a looking-glass. You are obliged to learn to think first and foremost of appearances; you must unceasingly project yourself into the mind of your audience; and, as you learn how simple and few are the tricks that eternally impose, you become proud of your small clevernesses, and forget how small they are. Nevertheless, I do not accuse Mobarek of having yet parted with his dignity. Cynical he no doubt is, but that without meanness.

The Prince was now completely in his element, alternately shouting directions to the actors and exchanging witticisms with his friends. Such was the position when a dramatic incident took place.

A man whom I recognized as the sham suicide, Prince Dantawat, walked slowly down the empty theater and went up to the Prince in an endeavor to engage his attention; but Daniyal was talking eagerly to someone on the stage, and when at length he did turn to the poor wretch at his side, it was simply to wave him away. Dantawat, looking the picture of dejection, then walked slowly back again, but on reaching me he paused. "I think I know you," he said.

I replied as pleasantly as I could, for he excited my pity. There was a look in his eyes which made me think that his troubles must have affected his brain.

"Do you see that man?" Dantawat went on, still more strangely, and he pointed at Daniyal, who was standing about fifteen paces away. I turned my head, and, as I did so, the fellow put his other hand to my sword, snatched it out of its scabbard, and ran towards the Prince. But I also sprang forward, and reached Dantawat just in time to push him on the shoulder, so that he reeled to one side. Daniyal, whose back was turned, saw none of this, nor did those beside him, who were also facing the stage. Many others, however, scattered about the theater, witnessed the whole incident, and at once a tremendous clamor arose, and a rush was made towards Dantawat. It is significant that, when seized, he offered no resistance, but stood quiet, seemingly unaware of what he had just done.

Now, leaving the question of Dantawat's sanity aside, the point arises: did he really intend to kill the Prince, or was he merely making a dramatic gesture, not unlike his sham attempts to drown himself in the lake? This is the matter that directly concerns me, because on it hangs the question whether I must be regarded as having saved Daniyal's life. It is my firm conviction that Dantawat was not in earnest, and it is extremely annoying to me to be looked upon as Daniyal's savior. Yet that is the view that has been generally adopted, and I have been powerless to alter it. The situation, immediately after the incident, passed entirely out of my control, and out of Daniyal's too. It was the crowd of noisy, foolish, irresponsible onlookers who determined the significance of what had occurred, and they of course were governed by no other desire than to make the affair as sensational as possible. I blush with shame and disgust when I recall the ridiculous scene in which Daniyal and I had perforce to play the leading parts. In Daniyal's exoneration let it be said that I believe he was secretly almost as much annoyed as I. But he lacked the courage to take what might have appeared an ungenerous attitude. Being called upon to regard himself as having narrowly escaped death, and to hail me as his savior, he accepted the proffered role. From that instant the worst was to be expected; and indeed it did occur. First of all of course the Prince made an exhibition of sang-froid (perfect composure enlivened by light humorous sallies); then came gracious forgiveness and a compassionate regard for his assailant; next a hushing of the hysterical emotions of his adoring friends; and last but not least—a proper acknowledgment, a generous recognition, of my glorious part in the affair. As a climax—I shudder in recording it—he gave me a public accolade, an embrace—a kiss!

PART TWO

1

IT WAS NOT long after sunrise the next day that Mobarek and I started on our journey. We traveled comfortably in a double palanquin, which was borne by eight men. The road was wet and slippery, our pace slow, and the cold unusual for this season. Mobarek, however, was wrapped in furs, and as for me, I have become accustomed to the rigors of this mountain climate.

I made the most of the occasion by discussing the attitude taken up by Gokal towards the Din Ilahi. Mobarek said that from members of the Brahmin caste the Emperor would require no more than that they should declare themselves not in opposition to the faith, and should not discourage the lower castes from joining. I answered that no self-respecting Brahmin could do otherwise than discourage a man from pronouncing the words: "I . . . do utterly and entirely renounce and repudiate the religion . . . which I have seen and heard of my fathers, and do embrace the Din Ilahi of Akbar Shah, and do accept the four grades of entire devotion, to wit, sacrifice of property, life, honor, *and religion*."

After a long argument we broke off without reaching agreement, but I am left with the presentiment that Mobarek will advise the Emperor to make very important concessions.

About midday we met a messenger on the way up to the Camp, and a bunch of letters was handed to Mobarek. "Ha!" he exclaimed, "this is from the Khan." And a moment later with an air of great satisfaction he turned to me to say: "Rajah, I have good news. The Khan has been delayed by the rains and will not reach Kathiapur for several days yet. This means that instead of hurrying, we can continue our journey in a leisurely way."

An hour later we arrived at our first halt, which was a pavilion in the woods built by Daniyal for his coming and going guests. The sun was now shining in a clear sky; the trees sparkled with raindrops; and on all sides the flowers of the pink rhododendron carpeted the ground. Here one could enjoy to the full the quiet and freshness which the Camp so noticeably lacks.

While we were at our midday meal a runner arrived with a hasty note from Daniyal. As he read it Mobarek began to smile. "The Prince tells me that another letter from his father reached him this morning, soon after we had left. In order to avoid the appearance of having received it, he is going off at once on a hunting expedition into the hills behind the Camp. The Emperor's previous letter, which we have to regard as lost, contained, as you probably have guessed, orders that he should cancel his coming fête. The Prince suspects that this fresh letter repeats those commands. So he is off at once, nor will he return until the day before the festivities are planned to begin. 'For by that time,' he writes, 'it will be too late to stop anything. And mind you bring Lalita with you; for then I shall be able to say that it was impossible *on her account* to change our program.'"

We both laughed.

A little later Mobarek began talking to me about a certain European, Smiss, or Smish, whom we are likely soon to meet, as he is on his way up to the Camp. Unlike any of the Westerners that I have yet come across this man is an Englishman—and not a Jesuit. The object of his journey is to study the religious thought of the East. He has been visiting China and Japan, and intends to make a sojourn of some months in India on his way back to England. In his desire to learn he offers a pleasing contrast to the Jesuits, who come here exclusively to teach. Smiss, I think, must be an interesting man, and I am glad I shall have this opportunity of talking to him. He has already spent a few weeks at the Imperial Court, where Mobarek met him but did not have the leisure—or, possibly, the inclination—to cultivate his acquaintance. My impression is that Daniyal, who has also met Smiss, and who is always ready to pick up new ideas, may have been influenced by this European in directions which Mobarek considers undesirable. At any rate Mobarek speaks of Smiss, and of Daniyal's interest in Smiss, in a tone of disdain.

Early in the afternoon rain began to fall heavily, and we resigned ourselves, not at all unwillingly, to the prospect of spending the night here. I rejoice in my absence from the Camp. A day and a night there were enough to fill me with a weariness, which was not of the body, nor of the mind, but of the spirit itself. In the midst of the downpour two trains of bedraggled ladies and gentlemen arrived. Despite the cold and wet they were in high spirits, for an invitation to the Prince's festival is a highly valued distinction. When we told them that they could not expect to meet Daniyal himself for another week, they were slightly discouraged; however, bravely disregarding the weather, they pushed on.

A little later there appeared, all by himself, the Englishman, Smith. (This he tells me is the correct rendering of his curious European name.) It was remarkable to see him plodding along on foot, regardless of the rain and cold. I suppose he is accustomed to severe weather in his own country. I gave orders that he should receive every attention; and a little later, after his carriers had arrived and he had changed his clothes, we met in the common guest-room. Smith is a man of about forty-five, obviously belonging to the caste of pundits. He has the slight and stooping frame, the peering eyes and anxious expression of those whose pursuit of learning is inclined to be intemperate. Rather peculiar is his habit of fidgeting all the time he talks. Instead of the black cloth of the Jesuits he wears a gray costume of fine texture, but somewhat awkward cut. In address he is friendly, uncertain, and inquiring;— on the whole a not unpleasing personality.

We had the room to ourselves, for Mobarek was as usual dictating to his secretaries. One on each side of the brazier, we eyed each other with a not unsympathetic curiosity, and very soon the conversation became interesting. Smith won my regard at once by saying that he conceived the dominant note of India to be religion—a characteristic, he added, in which this country contrasted markedly with China. In order to show him where he stood with me, I lost no time in telling him that I was a Buddhist. His reply was that he venerated Buddha, Christ, and Socrates above all other men. This showed me that he was not a Christian, an inference which he himself presently confirmed with a good deal of emphasis. I also gathered that he is positively hostile to the Jesuits on account of their intolerance and the cruelties into which it leads them. Circumstances have forced him into the company of Acquaviva and Monserrate during the last few months; and I could see that he had conceived a dislike of both these gentlemen, but of Acquaviva in particular. He was soon questioning me about Buddhism, and I was happy to dispel some of the mistaken ideas that he had derived from the puerile Mahayana forms of the faith. He spoke with great appreciation of the beauty of the ritual in China and Japan, the amenity of the temples and their gardens, and the atmosphere of serene benignity which the priesthood respired. All this is very well, but of the eternal verities enshrined in the teaching of the Enlightened One he has, I regret to say, learned practically nothing.

Whilst we were talking Mobarek came in. His manner to Smith was, I thought, slightly wanting in cordiality; but this, I hope, Smith did not perceive. After our guest had retired, Mobarek said: "Daniyal has asked me to persuade this European friend of his to return to Kathiapur with us. He has some reason for not wishing him to arrive at the Camp before he is back there himself."

I expressed myself not displeased, since Smith struck me as a pleasant and intelligent man.

"Possibly," replied Mobarek, "but he holds very undesirable opinions. In his own country he is not much considered."

"How do you know?" I inquired.

"I have it from Acquaviva."

Here is an example of prejudice. Mobarek respects Acquaviva because he is of ancient lineage, being in fact the son of the Duke of Atri, one of the most influential nobles in the Kingdom of Naples, whilst the family of Smith is, I understand, not noble, although large and highly respected. Acquaviva and Smith are not on good terms, and Mobarek has accepted Acquaviva's account of the man, much of which is probably inaccurate. I cannot believe, for instance, that Smith really endorses the Nastika dictum: "There is nothing superior to fish, flesh, wine, copulation, and ritual,"— although, in a moment of antagonism against the somberly ascetic Acquaviva, he may have said so by way of a jest.

Here is a late entry before retiring for the night. I continue to like Smith, but he puzzles me increasingly. Our talk this evening before withdrawing to our rooms was about the Greeks and their view of life. The topic was introduced by Smith, who showed himself highly appreciative of all that was gracious and intelligent in that brief civilization. "The Greeks," he said, "discovered, first among men, the difficult art of enjoying the best things of life. They seem to have been without fear and without a sense of guilt. In Europe to-day a sense of guilt, consciously or only half-consciously felt, hangs over practically everyone. What but that has given the Jesuits their power? However," he went on, "the somber religion of Ignatius Loyola will certainly not prevail. It is fundamentally unsuited to the spirit of Europe."

Presently in answer to a question of mine, he continued: "In India I am not conscious of this sense of guilt, but I must confess that here a primitive fear inspired by the forces of Nature does seem to me to pervade the ordinary man's religion. The Greeks freed themselves from this fear by humanizing Nature. The gods were conceived as being of a nature akin to ours. His religion helped the Greek to feel himself at home in the world."

"In India," I replied, "Nature is sterner and more terrible than in Greece. Our primitive ancestors were animists like the Greeks. They made gods of the natural forces; in our Rigveda you will find them; but those gods are awe-inspiring; they are not brought down to human stature. Our race has always been less happy than were the boyish Greeks. But an unhappy childhood is in some respects advantageous. It teaches one to grow up. Our people have been forced to look overhead into the immensities and down into the profundities, which the Greeks managed to ignore."

At these words of mine, Smith, I remember, fidgeted most uncomfortably. "I don't think fear has ever borne good fruit," he protested. "I look upon the progress of the human race as a gradual emancipation from terrors—often imaginary. Religion has too often been the vehicle of superstition, a cause of intolerance, and an excuse for fiendish cruelties. But the Greek by *his* religion was made a good citizen and a reasonable man. It taught him how to enjoy the best things in life and made him at home in the world."

"It made him feel at home on earth," I replied, "at the cost of ignoring the universe. Do you not agree with me that in their escape from fear the Greeks left behind something of the utmost value to the spirit of man? Something which leads the spirit forth out of aestheticism and intellectualism into a true maturity."

"I don't think I quite follow you," said Smith, eyeing me coldly.

"Well, let me remind you that one of your own philosophers has said: 'All knowledge begins and ends in wonder; but the wonder that is the child of ignorance must be replaced by the wonder that is the parent of adoration.' The Greeks had a lively intellectual curiosity, but little capacity for wonder or adoration."

"If you mean that the Greeks eschewed metaphysics," replied Smith, "I certainly agree with you, but to my mind they were wise in so doing. The grandiose abstractions in which the Indian mind delights had no appeal for them. Yet you can hardly reproach them with superficiality! If you cannot attach value to their mastery of the technique of living, consider their philosophy and their art!"

Anxious that we should not sink deeper into disagreement, I took refuge in silence, and Smith presently resumed speech. "The Greeks turned away from metaphysics," he repeated with firmness, "and in so doing I think they were not unwise. You, as a Buddhist, will surely not differ with me here. Buddha was pre-eminently a realist and a rationalist. In the pure form of Buddhism which you profess, all superstition is rigorously rejected. Indeed you yourself have told me that nearly all speculation on metaphysical or cosmological subjects is forbidden as mischievous." Thus speaking, Smith fixed a persuasive look upon me through his glasses, and, as I still remained silent, he went on: "Guided by an inborn common sense, the Greeks excluded from their religion all futile and dangerous elements. Thus they lived wisely and happily, shut in from the abyss."

At this point we were interrupted, nor was it too soon, for I was beginning to feel bewildered by what appeared to me to be a willful superficiality on the part of Smith. I could not make him out.

Here was a man whose appearance proclaimed him a pundit; he had, moreover, undertaken an arduous journey for the sake of gathering religious information, and in our earlier talk he had shown what appeared to be a genuine respect for the Indian mind. "The Hindu," he had said, "does, I am sure, really believe that the true life is a spiritual life." But since then what had he done? He had persistently extolled a temper of mind quite different from—indeed contrary to—ours. It almost looks as if he thought it better to be humanistic after the fashion of the Greek, than religious in the fashion of the Indian.

2

THIS MORNING I had another talk with Smith, but it has done little to clear my mind. We began with a discussion of Christianity, which was started by some remark of mine about Sita and her view of the Buddhist faith. Oddly enough, it was not long before I found myself engaged in a defense of Sita's religion—a change of sides for me, as my part until to-day has always been that of objector. But I have been a sympathetic objector, whereas Smith is quite the reverse. The hostile gleam that came into his eyes as he denounced the faith of his fathers took me aback at the time, and I cannot recall it now without astonishment. I am certain that Smith is one of the most kindly intentioned of men, yet he nourishes his prejudices with the milk of hatred. The fact is that with sixteen centuries of Christianity behind him, to say nothing of a Christian upbringing, he has become incapable of taking an impartial view, or even of realizing that his view is lacking in impartiality. Just as he might have become a fighting bigot, so he has actually become a fighting apostate. Could he but read the New Testament in the same spirit in which he reads his Plato, it would move him to the profoundest depths of his being—just as it did me, when I first read it. Could he but consider the character of Christ as he has considered that of Socrates, he would be overwhelmed by its beauty. But this is quite beyond him; and, if he is prone to associate the names of Christ, Socrates, and Buddha, that is done, I fear, not with any intention of honoring Christ but rather in order to bring him down from the unique position that Christians assign to him. As I listened to Smith I began to understand better his praise of the pagan view of life. Alas, how often do we not discover that an enthusiasm which at first sight appears generous is but the obverse aspect of some private and petty antagonism. It was not long before Smith was insidiously suggesting to me that Socrates and Buddha had much in common, and that what they had in common made them much the superiors of Christ. Buddha and the Greeks, said he, were at one in rejecting dogma and deprecating all metaphysical vaporings.

"It is undeniable," I replied, "that Buddha was impatient of questions, which, when once the truth has been grasped, reveal themselves as meaningless, nor do I want to deny that his austere realism contrasts strikingly with the sprawling unrestraint of much speculative Hinduism. But the difference between the most undisciplined Hindu and the most disciplined Buddhist is as nothing compared to the distance that lies between the Indian and the Greek. The Indian, be he an illiterate Hindu peasant or an erudite Buddhist recluse, lives in an unceasing consciousness of the immensities around him, and this consciousness is intimately bound up with the conviction that (to use your own words) 'the true life is the spiritual life.' Unlike the Greek, he has never striven 'to make himself at home in the world.' Buddhism has shown, it is true, that the accomplished Arahat may attain to a state of bliss in this world, but that bliss is not *of* this world; it arises out of a sense of deliverance from it.—To my mind," I went on, "one might almost say that Christ stands for the heart, Socrates for the reason, and Buddha for the spirit, in man; and while the heart, unsupported, is childlike, and the reason, in isolation, is puerile, the spirit by its own proper nature moves towards a maturity, which is, in fact, a gradual apprehension of the eternal verities or spiritual truth. I can perceive, but I do not feel, the charm of the Greeks; it is too often boyish and immature; and Plato, I confess, sometimes seems to me nasty, priggish, and smug. You, yourself," I reminded Smith, "have said of the Greeks that by their religion they were 'shut in from the abyss.' Your words are true. The Greeks cultivated a little of civilization, they evolved a small but exquisite culture, at the price of ignoring the immensities in the midst of which men live. But to ignore metaphysical problems is not to abolish them; and in a sense it may be said that every man who thinks at all is, willy-nilly, a metaphysician. I mean that there are metaphysical assumptions at the back of every one of his thoughts. The Greek liked to think of himself as a member of a city community, but his city was, nonetheless, a point upon the wandering earth, and the earth is a point in the universe, and every part of the universe partakes of the metaphysical mystery of its being.

"However, to return to Christianity," I went on, "what I am going to say about it now may cause you some surprise, as coming from the lips of a Buddhist, but please do not think that I am trying to gloze over the opposition between the Christian and the Buddhist attitudes of mind. My point is rather that Buddhism, Christianity, and the Hellenic view of life are all utterly different. The opposition between Christ and Buddha is sufficiently stated when I remind you that the latter was insistent upon the absolute necessity of banishing from the mind the ideas of God, the soul, and immortality. Let us turn rather to the contrast between the figures of Christ and Socrates. One of my reasons for holding, as I do, that the first towers above the second is this: the Greek spoke primarily as one to whom the only means of discovering the truth about the world as a whole and man's position in it, were the means provided by the reasoning mind of man. The Jew addressed himself to men's intuitions and spoke in the language of inspiration. It is this that has given Christ's utterances their unexampled power. Such power the reason will never command, nor is it desirable in my opinion that it should."

As Smith listened to me, I could detect a stiffening of his whole being. "Well!" he said at last, "we have reached, I am afraid, a core of fundamental disagreement. I believe in goodwill guided by reason; intuitions I hold to be very dangerous guides, and an appeal to them is not easily distinguishable from an appeal to blind prejudice. Prejudice means unreason, and unreason is responsible for most of the cruelties and follies of mankind."

"I don't mind admitting," I said after a pause, "that Christian morality requires Christian dogma to support it. But does not every system of ethics require support either from intuitions, which you mistrust, or from metaphysics which you eschew, or from dogma which you will not allow?"

As Smith remained silent, I went on: "The Christian conception of God as a loving father, intimately near to each human soul, is to my mind a beautiful one. Very beautiful, too, is the idea of an incarnate God suffering death for the redemption of the human race—and as an example to it. Christianity gives brotherhood to men, and value to every human life. In the place of the Pagan view of the time-process as an eternal repetition, it introduces the idea of an end in perfection at last. I ask you: was it not the dryness and sterility of Greek thought that led to the expansion of the later Greek mystery-religions? The freshness, the hope, the tenderness, the courage, of Christianity—these are what I value; but when I have said that, I must add: I am not a Christian; I am a Buddhist."

I was sorry to see Smith withdrawing into himself, but I could not refrain from speaking thus. We looked at one another in silence and my companion's face told me that he was as much puzzled by me as I by him.

At noon we resumed our journey, Mobarek, Smith, and I; and, as we traveled in separate palanquins, I had plenty of time for reflection. I soon saw what it was that had most deeply alienated Smith. There is no doubt that the word "reason" has for him associations and a meaning that it does not have for me. On the other hand the word "intuition" fills him with mistrust and dislike. The reason he regards as sacrosanct, just as Daniyal does "Art." We all of us hold something sacred, even the cynic, to whom his cynicism is holy. Next, I must bear in mind that the European is generally imbued with a sense of the value and reality of the phenomenal world in and for itself. To him the affairs of this earth have an importance on their own account. Neither Christian nor unbeliever knows anything about reincarnation. For the Christian the soul of the individual is somehow generated on this earth and continues in heaven, its place through eternity being assigned to it by the individual's behavior in this one short life. To us such a doctrine is so fantastically childish in its want of perspective that it is difficult to keep it in mind when talking to Christians. To the European of an agnostic turn of mind (and it appears that Smith is one), the individual as a temporary psychic unity comes into being at birth, and ceases to exist after death. The lifetime of an individual on this earth is consequently of supreme importance to him in and for itself, for there is no higher significance to which to relate it. But, unless one holds that mind is merely a function of matter, the birth of a mind is not explicable as a mere process of cell development, so I begin to fear that Smith is a materialist, and afflicted with all the intellectual and moral obtuseness of materialists. Yet I am certain that he does not wish to be regarded in this light; he talks about "spirituality" and "religion" as if these words had an idealistic significance for him. Lastly I must bear in mind that certain peculiarities of Smith's find their excuse in the belief that for each individual one single life-experience is all in all. It goes a long way to account for his equalitarian ideas, to say nothing of his neurotic pre-occupation with intolerance, cruelty, and physical pain. To put himself into the mental position of such a man is almost impossible for an Indian; indeed, I shudder when I reflect how appalling this world must seem to him. I can hardly understand how one so kindly and sensitive as he is can retain his sanity at all. What a ghastly spiritual bankruptcy awaits those unfortunate Christians who lose their faith! Completely devoid of a true understanding of the moral and spiritual order of the universe, they are like children thrown out of the nursery into a wilderness.

How truly thankful I am that Sita's faith is impregnable, for that it surely is. I am glad, too, that although I have presented my views to her and criticized her belief, I have never attempted to undermine it. Sita's mind is distinctly of the European cast; she would find much in Smith that is sympathetic to her in spite of his rejection of Christianity. Even for Sita man is at the center of the universe; God, in the last analysis, is postulated by her as necessary to man. She cannot understand the Indian way of placing the Absolute at the center, and regarding the whole history of mankind from first to last as nothing but a ripple upon the surface of that Supreme Mind.

I have been reflecting sadly upon my failure to render the Indian point of view intelligible to her, and I blame myself for it. Contact with the Western mind, as represented by Smith, has had a disturbing effect upon me. It shows me too well how, from every other angle except that at which we Indians stand, my present intention soon to withdraw from the world must appear selfish, and this moment singularly ill-chosen. India is on the verge of civil war; I am needed in my capacity of ruler; my wife and son require guidance; and my best friend—the man upon whom I rely to give them guidance—is in danger of falling into disgrace. Of course my hope is that by the end of the next few weeks the basis for an agreement between Gokal and Mobarek will have been found, and that I shall have determined upon the proper course for my successors in government. Yes, that is my hope; but, alas, it is already weakening.

3

THE SLIGHT ANTAGONISM that sprang up between Smith and me yesterday has disappeared, and this gives some satisfaction; although I could wish that our renewed amity stood on a securer base. I am afraid that Smith nourishes a latent disapproval of me, and that it is only by comparison with Mobarek that I find favor with him as a companion. Whenever I watch him and Mobarek together it is borne in upon me that no two people could be less well-fitted to appreciate each other's good qualities or to excuse each other's defects.

Mobarek springs from an aristocratic stock; in him personal ambition burns fiercely but is subdued to an impersonal religious fervor; he was early disciplined to the hardness of worldly life, and to the rejection of pity—self-pity most of all. He has never been tempted to separate thought and action, to accept humanistic values, or to forget the non-human divine. Mobarek's self is focused by a strong will, whilst the self of Smith is diffuse. Smith has the sensitiveness and sensibility that Mobarek lacks, and probably a wider field of intellectual activity. But his intellectuality is not independent, it moves to the promptings of a nature in love with ease and superficiality. Thus he is inclined to rate sensitiveness and sensibility too high. It is true that society owes much to its more sensitive members, who shrinkingly—or, if they dare, arrogantly—direct it along the path of civilization; but it is certainly not from them, as a rule, that humanity receives messages of inspiration or the example of endurance and valor. It is well that people like Smith should exist, and it is perhaps inevitable that they should exaggerate their own importance; but it is also well that society should not give them even the importance they deserve. A world that honored them would be a decaying one. I am bound to say, however, that in the present circumstances my sympathy goes out to Smith, for Mobarek, who is an adept at inflicting small social humiliations, never misses a chance of slighting him. He even resorts to the rather threadbare device of mispronouncing our friend's curious European name. He pronounces it Smiss, whereas it should be pronounced Smith, the "th" being similar in sound to the "th" in Tirthankar.

It surprises me that Mobarek should not be content merely to ignore this man. Perhaps the explanation lies in the fact that Smith has been taken up by Daniyal, and that Mobarek expects to see, or already sees, some of his views reflected in the Prince. I cannot otherwise account for the irritation that Smith's behavior and conversation cause him. The most trifling incidents give rise to disagreement between them, and in these disagreements the whole extent of their incompatibility at once makes itself felt. For instance, this morning in order to spare his carriers, Smith insisted in getting out of his palanquin whenever there was a slight rise in the ground. This delayed us, causing Mobarek to expostulate; and when we halted for our midday meal there arose a polite but dangerous argument on the rights of man.

Worse, too, was to come. Early this evening, not long after we had pitched our tents, one of Mobarek's guards came in with a report that a corpse had been discovered in the brushwood not far off. Mobarek shrugged his shoulders, he was not interested; I, however, went off to investigate, and Smith was moved to accompany me. The body was that of a young man who had evidently been killed within the last twenty-four hours. He had been stripped of his clothing, and his face disfigured in order to make him unrecognizable. The sight was a painful one, and Smith was a good deal upset by it.

On our return Mobarek shrugged again, and said: "That probably is the work of a Mahommedan. There have been no general massacres as yet, but religious feeling is rising every day. Salim's agents are busy preparing the ground."

"Are the Hindus also murdering the Mahommedans?" asked Smith with a sickened look.

"Yes, certainly," replied Mobarek with indifference; and then added, "but on the whole they show less spirit."

Smith pretended not to hear this, and for a while the talk was about Salim. I was surprised to hear Mobarek declare with emphasis that a religious war was not only possible but imminent. He addressed most of his remarks to me, but I suspected that they were meant for Smith, and that he was hoping to scare him out of his intention to join Daniyal at the Camp. He went so far as to hint that all foreigners would do well to leave the country.

Now Smith, as I have said, had been somewhat unnerved by the sight of the mutilated corpse, and Mobarek's words made him look uncomfortable; but I think this discomfort was largely anger, which a just suspicion of Mobarek's object provoked.

"Being neither a Muslim nor a Hindu," he said coldly, "religious fanaticism will pass me by. Foreigners are probably safer than anyone else."

"Do you think so?" returned Mobarek suavely. "Well, I hope you are right."

Smith smiled. "I am not even a Christian. Why should I be singled out for assassination?"

"Because," replied Mobarek, "to the religious-minded there is nothing more odious than irreligion."

Smith did not answer, and in order to fill up an awkward silence I made the remark that Muslims ought properly to feel less hostile to Christianity than to other religions, for not only had they recognized Christ as a Prophet, but they accepted the Virgin Birth, and the Second Advent. And Christians, on their side, should look upon Islam rather as a Christian heresy than as an altogether alien religion.

Our choice of a halting-place this evening was not a happy one, even if the proximity of the corpse be left out of account. The place abounds in horse-flies; and, although these creatures have given little trouble to Mobarek or me, they have persecuted the unfortunate Smith. It is on them that I fix the responsibility for a serious blunder on the part of our guest. Overlooking the fact that Mobarek, although not a Mahommedan, has many attachments to Islam, he began talking with scant respect about that faith. I suppose he was not obviously at fault, for, as he afterwards pointed out to me, Mobarek, besides being conspicuously at enmity with that doughty champion of Islam, Prince Salim, is himself the foster-father of quite another religion. But the real point of the matter is that in attacking Islam Smith let it be seen that he was inimical to religion in general, or—if this is saying too much—inimical to all forms of God-worship. I think that there is no doubt that Mobarek did not err in finding this spirit behind his contemptuous remarks. They were followed by a silence, and I hoped that Mobarek had not heard them (for Smith has a trick of muttering, as it were, to himself), or that his attention had been elsewhere. But the next moment the camp-fire flared up, and upon Mobarek's face I saw a look that I can only describe as satanic. It made me feel that perhaps Smith had better not tarry in India too long.

It has been said that human affinities and antipathies are determined very largely by the sense of smell, although those concerned may well be unaware of it. In my opinion even more important is the religious sense, even when differences of religious disposition are felt rather than expressed. In the relations ruling between Mobarek, Smith, and me such differences have not remained hidden. They have acted disastrously between Smith and Mobarek, while Smith and I have succeeded in remaining friendly only by the exercise of forbearance.

My forbearance this evening did, I confess, nearly fail, when Smith again began praising the cheerful, good-humored, matter-of-fact temper of the Chinese, who, he says, are like his own countrymen in never doubting that an enlightened sociality is all-in-all. Similarly, he finds the Japanese less alien to him than we are, and he even hinted that the negro is more sympathetic. He is determined to make out that between the European and the Hindu there is a profound difference in spiritual outlook. His argument is that while the European believes that life in this world is, or should be, a good in itself, the Indian has always held it to be an evil, from the everlasting recurrence of which he aspires to escape.

Now this is only looking at the surface of things.[1] In the first place the Hindu, in common with all men, instinctively clings to life, and instinctively seeks pleasure and happiness while alive. It is only in his capacity as a thinker that he proclaims life evil; and if the European were capable of an equal philosophic detachment he would inevitably come to the same conclusion.

Why does the European fail in detachment? The cause is the difference of temperament—engendered to some extent no doubt by different geographical conditions. In a cold, even in a temperate, climate bodily exertion is pleasanter and more natural than in the tropics, and, unlike exertion in the tropics, it produces an agreeable fatigue and an increased capacity for exertion. A habit of body and mind is thus set up which directs a man's attention outwards and attaches his thoughts to material things. And, because man is a self-explaining, self-justifying animal, men whose minds are thus oriented will adopt a philosophy or view of life which makes their behavior seem right and reasonable in their own eyes. That the European lives as he does *because* he finds life good, is simply not true; it is because he lives as he does that he persuades himself that life is good.

The Indian is not thus deluded. He recognizes that life is appetition, and that appetition is unrest, anxiety, pain, and sorrow. Christianity by urging that the appetitive impulse should be directed to the benefit of others, does much to redeem it; and it is in Christianity of course that the truly religious spirit of Europe has manifested itself. It is absurd of Smith to maintain that Christianity is opposed to the spirit of Europe, when historical evidences are so overwhelmingly against him. It is idle to put forward that Europe has never adopted Christian practice, although Christian precept has been professed. No race, no society, has ever yet succeeded in living up to its religious principles,—the Hindu no more than the European. The difference between us is not one of religiousness but of spiritual insight.

I tried to persuade Smith of this, and ended up by saying: "I believe the Westerner to mistake his own values, his own in-

---

1. Here Rajah Amar expounds his own views, which, as he uses some three thousand words, I have decided to abbreviate.

centive, his own meaning. His mistake will very likely be of considerable value to mankind, because in his wanderings he may well find much that is of cultural utility. It is important, perhaps, that a part should go astray for the sake of the whole. I am very ready to admit that your pre-occupation with material things has developed your practical reason far beyond ours. Christianity, too, has developed your hearts. It is now time that you developed the spirit that is in you. The reason and the heart both speak a simpler language than that of the spirit. In one of our earlier talks I said that Buddha addressed himself primarily to the spirit in man. I wish I could persuade you to study Buddhism, for then you would see what I mean."

4

YESTERDAY WE MET two or three parties of Daniyal's guests on their way up to the Camp, and I was amused (perhaps also a little annoyed) by the greetings I received. These people showed me by their manner that news of the Dantawat incident had reached them; they imagined that I had been staying with Daniyal in the Camp, that I was a close friend of his, and that I was now standing very high in his favor. They accordingly hailed me effusively and treated me as one of themselves. It devolved upon me to undeceive them; and to do this quickly, effectively, and without producing embarrassment, has not always been an easy task.

An interesting light has been thrown upon Smith and his relations with Daniyal by the manner in which these people have greeted *him*. Not only have they been very polite, giving him the consideration regarded as due to one who has been taken up by the Prince, but they have also been at great pains to display themselves as intellectuals. Evidently Smith has some reputation as a thinker; and Daniyal's patronage of him has, I fancy, served to fortify his own claim to intellectuality, while at the same time making intellectuality itself more fashionable.

It has been interesting, too, to observe Smith's attitude towards these young and fashionable friends of Daniyal's, whose attempts at "intellectual" conversation have been slightly disconcerting. He showed himself anxious to think well of them, and I soon began to understand what kind of picture he had formed of the Prince's aesthetic coterie. I remembered some things he had said to me at our first meeting, and, whereas they had only bewildered me at the time, I now found them quite illuminating. Speaking of the festivals in ancient Greece, when beautiful youths, flower-crowned, disported themselves in the Palaestra, he confided to me how greatly he was looking forward to the festivities at the Camp. "I should not be sorry," he said, "to witness scenes of a slightly abandoned jollity." I remember having been uncertain what to reply to this, for I, on my side, had had preconceived notions about Smith; so that I wondered whether I ought not to prepare him for disappointment—or worse. Well, since then my conception of this strange European has altered: I am now quite ready to let Smith make what he can of Daniyal and his friends. After all, people only see what they want to see; and Smith is not likely to be fastidious—or over-fastidious—in just the same manner as I. Certainly, what I call spiritual vulgarity often passes without giving offense and even without being noticed.

What, I ask myself, is the innate intellectual and moral taste of my friend Smith? The fact that he is already so friendlily disposed to Daniyal confuses my judgment. On reaching middle-age men of a certain type are apt to make a private—and sometimes an almost unconscious—resolution that they will keep their minds open to the appreciations and enthusiasms of youth. They are anxious to win approval—their own approval possibly, as well as that of others—by remaining in touch with the young. Such men are wanting in loyalty to themselves and their life-experience. A determination to see and feel as their juniors do falsifies their judgments, and opens the road to a general intellectual snobbery. A man must be true to his own taste—yes, even when he is able to conceive that it may be limited or bad. And this loyalty is even more important in the moral sphere than in the aesthetic. There are faults more serious than an honest narrow-mindedness.

This train of thought was introduced by the events of the evening, when a party of strolling players gave us an insignificant and tawdry entertainment. Their performance in one respect was, in fact, positively displeasing, inasmuch as they distorted and vulgarized the ancient and highly significant mystery-play that was part of their program. Some of Daniyal's friends, who were camping beside us, derived from the entertainment a pleasure largely made up of amusement—the kind of pleasure which the sophisticated take in a simplicity that flatters their sense of superiority. Taking his cue from them Smith worked up an enthusiasm which I cannot but regard as factitious. It would be unfair perhaps to say of this enthusiasm that it rested wholly on self-deception and aesthetic snobbery, because Smith was after all looking at the performance through the eyes of an ignorant foreigner, and he could not see in what respects it was commonplace and merely bad; but in associating himself with Daniyal's friends in their eulogies of the play he was certainly wanting in intellectual honesty.

Later, when all was quiet again, he and I walked down the bare spur of a hill to a point from which we could look out over the plains. The night had been dark, but now the moon, which was nearly full, came out and hung above the low mists that lay like a sea beneath us. That ghostly sea was ruddy as if dust and mist were mixed up together; and it foamed against the globe of the reddening moon as she sank. Spectral and lurid she sank, and all that region of the sky about her became the scene of a silent symbolic tragedy.

We neither of us spoke; and I imagined that Smith felt the beauty of that spectacle as much as I. But, after a few minutes, as we were walking back again, he broke out once more into praise of the play and the players.

I was wise enough to make no definite response, but here I may as well express my true feelings: I was seized with contemptuous irritation. Perhaps, too, I should do well to make a more general declaration. Let me admit that I have no leanings towards Art— not even the art of letters—although I have dabbled in literature from very early years. Now, when I write, my words are the simplest expression of my thought—and nothing more. If I correct what I have written, it is in no spirit of vanity, but simply in order to remove redundancies, to give a sharper outline to what is vague, and above all to make sure that my pen has not swerved from the truth. Of course, in order to communicate one's meaning in the fullest sense of the word, one must convey the feeling that accompanies one's thought—for thought and feeling are one. If this is art, then it is an ancillary art, and ancillary art is the only art I know. When I contemplate Nature, the works of man—even the greatest of them—appear to me small both in conception and achievement.

If there were a Creator Him would I passionately adore; but just as the empty firmament extends illimitably beyond the clouds and colors of our earthly sky, so over and above even the purest hopes and longings of man's heart there spreads the calm of truth. My face I turn upwards, and whether the sky be light or dark, the rays of truth strike down; out of that emptiness there comes no voice, no breath—no, but into that emptiness I enter and with it I become reconciled.

5

LOOKING BACK OVER my talks with Smith, I now see that we have been divided on two important questions neither of which we have ever clearly formulated. The first is this: What is it that constitutes religious experience as distinct from aesthetic experience? And secondly: Is it possible and desirable to make aesthetic experience fill the place of the other?

This morning I placed these questions before Smith, and invited him to express himself. He did not do so with any great willingness, but eventually I gathered that by religious experience he would designate all those conditions in which a man enjoys a sense of interior illumination, of direct awareness of the Numinous, or of communion with the Divine. These states of consciousness, he went on to say, are without value to anyone but the subject himself, because they offer no content the truth or error of which can be tested. The religious or mystic bias, is on the whole unsocial, tending to separate a man from his fellows, yet it prompts him to set himself up as their teacher. The religious-minded have always been impelled to lay down the law in matters of belief and conduct. The artistic faculty, on the other hand, conduces to no such didacticism, since artistic creations provide a common ground for estimating the value of an aesthetic experience. Consequently there is, he says, a brotherhood in art, a communion of one man with another on the aesthetic plane. The Beautiful places itself beside the Good and the True as an ideal that men can pursue in common, under a common discipline, and to their common advantage.

It was not, however, his contention that religious experience was of an altogether different kind from aesthetic: no, there was evidence that the first transformed itself into the second with the social and cultural advance of the community. The best measure of the civilization of any society was the value which it set upon Art. He begged me to remember that Reason, which was the guiding light of civilization, had always been on easier terms with art than with religion—and this for various reasons, the most obvious being that art did not attempt to legislate outside its own province.

As I considered these words of Smith's it became clear to me that it was through art that he had received his most valued experiences, nor was it less clear that his religious sense was very inadequately developed. Further, I realized that my position in discussing these matters with him was complicated by my being a Buddhist, for Buddhism is not a religion in the sense usually attached to that word by Europeans. This I explained to Smith, adding that although I did not believe in God, I was more in sympathy with those who did than with him. Belief in God was indicative of an attitude of mind which I could not but regard as more desirable than his. "There is that," I said, "which is more important than civilization; and just as the individual cannot live for himself, so cannot society live for itself, but must keep a self-transcendental ideal before it. Society is not worshipful, nor is humanity. Over and above the immanent there is the transcendent."

"I see no reason why man should 'worship' anything," said Smith. "So long as men aspire after goodness, truth, and beauty, that is enough."

I was silent for a few moments. How could I, without giving offense, explain to Smith that goodness, truth, and beauty, as he understood them, were far from being of the first importance? By goodness he meant virtuous behavior; by truth he meant truthtelling and the pursuit of certain comparatively unimportant kinds of knowledge; and by beauty he meant the creation and appreciation of works of art. Smith is a Platonist, and Plato's influence in Europe has made itself felt in measure as the Christian has moved away from religion. It is not at Plato's but at Aristotle's feet that the Christian theologian sits; the disciple of Plato is the man of letters, the aesthete, the dilettante.

At last I said: "It is through his moral, rational, and aesthetic intuitions that man apprehends certain goods, but the apprehension of the spiritual order of the universe is apprehended by the spiritual sense, and by that faculty alone."

Smith fidgeted in his chair, and hesitated, then finally took the bull by the horns. "You Indians make a great deal of the distinction between the 'spiritual' life, which is a life focused upon the unseen, and our earthly life which you regard as doomed to be unsatisfactory. I cannot help feeling that this pessimistic attitude toward life on earth has sadly retarded your country's material and social development. India's spirituality had contributed little or nothing to the good of the world; and the veneration which Indians give to that spirituality in my opinion has been a mistake. What is the spiritual order of the universe, unless it be an order exemplified in the better and happier living of the whole of mankind?"

"It should be thus exemplified," was my answer, "but it does not consist in that. What I am concerned to defend is not the Indian's way of life, but his conception of spirit and of the spiritual order of the universe."

Smith looked down and away. "The Indian's spirituality," he muttered, "often appears to me to be nothing more than a lack of common sense."

"That lack," I replied, laughing, "is, alas, only too often allied to our spirituality. But let me point out that the same lack is evidenced, although in an opposite manner, in the European's concentration upon the mechanism of civilization, and his feverish activity which brings him no nearer to happiness. And just as you see common sense in only one of its aspects, so also you seem to us to have fallen into great confusion over the question what constitutes knowledge, and over the relative values of different kinds of knowledge. Knowledge at the lowest grade is merely a knowledge of nomenclature. For instance, the statement: Peking is in China, displays knowledge of that kind. Next comes particular information, such as is contained in the sentence: Agra has over a million inhabitants. After this we place general information such as that exemplified by the rules of arithmetic. Knowledge of this grade has great importance in its own sphere, which is the conceptual sphere; but, as it becomes more abstract, it also becomes less useful to the understanding. For this reason the Indian attaches less value to it than to knowledge that is part of the actual stuff of human experience. In popular parlance one says: 'I now *know* what it is to be in love.' To us this use of language is accepted as philosophically valid. Indeed, we consider that an implicit, if not explicit, refusal to recognize feelings and intuitions as constituting 'knowledge' is the cause of an immense confusion in the philosophic thought of the West. The assumption that experience of this kind is of an inferior status leads to the further disastrous assumption that it must not be taken into account in seeking an understanding of the universe. But is a man really nearer to the heart of things when working out a problem in algebra than when reading the Sacred Books or listening to a great tragic play? To us it is evident that just as a knowledge, but not an understanding, of polo is to be obtained by studying handbooks on the game, so only a knowledge, not an understanding, of the universe is to be obtained in conceptual or abstract terms. The approach to an understanding can only be made by the gradual apprehension of ultimate verities through the exercise of the spiritual sense."

"I have no knowledge," replied Smith stubbornly, "of a spiritual sense, nor of a special class of verities which it is its function to discover. You were speaking just now of tragedy. In tragedy the universe is interpreted to us by art; we need have no recourse to anything beyond art."

"Tell me this," I replied, "if the spiritual sense were indeed identical with the aesthetic, how would it be possible to judge between great art and art that is perfect in a lesser kind? Yet that distinction is admitted. Some of us consciously—others, like you, unconsciously—recognize that art becomes great in the measure that it makes itself the vehicle of spiritual truth. Great literature, great music, great pictures, expand the consciousness with a breath that is not the aesthetic afflatus, and still less related to morality or rationality; but is essentially of its own kind—spiritual. Great tragedy is pre-eminent in this power precisely because in tragedy— more directly than in any other form of art—the spiritual sense takes control and puts the aesthetic faculty to its own service. In tragedy we feel ourselves to be reached by the voice of wisdom; and what is wisdom, if it be not an apprehension of ultimate verities?"

"I do not yet see that you have established the existence of a spiritual sense. It is the harmonious interaction of aesthetic, rational, and ethical intuitions that produce wisdom."

"In our psychology," I replied, "we do not allow to those intuitions any such pre-eminence as you accord them. We include them in the general category of the *rasas*, along with the sense of the comic, the sublime, the petty, the incongruous, the tragic, the indecent, the pathetic, and so on. It is one of the functions of the spiritual sense to co-ordinate these other senses so that to the persons, circumstances, and events, presented to him in his life-experience the truly wise man may respond with perfect taste—which is also perfect wisdom. The spiritual sense, the faculty of spiritual discrimination, must function on a plane superior to that of the other senses or intuitions because it is the valuator of those other modes of valuing. It is the co-ordinator of judgments by standards that otherwise have nothing in common. It is the judge between the pronouncements of any two, or more, modes of sensibility, when they appear to be out of harmony. On any particular occasion it decides what elements, if any, of beauty, ludicrousness, pettiness, pathos, and so forth enter, and in what degree each enters. In this aspect it is more ordinarily recognized as Taste. But in making these judgments it may also be seen to be Wisdom, for no particular occasion can be judged without reference to the universe as a whole. It is thus that the wise man reveals himself as possessing a more intimate understanding of the universe than other men."

It was foolish of me to go on at this length, for I had already become aware that my task was as hopeless as that of describing color to a man who has been born blind. Moreover, Smith does not realize that his lack of a spiritual sense disqualifies him from arriving at a good or true philosophy of life. As for me, I do realize that my aesthetic sense is extremely limited, and that I must make allowances for this; but I cannot believe that my inability to take much interest in works of art *as such* is as dwarfing as Smith's disability.

6

EARLY NEXT MORNING, as I was starting on my customary stroll, I came upon Smith, who was setting out in like fashion, so that it was inevitable that we should go together. By common consent we avoided controversial topics, and our walk would have passed off quite agreeably, but for an unfortunate incident which occurred just before we got back. Smith's attention was attracted by some blossoms on a creeper a little way off the path, and, being something of a botanist, he plunged into the brushwood in order to examine them. He had not taken many steps, however, before he stopped and stood still. He stood motionless for long enough to make me see that something was the matter, and when at last he tramped heavily back to me, I was struck by the strangeness of his expression. His face was pale, hard, and unfriendly. For a moment he looked me straight in the eyes, then—"Another murder!" he said.

I was certainly startled; what I answered I cannot remember, but an unpleasant silence ensued, during which I became increasingly aware of the change in his attitude towards me. Then, recalling his conversation with Mobarek about the other murder, I saw what was the matter. He was associating me with Mobarek, and had already made up his mind that neither of us were people who could be trusted to deal with this misdeed in the right spirit.

After a minute we made a move towards the place where the corpse lay. The face of *this* victim had suffered no disfigurement, and I fancied that the features were not unfamiliar to me, although whether the man was a carrier of mine, of Smith's, or of Mobarek's, I could not say. He had been killed cleanly with a sword-thrust through the breast, and his clothes were intact.

As we were standing there we heard voices, and a moment later four men appeared from the direction of our encampment. They were carrying implements which showed that they were intending to give the body some kind of burial; but when they saw us, they looked embarrassed and withdrew. Smith gave me another look, which was even more significant than the first, and, as we were going back to our path, I said briefly: "You may rest assured that I shall inquire into this."

He cleared his throat. "Those four who appeared just now— they are Mobarek's men."

I could not deny it. Moreover they were known by Smith to be Muslims; and they had been chattering and laughing together, as if the burying of a murdered man was one of their everyday tasks.

We continued on our way, Smith walking behind me along the narrow path, when, on turning a corner, I caught sight of Mahomed Fazul, the Captain of Mobarek's body-guard, no great distance ahead. The path in front of me forked, and I obeyed a sudden impulse to avoid meeting Fazul. Instead of coming after me, however, Smith paused, peered with his near-sighted eyes in the direction of Fazul, and then deliberately went by the other way. With a sharp movement of annoyance and foreboding I turned and followed him. The next moment we had reached Fazul. He was kneeling by a little stream, washing a blood-stained garment, while his unsheathed sword was lying on the bank by his side.

As we came up, he rose and with perfect composure made his usual salaam. Smith did not acknowledge it; grimly he walked straight on. As for me, I said: "Mahomed Fazul, I shall wish to see you presently." And again Fazul saluted with an unmoved face.

During the brief remainder of our way home no word was spoken. I was too much annoyed both with myself and with Smith to be the first to break the silence; as for him, keeping his eyes fixed upon the ground, he marched grimly along at my side, and, on reaching his tent, dived straight into it without giving me so much as a nod.

Considerably put out, I sat down in my own tent and considered the situation. I saw it as inevitable that Smith should now become fixed in his worst opinion of Mobarek and me; and this filled me with a sense of frustration and failure; it seemed a poor conclusion to our companionship.

Yes, looking at the matter through Smith's eyes, this is what I saw: Mobarek kept in his employ a savage and fanatical Arab, who had recently committed a murder, possibly two, almost under the eyes of his master; and the murderer had just exhibited a cynical coolness, which was no doubt largely explained by the fact that Mobarek not only derided religious toleration but vaunted himself on being a bloody-minded old bigot. As for me, for some time past my intellectual and moral integrity had been appearing more and more suspect, and my recent action in trying to screen Fazul had shown me up in my true colors at last. I fancy my position appeared to Smith a particularly contemptible one. For, although a civilized human being (which Mobarek was decidedly not), I found specious reasons for rejecting the civilized view of life. So Smith was waiting to see what course events would take—waiting in grim expectation of seeing both Mobarek and me exhibit ourselves at our worst.

Such was my reading of Smith's mind; and now I will show the other side of the picture. The case for Mahomed Fazul rests almost wholly upon the character of the man himself. He belongs to one of those tribes of desert Arabs who spend their time in wandering over the harshest regions of the Arabian peninsula. Fifteen years ago Mobarek, returning from a visit to Persia, brought this man with him. For some years he served in the Imperial army, then was transferred to Mobarek's body-guard of which he is now the Captain. During the whole of our present journey, I had been greatly impressed by Fazul's appearance and bearing, and by the respect in which his men held him. In Fazul I recognized a product of the desert—that place where only brave men can live, and they only by matching its austerity with the austerity of their lives. I know enough of the desert to realize what the first twenty-five years of Fazul's life must have been like. I know those wastes of harsh sand, rough gravel, and sharp stones, scorched and bleached by day, swept by chilling winds at night. It is out of this desolation, out of this poverty-stricken and yet splendid aridity, that there springs, like the frankincense tree, an unequaled faith in God. From nowhere else upon the earth does a fragrance of such sweetness and purity arise. How can one describe a passion that is as taintless as that air, steely in strength, and incandescent like the desert sun? When I look into Fazul's face I see a patch of desert ground, a surface hardened by endurance, trodden by every hardship. A gracious thing it is not; nor is the level look of those eyes other than repellent. That face is an iron door behind which the worship of Allah flames.

When, after much thought, I sent for Fazul, it was merely to tell him that I had seen the corpse in the wood and felt obliged to report the matter to his master. Next I questioned my own servants, and learned that the dead man had mocked Fazul at his prayers.

Before going to Mobarek, I sought out Smith and did my best to present Fazul's character to him in a favorable light. I pointed out that Mobarek would consider that the killing had been done under unendurable provocation. Indeed, could one, I asked, expect Mobarek not to take the view that the dead man's behavior had been practically equivalent to suicide?

We were sitting outside Smith's tent, and the bright morning sun revealed every shade of expression that passed over his face. Without a doubt he regarded my pleading as very specious, and disapproved of the attitude of mind underlying it. Censure was legible in every line of his countenance, and the stony silence in which he listened to me was very disheartening. I persisted, however, until suddenly he could contain himself no longer. A hot light came into his eyes, his hands began to grip one another, and he inquired curtly who was going to judge in the case. My words, he said, seemed to suggest that Mobarek was likely to take that office upon himself. But by what right? Let Mobarek appear as counsel for the defense by all means, but judge he should not, and could not, be.

I remained silent, overcome by discouragement. Whereupon, in a still more challenging tone, Smith went on: "As it happens, in one of my last audiences with the Emperor I discussed this very question—I mean the dispensing of justice—and I found that his views were exactly similar to mine. He told me he was resolved that there should be a standardized procedure, and that neither race, nor caste, nor religion should be allowed to interfere with the impartial administration of the law."

The note of triumphant satisfaction in Smith's voice was so ridiculous in its naivety that I really did not know how to reply. What was the use of trying to explain that it was absurd to pay any attention whatever to the Emperor's public pronouncements—certainly not to generalities such as these—and uttered for the benefit of a foreigner! Hastily I tried to get off the subject, but Smith would not have it; and I saw that I must give him a warning. If he was thinking of bringing the matter up to the Emperor in his next audience, let him, I said, consider the question again; moreover, it would be unwise—very unwise—to mention Akbar when discussing the affair with Mobarek.

After making every allowance for his principles, I am convinced that Smith is prejudiced by a strong personal dislike of Mobarek and an instinctive antipathy for Mahomed Fazul. I think that what I told him about Fazul probably did more harm than good. People like Fazul, by the mere fact of their existence, give Smith evidence of the inadequacy of his conception of human nature, and arouse in him an unacknowledged hostility. Smith's intolerance of intolerance is nothing short of fanatical. He does not like to be disturbed in his comfortable belief that the whole human race, if it only knew its own mind a little better, would realize that it wants just what he wants and dislikes just what he dislikes. We are all of us apt to explain away other people's differences of taste as misconceptions on their part.

Now Fazul is typically representative of a race to whom civilization does not appeal in *any* of its actual manifestations. The Arab is found in two contrasting types; he is either splendid or squalid; but in neither case does he illustrate human nature as Smith likes to imagine it. As a chieftain going forth to war from the barbaric splendor of a Moorish palace, or as a sneak-thief in a slum, he is unmoved by either rational altruism or rational self-interest. The springs of his being are not those upon which civilization counts. He has no inclination to make himself comfortable in the world;

what he prizes and lives by is just that which the apostles of humanism are obliged to ignore or deny.

Having come to the end of my profitless talk with Smith, I went to Mobarek, whom I found alone in his tent, writing a dispatch with his own hand. His keen, little eyes fastened upon me shrewdly; I think he noticed that I was troubled. In my brief statement of the facts I hardly mentioned Smith, but, when I had done, he said with a smile: "I am sure this must have been very shocking to our excellent friend. But no doubt you were able to soothe him."

"Not completely. But I have pointed out that the affair is not his business."

Mobarek looked amused. "Rajah! how could you say that to a lover of justice, to the friend of all humanity!"

I laughed, but on Smith's account I was uneasy. "Why not suggest to the Emperor that Smith would do well to leave India?"

This was perhaps a tactless thing to say, for Mobarek frowned. "It is not as simple as that. The Emperor takes an interest in foreigners, and he has not yet discovered the ineptitude of Smith. Daniyal, too, has taken Smith under his protection."

After a pause he went on: "Little does Smith realize that for Daniyal he has only the interest of a novelty. A few months ago the Prince was busy learning magic from the witch doctors of West Africa; before that he was being indoctrinated with the lore of Ancient Egypt. In a few weeks, when the Prince is tired of him, Smith will be thrust into the background to take his place among the freaks with which the Camp is swarming—a place somewhere between the hairless cat from Kamtchatka and the troupe of little golden-skinned eunuchs that has just arrived from Cebu."

With these words his manner suddenly changed, he summoned a servant and sent for Mahomed Fazul, asking me to remain present while he questioned him. Fazul stepped into the tent with an air of perfect tranquillity, and, when questioned, gravely confessed to the deed.

"Why did you kill this man?" asked Mobarek. "Had he attacked you?"

"No."

"Had he insulted you?"

"Yes, but that was not why I killed him."

"Then why?"

"He mocked the worship of Allah."

Mobarek was silent, looking down at the table. When he raised his head his eyes were closed and his lips slightly pursed. Lying back in his chair he gave a short sigh. "Very well," he brought out at last. "It was fated. Go in peace."

A silence fell between us, which Mobarek was the first to break. He gave me a look, still satirical but friendly, and began to talk of other things. In a little while I got up and left him.

PART THREE

1

WE REACHED KATHIAPUR at sunset on the same day, and parted with one another on the outskirts of the town. Mobarek was met by the Governor; Smith by some friends of Daniyal's whose guest he was to be; and as for me, refusing an invitation from the Governor on the plea that Srilata had already made ready for my arrival, I wandered off by myself.

It was an evening of golden sunlight, the sky being very clear in the west, but dappled with pink clouds overhead. During the day we had traveled down through a country of old, gnarled trees and broken rocks, where the wild meadows were bordered with red and yellow azaleas and cut up by rushing brooks of ice-cold water. But with every step it had grown warmer, and gradually the brooks had turned into streams which were spanned by high-backed bridges and bordered by almond trees and banks of Persian lilac. The larger houses that we passed had deep overhanging eaves of carved cedar with projecting oriels and windows filled with pinjra work in arabesque designs. It was a prosperous valley, filled with the sound of bells from grazing flocks, a part of the world where a serene and silken life was flowing on. At last the silvered roofs of temples appeared among the leafage, and Kathiapur lay before us, a little town of many gardens, where each man had his own tree for shade.

For a while, I sat beside a well, looking up into the sky, and my thoughts turned to Sita. In my constant awareness of the evanescence of earthly things there is a calm neither glad nor sorrowful, but sometimes strangely poignant. At such times I share the longing of those lesser poets whose hearts are bent on capturing in words a fragrance that otherwise blows away. Surveying the scene as one who formed no part of it, the thought of Sita, whose spirit is not called upon to renounce earthly joys, hauntingly recurred to me. Sinlessly she belongs to this earth, this earth enrichingly to her; there is a great-heartedness in her acceptance of my different pre-destination, and I felt grateful to her for it.

I cannot hope to find in either Srilata or Ambissa a like understanding. Each will have her reasons for disapproval, and although Ambissa's remonstrances will be the more vehement, it is not hers that I shall find the hardest to ignore.

By the time I had roused myself from these thoughts dusk had fallen, and I had some difficulty in finding the house that Srilata is occupying. It is a pretty little dwelling that stands in the middle of its own garden in a retired quarter. Thanks to her, I myself am now established in a house of the same pattern not more than a hundred yards away.

After dining together, we went out into her garden and there settled down to a leisurely talk. It is not many months since I last saw her, and yet my attention was caught at once by her small foibles, just as though they were not well-known to me, or as if she could reasonably be expected to have cast them off. However, I am paying her a compliment when I say that it is her lapses in intelligence that I always notice with the most surprise. To begin with, I found that she had accepted, apparently without question, the prevailing belief that at Ravi my acquaintance with Daniyal had ripened into friendship. "Do tell me something more about your life up there," she said. "It must have been most amusing to have the Pleasance of the Arts—such a charming name, by the way, isn't it?—quite close at hand. At Agra you gave me the impression that you had taken a prejudice against Daniyal. You seemed even to disapprove of *my* being a friend of his. Perhaps you weren't giving me the credit of being alive to his faults. But of course I have always realized that at times he is very silly, and that perhaps

507

there is even a streak in his character that one can't altogether like. However, I do think he has a genuine love of beauty—and then, of course, he is so witty, such good company. I am sure you agree about that."

These words positively took my breath away. Then I realized that it was out of kindness of heart that Srilata was imagining this change in me. She has always lamented what she considers my eccentricity, my inability to accept current valuations. Whenever I differ from the world, she feels sorry; for she cannot conceive that anyone sufficiently wide awake to catch the latest taste might possibly still prefer his own.

I made haste to explain that my life at Ravi had not been at all what she imagined; and that I had seen practically nothing of the Prince. "I am afraid," I said, "that you are going to find me without news of any kind. On the other hand, I am expecting all manner of interesting news from you. To-morrow, as you know, I shall be seeing Ambissa; and I should like to appear as little behind the times as I can; so please do your best to bring me up to date."

With her never-failing amiability, Srilata made haste to comply, but, alas! in a very short time, I was reminded that people who live in society form a habit of fastening only upon the odds and ends of things that possess conversational value. Talk consists in the passing round of little bright coins, the worth of which is unimportant, provided that they come straight from the mint.

Srilata's political information was of no use to me, except as showing that everyone in her set assumed that Salim was no longer a person to be reckoned with. When I pointed out to her that Salim had, after all, a large army at his back and commanded the sympathy of the whole Mahommedan world, my words passed over her without producing the smallest effect. The possibility of an arbitrament by arms clearly did not come within the scope of her imagination. All she replied was: "Well, my dear, from what I hear Salim has hardly a friend left in Court, and as for the Emperor, he leaves everything to Mobarek nowadays. Everyone says that he has been falling to pieces very rapidly in these last months. I don't think it will be long before he hands the Throne over to Daniyal."

"These rumors about the Emperor's physical and mental condition are nothing new," I replied. "I rather wonder at your paying any attention to them."

"Well, I am only telling you what people say. For instance, Babilo Tud was having luncheon with me here a few days ago, and he assured me that when he met Mabun Das coming away from his last audience with the Emperor, Mabun was positively dismayed. Akbar, Mabun said, had been drinking his usual mixture of wine and opium all the afternoon, and seemed unable or unwilling to discuss anything except the suppression of the Secret Sects. I am afraid that he has become quite unbalanced on that subject. Have you heard that *another* three or four hundred people were executed only the other day? And Mabun Das, who is obliged to do the rounding up of these poor wretches, was in despair about it. He said that what with wine, and opium, and religion, the Emperor was becoming quite incapable."

I shrugged. I was thinking how curiously shrewdness and stupidity were mixed up in the world's current gossip. Moreover, this was all at second-hand. But Srilata might quote Mabun Das, Man Singh, Abu-l-Fazl, or anyone else she pleased, even at first-hand, and yet I should remain entirely unimpressed. If important statesmen were to say what they really think at fashionable luncheon parties, either the statesmen would soon cease to be important or the luncheon parties to be fashionable. Shallowness is an indispensable requisite in polite conversation. Srilata knows as well as I do that it has long been the fashion in certain sets either to make fun of the Emperor or to shake one's head compassionately over his supposed decline.

To change the topic I asked her to tell me something about the people I was going to come across at Kathiapur, and she complied with polite animation. The interest she takes in scandal and intrigue is unflagging, but it is also light and detached. That she was in the thick of the social life at Kathiapur was evidenced by the number of notes that came in to her during the course of the evening. It was really very good of her, I reflected, to have reserved all these hours for me.

"The Khan arrived a few days ago," she was presently saying; "but Mobarek need not worry; the old gentleman has been quite happy here; everyone in the place has been at his feet from the moment he came; Mobarek in fact will find him in a particularly genial frame of mind."

"And what of Lalita?" I inquired.

"She and her sisters are here too. They are living under Ambissa's wing; and she, as you know, is a guest of the Governor's. The Governor lives in a sort of park in which there are several guesthouses. Ambissa with the three girls occupies one of them. The girls, I am afraid, have all been running rather wild since their mother's death; and Ambissa's responsibilities as duenna here in Kathiapur are particularly heavy. However . . ." and Srilata broke off.

"Tell me something about the Khan's daughters," I said. "The only one I know is Lalita."

"Oh, so you *have* met her?" said Srilata quickly. "When was that?"

I had a moment's hesitation—caused by my memory of the snatched embrace that I had chanced to witness. "I met her," I said, "on my journey from Khanjo to Ravi. She was traveling down from the Camp with Mobarek."

Srilata looked interested. "Was Hari with you then?"

"Yes."

There was a pause, in which we both wondered how much the other knew. Then Srilata went on: "Well, as you have seen for yourself, Lalita is very pretty, and in my opinion, the others are prettier still, for Lalita is a little too big for my taste. I know that a good many people—mostly men, I think—admire these large-boned Hill women; personally I prefer a more finely made type. Mahil and Parmi are smaller than Lalita, but all three have the same lovely coloring. Nothing is more attractive to my mind than that tawny effect which you get when the hair is a shade lighter than the skin—especially when the eyes are blue. Some people don't care about a parti-colored head of hair, but I find those tresses in various hues of gold quite enchanting. Mahil, the eldest, is twenty-two, and married; but her husband, who is a soldier, is away on the Northern Frontier keeping his eye on Mahommed Ali. I think she is the least reckless of the three. Parmi, the youngest, is only sixteen, and, although she is much less mature than our girls are at that age, she already behaves badly enough. It is a thousand pities there is no one in the family to keep a firm hand on her. The one I am most concerned about, however, is Lalita—on account of her special position."

"But, gracious heavens!" I exclaimed, "do you really mean to tell me that Lalita would be such a fool as to compromise herself now?"

Srilata laughed, and said nothing.

Presently, as it was getting late, I made as though to go, but Srilata, accustomed to staying up all night, would not hear of my leaving her yet. "Surely," she said, "you ought to make some return for all my indiscretions?" And with that she began questioning me about Daniyal and Lalita. What was the general feeling among Daniyal's friends about this match? What did Mobarek think about it? Had I ever heard Daniyal refer to it, and if so, in what sort of tone?

My answers, I have no doubt, were disappointing, and I am afraid that she thought I might have been more interesting had I wished. But she is never insistent, and presently she led the conversation on to Hari, asking what had prompted him to return to Ravi, and why, on his way from Agra, he had made a detour to avoid Kathiapur.

"He came back to Ravi," I said, "because Gokal had taken a turn for the worse and was particularly anxious to see him. You know what devoted friends they are. As for his avoiding Kathiapur, I didn't know that he had. Hari is an unaccountable creature, as we all know."

Srilata looked at me pensively.

"The thought that Hari is at Ravi now is a great comfort to me," I went on. "I should hardly have cared to leave the place without some person in charge. The Camp has attracted all sorts of strange characters into the neighborhood, and the presence of someone like Hari is almost a necessity. Servants, however trustworthy, never know how to act in an emergency."

A little later, feeling thoroughly tired, I got up and took myself off to bed.

2

MY HOURS OF sleep were brief, and I awoke with a sharp distaste for the business that lay before me. Memories of long unsatisfactory discussions with Ambissa rose into my mind, and I
resolved to guard against falling into my habitual mistakes. But
immediately afterwards I remembered how often in the past I had
armed myself with similar resolutions, and all to no purpose; for
it seemed to make very little difference what plan of action I
adopted, or how strong-mindedly I adhered to it. Ambissa always
has some scheme in her head to which she wants me to be acces-
sory, and there is something about even her most innocent schemes
that I always greatly dislike.

In striking contrast to Srilata, who has a light hand, Ambissa
persists; she never absolves one from the necessity of explaining
oneself; this involves explaining her to herself; a thing which it is
impossible to do agreeably.

The fact that Ambissa is not a bad woman, only makes the
position more difficult. Although her aims are invariably worldly,
her strategy unscrupulous, and her tactics wanting in finesse, her
motives are rarely, if ever, reprehensible. The advancement of herself and her family is what she has in view; and social ambitions—
especially those on behalf of others—can hardly be called wicked;
so that I can easily be made to look over-particular for refusing to

help her, a person more regardful of his own fastidiousness than of the welfare of his kith and kin.

There is no denying that Ambissa has had a successful social career. Her position at Court is impregnable, and she has prepared an excellent future for her sons. If Daniyal has been a thorn in her side, if he has amused himself by sticking darts into her, if he has ostentatiously refused to admit her into his inner circle, no one doubts that this is just fun and that at any moment he may swing round. Moreover, just as after a certain age old people begin to take a pride in the number of their years, so Ambissa has acquired a reputation which enables her to glory in the thickness of her skin. Thus, if I understand her relations with Daniyal aright, a kind of camaraderie, as between insulter and insulted, has grown up between them.

To do Ambissa justice, however, it is greatly to her credit that she is able to think of Daniyal without hatred. Nay more, I think I can say of her that she is without malice, spite, or hatred in regard to anyone. Once, when I pointed this out to Sita, she replied that no man could serve two masters, still less three; and that Ambissa was so much taken up with the World that neither the Flesh nor the Devil stood any chance with her. But without question Sita is inclined to be hard on Ambissa who is possessed of many virtues. She is a devoted mother, and would have made a very good wife according to her lights, if Hari had ever given her an opportunity.

The sun was already hot when I strolled over to the Governor's Park. I passed through the gates without challenge, and moved towards some gray shingled roofs that rose against a background of tall trees. Dragon-flies were hanging over the lily-ponds that skirted the road, and fallow deer stared at me curiously from out of the shade. I came to a group of long, low houses, about one hundred yards apart; and still not a single human being did I see.

Mounting the steps to the first of these houses, I found myself face to face with a pretty girl who had appeared on the veranda. She took a good look at me before retreating through an open window into the room behind. I heard her announce my presence, upon which there was a considerable stir within, and a moment later Ambissa hurried out. She greeted me with a warmth which I felt to be genuine enough, although her expression of it was exceedingly mannered. This she cannot help; besides, she was smothering a momentary vexation. "Did my servants send you here?" she said. "Because they shouldn't have done that. No, no! this is not my house. Mine is the one over there. But never mind.—I do hope you haven't been kept waiting. We . . ." With a sudden frown she broke off, as, from somewhere behind her girls' voices rose in altercation. But only for a moment, the high notes died down into muffled laughter.

"Come over to my house," Ambissa went on, and somewhat precipitately she led the way. "Dear Amar, how glad I am to see you! I was quite afraid you might not come after all, and I have so much to say. Besides, I want you to tell me all about yourself. How did you leave the dear Prince? I hear he has gone up into the mountains for a complete rest. I am sure he needs it. The journey down here would have been very tiring. Lalita has had such charming letters from him.—Yes, here we are; and now I am going to take you to my private room where we shan't be disturbed."

She produced a key from somewhere, unlocked a door, and we went in. A large desk littered with her correspondence reminded me once more that her life is a very busy one.

"Now we can have a long, leisurely talk," she went on; "and how delightful to think that we have several days before us. You will stay here for a week at least, won't you? In Agra one never has a moment to oneself, but here . . ." While she was speaking her eyes wandered restlessly, and one could not fail to notice her intense inward pre-occupation. This symptom distressed me, for it was something new. Up to now it has been one of her triumphs that she has managed, even when driving herself most hard, to present an appearance of repose.

All at once, in the middle of a sentence, she got up, opened the door, and looked out into the passage. "Oh, darling!" she cried. "There you are! Yes, Amar is with me. Yes, isn't it delightful! And so you are going back now? Well, tell the Khan I shall be coming this afternoon. Good-bye, darling, good-bye."

Closing the door again swiftly and firmly, she waited for a moment, then came back, once more rearranging her expression. The smile she had put on for the lady outside was evidently not quite the same as the one she keeps for me. With me she feels that the serious side of her character must be in evidence,—quite a mistaken idea, for I don't need to be persuaded that she takes life seriously. No, no, the difference between us lies merely in our choice of what things to take seriously.

It was natural that she should begin talking about our mother's death; she lamented that she had been unable to be with us at that time; and again, although her words were conventional, I felt that they were not insincere. Had she allowed herself any leisure for grief, she would most certainly have grieved; but in her life grief is a self-indulgence for which she has no time. Few people, I fancy, are capable of such a stern subordination of the natural instincts as she; and, if she shed a few tears now, those tears were not a sign of grief actually felt, they were rather a tribute to the grief she has been obliged to forego.

Her next subject was Ali. She was anxious about the boy, for he certainly should have reached Kathiapur before now. But here she contented herself with a few brief questions, and, as soon as she saw I had nothing to tell her, she passed on. Very painstakingly she set about justifying herself in having sent him up to the Camp; and, as I listened, I felt that at last we were getting down to business. I knew that she wanted me to repeat these excuses to Hari on my return to Ravi. When at length she did pronounce Hari's name, something in her manner put me on the alert. Hitherto she has always talked of him in the tone of the aggrieved, but still forgiving, wife. Her accent to-day sounded harder—not exactly harsh, but firm with the firmness of one upon whom a stern decision has at last been forced. Now and then she would pause, waiting, I think, to see what my response would be.

"Amar," she said, after a longer pause than usual, "did you have any talk with Hari before coming here?"

"You mean, I suppose, any private talk?—No. He arrived in the evening. The next morning early I went over to the Camp."

She looked at me hard as if she were trying to read my thoughts. "He had been away for some days, hadn't he?"

I felt vaguely surprised at her knowing what Hari's movements had been; and now, having had time to think the matter over, I feel still more surprised; to-morrow, perhaps, I shall ask her to explain.

The answer, I made, was that Hari's return was fortunate, for I could hardly have undertaken this journey had there been no one to look after my household while I was away.

"You left them all by themselves—without Hari or anyone—at Khanjo," Ambissa observed; and for the next few minutes we talked about Sita, Ambissa evidently wishing to show friendliness in her regard. Then again her tone changed, and I felt we were getting back to business.

"I wonder if you realize how unfortunate this quarrel between Hari and Daniyal has been? It makes everything particularly difficult just now. In fact I am afraid it has been nothing short of disastrous."

"Oh come!" I answered. "I am sure you are exaggerating. The Prince talked to me about Hari only the other day, and as far as I can judge he isn't harboring any resentment at all."

These words should have been pleasant to hear, but a shade of annoyance appeared on Ambissa's face. "My dear Amar, I doubt very much whether the Prince would allow you to see what he was feeling. But I am not thinking about that so much as about Hari's attitude towards him."

I remained silent, and she continued to look at me impatiently. "I want you to consider very carefully the position in which Hari has placed himself. You don't realize, perhaps, how tense the political situation now is, and besides you probably look upon Hari as an irresponsible character, who has neglected his affairs for so long that no one now pays any attention to him. I assure you that is quite a mistake. People don't dismiss Hari as easily and good-naturedly as you do. For one thing they remember—which you do not—that Hari is a Border chieftain. That in itself is enough to make people keep a watchful eye on him."

Again she paused.

"You are leading up to something," I said. "What is it?"

"I am certainly leading up to something," Ambissa answered slowly. "I wonder if you know that for some time past Hari has been intriguing very dangerously?"

"Intriguing?" As I stared at her I wondered whether she had heard something about Hari's flirtation with Lalita.

"It seems that Hari has been intriguing with Mahommed Ali."

Ambissa spoke with great gravity. "And not only with Mahommed Ali, but also, more recently, with Prince Salim direct."

If I was taken back, I was also incredulous. "I wonder who told you that?" was my reply.

Ambissa leant forward, very much in earnest. "You want to know who told me?—Well, it was the Emperor himself!"

"Oh!" The tone of my voice was an admission that she had made her effect. I remember staring at her in a vain effort to decipher her peculiarly unrevealing expression. Was her news as grave as she wanted me to think it? I began asking questions; I pressed her closely; and, alas, couldn't escape the conclusion that Hari was in very serious trouble.

When Ambissa saw that she had made her point, she nerved herself to utter the words that were to be her climax. With a firm face she came out with the announcement that she had divorced Hari!

It was some moments before I was able to grasp exactly what she meant. Only a few months ago, when Hari had been full of empty threats about divorcing her, she had shown great distress and a quite unreasonable alarm. Now I had to get it into my head that *she* had divorced *him*. And then, how had she managed it? The Emperor is making divorce very difficult, and for a wife to divorce her husband is practically unprecedented. I had every excuse for amazement. But there was no getting over the accomplished fact. The Emperor had apparently regarded Hari's treasonable activities as sufficient grounds for divorce.

At last I understood—and only too clearly—why Ambissa had been so anxious to see me. I was to go back to Ravi and inform Hari, first about Ali's attendance upon Daniyal in the Camp, and secondly about the divorce. Nor was this the worst, because it presently came out that the Emperor was about to order him to retire for an unspecified period to his estates in Sind, a place where he would be well out of the way. He was to be forbidden on pain of death to return to his Border principality, which was to be put under "the temporary administration" of the Khan. Ambissa counted on me to convey this news to Hari in such a manner as to make him see the wisdom of submitting without any useless fuss.

By this time I had lost the desire to argue or even to comment. My eyes remained fixed upon Ambissa in a gloomy stare; and I am bound to say that she returned my stare with unwinking firmness. Truly, she is a remarkable woman. Her eyes, her whole expression, the straight line of her back, all informed me that she was well prepared for everything I had to say. I accordingly reserved myself for another talk later on. I merely pointed out that, Hari being the man he is, there would very likely be murder.

Ambissa never blenched. She raised her eyebrows a little, sighed a little, and looked a little pained. Vaguely and reasonably she talked about retribution, and the wisdom of bowing before the inevitable. Nevertheless, it made her very sad, she said, that things had come to such a pass; she had spent sleepless nights. But all that was over; and now there was nothing to be done but to resign oneself.

I got up to go. Our talk had lasted nearly three hours.

"When will you come again?" she asked quickly, and began turning over the leaves of her engagement book. "It would be so nice if you would look in this evening. I have a little party, and I want you to make friends with these three girls of the Khan's. Such dears, all of them."

I replied that I could not promise to come. It was not unlikely that I should spend my evening with Srilata.

She gave me a sharp look. "Srilata knows all that I have been telling you, but—please remember this, Amar!—to the rest of the world my divorce is for the present a secret."

3

I HAD INTENDED as an act of courtesy to call on the Governor, but now I dismissed the idea. Leaving the house, I walked quickly away; but after a moment footsteps sounded on the road behind; it was the Governor who was hurrying after me.

"How are you, my dear Rajah?" he called out in a tone of excessive cordiality. "I was sitting on the veranda with the young Princesses when I saw you pass. Do you mind if I accompany you as far as the gate?"

Feeling slightly guilty, I did my best not to fall behind my companion in amiability. Nevertheless my second view of this man confirmed me in the impression that there was something about him that I did not like. He is tall, well-built, and handsome—in a rather commonplace way; he has an air of geniality, he wears a smile that is frank and open; and yet he does not inspire confidence.

Falling into step beside me, he began chatting about this and that, but I felt sure he had something up his sleeve; and after a minute he said: "I was hoping to catch you after your talk with Ambissa Begum, for that European traveler, Pundit Smith, has just been in to see me about the two murders that have taken place up the valley. Quite an agreeable fellow, Smith,—but, I am afraid, something of a busybody. He appears to be determined to bring the matter up before the Emperor in his next audience."

These words made me feel sure that the Governor had already guessed pretty accurately on what terms Mobarek, Smith, and I stood to one another. I answered that I didn't suppose the Emperor would pay much attention to Smith.

"In ordinary circumstances," he agreed, "His Majesty certainly would not. But I am rather afraid he may take it into his head that the first murder was a sacrificial one, committed by the members of some secret sect. In that case there will be a great to-do. I wish we had some means of identifying the victim." He gave me a meaning look as he said this, but its significance was lost on me, and he was obliged to add: "I don't like to confess that Ali's disappearance is beginning to worry me considerably. Isn't he by way of having left the Camp two days before you did?"

"I believe so."

"Well, have you any theory about his disappearance?"

"It seems to me to be not at all unlikely that he made a detour in order to get in a little shooting."

"That is possible, I suppose."

I halted. I looked into the Governor's face, and could no longer avoid the idea which he was insinuating into my mind.

"Are you suggesting," I said, "that the disfigured body I saw in the wood . . . ?"

His grave look was sufficient reply. When I next spoke it was to give voice to anxious, painful conjectures. The body, I said, seemed to me to have been that of a bigger boy than Ali; but boys of Ali's age change very quickly, and, alas, I couldn't on that score give myself the reassurance I craved. However, I went on, Ali certainly had attendants; and, if an attack had been made, some of his men would have assuredly escaped to bring in the news. Moreover, robbery apart, no motive for attacking the boy could be conceived, nor was it likely that robbers would have thought Ali worth attacking.

Whilst talking, we walked up and down in the burning sun, and physical discomfort was added to my mental distress. I cannot say I had ever had any peculiar affection for Ali, whom I hardly knew, but I was filled with pity for Ambissa.

"In my opinion," I said, "it is quite unnecessary to speak about these murders to the boy's mother as yet. After all, Ali may turn up here safe and sound at any moment."

My companion gave a nod. "I also hope," he added, "that this mystery will be solved before Akbar begins to interest himself in it—or in the other mysteries connected with the Camp. It would be a pity if Ali's name was to be coupled with that of the girl Gunevati."

I looked up sharply. The mention of Gunevati took me entirely by surprise.

"Of all the secret sects Akbar naturally detests the Vamacharis the most," he went on, "and when it is reported to him that Gunevati is a member of that sect . . ."

"What . . . ?" I stopped short. "Do you say that Gunevati is a Vamachari? What reason have you to think that?"

The Governor smiled. "I know it."

"How?"

"My dear Rajah, there is no shadow of doubt. I have seen the dossier on that girl. Mabun Das left it here for me to study. Let me tell you, Gunevati is not merely a member of the sect, she is one of their Yoginis—if you know what I mean? She embodies the Goddess in their secret rites." He paused; his face was superficially inexpressive, yet I received very strongly an impression of inward gloating.

For a couple of minutes we walked along in complete silence. I was thinking that in the light of this information Gokal's association with Gunevati, which had looked bad enough before, reached the uttermost limits of scandalousness. For how long, I wondered, had the wretched girl been occupying the attention of people in high places? It seemed to me ridiculous. A dossier, indeed! And I didn't at all like the idea that this dossier was in the hands of the Governor.

"Anyhow," I said dryly, "Ali has nothing to do with the Vamacharis, and nothing to do with Gunevati, and consequently . . ."

"Ali," the Governor interjected sharply, "was not—I mean—is not unacquainted with Gunevati."

"They are both living in the Camp," I returned with anger. "More than that . . ."

"They have been seen in each other's company very frequently. And I suppose you know who it was that brought them together?"

"Who?"

"I am afraid that it was your son—Jali."

"Jali—you say?"

"Yes."

I mustered a smile, which, no doubt, looked sufficiently uncomfortable to give the Governor considerable satisfaction. "Please explain."

"Well, Gunevati, you must remember, was not a stranger to Jali, for he and she were close neighbors at Khanjo, and at the Camp that acquaintance was renewed.—But perhaps Jali's visits to the Camp were sometimes made without your knowledge?"

I tried to cover my inward disarray. "Yes. But his cousin being at the Camp, it was not unnatural . . ."

"Exactly," said the Governor, "exactly! And I don't for a moment wish to suggest that Jali was doing anything wrong." As he was speaking these last words, he turned to look behind him, and, following his example, I saw that Smith was hurrying along to overtake us. This, I decided, was the moment to bring our conversation to an end. Taking leave of the Governor with as much politeness as I had at my command, I left him to the company of Smith and walked rapidly away.

4

ON GETTING HOME I took some food and threw myself down on my divan. Dismissing the Governor from my mind, I turned my thoughts upon Hari in an endeavor to find a means of helping him. The blow that was about to fall was severe. Banishment to that property of his in Sind was virtually a sentence of imprisonment—and imprisonment under miserable conditions, for those lands bring in very little revenue. As for the revenue from his Border principalities, that would certainly flow into the coffers of the Emperor—after the Khan had deducted what he considered his due as administrator. Yes, I saw it clearly now; that administration was being handed over to the Khan as yet another bribe for his continued allegiance. The disaster that was overtaking Hari might, of course, be regarded as retributive justice; that was the way Ambissa looked at it; but personally I felt the punishment to be too severe. Then, too, there was something ugly in the part Ambissa was playing. I did not go so far as to suspect her of having helped to bring about Hari's downfall; but it did seem to me that she had been rather quick to snatch at this divorce.

In the midst of these reflections I fell asleep. No doubt the enervating air of this place accounts for it. When I awoke it was to see my servant standing by my side, and I saw from his apologetic face that it was he who had roused me. Srilata Begum, he said, begged that I would come to her house as soon as I conveniently could.

Not a little anxious I jumped up, and a few minutes later I was there. A confused clamor of female voices greeted my ears, and in the hall I was hustled by three overdressed women who were hurrying away. The next moment my eyes fell upon the figure of Ambissa, who lay stretched upon the floor in a little room just by the entrance. Lalita was fanning her, while Srilata and two girls, whom I took to be Mahil and Parmi, were hovering round with restoratives. I examined Ambissa, who was unconscious, but it was difficult to tell how ill she really was because of the paint on her face. On my appearance the noise had died down, and Srilata now explained that an hour ago Ambissa had been very much upset by news of some murders recently committed on the road down from the Camp. Thinking that the Governor was to be found here, and wishing to question him, she had hurried over in the heat of the day but hardly had she crossed the threshold before faintness had overtaken her.

In the midst of Srilata's explanations a doctor arrived, and he very wisely insisted that Ambissa should be left in quiet; so we all trooped out into the big room that looks upon the garden, and there my attention was at once engaged by the Khan's three daughters. Lalita greeted me almost as an old friend; indeed I was a little taken aback by her manner which seemed to assume the existence of a kind of intimacy. Then Srilata presented Mahil, whose caressing eyes looked into mine as if she could see at once that we were companion spirits. Next came little Parmi, with cheeks flushed and eyes eager, as if from the pressure of exciting secrets. These young creatures spread about them an atmosphere tingling with animal vitality. The stream of life running through them was fresh and clear. Very different was their animation from that of the women in Daniyal's Camp.

Taken all three together, however, they were decidedly overpowering. They have a trick of all speaking at once and of shouldering each other away from whomsoever happens to be the object of their attention. For the moment that object was me; and I felt as might one who had just been thrust into the cage of three friendly but over-vivacious tiger-cubs. Tawny, I remember, was the word

Srilata had used in describing them; and tawny I felt them to be in inward as well as in outward coloring. Their volubility was terrific; they poured forth talk about Smith, the Governor, and Ambissa. They were vexed with Smith, for it was he apparently who had spoken to Ambissa about the murders; they made fun of the Governor (at least Mahil and Lalita did); for Ambissa they expressed an appropriate sympathy. Whilst I was being thus assailed, Srilata stood by, looking resigned and helpless.

Presently the doctor came in and he was able to allay our anxieties. Ambissa's heart was perfectly sound; there was no cause for anxiety; but she was driving herself too hard, and ought by rights to take a complete rest for several weeks. The young tigresses, stirred into fresh excitement, seized upon the doctor for all the world as if he were a bit of raw meat; but after a while he took refuge behind Srilata, and very soon in her company made good his escape.

Left unprotected, I was wondering how I should fare, when, most unexpectedly, a pleasant hush descended. The tempest dropped to a gentle breeze, and it was not long before I realized that the three sisters had many other moods besides the noisy one they had just been exhibiting. The next quarter of an hour passed quietly and agreeably enough. And it was profitable too, for I picked up a good many impressions that are likely to be valuable to me later.

Our talk was brought to an end by the sudden appearance of the Governor. I looked up to see him standing in the doorway with something like a smirk upon his face. Whilst his glances were traveling over my companions, I gave him another critical survey, and I must say I found him more unattractive than ever. In the presence of these young women his mustaches seemed to gain an extra curl, his complexion an extra glow, his fine shoulders an extra swing. Coming forward he embarked upon a gallant speech, but was unable to get very far with it. Behind him an enormous shape loomed up, a large, fat hand thrust him aside, and the Khan, bulky, red, and self-important, strode into the center of the room.

"Greetings, Rajah, greetings!" he called out, glaring at me out of his prominent, blue eyes. "Where's your sister, Rajah? What's this I hear about Ambissa, eh? What's all the to-do?"

Rising in unison, the three sisters flung themselves upon their father simultaneously, and he received three loud and voluble explanations all at once. Inevitably, before the pressure of such an advance, he yielded ground; he backed, and went on backing until presently the Governor and I found ourselves alone in the room.

But were we alone? A moment later I discovered that we were not. Standing in the door that gave upon the garden was Mabun Das. How he got there I do not know, but he now came forward with quiet self-assurance, greeted me cordially, and suggested that we should have a talk together under the mango tree at the end of Srilata's little lawn. I followed him out of doors with willingness; not only was I glad to escape further conversation with the Governor, but Mabun has always interested me. I recognize in him a man of strong character and outstanding ability; and perhaps, if I understood him better, I should like him more. I know him to live a life of tireless public service, to take pride in efficiency, and to be devoted to the Emperor. And yet he gives me the impression that he is without any interest in ultimate aims and ends; I suspect him to be at heart a cynic.

Our first subject—not an uncommon one in this country—was the Emperor. The key, said Mabun, to the Emperor's character was his pride in the fact that the blood of both Jenghiz Khan and Tamerlane was flowing in his veins; and to this consciousness of pre-eminence by birth he added the consciousness of pre-eminence by achievement. Never had he met anyone who was his equal, nor could he in his innocence conceive that such a one might exist. His conscious mind was that of a very simple man. What was it but his simplicity—one might almost say his humility—that caused him to identify his greatness with God's? One had to remember that in him the reasoning or rationalizing self was not highly developed; he was not of the sort who ignore in themselves everything that does not lie open to their examination or under their conscious direction. No, Akbar went to the other extreme; he identified himself with the whole mass of those unknown forces from which he derived his individual inspiration and potency. Thus it was that, rejoicing blindly in the streams of energy that rushed up into his being from the primordial fountains of life, he was gradually losing the power to distinguish between himself and God. In his earlier days military campaigns had absorbed his energies; next, the organization of his conquered realm had occupied him; but this was a labor for which he had no particular taste, to say nothing of the handicap of being unable to read or write. It was little to be wondered, then, that he was at last yielding to his mystic bias, and permitting himself to believe that he was the possessor of the Absolute Truth with a mission to enlighten, direct, and sanctify the people that he ruled. Out of this conviction had sprung the Din Ilahi.

At this point I observed that there was some strangeness in Akbar's reserving a special hatred for the Secret Sects, which did at least refrain from openly challenging his pretensions to a spiritual dictatorship.

"At first sight this may appear inconsistent," Mabun Das answered; "but we must remember that Akbar is a man of intuition or feeling, and feelings have a logic of their own—a logic which is often more profound than the logic of reason. It is obviously impossible for Akbar to suppress either Hinduism or Mahommedanism, so he has persuaded himself that these religions, being elementary and partial aspects of his own, are inoffensive. He thus escapes the necessity of regarding the mass of his subjects as insubordinate. But those who follow their own secret path do impugn his authority; indeed, they commit a double offense. They reaffirm the existence of the Great Mystery which he is by way of having incorporated in himself, and they exclude him from the knowledge of what their worship actually is. As an all-knower Akbar is fanatically intolerant of what is secret. Just as materialists are infuriated by mystics, so is Akbar outraged by any mystery to which he has not given his sanction and his seal. These Secret Sects, standing outside the circle of his light, reduce it to a mere candle-glimmer in the dark. For the unknown, once admitted, encompasses the known and dwarfs it."

To hear Mabun talk like this was a surprise, but not so great a surprise as it might have been. I had suspected from the beginning that he contained within himself something more than what he had yet shown me.

"All the people in the world, except Buddhists," I said with a smile, "can be fitted into two classes: those who proclaim and love mystery, and those who deny and hate it. The Buddhist turns away from mystery. For him it is merely the haze on the horizon, beyond which human vision cannot go."

Mabun gave me a peculiar look. "So you turn away from mystery, Rajah?—Well, mystery is dangerous—but to turn away is dangerous too."

What exactly he meant by this I did not inquire.

"Of course there is another reason why Akbar detests the Secret Sects," he went on. "During the last year or so his personal interest in women has declined—declined rather abnormally for a man of his age and temperament. And with this change of life his moral ideas have become correspondingly strict. It is not too much to say that his feelings on certain subjects are so strained and violent that at times he becomes almost insane. One has to study him carefully to discover just what things will irritate the inflamed nerve."

"The rank and file," I said, "accept Akbar's genius without examination as being beyond their comprehension, and on the other hand they dismiss as equally incomprehensible his foibles, his extraordinary departures from common sense."

Mabun nodded. "Even those who are in close contact with him make that mistake. They look to see what mood he is in, without ever seeking to understand the mood itself. They all have axes to grind, and regard the Emperor merely as an uncertain factor in their schemes. Even Mobarek looks upon him as nothing more than a tool. The Emperor *as a man* does not interest him."

After a moment's hesitation I brought out what I had in my mind. "Mabun Das," I said, "I have been given to understand that Hari Khan is not in favor with the Emperor just now."

A smile appeared upon my interlocutor's face. "Do not worry too much about that. The Emperor has a liking for Hari Khan all the same." He paused. "As for me, I want you to know that I count both Hari Khan and Gokal among my friends, especially Hari Khan. I took a fancy to him from the first, and during his recent detention at Agra a real friendship grew up between us."

"I am very glad to hear that," I replied.

Mabun looked down at the ground and smiled to himself. "Rajah," he said unexpectedly, "I hear that you and Shaik Mobarek are now fast friends."

I did not quite like his tone. "Certainly—I have for Mobarek a great respect and liking."

"The Shaik," said Mabun, "is a man of character—also, he has religion. This gives him influence over the Emperor, for both are visionaries. But Akbar is a practical visionary; he keeps much more in touch with actuality, and he may find it unwise to let Mobarek continue to lead him. Mobarek is first and last for the Din Ilahi; the Emperor is first and last for the good of the Empire; he is a realist."

"Both you and Mobarek belong to the same party," I said bluntly, "you both support Prince Daniyal."

Mabun looked away. "Mobarek is a visionary," he said in an even voice. "I, like the Emperor, am a realist."

I had another question on my tongue, but it could not be asked. Moreover, Srilata had just appeared on the veranda, thus reminding us that we had been in possession of her garden for an unconscionable time. We got up and joined her.

5

IT WAS ABOUT one o'clock last night when I laid down my pen; but although tired, I felt little disposed for sleep. The air was heavy and electric; two or three brief, sharp showers had recently fallen; a languid breath of damp came in through the open window.

Rising from my desk, I blew out the lamp and looked out into the night. The trees, shrubs, and creepers that made a wall round my little patch of lawn melted invisibly into the sky that was itself invisible, except in those moments when sheet-lightning lit up the great cloud-masses hanging above and silhouetted the motionless curtain of foliage. An outline of fan-shaped palms and heavy, ragged banana leaves then loomed above the warm, dark tangle of vegetation surging beneath. Wind-instruments from a Hindu temple in the distance made a faint liquid sound that was overlaid by the shrilling of crickets, the humming of insects, and the wailing of small owls. The air was saturated with the perfume of night-opening flowers.

I turned from the window, and by the glare of the lightning made my way towards the next room where I slept. As I moved my servant's white-robed figure gleamed out beside me, and he murmured something that I took to be his usual inquiry whether I had any more orders to give. I replied: "All is well. You can go to bed."

My thoughts, indeed, were far away, and abstractedly I moved into the next room. A small, red-shaded lamp was burning beside my bed. This was contrary to my instructions, for any light attracts the insects of the night. Surprised, I was about to call my servant back again, when something much more inexplicable met my eyes. Lalita, lost apparently in deep and dreamy meditation, was reclining on a divan at the far end of the room. For several moments while I stared at her, she returned my gaze without moving,—at first expressionlessly and then with a gathering smile. When at last she sprang to her feet, it was to come forward with a rush, and hang upon my arm, and let loose a peal of laughter. "Rajah!" she cried; "for heaven's sake don't look so unwelcoming, or I shall have to go away! Rajah, you must forgive me, please! I *had* to come. I simply had to come!" And she kept on repeating, "Rajah, I simply had to come!" in a sort of refrain, while she fell to pacing up and down the room.

I don't know what reply I made, and she certainly didn't listen to it. She was possessed by a curious pre-occupation, and her thoughts seemed to be far away from the words that continued to flow from her lips. "It's like this nearly every night, and I simply can't bear it! Can *you* sleep when the night is hot and thick and heavy like this? Bagavan has given me some opium, but it does no good. Nothing does any good. And every night is like this—thick and heavy and dead. The lightning flickers, and the moths beat their wings against the walls hour after hour. I can't bear this lightning—without any thunder. It's the silence that is so dreadful,— the silence with nothing but the flapping of the moths against the wall. We have no owls in our park. Perhaps, if there were owls ..."

She stopped, looked at me, and burst out laughing again. "I have been watching you through the doorway. Oh yes, I have been here a long time. I told your servant not to disturb you. You look very severe as you write. Is it a book? Are you working out a new philosophy?—It is so pleasant and peaceful here, lying on that divan, I nearly went to sleep." She paused, but only for a moment. "No, I didn't really feel sleepy. I was thinking. Over there, in our house—it is impossible to think. The noise, the confusion, and people in and out all the time! You have no conception what the life is like! The others seem to enjoy it, but I am driven

531

almost mad. Unless one's mad enough to enjoy it, it's bound to drive one mad. You must understand what I mean, for you are a Buddhist. Surely you see what I mean? Rajah, it's enough to drive *anyone* mad."

Her trick of repeating her phrases over and over again has a kind of hypnotic effect. I stood staring at her;—we were looking at one another hard, and, remote as she indeed was from me, somehow I did not feel out of sympathy with her. Going to the window, she stood with her back turned to me, silent for a while. Then she came close up, and this time her voice was sharp and low. "Rajah, we mustn't be overheard. I have something to tell you. Will you make sure that no one can overhear us? Look in the next room,— Rajah, please! It would be terrible if someone overheard us."

I went into the next room, which of course was empty; I closed the door to the passage, and then my own door was well. "You can put your mind at rest. Only one servant sleeps in this house, and he is nowhere near."

She came up to me again. "I suppose you think me quite mad. Oh, yes, of course you think me mad." Shaking her hair back, she shrugged her shoulders and laughed. I was studying her with more attention now, and she seemed to enjoy my gaze. But I did not like her so well as in the afternoon. Painted, powdered, perfumed, tricked out with jewels and rustling Italian silks, she looked so little a creature deserving of compassion, that my feelings flew to the opposite pole. Moreover, the theatrical element in her behavior alienated me.

After a moment I think she guessed what was passing in my mind. "I can't go on until you have told me something," she said.

"What do you want to know?"

In a low voice she replied: "I want to know what Ambissa said about me this morning?"

"She said nothing about you. Nothing at all."

"Do you swear it? I have to know. I have a special reason for asking."

"She didn't even mention your name."

"Did she talk about ..." The sentence remained unfinished. Looking down and away, "What *did* Ambissa talk about?" she asked.

I smiled. "My dear Princess . . ."

"Lalita," she corrected me.

"My dear Lalita, why should I tell you what she talked about?"

"Did she tell you she had divorced Hari?"

After a moment's hesitation, I said: "Yes."

Lalita gave a brief laugh. "She has been keeping it very secret. I only heard by accident. She told you nothing more?"

"No.—At least . . ." Again I hesitated.

She looked at me searchingly. "I see—It didn't occur to her, I suppose, to tell you that she is going to marry my father?"

I stared, frowning. She snatched at my arm again and clung to it, laughing into my face. "Yes, she is going to marry father, and she's been keeping that more secret still. You see she hasn't even told *you*. Oh, Rajah, don't you see the whole thing? What a fool I've been! Ambissa's been taking me in. She's been taking everybody in. You, probably, just as much as everyone else.—And she hasn't finished yet."

Lifting her head, she looked deep into my eyes. "You're not angry with me? It's no use being angry. I know she's your sister, but—but why should I pretend? I'm so tired of it all. And, you know, I like Ambissa very much in a way. I mean I used to like her . . . but really, after all this . . ."

She drew away, and flung herself down on my divan. For quite a long while there was silence in the room. I was trying to collect my thoughts, but without much success. Looking through the window, I watched the garden flashing into lurid visibility, then darkening, then flashing out again. I took the red shade off the lamp, and stood in front of Lalita, looking down at her thoughtfully. She smiled. "I suppose you want to see whether I am lying?"

"Why are you dressed up like this?"

"Have you forgotten that we have a party?"

"Oh yes, of course.—How did you get away?"

"No one saw me. I slipped away."

I was still puzzled, and quite determined not to encourage her to make an emotional display.

"How long ago did you hear about—about all this?"

"Oh,—not long ago."

She didn't tell me *how* she had obtained her information, and

I abstained from asking her. By some means, I suspected, that she was not very proud of.

After a pause I said: "I can understand your being startled by this, but I don't quite see what reason you have to be—agitated." (She snorted angrily at this last word.) "You yourself are shortly going to be married, which means that you will be leaving your father's house. Mahil, too, has a husband; and as for Parmi she will certainly also be married soon. Besides . . ."

I was interrupted by her springing to her feet. "My God!" she cried out in a voice of despair, "how little you understand! Oh, Rajah, you don't in the least understand!" She came up to me again; her eyes were burning, her face set. These mid-Asian women have a quality of independence, self-assertion, and violence, which contrasts strongly with the age-long submissiveness of the Hindu. She met my gaze with fierceness at first, then closed her eyes and turned away. "Well, what does it matter? Nothing is any use now. I shall have to go through with it.—Where is my cloak? Please give me my cloak, Rajah. The palanquin men are outside. I will go home now. . . ." Her voice was dull and hard. She was hunting about the room for her cloak; but presently she remembered that she had not brought one. All at once I felt a stab of pity. Until this moment my mind—or rather my imagination—had failed to take into account the fact that she was about to be married to a man she cordially disliked. My excuse is that I had only Hari's word for it that she disliked Daniyal. It had been open to me to look upon her as a young woman quite ready to embark upon love-affairs with married men for her amusement, and equally ready to sacrifice that amusement to worldly ambition. But no! that is not quite fair. I am not justified in assuming that she was not really in love with Hari; and if, up there, in that lonely valley in the Hills, what Hari told me was true, on one occasion at any rate she had been ready to sacrifice ambition to love—or at any rate, to a romantic semblance of it. My memory of the part I had played on that night made me now feel slightly guilty—not for preventing the mad adventure, but because I had thrown her back upon this loveless marriage.

With an instinctive movement I placed myself in front of the door. "No, Lalita," I said, "I won't let you go like this. Perhaps I have been slow to understand you,—but you must not misunderstand me. You must wait a moment longer."

"Rajah, there is a party going on. I shall be missed. You *must* let me go."

"What did you mean by saying: 'Don't you see the whole thing'? What did you mean by accusing Ambissa of taking everybody in?"

She was obstinate, and at the same time preoccupied. "I must go," she kept saying. "I must go."

Frowning, I stood my ground. For a minute we stared into each other's eyes; then—"You had better come too," she said suddenly. "We can say you were just arriving and that we met each other outside on the veranda—and walked up and down in the Park. Please never tell anyone I came here to-night. Please promise me that!"

Impatiently I reassured her.

"We can both squeeze into my palanquin. Come quick."

"Very well. But before we leave this house you must explain yourself."

"Explain myself?—Oh, Rajah!" She gave a little snort of laughter, flung up her arms, and began marching up and down. "Why do you ask me that? What is the use? I know well enough what you think of me. Oh, yes, of course I know. You think me hysterical. You think I am always.... But what does it all matter? As I have said before, you don't understand. You don't realize what I have been through. You don't realize how terribly I dread . . ." Her voice had risen to a wail, but now all at once she let it drop. "God! If only you understood what Ambissa is responsible for!"

Perplexed and helpless, I followed with my eyes her rapid pacing up and down. Her movements were exactly like those of an animal in a cage. This long-legged, broad-shouldered young woman gave me a curious sense of contact with animal life; the violence of pent-up vitality in her was something to be reckoned with—in terms of simple emotion, and of its power to arouse simple emotion.

All at once she began laughing again, but gently and to herself; she stood still, with narrowed eyes, and laid a hand on my arm. "Think, Rajah!" she said in a low, quick voice, "Ambissa is going to be the mother-in-law of the future Emperor! The mother-in-law of the Emperor! Think of it!" She paused. "And you, I suppose, will be uncle-in-law. What a charming family party we shall be! Ambissa has got us all roped in! She has even found the right husband for Parmi, who is to marry Ali. That makes another link, you see. Isn't it splendid, Rajah! Our two families between them will simply rule the roost. Everything will fall to us! We shall have first places at Court,—we shall hold all the best offices,—money and honors will simply roll in." She gave me an oblique look, and added, "It's no use your trying to stand out, Rajah. Everything was settled long ago for *you* as well as for the rest of us."

I hope I didn't let her see the effect her words had on me. I am rather ashamed of the extent to which they took me aback. Why hadn't I exercised my imagination a little more effectively for myself? "I see," I said beneath my breath.

"But it all depends on my marrying Daniyal," she went on with a peculiar smile, "and a few weeks ago I had decided I wouldn't."

"And then?"

"And then Ambissa persuaded me to change my mind again."

"I see." My eyes were fixed on the ground. "Thank you, Lalita," I said at last. "Now, I suppose, we had better go."

I led the way out of the house. Her palanquin-bearers had gathered some friends about them, and by the light of their lanterns were playing a betting-game by the roadside. They got up, spat into their hands, and made ready.

"Take four men instead of two," Lalita said urgently. "And we don't need a lantern. Tell them to put it out. Give them plenty of money. Tell them to run."

There was no room on the seat for more than one, so Lalita sat on my knee. On our way I don't think we exchanged a single word. But, when we were about a hundred yards from the house, she told the men to stop and put us down. Together we strolled on towards the lights and the voices. On the veranda there was no one, and after running up the steps and looking into the room, she turned back to me and said in a low voice: "Come!"

From the comparative obscurity of the veranda, we studied the party indoors. On the other side of the room was Ambissa, talking quietly but earnestly to Mobarek, who nodded his head at times, and once burst out laughing and patted her hand. The plump,

straight back, her carriage of her head, the slow waving of her fan
—all were extraordinarily expressive. As for her face, that hard social mask with its impenetrable eyes, struck me with a certain
chill. Not far away, Parmi and Mahil, who had just finished singing,
were receiving congratulations on their performance from the Governor and two or three young officers. Ranee Bagavan, the Khan's
sister, was talking to Srilata and Smith. The Khan himself, with a
jug of wine by his side, was pretending to listen, but I think he was
more than half-drunk. A few faces turned in our direction, but my
late appearance in Lalita's company did not seem to excite remark.

To my great relief the party broke up very soon, and I was able
to go back home to bed.

6

THUS ENDED MY first day at Kathiapur, and it has left me with a great many disagreeable things to turn over in my mind. Are all my days in this unpleasant little place to be equally rich in complications and entanglements? As my sojourn here threatens to become more prolonged, it becomes in equal measure more distasteful. But I must not go away until I am satisfied that there is no object in my staying any longer. During this time I shall not dare to think—indeed, I *must* not think—about my own future. That I *shall* retire from the world before very long is certain; in the meantime I must possess myself in patience.

The above lines were written at noon. It is now evening, and again I have a good deal to record.

I called on Ambissa early in the afternoon and found her waiting for me in her small, private room. She had a purposeful air, and at first sight gave an appearance of perfect health and serenity. Her face was as smooth and fresh as massage, paint, powder, and a strong will could make it. But the morning light also made visible a kind of inward haggardness. This I put down chiefly to anxiety on Ali's account, for no news of him has yet come in. The maternal instinct in Ambissa is strong. Moreover, her ambitions are so intimately bound up with Ali, that the boy's death would leave them hanging in the air. But it is also true that her ambitions have a mechanical vitality of their own, and that no matter what sorrows overtake her she will live the life of the world to her last breath. I felt a great pity for her, and was glad to be able to say in all honesty that the Governor's apprehensions seemed to me quite unwarranted.

We then began talking about Lalita; and I was struck by the fact that, while she had made no attempt to arouse my compassion in regard to Ali, she now put on sad airs, sighed continually, and blinked as if to keep back tears. "Yesterday," she said, "I couldn't bring myself to tell you what a trial that girl has been to me. But now I really must."

"What is the matter?" I asked.

"Well, she has taken it into her head again that she won't go up to the Camp."

I compressed my lips and looked away. Ambissa's eyes made me suspect that she had got wind of Lalita's midnight visit to my house.

"I expect Mobarek will be able to talk her round," I replied dryly.

"I think *you* might be able to talk her round."

"I?"

"Yes. I am sure you could help, Amar. She has a great respect for you, and—and she is the kind of girl who will only listen to a man. I do wish you would use your influence with her."

"But . . ."

"Listen, Amar!—I daresay you were a little surprised when I wrote to you about a week ago to suggest that Lalita should stay with *you* at Ravi instead of actually staying in the Camp. The fact is that she was then complaining that the Camp tired her too much, that she couldn't get a wink of sleep there, and so on. My suggestion that she should stay with you took the wind out of her sails, you see. In fact, it did more: it acted as a positive inducement."

"My dear Ambissa, there is a mistake somewhere. Lalita and I are the merest acquaintances. The pleasure of staying in my house could not possibly be strong enough to overcome—could not, I mean, be of any weight."

"Oh, then she has talked to you about her marriage—about Daniyal?"

"No. Everybody knows she dislikes Daniyal."

Ambissa was studying me with a speculative eye.

"You see," she said at last, "that child has a very difficult temperament. For instance, she thinks she didn't get on very well at the Camp on her last visit. She is over-sensitive, and easily takes offense. One must do all one can to help her, to give her self-confidence. With a little more self-confidence she would be perfectly happy, and able to fill her position quite well. I should like you to talk to Mobarek about this. He is confident that the marriage will be a great success."

My inward irritation caused me to reply bluntly: "A success, you mean, from the political point of view. But, personally, I doubt it. The situation might be made more difficult still."

"Oh?" And Ambissa raised her eyebrows.

"If Lalita were to fall out with her husband, the consequences would be serious. I am quite sure her father would take her part in almost any circumstances. Of all his children she is his favorite, and I hear on all sides that she can twist him round her little finger."

This, I am afraid, was rather malicious, but I wanted to goad Ambissa into greater candor. If she was really intending to marry the Khan, why didn't she tell me so? My words brought a warm flow of blood to her face; her eyes sparkled, as she replied: "Oh, the Khan is not the man to be twisted round *anyone's* finger, I assure you. You must get to know him better, Amar. It is no exaggeration to say that the future of the Empire lies in his hands." And her already upright back stiffened as she spoke.

I felt a touch of compunction. I bethought me that she had probably persuaded herself that she loved the Khan; and it was no less likely that he fancied that he loved her. Looking at her through this elderly lover's eyes, I saw her as a very well-preserved and handsome woman, and still comparatively young. She would adorn the Khan's various palaces, she would make a perfect hostess, the match was an eminently suitable one; but who could say that it was not a love-match as well?

Ambissa smiled at me sweetly. "With the Khan—and Mobarek—

540

to guide and help him, Daniyal's character will certainly develop along the right lines. I am sure he will make a kind husband." She paused. "But I should like the Prince to come under *your* influence as well. You could supply something that is all your own."

Now it is when Ambissa says things like this that I have much difficulty in not being positively rude to her. Swallowing down my exasperation, I replied: "Don't, please, interpret anything that I have said as uncomplimentary to the Khan. His fondness for his children illustrates a charming side of his character; and, if he has no great liking for Daniyal—well, two people less fitted to get on together I have never met. Besides, the Khan is a man of great pride, and—if I am to believe Mobarek—Daniyal has treated him on more than one occasion rather uncivilly. I put it to you: in the event of a quarrel between Lalita and Daniyal . . ."

"There won't be any quarrel, and I can hardly imagine any girl being such a fool. . . ." Ambissa interrupted with some heat, but she managed to check herself and made a fresh start. "My dear Amar, aren't you rather forgetting what a magnificent marriage this will be for Lalita, and how much she would have to lose by trying to make trouble between her husband and her father? I don't mean to imply that she is worldly-minded, but, believe me, she is not wholly blind to the advantage of becoming the wife of the future Emperor. If she has persuaded you that she *is*. . . ." And Ambissa ended with a shrug.

I laughed. "She has not had much opportunity to persuade me about anything, but . . ."

"Well?"

"By all accounts she has a romantic disposition . . . And Daniyal . . ."

Ambissa took a deep breath, and her face changed. "Ah yes, I understand." She eyed me comprehendingly. "Amar, let us be frank. You are thinking about that affair of hers with Hari."

I feigned astonishment. "With Hari, do you say?"

"Yes, yes!—Listen, Amar!" She leant forward confidentially. "I know all there is to know about Lalita's past love-affairs— real and imaginary. She herself has told me all about them. Oh yes, my dear, you needn't look surprised. She has talked to me about Hari by the hour. It may seem odd to you that she should have turned to me, Hari's wife, for consolation. But there it is! And I think it speaks very well for me that she should have done so."

I nodded.

"Hari of course behaved very wrongly. The fact that she was already engaged to the Prince should have deterred him—if nothing else could. They had a flirtation. It was very foolish, and—in the circumstances—very dangerous. Not that it went very far—oh no! But when one is engaged to a Royal Prince..."

"And that romance is now all over?"

Ambissa did not answer at once. Her eyes slid past me, and to give herself time to think she rose and let down one of the sunblinds. "The trouble," she said, "is that Lalita's visit to the Camp a couple of months ago upset her a good deal. And then—in order to restore her self-confidence—what did she do but revive the idea that Hari was in love with her still! Some silly girl had told her, I think, that he remained languishing,—and *that*, you see, was more than enough!"

"I think," Ambissa went on, "you can now understand one of the reasons I have had for keeping my divorce secret. I have been afraid lest Hari's new freedom should encourage Lalita to indulge in heaven knows what ridiculous day-dreams."

"But..." I broke off, and then a sentiment that I really cannot define won the day. "But why shouldn't she and Hari marry?" I asked.

For the second time that afternoon Ambissa flushed, then, conquering her anger, she gave me a strained and patient smile. "I don't think you can seriously regard Hari as a suitable husband for her—quite apart from..."

I remained silent.

"Well!" she continued, once more brisk in tone, "for about a week Lalita was in a dreadful state of mind. Thank heaven, I was there to comfort her—and talk reason. Like so many spoilt young women she enjoys emotional scenes. However, in the end, she gave up all her nonsense about refusing to marry the Prince. In fact, my dear Amar, if Daniyal were now to turn round and say *he* wouldn't marry *her*, I truly believe she would die of mortification."

While Ambissa was speaking a question had shot into my mind.

"By the way," I said, "when you suggested to her that she should stay in my house, did you contemplate Hari's being there too?"

Ambissa hesitated, then smiled as one confessing the truth. "I couldn't be sure whether he would be at Ravi or not, but I was convinced that if he *was*, it would do no harm. Lalita would see for herself that he was far from breaking his heart over her."

"Surely you were taking a considerable risk?"

She looked away, then took a sidelong glance at me, then looked away again. "I didn't really think he *would* be at Ravi."

"But you let Lalita think so?"

"Well—yes."

I was silent and annoyed. It was impossible to tell what was going on in Ambissa's mind. I was wondering what line to take when the sound of girls' voices came in through the open window. We both turned, and there, vivid in the sunlight, were the Khan's three daughters standing in a group about half-way between their house and ours. As usual they were all talking very loud, very impetuously, and all at the same time. I caught the sound of my own name, and was straining my ears to hear more, when Lalita suddenly looked round, said something in a lower tone, and after that their voices all dropped.

Taking a glance at Ambissa, I detected an inward shrinking, and I must confess that I shared, in some degree, her apprehensions, for it looked as if these young women were arranging to deliver an attack upon the two of us together.

At length Lalita detached herself from her sisters and walked resolutely in our direction.

A low murmur of annoyance came from Ambissa, and her eyes, passing over me, wandered round the room as if she were wishing she could thrust me into a cupboard or anywhere out of sight. I lay back in my chair with a false air of composure and waited.

"She seems to be coming here," said Ambissa, "I hope. . . ."

I said nothing.

Ambissa was frowning. Once again she opened her mouth, but closed it without speaking. It was not until the girl was actually to be heard in the passage outside that she hurriedly murmured: "Amar, do please remember! I absolutely count on you to. . . ."

Lalita entered swiftly, and, after closing the door behind her, stood leaning back against it and looking down at us with a faint smile. She was clearly very self-conscious, the flush on her cheeks and the brightness of her eyes belying her apparent self-possession.

"Darling," said Ambissa, brightly, "we were just talking about you, and now you are here to help us. But first of all do tell me whether you slept better last night. I am afraid your nerves. . . ."

"Thank you so much, Ambissa. I slept beautifully." Lalita's smile became frankly ironic and then flickered out. "You say you were talking about me—yes, of course! I knew that already."

Ambissa had no reply ready, and Lalita went on: "But haven't you discussed me long enough yet? I do rather object to it, you know."

"My darling!" began Ambissa in expostulation.

"No, no, no!" And with a sudden passionate gesture the girl waved Ambissa's words away. "For God's sake, don't let's go on any longer with that kind of thing! I can't stand it! Besides, Ambissa, it's no use now . . . You see, I know everything."

Lalita pronounced these last words without any emphasis, her voice, in fact, was both husky and low. For a few moments an uncomfortable silence reigned. Ambissa, prudently, was doing no more than look up with a pained and puzzled air.

At last Lalita turned to me, drew a deep breath, and went on: "Rajah, I am not treating you well, I know. I mean I made things difficult for you by extracting a promise not to tell." She gave an unhappy laugh, and then added: "I suppose *she* hasn't yet come out with the truth, has she?"

My answer no doubt was legible upon my face, for in a harder voice Lalita went on: "No, evidently not. But then—what a comedy! Here are you and she sitting together for hours, and all the time . . ." She laughed again, but fiercely this time; indeed I noticed that she had become pale and trembling. "Ambissa, I know you like to give people your own account of me and my affairs, but I wish that you would have the courage to tell them about yourself as well. Why are you hiding from the Rajah that you divorced Hari in order to marry my father?"

Ambissa blenched and drew herself up.

"You see; I know everything," the girl went on breathlessly. "And what is more I told the Rajah all about it last night."

Ambissa's face had become very hard. "My dear child, it seems to me that so far from *my* meddling in *your* affairs. . . ."

"But isn't this my affair too?"

"No, certainly not! My relations with your father do not concern you. I have a perfect right . . ."

Lalita laughed harshly. "Do you really mean to maintain that . . ."

"Lalita, please!" Ambissa, herself now very pale, got up from her chair.

"My God!" cried Lalita, stamping with her foot on the floor. "She says this is not my affair, when for the last three months she has been tricking me. Why has she been so bent on my marrying the vilest man on earth? Why has she spent days and weeks, arguing and wheedling and coaxing me? Why, a month ago, when I had summoned up enough spirit to say *I would not* marry that man—why did she begin crying, and almost go down on her knees to me? I tell you, Rajah, she went on and on until I was so sickened with the whole affair that I said yes just in order to get peace. Why did she do all this? What does it matter to her who I marry? There is only one answer—and I know it, and she knows it, and you know it, Rajah, too. You know it because I explained everything to you last night. For God's sake let us be honest at last. I have got to marry Daniyal because the marriage is a part of her scheme. It is an absolutely essential part of her scheme that I should marry that cad. I have got to marry him. There is no way out now, and that's the beginning and the end of it."

"My dear," said Ambissa dryly, "you speak as if I had been the one first to suggest the match, but you know very well that the proposal came from the Emperor himself, and that I had nothing whatever to do with it. The Emperor approached your father, and your father did nothing before obtaining your consent. You agreed to the marriage—quite readily, I have been told. Nor is that very surprising after all. There is not a girl in the country who doesn't envy you."

Lalita ignored this; she kept her face turned to me, and, looking straight into my eyes, she said: "Rajah, I have been a fool. I know that as well as anyone. But the fact remains that Ambissa has been deceiving me. I may marry Daniyal or I may not. We shall see.

But . . ." here her voice became shrill with fury, "but let her understand once and for all that I am not going up to the Camp again. Please make her understand that:—I am not going back to the Camp."

I inclined my head, and I think she felt that in this at least she would have my support. Looking round at Ambissa, I saw her biting her lips. She was angrier at this moment than she had been yet, and the swelling of the veins in her forehead alarmed me, for her temper, when once out of control, is very violent. It alarmed me, too, to observe that Lalita was meeting her looks with looks almost equally grim. Never again, I reflected, would these two women be able to patch up any but the sorriest semblance of amity, and I felt a flash of sympathy for the poor Khan. The silence which now reigned was a dangerous one, I made haste to be the first to break it.

"Come along, Lalita," I said, rising. "You have said your say, and that is enough."

Stepping in between the two women, I turned to Ambissa. "Good-bye, I will come again to-morrow morning—unless you would prefer to visit me in my own house?"

Then, without waiting for an answer, I opened the door for Lalita, took her by the elbow, and set her in motion. For the fraction of a second she resisted, then gave a little laugh and walked out.

Together we went slowly across the lawn, and not a word was spoken on the way. On reaching her house, however, she looked up into my face with a smile of genuine amusement.

"I am sorry, Rajah," she said, and ran up the steps.

7

A S I W A S leaving the Park, I came upon Srilata. She was walking slowly along with her eyes fixed on the ground; so pensive was
she, indeed, that she might have passed me by unawares, had I not
stood straight in her path. The moment her gaze fell upon me,
however, she assumed an air of cheerful composure;—and this had
the effect of putting me out of patience. I often feel that Srilata
carries circumspection too far.

In the brief conversation that took place I came near to upbraid-
ing her. It is not flattering to be treated as a fool in whom no confidence is to be placed. I forget how we began, but before half a
dozen sentences had been exchanged I found myself saying: "One
thing at least I see clearly, you are all united in a close body behind
Daniyal; you all share the same blind confidence in his future—a
confidence which seems to rest largely upon the prospect of his
marriage to Lalita. But I think you are all being both over-confident
and—and . . ." I could not find the word I needed, so I went on:
"Anyhow, I greatly doubt whether the marriage will come off. And
I don't think it would be a success, if it did,—not from any point
of view."

Rarely have I spoken more impatiently, and poor Srilata looked
quite disconcerted. "Why do you think the marriage won't come
off?" she asked.

"It is only by leaving both Lalita's character and Daniyal's completely out of account, that you all succeed in believing that it will."

Srilata was not much impressed by this reply; her face took on an air of relief, which of course further annoyed me. As I said nothing, she began talking vaguely about Lalita's character, although it was clear that the subject didn't interest her. Young girls as such do not interest her. It was solely as Daniyal's fiancée that Lalita occupied her attention at all.

Presently, in another burst of irritation, I quoted Lalita's actual words about Daniyal. A cad and the vilest man on earth—that, I said, was what she had called him.

"But she was talking nonsense," exclaimed Srilata, actually flushing a little. "And only a very young girl suffering from wounded vanity would ever talk in such a fashion. Daniyal has a witty tongue, and it sometimes runs away with him. He may have *said* one or two rather unkind things in the course of his life; but what has he ever done to justify such language on her part? No, no; Lalita is suffering from pique. You see she really isn't at all on Daniyal's intellectual level. I don't think she takes the smallest interest in art or literature; and Daniyal is completely wrapped up in them. His own work," she added, to protect herself, "may not be very important (although some of it *I* consider quite charming), but without a doubt he has a whole range of perceptions and appreciations which she is quite unable to share."

"Poor girl!" said I.

This was not the first time I had noticed that Srilata's taste in human beings had been vitiated by an excessive respect for the shallow intellectualism of her set. She is inclined to think me priggish in that I make no secret of valuing character above wits. But isn't it made plain to us every day that sharp wits and aesthetic sensibilities, where there is no worth of character to control them, turn people into fools or cads, or both? For my part, I cannot but regard Srilata's attitude towards art and literature as a kind of inverted priggery. Man is born to reverence; his spirit cannot but fly upwards; and when he fails to revere great things, he falls into the absurdity of revering small ones. I know people who revere their own petty cynicisms. When Art is great, it is by virtue of something that is not itself; worshiped in and for itself, both it and its worshipers are apt to look a trifle ridiculous. To bicker with Srilata, however, was the last thing in the world I wanted to do. If she tries my patience, I most decidedly try hers. All of a sudden, feeling on both sides that we were behaving like children, we looked at one another and began to laugh. We parted on good terms.

It is after midnight. As usual the atmosphere is heavy and electric; I stare out of the window, and my thoughts flit bat-like to and fro. Thirty minutes ago, I laid down my pen to open three notes which were brought in to me together. One is from Mobarek, and contains astonishingly satisfactory news. He tells me that on all the points upon which I have been standing out on Gokal's behalf the Emperor has given way. Unless Gokal proves unexpectedly hard to satisfy, there need be no more dissension between Akbar and the Brahmins on the subject of the Din Ilahi. I will say no more about this now.[1] The second note is from the Governor, who asks me to come and see him to-morrow afternoon; the third is from Lalita. She tells me that she and her sisters are going for a ride again to-morrow morning, and invites me to accompany them. Shall I do so?—Yes. It is desirable that I should get to know Lalita better.

Our ride did not take place. I woke the next morning with a severe headache and a high fever; but, as an attack of this kind nearly always overtakes me on first coming down from the Hills, I was neither surprised nor alarmed. I knew that in twenty-four hours I should probably be on my feet again.

Lalita and her sisters arrived at my house soon after the sun was up, for we had arranged to avoid the heat of the day. I heard the jingling of their horses' bits, their laughter, then their exclamations of disappointment and commiseration, as Vagira, my servant, told them of my condition. They wanted to come in, but I had foreseen this and given him instructions that on no account were they to be admitted. Lalita left word that she would call again in the evening to see how I was doing.

In the course of the day I received a visit from Srilata, and was

---

1. Rajah Amar actually continues to discuss the subject at very considerable length.

feeling so much better that I was able to invite her to stay and talk. "What I propose to talk about," I added, "is *myself.*

"As you know," I went on, "for several years I have cherished the idea that one day I would retire into a monastery; and now—now the moment is very near. This visit of mine to Kathiapur is a preparatory one. My object is to look round me at the world of men and affairs, consider what is best for Sita and Jali, and place their feet upon the right road."

Srilata was leaning forward with a startled air. "But you can't go away all of a sudden—especially not just at this time. My dear Amar, how can you think of it?"

"I am not going away all of a sudden, and whatever time I choose is likely to seem ill-chosen."

Upon this the inevitable discussion arose; but, quicker than might have been expected, Srilata recognized the fixity of my decision. I then pointed out to her that in some respects my departure might make things easier, because Sita, being a woman, might well be able to maintain a neutrality that would not be allowed to me.

As for my own future, the fact that in a few weeks or months I would be a yellow-robed monk with a shaven head and a new name, sitting in a monastery garden in Ceylon—this fact meant nothing to either her or me at this time. The mind cannot function simultaneously on two different levels of feeling. It meant nothing to either of us at this moment that we should soon be separating for ever; and Srilata showed good taste and good sense in not pretending to be more stirred than she was.

She did, however, point out that I was taking this step unusually early in life. She asked, too, whether I had considered how young Sita was, to be left, not a widow, but husbandless. Her large, dark eyes rested upon me curiously as she spoke, and yet to my reply she seemed to give only one half of her mind. I said, briefly, that when a spiritual call was sufficiently urgent, all mundane considerations became of secondary importance. These words, I knew, would convey little to her; she could see only what I was leaving behind, nothing of that towards which I was moving. My retirement in her eyes was as flat and dull as suicide.

On the other hand, in discussing the future of Sita and Jali she displayed a keen interest. Although she doesn't know Sita well, she is disposed to like her; and I truly believe that on Jali she could easily bestow much of the affection she would have bestowed on a child of her own. We talked for a long time, and now at last I felt that I was getting the best of what she had to give. Quick to understand how deep my concern was for those I was leaving behind, she plunged deep into a consideration of my problems. When I told her I was hoping that it would be possible for Gokal to take his place as Sita's chief counselor, she asked me a little dubiously whether he would lend himself to a policy favorable to Daniyal. Wasn't he rather unsympathetically inclined not only towards Daniyal but the whole of the Prince's party? I had to admit that this was at present a difficulty; but Gokal, I added, had great powers of detachment; moreover he was a man of remarkable finesse, and no one would be more skillful in steering a difficult course and protecting Sita from intrigues emanating from the Court, or from interference on the part of Ambissa, who would certainly try to get a finger into Sita's affairs as soon as I was out of the way.

Srilata understood my point of view; but she remained, for all that, dubious. Her last words to me, spoken with great earnestness, amounted to this: the fact that I was intending to go away before the conflict between Salim and Daniyal was settled, ought to simplify my decision, because now my personal likes and dislikes, which might have been allowed some weight had I been remaining on the scene, should not be permitted to interfere in my judgments. "And let me add this," she said. "You cannot be too careful not to alienate Daniyal. The Prince is very greatly swayed by *his* personal likes and dislikes. Were he to feel unfriendly towards you, his whole attitude toward Sita and Jali might be altered."

After Srilata's departure I got up and paced to and fro in the garden. My thoughts dwelt upon Sita; for I was slightly disturbed at not having yet received any letter from her. As the evening wore on, I began to think that Lalita wouldn't come after all. My headache and fever had left me, but I felt tired, and at last—at about midnight—I went to bed.

A little later, when already half-asleep, I became aware that a conversation was going on in my sitting-room. The voices were low, but I recognized one as my servant's and the other as Lalita's. Vagira, I supposed, was telling Lalita that she had come too late and consequently could not see me. As I lay there, however, heavy with sleep, I remained conscious that the low talk was continuing. It went on and on, until at last I roused myself; I drew on a robe, and looked through the door that was ajar.

Lalita and Vagira were standing by my writing-table, all the drawers of which to my astonishment were open. Presently they moved to an adjoining room, and I heard all the drawers and cupboards in that room being opened one after another. Going into the sitting-room, I waited for their return.

"Ah!" cried Lalita, as she came back, "so you were not asleep after all, Rajah!" Her voice expressed the greatest satisfaction. "I am dreadfully sorry to have come so late," she added.

I sent Vagira for some tea and sweetmeats.

She pointed to my writing-table. "I am glad you keep no papers there, Rajah. Vagira tells me that you have chests of your own, locked, and with secret drawers. You are wise. In this town there are no papers or letters that the Governor doesn't read."

She laughed. She seemed to be rather excited. "Do you know what I was doing in the other room?"

"What, I wonder?"

"I was looking for something I might have left behind. Did you know that our first night in Kathiapur was spent in this house? And that room was my bedroom. The room you are sleeping in was occupied by Mahil and Parmi. Parmi spilt a bottle of scent into the bed. Do you smell it at night?"

"I did. I had the bed changed."

She laughed. "I have found one of the things I left behind." And she held out a tightly closed hand. "Are you curious?"

"You want me to say yes."

"Perhaps you are not curious enough," she replied with a touch of malice.

Vagira came in with the tea. While he was arranging the tray, Lalita sat opposite, her gray-green eyes resting on me thoughtfully. She was dressed more simply to-night in a robe flowing from neck to ankle, but caught in by the girdle of the hill-women, which defines the line of the hips. The dress was of a purple so dark as to be almost black, and the girdle of black plaited horsehair hung down in front with long tassels of dark green and gold. Her necklace and ear-rings were of jade green. Unobservant of these things as a rule, on this occasion I noticed her dress because it made her look different.

"Do you know my country, Rajah?"

I shook my head.

"Ah! You should see my country! You should see it in the Spring. There is no Spring anywhere in the world like the Spring in the high valleys of Turkestan."

I thought of the Springtime in the Caucasus. I thought of Sita.

"Do you believe in our shamans, Rajah?"

"Of course not."

She looked offended. "You have never met them."

"No."

"They can tell you what you want to know.—Is there nothing you want to know?"

I laughed.

"Wouldn't you like to know what Sita is doing at this very moment?"

"As a matter of fact I have been thinking about Sita a good deal to-day. I was expecting a letter from her."

"Shall I tell you what Sita is doing? And Jali?"

I began to suspect what she was about, and I frowned. But she was not looking at me. She had picked up a small bowl that contained sweetmeats, and, emptying them out on the table, she filled the bowl with water from a jar.

"I want you to hold this for me on your knees," she said. "Yes, like that. And now . . ." She threw herself down on the floor beside me, and opening her hand, showed me what lay in the palm. It was a small black oblong cake of a substance that might have been opium. "Dried dragon's blood!" she said laughingly, and, breaking the cake in two, threw the smaller part into the water, which she began stirring with her middle finger, whilst she murmured some gibberish under her breath.

"I am sorry you are so superstitious," I said.

She looked up at me with serious eyes. "Everyone who knows our shamans believes in them. If they had told you the things they

553

have told me, you would believe in them too. Do you know what they are like? They are dwarfs, and very merry, and very dirty. One cannot help liking them, although they sometimes do wicked things. They are not wicked like Daniyal."

I felt that this was not the time to argue, nor could I stop the performance that had already begun. The hold that Shamanism has upon even the most enlightened of Lalita's countrymen is quite astonishing.

Under Lalita's stirring the water in the bowl became first pink, then a muddy crimson, and at last so thickly red as to look like fresh blood. "What do you say to that?" said she, putting her finger into her mouth first, and then wiping it on her handkerchief.

"It is a kind of chinese ink, mixed with powdered chalk. I should have thought you could have told that by the taste."

"Oh no, Rajah, dragon's blood!" she cried out, laughing excitedly. "It is, it is!" Getting up, she took a few steps to the window and stood looking out. "Anyhow, it doesn't much matter, does it? The question is: What shall I see in the bowl?" I became uneasily aware that she was struggling with a certain agitation; nor did it require much perspicacity to guess that this agitation was caused by the things that she had already prepared to say.

At last she gave a shiver, came slowly back, and knelt once more on the floor at my feet. "I want you to look into the bowl with me."

For a few moments I did so, then drew back. Her arms resting upon my knees, her face almost touching the surface of the water, she remained silent for two or three minutes; her shoulders beneath the thin silk of her dress were heaving very noticeably.

"I see the lake, and Ali crossing the lake." One of her hands tightened upon my thigh; she lifted her head and gave me a veiled look. "That means he is not dead."

I said nothing.

"Aren't you glad?"

"I have never thought he was dead."

She bent down again, and there was another long silence. "I have been seeing Daniyal," she said without looking up; "but I can't tell you all that I have seen. . . ."

"That is enough, then," I said. But, although no longer looking into the bowl, she continued to lean upon me with her arms, and I was constrained to keep still.

"I suppose you know how violently Daniyal hates you?" she said, still without moving.

"Hates me! Nonsense. Why should he? He doesn't trouble his head about me at all."

"Of course he hates you."

"Owing to the Dantawat incident? For having been by way of saving his life?"

"He hated you long before that."

"I think you must be mistaken. We had hardly ever met."

"Don't you remember the evening when he called at your father's house, and went round the room looking at the pictures and the furniture?"

"Now how on earth . . . ?" I began and then stopped. Obviously either Hari or one of the Prince's gentlemen-in-waiting had taken the trouble to give Lalita a description of that evening. But what trifles people take the trouble to report! One's surprise, on these occasions, is always proportionate to the insignificance of the matter reported.

Still in the same muffled voice Lalita went on. "Daniyal is less stupid in some ways than you think, Rajah. Do you imagine he didn't see how much you were despising him?"

Again I was quite taken aback. "You imply that my manners are very bad. Or that I am singularly inefficient at hiding my feelings."

"I think you are often unaware of what people are thinking about you. And you evidently don't understand Daniyal in the very least. He is frightfully sensitive as well as frightfully petty, and—unlike you—he is also frightfully cunning. *He* knows well enough what you are like. Quite apart from that evening, five minutes in your company would be enough to make him hate you like poison."

Is it possible that Lalita is right? I shall have to think about this.

"What does Ranee Sita think of Daniyal?" she inquired suddenly.

"Sita doesn't know him."

"I think she does know him—now."

"What do you mean?"

"When I first looked into the bowl I saw Ali crossing the lake. He was coming to your house. And then I saw another boat crossing, and in it were Daniyal and several friends of his."

"They were going to my house, do you say?"

"Yes."

"Go on."

"You understand, Rajah, that I only see glimpses of things— a scene here and there,—then the bowl clouds over again. I can't tell you all that has happened. But for one moment I saw Sita, Jali, Ali, and Hari, all together. Then I saw Hari and Ali alone, and Hari was beginning to get angry,—and then Sita came in and pointed to the lake. And the next thing I saw was Daniyal walking up to the house, and Sita standing in the door to receive him."

"And Hari, where was he?"

"He was standing behind Sita—with Ali."

Lalita was now calm, but her voice was low and strained. My own heart, I must admit, was beating rather harder than usual. Either this was all nonsense, or Lalita, having just received a letter from the Camp, was amusing herself by mystifying me. I felt a certain annoyance.

"When exactly did this visit of Daniyal's take place?"

"The day before yesterday."

This answer staggered me, because, if what she said was true, it was impossible that she should have received the news by ordinary means.

"I think we shall find that it took place earlier, if it took place at all."

"No. It took place the day before yesterday."

"Have you told Ambissa that Ali is alive?" I asked.

The question caused her to betray herself. She gave just a tiny shake of the head which showed me that her knowledge, or pretended knowledge, of Ali's existence, did not date from just a few minutes ago. However, the next moment she said quickly:

"How could I have told her? I have only just seen Ali in the bowl. Or rather, I did see him once before, but was not sure I recognized him. Do you think I ought to tell Ambissa? I am afraid she wouldn't think what I say is worth believing."

"Say nothing," I replied shortly.

After a minute she sat upright, but the bowl was still on my knees, and she still kept one arm firmly across them.

"I could tell you some more," she said, giving me a challenging look.

"I have heard enough. I don't believe in your magic, and you know it, Lalita."

Her face did not change. "Wouldn't you like to know something more—about Ranee Sita? or Jali? or Hari?"

I made no reply, and all at once she took the bowl, got up, and emptied it out of the window. Her expression was now one of intense pre-occupation, the eyes widely open, the brows slightly knit. She began walking up and down the room.

After a while, halting in front of me, "Rajah," she said, "I am glad you didn't see the faces of Daniyal and his friends, as they were sailing back across the lake . . . They were laughing, Rajah!"

"All this is nonsense," I said with an air of finality. "You are indulging your fancies too much, my dear. I don't want to hear any more."

Her eyes narrowed as she looked at me. "Is it only my fancy that Daniyal is wicked?"

I made a gesture.

"Is it only my fancy that I love Hari?" She paused, then turned away. "I love him! I love him! I love him!"

Still I remained silent.

She sat down on the divan and stared at the floor. Except for a curious twitching of her nostrils, she was motionless.

"Do you love Sita? Do you love her?" she asked in a dull voice.
"I do."

She gave a little laugh.

"Lalita," I said suddenly. "What is the meaning of all this? What do you want?"

"I want you to take me to Ravi."

"Now at once?"

"Now at once."

"But why?"

"Because you must—you must!"

"But a few hours ago you were refusing to go there. And if you go to Ravi—I mean to my house—you will be close to the Camp. You will have to spend your time in the Camp."

She kept her eyes fixed on the ground. "You *must* take me there," she said obstinately. "You must. You must."

"But how can I while Hari is there? You have made it impossible for me. I don't know what your ideas are, but I can't in any case be a party to...."

Whilst I was hesitating, she threw back her head and gave a laugh.

"Have you any reason to believe that Hari is still in love with you?" I put this question in a perfectly matter-of-fact way.

"Yes, I *know* he loves me," she murmured.

"How do you know?"

"I have had letters."

"Letters! That is very unwise."

"I meant to bring a letter of his—to show you. But it has disappeared."

"Good God!" I cried. "Don't you realize how serious that is?"

"I don't know ... The Governor probably has it,—in which case it really doesn't much matter. In fact, if it were to stop that man from making love to me, it might be a good thing." She began laughing again. "Last night it came into my head that I might have left it in one of the drawers here. I was looking for it when you first came in. But no! I couldn't really have been as careless as that," she added reflectively. "I can't understand it at all."

I turned, went to the window, and looked out into the night. I had some very difficult thinking to do. The truth is this: my memory had resuscitated a vague and momentary impression which I had received in Ambissa's room the day before. I seemed to remember that in letting down the sun-blind she had brushed some papers off her desk on to the floor, and that the corner of one of the papers thus disturbed had revealed a piece of Hari's handwriting. I seemed to remember having said to myself: "No, that can't be Hari's writing, but it is very like it."

"When did you lose this letter?" I asked.

"I only missed it to-day."

"Are any other letters of his missing?"

She hesitated, then said: "No."

"When was the letter written?"

"From Agra—towards the end of his time there."

"Was it the kind of letter, which—if it fell into the wrong hands . . . ?"

"Yes, it certainly was!" She laughed. "It showed that he still loves me. It was on account of me that he insulted Daniyal and got sent to prison."

I asked no more questions, although Lalita's answers left me far from believing that I had reached the truth.

"Will you take me to Ravi?" She had fallen back into her state of pre-occupation and was speaking in the low, strained, monotonous voice that always accompanied it. "Will you take me there, Rajah? Will you take me there at once? Please, Rajah, at once!"

"My dear child, it is impossible."

"But if I arrange it, will you take me?" She got up and laid her hands on my shoulders. "Rajah, it is terribly important. Much more important than you know."

I cannot tell what was in my mind during those moments, while she continued to supplicate. We were looking straight into each other's eyes with a curious absence of self-consciousness—a curious pre-occupation—with what I cannot say.

"I must see you again," I said, and disengaged myself and moved away.

"Yes. To-morrow." And with that, abruptly, she made ready to go. "We have arranged to ride again to-morrow morning. You must come. Will you be well enough to come? I shall want to show you something."

Show me something? I had no idea what she was talking about; but I said I would come. She went away in a hurry, leaving behind her the half cake of "dragon's blood."

8

THE NEXT MORNING I rose at daybreak. My night had been full of dreams and presentiments, nor was I surprised when a messenger arrived with a letter from Sita. I opened it hastily, and found that it contained a confirmation of all that Lalita had told me. I examined the seal; it was intact. I counted the hours the messenger had taken, and was more puzzled than ever by Lalita's performance of the evening before.

But to turn to the news itself. It appears that Ali, having heard that his father had arrived at my house, came across the lake to obtain permission to accompany Daniyal up to his hunting-lodge, some twenty miles farther up the valley. All had gone well between him and Hari at first, but after a while Sita heard Hari's voice raised in anger, and, following a decision she had already made, she lost no time in joining them. They were on the veranda; she stepped out of the door, and then it was—but I will use her own words: "And then it was that I received the surprise of my life, for, coming up the garden path, was an unbelievably sleek young man dressed in sky-blue and silver, and behind him were two other men in pink and gold, and a woman swathed in flowered muslins. I could only stand and gape, my astonishment making me quite forget that I myself was in one of my oldest dresses, with my hair in disorder and my hands covered with mud, for I had been planting some new irises in the water-garden. Hari had to pull me by the sleeve and whisper in my ear: 'Daniyal!' before I recovered my senses. Why didn't you ever tell me what a comic figure the Prince is? I didn't know whether to retire into the shades of the zenana or do the honors of the house for you. I think I should have turned and run, had there been time; but the next moment the Prince was bowing low before me. Then he turned to Hari, and him he greeted with a quite disconcerting effusiveness. Ali he patted on the shoulder. To my intense relief Hari behaved very well; he joked with the Prince, and was very gallant with the lady. In fact he and she embarked almost at once on a flirtation, and presently he took her off to look at the water-garden. The Prince sat with me on the veranda, drank some of our home-made sherbet (which, as you know, has a very odd taste), and pretended to like it. I can't tell you how dreadful he was in spite of his politeness. But fortunately Hari and his lady soon came back, and then the Prince took Hari by the arm and they strolled round to the front of the house 'to see the view over the lake.' What passed between them I don't know; I can only tell you that they still appeared quite friendly on their return, and that Ali was allowed to go back with the Prince. If this is to be the last that Hari and Ali will ever have to do with one another—well, that is not my business. Anyhow, I am thankful that Ali is not *our* son. Jali sends you his love. He has not been very well these last few days. But it is nothing to worry about."

This letter has left me a little uneasy. The more I think about it, the more I feel that a good deal is left unsaid. Besides, the tone is certainly not quite natural. This morning I was not given time to read it as carefully as I should have liked, for a few moments after its arrival Vagira came in to say that Lalita was waiting for me outside.

I found her on horseback in the road, and my own mount stood there too. She appeared to be in the best of spirits, but I detected a watchfulness in her eyes, and after a moment she said: "Ambissa had news of Ali early this morning. The Governor sent word to her that he was safe."

"I, too, have had a letter," I said.

"From Sita?"

"Yes."

We both paused. Mahil and Parmi were coming down the road, and there was not time to say much more.

Lalita leant down over her horse's neck. "The things that I told you—do you find they are true?"

"Yes."

I said this in a tone of voice that made her feel uncomfortable. "You think there is some trickery," she muttered. "And you are angry."

"No, no.—We will talk about it later."

I got on to my horse, and the next moment we were all cantering out of the town. Our way ran along a dyke under the spur of the hill that runs steeply up on the south of Kathiapur and juts out for two or three miles into the plain. The country in front of us as far as the eye could see was flat and green—green with the delicate coloring of young crops. For a quarter of an hour we went on thus, then the hill came to an abrupt end, and the new view that opened out took me entirely by surprise. In this direction the plain became a desert. Right up to the distant southern horizon there was nothing but hard, pebbly sand. And a hot dry wind came off this sand,— a wind that was delicious to me after the enervating air of Kathiapur. I gave my horse a touch of the spur and was off at a gallop.

It was not long before the three girls drew abreast of me, and after about ten minutes of galloping we came gradually to a halt. Already, to all appearances, we were in the midst of the desert, for a blue haze hung over the damp lands that we had left behind, veiling them from view. Overhead, the sky was streaked with thin, lofty clouds, which the sun, still low on the horizon, tinted faintly with pink and gold. The silence was broken only by the heavy breathing of our mounts. After a few minutes my horse began snuffling after tufts of a sweet herb that grew scantily here and there and I let him take me a little apart. Thoughts of the future had sprung suddenly into my mind; with an unwonted pang I reflected that in Ceylon there would be no more of this: no more riding over the desert, no more delight in physical energy, never again the feel of hot, dry air rushing past one's face . . . I should possess profounder joys, but life—life would already be a thing of the past.

Strange it was that at this period in my life I should have reverted—even for a moment—to such emotions as these.

Looking at my companions, who stood silhouetted against the east, I marveled at the nobility of those living forms. On this bare, level earth, under this pale, lofty sky, the forms of horses and riders had a noble—if inexplicable—significance. The present was full of beauty for me,—a beauty which was not impaired but enhanced, when I perceived, coiled up upon a flat rock close beside me, one of the largest poisonous snakes that I had ever seen.

Leaving her sisters, Lalita rode up to me, and together we moved slowly towards some low rocky bluffs, under which, about three miles away, I descried a ragged encampment.

"Did you see that snake on the rock?" she asked, and when I told her I had, she went on, "My brothers would have killed it."

"Yes. But they are not Buddhists."

She laughed. "We have no name for our religion. But we believe in Powers of Good and Evil. My brothers have killed not only snakes but men."

To this I said nothing.

"Some men are more evil than snakes; don't you think so, Rajah?"

I could guess what was coming; I said nothing.

"What about killing Daniyal? Would you blame anyone for doing that?" She was laughing as she spoke, but the next moment she stopped abruptly. "Was I right in saying that Sita had been visited by Daniyal?"

I nodded.

"And did she like him? Tell me, did she like him? I can see by your face what she thought of him. Oh yes, you don't need to tell me. I know. I know."

We rode on in silence for a while. Her eyes were fixed upon the encampment in front of us, and I got the impression that this was her goal. We had not gone much farther, however, before I stopped and made her stop too. Sniffing the air, I said: "You are not proposing to take me any nearer, I hope?"

"Oh, but you are a Buddhist. You don't mind. . . ."

"I am a Buddhist certainly; but why should I offend my sense of cleanliness? Why should I approach nearer to people who eat carrion?"

"They are not Aghoris," she murmured, slightly disconcerted.

563

"Perhaps not, but they are low enough."

From a distance of five hundred yards the encampment polluted the air; my eyes, too, told me that everything there was filthy; the children who were running out to look at us were covered with unwashed sores.

I looked at Lalita with curiosity. "Are you in the habit of coming here? And, if so, why?"

Mahil and Parmi had joined us, and the three sisters exchanged glances. "*I* don't come here," said Mahil, and gave a yawn. Parmi smiled enigmatically into my face, and her smile was that of a child.

"I have brought you here to show you something," Lalita cried out in a voice of irritation. "Go away!" she added, turning to her sisters. "I want to be alone with the Rajah. Go and wait over there."

For several minutes she and I sat on our horses in silence, staring at the ragged huts. At last an adult figure emerged, looked at us, and disappeared again. The existence of an encampment of outcasts in such a place as this struck me as exceedingly odd. Neither food nor water nor employment appeared to be available here, and yet the place showed signs of having been occupied for some time. Curiosity made me ride a little closer; and then an old woman came out from among the tents, and hurried up to us with a broad smile. In her hand under the folds of her voluminous and filthy garments she carried something with a good deal of care. Lalita greeted her like an old friend, dismounted, and introduced me as one from whom there was nothing to conceal. Reassured, the old woman took from under her dress a cup half-full of what Lalita called dragon's blood, planted it firmly in the sand, squatted down over it, and, pulling a hood over her bowed head, became completely still. Lalita crouched down beside her and waited. Soon a voice came through the folds of the hood, but I was unable to hear what was being said. In order to show that I was taking no part in the proceedings, I moved a little way off.

I was gazing absent-mindedly before me, when two pigeons, flying very fast, appeared over the bluff. After circling round once, they alighted somewhere amongst the tents, and almost at once an idea flashed into my mind. They were carrier-pigeons! and Lalita's second-sight was explained. While she obviously obtained her information from the old woman, it was now equally obvious that the old woman obtained hers from these birds. But the mystery of the encampment remained, and I was still puzzling about it, when my eye fell upon two men who were strolling along under the bluffs. One, a tall man, I recognized almost at once as the Governor; the other I did not recognize until they had drawn much nearer, and then, to my surprise, I saw that it was Mabun Das. The reason I had not made him out before was that, if not disguised, he had at any rate made himself look very different. Instead of the costume proper to his office he was wearing a dress that would have passed inconspicuously in any bazaar crowd. Seeing that Lalita was too much engrossed by the old woman to observe their approach, I gave her a call. She lifted her head, a look of annoyance passed over her face, and, after saying something to her companion, she got up and came towards me. The other got up, too, gathered herself together and shambled off towards the tents. A few seconds later the four of us were chatting together, while a groom rode up to take charge of our horses. Then I fell into step beside Mabun Das who led me in the direction of the bluffs, Lalita and the Governor remaining behind.

We sat down on a rock in a gully behind the encampment. Here, in the shade and to windward of the tents, the air was cool and sweet. I waited with no little curiosity for what Mabun Das would say. He took counsel with himself for a few moments, eyeing me with a faint smile, and tapping nervously with slim fingers upon his knee. "Rajah," he said at last, "it was no part of my plan, to meet you here like this. But now that it has happened, I'm not sorry. No, no!" And in his gentle, purring voice he began telling me what I needed to know. "As you are probably aware, I am responsible for the security of the Camp; and what you see here"— he waved his hand towards the tents—"is a part of my arrangements for keeping myself well informed. These people are runners, and in combination with them I have a service of carrier-pigeons." He paused. "I like to keep the existence of this place more or less secret, so I should be glad if you would say nothing to anyone about it—or about having met me here."

I nodded, and, after we had talked a few minutes more, he seemed to come to a sudden decision. Laying a hand upon my arm,

"My dear Rajah," he said, "allow me to give you a word of warning. Don't leave your family at Ravi very much longer. Salim, as you know, has commenced operations on the plain; and the possibilities of a raid in that direction, although remote, are not altogether negligible."

"How promptly should I act?"

"Oh, there is no great hurry. But I think you would do well to move within the next three or four weeks."

I looked at him wonderingly; and my look was full of interrogations; but all that he did was to smile and add: "Not a word of this to anyone, please!"

A silence fell between us. I stared out over the plain.

At last with intentional bluntness, I made the remark: "Of course, then, the Prince will be leaving the Camp quite soon?"

Mabun Das held up a hand and waved it slowly before my face. "Never mind what Prince Daniyal does—or does not do. Take the advice of a friend, and do not stay up there too long."

The possible implications of this last sentence were so astonishing that I could not embark upon a consideration of them. Another silence fell between us, during which Mabun Das kept his eyes fixed upon me, stroked his mustache, and appeared to be deliberating. When he next spoke, it was in a brisk and matter-of-fact tone.

"Of course, the world thinks I am a partisan of Daniyal's. I am officially supporting his party—that's true enough! I have appearances to keep up. Yes! And if"—he laughed gently—"if you were to go back now and tell the world that I am a traitor to Daniyal's party, no one would believe you. No, not a soul, excepting, possibly..." He broke off. "Anyhow, Rajah, I trust you to keep your own counsel. You may do so without any qualms. Trust my good sense and my good intentions, just as I trust yours."

With that he got up, and our conversation was over.

About our ride home I have nothing to say. On reaching my house I invited my companions to come in, for we were all four hot and thirsty,—and Vagira has the secret of a delicious beverage—an infusion of mountain-herbs, which he sharpens with lime-juice and sweetens with black honey. To me this return into the atmosphere of Kathiapur was like plunging into one of the steamy jungles of the Deccan; and in my rooms the heaviness of the air was intensified by a languid scent which the three young girls were using for the first time,—a present from the Governor. Their thin silks clinging to their warm, moist, golden bodies, they lounged about and chattered; and I—I watched them. Suddenly transported out of the present, I felt weary not only of life but of my efforts to be liberated from it. Nirvana, I thought, alas, how far away!

And now again, in this room that is still faintly redolent of their presence, I separate myself, I strain towards my former solitariness, which was a step towards the solitude of the immutable.

Even these few days of contact with the world have left their mark upon me. A depressing sense of isolation enfolds me. Or perhaps I should say that the isolation into which I have been gradually withdrawing myself has suddenly turned into loneliness. Gokal my most intimate friend, and Sita my wife, both seem to be far removed—and by what I hardly know, unless it be fundamental differences of temperament, outlook, ideal, and hope. There is no current of human sympathy flowing between myself and the rest of mankind. I still hold firm to my decisions—but not easily, not without doubts. Once more the fascination of Being uncoils like Kundalini within me. Life's energies and desires fascinate me—not as temptations but as mysteries.

As an energy of the inscrutable Maya, by far the most interesting of the three girls is Lalita, for it is in emotion that the flesh and the spirit unite to create that beauty which is this earth's last lure. Sometimes I think that Woman as Woman is irretrievably bound to the Wheel. Yet surely in Sita emotion has never been a blind tempest, nor womanhood a hidden, persistent domination.—No, no! a flower-scented wind in the face of the wayfarer—surely Sita knows that love is no more than that? And I, have I not passed beyond it? Have I not climbed into the region of snows? Am I not nearing the dark? Am I not in sight of the last needle-tip of ice, beyond which there is nothing?

Here the Rajah's diary breaks off, and there is a considerable lapse of time before it begins again. At this point, therefore, I continue the narrative in my own words.

PART FOUR

1

THE MOON, ALMOST full, was blurred by tenuous clouds, and a mist hung in white layers about the little town. The tangled trees of the Rajah's garden stood motionless in the milky obscurity. From beyond—from deep in the sacred grove—there came the tap-tapping of a stick upon the ground, where someone was making his way along the snake-infested path to the Hindu temple.

Round and about the Rajah's house, in and out through the open door, glided Vagira, moving restlessly, thoughtfully, and silently, on bare feet. Sometimes he peered across the garden into the darkness beyond, sometimes he stopped and listened, sometimes he crept round the side of the house to watch the under-servants who were loitering round the embers of a cooking-fire. At last he went out on to the road, and stood, gazing up and down, as if he was expecting someone. But all this was merely restlessness.

Presently an old man came drifting along, stopped, and wished Vagira good night. He spoke little above a whisper, and was answered in the same tone. The two stood looking up at the moon which hung above, a pale blurred disc.

"Your master's fever," said the old man, "I doubt not, it is worse."

Vagira made a gesture that might have meant anything.

"Kathiapur," said the old man, "is a place where men die easily."

"And live easily too," said Vagira.

"Yes; it is a place where men live easily, love easily, and die easily."

"What could be more satisfactory than that?" said Vagira.

"It is the climate," said the old man. "And you are lucky not to be here in the bad season, for then the insects, especially moths and butterflies, fill the air, the fat kine in the pastures turn and gore one another, fishes float belly-up in the ponds, and the burning-ground is like a forest, so many are the columns of smoke going up into the air. The smoke rises twice the height of a tall tree and there spreads out into a roof, upon which sit ghouls and vampires of different sorts, which can be plainly seen at night by anyone who looks down from the hill-slope yonder. Many a night I have watched them copulating by the hour. To-night the moon is hardly bright enough to make the climb worth while."

"What you tell me is most interesting," returned Vagira with politeness. "But my duties, I fear, would in any case prevent me from leaving the house."

"How long does the Maharajah intend to stay here?"

"Not long, I think."

"For him that is fortunate. In this climate . . ."

"Good night," said Vagira, stepping back through the little gate. "I congratulate you on having survived the climate for so many estimable years."

"I was born here," said the old man simply. "And to the dung-beetle the dung-hill is . . ."

But Vagira was gone; he had slipped back into the house and was peeping in between the curtains into the sitting-room, where the Rajah was seated at his writing-table. "He sits for many minutes without writing a word," said Vagira to himself. "That again is a bad sign."

Going a little way down a side-passage, he squatted on his heels in the dark and continued along a vein of unquiet thought. All the evening the Rajah had been particularly easy in manner and speech. He had worn a contented look, moved about with an air of relaxation, chatted at his meal. "All this is bad," thought Vagira. "It is thus that he tries to deceive not only others, but himself."

All at once there was the sound of voices in the road, and Vagira sprang to his feet. He was standing in the porch as the Governor mounted the steps, and beside him—somewhat to Vagira's surprise—there came a small wizened yogi. Vagira bowed low, the bow hiding a face of contemptuous dislike. After a moment of well-concealed reluctance he ushered both visitors into his master's presence, and withdrew—but no farther than the other side of the curtain.

The Rajah, the Governor, and the yogi sat together and talked. The room was in semi-darkness, the red-shaded lamps giving very little light. All three were fanning themselves, and their fans, as they went to and fro, beat against the fat moths that streamed in through the window. The Rajah's face was pale and his eyes had a glitter; his tone was amiable, almost playful, and Vagira listened to it with dismay.

Opposite to him sat the Governor, who, although shabbily —not to say strangely—dressed, was bearing himself with more than his usual swagger. The little yogi, crouching low on his chair, turned his head from side to side to study the faces of each speaker in turn; his sharp, beady eyes, the forward poke of his neck, made him the very picture of malevolent attentiveness.

"Vagira!" the Rajah called out; and, after creeping back for a few yards, Vagira pattered audibly towards the door and entered.

"Yes," the Governor was saying, "we now suspect that the murdered man was Prince Dantawat. He had been given datura. Under the influence of the drug he might have wandered far; he might have committed any folly. Whoever intended to murder him gave him the drug first in order to confuse subsequent investigation. This trick, as you know, is very common."

"Bring something to drink," said the Rajah, and Vagira bowed and went out.

To conceal from his guests the fact that they were most unwelcome was causing the Rajah an effort which he felt to be almost beyond his strength. His head was aching, the pains in his back were intense, but worst of all was the strain of keeping his mind in contact with reality instead of letting it wander in delirium.

Presently, to his surprise, he heard the yogi explicitly charging Daniyal with the responsibility for Dantawat's murder. Who was this little man, and why had the Governor brought him? Never before had he seen a human being the whites of whose eyes were so brilliantly yellow. Whilst the yogi was talking, he fixed upon him a look of polite interest; but whatever object his eyes rested on for more than a moment enlarged itself until it occupied the whole field of his vision. The result was nightmarish.

"Bah!" said the Governor, laughing coarsely. "What does it matter! The Prince had already changed Dantawat from a young man of good health and fabulous wealth into a penniless and besotted idiot. If he finished his work by causing him to be murdered, so much the better. The case of Dantawat from first to last is without any importance. If I disapprove of Prince Daniyal, it is on weightier grounds."

"On weightier grounds!" The yogi nodded solemnly. "And so does Pundit Gokal—on weightier grounds."

The Rajah suppressed a movement of surprise, but not quickly enough to escape the yogi's notice.

"Pundit Gokal is an old friend of mine," he said, giving the Rajah a sour look. "On my way through Ravi I had a long talk with him."

The Rajah, inclining his head with courtesy, exclaimed inwardly: "An old friend! Never!"

"A long talk!" the yogi repeated with an air of challenge. "And Pundit Gokal suggested that I should tell you what we talked about."

"I shall be very interested . . ."

"We talked on the subject of religion."

The Rajah inclined his head again. He was thinking that the conversation threatened to become quite intolerable, for he now felt quite sure that both his guests were drunk.

"We found that we were substantially in agreement," the yogi added with a spiteful leer. "That girl Gunevati has taught your friend a good deal."

At this the Governor gave a loud guffaw, then drew himself up and assumed an air of dignity.

There was a pause. The yogi seemed to have lost the thread of his ideas. At last he said: "As you have perhaps already heard, I was able to give the Pundit some medicine that will certainly cure him."

The Governor nodded. "That is true. Gokal is already very much better."

"Very much better," echoed the yogi. "I saw him twice. The first time alone. The second time Hari Khan was there too." He waited a moment, then added: "And I also saw Ranee Sita."

The Rajah smiled politely. "It is remarkable that you should have been able to discover just the right medicine for Gokal."

The yogi assumed a majestic air. "I live in contact with reality."

"Ah!" said the Rajah.

A snigger came from the Governor. After throwing a venomous glance at him, the yogi pronounced once more: "I live in contact with reality."

The Rajah leant forward over the tray. "Let me give you a little more sherbet?"

"No thank you," returned the yogi sourly. "I was able to doctor Pundit Gokal so successfully, because I got the right medicine from the woman who supplied the poison—an old woman who belongs to the . . ."

"Hush, hush!" interrupted the Governor.

"From an old woman who—who lives at Khanjo. Hari Khan could not get anything out of her. You certainly . . ." he held up a trembling finger—"would have got nothing out of her. Those who do not live in contact with reality can do nothing—nothing to promote either evil or good."

"That," said Amar, "is true."

"But you don't mean it," said the yogi rudely. "You mean something different."

"Surely," said Amar politely, "there are different levels of reality. The reality which I am striving to . . ."

"Spirit and flesh are one," said the yogi, as if enunciating a new truth. And the Governor leant forward in his chair, looked at each of the disputants in turn, and grinned with amusement.

"Pundit Gokal and I agreed on that point," said the yogi complacently.

"Yes, they agreed on that point," echoed the Governor, and again he guffawed—but this time with amiable intention.

"There is only one religion that is real," said the yogi, his voice rising shrilly. "Only one that proclaims the spiritual truth which actual life exemplifies. When you want to know a man's religion, do you ask him what it is?"

"Well, that would be one way of approach," said Amar.

The yogi gave a slow, cunning smile. "A man's words are nothing. I watch a man's behavior. I read his thoughts and his desires. The true religion of a man is that which he lives,—and that which all men live is the religion of Creativity, the religion of Sex. Knowingly or unknowingly all men worship Woman, and all women worship Man. To understand this in its simplicity is to grasp the truth; to grasp truth is to be in contact with reality; and to be in contact with reality is power."

"Rajah!" said the Governor with sudden fire. "That man"—and he pointed to the yogi with his foot—"that man is right."

There was a silence, in which Amar groaned inwardly. How was he to bring this visit to an end without giving offense?

"Rajah!" the Governor went on, "the Din Ilahi is a thing of emptiness and air. And Prince Daniyal supports it because he is nothing more than flatulence himself. Islam is a fine religion in its way, it gives sex pre-eminence. I have no quarrel with Islam, nor with Prince Salim. But the true religion . . ."

"The true religion," the yogi broke in, "is that which has run like a hidden vein of gold through the history of this country from the earliest times. Underneath all the shams and inventions of false shame, pedantry, and hypocrisy, there has lived amongst us Hindus the ancient verity that Sexuality and Religion are one. You, Rajah, are an ascetic, and it may pain you to listen to these words; nevertheless in your asceticism you recognize their truth. Chastity is a noble way of recognizing the divinity of Sex. But there are other ways."

Here the Governor, who had been fixing the yogi with admiration and approval, rose and struck his breast. "I would die for my religion. I would willingly die for the Great Goddess.—And," he added with a sudden drop into bitterness, "I very likely shall."

Gloomily he sat down again, and in so doing broke the fan with which Amar had supplied him. The movements he made in trying to pick up the pieces showed the Rajah that he was under the influence of drugs rather than drink.

"I offend you," he went on after a pause, "but I offend you less than Prince Daniyal,—because he is corruption itself. I offend you less than the hosts of the godless.—This creature here—I beg your pardon, yogi!—this yogi is more remarkable than you think. You should see him . . ." He broke off and grinned.

The yogi, after a moment's hesitation, grinned too. "If he likes to come to the temple, where there are girls . . ."

The Rajah put his hand to his brow. "Alas!" he began, "I very greatly fear . . ."

The yogi threw out an arm. "I know, you have fever. You have a headache. But I will cure you."

Searching in the folds of his robe, he produced a little wooden box, from which he took two pills. "Swallow these—unless you are afraid."

The Rajah took them in the palm of his hand. "You say they will cure me?"

"Yes."

The Rajah tilted his head back and swallowed the pills.

"In three minutes," said the yogi, "you will feel well."

There was a silence. And then from outside the Hindu temple in the grove a louder music floated into the room. The Rajah listened to it with interest; it was different from what he had heard on the other nights. He noticed his two guests exchange glances.

"We must be going," said the Governor in a changed voice. "I think," he added, as if supplying the reason, "I think Princess Lalita is coming to pay you a visit."

The Rajah was lying back with closed eyes. His headache had left him, and it seemed that his fever was leaving him too; but he did not feel drugged.

"Yes, you have cured me." He looked at the yogi curiously. "It is very remarkable."

"Here is another pill," said the yogi. "This will finish the good work."

The Rajah took it, looked at it, and said: "Another medicine?"

"For Kundalini," said the yogi, grinning.

The Rajah swallowed the pill. "I have reason to be very grateful to you. I feared that I was in for several days of sickness. Is the relief temporary or permanent?"

"I am not a magician; I am a realist.—Your fever will return, because it is in your blood, but less severely." He put some more pills into the Rajah's hand. "If you will take these to-morrow, you will soon be well."

2

AFTER HIS GUESTS had left him the Rajah stood looking down
at Sita's letter, which lay upon the writing-table. Several times
during the afternoon he had picked up his pen to answer it, but
something had stood in the way. He read the letter over again, trying to find what it was that struck him as unspontaneous and unnatural.

The glimmer of a lantern showed among the trees at the bottom of his garden, and he heard the tapping of a stick on the ground.
"It is those men on their way to the temple," he thought. "What
Vagira told me about that temple is obviously true.—The yogi is a
clever doctor. Cleverness and meanness too often go together. The
music of that temple has beauty. I wonder how far away it is ... I
think the instruments must be inside—all excepting one, that
faint wind instrument, which is not quite like ... "

After listening for several minutes, he called:

"Vagira!"

"My Lord?"

"Have you been down to that temple?"

"By day, my Lord—yes."

"There is a ceremony to-night?"

"Yes, my Lord."

The Rajah walked up and down the room. "I have been given

some medicine that has cured me—at any rate, temporarily. I had a touch of fever.—What do I hear being played outside the temple? Three hundred yards away? What is it?"

"It is a flute, played by the leper who sits outside."

"Why a leper?" said the Rajah dreamily.

"Perhaps because he is already half an animal; his face is the face of a tiger, as must always be. He lives in a hut in the grove, and the priests feed him."

"Have you entered the temple?"

"God forbid! Inside it at this moment they are playing music that is forbidden by the law; but the temple has very thick walls and triple doors, and the music within cannot be heard."

"The path to the temple lies at the bottom of this garden?"

"Yes, my Lord."

"Bring me something to drink, well cooled with snow."

Vagira withdrew.

The Rajah suddenly took note of the fact that one part of his brain was very clear. "The other part of it," he thought, "is dreaming, but I can watch my dreams as one watches a play. The last pill given to me by the yogi was very likely an aphrodisiac. I thought it at the time. Poor fool! He probably considers himself a very humorous fellow."

The Rajah went into the next room, and out into the garden.

"My Lord! My Lord!" called Vagira hurrying after him across the lawn.

"I am going to the bottom of the garden. The music inside the temple is so muffled that from here I can hardly hear it."

"But you cannot hear it at all, my Lord—neither from here nor from the bottom of the garden. Nor must you proceed until I have driven away the snakes."

"I can see well enough not to tread on snakes. But do as you please."

The Rajah turned back, leant against a pillar of the veranda, and looked up at the moon which had grown larger and more yellow. The music from inside the temple struck him as very curious, and the little, faint flute outside had a sweetness that was devoid of melancholy, because wholly impersonal.

There came into the Rajah's mind a vivid memory of the music that had been played in the Christian Church of the little town in the Caucasus, where he had married Sita. The contrast made him smile; and his smile deepened as he recalled how startled he had been at the time. What a volume of sound! And how simple and barbaric! And yet it gave pleasure to people who were quite cultivated in their way. He remembered the round fresh strong voices of ruddy-cheeked children; and the booming and roaring of big, bearded men. And afterwards, on coming out of the dark, incense-dim, re-echoing church into the quiet, clean-smelling air, how dazed he had felt! Fourteen years ago, and Sita had then been eighteen! Pink-cheeked like a child, and clear-eyed, and slender, and with what a gentle buoyancy of spirit. There had been frost upon the grass under the trees. There had been almond-blossom lower down in the valley. Crispness and brilliance. . . .

"The garden is now safe, my Lord."

"Thank you, Vagira."

The Rajah walked up and down very slowly on the coarse grass, which had recently been cropped by sheep. Presently, picking up the lantern that Vagira had left on the veranda steps, he crossed the lawn and made his way down the narrow path through the trees. He reached a broken-down fence of interwoven palm-leaves on the other side of which ran the track to the temple. Putting his lantern down, he leant against a tree-trunk and fell yet deeper into thought. He saw quite clearly now that already after the first four years of their married life he had begun to detach himself from Sita. And this process had been inevitable, for he had been straining towards something that lay beyond human relationships. Had this marriage been for her good?—or for his?

The leper's tune had changed. Perhaps, too, the temple doors had been thrown open, for a fuller music came through the trees, and forthwith the Rajah lost the sequence of his thoughts. "Sita," he murmured, "I have loved you; let that suffice! No memories now! The time has passed; youth has passed. Let me cling to the truth—*my* truth. But what can that truth be which women seek?

"Certainly there is a beauty in women's nature which is not the beauty of men's. And the difference is not merely a difference of color, but of essence. In a world filled with the brutality, the harshness, the pedantry, and the hypocrisies of men, are not women a saving grace, and a fragrance and a light?"

From the house there came the sound of people talking. The Rajah drew himself away from the tree-trunk, staggered slightly, and began walking back along the tunnel-like path to the house.

Two forms were visible from across the lawn. "Lalita?" he called out.

"Yes, Rajah. It's me." And the girl advanced to meet him.

"I wish we could stay out here!" she said, as they stood side by side in the middle of the lawn, looking up at the moon.

"If you like . . ."

"No." Her voice was lowered. "We couldn't be sure that we were not being overheard."

Together they went indoors. The little sitting-room was oppressively hot. Lalita went up to the tray.

"No palm-wine? Only sherbet and fruit-juice? I should like some palm-wine." She gave a little laugh. "Or, better still, some rice-spirit."

Amar made a sign to Vagira, who was hovering in the doorway, and as soon as he had gone, Lalita came up to him and said in an undertone: "When Vagira comes back will you please send him somewhere where he can't possibly overhear us.—Rajah, answer!" And she pulled at his sleeve.

"I beg your pardon; I was listening to the music."

"What music?"

"The temple music."

Lalita listened for a minute. "I can't hear anything."

Vagira came in, and set down some decanters on the tray.

"Please close the outer doors," said Amar, "and then go upstairs to your room, and stay there till I call."

Vagira bowed and withdrew.

"Yes. I hear it now," said Lalita. "But it is very faint. You must have extraordinarily good hearing."

Amar knit his brows. "Have you put on more scent than usual?"

"No."

"My senses are very acute to-night." He smiled. "And I think I know why."

Lalita was not listening; she went to the doorway and peered down each passage in turn. Meanwhile the Rajah poured out some palm-wine, which he handed to her.

"Thank you.—It so often happens that I forget myself and begin shouting." She laughed. "And anyhow, this is a country of eavesdroppers. You can't deny that, can you, Rajah?"

She took him by the arm and drew him to the window. "How dark it looks outside. Most likely the garden is already full of people listening." And she laughed again.

As they were leaning out together over the sill, he felt her body warm against his. He felt her leaning more and more heavily. "I, too, am thirsty," he said, and to give himself an excuse for moving he went and poured out another glass of palm-wine.

Lalita remained by the window. Looking at her, the Rajah thought: "How greatly she values her beauty! How deeply she lives in it, how unceasing her consciousness of it! But it will fade, and then what? The strange thing is that the answer to this question is the very reverse to what one would expect."

Lalita moved away from the window. "I am no good at intrigue," she said suddenly, "but when Ambissa and my father came to me this afternoon to persuade me to go up to the Camp, I pretended for about an hour that nothing would induce me to go. Then, when Ambissa suggested again that I should stay with you, I gave a grudging consent. Poor Rajah! You will soon have my father and Ambissa both beseeching you to take me in."

She was now standing by his writing-table. "What is it that you write here for so many hours at a time?"

"My journal."

"Shall you put down what we are saying to-night?"

"Yes."

"I wonder."

"I shall put it all down."

"Ah! You say that in order to . . ." She turned away.

"Do you write your thoughts down as well?" she asked in a low voice.

"Some of them."

She gave a little laugh that was slightly mocking. "You can't write them *all* down. I tried once. It is impossible."

She fell into a muse. As he looked at her, a wave of admiration swept over him. Taking flesh and spirit together as one, he found her somehow beautiful; and this in spite of her being self-centered, vain, and engrossed by the emotions arising out of sex.

"The trouble is that you don't believe anything I say." She lifted her head to give him a smile. "To begin with, let me tell you about the dragon's blood. . . ."

"Oh, never mind about that!" he interrupted.

"Very well. But when I am with the old woman I really do see things in the bowl. It is stupid not to believe in second-sight. So many people have the gift. Parmi, for instance, can see much more than I." She paused. "Do you know why, Rajah?"

"Why?"

"Because she is a virgin."

The Rajah's face was expressionless. "The old woman gets her news from carrier-pigeons," he said.

"Some of it. I know. But not all. And not knowledge of the future."

There was a pause. He noticed her breast rising and falling. She poured herself out some rice-spirit and drank it quickly.

"Do you attach much value to chastity?" she asked.

"I believe," he answered slowly, "that there are certain spiritual experiences which the unchaste cannot obtain."

Abruptly, and as it were involuntarily, she gave a loud, mocking laugh. "There are also certain spiritual experiences that the chaste cannot obtain."

After a moment she came up to him—so close that he could see the perspiration standing out upon her temples. "So you believe in chastity," she murmured. "And Sita too?" She was looking down through half-closed lids. The Rajah made no reply.

"You don't believe in my love for Hari," she said quickly, "nor in his for me."

"I think you have both been very strongly attracted to one another."

"Have been?—Do you know that I have been his mistress?"

"No."

"And you doubt it now.—That evening in the Hills after you had stopped Hari from coming to my tent—how do you know I didn't go to his?"

"I don't think you did."

"And how do you know I wasn't his mistress before that?—As a matter of fact I was. Long before."

"Let us drop this, Lalita."

"Very well." There was a note of anger in her voice. "Shall we talk about Sita?"

"If you like."

"I saw her for a moment at the Court—in Agra. I thought she was lovely." These last words were spoken in a low voice and sadly.

"Are you aware that her mind is set on religion—no less firmly than mine?"

Lalita gave the Rajah a peculiar smile.

"My dear child," he said after a pause, "I am going to tell you something about myself." Again he paused, his looks were thoughtful, and he passed his hand over his brow. "Briefly, it is this: I am going to retire completely from the world. In a few weeks I shall be setting out for Ceylon, where I shall go into a monastery—and so end my days."

Lalita's eyes, which had opened widely, rested upon him in a horrified stare. "In a few weeks?" she murmured.

"A very few weeks." And then, most strangely, he found himself saying: "Perhaps even in a few days."

Lalita had grown very pale, and her eyes continued to fix him in the same unblinking stare. He managed to maintain his gentle, kindly smile, although his heart was now beating hard.

Lalita suddenly looked haggard. "You can't do that! You can't do that!" she muttered.

The Rajah said nothing, but kept his gentle smile.

"You don't understand . . . How can you leave Sita? You told me you loved her."

"Yes. I do.—We love each other, but she agrees that I must follow my Path."

"She agrees!" Lalita caught up the words with a wince of pain.

For a few moments she kept an ominous stillness, then said: "Sita is in love with Hari."

The Rajah received this with perfect quiet. "I was afraid you might be imagining something of that kind," he said gently. "But let me assure you . . ."

"Fool!" said Lalita under her breath, and turned quickly away.

Whilst Lalita's face was turned away, the Rajah's gaze rested upon her with a look that was cold, hard, and calculating.

"Hari has been very deeply attached to Sita for some time," he said, and his voice was gentleness itself. "She gave him sympathy and comfort when he was feeling unhappy on account of you. But, believe me . . ."

Lalita gave a cry, and wheeled round again.

"Rajah!" she said in a low, hurried voice, "Sita is still young— not much more than thirty, I think? And she is lovely. And—and surely she must still want to be loved? Don't you understand what I mean, Rajah? How can you leave her just now? You can't really believe that she . . ."

The Rajah, looking past her, compressed his lips. "People are not all as you think," he said dryly, then paused, and went on in a gentler tone. "If you knew Sita as well as I do, you would understand better how it is that I am able to take this step. The way that she has been following—the ways she intends to follow—are not really very different from mine."

Lalita shook her head.

"Sita," continued the Rajah, "has a longing for saintliness, a longing which you at your present . . ."

Lalita raised her head; her jaw was clenched, with the lips drawn back. She opened her mouth to say: "That's enough. Sita has been Hari's mistress for some time. And I think you should know it."

The Rajah gave her a look of cold rage, and made a sound of contemptuous disbelief.

"I know it! I know it!" Lalita cried; and suddenly, walking up and down the room, she began to laugh. "Of course she's his mistress. I should have known it without their all telling me. It began at Khanjo; then there was an interval; and now they have begun again. Now they are alone together in your house. And you—you stop here—talking!"

The Rajah, very pale, was looking at her with the same hard, calculating eyes. With a trembling hand Lalita poured herself out some more rice-spirit and drank.

"I didn't want to tell you, but I had to at last. Don't you see that you can't let all these things go on? You can't want me to marry that loathsome cad Daniyal, when I love Hari, and Hari really loves me. You can't really want Daniyal to become Emperor of India, you can't really want me to help him on to the Throne. You can't approve of Ambissa's divorcing Hari—just in order to spite him, and because she wants to become the mother-in-law of the future Emperor. Answer me, Rajah!" And, as Amar remained silent, she went on: "Hari only makes love to Sita, because I'm not there. You can't let him go on. You can't leave all these things to happen! They are abominable.—Don't you see that you can stop everything by helping me to run away with Hari? Take me to Ravi and then you will see for yourself whether I am speaking the truth or not. For God's sake, take me to Ravi, Rajah! Hari admires Sita,—he worships her, if you like; but she is not his kind. You know it, Rajah, as well as I. But Hari and I, we are of the same kind—the same hopeless kind—and you must let us go to perdition in our own way."

The Rajah stood quite still for a minute after she had finished, and his expression was indecipherable. Then he moved about the room, absent-mindedly, as if looking for something. She watched him with a look of terrible anxiety in her eyes.

"Listen, my dear Lalita," he said at last, and his voice was calm. "I don't want to say anything to wound you, but . . ." He stopped. He seemed to be mustering all his resources. Gradually his face assumed a look of kindness. "Lalita, my dear child," he began afresh. "Forgive me for saying that the feeling you cherish for Hari at this moment is very largely artificial. It is a reaction from your dislike of Daniyal. And your feeling about Daniyal has also been undergoing a great deal of exaggeration and distortion in your mind of late. It is not necessary nor inevitable that you should hate Daniyal as you now fancy you do. You are romanticizing the whole situation. This is especially evident in your persuading yourself that Hari is still in love with you, and that Sita is in love with him. All that is nonsense.—And as for the rest of the picture you have drawn, it is so extravagantly colored, so grossly distorted, that it ceases to be anything like the truth. No doubt Hari has made love—and is now making love, if you like—to Sita. But where is the woman that he does not make love to? No doubt there are times when you regret having dismissed him, but—your love for him, Lalita, was never deep enough to cause you to break off your engagement to Daniyal, and . . ." Here the Rajah made a pause—"I feel pretty sure that you have never at any time been Hari's mistress. There is a serious element of untruth in all that you have been saying. And you have been deceiving yourself with your own misrepresentations. In regard to Sita in particular, you are inexcusably and willfully wrong. You have absolutely no grounds for saying . . . You have no reason to believe . . . that she has given way to Hari. And even if there is gossip to that effect, gossip is no evidence of truth. Perhaps that old woman with her dragon's blood has been inflaming your imagination with wild tales; very likely she has been cunning enough to invent just what was most likely to agitate you, and make you give her more gold. Your fancy has been running riot; it is time you checked it. Look reality in the face! Your marriage to Daniyal will not be ideal, but you knew that six months ago, when you became engaged. No doubt you then argued that Daniyal would not obtrude himself upon you as a husband, and that your position as Empress would bring compensations. Nothing of any importance has happened in the meantime to afford grounds for a change of view. Has Hari really sent you ardent love-letters? I venture to doubt it. He may have written once, but that doesn't mean much. In any case, he is *not* languishing. Lalita, you must come back to reality."

During this speech of the Rajah's Lalita had not stirred. Alone her expression had changed. Little by little the light had gone out of her face, which now looked heavy and dull—and almost ugly in its dull heaviness. She looked down and clenched her teeth. For a moment the Rajah thought she was going to reply, but no words came, and presently she walked slowly to the door. The Rajah followed her. They went out, and through the hall and down the steps into the road.

As she stepped into the palanquin, he took her hand and pressed it. "Lalita . . ." he began; but she caught her breath and cried out to the runners to start. The Rajah fell back. For a minute he stood in the road looking after the retreating palanquin, then went back into the house.

3

TWO DAYS LATER the Rajah was on his way back to Ravi, and this time he was traveling on horseback and without companions. Riding ahead of his train, he was able to give himself up to musings that were often so deep that, had he suddenly asked himself what he was thinking about, he could scarcely have found an answer.

Lalita he had not seen again. During the whole of his last day at Kathiapur he had remained in his own house, but there he had been visited in turn by Srilata, Mobarek, and Ambissa. Srilata had gone far towards convincing him that Ambissa's divorce from Hari was not to be interpreted discreditably; and as for Hari's banishment, that, she said, would certainly come to an end with Lalita's marriage to Daniyal, which would also end the existing crisis. At first Amar had hesitated to accept this view; but Mobarek, when he came, had given her his support. Finally, at the end of the day, Ambissa had bustled in with the tidings that the program of festivities at the Camp had been definitely abandoned, and that the Prince would very soon join Lalita in Kathiapur. As for the girl herself, she had "quite got over her attack of nerves," and was now "perfectly reasonable."

All this was eminently satisfactory. The Rajah had been able to leave Kathiapur with the feeling that a longer stay was unnecessary—perhaps even undesirable.

The forest through which he was now traveling reminded him of the ride from Khanjo to Ravi that he had taken with Hari some four months ago. Well he remembered that damp, silent, windless path under the tall trees, and how, as he had ridden in front wrapped in meditation, he had gradually become conscious of Hari's eyes fixed upon his back. Once again Hari's personality became intensely vivid to him. As clearly as if Hari had been at his side, he saw that figure, sparely and not inelegantly sturdy, that well-shaped head and rather broad face, in which the eyes were set widely apart. Had he, he asked himself, had he already suspected in those early days that Hari was under the influence of Sita's charm? Was it on that account that he had disclosed his intention to retire from the world? It had been a talk full of unspoken tussling, temperament struggling silently against temperament; and he had been conscious of a cold, impassible strength in himself, and the power to quench and make still. Yes, after a little while the fire had gone out of Hari; for, just as a python is powerless to exert its strength unless anchored to some rock or tree, so did man depend upon his grip on reality. Reality had a cold breath that extinguished the fire of all emotions that did not take proper account of it. Poor fools, the Governor and the yogi, who counted him no realist! Could he not have taken the fire out of them too? Could he not have bleached and wilted their vain fancies—even as he had bleached and wilted those of Hari—and of Lalita?

Then, in the midst of these thoughts, he suddenly reined in his horse, drew in his breath, and frowned. He realized that his face had been distorted by a cold and cruel smile. O grace of the Enlightened One! What anger, what ill-will, was there not lurking within him? Had he, indeed, enjoyed crushing Lalita?

For a while he brooded upon this, then cried out within himself: "What has become of my solitude—my communings in an immense heaven of calm, when the world was seen from so great a distance as to be small and silent? By what fatal weaknesses have I been snared? Alas, not only by jealousy and anger, but by doubt. I am filled with confusion and speculation where no confusion or speculation should be. Invasive and insistent, persuasive and clinging, appealing to pity, piteous with the transient beauty and animal pathos of Maya, such is the feminine spirit. To detach one-self from women is wisdom, but to fly from them is cowardice. Am I not thankful that there is no place even for love in Nirvana?"

This unrest inspired him with a craving for self-sufficingness such as he had never known before. His longing for solitude, for withdrawal, for peace, was overwhelming. And yet, at night, be-tween dreaming and waking, he found himself composing letters to Sita, the emotional tone of which embarrassed him whenever a memory of them drifted across his consciousness during the day. "Sita, my beloved," he would say, "how can I leave you without making you understand? I love you, and must pour out my love as a libation—down to the last drop. This I now do for your sake, that you may see the extent of my love; this I must do for my own sake, for I have to go my way emptied of all earthly passions. Only the love that is unearthly can I retain, the love that is an aspect of the Eternal contemplating itself. And you—although you do not recognize the Way, your Spirit nevertheless is advancing towards the Goal."

The detection of a hidden dream-activity within him, his dim consciousness that he was following underground trains of thought, inspired him with an anxiety that sometimes rose to the pitch of terror. Ignorance was one of the heaviest fetters of the spirit; and what ignorance could be more dangerous than that of one's own hidden mind? "While my hidden mind is uncoiling like a slow ser-pent what have I to do? What dare I do but follow the dictates of my will? And my will must be guided by such knowledge as I have. Yet both will and knowledge seem to me to give very little real power."

On the day of his arrival at the last stage of his journey it had been raining; a great storm had swept over that part of the forest in the night. Daniyal's guest-house—the one in which he had first met Smith—was glistening in the afternoon sun; the trees round it were still dripping, and from the ground there rose a gentle steam. Gone were the pink rhododendron flowers that had carpeted the earth on his last visit; indeed, the whole place wore an altered, storm-swept look. The fall of three great trees had enlarged the clearing and let in a good deal more light. From the broken trunks and torn branches there came a smell of resin which hung in the warm moist air.

Reflecting that he was now actually not more than fifteen miles from his own house, he wondered how his garden had fared, and whether Sita had not passed a very disturbed night. She must have been listening to the roar of the wind, afraid for the security of Hari and Gokal,—and yet their tents, to be sure, were pitched in so sheltered a spot that no tempest could do them much harm.

Beside his camp-fire, the evening before, he had come to the decision that he would go—not to his own house, but to the Camp. "From there," he said to himself, "I shall send a message to Gokal, asking him to come to me. He and I must talk together before anything else is done."

But even as he was making this decision he was seized with a keen desire to go straight home. Not to do so made him feel like an outcast and an exile. There even came into his mind the fantastic idea of spying upon the house and grounds from the hill at the back. From there, he reflected, he would be able to look down upon Gokal lying in the sun outside his tent, and Sita busy in the garden, and Jali, and Hari . . . He would see them all—as they were when he was not there. And to see people under such conditions— or to see any man as he is when he believes himself to be quite alone—is more than the fulfillment of a special curiosity; it is the indulgence of an unrighteous craving after secret knowledge and the power that such knowledge brings. Mabun Das, thought the Rajah, had too many opportunities for indulging this craving, and could scarcely fail to be corrupted by it. For a while his thoughts rested uneasily upon Mabun Das; then he rose, and, after visiting Vagira, who was down with fever, went to his own room and stretched himself out on his bed.

He had not been there long before the guest-house was astir with fresh arrivals, and he recognized the voice and laugh of Churaman. A keen curiosity to learn from Churaman whether he had been one of the young men who had accompanied Daniyal on his visit to Sita was held in check by an equally sharp disinclination to renew his acquaintance with Churaman at all. He found himself wondering once more what it was that Daniyal had been laughing about on his way back over the lake; and again he drew himself up with annoyance. The voices, male and female, that came through the thin partition awakened vivid memories of the afternoon that he had spent with Daniyal at the Camp; he decided that he would have his evening meal served in his room.

Dusk fell, and gradually, as he lay there, it was borne in upon him that he was once again in the grip of fever. His thoughts became more and more disordered, until at last he lost himself in delirious dreams.

When next he returned to a consciousness of his surroundings it was to realize that a considerable period of time had elapsed, and that he had become very weak.

"This has been a really bad attack," he said to himself. "I wonder how many days I have been lying here."

There was someone in the room outside the range of his vision. "Vagira!" he called feebly.

The answer came in a brisk, cheerful voice. "Yes, here I am." And Churaman's bulky figure appeared beside the bed.

Amar looked up at him, dismayed.

"Vagira has not recovered yet," Churaman went on. "But you, I can see, are well on the mend."

"How long have I been here?"

"Two days."

The Rajah closed his eyes, drank what Churaman held to his lips, and then with a sigh of weariness went to sleep again.

The next day when he awoke it was to feel himself truly convalescent. He sent for Churaman and said: "I am surprised at Vagira's not having dispatched a message to my wife. Is he still very ill?"

Churaman hesitated. "I am sorry to say he is dead."

The Rajah closed his eyes again. Between him and Vagira there had never been much speech, but the bond of affection had been none the less strong for that.

"Rajah," said Churaman, sitting down on the foot of the bed, "I congratulate you on your quick recovery. You will be able to continue your journey in a day or two, provided that the weather improves. For the last two days it has been almost impossible to travel. That is why I have abstained from sending a message to Ranee Sita to tell her you were lying ill here. In the circumstances I felt you would rather I did not disturb her peace of mind to no purpose. You were not sufficiently ill. . . ."

The Rajah stopped him by holding up his hand. "You were quite right. Nor do I wish her to be sent for now."

As he lay in bed, he allowed his thoughts to wander. It was dark and dreary in this little room, with the rain drumming on the roof, and a soughing of the wind in the trees. The death of Vagira and a sense of separation from home and kith and kin brought his spirits to a very low ebb; nevertheless he dwelt upon his loneliness with satisfaction, thinking that if he were to die, here in this inn, unconsidered, without any of the attentions commonly accorded to one of his rank, or the comfort of friends and family, or the brotherly ministrations of fellow-priests in a monastery—if he were to die like this, it would be a good death, offering him an opportunity to atone by humility and fortitude for some of the many errors of his past life.

The next day Churaman came in to pay him a farewell visit, for the weather had so far improved that he and his friends had decided to resume their journey to Kathiapur. In the course of the ensuing conversation it came out that Churaman *had* accompanied Daniyal upon his visit to Sita, and that he had subsequently been sent over as a messenger to her with an invitation to visit the Camp. This invitation had been accepted, and Sita had been entertained at luncheon by the Prince.

"In the afternoon," continued Churaman, "I had the pleasure of escorting Ranee Sita back across the lake, and she invited me to come up to the house. There we found Hari Khan and Gokal deep in conversation with a yogi who had come down from Khanjo, where he had been visiting his brother."

"I know the man," said Amar. "I met him at Kathiapur."

Churaman paused a moment, then said: "Do you know, Rajah, I consider him a rather dangerous fellow."

"Dangerous?"

"I mean indiscreet."

At this moment, given a little encouragement, Churaman might have said more; but Amar smiled and changed the subject; and before very long good-byes were exchanged.

Churaman's departure left the Rajah meditative. "During the last three days," he said to himself, "that man has given proof of the greatest kindness of heart; and what he has done for me he would have done for almost anyone else with a greater natural readiness. What conclusions am I to draw?"

The next day he was carried in a palanquin up to the Camp, and there he took up his quarters in Mobarek's house.

4

ALL THE MORNING it had rained; the afternoon was dull and dark. Clinging to a cloak that he had thrown about him, the Rajah stepped out into the blustering wind and looked up into a sky craggy with torn and ruinous clouds. All was gray, save in one place where a patch of gentle blue appeared beyond the wrack. The lake was rough, and the opposite shore no more than a blur upon the mist.

Going down to the water, he waited, gazing in the direction where Gokal's boat would appear. Soon he saw it—an indistinct, lonely speck; and the thought that this was Gokal, coming to him in answer to his call, made his heart swell with an unexpected emotion. "Perhaps," said he to himself, "I have never realized until now the depth of my affection for that man." His memory went back to the Gokal of fifteen years ago, a big man, well covered with flesh, but vigorous in spite of his sedentariness,—a man, too, with a head that both looked, and was, a fitting complement to the massive body beneath. There were many years of serene friendship to pass under review, before Gokal had fallen a victim to melancholy; and Amar sighed, thinking how it was simply as an escape from that melancholy that his friend had at last suffered himself to fall under the spell of Gunevati. During the last six months how sadly Gokal had changed! In that little boat there crouched a heavy-bodied, ill-complexioned man, whose eyes held a look of re-pressed anguish. Yet, even in Gokal as he now was, there lived a noble spirit, and his mind, although neglected and ill-used, was still, the Rajah believed, essentially unspoilt.

Turning, he cast a glance over the rain-drenched promenade. It was deserted, and the houses behind looked derelict. Scarcely could he bring himself to believe that the Camp still contained Daniyal and the greater part of his company.

A few minutes later the boat came in to the jetty, and Amar ex-amining Gokal with anxiety, found him looking very much better than he had dared to hope. In their greetings the two men betrayed a certain self-consciousness, but all at once, moved by a common impulse, they embraced—a thing they had not done for many years. The wind was behind them as they made their way up to the house. Exchanging superficial news, they walked slowly, half-afraid of the privacy that was awaiting them indoors.

Before entering, Gokal stopped and cast his eyes about him. "Have you heard the local legend concerning the shores of this lake?"

"Yes. It is said to be studded with ruins that lie buried beneath the silt."

"Hardly ruins! Say rather the shells of pleasure-houses like these."

Amar gave a little laugh. "Well, look about you! From the Pleasance of the Arts, too, the glory is already departing, as you can see."

"It will come again," returned Gokal unexpectedly.

Amar was silent for a moment, then said: "The Prince is going away in a few days. Perhaps he will return next year—perhaps not. Who can tell?"

Gokal looked down the lake-front. "A little flimsy. A little flimsy.—But the air and water of this place are said to preserve everything. It all sinks slowly beneath the silt, and there lies ten-derly preserved."

The Rajah was puzzled, then opened his mouth to speak, but the wind, sweeping in a fierce gust round the corner of the house, gave an excuse for silence. Together they went indoors.

The big room, now filled with dusk, looked larger and barer

than ever. Apologizing for its inhospitable aspect, Amar took his guest across to the wide window overlooking the lake. "Sit you down!" he said, and, after placing a cushion behind Gokal's back, turned and stood staring out over the empty promenade and the gray water.

"First of all," he pronounced at last, "I am going to give you a brief account of my experiences since leaving you." And with that he launched forth.

By the time he had finished the dusk had thickened. The expression on Gokal's face was hidden by the obscurity. Whilst Amar was talking, he had sat as still as a rock, and scarcely opened his lips. Presently Amar summoned a servant and oil-lamps were placed one at each end of the room.

"Just now," the Rajah said, "when I was speaking about Gunevati, you let me see that what I was telling you was not new. I suppose you had already heard something about her from Jali?"

Gokal nervously smoothed out his robes. The flickering lamp illuminated the large oval of his face, but the hollows of his eyes were dark; and yet those eyes seemed to Amar to be fixed upon him with an anxious, speculative intensity of gaze.

"Very well," the Brahmin replied in an uncertain voice. "We will talk about Jali, but—there will be more to say later."

A servant came in and set some wine down on the table before them.

"Where is Vagira?" inquired Gokal absently.

"Dead—as I have already told you."

"Ah!" Gokal sighed, made a gesture of apology, and shaded his eyes with his hand. "You will miss him."

Amar was silent.

"You are looking ill," said Gokal sadly. "It is the fever. You must be careful."

"All that is over," returned the Rajah shortly.

Gokal fidgeted, and then with forced utterance began to speak. "It was only a very few hours after you left the house that Jali came. . . ."

At that moment the lamp at the Rajah's elbow was blown out by the wind, and the door at the end of the room slammed with violence. The Rajah was about to call a servant, but Gokal with

595

a gesture stopped him. "Do you remember?" he went on. "It was a particularly beautiful morning. You were sailing across the lake to this place . . . As for me, I had had a bad night, and was sitting before my tent in the sun. Hari was still asleep. Sita had gone off to gather anemones on the hill behind the house. And then Jali appeared."

Here Gokal paused, smoothed his robes, and seemed to find difficulty in going on.

The Rajah said at last: "I cannot imagine why you find it hard to speak. Surely you don't suppose . . ."

"No, no," replied Gokal hastily. "My difficulty is that I shall not be able to avoid appearing fanciful and foolish. And yet I feel it to be important that you should not be too hasty in concluding that ill-health has weakened my intellect, because then nothing that I have to say will carry any weight with you."

"My dear Gokal!" exclaimed Amar. And he added: "Anyhow, what I think, that will I say."

"The night before you left," Gokal went on, "I fell into a kind of trance, and I was still in a tranced condition when Jali came and stood before me. He stood there in the sunlight looking very wan and pitiful. We looked at one another in silence. I already knew—partly by intuition and partly . . ." Here he broke off, and, after giving a kind of groan, made a fresh start. "Amar, I know that a belief in the supernatural is repugnant to you, and yet I am obliged to state my conviction that something outside the ordinary course of nature took place in the neighborhood of your house that morning. I was not alone in feeling it. As I have said, there was Jali standing before me; and, as I looked at him, I saw gathering in his eyes a look of astonishment and, finally, of terror. How long we continued thus I do not know, for something happened to change the whole scene. It was a morning of the hottest, brightest sunshine, as you know; every ripple on the lake, every leaf upon the trees, was sharp and clear; the face of nature was distinct with a hard definition of outline, and yet—and yet this same face of nature shivered and trembled as might its own reflection upon the surface of the lake. The thinness of the crust of tangible things, the emptiness of matter, the superficiality of appearances, suddenly were revealed. I tell you, Amar, everything wavered as if it were threatened with the loss of its flimsy surface actuality. I think this had something to do with Time, for Jali has since told me that, as I sat there before him, he saw me with my face changed and my eyes closed, as I shall be seen by him one day when I am dead. As for me, I was seized not so much with fear, as with an intense disquiet, a deep-seated uneasiness, caused, I think, by my sense of a slight but deep disturbance at the foundations of our common phenomenal world. And, while this was going on, I smelt the half-sweet, half-putrid smell of water-lilies, and then I was startled and deeply confounded by hearing the near-by trumpeting of an elephant. This sound came as a climax; and it startled me out of my trance—if trance it was. I got up to go to the assistance of Jali, who at that same moment had fallen to the ground in a faint. My servants came rushing forward with looks of bewilderment and alarm; and Hari burst, stark-naked, out of his tent. Hari has since told me that he was asleep and dreaming fearful dreams, when the trumpeting of an elephant awoke him. He started up out of his tent without knowing what he was doing, and the next minute, bewildered and vexed with himself, went back again.

"As you know, Amar, there were no elephants within hundreds of miles of Ravi at that time. But now—this, I expect, you do not know—there is *one*—one which arrived in the Camp a week later. It had been brought here at great trouble and expense by Daniyal, who had some idea, I believe, of introducing it into some scene in his play. But it has turned savage—from what cause I do not know—and it trumpets with rage very frequently. However, its trumpetings have never yet been audible across the breadth of the lake.

"But to go back to Jali. He remained unconscious for some time —perhaps half an hour. Knowing that I was the person to whom he wished to unburden himself, I kept him by me. He was carried into my tent; I was with him when he came back to himself, and he remained with me, sharing my tent, for the next few days. During that time he told me all about his recent experiences at the Camp, including all that he knew about Gunevati. He told me many other things besides . . . things which in time I shall let you know. My sense of guilt in regard to him is great."

Listening intently, the Rajah had not stirred; and, after Gokal had finished, he still remained silent. A servant now came across the room to announce that the evening meal was ready.

They went into another room, and, whilst eating, talked about the Din Ilahi. On this subject the Rajah had already written to Gokal at some length, so that the main features of the situation were known to him. But the Brahmin seemed unable to take interest in the various minor points that remained to be discussed. He was absent-minded and ate little, and the meal was soon over.

When they were back in the big room again and once more by themselves, Amar, standing by Gokal's chair, looked down at him and said: "Naturally enough your strange experience at Ravi baffles my comprehension." He paused. "How many persons in all heard the trumpeting of an elephant?"

"Ten people at least were sensible of a strange occurrence. But the actual trumpeting of an elephant was heard only by one or two besides Jali, Hari, and myself."

"Do you connect this thing in your mind...?" The Rajah stopped, hesitating.

"With Gunevati—yes. Only those who know Gunevati heard the trumpeting."

The Rajah was silent for a moment. "But what have we to do here with water-lilies? And anyhow," he added impatiently, "what is the connection between elephants and Gunevati?"

Gokal laid a hand on Amar's arm and gave a long sigh. "You shall know all I know—but we need time."

Amar smiled. "We have the whole night before us. And all to-morrow, if need be. Have we not got, in fact, as much time as we choose?"

"I doubt it," murmured Gokal.

Together they were looking out into the warm darkness. The wind had fallen to a dead calm. Suddenly Amar said: "The water-lilies, or the lotus, stand for the goddess Parvati... and then there is the elephant-demon Gajasura... Has that old myth been running in your head?"

Gokal laughed. "In the ancient mystery-play..."

"On my way down to Kathiapur," said Amar, "I happened to witness a very poor performance of it in company with Smith."

"I have a good deal to say about Smith," murmured Gokal.

Amar was surprised, but said nothing. Seating himself by the big, low window, he looked out over the lake, which was beginning to catch a faint brightness from the rising moon. The silhouettes of one or two strollers were to be seen on the lake-front. All at once there came to his ears the faint trumpeting of an elephant; but he said nothing, for he was not sure that Gokal heard it.

"What did Sita have to say about the Camp?" he asked. "Her visit must have amused her. Did the Prince make a more favorable impression?"

"She was amused," said Gokal slowly.

The Rajah laughed. "I think that in her eyes Daniyal will always be, first and foremost, a comic figure. And that is as it should be. I don't want her to take him too seriously."

Gokal turned his head to gaze straight into the Rajah's face, and in so doing he placed his own in shadow. His expression was indecipherable. He said: "Are you sure you are not shutting your eyes . . . ?"

"To what?"

Gokal continued to gaze at him.

"Let us be practical," said the Rajah with a change of voice. "I take it that you agree with me in regarding Daniyal's accession to the throne as assured. Well! had you been at enmity with Mobarek, or unable to countenance the Din Ilahi, your position would have been awkward, because unfortunately, your enemies have a handle against you. But, as I have explained, your way seems to have smoothed itself out, and this pleases me very much, not only on your account, but because, as you know, I want you to be Sita's chief counselor after my retirement. The position as it is now . . ."

At this point Gokal suddenly threw out his hand. "You are going too fast."

The Rajah frowned.

"What about Hari?" said Gokal.

"I was just coming to that," the Rajah replied quietly. "I think that the few months which Hari will have to spend in Sind will go a long way towards bringing him to a sense of reality. In his relationships with women Hari is apt to let his emotions run away with him. His sentiment for Lalita contained a great deal of unreality, as does hers for him at the present time. For Sita his feeling is no doubt of a different quality, but . . ." The sentence remained unfinished. "I hope," he went on after a moment's pause, "I hope that that feeling will form the basis of a true friendship. As for Sita, the responsibilities of government after I am gone, the duties imposed on her by her position, the care of Jali—these things will necessarily distract her mind from him. That romance"—and the Rajah smiled—"will accommodate itself to circumstances. A sentimental friendship—I don't use these words cynically—is what the future will bring forth."

Gokal took a deep breath. "Amar, are you still quite determined?"

"Yes."

"You are sure that you are inwardly prepared?"

"I am not so sure as I was." The Rajah's voice was bitter. "But, prepared or not, I am determined to delay no longer. Is it possible that you, too, are going to try to dissuade me? Are *you* going to use the argument that my secular duties come first?"

Gokal passed his hand over his brow. "I don't know . . . Let us begin by examining the position that you assign to me. I am afraid I am about to appear both unreasonable and ungrateful; but, alas, that cannot be helped. Amar, I find—to my own surprise and dismay—that, in spite of all the concessions Mobarek has made, I cannot associate myself with him in any way. Although Mobarek and I have much in common, although with him I believe that Life is governed by something outside what we commonly designate as Nature, and is transcendently oriented towards a supernatural goal, yet there is such a difference between his ideals and mine that I have to count him an antagonist.

"This difference between us is sufficiently illustrated by his attitude to Daniyal. His conscience allows him to ally himself with Daniyal in order to obtain for society the ultimate structure he desires. I could not do that. I believe it to be wrong to associate oneself with Daniyal even as a measure of expedience. Moreover," added Gokal reflectively, "I believe Mobarek's policy to be ill-judged."

He seemed to have finished, but all at once with sudden agitation he added: "Sita will never associate herself with Daniyal either. Make no mistake about this, Amar. It amuses her to laugh at him now,—so far she has had no occasion to do otherwise; but if you ask her to accept Daniyal, to give him even the semblance of her co-operation or goodwill, you will encounter an obstinate resistance. Neither Sita nor I can be left in the position in which you propose to leave us. Furthermore, for your own sake, I implore you not to retire yet."

Amar rose to his feet, and, after staring at Gokal for a few moments in silence, began pacing slowly up and down the room.

"This, I admit, is disconcerting," he said at last.

"I am sorry to have disappointed you."

Amar continued to pace up and down.

Gokal sat with bowed head. After a while Amar stopped and looked at him. "What you have been saying is, I think, only a part of what is in your mind."

Gokal remained dumb, and his silence was obstinate and somber.

"Since we began talking," Amar went on, "I have gradually formed the impression that certain features of the situation are greatly magnified and distorted in your imagination." His voice was cold and hard; Gokal raised his head, and his face now showed distress. "Perhaps," Amar continued, "it will relieve you to hear that I intend to tell Sita that my withdrawal will leave her free to enter into any relations with Hari that she pleases. Naturally, however, I shall say what I can in the way of advice and warning. I think that the feeling which has kept her from giving herself to Hari as yet is more complex than she knows. I shall suggest to her that loyalty to her own ideals enters into it no less strongly than her sense of loyalty to me. In her heart of hearts she is aware of the transitoriness of all human passions. I shall explain that I can contemplate with perfect equanimity—so far as *I* am concerned—her forming an alliance—possibly even a formal marriage might be arranged—with Hari. I shall not be jealous, and of course I shall have no right to be jealous. The love that has existed, and does still exist, between her and me will not be degraded nor diminished. In Nirvana all human lives and loves are lost; but the love of human beings for one another is the last of the fetters that men are called upon to cast off."

During this speech Gokal's discomfort, after reaching a climax, seemed to have subsided into a heavy, lifeless dejection. For several minutes Amar walked slowly up and down the room. When he halted before Gokal again, it was to ask: "Can you doubt that what I say is true?"

"Yes," said Gokal.

Amar turned aside and went to the window. The moon had now risen high above the lake, silvering the water. Amar stood looking at it, but not seeing it.

At last he heard a faint stir behind him and felt a hand laid upon his shoulder. "Let us go out," said Gokal in a low voice close to his ear. "I feel the need of air."

Amar turned. The look of affection, perplexity, and distress upon Gokal's face softened him. Together they left the house and walked down to the edge of the water.

5

STANDING BY THE moon-lit lake, Amar was reminded of that evening in the Royal Hunting Grounds near Agra, when a sense of the wonder and tragedy of human life had so deeply penetrated him that those few moments stood forth as a landmark in his life. But, he remembered, a little later he had been unable to express his own feelings or to give utterance to the sympathy that Gokal's grief awakened in him. Some channel of communication had been blocked. "It must not be like that again," he now said to himself.

A few steps away stood Gokal, white-robed, massive, and motionless, with his eyes fixed, not upon the lake, but upon a glow of yellow light that dyed the sky above Daniyal's theater. He appeared to be giving ear to the faint strains of music that came from that direction.

"If we walk a little farther," said Amar, "we shall find a grassy bank with a willow hanging over the water; there we shall be able to fancy ourselves on our own side of the lake." Scarcely had he finished speaking when a sound other than the music reached his ears—a sound, not loud, but too clear and unmistakable to admit of his ignoring it. He said: "When elephants trumpet in that particular way, they should be destroyed. It is a sign of madness in them."

"I have heard that trumpeting at intervals during the whole evening," Gokal replied in a low voice. "Have you not heard it too?"

"Perhaps. I am not sure."

When they had come to the willow-tree and seated themselves, Amar said: "Now it is your turn to talk, and I want you to speak first of all about yourself, for I see a great change in you."

Gokal laughed gently. "It is very simple. Whilst I was ill at Khanjo, with Sita nursing me, I moved a step farther upon my way."

Amar, silent, continued to question with his eyes, whereupon Gokal went on: "I freely admit that Sita has influenced me very deeply. You see, my mind had been prepared by a study of Western philosophy and Christianity. In fact those studies, by opening my eyes to the limitations and inadequacies of the oriental way of thought, were the first direct cause of my melancholia. I gained from them nothing positive. What I needed was contact with such a personality as Sita's."

Amar knit his brows.

"It is difficult to get from books anything but information. Westerners get little or nothing from our Sacred Books. And so it was with me."

"My friend," said Amar pensively, "consider how many years Sita and I have lived together, and yet . . ."

"Oh, you have apprehended, but recoiled."

"And she?"

"Has not apprehended," said Gokal, "but . . ." he smiled, "why should she?"

Amar was silent, and his face in the moonlight showed him to be puzzled. Still frowning, he looked out over the lake.

Gokal leant forward. "Is it not extremely significant that you fell in love with a Westerner—a woman, too, of so distinctive a caste of mind? Does it not mean that there are two natures in you? Your character, as I see it, and your life, as I pass it under review, persuade me that your philosophy gives a misleading interpretation of you— an interpretation misleading to yourself. Amar, I believe you to be a man with a deep intuition of godhead, and a craving to address himself to a personal god. Your philosophy I believe to be the reaction of another part of your nature against this basic tendency. In its peculiar character the Buddhism you profess satisfies the peculiar demands of your theorizing self. It would hardly be an exaggeration to say that your Buddhism is your own invention. The energies and impulses that gave it birth are personal, jealous, feminine,—so that in point of fact this cold impersonal philosophy of yours is the child and darling of an all-too-human heart.—Amar, when you refuse to the world the dignity of an arena for the very highest moral and spiritual struggle, your devaluation of life goes further than you see. It brings you very close to the position of such a man as Smith, who maintains that by tolerance, benevolence, and justice—combined with a devotion on the part of the *élite*, to art—the world will be as good as anyone could require.—No! I do not mistake you here: I have not lost sight of the difference between you and Smith. Whereas for Smith the spiritual is unreal, for you it is so real, so valuable, that it must be placed outside our common human life. Nevertheless it remains true to say that in regard to life on earth your attitude approximates most dangerously to Smith's. And I beg you to take this as a sign that your philosophy is fundamentally wrong."

There was a pause, at the end of which Amar said dryly: "You choose this occasion to say these things to me, because . . . ?"

"Because I see you standing at a division of the ways. Decisions of critical importance lie before you, and I believe that if you allow yourself to be guided by your philosophy instead of by your intuition, disaster will ensue."

Amar gave a little laugh; and when he spoke it was in an altered tone. "Let us cease from arguing in general terms, which are very apt to mislead through vagueness. I want to come down to the actual questions at issue. You hold, I think, that I should allow myself to be governed by my instinctive dislike of Daniyal even to the point of refusing to acquiesce with good grace in the success which I am convinced is assured to him."

"Yes, that is my opinion; the present crisis compels me to give utterance to feelings that have been gathering force within me for some time. I want you to obey your instincts in regard to Daniyal. But first you must see them as they are. Then, seeing them as they are, you will change your attitude from one of frigid and contemptuous self-withdrawal accompanied by outward acquiescence into one of hot anger and non-acquiescence."

"This is most strange!" exclaimed Amar. "Are you so changed

that you cast aside the doctrine of self-detachment that lies at the base of all."

"Beware of error here!" interrupted Gokal. "Do not confound self-detachment with what the Greeks called ἀοργησία, the incapacity for righteous warmth of feeling, and what Panjali himself condemns."

The Rajah gave a short laugh. "Is Daniyal then a fit object for wrath?"

"If you hate him, it is better to . . ."

"Hate him!" The Rajah checked himself. "My dear Gokal, are you seriously suggesting that I hate Daniyal—or that it is my duty to hate him?"

His head held proudly, his eyes half-closed, Amar looked out over the lake. Gokal peered at him out of the shadow of the willow-tree, and hesitated.

"You possess," he replied at last, "a particularly strong and fine sense of spiritual values. Now it is almost impossible to conceive of spiritual values as existing apart from personality; thus, although you yourself may not be aware of it, personalities are very significant to you."

"I will not argue the point. It is enough if I say that Daniyal's personality seems to me quite insignificant."

To this Gokal answered only with a sigh.

"Listen, Gokal!" the Rajah went on. "Ever since I left my own State, more than six months ago, I have been collecting information about Daniyal, ascertaining the opinions of others, and forming a judgment. Also, having met the young man myself, I have studied him with attention. I freely admit that he inspires me with a strong personal antipathy, but that does not affect my conclusion that he is completely trivial. When that has been said, everything has been said. Do not dignify Daniyal, I beseech you, by calling him wicked. Daniyal is simply negligible—excepting of course in so far as he offers Mobarek a very useful figurehead."

Gokal looked at Amar with curiosity. "I have not yet said that Daniyal is wicked."

Amar paused. "My mind must have been going back to a conversation we had on the terrace of the Agra Palace some six months ago."

Gokal inclined his head, then replied: "If triviality takes an important place in the world, if it is the chief barrier between men and God, then triviality is important."

Amar remained silent.

"No corruption is more easily spread than that of trivial-mindedness," Gokal went on. "It is more wicked to be heedless of good and evil than to say: Evil be thou my good! The man who defies God thereby acknowledges Him, and for him salvation waits; but the man who ignores God, the man who is incapable of an emotional response to the universe in its august or divine aspect—that man is indeed beyond the pale."

"In some people," said Amar, "an incapacity to respond denotes merely . . ."

"Amar," said Gokal quietly, "please do not speak without sincerity. Do you deny that the 'incapacity' we speak of might not just as well be called refusal? There is of course what men call moral insanity, but the term is fallacious. In organically diseased brains the very last faculty to disappear is the power of moral discrimination. Moral insanity is trivial-mindedness running riot in an intellect *otherwise* weak. In Daniyal the intellect is not weak; few of the people in this Camp are morally insane; they are trivial-minded, they offend God, and produce evil."

"I think you go too far," said Amar.

Gokal shook his head. "Trivial-mindedness in individuals or communities is responsible for practically the whole of what I mean by evil. Incidentally it leads to cruelty and other wickednesses, but these are only signs that evil is present. They do not constitute the evil of which they are the symptoms."

"This requires explanation," said the Rajah.

"Certainly. I will begin by explaining that I define evil as an offense against the Spirit of the Universe or God. Wickedness is an offense against man, and thus also an offense against God—but only indirectly. Evil is a characteristic of certain states of affairs, certain conditions of society; wickedness is a characteristic of certain persons. Badness is the characteristic of the acts of wicked persons; and suffering, mental or physical, is often the result. But suffering must not be confused with evil.

"Let us consider wickedness first; in its simplest form it is the blind, unthinking gratification of one's own appetites without consideration for others. A higher quality of wickedness is manifested in acts of revenge, injustice, and malice, directed against particular persons who have aroused enmity. A further step in wickedness is marked by pleasure in the suffering or humiliation of others without discrimination between persons and without particular incentive. This is pure cruelty, and here evil begins to enter in—not merely indirectly, but directly. With cruelty we approach the concept of wrong done not merely by persons to persons but *through* persons by the diabolic to God. Note the quality of impersonality in cruelty. In its essence it is spiritual. Note also the quality of sexuality in cruelty; cruelty, sexuality, and religiousness are kindred manifestations of spirit. Do we not find them associated in every time and clime?

"There are three kinds of wickedness to be distinguished: offenses against oneself, offenses against other persons, and offenses against God. The last is the highest and most subtle form of wickedness, because it is pleasure in the purest evil, sought in the directest way. What will be the nature and the characteristics of this, the wickedest type of man? He will not, as I have already explained, be merely regardless of other people, he will not be merely unjust and brutal; it is by no means certain that he will take pleasure in acts of physical cruelty; he may indeed be so constituted that such scenes will be abhorrent to him. But the mental suffering of others will always give him pleasure. Here, however, we must again particularize. To give him the highest pleasure this mental suffering must fall upon particular persons, not in their capacity as persons, but in their capacity rather as creatures of God, who do not merit those sufferings. What the wicked man looks for in human suffering is the spectacle of God being mocked, rightness being set at naught, the world being made to seem a place of purposeless evil, a triumph of the diabolic over the good." Here Gokal paused; and to his intense astonishment Amar saw that he was trembling.

"Yes," continued Gokal, "what the wicked man desires is this: that the gentle and the innocent, the kindly and the wise—all those to whom goodness is dear—should be offered a spectacle of the world such that they sicken at heart—sicken with a horror far more awful than any that could be caused by personal affliction. The wicked man likes to think that the good man is whispering within himself: 'How can such things be?' He wishes the good man's spirit to sicken—not on his own account, and not for others—not for the lot of any creature, but for the offense offered to the Creator, for the humiliation done to Goodness Itself. The wicked man knows Goodness only from the strange deep joy he receives from the idea that it is being mocked, and that those who trusted in it are being cast into despair.—Heaven forfend," Gokal added beneath his breath, "that you in your own experience should ever . . ."

The Rajah turned his head and fixed upon Gokal a deeply bewildered and troubled look. "Do you mean that you fear lest I should become an instrument . . ."

"No." He hesitated. "But . . ."

The Rajah was silent. Studying Gokal's face by the moonlight, he noticed that it was glistening with sweat and wore a look of profound exhaustion.

After a few minutes of gloomy abstraction he got up, and helped Gokal to rise to his feet. "Enough for to-night," he said.

6

THE NEXT DAY, when Amar and Gokal met, the sun was pouring in through the window of the big, dusty room. The morning had a hard brilliance, unusual to the valley, which was generally over-arched by a sky of milky haziness. With his back to the window Amar stood looking down at Gokal, who was sitting in the chair that he had occupied the evening before.

The two friends had come together in a changed mood, and this they both knew. "He has armed himself against me," thought Gokal sadly, "and, I suppose, it was inevitable, for how could I expect him to abandon in a moment the way of thought, and the projects, of years?" Presently, with a sigh and a smile, he held out his hand, in which lay two gold pieces. "Here is what I owe you," he said.

Amar returned his smile. "I think you owe me some kind of explanation as well. I woke up this morning feeling rather curious."

He was referring to an incident that had occurred as they were walking back the night before. A figure had emerged out of the shadow beside the path, had approached Gokal with a cringing air, and whispered something into his ear. For a moment Amar had thought that it was a beggar, but his next impression had been that the man was delivering a message, and instinctively he had moved out of earshot. A minute later Gokal had come up to him and asked for the loan of two gold pieces. After handing this money over, the Brahmin had received something in exchange, and upon that the man had vanished again. At the time Amar had been so deeply engrossed by the train of thought previously set up by Gokal that he had given the matter little attention, but in the course of a wakeful night his mind had reverted to it several times.

"Yes," he now repeated, "I am decidedly curious."

Gokal replied: "In exchange for that money I received a packet of letters addressed to Smith."

Amar gave a stare of surprise.

"It was a strange thing to happen," Gokal went on, "and all the stranger for happening at this particular juncture.—Here are the letters." He paused and drew out a packet from under the folds of his robe. "I want you to take them."

"And what am I to do with them?"

"That will be for you to decide, after I have told you my story. It begins from the visit that the yogi paid to me not long ago—the visit that you have already heard something about."

"Yes. The yogi told me that you and he had discussed religion together. I found it difficult to believe that he was speaking the truth."

Gokal smiled. "I assure you I found him not uninteresting. He expounded his Sakti views with a good deal of subtlety."

"That confusion of religion and sexuality is particularly distasteful to me."

"I think," said Gokal slowly, "I think one should beware of placing too great a distance between the two." For a moment he paused, then added: "The yogi also talked about Daniyal."

"With Churaman there!"

"I was careful, of course. So was Hari, who was also present. The yogi, on the other hand, was singularly indiscreet. He launched an attack upon Daniyal. After distinguishing between the different degrees and kinds of homosexuality, he maintained that Daniyal was to be put into the worst class. In Daniyal, he said, there was such grave aberrancy that the whole character of the man must necessarily be vitiated. The most potent of all human instincts could not deviate so widely from its proper channel without bringing about a distortion and disordering of the entire nature."

"Did he actually say this in the presence of Churaman?"

"No. When Churaman arrived we had passed on to a discussion of Smith,—but he spoke in just the same vein against Smith. He maintained that humanism and homosexuality were kindred manifestations of an arrested or distorted spiritual life. Was it mere chance, he asked, that Plato was the chosen teacher of humanists and homosexuals alike?"

"Perhaps he was under the influence of drugs."

"I think he is not quite sane."

"What does he know about Smith?" asked the Rajah after a silence. "And, apart from what I have told you, what do *you* know about him?"

Gokal smiled. "As a matter of fact I know a good deal. Acquaviva and I were sent by the Emperor to welcome him on his first landing in India. He came in the company of a man called Jones, whom the Emperor expelled from the country very soon after his arrival. Smith's friendship with Jones throws a revealing light upon his character. As for the yogi's connection with these two men, I can tell you nothing about it, but the other day to my surprise he produced certain letters written by Jones to Smith, and read a few passages aloud to us. It was an unwise thing to do in the presence of Churaman, because Smith and Daniyal are, as you know, friends, and these letters are such that, should they fall under the eyes of the Emperor, Smith would certainly be expelled from the country, just as Jones was."

Picking up the packet, which was lying on the table by his side, Gokal extracted a letter, and, after casting his eyes over it, went on: "Here is a passage that I came upon last night. 'To argue with a man who believes himself to be the Vice-Regent of God on earth is obviously a useless procedure. As long as India continues to lie under the heel of an autocrat in his dotage, her case will be hopeless. What is one to expect of a man who allows his official biographer to open with a sentence like this: "The most holy nativity of His Majesty from the sublime veil and consecrated curtain of Her Highness, cupola of chastity, and tap-root of the umbrageous trunk of happiness, occurred when the altitude of the lesser Dog-Star was 38° and when eight hours and twenty minutes had passed from the beginning of the night of 8th Adan 464." No, I say! India's salvation lies in Daniyal. I want you to tell me about this young man, whom *I* have only met once. Your accounts lead me to believe that he is unusually intelligent and liberal-minded. I hope you have explained to him that the only way to fight religion in India is to disintegrate it. I mean that polytheism must be encouraged, and religion divorced from philosophy. If the Indian must be metaphysical let him bombinate strictly *in vacuo*. Religion must become increasingly an affair of festivals, ritual, and fairy stories. The little godlings in their thousands are harmless. They become, as you have pointed out, familiar and friendly. The sentiment of awe vanishes; mystery vanishes; that old vestigial sense of godhead fades away. Godlings that you dress in the morning, give breakfast to, and then put to bed in the evening—these cannot do anyone any harm. Let us nourish the pious hope that Daniyal will discard that wicked old creature Mobarek as soon as he is well established in power.'"

The Rajah gave a laugh. "This all goes to confirm me in my opinion of Smith. Was the yogi intending to use these letters against him?"

"I think he was. And, if so, he acted foolishly in displaying them before Churaman. For this is what happened: twenty-four hours later he was knocked on the head and stunned, and the letters were taken from him. On hearing this, I assumed that they had passed into Daniyal's hands. But I was wrong. For, lo and behold, here they are!"

"Who is the man who sold them to you last night?"

"I have no idea—nor do I know why he thought I should be interested in them."

Amar pondered for a while. "You are not going to suggest that I should take these letters to the Emperor? This whole business is very distasteful to me."

Gokal smiled. "Daniyal is also most distasteful to you, and yet..."

The Rajah made a gesture of impatience. "Enough of Smith! Why should you or I trouble ourselves about him?"

"Amar," said Gokal with seriousness, "as a factor in the present situation Smith, I believe, is of considerable importance. There is a grave danger that Daniyal will adopt Smith's ideas. I first saw signs of this in Agra several months ago; a few words dropped the other day by Churaman gave me food for serious thought; and my thought has brought me to the conviction that Daniyal's genius for evil is going to lead him in the direction of Smith."

"Surely you are being a little fanciful? Besides, one can hardly regard Smith and Daniyal as likely to form a very powerful combination." And Amar laughed.

"There are epochs in history when power and influence belong not to the strong but to the cunning. My fear is that Daniyal, once established on the Throne, will discard Mobarek in favor of Smith. After all, the present alliance between Mobarek and Daniyal is artificial, for there is no real congruity between their ways of thought. An alliance between Smith and Daniyal, on the other hand, would rest upon a deep affinity. The fact that the true nature of their affinity is ignored by both is irrelevant. It matters not that Smith, in his own view, would be working for the welfare of India as the enlightened adviser of a liberal young prince. It matters not that Daniyal's view, although not quite so simple, would probably be not very dissimilar. Nor is it of importance that an adoption of Smith's ideas might well bring about—as its first immediate result—a general betterment of material conditions. No; what does matter lies beneath appearances, beneath the shallow surface of things. And in this case the truth would be that the powers of corruption would have won a victory. As you know, it is not the machinery of civilization but the informing spirit of the social unit that keeps it alive and in health. Even the era of material prosperity inaugurated by Smith would be brief. The virtues of justice and altruism, upon which he relies, unless working under the inspiration of a transcendent ideal, are working for ill. As Lao Tse has said: 'If the wrong man uses the right means, the right means work in the wrong way.' Justice and altruism too often draw their energy from envy, jealousy, and disguised self-interest. Smith does not understand this. Still less does he understand that lovers of mankind in and for itself are primarily haters of God. He does not understand that it is on these grounds that he and Daniyal meet. How much does Daniyal understand? I cannot tell you. Up to now he has been youthful enough to parade a frivolous, non-moral aestheticism; but he is also clever enough to realize that as an

Emperor the pure aesthete is not unlikely to end like Nero. Smith has arrived at the right moment to suggest another path."

During this speech Amar sat very still, with folded arms, and his expression was somber. When Gokal had finished, he raised his head; and Gokal met his dark stare unflinchingly.

"Well!" said Amar at last, "and if you are right, what then? Can I change the course of destiny?"

Gokal leant forward, a light came into his face, but just as he was about to speak the door at the end of the room opened and a servant advanced with a letter.

"From His Royal Highness to the Maharajah! And the messenger awaits a reply."

Amar took the letter, read it with an expressionless face, and said: "When I clap my hands the answer will be ready. Request the messenger to wait."

After the servant had gone, he turned to Gokal. "Daniyal wishes me to come and see him as early as possible."

Gokal's face had darkened; it now took on a look of extreme anxiety. "You must find an excuse for delay."

"But why?"

"Is it impossible to find some excuse? Let us consider."

"But I have no objection to going."

"You have not yet seen Sita. You have not yet had time. . . ."

"Are you afraid lest I should pledge myself—or her?"

Gokal made a vague gesture.

"Put your mind at rest. How can I make promises for Sita—or for you?"

So speaking, the Rajah drew up to the table, took a pen, and wrote. Presently the servant entered again to receive his reply.

Gokal rose from his chair, went to the window, and stared with vacant eyes across the lake. "What have you said?" he asked.

"That I will be with him in an hour or less."

Gokal gave a little laugh, and it was so bitter that Amar winced inwardly.

"Tell me, Gokal!" he said, "what, actually, do you want of me?"

Gokal faced round. "Actually," he said, "Prince Daniyal is not yet upon the Throne. Well, why not fight him?"

"Do you suggest that I . . ."

"Yes!"

"I was going to say: do you suggest that I should lead my little army out to join the ranks of Salim?"

"I do suggest it."

"My dear friend, you must be mad."

"I believe it is the only right course for you."

"For *me*!"

"Being what you are—yes."

"I am mystified," said Amar, whose eyes were now burning darkly.

"You are angry," said Gokal.

Amar compressed his lips, then opened them to say, "Right action, as I see it, always demands a recognition of what is practicable, and in this case . . ."

"No. That is where you are wrong. The world is such that no man has the right to think he knows what is practicable."

Amar shrugged.

"Man is under an obligation to act—under a psychological necessity that is also a spiritual obligation. And somehow in his action he must reconcile the pursuit of his own small, definite, and rightful ends with the working out of an inscrutable purpose. He must not forswear his intimate knowledge that he is the chief instrument of the *supernatural* energy determining whatever in time shall come to pass."

"The action that lies before me now," said Amar, "is to pay my respects to Daniyal. That done, I shall return."

7

AMAR WALKED OUT into the bright sunlight, and swept a glance around him. The promenade was now covered with gaily dressed figures. His eyes rested upon them in a dark, distant stare, whilst his thought dwelt somberly upon his recent conversation with Gokal, and went forward no less somberly to his coming interview with the Prince. The unusual clearness of the atmosphere made the opposite shore of the lake plainly visible; and presently, as he gazed across the glittering water, his mind was flooded with images of Sita. "I am cut off from humanity on the one side, just as I am cut off from inhumanity on the other," he reflected with bitterness. "The way of life is much simplified for those who throw their emotions into the scale."

With a lowering countenance he set off down the promenade, unconscious of the looks that were thrown at him as he passed. "Yes," he was saying to himself, "come what may, I shall withdraw; and no man shall stop me. Sita, Hari, Gokal—they must order their lives according to their own lights. If, after I am gone, Sita chooses to espouse the cause of Salim, let her do so! Moreover, I shall withdraw *at once*. Gokal's words have but precipitated my action."

So deeply engrossed was he by these thoughts that some moments passed before he became aware that a sprightly little figure was tripping along at his side, and throwing looks of smiling inquiry up into his face. He halted in astonishment. "Prince Dantawat?" he stammered. "You are not Prince Dantawat?"

"Certainly not, I am Shanta Shil, the Quietist." And the speaker put his head on one side coquettishly.

The Rajah was completely puzzled. "Then I don't think we know one another," said he. Still absent-minded and resentful of the interruption, he stared at the stranger with a frown. Surely this *was* Prince Dantawat? And yet Dantawat had been reported dead. Was it not, indeed, Dantawat's corpse that he had come upon in the forest? Moreover, how could this plump, smiling, little man be the same Dantawat that had presented so pitiable an appearance only three weeks ago?

"Oh, but we do know one another, Rajah,—indeed we do! Only you mustn't talk about Dantawat to me: I am a new man now. See, what lovely clothes! And how well I am looking, am I not? This is all the work of the dear Prince. He is taking care of me."

The Rajah, aghast, was now walking rapidly on; but Dantawat, to his extreme discomfiture, trotted by his side. "Rajah, do you remember, it was almost on this very spot that you saw me that morning when I threw myself into the lake. Oh, that was naughty of me, wasn't it? But rather brave, too, don't you think? Of course I always chose a place where there were plenty of people to pull me out. But all the same, when one doesn't know how to swim . . . Oh, I *was* unhappy in those days! and Daniyal had been so unkind! All my money gone, too! Not a penny left, and he wouldn't do anything to help me!"

The Rajah stopped, and examined with a long and horrified stare the man who stood before him. Dantawat's face, which had always been round and childish, now looked strangely puffy, and his cheeks were powdered and rouged. His cherubic aspect was rendered additionally comic by the fact that he had become almost bald. His body looked plump, under his tight-fitting brightly colored clothes. Far from resenting this stare, Dantawat looked coyly down upon the ground, his head a little on one side, and shifted his weight from one rounded hip to the other.

The Rajah removed his eyes from Dantawat to look around him for some means of escape. How was this unhappy lunatic to be

shaken off? To his unexpected relief, he found himself being ac-
costed by a lady whom he dimly remembered having met in the
Palace at Agra. Yes, it was Ranee Jagashri, a woman he disliked,
but was only too glad to enter into conversation with now, for he
took it for granted that she would ignore his companion, who
would then be obliged to withdraw. In this, however, he was
completely mistaken, Ranee Jagashri seemed to find it the most
natural thing in the world that he and Dantawat should be
strolling on the lake-front together, and she not only included
Dantawat in her conversation, but listened to his chatter with a
gay and cordial interest.

"Oh, look! There go Babilo Tud and Mansur! Poor dears, they
did try so hard to slip away last week, but the Prince caught them.
Of course, it's very trying for him when his actors run away; but
I did sympathize with them too. I'm not brave, like you, Ranee
Jagashri. What *should* I do, if Salim's horsemen were to come dashing into the Pleasance! I lie awake at night thinking about it.—
But of course I can't leave the dear Prince. Look at the way he has
treated me since I was so wicked as to . . . but we won't talk about
that! All I mean to say is that anyone but the Prince would have
been very angry with me. Most people are still so barbarous. They
don't understand how unfortunates like me should be treated.
But the Prince is showing them, isn't he, Ranee Jagashri?" To this
Dantawat received no reply, because the Ranee, having caught
sight of other acquaintances, had strolled on.

Laying a hand gently on the Rajah's arm, Dantawat invited him
to move forward again. "I know where you're going," said he with
a sly smile. "And you mustn't keep Daniyal waiting. Come along!
I will show you the way."

"I know the way, and I don't need you."

"But Daniyal isn't at his house. You don't know where he is."

"Where is he?"

"Never mind. I'll take you to him. I expect he's at his theater.
Of all the arts I love the stage best, don't you? Of course, you
know, we're all lovers of the arts here.—Oh look! did you see that?
What a splendid man! What muscles! Oh, doesn't he make one's
heart beat!" Dantawat was looking back over his shoulder at an
immense negro, a member of Daniyal's black body-guard.

Grimly Amar stalked on.

Tripping and skipping at his side, Dantawat kept throwing coquettish little glances up into his face. "Rajah, I believe I've guessed a secret of yours—shall I whisper it to you? I believe you don't really like the Prince! There! Am I not right? But, really, Rajah, fancy not admiring Daniyal. Doesn't his lovely smooth skin appeal to you?—No, not that way, Rajah. I do believe you're trying to run away from me! But it's no use; without me you'll never find Daniyal.—Now we go down this way, and there's the theater in front of you,—only you won't be able to get in by the main entrance, because . . ."

Unheeding, the Rajah stalked on. The large doors were, as Dantawat had said, closed, so he turned in the direction of the stage-entrance, and was half-way down the alley leading to it, when a familiar voice, sounding just above his head, caused him to look up.

There was Daniyal at one of the windows, smiling down upon him with eyes in which there was a glint—or so the Rajah thought —of malice. He stopped, saluted the Prince, and received a gay greeting in return. The big, low window revealed Daniyal almost at full length, sitting upon the corner of a table, which was covered with papers. The sun shining full upon him, his jewels all aglitter, he made a brilliant picture against the shadowy space behind.

"Smooth and voluptuous does he look," thought the Rajah, "but with what grossness in the curves of feature and figure alike! Yes, he is becoming more repellent every day."

He stared up, blinking in the clear sunlight, and smiling a strained smile, while Daniyal poured out an unbroken stream of chatter.

"His mind," thought the Rajah, "seems careless and detached. He cultivates a light intoxication of flippancy. He looks upon himself as moving in a world of arbitrary inclinations—inhuman with the inhumanity of those who have no affections, no pity,—and perhaps no fear. And yet . . ."

Daniyal turned away for a minute to address some remarks to a person inside the room. Lowering his head, the Rajah chose this moment to throw a frowning look upon Dantawat, who was crouching like a monkey beneath the window out of sight of the

Prince. "Go away!" he said beneath his breath; and Dantawat, grinning and grimacing most strangely, got up swiftly and ran off.

"So you are just back from Kathiapur?" said the Prince, facing round again. "I want you to tell me all about your doings there. I had a letter from Ambissa Begum this morning. She says that you and Lalita have become fast friends. I adore your sister, Rajah. What character! What pertinacity! And what a handsome woman! Do you know, as I look down on you from this angle, I can see such a strong family likeness. Come here and look at the Rajah, Dantawat, and tell me if you don't think . . ."

Dantawat's puffily cherubic countenance appeared in the window. He smiled and nodded; his little chirrup filled up the brief pauses in the Prince's flow of speech.

While he was talking, Amar's eyes rested upon Daniyal with a singular intentness. Daniyal's skin was shining golden, his light blue, slightly protruding eyes, which were often sleepy, had a light in them which the Rajah had never seen before. He was wearing a costume that matched their color.

"But what am I thinking of, to keep you standing there!" the Prince now suddenly exclaimed. "You must come in, Rajah. Dantawat, go and show the Rajah the way in."

With these words he got up from the corner of the table, and the sound of his footsteps on the boards showed him to be walking away. For the last minute a light breeze had been playing among his papers and the movement he had just made was sufficient to send several of them fluttering down into the street. The Rajah picked the papers up, and, when he raised his head, found it quite close to Dantawat's, for the latter was craning out over the sill.

"It's all right. He's gone," the little man chuckled confidentially. "He's talking to someone at the other end of the theater."

The Rajah held out the papers he had collected, but instead of taking them Dantawat gave a giggle, and, after glancing over his shoulder, said: "I should read them if I were you. They might be amusing." Then, drawing himself back into the room, he hunted rapidly through the papers on the table, selected one or two, and threw them down into the street. "Quick!" he said. "You'll find a letter from Ranee Sita there."

Flushing deeply with anger, the Rajah stooped, gathered the

letters up, and moved away in the direction of the stage-door. Entering, he soon lost himself in a maze of ill-lit passages, but was presently joined by Dantawat, who in an excited voice said: "Follow me, Rajah, follow me!" Amar had no choice but to obey, and presently he came out upon a wide, dusty expanse of floor, which was evidently the stage, for close beside him there stretched the lowered curtain.

Dantawat stepped up to one of the peep-holes and looked through. "Yes, he is still talking to the same man,—and it is something serious."

Drawing back, he laid his hand upon the Rajah's arm, pressing him forward. "Look!" he said urgently.

The Rajah stooped and looked. The big auditorium was divided up into strips of light and shade, as the sun's rays struck through the high upper windows, which, on the south side, had been unshuttered here and there. In one of the shafts of sunlight, some fifty feet away, stood Daniyal, an expression of extreme sulkiness upon his face. Beside him were two of his habitual followers, and both wore looks of undisguised consternation. They appeared to be cross-questioning a shabbily dressed man, whom Amar conjectured to be a member of the Prince's Secret Service. Only one of the lower windows of the hall was unshuttered; and Amar recognized it as the one beneath which he had been standing.

As soon as he removed his eye from the peep-hole, Dantawat took his place.

"Oh, Rajah, Daniyal's got a very funny look. He has just sent the others away and is talking quite alone to his spy. Come and look again, Rajah."

"No.—Show me the way round into . . ."

"Hush!" Dantawat, still with his eye glued to the hole, held up a warning hand. "Hush, hush!" he whispered. "Daniyal's coming this way. He's walking up and down. Be quiet, or he'll hear us."

The Rajah, frowning uncomfortably, remained silent. Then, laying a hand on Dantawat's shoulder, he wrenched him away from the curtain.

Dantawat, his eyes glittering, pointed vehemently and repeatedly at the peep-hole. "Look!" he whispered with intense excitement. "Look!"

Amar turned on his heel and walked away.

"Oh, Rajah, you've missed something," protested Dantawat, trotting after him. "And it's such a pity! Do you know what you've missed?"

A short distance in front of him the Rajah saw a door. "Is that the way?" he asked.

"Yes, the auditorium is through there.—But wait a minute. Shall I tell you what you missed?" He giggled. "You missed a very unusual look on Daniyal's face."

In spite of himself the Rajah paused.

Dantawat giggled again. "Perhaps you think that Daniyal's never frightened? But you're wrong. I tell you he's *always* frightened—but deep down, so deep that he doesn't know it."

The Rajah still paused.

"I'll tell you something very funny," continued Dantawat, but his tone had changed. "Sometimes Daniyal is actually frightened of *me*! Fancy being frightened of a thing like me! But he thinks I'm slightly mad, you see. He treats me so well, he gives me such beautiful clothes,—look at this tunic! Feel this heavy gold embroidery! Isn't it lovely!—He always has me by his side, just because he likes to show me off. Everybody says: 'How brave you are! How generous and forgiving! Why, anyone else would have had the wretched creature tortured to death!' And of course they're quite right. Daniyal is splendid, isn't he? He has all the best modern ideas, you know."

As if suddenly starting out of a trance, Amar pushed open the door in front of him and stepped into the auditorium. The Prince, still talking to his spy, was standing some way off. Going across to the window in which the table stood, the Rajah laid the Prince's letters down upon it and waited.

Presently Daniyal came up to him. "More trouble from dear brother Salim," he called out gaily. "He is sending out raiding-parties, I hear. I am going to pack up. Do you know, Rajah,"—and his voice became serious—"I've some of my most valuable things here,—all sorts of silks, embroideries, and carpets, to say nothing of jewelry. They must be packed up at once. They must be on their way down to Kathiapur before nightfall.—Babilo! Mansur! Do you hear what I say?" And he proceeded to give detailed orders.

"Ah!"—he had turned to Amar again—"but Salim little knows what I have in store for him! That dear child Gunevati has made a full confession. Yes, in writing of course; and, my dear, a more scandalous document I never saw. When my father holds his next court for dealing summarily with the Vamacharis out will come my evidence against Salim! Can you imagine the scandal! But we must keep Gokal's name out, mustn't we?" And his eyes twinkled.

Whilst he was speaking, the stage curtains had been drawn aside, and dim figures could be seen hurrying about; in the auditorium itself a few people had appeared. There was a girl in the distance who looked like Gunevati; but the Rajah could not be sure it was she. Presently Babilo Tud and Mansur returned, and Daniyal's attention was claimed once again. "Forgive me," he called out over his shoulder, "I shall not be more than two minutes," and he moved towards the back of the stage.

The moment he had gone Dantawat bobbed up out of the shadows. "Do you know, there's another man wanting to see Daniyal now. Such a fine fellow! He must have been in the army once, I think.—Oh, there goes that horrible elephant again! The mad ones are used for crushing Vamacharis to death, you know. I can't bear the noise they make, can you, Rajah?"

"Why does Daniyal keep this one?"

"Oh, just to frighten Gunevati with, I suppose. It's a dreadful animal. The other day . . ."

The Rajah moved away. A sudden impulse had seized him. *Was* that Gunevati sitting there in the corner of the hall? He wanted to know; he wanted to look at her; he wanted to see . . .

The face raised at his approach had such a delicate and melancholy beauty that his recognition was delayed. This couldn't be Gunevati—and yet it was! The girl stared up at him without interest. Her eyes showed that she knew him, but they also showed that she was living in the detachment of an unhappiness so deep that the exterior world was hardly present to her. The degree of her remoteness was brought home to the Rajah the next moment by the approach of Daniyal. Her big, dark eyes rested expressionlessly upon the Prince, as, gesticulating and talking gaily to Babilo Tud, he strolled over to her corner of the hall. From her dejected position she rose languidly, and, as she stood before him, no emotion of any kind was visible on her face. The Prince gave the Rajah a smile, and turned to pat her in kindly fashion on the shoulder. "My poor dear! You mustn't mope. You really mustn't.—Tell me, Rajah, what am I to do with the child?"

Thrusting his arm through Amar's, he drew him gently away. "Now I want to ask you something," he said. "Is it really true that you are intending to retire from the world? Rajah, I can hardly believe it! I shall not believe it until you tell me so yourself." And, stepping back, he looked the other up and down with an expression of amusement.

Amar stiffened and grew slightly pale. "Yes, I intend to retire."

"Soon? How soon?—No, no, Rajah! I don't think you really mean it."

Amar was silent.

Daniyal shook his head smilingly. "And leave that charming wife of yours? Who will look after her? Gokal? Hari?" He paused a moment, then laid a hand on Amar's arm: "Well, I couldn't believe it, until I had it from your own lips. But now that you have confirmed the news, let me tell you that you have my blessing. I see no reason why everything should not work out admirably."

There was a brief pause, but a pregnant one. The Rajah's face might have been cast in metal so lifelessly still was it. At last he inclined his head. "I thank Your Royal Highness. My intentions being what they are, I have nothing now to do but to commend to your favor those I leave behind." And with another and a deeper bow he signified his desire to withdraw.

The Prince ignored this movement. "If anyone is going to cause us trouble, it's Gokal, isn't it? Tell me frankly, what is Gokal's attitude?"

"I am afraid . . ."

"Exactly," interrupted Daniyal. "But it's too absurd, isn't it? For his own sake you simply mustn't let him be foolish. And, if your influence fails, no doubt Ranee Sita will be able to bring him round.—Oh, you can retire to your monastery quite happily! You know, Ranee Sita did me the honor of taking luncheon here with me the other day, and we reached a perfect understanding. I had to tell her about the threat of banishment that is hanging over Hari. Poor dear lady, she was of course rather distressed. But—oh, just look at the way they are treating those brocades!" He pointed to a group of men who were occupied in packing up. "What barbarians!—Well, never mind! What was I saying? Oh yes, Ranee Sita was naturally upset. But I was able to reassure her. I said: 'Now listen! If you make Hari reasonable and keep him reasonable, he shall *not* go to Sind. He shall stay with you. I give you my promise. There!'—And when she asked me what I meant by reasonable, I answered: 'Merely this; Hari must give up flirting with Salim and my other enemies, and he mustn't interfere any more between me and Ali.'—She shook her head at first, and said that Hari was rather obstinate; but of course she can make Hari do what she pleases. Women manage these things much better than we do; and, as a matter of fact, I had a letter from her only this morning—a charming letter—in which she says that Hari is going to be good. Don't trouble about Gokal, Rajah! She will make him see reason too; of that I have little doubt. Oh yes, we shall all get on famously together.—But to think of you all by yourself in Ceylon! Rajah, are you sure that you won't change your mind? I know that for some people religion is a necessity. I am not narrow-minded on the subject. But, really, to run away to a monastery at your age!—And to leave one's pretty wife behind! Are you sure you want to go as far as that?"

Amar, who had listened to this without the smallest change of countenance, now took a step forward to place himself in front of the Prince, made a formal bow, and then turned in the direction of the door.

But Daniyal caught hold of him by the arm. "Do you see that man over there?" He gave a little laugh. "Not a friend of yours, is he?"

Standing by the entrance was the Governor, and Amar noticed with a shock of surprise that his arms were bound to his sides. Furthermore, two negro soldiers were mounting guard over him. Not far off, evidently waiting to be summoned, was the shabby little spy who had been talking to Daniyal before. At a sign from the Prince he now hurried up.

"Rajah, I want you to wait a minute," said Daniyal carelessly. "I may have something interesting to tell you."

626

8

AMAR DREW ASIDE. For about five minutes the Prince and his interlocutor conferred together in low tones. Occasionally they both looked across the hall at the Governor; but the latter, his eyes fixed upon Gunevati, seemed to be unaware of their existence. At last Daniyal gave a little laugh, and his last words, spoken over his shoulder as he rejoined Amar, were loud enough for the Rajah to overhear: "Very well, take him away, and lock him up for the present."

During these minutes Amar had stood motionless, and it was difficult to tell from his expression whether he was observant of his surroundings or not. Behind him on the stage men were hurrying about busily; by the table in the window sat Dantawat, who appeared to be sorting papers. In her corner not far from the main entrance was Gunevati, and the Governor's eyes were still fixed upon her in an avid, sensual stare. The girl seemed to become aware of this after a while, for she raised her head and her glance passed fleetingly over him. There was neither pity nor curiosity in her look, only an immense weariness, an immense indifference. And yet, the next moment, she smiled; she was bending forward and putting out her hand, and a smile of ravishing beauty passed over her face. A large, white Persian cat ran and leapt on to her lap. She sank back at once into her former posture, the smile faded, and while her hand stroked the cat her thoughts evidently were far away.

For a moment the Prince stood looking at Amar with a smile. "Yes, I am afraid there is no doubt about it. The Governor is a traitor . . . in the pay of my brother Salim." His manner was as carelessly good-humored as usual, and yet something in him had changed. "A Vamachari, too, I expect! Altogether a disgusting creature! And yet Mabun Das has often spoken very well of the man. Isn't that rather odd, Rajah? Tell me, what do *you* make of it?"

"Your Royal Highness, I am very little acquainted with either the Governor or Mabun Das."

"You saw something of Mabun at Kathiapur," returned Daniyal, smiling, "and I appeal to you as a judge of character. Come, what do you think of the man?"

Amar was silent.

"Well! Tell me this at least," Daniyal went on, "how is it that Mabun and Hari became such friends at Agra? What brought them together, do you think? Come, Rajah, you have a knack of getting at people's secrets. You are so sympathetic. Ambissa Begum tells me that Lalita made you her father-confessor. She must have told you all about her flirtation with Hari. Dear me, what a romantic affair that was! It is wonderful, the way Hari steps out of one romance into another!"

As he spoke, Daniyal was pacing slowly up and down the hall, and on one of the scattered seats there lay some colored cork balls such as jugglers use; three of these he now picked up, and, whilst continuing to talk, kept them dancing in the air. "Do you know, Rajah, I have often wondered why Mabun never reported to me that my darling betrothed was carrying on—I think 'carrying on' is just the right expression here!—with another man? It isn't as if Mabun had been great friends with Hari in those days. And yet not a word did he ever say to me!—That Mabun *did* know all about it I have from Gunevati, and she knows because she informed him herself. Besides, her story of how she came to inform Mabun is *most* curious. I am inclined to think that she hasn't yet told me the whole truth. Perhaps she is afraid of giving Mabun away? Perhaps . . . Anyhow, her story is a very odd one. It appears that one evening when Hari and Lalita were having a secret meeting in the Royal Hunting Grounds at Agra, Lalita's horse knocked a man down—and that man, as it happens, was none other than my dear brother Salim! You see, Salim and Gunevati and some other Vamacharis were on their way to a deserted pavilion where they were going to have a little orgy together. Well! in the confusion of the accident poor dear Lalita dropped her riding-whip, and Gunevati picked it up, and then, somehow or other, the whip was traced into her possession by Mabun. It's a long, complicated story; and, as you see, parts of it are still missing. But the long and short of it is that Mabun has not been open with me. In fact, I find it difficult to believe that he has not been actually conniving with Salim."

Scarcely had these words left Daniyal's lips when shouts and screams were to be heard in the distance, and this was followed by a thudding of hoofs upon the planking of the promenade.

Daniyal and Amar each stiffened into immobility. Over the whole theater there fell a deep hush. Gradually the clamor died down, the hoof-beats faded into the distance again, and everywhere a deep silence reigned.

Abruptly Daniyal turned away, gave his shoulders a twitch, and swept a glance around him. "Dear me!" he cried, and again "Dear me!" His intonation was exaggeratedly nonchalant. "That sounded like a bit of life in the raw, didn't it? I was half-expecting brother Salim to put in an appearance here."

The sound of his voice was the signal for a general hubbub. There was a rush to the door on the part of some, while others craned their heads out of windows. Daniyal and Amar remained in the center of the hall; their looks met, then each turned away.

"Well?" the Prince called out. "Has no one anything to report?"

An answer came almost at once from Dantawat, who was at the window. "Yes! Oh yes!" he cried in a high excited pipe. "Your Royal Highness, there is somebody running! Oh, I declare it's Mansur! Poor Mansur, how frightened he looks! Now he's coming in by the stage-door." And Dantawat hurried up to the Prince's side. "Your Royal Highness, he will be here in a moment. Isn't it terrible! Did you hear those screams!—Rajah, why do you look like that? Your expression is really quite wicked. Aren't you sorry for . . ."

The sound of footsteps was now heard at the back of the stage, and Daniyal swung round on his heel. Exceedingly red in the face, and wearing an expression of the sourest disgust, Mansur came trotting forward upon his short legs. Having reached the Prince, he closed his eyes and pressed both hands upon his heart.

"Well?" said Daniyal with some impatience.

"Your Royal Highness . . . my heart!" and Mansur opened his mouth to pant like a dog.

"Nonsense!" said Daniyal.

"I was walking with Babilo along the lake-front, when suddenly a lot of horsemen appeared and began riding us down as if we were so many—so many—I don't know what. For about a mile along the promenade they went, trampling down men and women alike, and doing it on purpose, too! I never heard of such a thing!— Your Royal Highness should have closed the Pleasance weeks ago. Your Royal Highness isn't safe here. I should think fifty people must have been killed. Please, have I permission to go and pack up my things?"

Daniyal laughed, but in a tone of vexation. Turning his back on those who stood beside him, he moved a few steps away.

"Rajah!" he called without turning his head.

"The defense of the Pleasance is in the hands of Mabun Das. That man is a traitor, and I have always suspected it." For a few moments he stood looking straight before him. Amar stared into his face with a kind of greedy fixity; his lips were compressed in such a manner that he seemed to be wearing a smile. When the Prince began walking in the direction of Gunevati he remained by his side.

Rocking himself on heels and toes before her, Daniyal looked the girl up and down with half-closed eyes. Strangely enough Gunevati had not risen at the Prince's approach, and even now she remained seated. The reason, however, was apparent; she had watched the Prince coming towards her in a daze of fear; and now there was blank terror in her eyes.

"My dear," said Daniyal carelessly, "I am afraid your confession was incomplete, after all."

Gunevati was silent.

Daniyal gave a little shrug, and then looked sharply towards the main entrance. A fine-looking young man, in the uniform of a lancer, was approaching. Coming to a halt, he gave the Prince a military salute, and waited for permission to speak.

"Well?" said Daniyal.

"Your Royal Highness, I have the following report to deliver. Six horsemen rode into the camp half an hour ago. After being driven off from the military jail, from which they were evidently hoping to release the Governor of this district, they made off for the woods to the south-west. One of their number was killed outside the jail. Our casualties are one man killed and one wounded."

"Where is your superior officer?" asked Daniyal after a pause.

"He is coming. He sent me ahead to report, so that Your Royal Highness should not be left too long without knowledge of the affair."

"I shall talk to him outside," said Daniyal, and he moved rapidly towards the door, but on his way he stopped and turned. "Stay here, all of you," he ordered, and his eyes traveled across Amar's face.

For several moments after he had gone there was silence, then the lancer stepped up to the Rajah and said in a low voice, "Something of this kind was bound to happen sooner or later. Why on earth doesn't the Prince leave this damned place? To defend it against raids such as this is a sheer impossibility,—unless one puts up a stockade; and that the Prince won't allow."

"He says that Mabun Das is betraying him."

The young officer flushed with anger. "His Royal Highness has no right to speak like that. We are all loyal men—God help us!"

These last words, spoken in the manner of an aside, brought a faint smile to Amar's face.

The lancer folded his arms, and, after throwing a swift contemptuous glance round the theater, dropped his chin upon his chest in moody abstraction. Silent and motionless the Rajah also stood. For several minutes the silence of the building was such that the contented purring of the cat on Gunevati's knees was distinctly audible. The girl's fingers were scratching its head, but the look on her face showed her mind to be far away.

To Mansur and Dantawat this silence soon became oppressive. Mansur, who had been mopping his brow with a silk handkerchief, now blew his nose loudly several times in succession, while Dantawat began shuffling about with his feet. "I wish you'd put that handkerchief away," he said at last. "I wish you'd talk to me. Did you notice Daniyal's expression? Oh, it was very odd! It was indeed! I don't think I have ever seen him look quite like that before. Someone, I'm sure, is going to catch it!"

As Mansur completely ignored this, Dantawat glanced round appealingly at the others; but nobody showed a sign of having heard him.

Plucking at Mansur's sleeve, he went on: "I *am* glad I'm not in somebody's shoes, aren't you? Somebody's going to get into trouble, I'll swear. Who do you think it will be?"

Mansur turned away, and, without addressing himself to anyone in particular, observed in acrid tones: "Our casualties are reported as one killed and one wounded! Why, out there on the lake-front I should say there are half a dozen killed and certainly a score of wounded. These military people are all the same! To them civilians are no more than flies—their death doesn't count."

Dantawat giggled. "They might have killed you. But I don't think *that's* what's worrying Daniyal."

"Not a day longer shall I stay here," grumbled Mansur. "Not a day!"

"It's the treachery of Mabun Das," Dantawat went on brightly, "*that's* what he minds. Fancy Mabun being a traitor! But so many people are treacherous, aren't they? I mean just a little bit treacherous," and he tittered self-consciously.

"Mansur, come here!" he went on after a minute. "I want to whisper a secret."

Dragging at Mansur's arm until they were a few steps away, he whispered: "Have you looked at the Rajah's face? No? Well, look now! Look!"

Mansur looked and shrugged.

"Oh, you should have seen him and the Prince a little while ago! He doesn't like Daniyal, you know. He never did. They were walking up and down and talking together, and as they talked..." He broke off, for Daniyal's voice had become audible through the curtains that hung over the doorway.

For the next two or three minutes no one in the hall spoke, all were listening to the sound of a conversation between Daniyal and some people in the vestibule. Daniyal appeared to have all his usual calm, and to be furthermore in a witty vein, for his remarks were greeted by the laughter of his hearers. When the moment came for taking leave of his audience he could be heard doing so with all his customary flourish.

Suddenly the curtains were drawn apart by two negroes, and he made his appearance. He was accompanied by his secret agent, to whom he was speaking with a gay volubility. Instead of coming forward he remained by the entrance, taking a few steps now to the right and now to the left, and presently, whilst talking, he held out his hand to one of the negroes, who put into it the three colored balls which he again began to juggle with.

At last with a nod he dismissed his interlocutor, and, still keeping his balls dancing in the air, advanced slowly towards the waiting group. All remained where they were; but the white cat, which had got up from Gunevati's lap, was yawning and stretching itself. It now came running across the floor, and, on reaching Daniyal, rubbed itself against his legs, causing him to miss one of the colored balls. Then it threw itself down on the ground in front of him, lying on its back, and with a mew invited him to play with it. But Daniyal had frowned when the ball dropped, and now, lifting the sole of his right foot, he placed it on the cat's head. Then with a swift and smiling glance at his spectators he slowly pressed his foot down. One after another the bones in the cat's head could be heard to crack, and, when this sound came, the Prince's eyes glanced for one smiling second into those of Gunevati. The cat's paws were beating the air; its body rose stiffly in an arc and then collapsed in spasms; a little pool of blood spread out upon the floor.

Very slowly Gunevati slipped off her seat and lay upon the ground prostrate.

"Oh, what a shame!" exclaimed Dantawat with a nervous giggle. "Poor pussy! Such a lovely pussy!"

Daniyal's bright, blue gaze flickered once more over the faces of his audience, and the smile about his lips remained the same. The young lancer, coming suddenly out of his immobility, went forward, picked Gunevati up from the floor, and moved towards the doorway. At the same time Daniyal beckoned to his two negroes, one of whom took the cat up by the tail and carried its twitching body away; to the other he said something in an undertone, and this man remained by him.

During this scene the Rajah had stood completely motionless, except for a swelling of the muscles of his jaw, and a twitching of the fingers of his right hand. The veins on his forehead had also swollen; but these signs of emotion very soon disappeared. His eyes remained fixed upon Daniyal, darkly but expressionlessly, as the latter now came sauntering towards him.

"My dear Rajah," said the Prince, "you have been very patient. I know it's dreadful, the way I keep people waiting. It's one of my failings. But really, on this occasion . . ."

Slipping an arm through Amar's, he made as though to start off once again on a march up and down the floor. But Amar's body remained rigidly unyielding; so there, close up against one another, the two men stood, Daniyal smiling into the Rajah's face, towards which his own, uptilted, came gradually nearer and nearer.

"My dear friend," he murmured, "surely you are not . . ."

Suddenly, with a movement of great swiftness, Amar's hand went to the hilt of his short sword, and the blade was half out of its scabbard before the negro, who had stationed himself behind him, and was watching his every movement with ready alertness, brought down a metal elephant-goad on to the top of his head. The Rajah crumpled to the ground.

Stepping back, Daniyal surveyed the body on the floor with pursed lips and raised eyebrows. To Dantawat and Mansur, who had come running up, he said: "Another minute, and I really believe he would have run me through. A very hot-tempered gentleman!—I hope you haven't killed him?" he added, turning sharply to the negro.

"Not unless his skull is very soft," replied the man with a grin.

"Have I Your Royal Highness's permission to retire?" asked Mansur in a querulous tone. "I am feeling very unwell after what happened on the lake-front this morning."

Daniyal laughed.

"I take it for granted," continued Mansur sulkily, "that I am now allowed to pack up and leave the Pleasance? With Your Royal Highness's permission, I shall draw my salary and leave this afternoon."

Daniyal pirouetted on his toes, rubbed his hands together, and laughed again for quite a long time. "What nonsense! But you can run away now.—Only remember!" And he held up a warning finger. "There is a rehearsal this afternoon at five o'clock."

"A rehearsal?" cried Mansur in dismay. "But surely we're all packing up?"

"Yes, at our leisure. I find there's no hurry. Things are not as bad as I thought, and I am going to stay here another week at least. I shall do it, if only to annoy that wretched brother of mine." With a light step he moved towards the stage. "Come along, Dantawat, we must see what these men are doing. The way they are handling my things is really too barbarous!"

In another minute he would have disappeared, but the negro was hurrying after him. "What shall I do with the gentleman?" he asked with the same broad grin.

"Oh, let him be sent back to the house of Shaik Mobarek. He has a friend there."

9

IN THE EVENING of that day Gokal sailed back across the lake, with Amar stretched on a mattress at his feet. The boat moved very slowly, for the air was hardly stirring; the bows made no sound as they cleft the glassy water.

Every now and then Gokal would bend down to look into Amar's face, and at regular intervals he placed upon his head a fresh towel, wet and cold from the water of the lake. Amar's eyes were closed, but his face did not wear the look of relaxation that usually comes with sleep. His brows were slightly knit; he looked haughty and aloof.

Very slowly did the Pleasance of the Arts recede into the haze that was beginning to fill the valley. The sun, which had just set behind a spur of the hills, was making the air golden and spreading an iridescent film over the water. Not until the boat was nearly half-way across did Gokal cease to cast nervous looks behind him, for he was pursued by an unreasoning fear lest Daniyal should change his mind, and send out a boat to demand that Amar be brought back.

What exactly had happened was as yet unknown to him, but the men who had carried Amar unconscious to his door had said enough to show that *this* was what he had been obscurely foreboding, the fulfillment of a destiny that had perhaps been inescapable.

As a culmination and a fulfillment this calamity even brought with it a certain peace—just as the crisis of an illness is welcomed as ending a period of suspense.

A surge of pity and tenderness swept over his heart, as he bent down to gaze into Amar's stern, unseeing face. "Either he will die, or he will enter into a state of health and strength better than any before." With this thought he tried to comfort himself, as he wrung out another fresh towel in the water of the lake. Nevertheless, beyond the melancholy peace of the present hour, he saw no certitude anywhere. The dramas of real life, he thought, are not like those of the stage, for the imagination of the gods is never-ending, and of finality there is none.

Raising his eyes, he peered at the line of shore where the Rajah's house stood. It seemed to be getting hardly any nearer; for, as the distance diminished, the dusk deepened, and the outlines of things grew more dim. But the boat's slow progress no longer troubled him; out in the solitude of the lake he was free of his former fears. With the bats flying low over the water, and the colors of earth and sky all gently fading into a misty dusk, the tranquillity of earth penetrated him, and none of the impatient, reproachful questions that men ask of Fate seemed to him to need an answer. He noticed, not for the first time, that there is a moment when, by its very closing in, the evening expands itself, and the great dome of the sky hangs with a new spaciousness over the darkening earth. The silence, too, of the evening seems to possess this same spaciousness, so that even when sounds break it, they are of no account. "They are engulfed," he thought, "they are lost—like that flight of ducks, moving very high up, which in another moment will be gone."

Now the gray patch of the Rajah's roof was no longer visible, although the boat was close under the shore; nor were there any lights showing in the windows to mark the place where the house stood. Gokal looked down at the man who lay stretched like a corpse at his feet, and, thinking what a herald of sadness he was, his heart sank within him. All unconscious of what awaited them —for Amar had asked that neither Sita nor Hari should be informed of his arrival at the Camp—those two lovers were even now in the full enjoyment of their happiness. Somewhere no doubt among those dark trees they were sitting together and talking, or perhaps they were loitering on the grassy path by the lake; it might be that they had noticed his boat approaching and would be on the landing-stage to greet him.

"Nearly four weeks!" he said to himself. "They have had nearly four weeks." And he tried to take comfort in the thought that the beauty of a personal relation, no matter how brief in time, in eternity is everlasting. There are moments, he thought, when feeling rises to an intensity which causes it to leave an imprint upon something more enduring than individual memories. Lovers are dimly aware of this even in the engrossment of their personal happiness. They should remember it afterwards. . . .

Reflecting upon his own experiences of love—how enticed, and thwarted, and tricked, and self-betrayed he had been—he saw that even in his pitiable errancy there had been some profit, for it was to these experiences that he owed at least some part of his present understanding of what love might be,—some part too of his intuition concerning the loves of Sita and Hari. He needed the assurance that they did indeed love one another well to lift him above a sense of disloyalty to Amar. During these days he had been able to derive a kind of exultation from their love, but in his heart there had also been much sadness and not a little fear.

Strange, quiet days! when, living in the constant companionship of Jali, he had sat talking outside his tent, or wandered meditatively along the lake-shore, or gone out fishing on the lake. One after another, radiant mornings had blossomed into warm windless noons, the mellowness of which had lasted until the fall of night. And all these days he was listening with his inner ear to the soundless music that the lovers seemed to spread around them.

With a slight jar the boat came up against the wood of the landing-stage. Gokal felt a sudden shock at his heart, and he stood up. The two boatmen got out of the boat and squatted on the bank waiting.

Gokal stood quiet for some time, looking round him into the obscurity. He could see a little way over the lake and a little way along the lake-path, but wherever there were trees the darkness was complete. He sat down again and looked at Amar, whose corpse-like immobility now made him feel helpless and afraid.

What was he to do? what was he to say to Sita and Hari? The blow that he was about to deal them made him feel guilty and sick. This was such a sudden and violent end to their brief period of happiness. An end, yes!—but it was also a beginning.

Looking down at Amar, he envied him his unconsciousness. The thought came into his mind that if Amar were to die without recovering consciousness, it would be a good thing. But he condemned that thought.

There was no lapping of the water against the sides of the boat,—only absolute quiet! There were no lights in the house. No lights or sounds anywhere. In a moment of confusion and panic he asked himself whether the place were not deserted . . . whether Hari and Sita had not run away?

He got up and stepped clumsily out of the boat. "I am going up to the house," he said to the two boatmen. "Watch over the Maharajah while I am gone."

As he went up the path under the trees, he heard Hari, Sita, and Jali talking and laughing together in the veranda.

TITLES IN SERIES